# THE RAGING OF THE SEA

Also by Charles Gidley
*
THE RIVER RUNNING BY

# CHARLES GIDLEY
# The Raging of the Sea

'O Eternal Lord God, who alone spreadest
out the heavens and rulest the raging of
the sea; who has compassed the waters
with bounds until day and night come to
an end; be pleased to receive into Thy
Almighty and most gracious protection
the persons of us Thy servants, and the
Fleet in which we serve ...'

From the naval prayer

ANDRE DEUTSCH

FIRST PUBLISHED 1984 BY
ANDRE DEUTSCH LIMITED
105 GREAT RUSSELL STREET, LONDON WC1

PHOTOTYPESET BY FALCON GRAPHIC ART LTD
WALLINGTON, SURREY
PRINTED AND BOUND IN GREAT BRITAIN BY
HAZELL WATSON & VINEY LIMITED,
MEMBER OF THE BPCC GROUP,
AYLESBURY, BUCKS
ISBN 0 233 97647 7

# CONTENTS

Part One
# FATHERS AND SONS

# 1

The accident happened on one of the few sunny mornings during the otherwise wet and windy summer of 1931. Captain Yarrow was trying to break a foul anchor out of the seabed by using HMS *Winchester*'s main engines. Unfortunately he had omitted to inform the fo'c's'le of his intention. The result was a crack like a rifle shot as the cable parted and a hail of forged steel that hurtled back across the deck leaving an able seaman in a mess of blood and brains under the triple gun turret.

At the inquiry afterwards, Captain Yarrow cleared himself of all blame. The cable had been one week out of date for its six-monthly survey and Lieutenant Jannaway, who was a torpedo specialist and had been standing in for the regular fo'c's'le officer, had failed to ensure that the cable holder was disconnected from the capstan when the ship started coming ahead.

Captain Yarrow's career in the Royal Navy was more important than Lieutenant Jannaway's, so Jannaway took the rap. Yarrow had already logged him for shaking his fists at the bridge in the confused moments after the accident, and this act of insubordination seemed to confirm, to the members of the board of inquiry, that Jannaway was to blame. As they say in the navy, if you can't take a joke, you shouldn't have joined.

All this might have been forgotten had there been no mutiny, but the following September Jannaway drew attention to himself again. While on passage north with the Atlantic Fleet to Invergordon, he approached the commander of HMS *Winchester* one evening to sound a warning about the possible consequences of the inequitable pay cut Their Lordships were agreeing with the government to impose upon the lower deck.

Jannaway's advice, like that of a better known lieutenant in the Mediterranean Fleet, was that it would be foolhardy to assemble the fleet and so allow the men to meet and plan what action to take.

Jannaway, being ex-lower deck with a Cornish accent and a hesitancy in the presence of his senior officer, was ignored and laughed at; but the advice of the better connected Lieutenant

Mountbatten was heeded and acted upon. The Mediterranean Fleet was dispersed on Mountbatten's advice and remained loyal; the Atlantic Fleet assembled against Jannaway's, and within three days the ratings were sitting on the fo'c's'les singing the Red Flag and refusing to take the ships to sea.

Now, the mutiny was over. The ships had been sent back to their home ports and lay in Portsmouth harbour, drab in the evening rain. The afternoon dockyard shift had just finished, and a crowd of workers issued from the main gate on bicycles. Among them rode Jannaway, his uniform trousers in bicycle clips, the tails of his Burberry raincoat flapping behind him and the patent leather peak of his uniform cap pulled well down over his eyes. It was unusual for a naval officer to bicycle home at the end of the day, but Jannaway was not a great observer of convention.

He – and a hundred others – cycled down the Hard, past Messrs Gieves Naval Tailors and the Keppel's Head and on through old Portsmouth to Southsea. The rain pelted down; everyone was in a hurry to get home.

It had been a bad day for Jannaway. He had been attending one of the many special investigations into what was now being called the 'refusals of duty', and he was taking sombre news back to his wife. Although Austen Chamberlain, the First Lord of the Admiralty, had given the House of Commons his solemn promise that there would be no post-mutiny reprisals, the elders of the navy had since taken it upon themselves to start a search for scapegoats, and Jannaway was just the sort of person they were looking for.

He drew up alongside a row of tall Victorian houses, dismounted and hefted the bike up the steps to the front door, parking it in the hall out of the wet and taking off his dripping raincoat and cap before entering the ground floor flat.

His wife, a bustling, dark, scatterbrained girl, welcomed him. The mutiny had come as a blessing in disguise for her because her first baby had been born only a fortnight before, and her husband's unscheduled return home meant that he could be on hand to share the first weeks of parenthood.

They had been married less than a year. Dora had been a primary schoolteacher in Cardiff when HMS *Winchester* visited the city, and Frank had been the officer who organised the children's party on board. They had met, discovered that both were Roman Catholics and had fallen quickly in love. Within two months they were

10

married and within three Dora was pregnant. It had all happened so quickly, and Frank had gone back to sea so soon after their four-day honeymoon that they still felt a little shy of each other.

She came to the door of the flat looking flushed and maternal, her dark hair escaping from a kirby grip and the sleeves of her home-knitted cardigan pushed up to her elbows.

'You're just in time to see Alan have his six o'clock feed,' she said, though it was already twenty to seven. She led the way into the small bedroom where Alan Francis Jannaway lay in a second-hand cradle. She lifted him up and gave him to Frank, who cupped the baby's head in his hand and held it against his cheek to feel the smoothness of it.

They went into the bigger bedroom and Dora sat down by the bed, glancing up shyly at Frank as she undid her blouse.

He handed the baby to her and she put him to her breast. Frank knelt beside her and held her spare hand, gazing at the baby, who was already taking her milk with the businesslike self-confidence of one who knows what he is about.

'Seeing you like that makes me sort of overflow,' he whispered. 'I feel all full of – of love and tenderness.'

She had dark, almost black hair, but his was fine brown. His face was lean and weatherbeaten: there wasn't an ounce of excess fat on him. He had eyes that were sometimes grey and sometimes hazel brown. She looked into them and smiled.

'I know,' she whispered. 'It shows.'

He asked her why he loved her so much, something he often asked, and she, as usual, laughed and said that goodness only knew.

But he was quieter than usual that evening. When she had first met him, he had seemed very dashing and rather the typical naval officer, the sort that gives the navy a good name. He had that half jaunty, half risqué manner, the twinkle in the eye, the twitch of the eyebrow and that brisk, make-way-for-a-naval-officer way about him that had ladies falling at his feet. She had never dreamt of marrying a naval officer, least of all a handsome, loving naval officer like her Frank. It had seemed a risk to marry so soon after meeting him too, but like many women of her generation who had seen fathers and uncles and brothers cut down in the Great War, Dora knew that her chances of remaining a spinster for life were high, so when her chance came she took it.

'So what have you been up to today?' she asked.

He smiled ruefully. 'I'm in trouble again!'

'Frank! What have you done this time?'

He sighed. Dora knew very little about the navy and he wasn't anxious for her to learn much more. She still asked delightfully naïve questions about it, and on the rare occasions when she had visited the wardroom of HMS *Winchester* she had been ill at ease among the polished public school officers and their ladies.

But she would have to know something of what had happened that day, so he began to explain.

'They want me to name names,' he said. 'And I've told them I won't.'

'Good for you, darling. Whose names do they want, anyway?'

He smiled sadly, still reluctant at having to accept the facts himself. He had joined the navy as a boy seaman in 1910 and had been utterly dedicated to the service ever since. Now, he felt disillusioned and betrayed.

'They want me to tell them the names of ratings who were at Holy Mass on board *Warspite*, the Sunday before the trouble began.'

'Why would they want to know that?'

'Well, I know it sounds ridiculous, but there was only one RC mass held in the fleet that Sunday, so men from every other ship had to go by boat to the *Warspite*. What they're saying is that the organisers of the mutiny used the RCs to pass a message back to all the ships telling people to go ashore to a meeting in the fleet canteen that night.'

Dora was suddenly filled with fierce Welsh anger. 'You mean they're saying that the Catholics organised the whole thing?'

'Not in so many words, no, but –'

'How can they say a thing like that? I mean it's not true is it?'

He shook his head. 'I don't think so. But it is possible.'

The baby sucked quietly for a while and the rain pattered against the sash window. Jannaway stood up and began to unknot his uniform tie. Dora said more quietly: 'Can they force you to tell?'

'No. But they can make things uncomfortable for me if I don't cooperate.'

She asked how, and he wondered how much he should tell her. She had been lucky to have an easy pregnancy and an easy delivery. It had been a joke between them that she had conceived and produced a son so readily. All the same, he didn't want to overburden her with his worries at a time like this.

...d never for one instant lost
...een interested in clock
...uited to the work,
...and trembler
...oduced.
...alled
...d

'Tell me,' she said quietly, her thumb going gently back and forth against the baby's cheek. 'That's what a wife's for isn't it? To share things?'

He stood at the window and looked out over the esplanade to the Solent. The outline of the Isle of Wight was just visible through the rain and a destroyer was rounding the Outer Spit buoy on her way into Portsmouth harbour.

'I may have to leave the navy,' he said quietly.

She said nothing for a moment. When he turned to see her reaction she said: 'Are you sure you're not making a mountain out of a molehill?'

She would have to know. Whatever happened, sooner or later she would have to know. 'They think I was involved in organising the whole thing. And unless I cooperate and tell them the names they want to know, well –'

She moved sharply and Alan lost the nipple and had to be put back to it. 'It's ridiculous!' she exclaimed. 'Why should they even think you had anything to do with it?'

He told her all the reasons: he told her about the reprimand he had received two months before, about his warning to the commander of HMS *Winchester* – even about how, during a wardroom cocktail party, he had incurred the commander's displeasure by becoming involved in a heated argument about the leadership qualities among senior admirals.

'I don't understand it,' Dora said, and she was close to tears now. 'Did you have anything to do with it? Are they right?'

He sat down on the bed again, pulling his black tie back and forth between his hands. 'No, I didn't organise anything. But in a way, they're right. If I hadn't been an officer I'd have been out on the fo'c's'le cheering with the rest of them.'

'Cheering? What would you be cheering for?'

It was necessary, he was discovering, for a married naval officer to live two completely separate lives. People outside the navy, and that included Dora, had not the first idea about what the navy was really like. Sitting on the patchwork quilt, watching her wind Alan and put him to her other breast, was like living in a different world from the world of routines and orders, watchkeeping and discipline.

'They used cheering as a way of signalling between ships,' he explained. 'They all went up onto the fo'c's'les and sat on the anchor cables so we couldn't unmoor, and cheered to each other across the water.' He laughed shortly. 'All part of service tradition you see, love. When we have a mutiny in the navy, everyone cheers.' He laughed again, bitterly now: 'Then like a fool I went and played their piano for them. They'd hoisted it up on deck because they were bored, and when Captain Yarrow heard I'd been playing "Yankee Doodle" for them he put two and two together and made five. Sounds more like something out of Hans Andersen really, doesn't it?'

Dora didn't know what to think. She had only known Frank a year, and they hadn't been together more than ten days at a time since the day she first met him. She couldn't help wondering if he might be a bad lot after all. You could never tell with men, she had heard that often enough.

'You're not telling me fibs are you Frank? I couldn't bear that.' She pushed aside a stray lock of hair and tried to smile.

He realised that he had perhaps told her too much. 'Nothing's definite yet,' he said, putting his arm round her shoulders to comfort her. 'I may not have to leave. But I may get a draft to the Persian Gulf or something.'

She was managing, valiantly, not to cry. 'And I thought they said there wouldn't be any reprisals!' she whispered.

'I'm afraid the navy doesn't work that way, love. That was just a political sop. No, they've got a list of ratings as long as your arm they want to get rid of. They're using this to weed out all the dross on the lower deck. They'll be out – Services No Longer Required.'

'That's lower deck, Frank. Not officers. It doesn't apply to officers.'

'Doesn't it? They have their ways of making heads roll. They don't make a song and dance about it, they just ease people out by making it too unpleasant for them to stay in. Everyone's sitting in their cabins writing pages and pages of reports and notes and memoranda about it all, scraping up every last bit of dirt to fling at someone else.'

She took Alan from her breast and buttoned her blouse. 'Well,' she said, angry again. 'I never thought the navy was like that. I thought it was – well, honourable. Fair.'

She stood up with the baby in her arms. She was in a fluster now, because of what Frank had been saying. Really she would have preferred to be able to feed Alan by herself. That was how the

Frank Jannaway re-joined th
no inclination to go back
have a better chance
if he volunteer

He wa
Quee
ha

midwife had advised her to do it, away from disturbance and chatter, just herself and the baby.

'Now look what I've done,' she said. 'I've gone and fed him before his bath. I knew there was something I was doing wrong.'

'My fault,' Frank said. 'I've upset your routine.'

She gave the baby to Frank to hold while she went to the bathroom to prepare the bath tub. She tested the water with her elbow and made sure the baby soap, the towel, the powder and the Harrington's nappy were to hand, then came back and collected Alan.

Frank came to the door of the bathroom and watched. Dora sat down on a stool with the baby on her knee. She had taken off her rings and had pushed the sleeves of her cardigan up above her elbows. She undressed the baby and put him in the water, supporting his head with one hand and lapping the water over him with the other. Frank put his hand on her shoulder. He could still not quite get over the fact that he was a father and that this perfectly formed child was his son.

Dora looked up. 'I think he'll be a long distance swimmer, this one.'

They gazed adoringly at the baby for some time before Dora asked, 'Do you really think you'll have to leave the navy?'

'Let's not worry about that until it happens,' he said gently.

'But what would you do, Frank?'

He grinned and kissed her cheek. 'Drive the Gosport ferry maybe?'

'Be serious.'

He mused a few moments. 'I know what I'd like to do. I'd like to keep a little watch and clock shop. I'd like to restore old clocks. I could enjoy that.'

She shook her head in mock despair. 'Clocks! I'll clock you if you don't look out, Frank Jannaway!'

He went back to the bedroom to finish changing out of uniform. Dora lifted Alan out of the tub and put him on the towel over her knees. She patted him dry, taking extra care over the little creases and folds of skin behind his knees, between his legs and round his elbows and armpits. The midwife had said that a properly dried baby didn't need any powder at all, and she was anxious to do everything right.

Just then, Alan was sick. He was lying face down over her knees so the mess went straight down onto the floor. 'That was my fault,' she murmured. 'I shouldn't have fed you first, should I? Next time you must remind me if I do it wrong, see?' She loved talking to him like that, as if he understood. Having trained as a teacher, she was full of plans and ideas on how to give him the best possible start in life.

In the bedroom, Frank Jannaway hung up his uniform reefer and trousers in the wardrobe and took out his tweed jacket and corduroys. He had not thought seriously about leaving the navy until now, but the idea seemed suddenly attractive. Twenty-one years was a long time after all, and it was unlikely that he would go much further now that he had landed himself in all this trouble.

He stood before the mirror and knotted a plaid tie, wrapped up in his own thoughts and hardly aware of Dora in the bathroom. Yes, if he left now, he'd have a small gratuity. He might be able to go into business in a modest way. He could settle down, raise a family, make a home, breed grandchildren . . .

'I could always get a job in London,' he called to Dora. 'Remember Jack O'Riordan? He offered me a job in marine insurance.'

'When was that?' she replied from the bathroom.

'Oh – a year or so ago.'

'Exactly. A year or so ago isn't today, is it?'

He put a comb through his hair and called, 'Well look at the alternative. Two years in the Persian Gulf!'

He heard her make an impatient noise. 'Why don't you just tell them the names they want to know and have done with it?' she demanded.

'Get thee behind me Satan,' he muttered to himself, and was just about to make a different reply to Dora when he heard her scream.

She was still screaming when he reached the bathroom. She was sitting with her legs wide apart, her head up under the handbasin, her hair down over her eyes. She was screaming at the top of her voice and the baby was face down on the linoleum between her legs.

She was shaking and screaming so much that he had to pick up the baby himself. He asked her what had happened, what she had been doing. She was barely able to tell him.

'He – he – he – was sick,' she sobbed. 'O God! He was sick! And when – and when – when I stood up, I slipped. And he hit – he hit his head – on the bath, this sharp bit – Oh Frank! Frank!'

She followed him into the bedroom, dropping to her knees and making the sign of the cross. 'O God, O God!' she babbled. 'O Jesus, Mary, Joseph and all the Saints! Please make him be all right! Please make him be all right!'

The baby was clearly not all right. He was very quiet and his body had already become cold and damp. Frank calmed his wife sufficiently to be able to leave her with the baby, and ran for the doctor; but when he arrived there was already a dull purple mark on the baby's head, and it was too early to say whether or not Alan would be permanently injured.

# 2

Dora never forgave herself that moment of carelessness. When it became clear that Alan would be permanently disabled, she told Frank that she would devote her life to looking after Alan and that she did not feel that God wanted her to have any more children. For six years, they practised the only method of contraception allowed them by the Church, but in spite of all their efforts there was a mistake, and the result arrived in the afternoon of 13 March 1938.

Frank was trying to keep calm downstairs at the time, and had taken on the job of boiling kettles and amusing Alan. Since leaving the navy, he had settled into civilian life as a marine insurance broker and was now the proud owner of a terraced house in Mill Hill East. He went back and forth between the kitchen and the sitting room and the dining room wondering whether to put on another saucepan of water, playing snatches at the piano and helping Alan with his reading.

Upstairs, the midwife picked up the infant by the heels and smacked its bottom harder than was necessary. 'Another boy,' she told the father when he was allowed into the bedroom.

Dora now lay against the pillows holding the child. Frank stooped to see the wrinkled face of his secondborn. There was a trace of black hair on the head, and the baby wore what appeared to be a grin.

'Look at that,' Frank said. 'He's smiling!'

The midwife joined a pair of damp hands across her stomach. 'Wind,' she said.

Frank went to the door. 'Alan! Come and look at your brother!'

Alan was six and a half years old, not badly disabled, only partially spastic. He had fine brown hair and hazel eyes like his father's. 'What's his name?' he asked.

Dora looked at her husband. 'He's called Steven. Steven with a V.'

'Steven it is, then,' Frank agreed.

'He looks funny,' Alan said. 'He's got a funny face.'

'Like his Mum,' Dora said. Now that the baby had arrived, she felt curiously elated.

Frank Jannaway re-joined the navy eighteen months later. He had no inclination to go back into uniform, but he decided that he might have a better chance of doing something that really interested him if he volunteered at the outbreak of hostilities.

He was not disappointed. A commander on the third floor of Queen Anne's Mansions looked at his service record, found that he had been a torpedo specialist, noted his hobby of repairing clocks and watches and sent him down to Portsmouth for training in mine disposal. It wasn't exactly what Jannaway wanted, but then war seldom comes up to expectations.

The Jannaway children were not among the million evacuees moved out of the cities at the beginning of the war. Frank didn't believe in 'bomb-dodging' as he called it, and considered that the house in Chestnut Road was too far from the city centre to be in any sort of danger. 'Better to sit tight,' he told Dora. 'It won't last more than a few months I expect, and then we can all settle down again.'

Dora was not quite such an optimist. She didn't like the gasmasks they had to carry about with them, nor did she like the Ministry of Information pamphlets about air raids. She wasn't sure exactly what her husband's job involved, but she had a feeling it might be more dangerous than he cared to admit.

Frank suddenly found himself having to work much harder than he had expected. He completed training at HMS *Vernon* in Portsmouth, and was sent up to the admiralty one morning to choose an assistant. He picked a man called Jock McCullen, principally because he had 'RC' in the religion box of his service certificate and partly because he had been serving in the *Warspite* at the time of Invergordon.

He trained Jock rather as a surgeon trains a theatre sister, and together they began disarming the new magnetic mines that were being dropped over the major cities and dockyards of Great Britain.

They made a strange looking pair. They would arrive on the scene of an unexploded mine in a three-ton truck, Jannaway wearing his lieutenant's reefer over a white polo-necked sweater and his trousers tucked into a pair of seaman's boots, while Jock, who had grown a thick beard that practically obscured his face, wore a bright blue woollen hat with a red pom-pom on top. Jannaway had long legs and Jock had short; the one would stride purposefully over the rubble and the other would trot.

The early mines were comparatively easy to defuse provided you

19

knew exactly what you were doing, and never for one instant lost concentration. Jannaway had always been interested in clock mechanisms and found that he was well suited to the work, becoming intrigued and challenged by the time delay and trembler mechanisms which the weapon designers in Germany introduced. What intrigued him even more was a twenty-year-old Wren called Betty Simpson, who worked in the Portsmouth Signal Centre and proved of great comfort to him in his evenings off duty.

Life was without such comforts for Dora. She had to cope on her own like every other war wife, with the additional difficulty of having to help Alan overcome his disability. Prodded into action by national propaganda, she started an allotment and grew cabbages and potatoes, and later persuaded her husband to build a chicken run. She became part of another army, the army of women who gave support to their menfolk and who 'managed'.

'Invention is the necessity of mother,' she used to say, shovelling a concoction of mashed potato and dried egg into Steven's mouth like a stoker at the boiler face.

The dark years of the war dragged by. Steven turned from a mewling, dribbly infant into a very small boy. The grin his father had remarked on his birthday had become more or less permanent: he gurgled and kicked in his cot, explored every corner of the house as soon as he could crawl, and ate coal whenever the opportunity arose.

Frank Jannaway's short periods of leave were nearly always surprise arrivals. The three-ton lorry would draw up outside number fifty-nine Chestnut Road and there he would be, his cap tipped over his eyes and his pockets full of black market butter and sugar. Home was the sailor, home – not exactly from the sea, but at least from the comforts of the officers' mess in HMS *Vernon* and the tender embraces of Betty Simpson.

Dora would rush to welcome him, flinging herself into his arms, and Steven would stand in the hall, a finger in his mouth and awe in his eyes at this semi-stranger in a brass buttoned reefer, who winked at him and scruffled his short black hair.

'How's Alan?' he would say, putting his arm round Alan's shoulders. 'And how's Captain Oates?'

He hoisted Steven up and gave him a hug. He was four and a half now, and recognised his Dad. He didn't know why he was called Captain Oates but he liked being called it all the same. He also liked the smell of tobacco and the easy sense of security his father brought into the house with him.

'So what have you been up to young man?' Frank asked one morning in January '43 when he turned up on the doorstep without any forewarning at all.

'Having breakfast,' Steven said, and didn't understand why his parents laughed.

'Would you like some?' Dora asked. 'Only porridge and toast I'm afraid.'

'I don't mind if I do,' said Jannaway, mimicking a current comedian. He took off his greatcoat and shook the snow off his shoes. He had recently been promoted to lieutenant commander, and wore two and a half gold rings on each sleeve.

Dora dashed into the kitchen to make more toast and tea. She stirred up the last of the porridge, which had congealed in the pan.

'You're looking thinner,' she said when he came to the door. 'You aren't eating enough.'

'You're looking younger and more beautiful,' he lied. 'I'm not seeing you enough.'

He kissed her and she burnt the toast. She scraped off the charcoal into the sink.

'Mummy's always doing that,' Alan stuttered.

They sat and watched him have his breakfast. He was like a returning hero to them, and he knew it.

'Will you shave now?' Steven asked him when he was finishing.

'He's very anxious to see you shave,' Dora explained.

'I've already had a shave, Captain Oates. You'll have to wait until tomorrow morning.'

Dora put her hand on his arm. 'I want to take a snap of you before you change. When you've finished your tea, no hurry.'

'What do you want a photograph of my ugly mug for?' Jannaway laughed. 'You don't want a photo of me!'

Steven pushed his forefinger into the curl of gold braid on his father's sleeve. 'Yes we do,' he said earnestly.

They went into the narrow back garden. There was snow on the ground, and the apple tree, which grew beside the coal bunker, was covered in hoar frost. Steven ran about making new footprints in the snow and pretending he was a railway engine by blowing out steam.

'Put your cap on,' Dora said. 'I want you with your cap on.'

21

She opened up her concertina Kodak and Frank tipped the peak of his cap down over his eyes and grinned obligingly. The shutter clicked. 'Lovely!' she said.

'Now me!' Steven demanded.

'I'll take one of all three of you. I've only one left.' She pushed back a wisp of hair that had escaped her bun. 'You in the middle, Frank, that's it!'

'All your menfolk!' he joked.

She took the picture and they went inside. Upstairs, Frank and Dora closed the bedroom door and greeted each other again. He changed out of uniform into his corduroys and tweeds, remembering to transfer his wallet from his uniform to his hacking jacket before giving Dora the uniform to press. That was important, because there was a letter from Betty in the wallet which he hadn't yet had the heart to destroy.

'Horrible thing!' Dora said, taking the uniform from him. 'I'll be glad when you never have to wear it again!'

Downstairs, he rubbed his hands together and said, 'Now then, what's for mending?'

He adjusted the brakes on Dora's bike and put a new washer in the kitchen tap. He put a shelf up in Alan's room (Alan was reading more and more these days) and had a look at the leak in the loft. The house filled with the smell of his tobacco and the sound of his voice, and after lunch Steven said, '*Now* will you shave?'

He took him on his knee and played This is the Way the Gentlemen Ride until he was helpless with laughter. Steven whispered conspiratorially into his father's ear, 'Can we go bogonning?'

'Bogonning?'

'He means toboganning,' Dora said. 'We haven't got a toboggan,' she told Steven. 'So we can't.'

'What about trays?' Frank asked. 'Just as good.'

So they all went toboganning. Steven was dressed up in his leggings and his mitts and Frank carried him on his shoulders all the way down the cinder track to the gap in the railings. They went down the path to the stream, which was frozen at the edges, and on the way across the bridge Steven was dangled over the water until Dora told his father that was enough. They went over the deserted golf course and up to the steep bank by the railway line. The sun broke through the mist and glinted on the snow.

Frank had to be first. He lay down on a Coronation tray and went skittering down head first. Dora sat heavily down on the other tray, which refused to budge. Alan took over his father's tray and fell off after twenty yards.

Steven had climbed to the very top of the bank.

'Not from up there,' his mother called. 'Start further down!'

But he was already accelerating down the piste, a red faced, black haired, small-bore bullet, whistling past them at great speed, becoming airborne as he topped a hillock and disappearing from view as he went on down to the stream.

Frank and Dora chased after him. Frank slithered down a steep clay bank and found his son in two inches of nearly frozen water, still clinging to the tray, his button nose a few inches from a discarded cistern. He picked him up and put him under his arm like a pig for market.

'We'll have to have another go at that, won't we?' he said, putting Steven down. He took his hand and ran with him all the way to the top of the bank.

'Frank!' Dora called. 'Don't be silly, Frank!'

But Frank bent and looked his son in the eye. 'We're not being silly, are we? You're not afraid, are you?'

Steven didn't know what being afraid was like, and it was a nice feeling to be doing something his father wanted him to do which his mother said was silly.

Frank aimed him in a different direction and told him how to dig his toes in if he wanted to slow down or change direction, then he gave him a push and he went hurtling off again, coming finally to rest a few yards from the third hole.

There was no stopping him after that. For an hour he ran up and slid down the hill. Watching him, Dora leant against her husband and admitted he had been right. 'I suppose it's like going up the mast again after you've fallen off, isn't it?' she said.

She walked between Alan and Frank, her arms linked in theirs, while Steven tried to keep step with his father by jumping along in big strides. The sun turned crimson and settled over the chestnut trees. Dora hung up the wet clothes in the kitchen and Frank lit the fire.

They gathered round the piano and he played the songs they had sung before the war, nostalgic songs they both loved, songs that Steven had never heard before. When Frank sang 'Lily of Laguna',

Dora's eyes filled with tears and she had to borrow his handkerchief.

Steven had to be carried up to bed. His father hoisted him over his shoulder like a sack of potatoes and pretended he was going to let him slip when they were halfway up the stairs. Steven hung head down, held by the heels, and watched the stairs receding behind him.

His father didn't know that Panda was supposed to clean his teeth as well or that the monkey with the half-peeled banana was supposed to join in the prayers. Dora and Alan came up and sat on the bed, and Frank read *The Tale of Pigling Bland*, which Steven had chosen because it was the longest of all the Beatrix Potter stories and he liked the picture at the end.

His father kissed him on the cheek and told him to be a good boy and go to sleep. Steven lay in the bed looking small and pink and innocent. 'Tell me when you're going to shave,' he said.

They switched out the light and went onto the landing. 'I think he'll remember today, won't he?' Dora whispered.

There was an air raid in the night, but they didn't bother to move downstairs, and Steven slept through it without waking, exhausted after his afternoon on the snow. When the lorry arrived outside the front door, Frank was awake immediately. It was just after six, and still dark. He rubbed his fist on the window pane to get rid of the frost. 'It's Jock,' he said shortly, and hurried downstairs to open the front door.

Dora got out of bed and put on a dressing gown. She went down to the hall: the black bearded able seaman had left the door open and a chill draught had followed him in. Jannaway was looking boyish in his pyjamas, his hair standing up on end.

'I'm being called out,' he said. 'Sorry.'

She made them a cup of tea while her husband changed into uniform. He came down in five minutes, his reefer buttoned over his white sweater. He gulped his tea down and prepared to leave.

'When will we see you again?' she asked.

'Can't promise,' he said. 'But I'll try and get tomorrow off.'

He kissed her goodbye and she stood at the window in the front room to watch him go.

As the lorry drove off, its roof scraped against the branches of the birch tree, brushing the hoar frost off and leaving behind it a

pale silver cloud that hung for a moment outside the window.

Frank Jannaway realised he had left his wallet behind when they were driving down Archway Road. The discovery came as a dull shock. It was unlikely that Dora would look into his wallet, but it was just possible. He lit two cigarettes and gave one to Jock, who sat hunched over the wheel, peering ahead at the patch of light thrown by the dimmed headlights.

'Forgotten my dratted ID card,' Jannaway said.

'I doubt you'll be needing it,' Jock replied.

They went slowly on through Holborn to the city. Jock had been given an address near the East India Docks where a mine had fallen and failed to explode. Jannaway took out a road map and gave him directions as they neared the scene. They turned left into Aberfeldy Street and right into Blair Street, drawing up beside a road block manned by an ARP warden and marked by a notice announcing the presence of an unexploded bomb.

'Number seventeen,' the warden said, pointing along the row of slums to a terraced house with a demolished roof. 'We've evacuated the area and they've promised to stop the trains.' He nodded his head. 'There's the gas works across the way. Will you have a cup before you start? The WVS van's here.'

'We'll take a look first,' Jannaway said, and he and Jock set out along the road.

They found the mine as directed, in the front room of number seventeen. Its parachute had snagged on the chimney, and it hung nose down, a crude, black sausage-shaped piece of cast iron.

There was a china dog on the mantelpiece and a saucer of milk by the grate. A framed wedding photograph stood on the dresser.

'Type C,' Jannaway said very quietly. It was the sort of mine that could be set off by vibration or a magnetic field. When it was set off, a timing mechanism ran for twenty-two seconds before an electrical connection was made to a small charge, called the gaine. The gaine was set off by an electric detonator, and the explosion of the gaine in turn caused the explosion of the five hundred pounds of high explosive. It was impossible to tell whether the timing mechanism had been started and had stuck, or whether a further time delay had been fitted. All that could be said positively about it was that it might or might not go off at any second, that it might or might not contain a booby trap or a trembler device to prevent disarming and that if the timing mechanism was activated by some slight vibration or jolt, there was anything from nought to twenty-two seconds in which to run for cover.

Jannaway and McCullen picked their way carefully out of the house and retired to a safe distance.

'We'll not be using drawlines on this'n,' Jock said. 'Unless you want to turn her.'

Jannaway nodded his agreement. The access plate to the timer was almost turned to the wall. A tool was available which could be attached to the timer so that it could be unscrewed using remote lines, but this one would have to be taken out by hand.

They walked back to the WVS van and accepted mugs of tea. The ARP warden and the WVS lady watched them as they stood discussing their tactics.

'We'll build a good bolt-hole, Jock. In the next door garden.'

'I'd rather further away.'

'Further away's further to run.'

They worked methodically through the morning. They built a thick wall of sandbags in the next door garden, five high and five deep. They carefully wedged the mine with more sandbags so that it would not be able to move while it was worked on. They moved furniture and rubble out of the way, and spread a sheet on the floor beside the mine. Jannaway set out his non-magnetic tools, his screwdrivers, his spanners and his long-nosed pliers on this sheet, and Jock McCullen was ordered out to take shelter while he started work. There was only one shouted order that he had to listen for: the single word, 'Run'.

Alone in the room with the mine, Frank Jannaway closed his eyes and made the sign of the cross. When he opened them, a tortoiseshell cat was looking at him through the broken window. He remembered the saucer of milk. He didn't know much about cats, but this one looked as though it had remembered the saucer of milk as well. He carried it out of the hall and set it outside by the front door. The cat leapt down and ran to it, its tail swishing from side to side in appreciation.

He returned to his mine. He felt unsettled. He liked to start work as soon as he had made his peace with God, and he couldn't quite stop thinking about the letter he had left behind in the inside pocket of his tweed jacket.

He held a stethoscope to the mine and confirmed that no time delay was in action. He took a screwdriver, and started to remove the access plate, loosening all the screws by one thread in turn so that it came off evenly. From time to time, he stopped to wipe his hand on the towel he kept round his neck. It was surprising how much you could sweat, even on the coldest day.

The access plate came off cleanly and he laid it to one side. He made a minute inspection of the head of the timer, and wished that he had decided to turn the mine after all and use the drawlines. He had taken a long time to get as far as he had, and he was loath to continue. He had disarmed mines like this before, and in more difficult conditions, but there was something about this one ... no, he mustn't start thinking like that. This one was just the same as any other. There was no such thing as a mine 'having your name on it' as some people believed.

He went out to Jock.

'It's a straightforward Type C,' he said.

'You mean you've done it? She's safe?'

'Just about to start.'

He ignored McCullen's look of surprise. 'Go and get yourself a bite to eat. It won't take me long now.'

He went back into the front room and wiped his hands on the towel. He looked at his hands: they were shaking, and they had never done that before. He knew that such things happened, and that there was a ward in Netley Hospital where they looked after men who screamed at the sound of a ticking clock.

At the end of the street, the small group of firemen, wardens, the WVS lady and Jock McCullen warmed their hands at the brazier. The minutes went by, and at midday the silence caused by stopped traffic and trains was shattered by a factory hooter. For the seconds while it lasted, they waited for the explosion, but no explosion came.

'Taking his time,' the warden said eventually.

'Ay, you would an' all,' McCullen replied.

Jannaway nearly had the timing device out. He was turning it gently in his hands and it was emerging, thread by thread, from the cast iron side of the mine. One last turn, and it was out: he took the weight of it in his left hand, holding it close up to the mine while he picked up a pair of long-nosed wire clippers with his right. A dribble of sweat went down the side of his face, but this was no time to think about that. He slipped the clippers in behind the timer, and at the same time the cat appeared at the window, its back arched and its tail high. It looked in at him with yellow eyes. They stared at each other, cat and man, and without warning, it leapt.

He lurched forward as it landed on his shoulders, and immediately he heard two sorts of purring: one was the deep contented purr of the tortoiseshell cat, and the other the steady whirr of the time delay.

The staff car arrived at the door at seven o'clock that same Sunday evening, when Dora had just put Steven to bed. She went to the front door and opened it to a naval commander in his best number five uniform.

'Mrs Jannaway? May I come in?'

She knew straightaway why he had come, but it was somehow better to let him tell her in his own way. She led him into the sitting room and turned off the wireless. She asked Alan to leave them alone for a few minutes, and when the door had closed behind him she turned and smiled, and offered the commander a seat.

He held his hat in his hands and looked nervously about the small, cluttered room.

He seemed unable to start, so she helped him. 'It is bad news, isn't it?'

'I'm afraid so.'

'Is he dead?'

'Yes.'

How unbelievable it seemed later, when she thought about the way he had told her and the calm manner in which she had accepted it. They sat in silence, he looking down at his cap, she sitting bolt upright in the armchair by the fire, with the bookcase and the wireless at her back and the mending she had been doing over the arm.

'I expected this,' she said. 'Sooner or later.'

The commander nodded as if he had, too. 'He died in very courageous circumstances,' he told her.

She smiled. Yes, she was not surprised at that, either. Her poor overgrown schoolboy of a husband.

He began telling her other things: pieces of useless information about pensions and benevolent trusts, which were unlikely to bring her husband back. He said the officers' society to which her husband had belonged would be in touch, and then he was on his feet, in an almost obscene rush to be out, she felt, to leave this tragedy behind him and get on with his war.

When he was gone, she called Alan and Steven in. She held their hands, and they sat either side of her on the arms of the chair. She was determined not to break down. She felt that she owed that to Frank. He would want her to be brave, as he had always wanted Alan and Steven to be brave.

'Let's talk about Daddy,' she said.

She came into the bedroom and closed the door gently behind her. She had put Alan and Steven to bed, and the house was quiet. Outside, it was snowing softly; from time to time a gentle tap on the window could be heard, as if someone were secretly asking to come in.

She had not told the boys yet. She thought it best not to: there was time enough for that tomorrow, when she could be with them for the first few hours and cushion them for the shock.

Shock? She had not experienced it yet herself. She believed, she knew that Frank was dead, but somehow he was not dead, or at least some part of him lived on in her. She had spoken lovingly of him to the boys, and they had talked about holidays they had had before the war, when Alan was three and four and five, and they had gone down to Studland. She had asked each of them what they could remember about their father, and Steven had said, 'Shaving'. Alan had looked at her a little oddly: he was an intelligent child, and she wondered if perhaps he had already guessed the truth. She was much closer to Alan than she was to Steven. They had fought together through the years to conquer as much of his paraplegia as possible, and they had won nearly every battle. He was able to write as well as read, though the process cost him great effort, and he would be starting at the Salesian college next year. What she admired most in him was his lack of jealousy – especially for his younger brother. She had never dared hope that they would get on so well, that Alan would turn out to be such a wonderful elder brother; she believed that perhaps this was the blessing in disguise that had come with his paraplegia, and that his generosity of heart was some God-given compensation for his lack of muscular control.

How quiet it was! She looked about her, at the photograph of Frank on the mantelpiece over the gas fire, and their wedding photograph on the chest of drawers. She felt that perhaps it would be a good thing to weep now, deliberately to let the tears come, and a few did. She let her eyes fill, a little ashamed of herself because

29

she felt that she was acting; she opened the wardrobe, and stared in at the clothes he had left behind.

She sat on the bed and covered her face with her hands, and the tears began to come of their own accord. But even in this sorrow, she was aware of how lucky she had been to be his wife, to share his funny, unsuccessful life, to be at his side when his naval career crumbled, and to help him start again as a civilian. And wouldn't he have wanted to die like this? Courageously, the commander from admiralty had said. He had sent the other man away, perhaps knowing that the chances of success were small, perhaps deliberately exploding the mine so that it would kill only one.

She stood up and lifted his tweed jacket from the back of a chair where he had left it that morning, and saw the wallet. It was a very natural thing to do to take it out now, because she knew he kept her own photograph in it. She looked sadly at herself, the Dora of ten years ago, in a cotton dress and a sunhat, looking glamorous and fancy free.

She found the letter then, and saw the strange handwriting that began, 'My darling . . .' She found herself reading it and wondering at the same time how it could possibly have come into his possession. She stared at the last line, in which the writer had said that she was not a two-way Bet or a side Bet but his safe, one and only Best Bet and that if he laid it all on her they would come romping home together.

She found herself shaking so much she had to sit down. She had not had the slightest suspicion of this and would not have believed it of Frank even if she had been told. It was just not in his nature. He was her husband, they were one, he could not belong to anyone else.

She sat for a long time on the bed, staring at the letter in her hand. She thought of all she had said to the boys that evening, how she had deliberately built up their father into a memory to be cherished, an example to follow; and slowly, her thoughts cleared and she knew what she must do: she must never mention his infidelity, or even hint at it. The boys must grow up to believe in their father just as she had believed in him and trusted him.

She knelt by the gas fire and struck a match, and carefully burnt the two pages of the letter. When they were burnt, a sudden whiplash of anger overtook her: she could still see the words on the burnt paper, so she took the ashes in her hands, her hair falling over her face, and crushed them to powder.

The investiture took place four months later. She put on her black suit, her pearls and her hat whose brim dipped over her eyes, and bought a grey suit for Alan, who was now tall enough to go into long trousers. She bought a tie for Steven – his very first tie – and put water on his hair to make it stay down when she brushed it.

They travelled to the palace by taxi, and they were conducted along carpeted corridors and up gilded stairs. On their way, they saw one of the corgis, which waddled along in the opposite direction, ignoring them completely.

A naval officer came and talked to them. He tried to put her at her ease, and told her how to address His Majesty.

They were beckoned through into a high-ceilinged room and were presented. She was surprised to find herself as tall as the King and taller than the Queen.

'Your Daddy was a very brave man,' the King said to Steven, who gazed up into his eyes. 'You won't forget will you?'

Steven replied by solemnly shaking his head, and after the investiture, when they were walking away, he asked in an all too clear voice, 'Mummy, was *that* the King?'

Outside the palace gates they were met by a barrage of press reporters and cameramen. Dora posed for them with Alan and Steven on either side.

'Can we have the little boy on his own, Mrs Jannaway?' one of the reporters asked. 'On his own, with the cross.'

Steven was shown how to hold the box with the medal inside. He stood with his back to a Grenadier Guard in a sentry box.

'Look up here, sonny!' the cameraman said. 'Look up at my hand here!'

The shutter clicked, and in the morning Steven Jannaway appeared on the front page of the *Daily Mirror*. SON OF A HERO was the headline, and underneath, the little boy holding the George Cross looked perplexedly up at the sky.

# 3

Being the son of a hero was exciting at first because whenever he went out with his mother or Alan, or took his bike out in the road, or went shopping, he always knew that people were looking at him and talking about him. It made him extra special. His name was Steven Jannaway and people said oh, the son of Frank Jannaway, the G.C.? and he said yes, and looked them in the eye the way his mother said he must because that was the way his father would have wanted him to behave. Not that it was always easy, being the son of a hero. In the early days, that autumn when the stream flooded and he had just started at his first school, he had to learn that he mustn't shout in the road or interrupt his mother when she was talking, or cling, or say Big Jobs in the meat queue. He had to learn how to behave like a sort of hero himself, and she had to be a father as well as a mother. She didn't cuddle him so much and she always made him do his best. He had to go for a haircut on his own and do without having the landing light on. He had to speak the truth even when it meant owning up about stealing matches or playing mothers and fathers with Hetty Ringrose, because the one thing she would not tolerate was deceit. She wanted him to be the good Catholic boy his father would have been proud of, and because she was a schoolteacher now she knew how to make him do things properly. She leant over him and smelt of coal tar soap and ticked his sums with red crayon, tick tick tick, until the crayon stopped and looked at the numbers and instead of a tick put a red dot by the place where he went wrong and she said no, Steven, that's not right is it? Can you see where you have gone wrong? You'll have to do that one again, won't you?

She would have liked to send him to a better school but she couldn't afford it because she only had her widow's pension and her teacher's pay, and that wasn't enough to feed and clothe them as well as she would have liked, let alone send him to Byron House. So he went to the local primary where she was a teacher and every afternoon they walked down Dollis Road together and had tea. The leaves blew off the birch trees in Chestnut Road, and the stream made a great flood over the allotments. There was Good News from Africa and when he said are we going to win the war? she said yes, because Hitler was an evil man and Good must surely triumph over Evil. He said why is Alan a spastic? and her face went wild and angry. Who's been asking you about Alan? she wanted to know, but he didn't like to tell her about the spastic jokes they had been telling him and how he had said that Alan wasn't a spastic at all and how they had said he is, so. He is a spastic, isn't he? he said, and she looked away and said I don't want to discuss it, Steven. But she had to discuss it later because he came home with a bruised lip and the arm torn off his windcheater. They had said his brother was a spastic again and he had said he didn't want to discuss it. He is a spastic isn't he? he asked and she sighed and looked at the gas fire and said, all right, I will tell you about it. They sat in the dining room and people went along the road outside on their way home from work, looking in at Steven and his mother having tea. All right, I will tell you. It was an accident. It happened when he was a tiny baby. She couldn't go on. She cried without making any noise. She had cried before, when his father had died, but he hadn't seen her cry, only known that she had been doing it. She turned her face away from him and bent her head. She wasn't soft and motherly any more but wild and angry. I dropped him in the bathroom, she said. It was an accident, but it was my fault. I was careless. Her words came out in between hiccups and he wanted her to stop. He didn't want to hear anything more about Alan being a spastic, but she went on and on. I dropped him on the bathroom floor because I was talking and I wasn't paying proper attention. He hit his head on the bath because I was careless and it was my fault.

Later, when she was better, after she had had the 'flu and they had been looked after by Mrs Groves from three doors down, who made porridge with lumps in it and had a smelly dog who was always doing your leg, his mother said a little more about Alan. She lay in bed with her hair undone and said yes, he will always be a spastic, but he isn't nearly as bad as he might have been and he is very brave and is doing his best to overcome his handicap. But you have all your faculties, do you know what faculties are? They are all the easiness of running and jumping and skipping and laughing and singing and talking. You have a perfect body and you must never forget that. You must always do your very best and make the most of what you have got. You must try your best at everything, for Alan's sake.

After that, if ever he said he had nothing to do, she set him sums or a piece of the Imitation of Christ to copy out. It was like being at school all the time and nothing he did was ever quite good enough. The only person he could talk to about school was Alan, who was six years older and wore pebble glasses and whose hair would never lie down because she had to cut it instead of a barber. Alan was the person who could answer most of his questions, especially questions about his father. He could remember a holiday they had had before the war. He could even remember seeing Steven on the day he was born. He said that his father was always having good ideas and saying funny things and shocking his mother, and that when he was at home people were always laughing and enjoying themselves. Alan tried to be like his father, and used to think up games and dares for Steven to do. He shared his presents and let you sit on the big tricycle he had when he was fifteen. He had lots of books about the navy and had the Sea Cadet magazine every month. If he hadn't been spastic he would have joined the navy and worked his way up from the lower deck, and when he talked about battlecruisers and sub lieutenants and explained how to take bearings and fix the ship's position (which Steven never understood however often it was explained) you couldn't help feeling a little bit enthusiastic too. Both the boys had the framed photograph of their father which Mrs Jannaway had taken on his last day at home, the day they went toboganning. It had come out quite well, but was a little bit blurry. He had his cap tipped down over his eyes and he looked as if he had just made a very naughty suggestion. Sometimes Steven looked at it for a long time, trying to make him come back alive again, and then, if his mother was out, he went into the front bedroom and found the medal in the wardrobe drawer. He took it out and looked at the silver cross and the words For Gallantry, putting it back very quickly when his mother came in from doing the hens and he heard the kitchen door slam. She didn't like him looking at the medal. He didn't know why, but she just didn't.

Sally had short pigtails done in elastic bands and brown eyes. She sat by the window four desks away and everyone liked her and tried to walk with her in the crocodile to the Squires Lane Baths or on nature walks when they went by bus to Hampstead Heath. She wouldn't lick tongues with anyone but she was good at tennis ball

34

footer in the playground and she shared her coffee essence at break, putting a little drop in your milk and stirring it for you with a straw. She had a younger brother and at the end of the day they went home holding hands. Why haven't I got a sister? he asked his mother one day, and she said that it just didn't work out that way. How does it work out? he asked, and she said all right, Steven, I'll tell you, and she explained how two people who were married and loved each other very much could sometimes make a baby and that the seed had to be planted in the mother's body by the father and that every time that it happened it was a miracle worked by God, and he wanted to know where the seeds came from and she didn't take it seriously and said he would find out all in good time. It still didn't explain why he didn't have a sister, so he asked her again and she said they were lucky to have him, he was a surprise, and he thought about that for a few more days before asking her, was I really a surprise? and she said not so much a surprise, more a mistake. She was doing out the grate in the sitting room and she looked back at him and saw his expression. She gathered him into her arms because he was still only small. No, I didn't mean that, she said. I didn't mean it, I didn't mean it. Her hair was going grey and there were lines on her forehead where she worried. Her hands were chapped from washing up and working on the allotment and making hen food. She held him in her arms with his cheek against hers, and it made him wonder which was right, whether he was a surprise or a mistake.

The milk arrived very early in the morning, on a horse-drawn milk float, and the milkman's name was George. Sometimes they went for a long walk all the way up to Partingdale Lane, and visited the Express Dairy Rest Home for Horses. As you walked up the lane towards it, you could hear the smith at work in his smithy, the hammer on the shoe ringing and ringing and ringing, and you could watch him pumping the bellows and the coal going white hot and the shoe coming out, or see the shoe going onto the horse's hoof, making it hiss and smoke and giving off a strong smell that made you cough. The war was over and he was reaching the age of reason. It was possible to take the middle out of the cardboard milk bottle top, lick the cream off the bottom and then throw it like a miniature discus that went flying up over the house. He had to go to catechism class with Hetty Ringrose, who had glands, and learn why God made him. That was the summer he played mothers and fathers with her behind the new tennis pavilion at the bottom of the allotments, the one that had been built to replace the one that the V2 destroyed. She let him put his hand all round her bottom and she felt up his trousers with hers. It was something he had to tell Father Longstaff for his first confession. Father Longstaff had thick black hairs growing out of his left ear, the one you said confession into, and he smelt of Senior Service cigarettes. He coughed and said well done my child, now for your penance say one Our Father and one Hail Mary and make a good act of contrition O my God because thou art so good I do most sincerely beg pardon of thee. He felt holy and pure the next day, at his First Communion, and wore a white shirt instead of the usual grey one. The wafer was a disappointment because it tasted of nothing at all and he didn't believe that it was the body of Christ, although he tried hard and pretended to himself that he did. But it obviously wasn't because it had been stamped out in a machine. *Corpus Domine nostri Jesu Christi custodiat animam tuam in vitam aeternam, amen*, said Father Longstaff, and he went back to the front row with his hands together under his nose, and Hetty Ringrose looked at him out of the corner of her eye. Afterwards, there was real roast lamb for lunch because Mrs Jannaway had saved up the coupons for weeks so that they could celebrate Steven's first communion, and when they had finished and made the sign of the cross, she said why don't you and Alan go for a nice walk by the stream? so they did, and they found some children swinging on a rope. It was attached to a high branch and they were swinging right out over the stream. Alan said go on, have a go, why don't you? so he did. They caught the rope and showed him how to sit on the big knot at the bottom. He started at the top of a steep clay bank, and when they let him go he went rushing out over the water as if he were flying. The rope was hard and thick between his legs and his thing rubbed up against it and gave him the funniest feeling he had ever had, like wanting very badly to go to the lavatory when you knew you didn't, and it was such a strange feeling that all he could do was hold onto the rope until it stopped. What was it like? Alan said. Tell me what it was like. That was what he often said when you did things he couldn't do. But it was impossible to say what it was like because you had to do it yourself to know. After that he often went down and swung on the rope and although he knew it had something to do with mothers and fathers

36

and touching Hetty Ringrose's bottom and sin, nobody had ever said you couldn't swing on a rope or that it was a mortal sin, so it wasn't worth confessing. Instead, because he never did any real sins, he thought up a few interesting ones to whisper into Father Longstaff's ear, and because he went to confession every Saturday afternoon and Communion every Sunday morning everyone said what a nice little boy he was. He was in a State of Grace, and that meant if he fell on the live rail at Mill Hill East or got run over by a trolleybus in Regent's Park Road, he would go to heaven, because he wasn't old enough to have done anything really bad and anyway he had a plenary indulgence for saying a special prayer in front of the crucifix, and that let him off Purgatory.

Sometimes he had a dream. Lots of people came to watch him and Alan was there encouraging him and saying go on, you can do it. He clenched his fists tight and jerked his arms down, and went straight up in the air, right up, higher than the trees by the stream, so that he could look down on the crowds of people, the golfers on the golf course, the allotments, Chestnut Road, the big brick viaduct and the tube trains crawling back and forth between Finchley Central and Mill Hill East. Providing he kept his fists tightly clenched, and concentrated the way he was supposed to at school, he could keep himself up there, hovering just below the clouds. He could look down at Alan, who was shouting up to him Well done! That's the ticket! Keep it up! and eventually swoop down like a Vampire Jet and fly a few feet off the ground so that people's faces went into a blur; then he would land and Alan, who was not a spastic, would slap him on the back and shake his hand and the King would be there somewhere but he never quite managed to meet him. It was such a real dream that sometimes he felt that it had really happened. When he told his mother about it she said oh yes. Everyone has dreams like that. It's when your heart misses a beat.

Uncle Roland wasn't an uncle at all, but a man their mother met and brought home to tea. She said he was a Very Clever Man. He was an engineer and wore brown suits and large, pale brown shoes. He wanted to marry their mother and started giving them presents to make them like him. He gave Alan a camera and Steven a Meccano set. He used to bring along a bottle of sherry and make Mrs

Jannaway laugh. He was always saying happy days and if I remember rightly. He read Steven's report, which said Steven should concentrate less on diverting his neighbour and more upon the subject in hand. He said come on, Old Man, I'm sure we can do better than this, can't we? Steven wanted to saw his fingers off with the new hacksaw Alan gave him for Christmas. He didn't like being called Old Man and he didn't like having to play with his Meccano set when Uncle Roland came so that Uncle Roland saw how much he liked it. He didn't like the way his mother changed and went silly when Uncle Roland came to the house, and once he caught them kissing in the kitchen. What would you say if I married Uncle Roland? his mother asked him, and he said I wouldn't say anything, and slammed the kitchen door when he went out to bike round the stream.

That September, Alan was seventeen and Uncle Roland gave him a pianola. Alan's voice had broken. He had a cracky sort of laugh, and usually he wore a tweed jacket and brown corduroy trousers, which was what their father had often worn. He fed the hens every morning and read books in his room at night. He knew the whole of the morse code because Uncle Roland had given him a morse buzzer and a set of teach yourself morse cards for Christmas. He was mad on the navy and had books on sailing, and had gone in a dinghy with Uncle Roland on Regent's Park lake. He also had their father's old gramophone and a case of records, most of which were scratched because he had difficulty putting the needle on properly at the beginning. He liked music and as well as wishing that he could have joined the navy, he also wished that he could play the piano, and that was what gave Uncle Roland the idea. It had come in a Selfridge's green van on a Saturday when Uncle Roland was there. It took up a lot of room because it had to go up against the piano in the dining room and the dining room table had to be moved closer to the gas fire. Uncle Roland asked the men who delivered it exactly how to work it, and then he put a roll of paper in it and sat down at the piano stool, putting his big feet on the pedals. He sat back as if he were riding a bicycle with no hands and pumped his feet on the pedals. The roll of paper moved up through the machine and the piano began to play as if there were a ghost playing it and Steven, who was ten, hated it because it was like cheating. The person who was most pleased with this present was Uncle Roland, because it was his idea. Come on Al, he said. Your turn. Sit yourself down, that's the way, feet on the pedals and off you go.

The trouble with the pianola was that Alan couldn't work it properly. He could pump the pedals, but he couldn't pump them evenly the way you were supposed to, and as a result the music came out as if it were being played by an idiot. Alan liked music and he knew that he was doing it wrong. The harder he tried, the worse it got for him, because he knew what the Polonaise in A or the Rondo Alla Turca or the Moonlight Sonata should sound like and he couldn't make the pianola do them properly. Eventually he got so angry with himself that he lay down on the floor and pushed the pedals with his hand, and when Mrs Jannaway went into the dining room to say well done, there he was. After that you could hear him crying in his room. He didn't sound like anything at all when he cried because his voice had only just broken. If he sounded like anything it was a donkey braying. Steven went and cried in his bedroom and Mrs Jannaway went and cried in the hall. Later, she went into Alan's bedroom and Steven heard her talking to him in a quiet voice for a long time. The next day, Alan was different. He wasn't going to have to try to play the pianola any more. Steven looked at him and asked, are you grown up now then? and Alan looked back and smiled in the nice lopsided way Steven liked and said, yes, maybe I am. He liked Alan a lot after that and they used to sit in his room at the back of the house and listen to records or talk. They talked about almost anything because Alan was always reading new books and could tell Steven about them and explain things; but he knew, now, that there were some things in life that he would never be able to do, and that Steven would have to do them instead.

He had a Rocket-a-Copter which had folding wings made of balsa wood, which you shot up into the air and which then opened up and came spinning down, and he was playing with it when his mother called him in and told him that Alan had made a very generous suggestion. She said that they could return the pianola to Selfridges and have the money from it. Alan thought it would be a good idea for the money to be spent on piano lessons for you, she said. What do you think? Would you like that? He nodded and said yes, because almost anything Alan suggested was a good idea, so a few weeks later he started with Mrs Winter in Chesterfield Avenue. She had blued hair and pearls and she made him leave his shoes in the porch. She gave him floury scones and weak tea and made him find the notes she sang on the piano. She said he was a lucky boy because he had perfect pitch, and she was surprised and pleased that he did his exercises so well. The reason he did was because his mother made sure he did. She said that if a thing was worth doing it was worth doing well. Alan had been very generous to give him these piano lessons, and he mustn't waste them. You must strive for excellence in everything you do, she said. You must never accept second best. He started at the Salesian College and biked to school. He had the sex talk from Brother Dominic and was told about the sanctity of marriage, and the respect and courtesy due to women. He did his homework on the dining room table and connected the aerial of his crystal set to the bed springs. He started Latin and Greek and was encouraged by Father Longstaff, Mrs Winter, the headmaster, Uncle Roland (who didn't come so often now) but most of all his mother. His first report arrived and it said that it was a pleasure to teach such an enthusiastic, attentive boy who so obviously enjoyed classical studies: well done.

But he knew, secretly, that he wasn't attentive or enthusiastic because he wanted to be but because he had to be. He knew that what interested him much more than school work or the piano was girls. He thought about them almost the whole time. He knew now that if he were suddenly killed he would probably go to hell, because he was beginning to have the seed and it shot out like a blob of spit, frightening him at first because it was the stuff that could actually make babies, and he was guilty of the sin of Onan. He led a double life: that of the good-boy Steven and the filthy, self-abusing, mortally sinful and almost certainly damned Jannaway, the Jannaway whose underworld life was frequently punctuated by dreams about doing it with girls, usually when he was swimming so that it didn't matter about spilling the seed until you woke up and found that you had.

1952 was an important year because the King died and they went to see the funeral march. It was a gloomy day in February, and the coffin went by on a gun carriage pulled by rows and rows of slow-marching sailors. Uncle Roland stood to attention and Mrs

40

Jannaway cried. Steven was nearly fourteen and his voice was beginning to break. He was going to be tall, but he wasn't tall yet. He looked at Alan and he knew that he was wishing he could be in the navy instead of working as an assistant librarian, so that evening, after Uncle Roland had gone, he said that he thought he would like to join the navy in a few years, and he could see by Alan's face how pleased he was. His mother warmed her hands at the gas fire and said oh, Steven darling please don't get that idea into your head. She sighed and said all right, I'll tell you why. Your father was only in the navy because he joined up for the war. He joined up again because it was his duty, that was all. He didn't like the navy. How do you know he didn't like the navy? Steven said. She sighed again and told him all about the mutiny up in Scotland when the Atlantic Fleet refused to go to sea because of a pay cut. That was why your father left the navy in the first place Steven. He refused to give the names of the ratings who organised it. He was at Mass on the Sunday before, and the Catholics were the ones who took the messages back to their ships about meeting ashore and planning to refuse to do their duty. Your father knew who they were, but he wouldn't tell, understand? That was why he left the navy.

He didn't believe it. The story sounded as though it might almost be true, but whenever his mother talked about his father, he always had a feeling she wasn't telling the truth. Usually she looked you exactly in the eye, but when she talked about his father, she looked at the gas fire. He talked to Alan about it, and Alan said that his father had talked to the ratings too much during the mutiny, and that the ratings in his ship (you always said *in* a ship, never on) had hoisted a piano up to the fo'c's'le and had cheered when Lieutenant Jannaway had played it for them. There had been a lot of cheering during the mutiny, and that was why people said Cheers to each other when they had a drink. Alan knew all about that sort of thing – anything that had a connection with his father or the navy or ships or the sea. Why don't you join the sea scouts? he suggested, so Steven did, but he knew they were a waste of time almost straight away. Everyone shouted and gave orders and pretended they were tin Hitlers. They played High Cockalorum and Mounted Horse and British Bulldog. Mr Kendrick the scoutmaster had asked Mrs Jannaway what nickname he might like, and Mrs Jannaway had said he used to be called Captain Oates when he was very small, so Mr

Kendrick tried to call him that. He got his Second Class and his Shooting Badge, and then one evening in November a few months after he had joined, he was met by the Woodside Parkers on his way home. The Woodside Parkers were sea scouts, but they were also a private gang led by a boy called Eddie Lutt, who was going to be an artificer apprentice in the navy the following year. They had left early, and when Steven biked down Holden Road, they stopped him. You're coming down the park, Lutt said, and when he said no, he was going home, Lutt said you're coming down the fucking park. There were five of them, and he didn't have a three speed on his bike. He went down the park with them and they frog marched him through the mist to a disused air raid shelter. Ever been milked? Lutt asked, and he pretended he didn't know what that meant. They pinned him against the wall inside the shelter, and undid his flies. They tried to milk him but it didn't work and some of them lost their nerve and cycled off. He punched Lutt in the face and ran for the doorway, riding off through the fog, the dynamo screaming on the back wheel. What've you been up to? his mother asked when he wheeled the bike into the hall. Running the marathon?

She didn't have a set evening for doing the ironing because there always seemed to be ironing to do. Usually she did it in the kitchen, and the piles of pants and sheets and pyjamas used to topple off the dresser. She wasn't a tidy person at all, and was always hoarding things like string and newspaper cuttings, buttons, paper bags, rubber bands and jam jars. All the sideboards and mantelpieces were crammed with things she couldn't find and didn't want to lose. What do you mean you're not going to scouts? Of course you are! she said when he came down and told her. Her hair was going grey and she wore glasses. Her mouth worked as she ironed one of Alan's white shirts, and she spoke as if she were reciting something she had learnt by heart. You can't give up things like this, Steven, she said. You've got to learn to persevere. That uniform cost money, do you know that? Money doesn't grow on trees, does it? What would Alan say? You're lucky to be able to go to sea scouts at all, aren't you? Life isn't all roses you know. You've got to learn to take the rough with the smooth. Just because you didn't enjoy it last week doesn't mean you can give it up. She picked up the piles of ironing and took them upstairs to put in the airing cupboard, and she told him to go and get changed that minute, otherwise he would be late.

He came downstairs in his sea scout uniform and she said that's better, you'll enjoy yourself once you get there, you see. (She watched him wheel his bicycle out of the hall and when he had gone went back into the kitchen and found that the leeks had boiled over. She worried about Steven because he was being lazy at school and difficult at home; she worried about Alan because he spent so much time reading, and she worried about Roland because she knew that they would not get married because he didn't get on with Steven. She stood in her kitchen and mopped up the spilt water on the top of the gas stove, wondering why Steven had taken a dislike to sea scouts, and a little glad in her heart that he had, because she hadn't really wanted him to join in the first place.)

Steven wheeled his bike out of the hall and pulled the front door shut behind him. He rode off in the wrong direction, along Dollis Road and up Bittacy Hill. He freewheeled down Partingdale Lane, the dynamo humming and the front light stabbing the darkness. He made a circuit, coming back along Frith Lane, under the railway bridge and along Holders Hill Road. He cycled on and on, round and round and when he eventually arrived home his mother said, you're early back! and he said yes, well, we finished early didn't we? She gave him a look and the following week he made sure to stay out longer. He did the same thing four weeks running, and when she asked if he was enjoying scouts more now, he said they're all right. He wasn't sure if she believed him, and when he was practising on the piano a few days later Mr Kendrick arrived on his motorbike. He came into the dining room without taking off his duffel coat and scarf. Mrs Jannaway made him a cup of tea and gave him a Garibaldi biscuit. He sat down and looked at Steven and said, well, Captain Oates, and where've you been these last four weeks?

The photograph of his father still hung at the foot of his bed. It was the first thing he saw when he woke up every morning. He stood in his room and looked at it, listening to the voices of his mother and Mr Kendrick as they came out of the dining room into the hall. He heard the front door open and close, and saw the scoutmaster go out to his motorbike, kick the starter and ride off. When the noise had died down, he realised that his mother was standing at the door behind him. She said she wasn't just cross, she was ashamed and disgusted. She said he had deceived Mr Kendrick, deceived Alan and deceived her, his own mother. Well, she said,

43

haven't you got anything to say at all? He shook his head, so she told him that she had promised Mr Kendrick he would be at sea scouts the following week. Well I won't be, he said, to which she replied yes you will, Steven, I'm telling you. You will. You can't force me, he said, and she said we'll see about that.

In the morning when he was getting ready for school she had another go at him. If you're not prepared to stick at sea scouts, I don't see why Alan's money should be spent on your piano lessons. She bent to turn out the gas fire, and after a few seconds the flame went out with a pop. Well? she said. What have you got to say to that? Do you want to give up the piano? No, of course you don't. So you'll just have to go on with sea scouts. I'm not going back, he said. I've decided. Even if I have to give up the piano. Steven, she said. Aren't you being a little bit silly? Cutting your nose off to spite your face? I don't want you to give up the piano! But you must learn to stick at it. It's like going up the mast again after you've fallen off. I haven't fallen off any mast, he said. Yes you have, she replied. You've betrayed my trust. He didn't know why, but he wanted to hurt her. He was taller than she was and his voice was deepening. Her hands were all damp from washing up and the sleeves of her grey cardigan were pushed up to her elbows. If his father had been alive, none of this would have happened. His father would have been on his side, he knew he would have. He was sick of the way his mother was always insisting on him doing his best and asking him if he'd made a really good confession. What did she know about the world? Stuck in a classroom teaching six-year-olds every day. And she was frightened of him, you could see that in her eyes. She wanted to keep him in her cocoon, that was what it was, wrapped in her strong, silken threads. She wanted him to be a good boy and go to sea scouts, she wanted him to be a good boy and learn the piano, she wanted him to be a good boy and look after her, his little mother.

He had talked to Alan about what he wanted to do, and sooner or later he would have to tell his mother, so it might as well be now.

'All right,' he said. 'I'll give up the piano, definitely. I won't need any piano lessons anyway, because I'm going to join the Royal Navy.'

# 4

There are as many ways of becoming an admiral as there are of climbing a mountain, but they fall into two main categories, one being to climb all the way yourself, and the other to persuade someone else to carry you.

Henry Braddle was a believer in the first method, though he was not averse to a little assistance from time to time. Unlike those who follow a policy of finding a successful senior officer, latching on to the slack of his pants and hanging on for grim death, Henry had decided that he was capable of winning promotion through his own efforts. For many years, he had been scrambling with great determination up the naval mountain, and the rocks and boulders he had dislodged on his way up had crushed several of the climbers who followed in his footsteps.

He banged a hairy fist on the beige covered table in the Vice Chief of Naval Staff's conference room.

'No,' he said. 'I do not go along with that. With the greatest respect to Lord Louis, that is balls.'

He was one of several staff captains who had met to discuss future policy of officer training – a subject referred to at different times and by different officers as a well ridden hobby horse, a well kicked football and a hot potato.

'If you put cadets in small ships they'll spend their entire time smoking duty frees and spewing their rings up,' Braddle said. 'We'll end up with Fred Karno's navy.'

The Vice Chief of Naval Staff suppressed a smile. He knew that Braddle's son was due to go to Dartmouth in a fortnight's time, and that Henry was anxious that the boy should receive his sea training in a big ship, as so many young officers had before him. He glanced down the table. 'What's your view, Freddy?'

Freddy Sykes-Morris twirled a silver propelling pencil and selected his words for promotion. These conferences with VCNS could make or mar your future.

'My feelings are that we must look to the major threat now posed by the Soviet navy to decide the emphasis we should place on the various aspects of officer training,' he said. 'We can't ignore the submarine threat any longer.' He glanced at Braddle, who was bunching his lips in anger. 'We have to face up to the fact that the young gentlemen going to Dartmouth now will spend most of their careers grappling with the submarine problem – whatever specialisation they choose. As I see it, we therefore have no viable option as to choice of training ship.' He looked round the table, and then at the bushy eyebrows of the admiral. 'Frigates,' he said. 'Anti-submarine frigates, preferably the most up to date we can spare.'

In the pause that followed, the whistling of Braddle's breath among the hairs that grew in his nose could be clearly heard.

The Vice Chief of Naval Staff folded his hands on the table in front of him. He knew already that a squadron of destroyers or frigates would be formed; Mountbatten had already decreed that, and what Mountbatten said, happened. The purpose behind this meeting was simply to give the staff captains the impression that the decision had been taken as a result of their advice.

'Are we at least agreed that HMS *Triumph* is quite un-satisfactory?' he enquired, referring to the old aircraft carrier currently in use as a training ship.

All but the Director of Air Organisation and Training nodded their heads obediently. VCNS went on, careful not to look at Braddle. 'I take the point that there may be minor drawbacks as regards accommodation and administration of cadets in small ships, but I believe these can be overcome. I think the subject has been aired sufficiently and your views will of course be reflected in the minutes.' He looked at his watch. 'Well, gentlemen, I think we must draw stumps in order to give the Wren stenographer time to type this before the weekend. I'll have copies passed for information, of course.' He stretched his back. It was a Friday afternoon, and he was looking forward to getting home. 'Thank you gentlemen.'

The conference broke up. Henry Braddle gathered together his papers and put them in his black briefcase. He nodded a curt good-day to his colleagues and stamped out.

Third Officer Pam Wisely rose from her desk in his outer office as Henry Braddle stamped in. He took a pack out of his briefcase and threw it in his out tray. 'What do you want?' he asked her.

Pam Wisely was used to this abruptness and regarded it as entirely normal. The time to be on your guard was when Captain Braddle became quiet and courteous. 'Nothing, sir,' she said. 'I was simply wondering if there was anything you wanted.'

Braddle blew down his nose and said there was plenty but that he doubted whether it was in her powers to help. He took the packs out of his in tray and dumped them on his desk. As she turned to go, his telephone rang. He picked it up immediately and shouted into the mouthpiece: 'Braddle!'

He always answered his telephone in the same way. The name Braddle, like Jellicoe and Saumerez and Dreyer was part of the naval tradition. There had been Braddles in the navy since the eighteenth century, when Lieutenant Bartholomew Braddle won public praise for the accuracy of his gunfire at the Battle of the Saintes.

Braddle was a good name for a gunnery officer. It was reminiscent of that word, music to naval ears, which was sung out by the spotter when a broadside landed round the target. 'Straddle!' they used to call, and the gunnery officer, beaming quickly at his captain, would pass the order down a copper voice pipe to fire for effect.

The Braddle family had been quick to build on Bartholomew's reputation. There had been Braddles in the navy almost without a break since 1784, and each had added a little to the family reputation. It was the great grandson of Bartholomew, Thomas Braddle, who had finally secured a place in naval history for the family name. Serving in the China Fleet with Keyes and Tomkinson, he had been singled out as a man not only of determination and courage but one who had a clear insight into naval politics. He commanded a destroyer at Jutland and leapt up the promotion ladder, dodging the unpleasantness at Invergordon which did for so many careers in 1931 and eventually retiring in the rank of full admiral. He lived on now in retirement, writing the occasional memoir for the *Naval Review* or *Blackwood's Magazine* in the peace and quietness of his Hampshire estate.

His son, Henry, was a gunnery specialist as every other Braddle had been. He was a thickset man with short cropped hair that made his head look like a bullet. He had small ears that lay flat against his skull, and beady blue eyes that could shrivel a midshipman at a hundred yards.

'Hello darling,' said a gentle voice at the end of the line. 'It's me.'

'Me' was his wife, Clara.

Braddle did not believe in the niceties of husbandly courtesy. 'What do you want?' he said, in exactly the same blunt way he had addressed Pam Wisely.

'I've just had a call from Giles,' Clara said.

Braddle picked up a small brass cannon which he kept on his desk. He had made it himself as a fourteen-year-old cadet, turning it on a lathe in the Sandquay workshops of the naval college under the supervision of a retired artificer. He weighed it in his hand, admiring it. 'What about?'

'He wouldn't say, darling. But he did say he'd like to speak with you. I said I'd ask you if you could collect David on your way home this afternoon.'

Braddle blew out his cheeks and put his top lip over his bottom one. He put his cannon down and pulled at his nose. 'This is bloody inconvenient. I'm up to my arse in bumf.'

'Could you ring him darling? He was most insistent.'

Braddle sighed into the telephone.

'I need to know one way or the other, Henry,' his wife said. 'Because if you're not going to collect David I shall have to leave right away. Don't forget we've got this party tonight.'

'Oh, all right,' he said, and was about to ring off when Clara said, 'Can I take it you will collect David then?'

'Affirmative!' he shouted, and rang off. 'Pam!'

She appeared. 'Sir?'

'Get me the headmaster of Craybourne on the blower.'

'Service call, sir?'

'Better make it private.'

He sat down at his desk and glowered through the open door as Pam Wisely asked for trunks and put the call through. He was a member of the board of governors for Craybourne boys' school, and had been partially instrumental in appointing Giles McNee as headmaster two years before. McNee had come down from Edinburgh where he had been the headmaster of one of the better boys' prep schools, and was widely regarded as a man who had a flair for encouraging the young. It was largely thanks to Giles that Braddle's son David had scraped the entrance exam for Dartmouth.

The call came through a few minutes later. 'I've run into a rather tricky problem,' McNee said in his soft Inverness accent at the other end of the line.

'What sort of problem?'

'I can't discuss it on the telephone, Captain. I'm sorry.'

'You want me to come to you?' Braddle said, as if he were Mahomed recently invited by a mountain.

'Yes, I'm afraid I do. I can't let David leave until we've spoken.'

There was something quietly persuasive about McNee's tone, and although Braddle was naturally bombastic, some of that bombast was put on deliberately, to foster his image as a forthright, fire-eating gunnery officer and so increase his chances of promotion to flag rank. 'All right,' he said glancing at his Rolex. 'I'll be with you by five, will that suit?'

'Thank you, I'm most grateful,' McNee said, and they rang off.

'Pam!' The Third Officer sprang once more from her desk and appeared at his door. 'I shall be leaving shortly. Is there anything else I should see before I go?'

She stared at him in amazement. He hated anyone on his staff to leave early on a Friday afternoon, and always made a point of saving up packs in his in tray to look at so that he could be seen at work until the very last minute of the week. It kept everyone on their toes and made Braddle one of the most hated captains in the admiralty, which was precisely what he wanted.

She shook her head. 'I – no – I don't think so, sir.'

'Well don't look so bloody miserable girl,' he said.

She tried to smile. 'It doesn't make any difference this week-end, sir. I'm duty.'

He leant back in his swivel chair and laughed, and the sound of his laughter echoed down the polished corridors like a long burst of fire on an Oerlikon machine gun.

The dark green Rover saloon purred down the A4 and turned right at Maidenhead through the narrower country lanes of north Berkshire. It was a day of blue sky and showers, lambs in the fields, the country looking washed and clean. Now that he was away from the office, Henry Braddle relaxed, and allowed his thoughts to wander. He remembered his own last day at school thirty years before when he had left Stubbington to go as a thirteen-year-old cadet to Dartmouth. It was a damn shame they had introduced this new sixteen-year-old entry. He had opposed the idea, as had many naval officers of his seniority, with great vigour, getting his father to speak personally to Attlee about it; but the Labour government had been intent upon destroying every last vestige of elitism, and had declared that the thirteen-year-old entry discriminated against the working-class boy. Braddle had advised his son to wait until he was eighteen and join the navy as a Special Entry cadet – a Benbow as they were called – but the boy had wanted to join as soon as possible, and he had not liked to stand in his way. Now there was this business of sending cadets to sea in small ships. That would be a disaster: the advantage of the old training cruiser *Devonshire* was that she introduced the young officers to the structure and traditions of the service. He accepted that she had had to be replaced, but why not by one of the cruisers like *Belfast* or *Sheffield*? Small ships were all very well for building team spirit and inspiring recruiting films like 'In Which We Serve', but as far as Henry Braddle was concerned, they were no good for training officers.

He turned right off the main road and up a straight avenue of mature elm trees, at the top of which stood the Georgian main building of Craybourne School. He parked the Rover outside the pillared entrance and walked in through the marbled hall, the heels of his highly polished black shoes clicking sharply as he went, his city suit immaculate, his Whale Island tie neatly knotted in his cut-away stiff white collar.

He rang the bell outside the headmaster's flat, glancing at the oaken board upon which his own name appeared as one of the school governors. The door opened: Giles welcomed him. 'Captain. Come in. Kind of you to come personally.'

They shook hands: McNee much taller than Braddle, with an academic stoop and leather patches on his tweed jacket. They went along a passage and into the study where a log fire burned in the grate and McNee's books and university photographs lined the walls. A man Braddle vaguely recognised rose to his feet as they entered.

'Do you know Doctor Blakely?'

'I know you by sight, Captain, but I don't think we've met.' Blakely's handshake was limp, and his eyes were magnified by a pair of pebble-lensed spectacles. He wore a hand-woven tie and suede shoes. 'I must admit I'm as much in the dark about this as you are,' he said and then added quickly, 'That is I presume –'

Braddle ignored him. He had just remembered who he was. He was the thin streak who had argued the toss at a parents' conference a year before. A psychiatrist or a psychologist of some sort.

They sat down, and McNee poured tea and offered biscuits. He was better at dealing with boys than with their fathers.

'I've already explained that David is due to go to Dartmouth next term,' he said to Braddle, 'and perhaps you should know that Julian Blakely looks all set to win a scholarship to Cambridge at the end of this year.'

Forgetting for a moment that he had been asked to attend because of some sort of crisis, Braddle beamed comfortably, expecting that McNee was about to propose some sort of joint celebration.

McNee placed his finger tips against his forehead and closed his eyes for a moment. 'Well go on, Giles, don't keep us in suspense,' Braddle said.

'I'm not sure if I should be consulting with you at all.' McNee looked as if he were suffering actual pain. Outside, a boy ran past the window carrying a tuck box. 'But I think I have no choice.' Whatever it was he had to say was disturbing him considerably. He looked from one to the other and then, in his quiet highland accent, broke the news that their respective sons had been discovered in bed together in the early hours of that morning.

It had started to rain. The downpour drummed on the car roofs in the quad where parents were arriving to collect their sons. Inside the headmaster's study McNee, Braddle and Blakely sat in silence for several seconds.

McNee broke the silence. 'I was up late – working on reports. Took a stroll through the school, something I often do on the last night of term.' He looked at Braddle. 'I found your son's bed empty. I heard movement in the sixth form rooms, went up to investigate. I don't know now why I chose that door.'

Braddle pulled at his nose. 'What were they doing?'

'Julian was making a very good pretence of being asleep. David was hiding under the bedclothes.'

Braddle's face took on an expression of solemn revulsion, the thick-lipped mouth turned down, the eyes darting back and forth as if watching for an attack. Blakely took off his spectacles and polished the lenses. His eyes seemed suddenly much smaller.

'Did you question them?' Blakely asked.

McNee smiled. 'I said, "What are you doing?" They just looked at me. I sent Braddle back to his dormitory. I spoke to them separately this morning.' McNee stopped a moment. 'All David will say is, "I'm sorry sir." Julian claims he was in bed asleep when David came to his room.'

Blakely said, 'There's – what – a two-year age gap?'

McNee nodded.

'Were you witness to any actual misbehaviour?' Braddle asked. 'I mean – sexual?'

'No.'

'What about a medical examination?'

'I considered it, but decided against it.'

'They aren't criminals, Captain,' Blakely said. 'They're boys.'

Braddle snorted through his nose. He looked at McNee. 'Are you going to expel them?'

'Is that what you would recommend, Captain?'

'I don't see that you have any alternative.'

'Wait a minute,' Blakely said. 'Let's not lose our sense of proportion. This is presumably an isolated incident.'

'That we know of,' Braddle put in. 'As far as we know.'

'We have no proof of actual misbehaviour,' Blakely went on. 'Everyone knows that midnight feasts go on at the end of term. They might have heard the headmaster coming and each rushed for the nearest bed. And if you expel one, you can't very well not expel the other.'

'If?' Braddle said. 'If?'

'Yes, if. All we know positively – if I understand you right, headmaster – is that the two boys spent some time in bed together. That in itself is not a crime, surely. I doubt even if it's against the school rules.' He stood up and went to the window, gazing out at the sports grounds, where the rugger posts were already being removed in preparation for the cricket season. 'If Julian is expelled, I shall seriously consider suing the school for damages. He is at a point in his academic career when a disruption of this sort could mark him for life. I might not win my case, but I would certainly do considerable damage to the reputation of the school. I would not like that, but if my son's future is to be sacrificed because another boy got into his bed while he was asleep in the middle of the night –'

'Wait a minute,' Braddle said. 'Wait a minute –'

'May I –' McNee started. 'May I say something?' He waited for their attention, and continued: 'It was within my powers to expel both your sons out of hand. I have complete freedom from the board of governors to act as I see fit when such incidents as these arise. But I believe that my aim in this case must not be to lay blame and punish but to find out what is the best course of action to follow. That is why I thought long and hard before asking the two of you to come here this afternoon. What I want to avoid above all is the wrangling and counter-accusation these cases so often involve. Our first responsibility must be towards the welfare of these two boys. It is their careers – their lives – that are at stake. If I expel them there is no question of David going to Dartmouth next term, and I doubt too whether Julian would be able to cope with such an abrupt change in his academic curriculum and achieve the success we hope for him. So all I ask is, let us consider the boys and let us consider the school. Let us be very sure that whatever action we take will be constructive rather than damaging.'

Braddle sat bolt upright, his hands clenched on the leather arm rests. 'What are you suggesting? That we say no more of it?'

As soon as he had spoken, all three knew that although there might be a great deal more talk, a decision had been taken, for the headmaster had been wrong in one small detail: there were not two careers at stake that afternoon, but five.

Driving down to Meonford with his son sitting in the passenger seat beside him, Henry Braddle wondered what the devil he could say. In the quiet of the headmaster's study, Blakely had expounded his views on adolescent homosexuality, quoting his own book on the subject and emphasising the need young people had for love and parental understanding. He had used all the psychology jargon Braddle detested, stressing what a devastating effect a parent's attitude could have, and how a brilliant boy could be marked for life by a wrong attitude or a negative approach. Henry Braddle didn't go along with all that rubbish, but he could not avoid the fact that he was going to have to say something to David before they arrived home, and whatever he said must put the fear of God into the lad and make one hundred and one per cent sure that there wasn't so much as a whisper of this sort of thing from him again.

The damnable thing about it was that the boy was so young for his age. He looked closer to thirteen than sixteen. Clara had begged him not to allow David to go through for Dartmouth, but he had said that he wasn't going to be the first Braddle in a hundred years to forbid his son to join the service. So David had been coached and prodded into studying for the exams and had scraped in with pass marks; once he got to the interview, with a name like Braddle, he could hardly fail.

But what in hell am I going to say to him? Braddle wondered as the car sped southward through Alton. He glanced at the boy, who gazed ahead without giving any sign of what was going on in that young mind of his.

Braddle had never really known his son. His naval career had kept him at sea for most of the war, and David's personality had been somewhat swamped by that of his sisters, Sarah and Julietta. Bringing up the children was Clara's pigeon as far as Henry Braddle was concerned. He had done his bit of course, taking David along to the Royal Tournament whenever he had complimentary tickets and having him shown round his various ships. He had taken him sailing, too, in the Whale Island fifty square metre yacht, and had presented David with a succession of weapons on his birthdays and at Christmas: toy pistols and popguns at first, bows and arrows later, air pistols and air guns after that, until the most recent present, a single barrelled four-ten shotgun which they had chosen together at Purdy's.

McNee was right of course. It would have been madness to expel the boy. Chances were that even Blakely was right – that far more cases like this occur than are ever found out, and that if every judge, bishop, admiral and civil servant who had ever had a homosexual experience at school were to resign, the entire Establishment would founder.

He finally broke the silence just after passing through the village of Warnford. 'Time we talked,' he said, and pulled the Rover off the road into a lay-by. 'Shall we take a walk?'

They set off along a track that led through a beech wood. Even now he had no clear plan of what he was going to say. He was aware of David's apprehension as he walked along at his side and felt a momentary pang of sympathy for the boy. He knew he had to give some sort of parental pep talk, but his mind was devoid even of an opening line.

Then he had an idea. He stopped abruptly. There was no need for all that claptrap about isolated incidents and second chances. It was much simpler than that. He looked down into his son's cherubic face.

'I know all about it, David. And after this I don't want to hear anything more about it again. As far as I am concerned it will be over. It will never have happened, and it will not be possible for it to happen again. Do I make myself clear?'

The boy looked up into those piercing blue eyes.

'Well?'

David nodded. Braddle walked on, not satisfied that he had made himself clear. A pigeon flapped out of the branches overhead, and he mentally took aim and fired.

'Do you still want to go to Dartmouth?'

'Yes.' David's voice still showed no sign of breaking.

'Do you think I should allow you to go?'

'I don't know.'

Braddle quelled a feeling of impatience. Why was it that of his three children, his only son should be the smallest, the quietest and the most self-effacing? He scraped at the stubble on his chin, making a noise like sandpaper on plaster.

'You know what'll happen to you if you do anything like this in the navy, don't you? You'll be court-martialled and slung out.' Suddenly he felt emotionally moved that his son should have complicated their lives so irrevocably. 'Have you any idea what this means, David? Don't you realise that – that –' He was about to say that David would have to live with this for the rest of his life, but something Blakely had said echoed in his mind, and he stopped. He turned and grasped his son's hands. They faced each other under the arch of new leaves. 'Will you promise me – solemnly – that this will never happen again?'

David Braddle frowned and nodded, unable to look his father in the eye.

'Say it,' Braddle insisted. 'Give me your promise.'

The boy looked up into his father's face, and his self-control finally broke. 'I promise,' he whispered, and his eyes overflowed.

Braddle let go of his hands and turned away, suddenly moved by it all, wondering where he had gone wrong and how he might regain contact with this son of his who treated him like a distant relation. 'All right,' he said as they walked back along the track. 'Let's forget all about it. I won't even mention it to your mother. It's over. Dead and buried.'

They reached the car: the doors slammed, and a few moments later the Rover was accelerating away, its tyres hissing on the wet road.

Although the comparison may seem a little far fetched, naval officers are in some ways like bonzai trees: they do not grow naturally, but have to have their roots and branches expertly clipped if they are to attain the desired proportions. Left to himself, unclipped, untrained, unbrainwashed, the teenage boy will not grow into a naval officer; but there are some who grow into naval officers more readily than others, and Peter Quentin Lasbury was an excellent example.

His parents, Anita and Rex, had separated when he was at Eton. Anita had become a successful film actress and his father a South African tennis champion. Both were too bound up with their own lives and lovers to take much interest in the sole fruit of their union, and as there was plenty of money available, young Lasbury spent a lot of time in the charge of aunts, uncles and the friends of friends.

He was a stunningly good looking child from his earliest years, with thick, flaxen hair, and skin that went honey-brown on the ski slopes of St Moritz; and his school education ensured that his social poise and self-confidence matched his Adonis looks.

Nobody cared very much what Peter did with his life and as a result he eventually took the advice of his tutor and tried the navy.

Everything went right for him. He was the right size, the right shape and the right colour. His name was right, he knew how to dress, and the allowance his mother gave him meant that he could afford those little luxuries that mark out a gentleman from the herd.

He walked off with the King's telescope and the Robert Roxburgh Prize at the end of his naval training, and as a sub-lieutenant on courses proceeded to captivate the hearts of a large number of debutantes doing the season. He was seen at the Derby, Royal Ascot, Henley, Cowes, Twickenham (which he referred to as 'Twickers') and Cowdray Park. After a year in the fleet, admirals jostled to have him as their flag lieutenant, and he took his pick, becoming flag lieutenant to the commander of the Far East fleet and running his own – as well as his admiral's – social programme entirely to the satisfaction of the British colonials in Singapore and Hong Kong.

If he had made any mistake at all in his career so far, it was only a very minor one: as a midshipman in Malta he had accepted a wager to have the largest tattoo on offer by a local tattooist emblazoned upon his back. To the delight of his gunroom colleagues, he had settled for a tattoo of a prancing, snarling panther which was to extend from the nape of his neck, where its tongue curled upward, to that unmentionable part of his anatomy where its tail curled down.

The work took a week to complete. Every evening during the dog watches, Midshipman Lasbury lay like a fish on a slab while Mr Zammitt, a cringing, hand-wringing chain smoker, exercised his skill with the needle and the ink. The result was nothing short of a masterpiece: it was photographed, and until very recently was still on display in Mr Zammitt's parlour as an advertisement of his handiwork.

In the early mornings when the midshipmen went to PT, Peter Lasbury's panther would come alive, leaping and jerking as the beautiful body upon which it was drawn flexed, stretched and doubled on the spot. At cocktail parties in the tropics, dressed in the high collared tunic with brass buttons to the throat, Lasbury would sometimes intrigue a young lovely by mentioning his panther. Would she like to see it? She would? Bending down a little, he would pull out the back of his collar and invite the blushing girl to see if she could see the tip of its tongue; later in the evening, after a few of the special Pimms he was adept at mixing, the results could be quite astonishing.

Soon after his return from the Far East, he was appointed in command of the motor torpedo boat *Dark Swordsman*, based in Haslar Creek at HMS *Hornet* in the borough of Gosport. He was the youngest commanding officer in the Royal Navy, but this did not stop him turning his boat into his personal yacht, and his flair for dealing civilly with the most junior rating as well as the most senior officer made his year in command a resounding success. The seal was finally set on this success one afternoon when he was able to assist a member of the Royal Family whose boat was in difficulties off Cowes, and this secured for him a personal invitation to attend the Coronation in Westminster Abbey. It was there that his friendship with Sarah Braddle began.

Sarah's mother, Clara, had shared a flat with Anita Yarrow before the war and was Peter's Godmother. She had often mentioned the Lasburys to her children, and Peter had already become something of a living legend to them. Seeing Peter in his uniform across a crowded Abbey had convinced Sarah that here was her future husband, and within a few months of that first fleeting glance she was pushing him determinedly into courtship.

Lasbury was not all that anxious to get married because he wasn't too sure about the sex side of things; but as Sarah was the elder daughter of one of the most influential families in the Royal Navy, he decided that it would be foolish to end the relationship. Breaking the hearts of captains' daughters was not good for the career, and he had no intention of doing anything that might prejudice that.

He was waiting for Sarah on the down platform of Petersfield station on a Friday afternoon in early April. He had recently started the long course in communications at the shore establishment of HMS *Mercury*, which still regarded itself as the Mecca of the silk handkerchief brigade and had welcomed him to its top secret bosom. There he stood: his hand-lasted shoes gleaming, his cavalry twill trousers cut in the new fashion (nineteen inches at the bottom, no turn-ups), his hand placed casually in the side pocket of his dog's-tooth hacking jacket.

Sarah saw him as the Waterloo train jerked to a halt.

'Sarah!' he said. 'Super!'

'Peter!' she answered. 'Hello! Lovely!'

He led the way out of the station car park, put her suitcase in the back of his MG, waited while she knotted a silk headscarf under her chin and then, starting the engine with a throaty roar, whisked her out of Petersfield and into the budding countryside of that hotbed of naval families, the Meon Valley.

Julietta was in the loo when they arrived. She stood on the seat and looked out of the small window as the MG nosed in through the green gates of Meonford House and crunched its way up the gravel drive. She looked down upon the flaxen head of Peter and her heart tripped.

Clara had been seeing to the horses and came round the side of the house wearing gum boots with her twin set and pearls. 'Peter darling!' she said. 'Super to see you!' The dogs wagged and barked and grovelled, and as they went into the house, Julietta left her look-out post and went onto the landing to hear more.

'I'm putting you in with David,' Clara was saying in the hall. 'I hope you don't mind, but we are a bit of a houseful this weekend.'

Julietta slipped into her bedroom, took a quick look at herself in the mirror and timed her exit so that she met Sarah and Peter as they reached the top of the stairs.

She considered herself to be much more attractive than her elder sister. She had thick, dark eyebrows (Daddy's eyebrows) and glossy hair which she tied in a pony tail. She had been skiing in Austria the previous week and was generously tanned. Her yellow dungarees were straight out of *Vogue* Young Fashions and she knew how to look demurely up at a man without raising her head too much.

'Oh hello!' she said, and gave him a secret message by touching his palm with her forefinger when they shook hands.

'Hello, Juju,' Peter said. 'Lovely to see you.'

'You're in here,' said Sarah, ignoring her younger sister, and showed Peter into David's immaculately tidy room.

Julietta went back to her room and decided she wanted to cry. She was thirteen, and everything was beastly. Sarah was being snooty and Mummy was spoiling David rotten because he was going to Dartmouth next week. Daddy was grumpy because of the Cuts and she was starting the Curse. It had been exciting the first time because Mummy had made a fuss and Daddy had been nice and you felt important because you were really growing up. The second time hadn't been all that bad either because it was a confirmation and proved it. This time was different: she was headachy and the world looked like a jigsaw puzzle gone wrong: nothing quite fitted and people did the wrong things. Also there was this beastly mess to deal with and people made excuses for her like saying 'Julietta's got a little tummy ache' when it wasn't a tummy ache at all but a socking big something else ache, one that made her feel sick and horrible, and here was Sarah all glowy in her Jaeger get-up with this glorious man whose eyes saw right through your bra and whose voice made electricity down inside you when he came out of David's bedroom with Sarah, laughing in that lovely boomy way, his hand straying to his behind to pull out his trousers as he went downstairs.

Just you wait, thought Julietta. Just you wait. All of you. I'm better looking and I've got a nicer body than Sarah. Her bust's too big and mine's just right, and I don't need to stink of Chanel the way she does. One of these days I'll have someone better than Peter trailing round after *me*.

That was when the tears came properly because there was no one better than Peter Lasbury and never could be. She shut and locked her bedroom door and had a jolly good look at her breasts, holding onto them for comfort and letting the nipples pop out between her fingers.

'I'll jolly well start on him this evening,' she whispered. 'I'll jolly well take him off her, silly cow.'

Henry and David arrived back from Boarhunt at about five. They had been doing a bit of rough shooting with Suki the black labrador, and Henry came into the kitchen brandishing three pigeons, one of which was dripping blood from the head.

'David shot two,' he announced to his wife, who was busy supervising Mrs Hardesty while two naval stewards went in and out with bottles and glasses for the party that was to be held that evening.

'Jolly fine,' she said, 'But will you please hang them in the potting shed because they're dripping nastiness on my tiles.'

Henry handed the pigeons to his son, who took them a little reluctantly. He didn't mind shooting the things, but having to hold them by their clammy legs was a different matter.

'How is he?' Clara asked confidentially when David had left the kitchen. The previous week, Henry had told her that David had suffered a mild emotional breakdown as a result of the strain of the Dartmouth exams and interview. He hadn't liked deceiving her but had felt obliged to do so. Since his *tête-à-tête* with David the previous week he had tried to build up some sort of rapport with his son, but with little success: most of their afternoon had been spent in uneasy silence.

'Not too bad,' he said now, glancing at Mrs Hardesty who was making canapés at the other end of the kitchen.

'I had a word with Peter,' Clara said. 'I thought it might be an idea if he encouraged David a bit. You know, bolstered his morale.'

'Splendid,' Braddle said, and Julietta entered the kitchen.

She put her head on one side and stood on one leg. 'Mummy, what am I going to wear?'

Clara sighed. It seemed sometimes that the entire family relied upon her to take all their decisions for them. 'I should think your taffeta, wouldn't you?'

'Oh Mummy that's *awful*! New Look is right out!'

'In that case your dirndl. With your Austrian blouse.'

'Dreary old dirndl,' said Julietta. 'It makes me look like a barmaid. Wouldn't it be nice to have just a few decent clothes, don't you think?'

She was joined by David, back from the potting shed. Henry mumbled, 'Right, well, I think I'll make myself scarce,' and did so.

'You can wear your uniform this evening,' Clara told her son.

'Do I have to, Mummy?'

'Well I think you ought to, darling. Grandpa will be very disappointed if you don't.'

He made a face. 'I'll be the only one in uniform except the stewards.'

'Well jolly nice, too,' Clara said, 'and please leave those alone, Julietta,' she added, too late to prevent her daughter sampling a vol-au-vent.

The bathrooms filled with steam and the scent of Imperial Leather wafted about the landing. Julietta changed into her dirndl then into her taffeta and then back into her dirndl, getting very cross in the process. Peter and Sarah came back from walking the Jack Russells in the water meadows, and David was treated to a glimpse of Peter's panther.

'How's things then?' Peter asked, shaving himself carefully with a Rolls razor. 'Looking forward to the big day?'

'Oh yes,' David said. 'Tremendously!'

Their eyes met. David had unusually long eyelashes, which Peter found almost irresistibly attractive. 'Not wearing the uniform after all?' he commented as David put on a pair of grey trousers.

David shook his head. 'I know the feeling,' Peter said. 'One doesn't want to show off, does one?' He wiped the last traces of lather from his face and patted on after-shave. David had put on his suit and was ready to go. 'Don't wait for me, David, I'll be down in a jiff.'

Julietta waylaid her brother as he came out of his room. She was wrapped in a bath towel. 'I've had a super idea,' she told him in a low, urgent voice. 'Let's swap clothes again, shall we? You can wear my dirndl, and I'll put on your uniform. Okay?'

They had often swapped clothes when they were little, and although they were separated by nearly three years, Julietta was almost as tall as her brother, and there was a striking resemblance. They shared the thick Braddle nose and the protruding upper lip.

She took him by the arm. 'Come into my room. Quick! We'll use handkerchiefs to give you bosoms!'

But David was not enthusiastic. He pulled away from his sister and went along the landing under the oil portraits of Braddle ancestors. 'I'm not putting on a dress for anyone,' he muttered.

'Scaredy-cat!' she called after him, leaning over the banisters as he went downstairs. 'What's the matter, are you afraid of what Daddy would say?'

61

Henry and Clara divided their friends and acquaintances into categories: family, friends, dulls, oldies and children. It was usually necessary to invite people from each group to their parties, but they arranged matters so that the dulls arrived under the impression that the party was from six-thirty to eight, the friends pretended to leave, then hurried back through the back door when the dulls had gone, the oldies were matched with other oldies and the children (whose ages ranged from thirteen to the mid-twenties) had a dancing-to-records party in the cellar when the main party was over.

Nearly all the guests were naval or ex-naval, and David, handing round the pineapple and cheese squares, was repeatedly congratulated on winning his cadetship. Everyone wanted to know when he started term and which House he would be in and whether he knew Commander So-and-So's son who would be starting at the same time, which he did.

'Go and get your results, darling,' Clara told him. 'They're on Daddy's desk in the library.' Then she turned back to her circle and informed them confidentially: 'He didn't exactly sparkle in the written exams, but he really did awfully well at the interview.'

David was collecting the envelope with the Dartmouth entrance results in it when Julietta came to the door of the library. He turned, but before he could say anything, she had taken the key out of the door, shut it on him and locked him in.

She raced upstairs to his room, snatched the cadet's uniform from the hanger and rummaged in David's wardrobe for socks, shirt, tie and shoes. She couldn't manage the stiff collar so she used one of his tennis shirts instead. Trembling with excitement, she pulled on the trousers and buttoned up the reefer. She took his brand new hat from its nest of white tissue paper, gathered up her hair on top of her head, and jammed it on, pulling the shiny patent leather peak down over her eyes.

In the drawing room, like a hub for the entire celebration, Peter Lasbury was explaining the game of polo to the newly wedded wife of one of his contemporaries. 'Usually one has six chukkas, do you see,' he was saying. 'Each chukka lasts seven and a half minutes and there's a three-minute interval for changing horses. Hullo –' he added, seeing Julietta and thinking it was David. 'I see young David's put his glad rags on after all!'

'David!' roared Henry from the far end of the room. 'What the devil are you doing wearing your hat!'

'Darling!' Clara said to her husband. 'He's only put it on to show us!'

Julietta had cleverly not quite entered the room so that her face could not be clearly seen. But now she entered, and satisfied that all eyes were upon her, lifted the cap with a flourish so that her chestnut hair cascaded down over her shoulders.

Henry barged his way through the crowd, white lipped in fury. He seized his daughter by the neck and marched her from the room.

'One of Juju's merry japes,' Sarah said at Peter's elbow, and beckoned to a steward with a jug of gin and tonic to replenish his glass.

While the wave of fury broke about him, Henry Braddle was not entirely responsible for his actions. He ran Julietta up the stairs, past the oil portraits of bygone Braddles and into her room. His thick, blunt fingers picked at the brass buttons, releasing them from their stiff holes. 'Take it off! Come on! Off with it!' he said. She was only thirteen, and he didn't give a damn. 'I am going to put you over my knee,' he said 'and I am going to spank your bottom.' The image of it rose in his mind like an ancient tribal custom, a symbol of all that he believed was good about his own nursery days. He lifted the reefer jacket from her shoulders. 'And the trousers,' he insisted.

'Daddy – no! Please!' Julietta pleaded, but she obeyed all the same: she had always been her father's favourite, and now that he actually seemed about to carry out a much used threat, she was experiencing an unexpected thrill of anticipation. She stepped out of her brother's uniform trousers and cowered from him, David's shirt tails fortunately concealing her blue school knickers, which might have whipped up Henry's passions even further.

Now that the moment had come, Henry Braddle lost his nerve. He stared at his scantily dressed daughter and realised that he was getting himself into a situation he might later regret. Behind him, Clara came to the rescue. 'Leave this to me, Henry,' she said, and he backed away, clutching David's uniform as if it were a holy relic he had saved from desecration.

He went into the big bedroom whose windows overlooked the sloping lawns, the paddock and the river Meon. He didn't understand quite why the sight of Julietta in her brother's uniform had enraged him so much. Perhaps it was the combination of her brazen sensuality with all the tradition and discipline that David's uniform represented that had sparked off this wave of anger – he wasn't sure. What he was sure of, and what worried and shamed him, was that at the last moment, when Clara had intervened, he had wanted to put Julietta over his knee for a quite different reason: her wide, dark eyes seemed to have transmitted to him a desire, a willingness to be spanked which he had found titillating in the extreme. He felt that captains in the Royal Navy should not be titillated, and especially not by their thirteen-year-old daughters.

Clara came in. Clara was good for Henry. She was a calming influence. He wished he could tell her all about David and receive her approval for the decision he had taken. Domestic crises were very much more complicated than gunnery tactics, and he made a mental note to hold himself more aloof from his children in future.

'She's putting on a dress,' Clara said. 'I've had a little talk with her. She locked David in the library, the naughty girl. Come along, Henry. Let's just forget it happened, shall we?'

They went downstairs, and a little while later Julietta appeared in her dirndl. The dulls left on time, the oldies motored off in their pre-war motor cars, and the friends stayed on for soup and pâté.

Things ended towards two in the morning and the last people up were Peter and Sarah. Peter was suffering from an overdose of Braddles. He had been grilled by the old admiral, eyed by David, danced with by Clara, Julietta and Sarah and ribbed by Henry for joining the communications branch. The whole family seemed bent upon making him one of them, and he wasn't sure if he liked the prospect after all.

Sarah was beginning to have second thoughts about him as well. She had danced slowly with him in the cellar that evening, pressing her cheek against his to the husky voice of Eartha Kitt, clasping her hands at the back of his neck and wishing he would close his eyes and catch the romantic mood.

'Is anything wrong? Are you bored?' she had asked, and he had replied, 'How could I be bored in such excellent company?'

That was the trouble with Peter. He always said such nice things but seldom followed up his words with deeds. Up to now, she had presumed that he was too mature to indulge in teenage necking, but that evening she began to think that there must be some other reason for his tactful way of keeping her at her distance.

She had cornered him against the Aga in the kitchen. The guests had gone; David and Julietta were in bed, and she had him to herself. She put her arms inside his jacket and pressed her mouth upon his.

She was good at snogging: she had had lots of practice. She had even suffered from glandular fever the year she came out, and the ailment had caused her a secret pride when her mother had referred to it as the Kissing Disease.

She arched her neck back and moved her body against Peter's, going gently from side to side so that if he couldn't feel her breasts through his shirt and her coffee-cream dress there must be something seriously wrong with his nerve endings. But instead of responding as any male Sarah had ever known would have responded – instead of returning her kisses and making sure that she felt certain parts of his anatomy as unmistakably as he could feel hers, Peter leant backward as if trying to get away from her, causing Whisky, the cat, to jump down from his perch on top of the boiler.

Sarah drew away. 'Don't you like me kissing you, Peter?'

He frowned and blinked. 'One doesn't want to overdo it, does one?' he said.

She tried again, but with little success. Her open lips were met by closed ones. 'Have I got halitosis?' she asked. 'Or is it B.O.?'

He laughed gently, shaking his head and touching the tip of her nose with his finger. 'Of course not!'

'Well what is it?'

He kissed her in reply, but it was not a satisfactory answer. She stared at him for several seconds, and in the silence they could hear the hum of the refrigerator and the gentle lapping of Whisky as he helped himself from a saucer of milk. Suddenly Sarah wanted to test him, and she said what she had never said to a man before.

'Would you like to make love to me?'

She wasn't sure whether the look on his face was horror or surprise. 'We could,' she said. 'If you'd like to. Everyone's asleep. We could go down to the cellar.' She held his hands loosely in hers, looking up into his eyes, trying to fathom what was going on in his mind. 'And it would be quite safe too,' she whispered. She coloured a little, shocked at her own audacity. 'I've got something you could wear.'

She saw tiny beads of sweat break out on his upper lip. 'Sweetie,' he said. 'It wouldn't be fair. On you or your parents. Would it?'

She let go of his hands. 'Never mind,' she said. 'I'm sure you're right.' She smiled too brightly. 'I think I'll go to bed like a good little girl.'

Peter waited a few minutes before going upstairs after her. It wasn't the first time this sort of thing had happened, and there was a thread of self-doubt in his mind. Why was it that women had to thrust themselves upon one so?

He went quietly into David's bedroom and undressed by the washbasin light. He stood in his candy striped undershorts brushing his teeth vertically and horizontally, and while he did so saw in the mirror that David was awake and watching him from the camp bed.

Within a few minutes, this knowledge had aroused him more effectively than all Sarah's caresses and kisses. Pretending to be unaware of his audience, he stripped and arched his body back as if tired at the end of a long day, so that the tattooed panther seemed to gather itself for a pounce.

He manoeuvred himself into a position from which he could see David in the mirror again, and caught him with his eyes open. He turned back and looked down at the boy, admiring the long lashes on the closed lids – lids that were trembling deliciously.

Carefully, without making it at all obvious, he put on a little display for the boy, quite sure that he was being watched, and revelling in the knowledge of it.

He got into bed, switched off the light and lay back, listening to the beat of his heart. 'Goodnight David,' he said softly; and after a few seconds was gratified to hear the boy whisper back, 'Good night.'

Part Two
# A HERO OF OUR TIME

# 5

'Can I ask a favour?' Alan asked.

They were in Steven's room, and Steven was getting ready to go.

'What?'

'Will you try to keep some sort of record?'

Steven struggled with his tie. Every time he pulled it tight enough to conceal the collar stud it jumped out of the collar at the back, and if he left it loose the knot kept slipping down.

'What sort of record?'

'Impressions,' Alan said. 'So that I can really know what it's like. Just – put them in your letters. When you have time.'

'That'll just have to do,' Steven said, and took his uniform reefer off its hanger. The sleeves had a yellow lining and his name and the date were typed onto the Gieves label in the inside pocket. He did up the four brass buttons and squared his shoulders, fascinated by his own reflection.

'Will you?' Alan said. 'Will you try to write something down?'

Steven had wanted to join as a rating at first – to go in as a boy seaman, just as his father had done. It had been Alan who had convinced him that it would be better to take the exams and interview for Dartmouth, to try to enter as a cadet. It had been Alan, too, who had helped him stand up to the opposition of his headmaster, who had been convinced that Steven's interest and ability in the classics might one day win him a place at Oxford. He had told Steven that if joining the navy was what he really believed he should do he owed it to himself to insist upon doing it – whatever his headmaster, Father Longstaff or even his mother might say.

Once the decision had been taken, it had been Alan who had coached him for the ordeal of questioning and initiative tests he had to face at the interview. Alan had spent hours with him, firing questions at him, tying him up in knots about why he wanted to join the navy, why Britain needed a navy, whether it was right to build ships that were designed for war – even whether war could be justified. At times, Alan had made him wonder if he really did want to join; he had tested him so completely that when the moment

69

came and the admiral looked across the table and asked the question that was always asked – 'Why do you want to join the Royal Navy?' he had been able to answer with confidence. Because Britain depends on her navy for the defence of her shipping, and shipping is the arterial blood of her trade with the world; because the traditions of the service are a part of the nation; because being in the navy would give him opportunities he would not find in any other way of life – and finally because his father had been in the navy, and he, Steven, had always wanted to join the navy and had always been interested in boats and ships and the sea.

It was not an entirely truthful answer, but the confidence of that single reply had won him the cadetship. Many of the things he said and did during his day down at Dartmouth had bordered on unsatisfactory. He had fluffed his two-minute talk on Jazz; his performance in the gym, transferring the oil drum across an imaginary chasm, had ended in chaos and laughter; the psychiatrist had reservations about his temperamental suitability for a military career ('You'd have said the same about Nelson,' the admiral remarked) and the headmaster on the interview panel suspected that this young man with a shock of dark hair and a too confident grin had not read some of the books he claimed to have read. It had been his utter belief and confidence in the Royal Navy that had finally won the day for him: it had swayed the admiral, and the admiral swayed the board.

'Of course I'll write to you,' he said now, and looked round the small bedroom to make sure there was nothing he had forgotten.

Alan's face worked as he struggled for words. 'Not ordinary letters.'

'What sort of letters then?'

'Are you nearly ready?' Mrs Jannaway called from downstairs.

'On my way!' he called back.

He zipped up his grip, a brand new navy grip with his initials, S.J.J., on the side. He took his Burberry raincoat from the bed and put it on his arm.

'What sort of letters?' he repeated.

Alan struggled for words again. 'Tell me everything,' he said. 'So that I can live it.' He jabbed a finger against his temple. 'In here.'

'I may not have time, Alan.'

'Make time. It'll be good for you. Keep the old brain from ossifying.'

Steven grinned. He was the bigger of the two now, having broadened out and grown four inches in the past eighteen months. 'Well – no promises,' he said. 'But I'll try.'

Dora stood at the foot of the stairs, ready with his cap. She was wearing the suit she had worn for Roland's funeral.

'Well, put it on then, Steven,' she said.

'Mum,' Alan said. 'Your nose is red.'

She fumbled in her bag and dabbed on more powder from her compact.

'All the very, very best,' Alan said, gripping his brother's hand. 'And don't forget, I want regular reports.' He wasn't coming to the station with them. Steven didn't want to be seen with a spastic brother on his first day, he knew that without having to be told.

He stood at the front door and watched them go. 'You can pretend I'm an admiral!' he called as they were going out through the latchgate.

He watched them walk away along the avenue, Steven a full head taller than his mother, whose court shoes clacked quickly along to keep pace with his stride.

He came inside and shut the door. He went into the dining room and looked at the cluttered mantelshelf, the closed piano; he went upstairs to his bedroom and looked out over the allotments. The chestnut trees were putting out their first leaves; children were playing on a rope that dangled over the stream.

He stood there for a long time, until a tube train headed out from Mill Hill East, across the viaduct, made the house rumble as it went.

He needed to keep busy, take his mind off it all. Getting Steven into Dartmouth had filled his life for more than a year: suddenly the goal had been achieved, and the achievement of it had forced him, once again, to face up to the real meaning of being disabled.

He went downstairs to put on his brown overall coat. He took a bucket of feed and went down to the hen run, trying not to think of anything but the clucking Rhode Island Reds that ran for the food he threw down in the mud.

But it was no good. He upturned the bucket and leant against the wire netting.

'Pretend I'm an admiral,' he whispered, and sobbed aloud.

The college looked like a piece of Whitehall that had been put down

71

in a fold of the Devon hills above the River Dart. He saw it from the train on the last run in to Kingswear. There were battleship grey boats moored in neat lines, and a tethered ferry was crawling across the water. Further up the river, the trees came right down to the water's edge, and one of the hills was topped by a smooth, rounded expanse of brilliant green.

This is it, he thought as he walked down the platform with the other first term cadets. This is it. It's happening.

He boarded the ferry and stood on the deck. The lines were cast off and the ferry headed across to Dartmouth. Gusts of wind sent catspaws over the water; a fleck of spray was cold on his cheek. He glanced up at the college again. It dominated the whole scene. You couldn't help looking up at it.

The ferry turned and began its approach. The engines went astern as it went alongside the railway pontoon, and the tyre fenders squeaked as they were compressed. The cadets made ready to disembark.

The whirlwind was sudden and shortlived. It went along the waterfront lifting a piece of paper high in the air. It whistled in the stays round the funnel and lifted Steven Jannaway's cap, sending it away like a discus until it landed in the water astern of the ferry.

He appealed to one of the ferry crew for assistance. The man laughed, but not in an unkind way. 'Nothing I can do, my lover,' he said in his Devon drawl. 'You should've put 'er on proper.'

The other cadets had already disembarked. He hung back, watching his cap being taken away on the ebb. A voice barked at him. 'You! Cadet!'

It was a chief petty officer in a serge uniform. Jannaway ran up the ramp and onto the quay. A naval lorry was waiting: he handed up his grip, took hold of the rope that dangled from the roof of the lorry, and heaved himself up.

He sat down on the bench inside with the other cadets and watched the road go away from him as they moved off along the waterfront and on, up the steep hill. Looking out of the back of the lorry as it went up that hill, and seeing the town of Dartmouth and the river recede behind him made him feel as if he were looking back on his past life – a life that was gone and could never be recaptured.

The lorry stopped. They were at the back of the college, and this view of it was not so imposing. They jumped out of the lorry and handed each others' grips down. Four senior cadets in serge trousers and seamen's jerseys approached. The roll was called and they were divided into Houses.

Jannaway found himself in a group of nine. 'This way,' one of the senior cadets said, and they followed him into the college. Actually going in, wearing the uniform, walking along the main corridor with the faces of those who had gone before staring at you from their term photographs – he didn't know what it was like. He felt that he was stepping onto some vast, slowly turning wheel.

They went up two flights of teak stairs which smelt heavily of polish. The walls were tiled, and there were no banisters. They were led into a long dormitory. The senior cadet stopped.

'My name is Faber, and I am the fifth term cadet captain. You are in Grenville House, which is the best House. Don't forget it.' He licked his lips between sentences and looked at them as if daring each to challenge his words. 'Answer your names. Ainslie, Braddle, Carter, Courtenay, Jannaway, Livingstone, Munro, Whetting-steel, Whitelaw.'

'Yes, yes, yes, yes, yes, yes, yes, yes, yes.'

'This is your chestflat and these are your chests,' said Faber. 'Braddle?'

'Yes sir?' A small cadet with a pink face and lips like rosebuds came forward. One or two of the others grinned to each other.

'I'll use your chest as a demo,' Faber said.

There was a chest at the end of each bed. It had a top half and a bottom half. It was painted black with a white front, and your name was printed on a card in a polished brass card holder on the front. The bottom half of the chest had opening doors and two shelves. The top half had a flap that hinged down, with more shelves and a drawer with a brass handle and a lock.

'This is your private till,' Faber said and opened the empty drawer. 'It is to be kept locked at all times.' He licked his lips and glowered at them.

Each cadet's kit was piled on his bed. Every item had already been marked in black ink, the work of the House Chief, a naval pensioner.

Faber took a shirt from Braddle's pile of kit and held it up. 'This is how you fold a shirt,' he said. 'Watch.'

Jannaway watched. Faber had fingernails that were bitten to the quick. There was a shred of dried blood on his chin. Everything he said seemed to be in defiance of anyone who might presume to contradict him. 'Underpants here,' he said. 'Socks here. Folded. Like that. Collars here, with the tie in the middle. Like that.'

Each bed was at right angles to the wall. It had a white and blue counterpane on it into which was worked the admiralty fouled anchor. There were twenty beds in all, ten on either side, and the chests at the foot of the beds made a corridor down the centre. The parquet floor was bare, and apart from a thermometer by the door and a notice about Action in the Event of Fire, there was no other furniture whatsoever. A southwesterly wind blew in from the sea through the windows, each of which was exactly one third open.

Jannaway looked out of these windows. Below, he could see the parade ground at the front of the college, and the mast. Beyond that was the town of Dartmouth, the harbour entrance and a short stretch of horizon between two headlands.

'Are you paying any attention at all?'

He was jerked back by Faber's words.

Faber licked his lips. 'Well?'

'I'm sorry,' he said.

'You'll be a lot bloody sorrier if you don't know how to lay out your kit in a couple of weeks' time,' Faber said, and continued with his demonstration. He showed them how to stow their kit, fold their kit and lay their kit out for rounds; he even showed them which way up the counterpane had to go on their beds and how shoe laces were to be tucked into the shoes when they were laid out for inspection.

'Okay,' he said. 'Clean into working rig before you start, otherwise you'll get shit all over your number ones.'

They were left on their own.

'Start?' said Jannaway. 'Start what?'

When the senior terms arrived the college came alive. Until then there had been just the thirty-eight first termers doubling along empty corridors, learning to march and salute, finding out where their classrooms were, meeting their tutors and being given pep talks by the captain of the college, the term officer, the headmaster and the chaplain. It wasn't until the senior terms arrived that you began to realise you were in the navy.

They came into the chestflat on the Sunday evening calling each other Roddy and Buster and asking each other if they had had a good leave. One brought a wind-up gramophone back with him.

He set it up on top of his chest and Doris Day sang 'I Just Blew in from the Windy City.' Others of the second term, who shared the chestflat with the first termers, decided to play a practical joke. They removed the chest and bed of a cadet called Tomkins who had not yet arrived, and when he did feigned surprise. 'Chas! We thought – oh my God! We thought you'd been sacked! None of your stuff's here! Didn't you get a letter or anything?'

He believed them for a moment. He stood in the chestflat and his face went white. Then he saw one of his term mates trying to control his laughter and he said 'I say you chaps stop playing silly buggers, where's my gear?' and they relented and led him into the bathrooms where his entire kit was in one of the long, deep baths and his bed and mattress were vertical in the heads.

Later that evening there was a belly muster. Everyone had to stand by their chest and show their belly to the surgeon commander who went past in a bum freezer. When he had gone, Tomkins did a belly dance. Tomkins was the fool of the second term. He stood on his chest and writhed his navel round and round and in and out. Everyone cheered and there was a festive mood.

Just before Pipe Down the House Officer came into the chestflat. He was known as Basher Rudkin. He was a small man with shirt cuffs that stood two inches out from the sleeves of his mess jacket and he spoke an exaggerated version of navalese, which is an accent loosely related to Oxford, Knightsbridge and Buckingham Palace.

'You're Braddle, aren't you,' he said through his nose.

'Yes sir,' Braddle replied, trying to make his voice sound as if it had broken.

Basher Rudkin chuckled. 'I suppose you're going to be a gunnery officer, are you?'

'I hope so, sir.'

Rudkin nodded to himself as if all was right with the world, and strolled on down the chestflat to talk about the cricket fixtures with some of the second termers. He stood with his hands behind his back like the Duke of Edinburgh, and from time to time braced his shoulders.

Jannaway's bed was next to Whettingsteel's. 'Why do they always pick on Braddle?' he asked.

Whettingsteel was tall and wiry. He had a wry sense of humour that Jannaway liked. 'Haven't you heard of the Braddles?' he whispered. 'They've been admirals since the year dot.'

Jannaway looked across at David Braddle, who was sitting on his bed in a pair of green standard issue cotton pyjamas. It was difficult to imagine that a boy like that might one day become an admiral.

They were given a fortnight to find their way about the college, learn the Guff Rules and how to lay out their kit for rounds. During that time they could not be punished by the cadet captains but they were shouted at. They were told to brace up, smarten up and double up, and as the end of the fortnight drew near hints were dropped that they had better look out after next Sunday. Every evening they spent an hour in the gunroom after prep bulling their number one shoes, melting polish in a spoon over a candle flame, pouring it on their toe caps and gently polishing it with a duster and plenty of spit. Before Sunday divisions they learnt that it was necessary to spend at least half an hour working on each other with clothes brushes to remove every last fleck of dust from their number one uniforms. In the early mornings they queued up to take their compulsory cold baths under the eye of Faber, before washing and shaving at rows of metal basins.

A notice was chalked up on a blackboard in the gunroom at the end of the fortnight. It announced that Highland Games would take place at 1400 on Sunday and that all first termers were to attend.

The senior terms gathered for the event and there was a great deal of shouting and chanting. The wooden tables and benches were placed in a square and the first termers ordered into the centre. Harper, a fourth termer with a nose like a suitcase handle, took charge. He picked on Braddle first, not because Braddle was the grandson of an admiral but because he was the smallest.

'What's your name?' he demanded, and when Braddle replied the senior terms shrieked their delight in high falsettos, imitating David's unbroken voice.

Harper waited for the cheering and stamping to die down. The senior terms had put the benches on top of the tables and sat looking down into the square. 'Everything off,' Harper ordered, pointing at Braddle. 'Stark bollocky.'

Braddle looked back wide-eyed. The onlookers chanted. At the back of the building, Basher Rudkin slipped out for a long walk.

The first termers were made aware that it was their duty to strip Braddle naked, and Braddle was informed that he had to prevent them. But as they moved towards him, Jannaway separated himself

76

and stood in the corner of the square. 'No, I'm not stripping anyone,' he said.

'That's what you think!' someone shouted. Three third termers got him by the arms and held him. He struggled violently and others joined in. They pulled off his shoes and trousers and ripped his shirt. But suddenly, miraculously, Jannaway was free. He wore only his socks, torn shirt and voluminous admiralty elephant bloomers. He leapt onto the gunroom windowsill and lashed out with fists at anyone who approached him. His lip was bleeding, and spots of blood flew about and turned his teeth red.

He wasn't free for long. A dozen cadets rushed him and he was overpowered and forced to watch the proceedings, his face drenched in sweat, his black hair standing up on end and his mouth full of blood.

Braddle made little attempt at resistance at first, but this gave rise to jeering and whistling and shouts of 'Fight, you little turd!' After that he made a show of it, struggling while his term mates removed the plain blue blazer, grey trousers and white shirt that were worn on Sundays after lunch. He stood in his underpants and laughed, thinking it best to show he could take a joke, but the senior terms chanted, 'Everything off!' and a moment later he was naked, and they were singing the 'Rodean Song'; and 'Daisy, Daisy, Give Me Your Answer Do'. They made him scramble round under the tables and encouraged him from above with gym shoes.

It was Whitelaw's turn after Braddle, and then Carter and after him Whettingsteel. The idea was to choose the victims in order of ascending size so that the fights became progressively more vicious and equally matched. The early fights were more of a token demonstration of resistance on the part of the victims, but the repeated struggles, the cheering and singing and stamping of feet must have stirred up some sort of blood lust, for the later fights became much fiercer, with cadets struggling as if their lives depended on it, rolling about on the parquet, crashing into the tables, sweating, cursing and bruising. The last contest, between Courtenay and Livingstone, was won by Livingstone, a heavily built Geordie with short cropped fair hair and a physique like a bull. He got Courtenay face down on the floor in a half nelson, and wrenched off his trousers with his spare hand. The senior terms threw the clothes about and sang the 'Rodean Song' again. Tomkins leapt up on the windowsill and led a chorus of the navy version of 'Rule Britannia':

Rule Britannia, marmalade and jam
Five Chinese crackers up your arsehole
Bang-bang-bang-bang-bang!

After that, when Jannaway had been spreadeagled and blacked from his waist to his thighs, the newly initiated first termers were left to themselves. Braddle took a splinter out of Whitelaw's left buttock, Jannaway discovered that one of his front teeth was loose, and the wife and teenage daughters of one of the masters were hurried along the corridor, their eyes averted from the bruised, blacked and naked cadets inside the Grenville Junior Gunroom. The following day, the master concerned made a complaint to the Captain of the College, but no action was taken because everyone knew that initiation ceremonies took place in the college on the second Sunday of term, and the officers and staff had been advised to keep clear of the gunrooms while they were going on.

Britannia Royal Naval College
Dartmouth

3rd June 1954
Dear Admiral!
　　You wanted to know what it's like, so here goes. Well – I don't even know where to start. In the morning I suppose when they shout 'Turn out!' and thump on the chests and we all troop off to the cold baths. I've discovered that the only way to have a cold bath is to make as big a splash as possible. That way it takes the mind off the temperature.
　　After the bath (you only have to go under and out) you wash. Nasty little metal basins and not enough room, so you get your next door neighbour's tooth-cleaning spit on your shaving brush. Then there's a sort of count-down to clear chestflat. Don't ask me to explain everything, Admiral. You can blooming well work it all out for yourself (Sir!). So we all throw on our working rig and rush downstairs and along the main corridor (millions of photographs with millions of cadets looking at you from nineteen-oh-what-not) and along to the dining hall (porridge, bacon and beans, soggy toast, ancient pensioners dishing out tea, and a fussy lady who marches up and down telling us to drink up our milk).
　　Then divisions. Lots of bugle calls that echo about inside the college. I don't know what any of them mean. All I do know is that you have to rush across the parade ground and fall in and if you miss an order all hell breaks loose and you end up with cuts. (Did you know that no

one ever says 'Atten-shun'? It's always 'Ho' or 'Ha' or even 'Hun', but never 'Shun'.) (Also, all this perfect rifle drill you see the navy doing is a con trick. Someone clicks his tongue in the back rank to give the time!)

After divisions we go off to studies. You have to double everywhere, salute all the masters and officers and STAND TO ATTENTION AND SALUTE if the Captain goes by. All the corridors are polished with a special slippery polish so that it's a bit like running around on a skating rink with your arms full of books. My working rig trousers are becoming smooth and shiny already.

The masters are an extraordinary bunch. Most of them are about ninety and have yards of campaign medals from both wars, which they wear on Sunday divisions. The French master shouts, the Maths master farts and the Mechanics master has an uncontrollable temper which makes him quiver all over and go yellowy-white round the gills. They are all known by their initials, so we have Harry B and Oily P, Toothy D and Piggy C. We do quite a mixture of subjects: French, Maths, Parade Training, History, Gym, English, Seamanship, Mechanics, Signalling, Engineering, etc, etc. I was given three out of twenty for an English essay last week. It was about 'smartness'. I think I must have said the wrong thing!

You would like to see (and hear) the dinner call. Four cadets stand in line at the head of the quarterdeck (that's the sort of main hall, Admiral, in case you were wondering) and pipe it on bo'sun's calls. It goes on and on, lots of long trills and pips and highs and lows. Everyone thunders down the main passage and into the mess hall, and the Chief Cadet Captain comes in and says Grace. 'THANK GOD!' 'AMEN!' Like that. We all sit crammed together on benches and a bronze statue of Nelson looks down on us. The other day one cadet (Tomkins – a complete idiot) was forced to have his lunch sitting under the table as a sort of joke. It was all to do with his not knowing the difference between naval and navel.

We have something called Turn On after lunch. You have to lie on your bunk for fifteen minutes. After that you change into sports rig and rush off to play cricket or tennis or go down to the river. I usually go on the river. I've passed my Motor Cutter test and am now learning how to handle a picket boat. You collect the boat board and keys from the Chief at Sandquay and go out to the trot in the duty motor cutter. You start up the Gardiner diesels and spend the afternoon practising alongsides, picking up buoys (or make-believe men overboard) and doing boathook drill.

Tea's at four-thirty and after that we go to evening studies, which I detest. After that there's Evening Quarters, for which we wear Number

Twos. Most people buy second-hand reefers. Mine has five names in the sleeve and I bought it for four shillings (a week's pay!). There's one cadet here, David Braddle, who is the son of a captain, who is very small and has a reefer with thirteen names in the sleeve. The brass buttons are very wide apart and he looks like the Winslow Boy in it. We wear white lanyards with our reefers in the evening – across the lapels – and you can tell which term a cadet's in by the way he wears his lanyard. We first termers wear it straight across, second termers loosen it so that the turk's head is at the cross of the lapels, and so on down with the sixth termers having it dangling down to their brass buttons. Faber inspects us at Evening Quarters (which are held on the quarterdeck) and then we have supper, followed by prep in the gunroom. If you do a bad prep, the masters can give you a drill, which is doubling up and down with a rifle.

Where are we? Supper, prep, rounds.

Rounds are terrible. You have to lay out your kit in exactly the right way on your chest, and if anything's wrong you can get cuts. Also, just to make sure we don't have too much time, the chestflat has to be cleaned *by hand*, and that means by hand – no stupid things like dustpans or brushes. The chests have to be lined up into a perfectly straight line and the windows opened exactly the right amount. There's a last minute panic to get your chest sorted out, and then you hear the pipe and the rounds party comes through, led by the Duty College Cadet with a lantern. This is by far the worst moment of the day because you never know what they'll find wrong. Sometimes they'll go straight through, but if the Chief Man is in a bad mood he can take every chest apart just for the hell of it, and you end up with your kit jumbled up in a heap.

There's 'Time for Prayers' after rounds, and you *have* to kneel by your bed. After that the House Officer sometimes wanders through. He is an extreeeemely smoooooth officer and he always calls me Whettingsteel, which is a little worrying.

After he's gone through, Faber (our best-beloved cadet captain) dishes out cuts. I've had two lots of three so far. It's all a bit Tom Brown's schooldays (which I suppose the whole college is in some ways). Faber comes to the door of the chestflat and calls you out to the showers where you have to hold on to a bench while he 'administers the punishment'.

After that – Pipe Down. It's the best sound of the day. Two high pips, a high trill, a low trill and a sudden up turn at the end. You can hear it being piped all over the college, and the clock strikes four bells – ten o'clock.

Seven pages! I'm exhausted! But I haven't even begun to tell you what it's *really* like...

When he went home after the first term, his mother looked older and Alan smaller. Mrs Jannaway met him on Paddington station. She kissed him and squeezed his hand. 'Well are you enjoying it Steven?' she asked as they sat side by side in the tube train on the way home. He assured her that he was, unwilling to explain that naval training was not to be enjoyed but endured; that he was being hardened like steel, and that the process was necessarily painful.

He went up to his bedroom and found everything exactly as he had left it. He looked out along Chestnut Road, wondering if it might be possible to slip back into the person he had been before those boxes of uniform had been delivered at the door.

'Now then,' his mother said behind him. 'Have you got any washing for me to do?'

'No, I've sent all my dhobeying to the laundry.'

She looked him up and down, reacting to his new-found jargon. 'You have, have you? Well if you're going to get changed, don't be long because Alan will be back soon and he likes his tea as soon as he gets in.'

His new naval persona hung about him: he spoke with greater confidence and used his Dartmouth mannerisms and expressions half intentionally, in some ways proud of them and in some ashamed. He ate more and took more for granted. His voice had broken and his laugh had changed into a naval officer's laugh. He made gaffes like telling Alan to 'shake it up' when they were getting ready for Mass, or saying 'thank you Chief' to his mother when she took his pyjamas to wash them.

'I'm not your chief, Steven,' she said. 'I'm your mother.'

In the end it was easier to bow to the inevitable and play the part of the young naval officer on leave. He obliged his mother by wearing his uniform to Mass (however much she hated his being in the navy, she was still proud of his uniform) and walked along the aisle with his cap under his arm. He said good morning instead of hullo to the people he knew and linked his hands behind his back, looking you in the eye when he spoke to you, keeping his chin in and his shoulders braced. He avoided speaking to Hetty Ringrose and suffered agony when invited to feed the hens.

During the term, he had only managed to write one letter to Alan, finding it difficult to give his brother that vicarious experience of naval life he had requested; both tacitly acknowledged this, but the subject was not mentioned. Sometimes Steven saw in his brother's eyes a hint of regret mingled with the pride and love he had for his younger brother. They were still close, yes, but each knew that within the space of three months, the navy had driven between them an invisible wedge which made it no longer possible to be entirely at ease in each other's company.

He had not expected life at Dartmouth would be easy, but nevertheless the demands that were made on him came as a shock. It was necessary to experience the training to believe that naval officers really did speak with such grossly exaggerated accents, and that the business of looking smart, standing up straight, making your shoes shine and laying out your kit for rounds every evening could be taken quite so seriously.

There was an added difficulty, for while Steven Jannaway was a naval officer at home, he was much more aware of himself as Steven Jannaway at Dartmouth. However hard he tried to be like everyone else and accept the intensely competitive atmosphere and be moulded by it, he could never quite shake off a feeling that the whole business was a magnificent fancy dress charade. As a result, he felt like an interloper, an outsider who looked upon the cavortings of his contemporaries with an inward smile of contempt – unaware that many of them regarded him in exactly the same way.

Not for Jannaway the hard, gem-like flame that burns within the soul of every would-be admiral; not for him the passionate longing for golden rings upon his arm that was so accurately expressed by David Braddle's latest catch-phrase: 'My God! I can't wait to be a commander!'

This negative attitude of Jannaway's was all wrong. To be a success in the navy you had to be dedicated, professional and ultimately obedient. Jannaway had difficulty with each of these qualities, particularly the last.

He collected the nickname 'Shag' quite early on. Everything about him was 'shag'. His cap badge was seldom in line with the seam of his cap; his lanyard was never quite as white as it should be; his shoe laces had a habit of breaking, and wherever you went in the college, items of his kit floated about: a boot brush here, a pyjama top there, a towel somewhere else. If ever you found a piece of lost property in the college, it was almost certain to be marked S.J. JANNAWAY.

His performance as a cadet was remarkable for the knack he had of landing in disaster. It was Jannaway who dismasted a Dartmouth One Design dinghy during the Woodcock Trophy race, by sailing close hauled under the trees that lined the River Dart. It was Jannaway who tried to anchor one of the college yachts with an anchor that was not attached to its chain. When his tutor took him out sailing in his brand new National sailing dinghy, the Jannaway curse struck again: while putting the sail battens in, he trod with muddy gym shoes on the pristine white sail, so that when it was hoisted in full view of the Royal Dartmouth Sailing Club, the Jannaway footprints went on display for all to see.

If his performance on the river was disappointing, his academic showing was even more so. He had passed into the college on all the subjects that naval officers never use, could translate chunks of the Aeneid or quote Aristophanes in the original Greek; but invite him to prove the Cosine rule or apply Newton's laws of motion, and he was inclined to go to pieces. He came bottom or nearly bottom of his term with dismal regularity, and it began to dawn upon Their Lords Commissioners of the Admiralty that it might be kinder to both Jannaway and the Queen to admit that a mistake had been made, and invite him to leave.

He was given a series of pep talks by Basher Rudkin. He was told that he was lacking in officer-like qualities and that he must sharpen up. Pacing back and forth, Rudkin would stop from time to time, shoot a piercing glance in Jannaway's direction and say, 'I'm sure you can do it, Jannaway. I'm sure we can pull you through,' and Jannaway would nod and wonder where to put his hands and whether his tie had slipped.

It would be easy to depict him as a figure of fun, and it would be equally easy to make him out to be a loner, and destined for failure. In some ways he was both and in some he was neither: not quite tall, not quite dark and not quite handsome, he teetered continually on the brink of taking himself and life seriously, but veered away from doing so because of his need to keep the realities of life – Alan, his father, his school and his Catholicism – in the background.

It was his boast that the navy would never change him, that he would always retain his individuality, never cease to be the real Jannaway, the quintessential Shag. Within a few terms he knew that this boast was an empty one.

He changed and continued to change – he couldn't help it. The training was a most subtle piece of brainwashing: it taught young men that exercise was only good for them if it hurt, that a battle against superior odds was to be sought out and hoped for and that the importance of morale to material is as three to one. It inculcated an outward show of disrespect for certain rules and a slavish, inward adherence to others; it laughed at adultery as something that every red-blooded officer since Nelson had indulged in, and it grinned slyly at homosexuality, while maintaining an official horror at the very thought of it. It embedded that streak of ruthlessness that is an essential ingredient in the characters of military people – embedded it and then glossed it over with layer upon layer of panache, élitism and all the mannerisms and social graces which mark out a naval officer and make him a member of a most exclusive club.

By the end of his sixth term, the process was well advanced. Hours spent on the river had given him an easy confidence at the helm of a twenty-seven foot whaler or the wheel of a picket boat. He could take charge of a squad on a parade ground, could bark out orders, salute with a sword. Weekly classes on the polished parquet quarterdeck, clasped in the arms of Tim Whettingsteel, had given him the rudiments of ballroom dancing, and the end of term dances in the gym, with blind dates delivered chiffon-wrapped from the hills round Totnes had introduced him to the art of seduction.

Many of the lessons he had learnt were from his contemporaries, for derision was poured upon those who did not conform. If you had mannerisms or personal habits that were unacceptable you were ragged, debagged or ostracised until you put them right. Thus, in spite of Jannaway's boast, the training system largely succeeded in turning him from a Catholic schoolboy into a slightly rough and ready naval officer.

Two weeks after the beginning of his sixth term, in the third week of January 1956, Jannaway was summoned to the cabin of his Divisional Officer.

Since he had joined the college, radical changes had taken place in the methods of training and the buildings themselves. The sixteen-year-old entry had been acknowledged a failure, and cadets were now joining at the age of eighteen; the chestflats had been converted into cabins, the masters were known as lecturers and the Houses had been renamed Divisions. The naval college was being changed from a public school to a university.

Tommy Darnley, the new Divisional Officer, had joined at the beginning of the term, and was bent upon making his mark. He was a man with a ruddy face and a voice that could carry through a force ten storm.

'Jannaway,' he said. 'Come and have a word.'

Jannaway followed his divisional officer to the cabin at the end of the corridor and accepted a seat.

'Right,' said Darnley. 'What are we going to do about you?'

Jannaway recognised this preamble as the beginning of a pep talk.

'I don't know, sir,' he said.

'In that case I shall have to tell you. So pin your ears back.'

Jannaway sat awkwardly in the chair, his face reddened from the cross-country run he had been on that afternoon and the shower he had taken before changing for tea.

Darnley had opened his confidential file. He held it up for Jannaway to see. 'I've been reading your comic cuts, young man,' he said.

'Sir.'

'Your last term as a cadet.'

'Yes, sir.'

'Your make-or-break term, yes?'

'Yes, sir.'

'It's not just a question of passing exams, Jannaway, you realise that?'

'Yes, sir.'

'Not just a question of keeping your nose clean, either.' Darnley looked sideways at Jannaway, and Jannaway looked sideways back. 'It's your motivation that's weak, that's the trouble. Anyone told you that before?'

Jannaway shook his head.

'Well I'm telling you now, Jannaway.' He tapped the file. 'Lack of assertion. Lack of drive. Carelessness. Lack of self-discipline. They're all in here, and they all add up to the same thing. Lack of motivation.'

Darnley closed up the file. He leant forward over his desk and put his chin on his fists, staring deeply into Jannaway's eyes. 'We're going to have to do better, Jannaway. We're going to have to pull our finger out. Extractum digitum, as you might say.'

Jannaway had often been irritated by the references people made to his curtailed classical education, and it irked him that a language he had once loved should be casually murdered by his divisional officer. He tried to pay attention to Darnley's exhortations, but he had heard them all before, and his mind was inclined to wander. He glanced about the cabin. Lieutenant Commander Darnley's fishing rod and waders stood in a corner and there was a photograph of six motor torpedo boats in close formation on the wall.

'Don't misunderstand me, Jannaway, if you're to come back as a midshipman the term after next, you're going to have to convince us that it's worth the Queen's while to spend a very large sum of money on your further training.'

He looked at the Harrods portrait photograph of Lieutenant Commander Darnley's wife. It had been taken just after her Coming Out and she was as demure as every naval officer's wife should be: coiffed, pearled and powdered, she gazed out at the world from the security of her silver frame. Every naval officer had a wife like that. Jannaway didn't know where they came from: he imagined they were stored like orchids in cellophane, crated and warehoused somewhere behind Buckingham Palace, to be handed out with the Queen's Commission. He imagined them being removed from their individual crates by some liveried footman, dusted and set in line along the walls of the throne room so that as each newly promoted sub-lieutenant stepped forward –

'Starting today,' Darnley said, and Jannaway came out of his reverie with a jerk.

'Yes, sir. Starting today.'

He went back to his cabin, which he shared with three others. Tim Whettingsteel, who was a Supply and Secretariat cadet, was teaching himself to type. He was playing the march from 'Aida' on his record player, typing one letter at each beat. Jannaway stood behind him and watched for a moment before stretching out on his bunk.

Whettingsteel stopped typing and switched off the record player. 'What did our glorious leader have to say?' he asked.

'The usual. Nothing like a little Jannaway-baiting before tea.' He mimicked Darnley. 'We're going to have to pull our finger out!'

Whettingsteel leant back in the tubular chair at his desk and took off his admiralty issue spectacles. 'You know what your trouble is, don't you Shag? You haven't learnt the rules of the game.'

'Which particular game are we talking about?'

'The oily Q game,' Whettingsteel said, using the Dartmouth expression for officer qualities.

'Don't you start.'

'But I'm right, aren't I? Look at Barry Courtenay. He isn't particularly bright, but he always manages to give the impression he's on the ball.'

Jannaway gazed at the ceiling. 'On the ball. I hate that expression.'

'You should love it. You should make it your own.'

'Should I? Is that what you do?'

'Not exactly.'

'No, you don't. But you don't have to, do you? You have a brain, which is always an advantage.' Jannaway slowly raised his legs to the vertical and pedalled his feet in the air. 'I think they're going to sling me out,' he said.

'I wouldn't have thought that was entirely necessary,' Whettingsteel said.

'Oh thanks!'

'What you should do is join the Need to be Seen club, Shag. Push yourself forward a little. Curry favour.'

Jannaway sat up. 'Deliberately?'

Whettingsteel shrugged. 'Why not? Practically everyone else does it.'

'And how would you suggest I go about it?'

'Well . . . find out what Darnley does and do likewise.'

'Not quite as easy as it sounds, Tim.'

Whettingsteel went to the window and looked out over the parade ground and harbour. 'Yes it is. Just ask yourself – what does he do in his spare time? Play golf? Support the rugger team?'

'I have a nasty suspicion he follows the beagles.'

'Go beagling then.'

'My God! The pursuit of the uneatable!'

'It's in a good cause. Free scrumpy at the meets, too, they tell me.'

'There must be something else he does.'

'Go and look at the noticeboards. See what his name's down for this term.'

Jannaway leapt off his bunk. 'All right, dammit. I will. I'll start sucking up. Get a few Brownie points.'

He left the cabin, and returned five minutes later. 'Oh God!' he said, beating his head against the wall. 'What have I done? What have I done?'

Whettingsteel looked up from his desk. 'What have you done?'

Jannaway began to laugh. 'Guess what,' he said. 'I'm a beagler,

I'm a Scottish Country Dancer, and I'm singing in the Messiah!'

Four weeks later, in the middle of February, Steven Jannaway sprinted down the main corridor and skidded to an unsteady halt at the main entrance. He had been detailed off to meet the Gainsborough House choir that afternoon, and was very nearly late.

He stood on the granite steps in the main entrance and waited as the school coach drew up and the girls, in green mackintoshes and straw boaters, alighted.

Last out of the bus was the music mistress.

'Miss Eagles?'

'Yes, I'm sorry we're late, I made the driver go to the wrong entrance.'

Steven had the extraordinary sensation that he had already known her for some time, as if they were friends from that very first moment. Tall, with mousey-blonde hair, she had the kindest, friendliest eyes he had ever seen. They realised they were staring at each other at the same moment: he looked away, saw the single ivory bracelet at her wrist, took in at a glance the fact that she had a lovely figure as well as a lovely smile, swallowed, and stuttered, 'Right, well, I'd better lead the way.'

He showed them into the visitors' room where they left their coats. He heard the music mistress say, 'Do please get a move on, we don't want to keep the navy waiting!' and a minute later they were going along the side of the quarterdeck, a high roofed hall with galleries on either side that formed the architectural centrepiece of the college.

'Are we dreadfully late?' she asked.

'Not really. Haven't you been here before?'

She shook her head. He looked across at her and caught her eye. His heart started thumping and he had a feeling that hers might be doing the same.

They climbed several flights of teak stairs. Catherine Eagles noticed that her guide had started to limp. She wondered why, and glancing down saw the reason. Really! She wouldn't have thought he was old enough for that, but she couldn't help finding it rather flattering, all the same.

They reached the top of yet another flight of stairs. 'This way,' he said, and they turned left along a corridor that led to a pair of swing doors.

They pushed the doors open and stood on either side, holding them open as the sopranos and altos of Gainsborough House choir entered the college cinema, where the first full rehearsal was about to begin. They stood facing each other, both aware of a peculiar heart-stopping sensation that neither had known before.

When the last of the girls had entered, Catherine closed her side of the swing doors, and Jannaway released his to bang shut of its own accord.

For a moment, her face seemed to light up in an ecstatic expression; then she gave a yelp of agony, and he realised two things – first, that the door had slammed on her fingers, and second that he was in love.


He looked like an apologetic puppy, standing in the lobby of the college sick quarters when she came out of the treatment room. There were no bones broken, but she wouldn't be playing the cello, the flute or the piano for a week or two. Her finger was in a stall and her hand was in a sling.

He had been detailed off by Lieutenant Commander Darnley to look after her, and could still hardly believe his luck.

'I sent the transport away,' he said. 'I thought you might like to walk.' She gave him an odd look. 'It's not very far,' he reassured her.

They set out down the tarmac path that went downhill from the sick quarters to the college. There had been a light fall of snow, and Dartmouth, to their right, looked like a wintry picture postcard.

To their left, dogs barked.

'Beagles,' he explained. 'Would you like to see them?'

She realised that it was just an excuse to have longer with her. He had a rather rueful grin and dark, pleading eyes.

'A pack?' she said.

'Yes, a pack. They're just up here.'

She followed him up a path that led to the beagle kennels. They stood at the wire netting and the dogs pushed wet noses out to them, barking and wagging with joy at their arrival.

'It's a funny place to have beagles,' Catherine said.

'It's a funny place all round.'

'How many are there altogether?'

'Sixteen couples. You count them in couples.'

'Why?'

'I don't know really. When they're walked, you put a young one with an older one so that he can learn.'

'You seem to know a lot about them.'

'Oh I do. I'm a beagler. It's all part of the training.'

She put her head back and laughed, biting her lower lip in a way that made him want to wrap her in his arms then and there.

'I don't believe you!'

'Every Saturday,' he laughed. 'Yoiks tally-ho. It's what every good naval officer does in his spare time.'

They began walking back down the path.

'Can I ask you your name?' he said.

'Catherine. Eagles.'

'I'm Steven. Jannaway. People call me Shag.'

She let that pass.

'How's the finger?'

'Oh – throbbing nicely,' she said lightly, and saw him blush immediately.

'Perhaps we ought to be getting back,' she said.

He nodded. 'To the Halleluiah Chorus, yes. Never to meet again.'

They walked downhill beneath dripping beech trees. 'Sorry to rush things,' he said, 'But I would like very much to meet you again.'

This was the moment when she should gently but firmly tell him that that was out of the question. But she couldn't. It would be cruelty to animals. She smiled. 'You are rushing things, aren't you?'

He grinned his mongrel grin. '*Carpe diem. Quam celerrime.*'

'I'm afraid Latin was never my strong point.'

'I expect you've got plenty of others.'

'What does it mean?'

'Gather ye rosebuds while ye may. Roughly.'

'Very roughly by the sound of it.'

They had reached the rear entrance of 'D' block. 'Well,' he said. 'When are we going to meet?'

'I'll see you at the rehearsals.'

'That isn't what I call meeting.'

She looked down at the asphalt and shook her head. 'I think it'll have to do for the time being, won't it?'

They smiled; he wondered if her heart was going as completely out of control as his.

'I think we ought to go in,' she said. 'Separately, if you don't mind.'

He let her go in first, and when he followed her a few moments later she was safe among the altos and being careful not to look in his direction.

Being in love got in the way of everything. Just when he was supposed to be making the supreme effort to be 'taut', which in naval parlance means on the ball, efficient and bursting with officer qualities, he found himself mooning about in a dream, thinking of Catherine Eagles.

The rehearsals took place every Wednesday evening. He attended them all, singing his part in a glow of absentmindedness, waiting for that moment when Catherine's eyes would meet his and the week of waiting would become worthwhile.

He found it almost impossible to talk to her however: she was always surrounded by officers or lecturers from the college, and he began to feel that some campaign was being conducted to keep them apart. 'How's the finger?' he managed once, to which she replied 'Doing nicely' before being ushered away to talk to someone more important.

He wondered if he could invite her to the end of term dance, but as it was the spring term, this was not going to be much of an event, and he didn't want to embarrass her with an evening in the gym dancing to a noisy band. Besides, he was a mere eighteen (or very nearly) and she was what – twenty-two?

One thing he was sure of was that she was attracted to him. Sometimes when their eyes met, he was convinced that he saw a message in her expression which said, yes, don't give up, I feel that way too.

So he did not give up, and after a few weeks he found that he suddenly had a very important reason for staying in the navy, passing his exams and as Lieutenant Commander Darnley had put it, pulling his finger out. He began sending more collars to the laundry, taking greater care over his appearance and actually reading the College Daily Orders to make sure that he knew what was going on. Miraculously, Shag Jannaway ceased to be shag.

'I don't know what's come over you,' Whettingsteel said to him one Saturday evening when Jannaway was polishing his shoes for Divisions the next day. 'They've finally got through to you, haven't they? I never thought they would.'

Jannaway grinned, and kept the reason to himself. It was a source of great satisfaction to him that no one so much as suspected his passion for Catherine Eagles except Catherine Eagles. That he knew, for at the last rehearsal their hands had touched quite by accident, and she had said 'Hullo Steven.'

The end of term exams came and went; he hardly noticed them, and as a result did better in them than anyone had expected. Next term he would go to sea in the training squadron, and the term after he would return as a midshipman for another four terms at the college. If I can't get to know her in that time, he told himself, I don't deserve to.

Dartmouth was at its worst on the night of the performance. A gale was coming up through the harbour entrance and rain was battering against the long façade of windows. The college chapel was candlelit and the lines of brass memorials glittered and shone on the brick walls. The cadets wore wing collars and bow ties with their uniform reefers; the officers wore mess undress and the lecturers dinnerjackets. When the contingent from Gainsborough House arrived, Steven caught his breath at the sight of Catherine: she was in a dark green evening dress, and as she followed her charges up the aisle she looked back into his eyes and smiled in a way that told him everything he wanted to know.

The chapel filled with officers, lecturers and their families, as well as a few midshipmen and cadets; the orchestra tuned, the head of music tapped his baton and the overture began.

Steven had never sung in the Messiah before and had seldom entered a Protestant church; since coming to Dartmouth nearly two years before he had had little time for music and had never once touched the piano while at home on leave. But that evening, so close to Catherine that he could have reached out and touched her shoulder, when the triumphant solos and choruses filled the college chapel, he knew again that there was in him a love of music which could never be completely extinguished.

Afterwards, there was coffee and biscuits in the mess hall for performers and audience. He was one of the last to leave the chapel, and by the time he arrived Catherine was in conversation with the captain of the college. There was no hope of being able to talk to her. He saw her glance in his direction; he hung about and sipped his coffee, feeling more miserable every minute.

Quite suddenly, she left. One moment she was still talking, the next she was gone. He went quickly down the main corridor after her. She was with one of the senior members of the Gainsborough House staff. He followed them to the visitors' room and hung about outside, not knowing what he was going to say when they came out.

When they did, they were together.

'Goodnight!' Catherine said cheerfully, turning up the collar of her coat as she went out into the rain and wind.

He ran out after them. They were getting into a Morris Minor.

'Wait!' he called. 'Please!'

Her companion had already started the engine. Catherine wound down her window.

'What is it?'

'Can I write to you?' he blurted out. 'I'm going to be at sea next term, but I'll be back as a midshipman in September.'

Their faces stared at him in amazement. The rain was beating down and he was getting wet.

Then Catherine smiled. 'All right. Yes, you can write to me if you want to.'

He thanked her and stepped back as she raised her hand and the car drove off. He watched it go down the ramp above the parade ground and continue down the steep hill, into Dartmouth. He stood there in the rain, waiting to catch a glimpse of the rear lights as they went on through the college gates, then turned, went back to his cabin and began his first letter.

Dear Catherine...

He stared at the words. He didn't know why, but he felt quite sure that this would be the first of many, many letters, and that his life and Catherine's were, from that moment, permanently linked.

# 6

Peter Lasbury raised his King's telescope to his right eye and brought the three ships of the Dartmouth Training Squadron into focus. He studied them carefully: they were four or five miles off still, but the high, rounded bridges of the two frigates were unmistakable. Each was showing a bow wave that extended almost a third of the ship's length, and Lasbury estimated that they must be doing twenty knots.

He looked at his watch. It was twelve minutes to nine. They were due at the breakwater at 0900, and would be just in time, arriving at a smart pace, in accordance with normal practice.

'Bo'son's mate!' he said, closing up the telescope.

' Sir!' The bo'sun's mate was an ordinary seaman of nineteen. As a dutyman on watch he wore his white duck uniform with the crossed torpedoes on his left arm to indicate his specialisation.

'Go and tell the captain the DTS is in sight and approaching the breakwater.'

Ordinary seaman Palmer's face crinkled as he tried to take the message in. 'Yes, sir,' he said uncertainly. He made to go.

'Wait!' Lasbury ordered.

'Sir?'

'What's the message you're going to give to the captain?'

'Er – the – er – Captain D is in sight near the breakwater, sir.'

'No, Palmer. Listen. The D-T-S is in sight and approaching the breakwater. Do you know what the DTS is?'

'Sir?'

'It's the Dartmouth Training Squadron.'

'Yes, sir.'

'Right. Go and tell the captain.'

'Yes, sir.'

'And Palmer –'

'Yes, sir?'

'When an officer gives you an order, you salute and say "Aye aye, sir". Got it?'

'Yes, sir.'

'Off you go, then.'

Palmer saluted. 'Aye aye, sir.'

Lasbury watched him double away, pleased to have been able to put him on the right track. He paced up and down the quarterdeck of the cruiser, which lay alongside at Gibraltar. He was the officer of the forenoon watch, and wore full whites, with a sword belt at his side. He went twenty paces aft and twenty paces for'd, twenty paces aft and twenty paces for'd, then stopped, extended his telescope and looked again at the approaching ships.

Young Braddle was in HMS *Gazelle*, of course. He hadn't seen him since that rather awkward evening with Sarah. All in all, it was better to have ended his friendship with her. It had not been founded upon affection, he knew that now. Of the two girls, Julietta was the more interesting. He smiled, remembering her extraordinary appearance at the party, dressed up in her brother's new uniform. She had sent him a Christmas card two years running, and a picture postcard from Switzerland. He had not bothered to reply, but had been warmed by the enthusiasm of her greetings and the little row of kisses she had put under her name.

Lasbury saluted as Captain Sykes-Morris came to the quarterdeck. Sykes-Morris was a contemporary of the captain of the Dartmouth Training Squadron, and was interested to see how his old term mate handled his command. He raised his own telescope and studied the approaching ships, which were coming up fast. Standing a few paces behind him was his yeoman of signals, ready with clipboard and signal pad in case he wished to make a signal; on the other side of the quarterdeck the quartermaster, bo'sun's mate and Royal Marine bugler also stood waiting. The bugler blew gently down his instrument to ensure that when the moment came it would sound true.

The three ships – two frigate conversions and an old destroyer – entered the harbour between the breakwaters and slowed to make their approaches to their alongside berths. As each steamed past HMS *Durham*, a bo'sun's call piped the 'Still' and the voice of the first lieutenant could be heard calling the ship's company to attention.

'Sound the alert!' Lasbury ordered, and the bugle notes brayed out over the water.

'Attention on the upperdeck,' announced the quartermaster on the ship's loudspeaker system. 'Face to starboard.' All along the upperdeck of the cruiser men working with mops, scrubbers or paint brushes stopped work and faced to starboard, while on the quarterdeck Captain Sykes-Morris, who had been promoted to captain a year before his old term mate, returned the salute of his junior.

The three ships berthed ahead of HMS *Durham*, under the huge grey sheerlegs that towered over the harbour. These sheerlegs were like the captured tusks of some prehistoric monster, and were as much a part of Gibraltar to naval people as was the Rock itself.

When the three ships had saluted in turn, and Captain Sykes-Morris had returned to his cabin, Peter Lasbury went for'd to watch the berthing operation. The first two ships went alongside with comparatively little fuss, with the head and stern ropes being passed to the dockyard workers on the quay and the cadets working under the direction of petty officers to make them fast. The third ship, HMS *Gazelle*, had more difficulty. She had to fit in between the bows of HMS *Durham* and the stern of HMS *Venus*, and with a stiff breeze blowing off the berth was unable to slide in alongside as easily.

A hail of heaving lines snaked away from the bows as she made her approach, most of which fell in the water. The propellers churned up black mud from the bottom of the harbour, and the voice of the first lieutenant issued orders in rapid succession over the ship's broadcast.

'Check away head rope, check away back spring, down slack fore spring, down slack stern rope!' The words boomed and echoed against the dockyard buildings, and faces appeared at the windows of the Flag Officer Gibraltar's offices, for nothing fascinates a naval officer more than the sight of another naval officer mishandling his ship.

'The ship is coming astern eight feet!' announced the voice, and the water churned again under the stern. Peter Lasbury raised his telescope. The figures working on the quarterdeck of the destroyer were only a matter of seventy yards away, but it was interesting to see them in close up and there was always the possibility that he might pick out young Braddle.

And there he was: acting as port screwflagsman, a green flag in his right hand and a red in his left, indicating to the bridge whether the lines were clear of the water aft. He was on the port after Bofors gun deck, standing bolt upright in the way short people often do, and in exactly the same way as his father and grandfather did.

'Hold on to the back spring,' the first lieutenant ordered, and when the order was not immediately obeyed, repeated, 'Hold *on* to the back spring!' The quarterdeck party heaved in the slack of the wire hawser and took turns on the double bollards aft. The strain came on very quickly as the ship moved aft, and the cadets were unable to hold it. 'Hold on to the fucking back spring!' bawled the petty officer, and four more cadets raced to back up the others. The wire rose dripping out of the water, tautened and vibrated hard.

'Surge! Surge! Surge!' shouted the quarterdeck officer.

'HOLD ON, I say again, HOLD ON to the back spring,' said the first lieutenant.

Lasbury smiled, enjoying the spectacle. Up and down the port side of the destroyer, cadets scurried about with fenders and lines. Orders were shouted and countermanded. The destroyer see-sawed back and forth, trying to get her position alongside exactly right, the attempts of the captain to manoeuvre with engines being repeatedly frustrated by the forecastle and quarterdeck parties, who seemed unable to hold on when ordered to hold on or check away when ordered to check away.

Eventually the officers on the bridge of the destroyer decided that the ship was in the correct position, and the order 'Double up and secure' was passed: you could almost hear the ship sigh with relief.

Lasbury strolled aft. He went to the quartermaster's desk and took out a signal pad and pencil. FROM LIEUTENANT LASBURY TO CADET BRADDLE, he wrote. RPC TOMORROW SUNDAY 1230 FOR LUNCH AND WALK UP THE ROCK.

He tore the sheet off the pad. 'Bosun's mate!'

'Sir!'

'Take this to the officer of the watch aboard *Gazelle*.'

'Yes, sir.'

'Palmer!'

'Sir? Oh. Sorry, sir.' Palmer saluted. 'Aye aye, sir.'

Lasbury watched as the bosun's mate doubled away down the brow and along the quay to HMS *Gazelle*. He achieved a curious satisfaction from training the young, and always had. He knew that his request for the pleasure of David Braddle's company would flatter him, and that David would regard it as something of an honour to be invited to lunch by a lieutenant.

He paced up and down, his telescope under his arm, enjoying the sunshine and the breeze. After a few minutes, Palmer returned. He doubled up to Lasbury and saluted.

'From Cadet Braddle, sir, WLP.'

Lasbury chuckled. 'Not WLP, Palmer, WMP.' Palmer looked blank. 'Do you know what it stands for?'

'No, sir.'

'Have a guess.'

'I – I wouldn't know, sir.'

'With much pleasure, Palmer. You ought to know that by now.'


David Braddle went on a run ashore that evening. Normally he would have gone ashore with his friend Chas Tomkins, who had been back-termed and with whom he had struck up a camaraderie, but Tomkins was under stoppage of leave for loafing in the heads when the hands were turned to, so Braddle went ashore with Courtenay, Jannaway and Whettingsteel instead.

They walked through Gibraltar dockyard in their Harris tweed hacking jackets and cavalry twill trousers, Braddle striding out to keep up with the others, and dropping back when there wasn't room to walk four abreast. He had grown up a bit since joining Dartmouth, but was still regarded as a 'wet' by his term mates, and had been allowed to accompany them on this run ashore on sufferance.

David was conscious of the mild contempt in which he was held and was anxious to be accepted by his peers, but he seemed unable to throw off the prep-school personality and lavatorial humour which was amusing for no more than about three minutes.

He was like one of those small, pink india rubber balls sold in pet shops to the owners of little dogs: the harder you crushed him, the higher he bounced back.

The other members of this quartet also had their roles to play. Whettingsteel was the natural leader: tall, quiet and dispassionate, he was the one who had the common sense to keep them out of trouble without appearing to boss. Courtenay was the heavy-weight centurion, the natural first lieutenant, and Jannaway was the romantic, his thoughts full of Catherine and his wallet full of her letters.

'So what will happen to you tonight, Daisy?' Courtenay asked as they walked down the busy High Street. 'Are we going to have to carry you back? Will you be sick in the taxi?'

Braddle laughed and rolled his eyes. He managed to sound tipsy without having had a drink. 'My behaviour will be as impeccable as it always is, gentlemen,' he said.

They did some shopping. Jannaway bought a teaspoon for his mother and Courtenay bought a cigarette lighter for himself. Braddle found a ball point pen with a girl on it, whose swimming costume magically disappeared when he held it point upward.

They sat in the Trocadero and drank fourpenny Malagas, and David Braddle regaled them with an inexhaustible stream of anecdotes and shaggy dog stories, most of which they had heard before. The bar filled with sailors, who sat round the tables with pints of beer, their sleeves pushed back off their wrists and the front flap of their trousers unbuttoned.

After Braddle had told a particularly unsavoury joke he had heard from the messdeck petty officer while scrubbing out the cadets' heads the previous day, Jannaway took out his latest letter from Catherine. It was the first he had had from her since the ship had sailed from Devonport a month before, and he had only had time to read it once.

Braddle panted like a dog and licked his chops. 'Come on, Janners, let's have a look at the sports page.'

'Shag doesn't descend to the level of sports pages,' Whettingsteel said. 'He lives on a higher plane.'

Jannaway grinned amiably. Although he did not like talking about Catherine, he enjoyed being seen to have a letter from her.

'What's that, the fourth this cruise?' Courtenay asked.

'Second, actually.'

At the far end of the bar, two sailors were trying to dance a flamenco amid the cheers and laughter of their shipmates.

'Who's shout?' Braddle said. 'Or are we moving on?'

They looked at Jannaway. He put his letter away and bought four more Malagas. Braddle downed his in one, and his eyes watered at the sudden influx of alcohol. 'Here we go,' Courtenay said. 'Daisy's off.'

David Braddle beamed and tipped his chair back, swinging his short legs to and fro. 'Two letters in two months,' he said. 'That sounds a bit piss poor to me, Janners. She can't be exactly hot to trot, can she? You'll have to sharpen her up.'

At the end of the bar, the flamenco dancing sailors had collapsed upon each other, arms round each other's necks, one trying to lead the other in a tango.

'Two letters in two months,' Braddle said. Jannaway was one of the few people he felt confident enough to bait. 'And I bet I know why, too.' He tipped his chair back against the wall, touching his upper lip with the tip of his tongue.

'Go on, tell us why, Daisy,' Courtenay said.

Braddle glowed with alcohol and the knowledge that he had their attention. 'Okay, I will.' He turned to Jannaway. 'Bet she writes once a month, doesn't she?'

'What if she does?'

'Once a month, the same time every month, I bet she does. Doesn't she? That's what it's all about, Janners. It's chemistry, not love. You haven't got any sisters, have you? Well I have, and *I* know they go broody every four weeks. I mean – if I had a popsy who only wrote once a month –'

'Fat chance, Daisy,' Courtenay put in.

'I'm saying *if* I did, I'd get a bit bloody suspicious.' He pointed at Jannaway. 'I bet if you look at the dates on her letters you'll find I'm right.'

Jannaway pushed back his chair and stood up. 'What a dirty minded little boy you are,' he said. 'You're not even worth hitting.'

He waited just long enough to see by Braddle's expression that his words had struck home before walking quickly from the bar, making a detour round the belching ratings who swayed and tangoed, locked in alcoholic embrace.

Outside, he took a side street to get away from the bustle of the main street, walking fast, angry with himself for over-reacting. He stopped somewhere near the fleet sports grounds, feeling a wave of nausea that was caused as much by his dissatisfaction with life as the quantity of Malaga wine in his stomach.

What would Alan have thought if he had heard David Braddle's conversation, he wondered. He pictured his brother feeding the hens every morning, pedalling laboriously up the hill to the library, working slowly and painstakingly at his typewriter up in his room. What would he have thought, and what would he think if he knew what the navy was really like?

Then he thought of Catherine. She had replied promptly to his first letter, writing to him at home. Yes, she had said, I wanted to speak to you, too, that evening. Why shouldn't we write? She could imagine that it might be lonely away at sea, because her parents were in Kenya and during the school holidays she had to stay with her brother in Clapham. What was it like in the training squadron? She told him to write and tell her all about it. He had been amazed at how ready she was to write and how her letter seemed to presume that they knew each other far better than they did. He wrote back and told her something of himself, avoiding the fact that he was a Catholic and that Alan was a spastic. He said how good it was to get her letter and that he too sometimes felt alone in the world. In her second letter, she told him that she was an adopted child. This latest letter, her third, told him about school life, the characters in the common room, the headmistress, Miss Lucknell.

He took the three letters out of his wallet and looked at the dates. 6th of April, 3rd of May, 11th of June. Was Braddle right? And if he was, did he care? He didn't know. Although he had kissed blind dates at Dartmouth dances, he had never felt so close emotionally to a girl before. Catherine and he belonged together, it was as simple as that. Until he met her, he had not realised how much he needed the gentleness and affection she was already bringing into his life. Here was someone who seemed to know him and to share his thoughts from the very moment of their first meeting. No, he did not believe it was chemistry rather than love. And what if it was? She was a woman and subject to forces which he did not understand. Even if Braddle were right, he would still feel the same. Perhaps he would feel more strongly about her because she would be 'more of a woman'. He didn't understand his own thoughts, so how could he possibly hope to understand hers?

He wondered what he was doing, where he was going and whether it was all worth while; and in this solitary mood, wandered slowly back to the ship.

Later that night, when Jannaway had turned in, Courtenay and Whettingsteel brought Braddle down to the messdeck. They sat him on a bench, unbuttoned his shirt and his trousers, stripped him to his Y-fronts and lifted him into his hammock, turning him on his side so that if he vomited in the night he would not choke; and the following morning, over devilled kidneys on fried bread, which is known in the navy as 'shit on a raft', everyone heard how the largest of all the whores in Gibraltar had sat upon Daisy Braddle's manly knee; how he had been thrown out of a night club for making objectionable remarks about the Bols, had been sick in the road outside the Governor's residence, had insulted the Indian taxi driver and had lost his Burberry raincoat, his paybook and his month's ration of tobacco coupons.

101

There was a compulsory church parade that morning, for all but the Roman Catholics and Moslems. The cadets put on their best uniforms and were marched in threes to the cathedral. Afterwards, David Braddle went straight back to the ship to change out of uniform for his Sunday lunch with Peter Lasbury. He put on his tweeds and twills again, and decided that this was a suitable occasion upon which to wear his brown trilby hat, which he had been advised to purchase by his father. This hat he raised solemnly as he reached the top of the brow to HMS *Durham*, in reply to the quartermaster's salute.

He was shown for'd by the bosun's mate, and after entering the ship's superstructure by a watertight door, went along a highly polished passage, through two more bulkhead doors, down a double accommodation ladder to the wardroom lobby, where a glass fronted cabinet contained the trophies that HMS *Durham* had won during her commission.

The bosun's mate knocked on the teak door frame, and a chintz curtain was drawn aside. Peter Lasbury looked up from the sofa.

'David! Come you in!'

'Shall I leave my hat –'

'Yes, of course. No, not there, old boy, that's Chief's peg.'

David Braddle hung his trilby on an acceptable hook and entered. There were one or two officers sitting in the chintz covered armchairs, reading the Sunday newspapers, but none of these took any notice of him. 'Now then,' Lasbury said, ' What'll you have?' He indicated the bar, where a large Maltese steward stood ready in a freshly pressed white front.

Braddle hesitated. 'Well – perhaps I'd better have a beer, sir,' he said.

Lasbury lowered his voice. 'You can have a short if you want, David. And less of the sir, eh?' He smiled reassuringly, and Braddle relaxed a little.

'Could I have a horse's neck?'

'Certainly, you can. That's one horse's neck, one G and T, Grech.'

Steward Grech mixed the drinks, and they took them to a corner of the anteroom away from the newspaper-reading officers.

'So how's life treating you?' Lasbury said, offering the saucer of salted peanuts and helping himself. 'Enjoying the cruise?'

'It's absolutely super,' David said. 'Better than I expected.'

'Was that you I saw in the main drag last night?'

David blushed. 'It may have been.'

The commander entered the mess. Lasbury stood up and introduced David. 'Cadet Braddle, sir,' he said, emphasising the name, so that the commander should be aware exactly why the young gentleman had been invited aboard.

The commander was a lean, keen man, with fair hair and red eyelashes. He looked closely at Braddle as if examining an interesting specimen, which of course he was. 'Which one are you in?' he asked.

'*Gazelle*, sir.'

'Are they teaching you anything?'

'A bit, sir.' Braddle tried a little humour. 'Not enough gunnery!'

'Guns!' said the commander. 'Guns! Don't talk to me about guns! They're a thing of the past!' And with that he moved away to order himself a gin and water.

Lunch was served at one o'clock by the Maltese staff: roast pork and crackling, buttered carrots, roast potatoes that had gone soft and watery cabbage. The officers ate off white plates which bore the blue admiralty badge, and each plate had to be set down so that this was at the top and central. If a steward set a plate down askew, the officer concerned adjusted it without any interruption to his conversation.

Peter Lasbury maintained an easy conversation throughout the meal, ribbing his colleagues about incidents or situations Braddle knew nothing about, but managing to make him feel included all the same, living up to his most recent confidential report, in which his commanding officer described him as an officer of great charm.

There was coffee afterwards, and when that was finished Lasbury said, 'Right. Let's take a wander up the Rock.'

Braddle nodded enthusiastically: in Lasbury's company he was quite a different person from last night. He liked Lasbury immensely, looking up to him as to a superior being, and as they set out in the blazing sunshine, he hoped that some of his term mates would see him, quite unaware that he looked more like a small boy being taken out by an uncle than a young naval officer out for a stroll with a friend.

'Just remembered,' he said as they went out through the dockyard gates. 'I've left my hat behind.'

'David! How terrible!' Peter laughed, and for a moment their eyes met in a look of happy anticipation.

'What would you say to an ice cream?' Lasbury suggested as they walked up the hill towards the Rock Hotel.

'Super!' David said.

'I've always liked ice cream,' Lasbury said, and led the way up to the terrace. They sat down at a table with a parasol, and Lasbury took off his jacket so Braddle followed suit. The waiter brought chocolate and vanilla ice creams, and David waited for Lasbury to take the first mouthful before starting himself.

'What news from home?' Lasbury said. 'How are those sisters of yours?'

'Julietta's gone all sporty. She's got a horse.'

'And Sarah?'

'She's got a job in Amsterdam.'

'Has she indeed. What about you? You go back to Dartmouth next term, do you? Looking forward to it?'

'I'd rather be at sea.'

Every now and then their eyes met, and Braddle was aware of a feeling of anticipation, as if his drinks before lunch, the lunch, the coffee and now this walk up to the Rock Hotel and the ice cream were all a preparation, an overture.

They went on up the hill. Lasbury carried his jacket over his shoulder, and David did likewise. From time to time they stopped to admire the view. The breeze had dropped away, and it was hot. To the south, a thunderstorm muttered over the Atlas mountains.

'Let's take a short cut,' Lasbury said, and they left the road to follow a path that went up between bushes and boulders. After a few minutes they came out on a spur of rock below which the mountain dropped away sharply to the road several hundred feet below.

They stopped. 'What a view!' Braddle said.

Peter Lasbury folded his jacket and sat down. 'Far from the madding crowd,' he said. He leant back, using his jacket as a pillow. 'Shall we take a breather?'

They sat in silence for a while, looking out over the Straits, where a steady procession of ships went in and out of the Mediterranean. To their right, a ferry headed across the bay towards Algeciras.

'In the rich midnight of the garden trees,' Lasbury said. 'Something something on those mingled seas. How does it go?'

'I've no idea.'

'Ha!' Lasbury said a little later. 'Look at that!'

'Where?'

'There, right in front of you!'

It was a chameleon, clinging motionless to a bush, its hideous eye swivelling and blinking.

'I think I'll do a bit of bronzey-bronzey,' Lasbury said. He took off his shirt, hesitated, then removed his trousers also, to reveal a pair of pink and white striped Gieves undershorts. He saw David's face and laughed. 'Ah. You're admiring my panther. That was the result of an evening's foolishness, I'm afraid to say.' He lay down and put his hands behind his head. An insect chirruped nearby. Braddle took off his shirt and glanced enviously down at the mat of golden hair on Lasbury's chest and navel.

'David,' Lasbury said after a while.

'Yes?'

'Would you object most terribly if I stripped off?'

Braddle laughed uncertainly. 'No!'

Lasbury stood up and looked round. 'I don't think we'll shock any natives, will we, and one doesn't often get the opportunity.' He stepped out of the shorts and lay down again. 'Hope I'm not shocking you,' he said.

Braddle sat beside him, as if on guard. It wasn't all that odd that Lasbury had stripped off so unselfconsciously. Nakedness in the navy was a commonplace. You swam a length of the bath naked after gym at the college, showered naked before every run ashore and swam naked over the ship's side when hands were piped to bathe.

Lasbury opened one eye and looked at him. 'This is glorious,' he said. 'People pay thousands on the Riviera to do this, did you know that?'

David Braddle laughed. He was trembling all over.

'Go on, David,' Lasbury said. 'Live dangerously. Or are you shy?'

David Braddle's naval training had not been all in vain. He knew that naval officers weren't supposed to be shy. They had to be self-assertive, confident, keen, efficient, enthusiastic, unflappable and good company.

He grinned quickly, and accepted the challenge.

Lasbury watched him through half closed eyes. Braddle was sitting beside him, his knees drawn up, shaking visibly.

'What's wrong? Are you frightened?'

'No,' Braddle almost sobbed.

'Well stretch out then. Go on.' Lasbury put out his hand and touched him. Braddle jumped as if he had been touched with an electric probe. Lasbury laughed gently. 'Oh, come on, David! There's nothing to be afraid of!'

So David lay back, and as soon as he did so Lasbury whispered, 'Oh, yes, I thought so,' and the pretending was over.

Peter Lasbury pulled on his trousers and tucked in his shirt. He looked down at Braddle, who was weeping. 'Are you coming up to the top?' he asked.

Braddle shook his head, unable to speak.

'For goodness sake! You loved it!'

Braddle looked up at him. 'You bastard!' he sobbed. 'You bastard!'

'Don't be wet, David. You weren't forced into anything at all, and you know it.'

Braddle sobbed, his head bent, his arms crossed about his middle in an attempt to hide his nakedness. Lasbury looked at him, sorry for him but unable to help. There was no point in trying to talk him out of it now; he would probably prefer to be left on his own. He slung his jacket over his shoulder.

'I'm going on up to the top,' he said, and went off up the path.

He needed the exercise now and climbed fast to the ridge, pushing himself physically to take his mind off the unsatisfactory ending to his afternoon with David. He reached the ridge, and continued up to the fortifications, where a massive gun pointed out over the Straits. He paced about on the reinforced concrete, rationalising what had happened in his mind and convincing himself that Braddle had all but begged him to do what he did. How ridiculous of him to break down like that! One thing he was sure of: David would say nothing of it. But what if he did? If he does ... if he does, we'll both go down together, Lasbury said to himself, the wind in his fair hair and the sun sparkling on the Mediterranean below him. I'll drag the name of Braddle so low it'll earn a place in the history books.

But he didn't want that. No, he would much rather be able to make it up with David and develop the friendship. They could be useful to each other after all; such relationships had worked excellently in the service before, and he saw no reason why they shouldn't work again.

Three hundred feet below, David Braddle collected his clothes and put them on. He wanted to gain control of himself, but each time he thought that his tears had finally subsided, a fresh wave of emotion broke over him: emotion borne not so much of remorse or guilt, as of the knowledge that what Peter Lasbury had said had indeed been true: he had loved it; and what had happened that afternoon high on the Rock of Gibraltar had been the inevitable consummation of his cadetship in the Royal Navy.

He never went to the top. He retraced his steps and hurried down the hill, seeking refuge in side roads where he would not be seen by people he knew. He walked aimlessly, and after a while found himself on the other side of the Rock, passing beneath the water catchment and continuing past the bathing beaches to the border post on the road to La Linea.

He stood by the sea, hiding his face from the jostling holidaymakers. He tried to pray but didn't know what to say or even who he could pray to. It seemed to him that no one had ever experienced what he was experiencing, or suffered the internal torture he was suffering now.

On his way back, past the Officers' Pavilion, he saw a crowd of junior officers with their women friends – nursing sisters from the military hospital. He watched them from a distance, wondering why he could not be as they were. Why was it that he enjoyed so much what others condemned? And how was it that Peter Lasbury could take it so lightly and shrug it off so easily?

The thunderstorm rolled in over Gibraltar later that evening, when David had entered the dockyard and was sitting alone on the breakwater, looking across the Strait. The lightning flickered and the claps of thunder roared, echoing against the Rock. A squall whipped up the water between Spain and Africa, and the sea became white-capped and angry. Caught in the downpour, he was quickly soaked, but he remained where he was, watching the forked lightning split the sky and waiting for the crashes of thunder.

Eventually, he made his way back to the ship. The enclosed atmosphere of the messdeck was oddly welcoming, and it didn't seem to matter that Jannaway saw that he had been crying. 'Where did you get to, David?' he asked kindly, and he replied, 'Oh, just a quiet run, you know.'

He heaved his hammock up to the steel bar and made it fast with a clove hitch. He undid the seven marline hitches, and as the last one loosened, a small brown envelope fell to the deck.

He picked it up. It had his name, 'David' on it, and he wondered if it might be from Peter. But it wasn't: there was just a short note inside, written in capitals and unsigned: YOU WERE SEEN THIS AFTERNOON. SUGGEST YOU WATCH YOUR STEP OTHERWISE THE BUZZ WILL GO ROUND.

He stared at the words in horror, then quickly crumpled the note and put it in his pocket. He undressed and lifted himself by the steel bar into his hammock. He lay on his back and listened to the murmurings of other cadets returning from shore, the hum of generators and the steady whispering flow of air from the punkah louvres.

He thought of past happinesses he had known: days just after the war when he was seven and eight years old and his father, a cheerful lieutenant commander with the DSO and DSC, was back from the war. He remembered his mother sitting on his bed reading the *Little Black Sambo* stories to him, and those nights when Julietta had come into his bed for comfort; and thinking these things, he stifled his sobs and fell into a fitful sleep.

He knew what he had to do the moment Call the Hands was piped and the voice of the training petty officer shouted 'Turn out!' but he was determined to give no sign of his intention. Having taken his decision, and knowing what was going to happen, made it all easier and in a strange way almost enjoyable because he was quite sure that what he was going to do was right.

He lashed up his hammock and washed in the bathrooms as usual, going up on deck after breakfast to fall in with both watches. He collected the bucket and scrubber from the washdeck locker and scrubbed the spurn-water beading, enjoying the physical effort of moving the scrubbing brush and the way the suds foamed up over his hands. Everything that happened that day was of special importance to him, because each was an experience that he was saying goodbye to. 'Hands fall in for leaving harbour,' the quartermaster piped, and he stood up on the upperdeck in line with Jannaway and Whettingsteel and Courtenay and Abdul Aziz and Ainslie; he stood with them and was prouder than he had ever been before of being a cadet in the Royal Navy; and as the destroyer and the two frigates slipped out of harbour, it was as if everything was new again: as if he were seeing the white ensign flying and feeling the deck moving under his feet for the first time. The ship carved a white wake in the dark blue water and salt spray whipped back into his face; the four-point-five gun crew was piped to close up, and David was the first to fall in beside the mounting, the trousers of his number eights tucked into his socks, the sleeves of his anti-flash gloves pulled well up, only his eyes showing under the khaki helmet. He looked up at the racing clouds and was first to spot the RAF Meteor aircraft towing the sleeve target; he heard the gunnery officer's voice on the loudspeaker: 'Four-fives, stand-to!' 'Four-fives, aircraft!' 'Four-fives, engage!' He handled the cordite and the shell, rammed them home into the breech with his fist, saw the breech close, the gun recoil, the puffs of white smoke trailing the target; and afterwards, when the empty cordite cases had been stowed away, he enjoyed the mad rush down to the messdeck because everyone knew it was 'baby's head' for dinner. He joined in the imitated cries of hungry seagulls, the shouted curses and goodhumoured repartee. 'Come on, you bloody shitehawks, give us a look in!' he shouted, and elbowed his way between them, scooping up an extra steak and kidney pie, more mashed potato, more boiled carrots. A wave crashed against the scuttle and the ship heeled. 'Hands to dinner, starboard thirty!' he shouted with the rest, spreading his arms to catch plates, jugs, trays and bottles of tomato ketchup as they slithered across the mess tables. He was glad, too, to have the afternoon watch, to see the weather worsening, to help the watch on deck rig the lifelines; he stood on the irondeck and looked out over the waves that were streaked with white, and the sight of them strengthened his resolve. After his watch, he ate four pieces of toast and peanut butter, swilling it down with tea, sweet tea, cup after cup of it. He sat at the mess table and joined in the game of liar dice, spitting on the dice, holding them to his ear, whispering 'Speak to me bones!' He didn't mind when they pulled his leg, called him Daisy, or imitated his voice, because he knew that it was right, and that everything, every single thing that happened to him that day would be remembered, would be special. When the first lieutenant announced that the ship had been ordered to proceed at speed to stand by a ship that was in difficulties, it seemed to him that even this had been predestined, for as the ship increased speed, so did her motion: the bows plunged harder, the rivets creaked and groaned, and water slammed against the messdeck scuttle. So he slung his hammock for the last time, to take some rest before going on watch at midnight; he hoisted himself in and lay back, enjoying the sensation of swinging back and forth as the ship rolled; for only a few minutes, it seemed, he fell asleep, and then there was the face of Tomkins, who was dressed in oilskins with a towel round his neck, saying, 'It's blowing a fucking hooligan up there, mate' and it was time to turn out for the middle watch: time to report to the petty officer, to be detailed off as one of the seaboat's crew; and the hot sweet Ki was good to drink and the potatoes baked in the boiler room asbestos tender and warming; it was good to eat and drink like that, in the company of old Ainslie, Barry Courtenay, Tim Whettingsteel, and it didn't matter that they took the micky because everything they said would now hold extra meaning, later on. They would remember and they would be full of regret. An hour as seaboat's crew, an hour as lookout: up he went, up two ladders and onto the bridge wing, where Abdul Aziz hugged a bucket and retched into it; he slung the binoculars round his neck and focussed them on the dark sea, picking out the light of a distant ship and taking pride in reporting it: 'White light, green two-zero, far, sir!' he shouted, and the officer of the watch replied, 'Very good,' and he laughed and looked straight down at the sea and whispered, 'Very good, very good,' and tried not to think of Peter, the panther that seemed to come alive, or his own helpless climax as Peter's head nodded back and forth. He tried to forget that because there wasn't much time left now, not long to go because he had made a promise to himself that he would do it and would not be afraid. When his relief took over the binoculars, he almost said 'Goodbye,' but he managed not to; he went to the officer-of-the-watch and reported, 'Starboard look-out relieved, sir, one light in sight, reported, binoculars correct.' He left the bridge and went down the ladder to the ops room flat, and now the moment had come. 'I think something's broken loose on the fo'c's'le,' he told one of the petty officers, and when the petty officer had gone, he went out into the night.

The stars jerked and wheeled, and the spray flew. He had a key to the deck locker, and he was careful to relock it after taking out the mooring shackle and a length of cod line. He sat on the sloping foredeck, huddled against the locker, weeping and praying. But it was no use; there was no going back now. He had thought it all out and it was better to do it this way so that no one would ever know what had happened.

110

He tied one end of the line to his ankle with a round turn and two half-hitches, and the other to the shackle with a bowline. He crawled down the deck to the guardrails, and climbing over, carried the shackle with him, making sure that it would not snag; then he stood for a moment as the destroyer leapt up out of a wave, and as the bow plunged down again into the next, he jumped.

## 7

Catherine Eagles watched Steven put a dollop of Devonshire cream onto his scone and bite into it.

'No jam?' she asked.

He shook his head. 'Spoils the taste for a purist,' he said.

She had walked up the hill from Gainsborough House, and they sat under the oak beams of a café that specialised in cream teas. It was the first time they had met since Steven had returned to Dartmouth as a midshipman: he had arrived on an elderly motorcycle looking red faced and windswept, his cavalry twill trousers speckled with mud.

'That's what you are is it? A purist?'

He put on a Devonshire accent. 'That's right, my lover.'

She glanced back at a waitress who was eyeing them from the door to the kitchens. 'I'd rather you didn't call me that, Steven.'

'I'd rather you didn't call me Steven.'

'Well I'm definitely not going to call you Shag.'

'Steven's what my mother calls me,' he said.

'Well what's wrong with that?'

He smiled and shook his head. She saw that he was a little embarrassed, and decided to change the subject. 'So. Midshipman Jannaway. What does it feel like?'

He laughed. 'Not you as well!'

'Now what have I said?'

'Well. My brother's always asking me what it's like.'

'You haven't told me much about your brother,' she said.

'No, well. Not much to tell. He leads a rather mundane life. He's a librarian.'

'Being a librarian isn't necessarily mundane.'

'No, I didn't say it was. But Alan does lead a pretty dull sort of existence.'

'Is that his fault?'

'Not really.' He looked at her oddly, as if making up his mind about something. 'He's a spastic,' he said abruptly, and looked challengingly into her eyes.

She sensed that this was a delicate subject with him, something he did not normally discuss. She felt it would be better to talk about it in a matter-of-fact way than to gush sympathetically.

'Is he badly handicapped?'

He shook his head. 'Not very. He's one of the lucky ones. At least, that's what he says. It's ... just down one side, mainly.' He opened his hand and looked at the palm, then closed it again, looking back at her. 'My mother dropped him when he was very small.'

She felt her eyes fill with tears.

'Sorry, I shouldn't have told you,' he said.

'No, I'm glad you did.' She blinked quickly to rid herself of the tears.

He topped up the teapot with hot water and poured more tea for himself and for her.

'Does it make a big difference?' she asked.

He stopped, teapot in hand. 'Being a spastic? I should imagine so, wouldn't you?'

'I meant for you. Having a spastic brother.'

He shrugged and put the teapot back on the mat. 'I don't know. I've never thought about it.'

She watched him stirring his tea. He had thick, dark eyebrows that sometimes gave him a puzzled look. He knew that she was looking at him – she could tell that. She felt that underneath the jocular and sometimes outrageous things he said there was a person who would be difficult to get to know but who would be worth making the effort to know.

'What about this walk along the cliffs then?' she said.

'Yes,' he said, and smiled gratefully. 'Good idea.'

She insisted on going halves with the bill. They walked out into the September sunshine. 'Modestine doesn't like hills,' he said, wheeling his ancient James motorbike into the road.

'Modestine?'

'*Travels with a Donkey*,' he explained. 'Stevenson. Get it?'

'I never read it.'

'I had to. It was a set book for the Dartmouth entrance exam.'

She gathered her tartan skirt between her legs and sat on the pillion seat.

'Arms round my waist please,' he said. 'Much safer.'

'Sounds like a good excuse.'

He grinned. 'Yes, it can be that too if you like.' He kicked the engine into life and they set out, fut-futting along high banked lanes. Going up a steep hill the clutch slipped and the engine raced. 'Paddle!' he shouted, and they helped Modestine along with their feet.

They topped the crest and Torbay came into view. The brakes screamed and Modestine came to a halt.

'All in one piece?' he asked.

'I think so.'

'Come on, then,' he said abruptly, and strode off ahead of her. She ran to catch him up and when she took his hand he looked back at her and smiled in a way she had not seen before, as if suddenly he had stopped being a midshipman and was himself.

They went down a narrow path. He picked a ripe blackberry and put it into her mouth. She hoped she wouldn't be seen with him by anyone from the school. It was silly to feel bad about being older than he was, but she did, she couldn't help it.

There was a warship anchored in the bay. 'What sort is it?' she asked. 'Come on, you should know.'

He scratched his head then peered through imaginary binoculars. 'Battleship. Japanese, I would say. I shall have to get back, the invasion's started.'

'You don't know, do you?'

He lowered his binoculars. 'It's a very boring little minesweeper called *Jewel*.'

They walked along the cliff top. He interlaced his fingers with hers, saying things to her with the pressure of his hand. When they sat down on the turf, he said, 'I like your hair,' and blushed.

'It's all over the place!' she said.

'I know, that's what I like about it.'

She didn't know what to say to him. He took her other hand and they sat face to face. He said, 'You look frightened.'

'Perhaps I am frightened.'

'You don't need to be frightened of me.'

'I'm glad about that, Steve.'

He lifted her hand and kissed it reverently. The wind flattened the sea grasses and the pinks. She looked away from him, out over the Channel.

'You still look frightened. Frightened mouse.'

'Perhaps I'm frightened of me,' she said.

114

He leant forward and kissed her for the first time. 'I feel as though I have been searching for you for years and years and years,' he whispered.

She look a deep breath, in ... out, unaware of the effect the taking of it and the rise and fall of her breasts had upon him. She avoided his eyes and said, 'I'm five years older than you are.'

'So what?'

They waited while a family out walking with a spaniel went by.

'Are you frightened of being seen with me?' he asked. 'Is that it?'

She shook her head.

'What then?'

She said nothing. He kissed her again, or rather, they kissed each other, gently, lovingly.

'What is it?' he asked. 'What is there to be afraid of? Have you some dark family secret or something?'

'Not exactly. You'll probably think I'm very silly. It's – I'm not a C of E, you see.'

He began to laugh. 'Well nor am I for that matter! I don't mind what you are! What difference does that make?'

'It does make a difference, Steve. I'm a P.B. – Plymouth Brethren. My parents are missionaries.'

'Well fine! That's all right!'

'I can't explain why it makes a difference –'

'Don't try!'

She was silent for a while, looking out over the sea. 'If only you knew,' she said.

'Tell me, then.'

She lay back and began talking about her upbringing, her childhood on a mission station in north-west Kenya. He didn't really listen to what she was saying. He propped himself on one elbow beside her, looking down into her hazel-grey eyes, allowing the backs of his fingers to brush lightly over her breast.

She stopped speaking and gently removed his hand. She was trembling and flushed. 'You have no idea what sort of effect that can have, Steve,' she said.

'Well. Don't you think it affects me, too?'

They walked back along the cliff path. 'I've never allowed anyone to do it before,' she explained.

'I've never done it before,' he lied. 'And I don't think I'll ever want to do it to anyone else.'

115

'Come on,' she said. 'I want to run. Blow all this lust away.'

They ran. 'It wasn't lust on my part,' he said.

'I just feel guilty, that's all. I'm old enough to know better. My parents would have a fit if they knew.'

He hugged her. 'Don't let's worry about your parents. Or the Plymouth Brethren. Or the Pope for that matter.'

'Why the Pope? You don't mean –' She stared at him, the answer dawning.

'I'm afraid so. I'm what they call a Holy Roller.'

They met at weekends, wrote love letters and walked along beaches that were deserted now that the summer was over. 'I'm terrified of letting things get out of control,' she said to him one afternoon when they were walking by the Slapton marshes. 'It would be so very easy to start, and so difficult to stop.'

A flock of starlings wheeled, darkening the sky. 'It's all right,' he reassured her. 'I don't want to spoil things either.'

'If only I wasn't so much older.'

'You wouldn't be you if you were younger. You would be somebody else.' He rubbed noses with her. 'I wouldn't be interested.'

In her letters home she told her adoptive parents that she had made friends with 'one of the officers from the college', concealing his age and religion because she knew that they would disapprove and bring pressure to bear on her to end such an unsuitable liaison. She continued to go to the Sunday morning meeting in the Brixham gospel hall, but she knew that she was already separating herself from the Plymouth Brethren.

Steven had suddenly found, through her, a direction and purpose in life. They belonged together – both of them knew it. They repeatedly found themselves voicing what the other had been about to say. 'Sometimes I feel that part of me *is* you,' he told her.

She wouldn't come to the Christmas Ball but he persuaded her to come to the summer one. She arrived in a grey-blue dress that went with her hazel eyes; she was twenty-four and he nineteen. He showed her how to do the Samba and the Charleston, ignoring the amused glances of his term mates, sure that she was the most beautiful, the most graceful and the most genuine person there. Specks of light whirled round and round the quarterdeck; officers and their ladies, midshipmen and their girl friends, cadets and their blind dates waltzed and quickstepped and tangoed.

116

Steven and Catherine paused to eat chicken salad and strawberry trifle. They wandered hand in hand, visiting the lecture rooms that had been turned into sitting out rooms, each decorated in a different style. They visited the Arabian harem, the fisherman's bistro, and the Hawaiian desert island, and then walked away from it all, out into the summer evening.

They stood under the trees and said hullo to the beagles. They looked down at the lights of Dartmouth. She leant her head against his shoulder, frightened again that things were going too far, too fast.

'Only one more term,' she said. 'Will you be sorry to leave?'

'After nearly four years? What do you think?'

They went across the cricket pitches to the sports pavilion and sat on the verandah. He told her about his first term, the initiation ceremonies, the cold baths, the cuts, the doubling and the fear of being withdrawn from training.

'Had you any idea it was going to be like that?' she asked.

'I don't know. Not really.'

She traced a pattern with her finger on the back of his hand. 'Had you any idea even why you were joining?'

He thought of the carefully rehearsed answer he had given at his interview, and laughed. 'It was a sort of mistake,' he said. 'Like me.'

Back in the college, he took her along the main corridor to the chapel. They looked at the roll of honour, which included the names of fourteen-year-old cadets killed at Jutland and Gallipoli. Inside the chapel, they read the inscriptions on the brass memorials. The memories of commanders, lieutenants, midshipmen and cadets were perpetuated here, each with his name engraved in polished brass.

'Here's the latest addition,' he said as they came to a brass plate which read:

In Memoriam
DAVID LAURENCE BRADDLE
CADET, ROYAL NAVY
Lost at sea
June 20th 1956


They decided not to stay for the end of the ball, but instead walked down to Dartmouth together, where Catherine was spending the night at the Raleigh Hotel. She had a front door key, and it would have been possible for him to go up with her to her room, but they agreed that it might spoil the evening for both of them if he did.

They stood at the water's edge by the pontoon where the Kingswear ferry berthed and looked down at the calm, black water; she thanked him for the evening and he thanked her for sharing it with him, for being the person she was. He was unable to say 'I love you,' but he felt that she understood all the same; when they kissed for the last time before she went inside, she whispered 'God bless you,' and the mutual acknowledgement of the existence of God seemed to bind them together in a much surer way.

It was a long walk back. He arrived in his cabin after two o'clock, when Courtenay was preparing for bed.

'Did you get a bit?' Courtenay asked.

Jannaway threw his cap on the windowsill and stretched out on his bunk. 'No comment.'

'Big love job is it?'

'Maybe.'

'I saw you,' Courtenay said. 'Creeping off into the moonlight.' He turned back to the washbasin and rinsed soap off his face. He had been selected as the Divisional Captain for the following term, which was their last. He towelled his face dry and looked across at Jannaway, who had folded his hands on his chest and closed his eyes.

'You know what'll happen, don't you? She'll grab you by the lower band, drag you to the altar and have your balls locked up with the housekeeping before you can say shag a rat. I'd watch out if I were you.'

Mrs Jannaway and Alan came down for Steven's passing out parade the following term. They arrived by train on a cold, clear December afternoon, leaving their luggage in the Queen's Hotel before meeting Steven for tea in the Butterwalk restaurant.

They sat by the latticed window under oak beams, and Mrs Jannaway cut up Alan's toast for him. This was the first time she had visited Dartmouth and she was ill at ease. 'Well,' she said. 'What's the programme for tomorrow, Steven?'

He explained in his lazily confident way: 'We all shamble on to the parade ground, and when everyone's had a good shout and some old buffer of an admiral's inspected us, we're given a pep talk. Then

118

they present the goodies – the Queen's sword and the telescopes – then after a bit more shouting the Royal Marine band plays "Hearts of Oak" and we all shamble off again. After that, you're invited to tea and stickies in the Captain's house.'

Alan laughed. 'Tea and stickies!'

Mrs Jannaway smoothed the jacket of her blue suit and looked across the restaurant at another family that was having tea. She wondered what her husband would have thought of all this. Would he have been proud? She didn't know. It was fifteen years since that naval commander had called at her door: fifteen long, battling years on the edge of hardship, never quite having enough. And here was Steven talking about 'tea and stickies' with a captain.

'Is Alan included?' she asked.

'Of course,' Jannaway said, wondering whether the captain's secretary knew about Alan and unsure whether he had been invited. It was something he would have to check.

After tea they walked together through the town, and as they came out of Christopher Milne's shop, met Tomkins with his grandmother.

Tomkins was anxious to talk. 'Shag!' he said, ignoring Mrs Jannaway and Alan. 'Have you heard? Tim Whettingsteel's jagging his hand in!'

'What do you mean?'

'Just that! I went into his cabin this morning and he was packing his trunk. He's not even staying for tomorrow!'

Jannaway was aware of his mother and brother listening to the conversation intently.

'Has he been chucked out?'

Chas Tomkins shook his head. 'His father's buying him out. I asked him why, but he wouldn't say. He went all aloof and said I wouldn't understand even if he explained.'

Tomkins went off down the street with his grandmother. 'What was all that about?' Mrs Jannaway asked.

'One of my term. It sounds as though he's leaving the navy.' He saw Alan looking at him, and deliberately made light of it. 'Oh well. Improves the chances of promotion, I suppose.'

He had booked a table at the Royal Castle for dinner. They had a glass of sherry in the cocktail bar before the meal and took their seats at a corner table. 'I say!' Dora Jannaway remarked when the waiter brought the menus. 'Nothing but the best, what?'

Alan managed very well. He chose ragoût of beef, and Steven saw his knuckles whiten as he fought to control the fork in his hand. Mrs Jannaway kept up a rather false conversation, telling Steven about what was going on in Chestnut Road. Mr Groves had recently died, and Hetty Ringrose was training as a physiotherapist. There were new people in the house next door with twins eight months old. This flow of useless information began to peter out when the coffee arrived, so she asked Steven where he had bought his new tweed suit. It was a Gieves one, he explained. He had opened an account with them. 'Catherine helped me choose the material,' he added.

'Catherine,' Alan said. 'That's your music mistress!'

'Well not exactly!' Steven took out his wallet and produced a photograph of Catherine he had taken at the beginning of the term. She was standing by the sea, looking back at the camera over her shoulder. 'There she is,' he said, and passed the snap across the table.

Alan studied it closely.

'Well? What do you think?'

He made a noise in the back of his throat. 'She – looks – lovely,' he said with difficulty, and turned to his mother. 'Doesn't she Mum?'

Mrs Jannaway took a cursory glance at the photograph and handed it back to Steven. 'Very nice,' she said, and there was in her eyes a burning ferocity that Steven had seen once or twice before.

'What about you?' Steven said. 'What about this writing?'

They had returned to the Queen's Hotel and Alan had insisted on buying him a late night brandy after their mother had gone up to bed.

Alan laughed. 'I can use a pad without lines.'

'I didn't mean that, you know I didn't.'

Alan shrugged. 'I keep trying.'

'Are you pleased with anything?'

'You can't be pleased with anything you've written yourself,' Alan said. 'Only relieved.'

'Well have you submitted anything?'

Alan shook his head. 'Nothing worth submitting. If I could get you to put down a bit more about the navy I might be able to scrabble something together. But four letters in four years . . .'

'The spirit is willing but the flesh is weak.'

'I know the feeling!'

Steven looked at his watch. 'Time I made a move.'

'I'll come up with you,' Alan said.

'You can't! It's an awful slog up that hill!'

'We'll go by taxi. I'll stand the fare.' Alan stood up. 'I'd like to, Steve. I'll enjoy the ride.'

They went out into the street together. It was nearly midnight and Dartmouth was quiet. Steven knew that Alan was doing something more than 'enjoying the ride'. He knew that his brother wanted – for a few brief minutes – to travel up to the college so that he could imagine himself in his brother's place.

On the way there they overtook two midshipmen who were staggering and running up the steep hill to the college, trying to get back before their leave expired.

'Let's give them a lift,' Alan said, and told the driver to stop. The midshipmen tumbled into the back seat, filling the taxi with beery breath.

'My God!' drawled one, gasping for breath. 'Oh my God!'

'Jesus H. Christ!' said his drinking companion, hiccupping and giggling and swaying from side to side.

The taxi reached the top of the hill and went up the ramp that ran round the parade ground, drawing up at the main entrance.

'Cheers dears,' said one of the midshipmen, and the other said, 'Thanks most awfully,' with an exaggerated accent. 'I think I'm going to puke,' said the first, and fumbled with the door handle. 'How does one emerge from this cabriolet?' He pushed at the door and it flung open unexpectedly so that he fell out into the road.

'You goon, McHaggistackle!' said the soberer of the two. 'You bloody spastic!'

The college clock struck eight bells and the drinking companions walked carefully into the college entrance. Steven Jannaway looked back into his brother's face. There was nothing that either could say.

In the morning, the newly promoted sub lieutenants fell in in a squad with their swords. The midshipmen and cadets paraded on either side and the Royal Marine band played selections from the shows as a senior admiral walked up and down the ranks, trailing his sword behind him. Fathers and mothers, sisters, uncles and aunts watched from the ramps, and the officers and lecturers stood in a line wearing their medals. When the inspection was complete the admiral stood on the stone bridge and addressed the passing out term.

'You young officers standing before me now will be joining the fleet at one of the most exciting moments in the history of the Royal Navy. As you know, plans are already well advanced to embark upon a building programme of a new generation of ships and aircraft. Those ships, those aircraft and you young officers will comprise the navy of the future. It will be a navy in which every officer will have to be highly qualified, highly professional and highly dedicated, and I have every confidence that you will preserve and maintain the very best traditions of the service to which it is your good fortune to belong.'

He went on in a similar vein for some while, and when he had finished the parade marched past. Orders were yelled, squads moved to the left and right in threes, and the drumbeat rolled and echoed against the college buildings, rendering it difficult to keep in step.

Afterwards, there was a bit of a rush. Steven went up to his cabin, which commanded almost exactly the same view as had the chestflat in his first term. He changed out of uniform and zipped up his admiralty grip. The college was emptying: taxis were departing and people were saying goodbye. Where do I belong? he wondered, and wished that Catherine had been there that morning.

He went down to the front of the college and was in time to see his mother and Alan come out of the captain's house. Mrs Jannaway was crimson with anger, and Alan was shaking his head.

'What's happened?' he asked them. 'Did something go wrong?'

'My fault,' Alan said.

'No it was *not* your fault,' Mrs Jannaway insisted. 'It was not. I won't have you taking the blame.'

'But what happened?'

Mrs Jannaway had taken Alan's arm. 'I don't want to discuss it,' she said.

'I made the captain's wife spill her sherry,' Alan said. 'When we shook hands.'

'She shouldn't've been holding her sherry and the glass was too full, silly woman,' Mrs Jannaway said. 'No, don't worry about us,' she told Steven when Courtenay and Ainslie came up. 'You go and say goodbye to your friends.'

122

## 8

'To Sub Lieutenant S.J. Jannaway R.N. The Lords Commissioners of the Admiralty hereby appoint you Acting Sub Lieutenant R.N. to Her Majesty's Ship *Syston* addl. and direct you to repair on board that Ship at Port Edgar on 12th January 1958. Your appointment is to take effect from that date. You are to acknowledge the receipt of this appointment *forthwith*, addressing your letter to the Commanding Officer, H.M.S. *Syston*, taking care to furnish your address. By Command of their Lordships, J.G. LANG.'

It had arrived shortly before Christmas. On his appointment preference form, he had asked for a ship on home sea service in order to see something of Catherine, and had expected to be sent to a ship based at Plymouth, Portsmouth or Chatham; instead, he had been appointed to a coastal minesweeper on Fishery Protection duties, based in Scotland.

It was a bitterly cold afternoon when he walked along the Port Edgar jetty towards his new ship, and a north-easterly gale was blowing under the Forth Bridge, making the waves look as though they were falling over each other in a desperate attempt to get away from the sea.

HMS *Syston* looked as if she had been designed as a child's toy: a single Bofors gun was mounted before the bridge and a twin Oerlikon abaft the upright funnel. The sweep deck was dominated by the large drums which carried the wire and magnetic sweeps, and on either side of the bridge were stowed secret devices for sweeping acoustic mines.

Steven knew what was supposed to happen when he arrived on board. According to the briefing he had received a few days before leaving Dartmouth, he was supposed to approach the officer of the watch, raise his trilby hat and say, 'Sub Lieutenant Jannaway come aboard to join, sir.'

His actual arrival was somewhat different. He had resisted all coercion to buy a trilby and arrived hatless and windswept in a Burberry raincoat and weighed down with an admiralty grip and a

Revelation suitcase. Nor was there any officer of the watch: instead, a large able seaman was warming his hands on a mug of tea.

He walked down the narrow brow, deposited his luggage on the wooden deck and saluted in the new manner recently introduced by Lord Louis, who had insisted that it made no difference whether the person saluting wore a hat or not.

'I'm the new sub lieutenant,' he said.

The able seaman had the grace to put down his mug of tea on an ammunition locker. 'Oh aye, sir? You'd best see the Jimmy. He's in the wardroom.'

He went aft and carried his luggage down a steep accommodation ladder to the sweep deck, entering the superstructure via a watertight door. Inside, there was a small passage with doors to cabins and the wardroom.

A curtain was pulled across the wardroom doorway, over which a notice announced THE SYSTON ARMS. From inside came the sound of laughter. Jannaway knocked on the lintel and looked in. Two lieutenants and two sub lieutenants were having tea. They were crammed round a small table in a room not much bigger than a railway compartment.

'Yes?' said one of the lieutenants, a man approaching thirty who was going prematurely bald.

'I'm Jannaway, sir.'

'How do you do,' said the lieutenant. 'I'm Lyle.'

There was a shout of laughter from the others. The other lieutenant, who had a deathly white complexion and a large mole on his cheek said, 'What do you want, laddie?'

'Come aboard to join,' Jannaway said.

'I see,' said Lyle and looked at the mole-face. 'Are we expecting a new sub lieutenant, Number One?'

'I believe we are, sir,' said his first lieutenant.

'What happened to the last one? Have we lost him?'

There was more laughter. Lyle, who had a face that looked as if it had been scrubbed with a wire brush, remained completely deadpan.

'Would you care for some tea?'

'Thank you, sir.'

'In that case be so kind as to hang your raincoat up before you come into the wardroom, thank you.'

Jannaway hung up his coat and entered.

'First Lieutenant?' said Lyle.

'Sir?'

'Introductions.'

'Aye aye, sir.' The mole-face turned to Jannaway. 'Lieutenant Lyle, the captain. My name's Gundry. Willie Johnson, who tries to navigate from time to time –'

'Objection!' interrupted Johnson.

'Overruled!' said Lyle.

'And Julian Devonald –'

'Our sleeping partner and chief purveyor of duff gen,' put in Johnson.

The sub lieutenants put down their hot buttered toast and shook hands.

'That's where you sit,' Devonald said. 'In the corner.'

'If you want some toast, there's a toaster in the pantry,' said Lyle. 'Do you want some toast?'

'Well – perhaps –'

Gundry took the lid off the teapot. 'There's no tea left either.'

'I don't mind,' said Jannaway.

'I do,' said Devonald.

'Can you make tea?' asked Johnson.

'What do we call you?' asked Gundry.

'Steven, sir. Or Steve.'

'Well even Steven,' said Lyle. 'You don't have to be crazy in this wardroom, but it helps.'

The others laughed at this as if it were a sparkling piece of wit and Jannaway thought it might be politic to join in, so he did.

'Right, okay,' said Gundry when the ensign had been hoisted at eight o'clock the following morning. His face had a puffy look and his hand shook when he put his fingers to his aching brow. 'Okay,' he said again. 'You'll be the assistant gunnery officer, the assistant wine and mineral caterer, the assistant tobacco caterer, the assistant sweep deck officer and the assistant divisional officer for the stokers and miscellaneous. Okay?'

Jannaway nodded. 'Yes, sir, I think so. Er – who will I be assisting?'

'Me,' said Gundry, 'but you'll be doing all the work, never fear.'

A wizened leading seamen called both watches to attention and reported them. 'Both watches of the 'ands mustered and correct, sir.'

Gundry rubbed his hands together and said, 'Thank you, Buffer, what do we want to do today?'

'I'll need the 'ands to check the loop, sir. We've got the BLO coming at nine.'

'All right, Buffer, carry on.'

'Sir.'

Gundry turned to Jannaway. 'Buffer's a bit of a rough diamond but he's jolly good value really. Okay. Better go and muster the booze, I suppose.'

He led the way down to the wine store, which was right aft by the tiller flat and they spent an hour mustering the considerable stocks of wardroom duty free liquor, minerals and tobacco. Jannaway had received no training at all in catering while at Dartmouth, but was informed that he would have to learn quickly. 'If you run out of Gordons Father will have your balls for bangles,' Gundry said. 'And if you run out of brandy or ginger ale I shall personally crucify you.'

In the afternoon, he was shown his division's service certificates and personal papers. His division consisted of two stokers, two electrical mechanics and a steward.

'Father wants Larkin to pass for leading steward next time round. All he needs is the educational test, but he can't pass, so you'll have to fix it.'

'How do I do that?'

Gundry snorted and touched the mole on his cheek with his finger. 'How do you think laddie? By making sure he gets the answers right on the exam paper, that's how.'

He was next seen by Lyle, who had the inevitable photograph of his debby wife in a frame on his desk. 'We're all learning in these ships,' he said. 'Even I am. Just make sure you learn quickly.'

Jannaway did as he was told. Within weeks of joining it dawned upon him that HMS *Syston*'s organisation was founded upon the ability of the officers to bend the rules and get away with it. He learnt that there was no point in trying to keep a faithful record of alcohol consumption in the wardroom because the officers refused to use bar chits and drew pictures on the slate. He learnt that no minesweeper tobacco caterer actually issued tobacco coupons to the ship's company because they were swapped, sold on the black market or lost. He learnt that it was impossible to get quartermasters and officers of the day to record the magazine temperatures or the times of issue of keys in the magazine log and that all such records were better compiled at the end of the month, when consumption could be recorded to fit in with the stocks remaining and inspired guesses made as to the wet and dry bulb readings in the for'd magazine and signatures collected for the issue and return of keys and the completion of inspections in accordance with the Naval Magazine and Explosive Regulations.

He learnt, in short, that this coastal minesweeper, this microcosm of the Royal Navy lived a double life: the official life, which was reflected in the fudged accounts and carefully worded reports of proceedings which were forwarded over the captain's signature to the Captain of the Fishery Protection Squadron, and another life, which went unrecorded.

This other life was one of lunch and late night drinking sessions, and parties that went on into the early hours of the morning. It included incidents and near shaves that so nearly but never quite landed the captain and his officers in what they called the kakky. Some of the incidents were hilarious, some were fraught with rancour and accusation, and others were thoroughly dangerous.

He slipped quite quickly into the routine of falsifying the records and returns, taking a certain pride in the creativity of his magazine temperatures and the skill with which the wine accounts were made to look as though they had been written up every day. At the end of each month he used the left-over tobacco coupons to purchase cigarettes up to the maximum allowance for the ship's company: in this way the wardroom was never short of extra cigarettes to offer at cocktail parties or to use as payment for services rendered. Only one month did this arrangement go wrong, and that was when Jannaway inadvertently destroyed a sheet of coupons; to cover up this error, it was necessary to perform a cunning piece of embezzlement devised by Lyle which could only have been found out if the customs authorities, the tobacco suppliers and the auditing officer from the shore base had compared their records.

He found that it was necessary to be aware of three sets of rules: first the official rules, the Queen's Regulations and Admiralty Instructions, the Admiralty Fleet Orders and the Fishery Protection Orders, the Home Fleet Orders and the welter of other orders produced by almost every staff officer above the rank of lieutenant commander; secondly the unwritten rules concerning which of the official rules could be broken; and thirdly – perhaps most importantly of all – a completely different set of rules, written or unwritten, that must never, on any account be broken. These included never referring publicly to any of the captain's several affairs which took place in the various ports of call up and down the coasts of Great Britain; never hesitating to call the captain at night – even if the ship you thought was on fire turned out to be the moon rising; never running out of gin and tonic or horse's neck; never admitting to a visitor that the captain was on board until you had confirmed with him that he was, and never disturbing the captain on a Sunday afternoon – even if one of the able seamen had suffered a heart attack on the football field.

Provided he stepped carefully through this minefield of rules, remembered to salute the first lieutenant in the morning before Colours, avoided being in the bathroom when the captain wanted a shower and continued to laugh when the captain gave them all the benefit of his considerable wit, Jannaway found that life was quite bearable.

After a few months, driven out by the smell of the first lieutenant's feet, he went to sleep in the charthouse; he struck up a friendship with Julian Devonald and later took over the running of the ship's office from him. More months went by: he became the navigating officer, bribed the dockyard chart depot with five hundred cigarettes to bring his chart corrections up to date and as a result was complimented by the squadron navigator on the efficiency of his department. As a result, Lyle forgave him when he put the ship aground at her berth in the Scilly Isles, broke the log while going to a buoy at Chatham and arrived one hour late at Bergen through forgetting to change time zones. No official report was made when the new acting sub lieutenant cycled into the docks at Milford Haven on the ship's bicycle, for on return to Rosyth another bicycle was 'found' and HMS *Syston*'s number quickly painted in.

He was the senior sub lieutenant by the time he left the ship. He called the first lieutenant by his first name and, like his predecessor, became extremely angry if the junior sub used a hard pencil on his charts. The once pristine gold ring on his arm became frayed and curled, and the silver thread on his cap badge earned itself a little coating of verdigris from the salt spray. In the evenings, sipping his horse's necks, he joined in the games of liar dice with the captain and the first lieutenant, becoming every bit as excited as they at the loss of a matchstick.

To Catherine, he tried to remain faithful. There were little incidents of unfaithfulness – no one could help that in the navy – little adventures with the daughters of trawler skippers, mayors or local businessmen in the ports of Fleetwood, Milford Haven, Cobh or Lerwick where the ship called from time to time. 'A little bit of a grope' was how such activities were usually referred to, and any red blooded sub lieutenant with a willing woman and the use of the chartroom could hardly forego such opportunities.

Lyle put his views on the ethical side of adultery one evening when they were playing liar dice. 'I look at it this way,' he said, his eyes de-focussing as a result of several whiskies. 'The average woman is like porridge at breakfast. You don't really like it, but it fills a gap. It's only when you go home to your ever loving one and only that you get your double eggs and bacon, grilled mushrooms and – and –'

'Hot tomato,' Jannaway suggested, and was rewarded by his commanding officer's laugh.

He was now, in the spring of 1959, just twenty-one. He was half an inch under six foot, a pound under eleven stone and a year away from promotion to lieutenant. He was also the officer of the afternoon watch, and sat in the captain's chair on the bridge of HMS *Syston*, looking out over an empty horizon.

The ship was returning to Port Edgar at the end of the spring patrol, which had taken them south down the coast to Ramsgate, across the channel to Den Helder and back via Boston in Lincolnshire. They had avoided collision, grounding and mutiny, and the married men had avoided petitions for divorce. It had been a successful three months in other ways, too: they had arrested a French trawler for fishing within the three mile limit, won a football match against their chummy ship *Wigton* and, during a NATO exercise, had succeeded in sweeping a dummy mine.

He stretched his shoulders and nursed his hangover. The first lieutenant had given a general make-and-mend, and most of the officers and ship's company were asleep.

The night before had been quite a party. Some of the nurses from the local hospital had come on board and there had been smooching to records in the wardroom. The captain had befriended the wife of an RAF officer who had been night flying and she had been persuaded in the early hours of the morning to submit herself for the perfect woman test.

Tony Lyle set great store by the distance between a woman's nipples, believing that the ideal measurement should be nine inches and that perfection was reached if each nipple was also a similar distance from the top of the sternum. It was a rare event for a lady to allow herself to be measured, and this one had been considered sporting to go along with it. 'No, let them hang loose my dear,' Lyle had said, holding up the ruler. 'You must be completely un-bowsed,' and when the measurement had turned out to be a little on the large side he had informed her, to the delight of the officers, 'I'm very sorry to say that you are not the perfect woman, my dear. But if you care to step into my cabin I may be able to help you overcome your disappointment.'

The ship lifted over a gentle swell. Down aft, the duty chef emptied a bucket of potato peelings over the stern and seagulls took off from the sea, flying low and fast over the waves to investigate.

Jannaway stepped down from the captain's chair. It was fifteen hundred, time to complete the log. He entered the course, engine revolutions, distance run and log reading, standing at the chart table under a canvas hood.

When he had made the entries, he took Catherine's latest letter from his pocket and still standing under the hood to keep out of the wind, read it over again.

He smiled to himself, hearing her voice and seeing her face in his imagination. She had agreed to come up to Edinburgh for a week-end, and he had a feeling that this time, at long last, she might allow him to make love to her. She hoped he was behaving himself and showing the flag with suitable aplomb. Was he involved in this silly cod war business with Iceland? Or wasn't *Syston* big enough for that?

Suddenly, as he turned from the fourth to the fifth page of Catherine's letter, something made him look up, and he experienced the feeling of a cold hand grasping at his heart. Less than two hundred yards on the starboard bow, a Russian fishing trawler was closing on a collision course.

He leapt to the voice pipe. 'Starboard thirty!' he shouted, and as the rudder went on the ship heeled violently, first to starboard, and then to port. From between decks came the sound of crashing crockery and angry shouts of protest.

Tony Lyle appeared on the bridge when he had altered back to his original course and was looking back at the trawler.

'What the bloody hell are you up to, officer-of-the-watch?'

The trawler was going down the port side, and a figure leant out of the wheel house and shook a fist. Lyle saw the letter on the chart table and picked it up. 'Were you reading this?'

'Yes, sir.'

'You are a cunt of the first order,' Lyle said. 'I'd have you reprimanded and logged if I thought it'd do you any good.'

'Sir.'

'That could have been the end of my career as well as yours, do you realise that?'

'Yes, sir. I apologise, sir.'

'Jesus Christ!' Lyle exclaimed, and tore the letter up. 'What the hell do they teach you people at Dartmouth these days?'

He threw the pieces of letter to leeward: they were caught in the wind, and as they settled on the grey water, more seagulls swooped, wheeling away as they discovered there was nothing to be scavenged.

'Do better, sub lieutenant,' Lyle said, and went back to his cabin to resume his afternoon sleep.

The summer of 1959 was an unusually hot one, and it lasted into the middle of October. In the first week of that month, Peter Lasbury drove from Hampshire to London in his E type Jaguar in order to call on Tony Fitz-Gibbons, the lieutenant commander who was responsible for the appointment of officers in the communications branch.

Visiting your appointer was something of an occasion, and Lasbury believed in dressing appropriately. His charcoal grey suit came from Savile Row, and he wore a stiff, white cut-away collar with a striped blue shirt. His black shoes had toecaps, which proved they were not service issue, and he carried a tightly rolled umbrella with a bamboo handle. A curly-brimmed bowler completed this ideal garb for the ambitious naval officer, and he walked with justifiable self-satisfaction through the courtyard and in through the front door of the admiralty.

Most officers are invited to take a seat in a waiting room before being summoned to interview by their appointer, but Lasbury had arranged things differently. Instead of having to wait nervously while pretending to read *Navy News* or the *Naval Review*, he walked briskly along a polished corridor, knocked at a door and went straight into his appointer's office.

Fitz-Gibbons looked up from a corner desk, a small, mole-like man with thinning black hair and an annoying laugh. On the walls behind his desk were various charts, rogues' galleries and pictures of by-gone warships. In an adjoining office a typewriter clacked furiously and a telephone rang.

After the social preliminaries, Fitz-Gibbons opened Lasbury's personal file and began to look serious. He placed the tips of his white fingers together and leant back in his swivel chair.

'So,' he said. 'What can we do for you, Peter?'

Lasbury had been promoted to lieutenant commander two years before, and had spent those two years as a staff instructor at HMS *Mercury*, the communications school near Petersfield. The appointment had suited him well: he had attended most social and cultural functions of note in the home counties, had added a large number of useful names to his address book, purchased his Jaguar and bought a flat in Chelsea. He had also managed to steer clear of any repetition of the lapse he had experienced with David Braddle. Life was going well for him, and he now intended that it should go even better.

'I shall be in the zone this time next year, Tony, and I don't want to stay in it any longer than I have to.'

Fitz-Gibbons plucked a hair from his right nostril. He had already been in the zone for promotion to commander for nearly five years. 'None of us do, Peter, I can assure you of that.'

Lasbury ignored this hint of bitterness and proceeded. 'I've had a shufti at the pink list,' he said, referring to a confidential document forecasting ship's programmes, 'and I see *Copenhagen*'s commissioning for the Third D.S.'

'That's right.'

'Come on, you miserable old bugger,' Lasbury said lightly. 'Who have you got earmarked to take command?'

Fitz-Gibbons laughed his simpering laugh. 'That would be telling, wouldn't it?'

'It's Johnny Tinnick, isn't it?'

'Is it?'

'You know damn well it is.' Lasbury crossed his legs and lit a cigarette with a Dunhill lighter.

Fitz-Gibbons shook his head. 'How do you do it, Peter? How do you do it?'

Lasbury blew a cloud of smoke and smiled triumphantly. He had

132

met Commander Tinnick in the Royal Yacht Squadron bar during Cowes week, and had caught wind of his appointment to *Copenhagen* then. It was a plum job. *Copenhagen* was one of those ships with a history: several serving admirals had commanded her, and it was a fairly safe bet that Tinnick, who had been promoted to commander at his first shot, was destined for stardom. The Third Destroyer Squadron would be based at Malta, and Lasbury liked Malta. He also knew that as first lieutenant he would stand an excellent chance of early promotion himself.

'Have you any takers for Number One?' he asked.

'Not yet.'

'In that case you needn't disappoint anyone, need you?'

Fitz-Gibbons rose from his desk and crossed to a dark green filing cabinet. He unlocked it and took from the bottom drawer a large bottle of South African sherry and two glasses.

'All right then, *Copenhagen* it is – if I can wangle it – but if I hear a squeak of a complaint out of you after this, I'll ship you straight out to the Gulf in a Loch class frigate.'

That was one of Fitz-Gibbons's little jokes, but for anyone other than Peter Lasbury (whose most recent report actually described him as a brilliant officer) he would have meant it.

Lasbury emerged from the admiralty at a quarter to one, and was just wondering whether to lunch at Whites or take a stroll down to Shepherd's Market when a familiar voice made him turn.

'Lasbury! What the bloody hell are you doing here!'

It was Henry Braddle, in a huntin' shootin' and fishin' tweed suit, veldschoen shoes and a hat that made him look like a red faced, rounded Sherlock Holmes.

'Sir!' Lasbury said, and raised his bowler. 'How very nice to see you.'

'Been to see your appointer, I suppose?'

'That's right, sir.'

'Get any joy out of him?'

'Well as a matter of fact I did, yes, sir.'

Braddle's penetrating blue eyes twinkled with unusual benevolence. 'I'm having a pie and a pint at the Nelson,' he said. 'Will you join me?'

Lasbury accepted with pleasure: neither he nor Braddle saw any connection between David's death and themselves, nor any reason why they should not enjoy each other's company. They walked up Whitehall and across the road to the Nelson, and Lasbury put Braddle into a good mood by asking him about the Sea Slug missile which was to be fitted in the new guided missile destroyers. Braddle, as one of the elder brethren of the gunnery branch, had witnessed some of the firings in Cardigan Bay, and apart from one missile, which failed to lock on and eventually landed somewhere in the Black Mountains, the trial had been an astounding success.

But there was another reason for Braddle's good mood for he had received some excellent news that morning – news that he longed to impart. Eventually, over his second pint of beer, he did so.

'Keep this under your hat, old boy,' he said, munching a slab of veal and ham pie. 'But they're giving me my flag at long last.' He looked hard at Lasbury, whose face lit up at the news of Braddle's long awaited promotion to rear admiral; and in answer to Lasbury's unasked question, Braddle added: 'Malta. Flag Officer Flotillas.'

Lasbury leant back in his chair and reached out a hand, placing it on the bottom of Lettice, who was collecting empty glasses and whose bottom was ideal for placing the hand upon.

'A bottle of Veuve Cliquot if you please,' he said, and when the girl looked blankly back explained: 'Champagne, in a green bottle, with an orange label, in a bucket, full of ice.'

Jannaway had left HMS *Syston* the previous August and had spent four months since then at HMS *Diligence*, a shore establishment on Southampton Water which was responsible for the large fleet of reserve minesweepers that were moored, two by two, under boxwood covers. This was the mothball era of the navy: Duncan Sandys had decreed that Britain's New Navy should be more compact and less reliant upon size or numbers than on quality and professionalism. National service was coming to an end; the last battleship had been placed in reserve and there was already talk of eventually replacing carrier borne aircraft by guided missiles.

During this time, Jannaway bought a 250cc BSA motorbike on which he rode down to Devon for many of his week-ends in order to be with Catherine. He was beginning to know her properly now and a new, deeper affection was growing up between them. They were happiest when alone together, seldom meeting in the company of others, and putting off the day when they would have to meet each other's relations.

It happened, eventually, at the end of that year. Catherine accepted an invitation to stay for a couple of nights with the Jannaways, and Steven met her on the wooden planks of Mill Hill East tube station on a Friday afternoon a week before Christmas.

She was in a grey overcoat with a high collar which set off her hair and the delicate colour of her cheeks. He took her suitcase and they walked down Bittacy Hill and under the viaduct.

'I'll take you the pretty way,' he said, and led her off the road and along the path by the stream. There had been a heavy frost and frozen fog in the night and the trees were still covered in a white tracery. The mud, churned up by children's bicycles, was frozen hard and ice was forming at the edge of a pond by the golf course.

'This is where I used to cycle when I was a lil' boy,' he told her, ducking his head under a low branch as they went single file along the path. 'How was your Oratorio?'

Gainsborough House had sung the Christmas Oratorio with the naval college at the end of term. She ran a few paces to catch him up, and caught his hand. 'Do you know it? Have you ever sung it?'

'Never.'

'Well I'm probably doing Bach an injustice, but I always feel with the Oratorio that it never quite gets to where it's supposed to be going. Do you know what I mean?'

He smiled back at her, his eyes dark with mischief and his face red with cold. 'You didn't manage to snatch any handsome midshipman from his cradle I suppose?'

'I couldn't get one to slam a door on my finger.'

They stopped under a hornbeam.

'You're trembling,' he said. 'Little mouse. What is it?'

She closed her eyes, breathing out. 'Blue funk, probably.'

'They're quite harmless. Mum may be a bit sharp, but you'll like Alan. All you have to do is –'

'What?'

'Just forget he's the way he is. Don't worry about how he speaks. Just listen to what he says. You'll like him, I'm sure you will.'

They went over a bridge and under the chestnut trees that bordered Lovers' Walk. 'There are the allotments,' Steven said, making conversation to put her at her ease. 'We had that one over there. They've knocked the henhouse down now. That's the new tennis pavilion. The old one was blown up by a doodlebug.'

'I think you've told me this before, Steve.'

'It's my heritage, you see. These are my silver spoons.'

They went along a cinder track that ran behind a row of terraced houses. There was a dustbin beside each back gate. He led the way up a narrow garden, past a concrete coal bunker and up four steps to the back door.

'Anyone in?' he called as he entered the kitchen. He saw her standing at the door. 'Come in, come in!' he said.

There was no one in, and yet she felt that the house was crowded with voices and memories. Following him through the kitchen and into the narrow hall was like visiting the set of a play you have read but never seen acted. He carried her suitcase up the stairs and said, 'Come on up.'

She followed him into the small bedroom at the front of the house. There was a bookshelf full of schoolboy novels, a poster of a battleship on the wall above the bed. On the opposite wall was the framed photograph of his father. She looked at it closely.

'You're not like him at all, are you?'

'Not really. Alan is though.'

A door banged downstairs. They jumped apart.

'Anyone in?' called a voice which she knew immediately must be Alan's.

They went downstairs. He was in the hall: he had a bookish look about him, leather patches on the elbows of his jacket, and heavy hornrimmed spectacles. His left hand curled in on itself.

'My brother,' Steven said. 'Alan – Catherine.'

He had a very firm handshake – almost too firm. He said, 'Very pleased to meet you,' as if with difficulty, but she discovered later that everything he said appeared to be said with difficulty.

'Catherine's to have my room,' he said, and when Steven began to say she could have his, added, 'No, I insist.' He heaved himself up the stairs and they followed him. Steven glanced back at her and smiled as Alan led the way into the larger bedroom at the back of the house.

Steven looked round. 'It's been redecorated.'

'I know,' Alan said. 'Mum and I did it.' He turned to Catherine: he had fine, pale brown hair and crows' feet when he smiled. Half of his face, the right side, was unaffected by muscle spasm, and if the left side had been similarly unaffected he would have been unquestionably good looking. 'The top two drawers are empty,' he was saying. 'Bathroom's next door. I expect you'd like to unpack

136

and have a wash, wouldn't you?' He ushered Steven out and she was left on her own.

She paused a moment, looking round at the Whistler reproductions, the shelves of paperbacks and the closed up typewriter on the table under the window. There was also a crucifix hanging by the bed.

She opened her case. On top of her clothes was a plain brown envelope: it contained the first of a series of pamphlets issued by the Catholic Truth Society, and represented for her the beginning of a path which she had known for some time that she would eventually explore.

Dora Jannaway freewheeled down Dollis Road and thought about what she had to do. She had ordered extra milk and the fish pie would have to go into the oven as soon as she got in. Some of Alan's socks needed darning (he had always been heavy on socks) but this girl friend of Steven's was coming to stay and she wasn't sure she wanted to darn socks in front of her.

She braked carefully, aware of the icy patches and turned right into Gordon Road and left into Chestnut Road, dismounting as she reached number fifty-nine and wheeling the bicycle down to the front door.

She heard their voices in the sitting room as she entered the hall. She propped up the bicycle and immediately busied herself with the lighting of the paraffin stove.

Steven came out of the sitting room. 'Mum?' he said.

She was down on her knees, still wearing her coat, lighting the wick with a match. She pushed herself to her feet, wincing at the pain in her knees.

'This is Catherine,' Steven said, and a girl in her twenties who looked far too mature for him came forward.

'I won't shake hands, they're covered in paraffin,' Dora said. 'Pleased to meet you all the same,' she added, and took refuge in the kitchen. Washing her hands at the sink, she hated herself for her abruptness. She knew that many years of keeping discipline in classrooms had soured her, but she also knew that there was nothing she could do about it. She could remember the sort of person she had been once, when Frank had been alive, but saw no way of becoming that person again. She loved Alan above all things, but still tortured herself over her own moment of carelessness; and she resented the fact that Steven had been taken from her by the Royal Navy and turned into the sort of person she instinctively distrusted – a member of the officer class.

She was putting the fish pie in the oven when Steven came to the kitchen door, and a moment later Catherine appeared behind him.

'Is there anything we can do to help, Mum?'

She looked at their faces, side by side. She had been happy like that, once.

'Nothing at all, thank you,' she said. 'It's all been done.'

They had supper in the front room. 'Fish, I'm afraid,' Dora said. 'I hope you don't mind, but it's Friday.'

'It looks lovely,' Catherine said. She had been given the chair nearest the gas fire, and looked flushed.

Mrs Jannaway helped herself last. 'Will you say Grace, Steven?'

'God save the Queen, bless our dinners, make us thankful,' Steven said.

Mrs Jannaway shot an angry look at him. 'Where on earth does that come from?'

Steven grinned. 'Dartmouth. Thought it'd make a change from "F'what we're about to receive".'

Alan changed the subject. 'You teach music,' he said to Catherine.

'That's right. Piano, flute and cello.'

'Steven used to play the piano,' Dora said.

Catherine felt an ankle touch hers under the table. She saw Steven looking at her, and looked quickly down at her plate.

'He was very good,' Dora said, 'but he's never touched it since he went to Dartmouth, have you?'

'Quite a bit before that,' Steven said.

'Mrs Winter said she believed you had perfect pitch.'

'That was a trick,' he said. 'My bicycle bell rang in E flat.'

Alan laughed. 'Now you tell us!'

'I tried to develop it once,' Catherine said. 'I could make a sort of F or F sharp when I breathed in through my front teeth, but it never seemed to work when I wanted it to.'

'Steven got it right every time,' Dora said.

'M-mozart could tell when his fiddle was an eighth of a tone flat,' Alan remarked.

'Lucky old Mozart,' said Steven.

There was a silence.

'You teach too, don't you Mrs Jannaway?'

Dora gave a little laugh. 'After a fashion, yes.'

Catherine removed a large bone from her mouth.

'Yes, I'm afraid you'll have to look out for bones,' Dora said. 'I didn't have as many minutes as I'd have liked this morning.'

They ate in silence for what seemed a very long time. Catherine began to panic inwardly. Please say *something* she thought. Anyone.

'More pie?' Dora asked.

'No – I really did have a lot. It's delicious.'

Steven's plate was heaped with a second helping, which he ate dutifully. 'Catherine's parents live in Kenya,' he said, trying to open up a new vein of conversation.

'So we gathered,' said Dora.

They waited for Steven to finish his second helping, then Dora rose to collect the plates. Catherine helped. She carried the pie dish out, and Dora directed her where to put it. Mrs Jannaway opened a tin of Cape gooseberries with a firm and practised hand and shared them between three plates. 'I'm not having any,' she said. 'There's not enough for four out of one tin.'

After the meal, Dora went out to make a pot of tea. 'How about playing for us?' Alan said. 'That piano could do with a bit of exercise.'

'I don't know about that,' Catherine said. 'I don't usually give performances.'

'Now now,' Steven said. 'Don't let's have any of that shy puritanical stuff.'

Dora came back with the tea tray. 'Catherine's going to play for us,' Alan said. 'Aren't you?'

She felt as if she were at an audition. Steven caught her eye, apologising with his expression for hurting her with that remark about shyness. 'Go on, Mouse,' he said quietly.

'What would you like me to play, then?'

'Anything you like,' Alan said.

Dora began clearing the table. 'Don't worry about me,' she told them. 'I'd rather do it myself.'

Catherine played an arpeggio. 'It's a lovely piano,' she said.

Dora paused at the door. 'I have it tuned once a year, but no one ever plays it.'

'Except this evening,' Alan said.

'Go on, Cath,' Steven said. 'We're all on tenterhooks.'

She flexed her fingers and launched into something she was sure they would recognise: Mozart's 'Rondo Alla Turca'. She had been teaching it to one of her pupils during the previous term, and was well practised. Playing it there in the little front room, with the gas fire flaring behind her, she was aware that she was having an almost electrifying effect upon them: Mrs Jannaway stood at the door with plates in her hands, and Steven and Alan sat at the table behind her. She became engrossed in the delicate mathematics of the melody, and found herself giving a better performance than usual. Pride had something to do with it: she wanted to 'show them', prove that she was more than just another music mistress.

She played the final chord, and turned on the piano stool, feeling that perhaps she had overdone it and should have played a shorter, more modest piece to begin with.

Dora went out to the kitchen without a word. Alan stood up, his face working. He said, 'That was wonderful,' indistinctly, and left the room.

'What's happened?' she asked. 'What have I done?'

'Poor Mouse,' Steven said. 'You couldn't possibly have known.'

'What couldn't I have known?'

He sat down on the piano stool beside her, taking her hand in his. 'Alan had a pianola once, but he could never play it properly. Ages ago, this was. He always wanted to play that piece on it, but it never worked for him. He ended up pushing the pedals with his hand. We got rid of the pianola after that.' He smiled sadly. 'Mum used the money to pay for my piano lessons.'

She looked down at the keys. 'I'm sorry.'

'There's no need to be sorry.'

'Yes there is.'

'Alan isn't angry. Just upset.'

'What about your mother then?'

'Don't worry too much about her.'

'I feel so guilty!'

'Mouse,' he said. 'Don't cry. Please.'

'I feel like a thief.'

He held her face in his hands. 'You're not a thief. You're the most important person in the world to me. I need you. I love you.'

The door opened unexpectedly. 'Oh,' said Dora. 'So sorry. I'll come back later.'

In the morning, Steven received notice from the admiralty of his next appointment. He was directed to join HMS *Copenhagen* in February. Alan brought his old copy of *Jane's Fighting Ships* down from his room and became very enthusiastic on his brother's behalf. HMS *Copenhagen* was a Battle Class Destroyer – a 'real ship' Alan called her – with twin four-point-five inch gun turrets and eight torpedo tubes.

'You're a lucky old toff,' he told Steven when they were sitting at the table after breakfast; and Steven, aware that his mother was watching, looked into Catherine's wonderful eyes and said 'Yes, I know I am.'

## 9

Sleet was falling over Devonport when he arrived at the barracks. He checked in with the hall porter of the officers' mess, put his bags into the room he had been allocated and went along to the ante-room for tea. He was helping himself to toast and peanut butter when Lasbury came up.

'Would you by any chance be Sub Lieutenant Jannaway?'

'That's right, sir.'

'Splendid,' said Lasbury. 'We're all over there by the fire. Come and join us.'

He followed Lasbury over. The officers of HMS *Copenhagen* had commandeered the electric fire, and sat round the bar fender. They all seemed to know each other extremely well.

'Steven, isn't it?' Lasbury said, and introduced him to his fellow officers.

'I gather you were in the fish squadron?' the navigating officer said. He was a small, muscular officer with crinkly hair and a Roman nose. Peter Wingrove. Jannaway was so busy trying to remember names that he had difficulty in listening to what people said.

'That's right. *Syston.*'

'Who was driving?'

'Lieutenant Lyle.'

'Randy Lyle!' Wingrove said. 'My God!'

On the other side of the bar fender a small, Devonian lieutenant with sidewhiskers (up from the lower deck, Jannaway guessed – an 'SD' officer) was arguing with the engineer officer about transport. The ship's company was still living in barracks, and the engine-room department was keeping a different routine from seamen.

'If the buses aren't back alongside the ship by twelve fifteen, my lads go without hot dinners,' the Devonian was saying.

'Balls,' replied the engineer officer. 'That's just balls.'

'It's bloody ridiculous,' stammered the other, his sidewhiskers twitching. 'If my lads get cold dinners with no choice again there's going to be trouble.'

'Children, children,' Lasbury said, and glanced towards the door, where a polished looking commander with thin, sandy hair and a gleaming complexion entered. The argument stopped abruptly and one or two officers stood up.

'Number One,' said Tinnick.

'Sir.'

'Welding sentries.'

'Yes, sir. Fixed. The Chief GI has a rota. It'll be on daily orders tomorrow.'

'Not good enough,' the captain said. 'There's welding going on in my cabin flat now. I've posted the leading steward as a sentry, but he'll have to be relieved.'

'Will fix, sir.'

Commander Tinnick surveyed the faces of his officers. 'Chief,' he said.

'Sir.'

'Evaporator spares.'

'Due tomorrow, sir. Fitted by Friday, with luck.'

Tinnick nodded, then saw Jannaway. 'Who are you?'

'The new sub, sir,' Lasbury said.

Tinnick nodded, as if being briefed by a voice that no one else could hear. He looked at his watch. 'Come and see me in my cabin at five thirty.'

When the captain had moved away to talk to some officers of his own rank and seniority, Lasbury drew Jannaway to one side. 'A word of advice in your shell-like ear,' he said. 'We set very high standards of dress in *Copenhagen*.' He glanced down at Jannaway's tweed jacket and worsted trousers. 'It wouldn't be a bad idea to change into uniform to see the captain. Start off the way you intend to continue. All right?'

He reported to Commander Tinnick's cabin on the dot of five thirty, having showered and changed into his best number fives.

Tinnick was working at his desk, checking the unbound copies of the Captain's Standing Orders which he had drafted personally. His uniform reefer lay on the bed and the picture of a ferocious admiral in white uniform stood on his bedside table.

'So,' he said. 'How do you feel about coming to HMS *Copenhagen*?'

'Very pleased, sir.'

'What did you do in your last ship?'

Jannaway was rather proud of what he had done. 'Just about all the jobs, sir. I started off with the wines and gunnery and ended up as pilot and communications officer.'

'What about watchkeeping?'

'Yes, sir. I've got my ticket. And ocean nav certificate.'

Tinnick nodded briefly, not looking very impressed. He opened the bottom drawer of his desk and took out a thin file marked JANNAWAY. Inside was a single minute sheet on the left and a single letter from the Director of Naval Officer Appointments on the right. He read this letter carefully, nodding to himself while Jannaway waited and tried to read the letter from where he was standing.

'Not married, are you?'

'No, sir.'

'Engaged?'

'No, sir.'

'Good.' Tinnick closed the file. 'What about sport?'

'Swimming, sailing and a bit of rugger, sir. And tennis.'

Tinnick said nothing for a long time. Then he nodded. 'All right,' he said.

Jannaway presumed he was being dismissed, and moved for the door.

'Where are you going?'

'I'm sorry, sir. I thought –' He stopped. Was that a glint of pleasure in Tinnick's eyes? He wasn't sure. Whatever it was, he didn't like it.

'Do you know the ship's programme?'

'Well – roughly, sir –'

'Do you know what your duties will be?'

'It's office boy isn't it, sir?'

'Correspondence officer. Does that please you?'

'It's a challenge, sir.' Jannaway coloured. Tinnick seemed to have cornered him, and appeared to be enjoying his discomfort.

'Very well, Jannaway,' he said, and he managed to make the name sound ridiculous. 'I hope you can rise to that challenge.' He nodded to himself, then, as if surprised that Jannaway were still present, added: 'You can go now.'

He travelled down to the ship at seven forty-five the following morning, jammed into a Utilicon van with the other wardroom officers.

HMS *Copenhagen* was at the bottom of a large dry dock. Swathes of electric cables and air hoses spewed out from her innards like entrails, and her decks were strewn with pieces of machinery. Dockyard mateys were working with pneumatic drills and hammers, and the dock echoed with whines and bangings. A mobile crane sounded its warning hooter and clanked along the dock edge: overhead, seagulls wheeled and cried despairingly.

Jannaway followed the others aboard. Keith Parry, the ship's supply officer, had been briefed by Lasbury to show the newcomer the ship, and he led the way under the port motor cutter davits and in through the screen door.

There was a different kind of chaos between decks. Pipes were being lagged, damage control markings painted and the blue light of a welder flickered in the passage.

'The ship's office,' Parry said, opening the door to a small compartment in the middle of the ship. 'This is your leading writer. Your new boss, Rudd.'

'Not much room,' Jannaway said.

'Even less with two in here, sir,' Rudd said lugubriously, and immediately a pneumatic hammer started up in the next compartment, making further conversation difficult.

'I'll leave you to it!' shouted Parry. 'Don't forget there's a meeting in the wardroom at stand easy!'

Parry left. Jannaway began a shouted conversation with Rudd. 'This my desk?' 'Suppose it'll have to be, sir!' 'How long have you been with the ship?' 'Nearly a month.' 'Got much work on?' 'This lot.' 'What are they?' 'Letters for typing, sir.' 'All these? Who drafted them?'

The hammer stopped. 'The skipper,' Rudd said. 'He likes writing letters.'

'So you're pretty snowed under,' Jannaway said.

'Pretty well, sir. Yes.'

'Anything I can do?'

Leading writer Rudd looked at this fresh faced sub lieutenant and resisted the temptation to tell him to stop asking bloody silly questions. Instead, he said, 'You can take over custody of the railway warrants if you like, sir.'

They set about mustering the warrants, of which there seemed to be a very large number. 'Do we really need all these?' Jannaway asked, and Rudd laughed a little mournfully and said oh yes, they needed them all right.

Steven discovered why soon after. The coxswain, a cheery chief petty officer, popped his head round the door and said, 'Morning Scribes. How are we today? In a good mood?' Then he saw Jannaway. 'I beg your pardon, sir, I didn't see you.' He introduced himself and produced a list of a hundred and twenty names, most of whom required a separate railway warrant for weekend leave.

Jannaway settled down to write them all out, pleased at having something positive to do, and when he went up to the wardroom for stand easy felt that he had made a good start.

Commander Tinnick arrived on board at ten thirty and was met by his first lieutenant, who accompanied him to the wardroom. The officers put down their cups and saucers and extinguished their cigarettes. 'Are we all here, Number One?' Tinnick asked, looking around at the expectant faces of his officers.

'All here, sir, affirmative,' Lasbury said, and Tinnick began.

In crisp, nautical sentences he told them that there were no bad ships' companies, only bad officers, and that he would not hesitate to replace any officer he did not consider worthy of the privilege of serving under him. He told them (quite brazenly, Jannaway thought) that it was his intention to become the First Sea Lord, and that he could not achieve that ambition without their wholehearted support. Twenty-four hours a day, seven days a week, that was all he demanded of them. 'Let us have no back-scratching on the way we did things in the last commission,' he said. 'Let us start out in the way we intend to continue. It's been said before and I'll say it again: a taut ship is a happy ship.' He went on to impress upon them the importance of good divisional work and the overseeing of the welfare of the men. He warned all the seamen officers that he would personally conduct a quiz on the Rule of the Road at Sea the following week, and that the pass mark would be one hundred percent. Then he broke the news that, because of recent delays, it would be necessary to extend the working day by an hour and a half and to grant only short week-end leave that week-end. Having fired this last broadside, the captain withdrew, leaving his officers in some confusion. The engineer officer had granted a large number of long week-ends to his staff as a reward for the extra long hours they had already been working, and Jannaway was aware that all the dates on the railway warrants he had so recently completed would have to be amended. Keith Parry, whose tan from a recent skiing holiday was rapidly fading, realised that the entire transport schedule would have to be reorganised. Peter Lasbury was particularly angered because the captain had taken decisions about the running of the ship without reference to him.

After lunch in the barracks mess, Jannaway was required to attend a session in the MASTU – the mobile anti-submarine training unit. This consisted of two long trailers which contained a mock-up of an ops room, sonar control room and bridge. Anti-submarine attacks could be simulated, and each of the seamen officers was required to demonstrate to the captain that he knew the rudiments of an attack and what to do if torpedoes were detected. Commander Tinnick took the whole business extremely seriously, and when Wingrove made the error of turning the wrong way and placing the ship's wake between itself and the submarine, he let fly, beating him over the head with a rubber sheathed microphone and saying, 'No, no, no, navigating officer. Echo moving left, port wheel. Echo moving right, starboard.'

Standing at the wheel, watching this going on, the coxswain winked at Jannaway and lifted his eyes to the heavens.

The work load increased steadily as the days passed. There never seemed quite enough time to do anything thoroughly. He was the correspondence officer, the sports officer, the assistant NBCD officer, the education officer, the transport officer and the boats officer. He felt like one of those music hall artistes who balance plates on sticks, darting from stick to stick to keep the plates spinning. Why wasn't the eight o'clock transport on time? What has happened to the damage control transfers we ordered? How much longer is it going to take the ship's office to bind and amend and distribute the Captain's Standing Orders? Why have we not completed the complement return? Where is the list of ratings wishing to take the educational test for leading rate?

He took the tray of correspondence to the captain every morning after Colours, and Commander Tinnick took pleasure in catching him out. Whereas in HMS *Syston*, Lyle had trained Jannaway to know the rules and know how to bend them, Tinnick was now bent upon teaching him to obey every written instruction to the letter – even to seek out new instructions to obey, so that the Captain 'D' of the squadron might be amazed at the efficiency of HMS *Copenhagen* and never have cause to send the dreaded hasteners which Jannaway learnt to fear above all else.

At first, his inexperience was edgily tolerated by the captain; after a few weeks, when the ship's company had moved aboard and the ship floated out into the basin, Tinnick's impatience became more marked. At one of his weekly planning meetings, he coined the phrase, 'Let's put a bomb under Jannaway,' which was taken up and quoted on later occasions when the sub lieutenant committed some other peccadillo or forgetfulness.

Gradually, the chaos and noise of the refit subsided, and the decks became less littered with chunks of machinery. The ship had to be painted, the brass polished and the corridors cleaned. The ship's boilers were flashed up and the engines tested. The compass was swung, the log calibrated and the programme of 'Hats and Sats' (harbour acceptance trials and sea acceptance trials) went ahead. The engineer officer fought with the electrical officer, the supply officer fought with the navigating officer and the captain fought with the Admiral Superintendent of the dockyard. The explosives accounting officer was taken away in an ambulance with heart pains, an electrical artificer committed suicide and the Chief Stoker was hospitalised with duodenal ulcers. Meanwhile Peter Lasbury walked about in an invisible cloud of after-shave lotion, charming the able seamen off the messdecks and training Sub Lieutenant Jannaway (whom he liked, because he was young and good-looking) in the ways of the navy.

The ship arrived at Portland for her work up in early March, and for six weeks exercised almost constantly. The Portland staff officers and chief petty officers arrived at seven o'clock each morning and left late at night. The noise and chaos of the refit was now replaced by new noise, and new chaos. Every conceivable role which the ship might be called upon to play was exercised and every possible catastrophe rehearsed. The ship was attacked by frogmen, nerve gas, nuclear fall out and jet aircraft; there was fire in the boiler room, fire in the four-five magazine, fire in the squid handling room. The ship was towed by her sister ship, HMS *Nile*, and took *Nile* in tow. The landing party landed to give aid to a civil power smitten by earthquake and flood, and the boarding party boarded a runaway liner, lining up the hijackers and bringing them aboard *Copenhagen* for questioning by the interrogation officer. At almost any time of day or night the alarm bells would sound: 'Fire, fire, fire! Fire in number two boiler room ...' The voice of the quartermaster would bring fire parties running down the main passage, the fire hoses snaking out, men donning breathing apparatus, the officer of the day trying to take charge, the telephones yodelling in the damage control headquarters and the Portland staff officers standing to one side, observing what was going on and making notes for the report that would be written up and presented, with recommendations, to the captain at the end of the week.

In the middle of all this, Steven Jannaway and his leading writer kept the flow of paperwork on the move, and it was not unusual for Jannaway to appear outside the captain's cabin with a tray full of correspondence towards midnight, when the staff had left and the captain came down from the bridge. This burning of the midnight oil suited Tinnick very well indeed, for he was at his sharpest in the early hours, and ready for the battle of wits which he fought each day with his correspondence officer. It was a battle Jannaway could not win, for if a return was made on time, a letter well typed or suggested action well thought out, Commander Tinnick would listen to his inner voice, nodding his head and saying – eventually – 'Yes. Good. This was Rudd's work I take it?' while if a return was late or a report incorrectly rendered, it was always Jannaway's fault. 'Do better, sub lieutenant,' Tinnick would say, and hand the offending document back.

But there was a greater disappointment for Steven, and this was a particularly keenly felt one. During his time in HMS *Syston*, he had been allowed to handle the ship during officer-of-the-watch manoeuvres and considered that, whatever else he was bad at in the navy, this was his strong point. He held a watchkeeping certificate which stated that he had 'proved himself in all respects competent to take charge of a watch by day or by night', but Commander Tinnick decided that this sub lieutenant was not capable of doing so in HMS *Copenhagen* until he had proved his ability to cope with emergencies like steering gear breakdowns, men overboard or sudden changes in formation at night.

'Man overboard!' he would suddenly announce, and a stuffed dummy would be hurled into the ship's wake.

'Sound five short blasts! Starboard lookout keep the man in sight! Flag oscar close up! Starboard thirty!' Jannaway launched into the routine, turning the destroyer back towards the man, reducing engine revolutions, ordering the seaboat away, dashing to the bridge wing to keep sight of the 'man' and passing engine and wheel orders to the quartermaster.

'Stop both engines! Starboard thirty! Midships!'

'Too late, too late!' Tinnick cried, rubbing his hands together at the prospect of seeing the sub lieutenant getting it wrong again.

'Half astern both engines, revolutions one two zero!'

'Oh no you don't, you're not in your minesweeper now!' Tinnick said, and took over from him, cancelling the last order so that the destroyer surged past the floating dummy.

The engine-room telephone rang and the artificer of the watch enquired if there was an emergency. 'You never told them, did you? You forgot to pipe man overboard! Nought out of ten, sub lieutenant. Not good enough, not good enough at all!'

Each practice produced a worse result. He began forgetting elementary actions and the tension that the captain built into the manoeuvre – which was essentially quite simple – became more of an emergency than the one that was being practised.

Jannaway's case was not an isolated one. The gunnery officer – the one with the sidewhiskers and the tic – was another of the captain's victims. Gunnery shoots became a nightmare for him, the captain demanding to know what the delay was when the guns didn't fire when they were supposed to, shouts and curses issuing from the transmitting station or the mountings, long arguments developing between the technicians and the operators. Sometimes the whole system would rebel against itself: the director would swing smoothly round, but the gun barrels would leap and jerk like mad things. This enraged Commander Tinnick more than anything else: the ordnance engineer officer, the electrical officer and the gunnery officer would be called to a conference in his cabin: they assembled in their white overalls and sat on newspapers to avoid dirtying the chintz. The skill of radar trackers would be called in question and in the middle of it all a signal would arrive from the Flag Officer Sea Training: IT WAS OBSERVED THAT YOU LEFT HARBOUR THIS MORNING WITH A FENDER OVER THE PORT SIDE. DO BETTER.

'I'm bloody pissed off,' Jannaway said one evening in the wardroom when the officers gathered for gin and crisps.

'The sub lieutenant is pissed off,' Wingrove said. 'Why are you pissed off, sub lieutenant?'

'I'm pissed off with being "taut" the whole time.'

'Start off in the way you intend to continue! A taut ship is a happy ship!'

Jannaway dipped a crisp into an egg cup of tomato ketchup. 'No,

150

you got it wrong, that's not what Father said at all. It's a taut *shit* is a happy *shit*.'

Peter Lasbury overheard this remark and smiled, aware that Jannaway had adopted something of his own lazy drawl, and pleased to see that the sub lieutenant was developing his sense of humour.

There was a wardroom cocktail party on the eve of the ship's departure for the Mediterranean. Catherine took the day off from Gainsborough House to attend it and was met by Steven at Plymouth. He took her case and kissed her as if he were already her husband and she reflected that every time they met he seemed to have changed in some way. There was something about this new self-confidence of his that was a little frightening and she suspected that some of it was an act he had picked up from his naval companions; but that was hardly surprising, was it? Perhaps, if she were honest with herself, the truth of the matter was that she wanted him to stay boyish, wanted him to need her as a sort of elder sister. That thought was much more disturbing than the first.

'We seem to spend our lives in hotel rooms, don't we?' she said, brushing her hair firmly and rapidly, seated at a guest house dressing table.

He stood behind her and their faces were reflected in the mirror. 'One of these days I'll carry you over the threshold. We'll have a cottage in 'appy 'ampshire. There'll be honeysuckle and roses round the door and hollyhocks in the garden. I shall call it Mouse Cottage and we'll grow lettuces and peas.'

'You'll be away at sea all the time.'

He went to the window and looked out over Plymouth Sound.

'How is that beastly captain of yours?'

'Beastly.'

She looked across at him standing there, wishing that she could know once and for all whether her attachment to him was real love, the sort of love that would last a lifetime and would grow.

He looked back. 'What are you thinking?'

'I was just hoping that you wouldn't change beyond all recognition by the time I next see you,' she said.

He grinned and came back to her, putting his arms round her from behind so that his chin rested over her shoulder. 'I shall come back the new Jannaway. I'll have a patch over one eye and a wooden leg. I'll sweep you off your feet and we'll get down to some serious breeding.'

He had slipped his hand in over her breasts and was kissing her neck. She suddenly wanted him much more than she had ever wanted him before.

'This time next year . . .' he said.

She looked at herself in the mirror and thought, I shall be twenty-seven. She felt a sort of panic inside her: had she been wasting time on him? Wouldn't it have been better to concentrate her efforts on finding a more suitable mate? And how cold and calculating she could be sometimes, thinking about him like that as if he were a business proposition, when his hand was going back and forth over her breast and sending electric messages that were already turning her to jelly down there . . .

She gently removed his hand.

'What's the matter, don't you like it?'

'I like it too much, Steve. Didn't you know that?'

He stared at her, and she knew that if he had simply taken her to the bed and made love to her, she would have given herself to him.

But he did not: his new-found confidence seemed to have deserted him. He was the shambling mongrel puppy again, the gauche midshipman with an uncontrollable erection.

He frowned. 'We could get engaged if you like. I mean properly. Now.'

She shook her head, smiling sadly. 'It wouldn't be fair on you Steve. You don't want to be tied down now. Not when you're just off to sea.'

'You sound as if you want me to go and sow a few wild oats.'

'Maybe I do.' She took his hands. 'But not too many, all right?'

'Perhaps you ought to, too. I know, why don't you come out to Malta and do the fishing season? You might hook a better catch. Some sleek, glistening lieutenant commander who fights every inch of the line.'

'That would make you the one that got away.'

'No. You never hooked me. I jumped into the boat, you'd have to throw me out.'

She changed into a dress for the evening and they took a taxi into Devonport dockyard where HMS *Copenhagen* lay alongside.

'She's looking clean, isn't she?' Steven said as he led the way up the starboard side, under the whaler davits.

152

'Who is?'

He laughed. 'The ship. Hadn't you noticed? We've had the chaps slogging their guts out to get her looking like this.'

She looked vaguely along the freshly painted green decks. 'I hadn't really thought about it. Yes I suppose she is looking quite smart.'

' "Quite smart"! Don't you realise she's the shiniest ship in the Andrew?'

In the wardroom, she was introduced to Peter Lasbury, who was wearing a black satin tie, his best doeskin uniform and gleaming mess boots. Steven excused himself to go and change.

'So how long have you two known each other?' Lasbury asked her when the Maltese steward had brought her a gin and bitter lemon.

'Oh – ages. It's about four years now.'

He surveyed her with condescending amusement in his Cambridge blue eyes. Other officers were coming into the wardroom. She was the only woman present, having arrived early to give Steven time to put on his uniform.

'Am I allowed to be here?' she asked. 'I'm afraid we came rather early.'

'Better to come early than not to come at all,' Lasbury said, and he seemed to be laughing at her for some reason which she did not understand. 'You're the one that's a teacher, aren't you?'

'That's right. Music.'

Lasbury snapped open a leather cigarette case and offered it. She shook her head, so he took one and lit up. 'Any particular instrument?'

'Piano, cello and flute.'

'I see.' He looked at his Cartier watch, then turned to one side and reached out his hand as if to play a tennis stroke. They were immediately joined by the electrical officer, whose pink face and spiky hair made him look like a schoolboy on a Sunday school outing. 'Bobby Minter,' he said and shook Catherine's hand. 'Will you excuse me?' Lasbury asked. 'Duty calls.'

The electrical officer's cocktail party technique was not as smooth as Lasbury's, but it was just as condescending. 'Where do you spring from?' he asked.

'Kenya.'

'Oh really? What do you do out there for goodness sake?'

'My parents are missionaries.'

153

'Oh,' he said, and his eyes glazed. He handed her on to the new gunnery officer, the old one having been removed from the ship as a result of the disastrous performance of the gunnery system during work-up.

She was glad when Steven rejoined her, but she couldn't help noticing that with the putting on of his best uniform he too had put on a cocktail party manner. 'Right,' he said. 'Sorry I was so long. How's your glass?'

The party got under way. The guests were ushered into the wardroom and the usual drinks were served from the usual silver tray. Trained by the first lieutenant, the officers circulated among the guests to ensure that no one was left unattended for more than a few moments. Catherine heard the same formula several times: 'Hullo, good evening, I'm Tommy Bloggins. How's your glass? I think we met briefly at the commissioning ceremony didn't we? Are you local?'

After a while she was joined by one of the wives, who wore her hair in a band and a naval brooch on her dress. 'Hullo, I'm Jill Parry. That's my other half over there. He's the pusser. We were wondering if you and Steven would like to come out for sups at the United Services Club afterwards? We might even go on to the sailing club for a jump up. Does that sound like a good idea?'

She had hoped to spend the evening alone with Steven, but he seemed enthusiastic about going dancing, so she agreed. They could not depart immediately however, because Keith and Steven were required to remain in the wardroom until the last of the guests had gone. Some of these – the dockyard managers who had been invited to the party as a way of saying thank you for services rendered during the refit – took a very long time to go, and eventually Lasbury told the petty officer steward to close the bar. The officers who were remaining on board loosened their ties and undid their brass buttons, and fried bacon and eggs that had been keeping hot in the officers' galley were served for those who were remaining on board.

Later, after a chicken salad supper at the United Services Club, Keith turned to Steven. 'Are you two fit for the Groin Exchange?' he asked.

'I wish you wouldn't call it that,' Jill said. She turned to Catherine. 'He means the Grain Exchange. It's where the sailing club has a sort of discotheque.'

'I'm on,' Steven said. 'Soft lights and smoochy music. Just the job.'

She sat with him in the back of Parry's Morris Thousand. The car sped downhill into a darker area of the city, close to the civilian docks.

The club was up a narrow flight of stairs in what looked like a sail loft. Filled with swaying couples and cigarette smoke, it was just the sort of place she had not wanted to go to on Steven's last night.

'Come on!' he shouted in her ear. 'Let's do something to this!'

They moved about on the bare wooden boards. He lifted her arms and made her put them round his neck so that she could feel him against her breasts. He pushed his knee in between her legs, and told her to relax. 'People don't care what we do here,' he said.

He had changed again: he was suddenly not Steven at all but just another randy naval officer, so that her delight in being in his arms froze up. Was she just a prude? Should she relax, should she try to behave like all these other clinging couples and indulge in this pseudo-love? No, it was no good. It was hopeless trying to pretend she belonged in this dark, deafening, smoky place.

'Something's wrong,' he said. 'What is it?'

She shook her head. 'I don't know if I can explain.'

'Do you want to go?'

'Can we?'

He nodded. They stopped dancing and went across to say goodbye to the Parrys.

Outside, a fight was going on. They were in time to see a youth take a running kick at another from behind. Blows and obscenities were exchanged.

They walked in silence up the hill. 'You're angry with me aren't you?' he said eventually.

'No, I'm not angry.'

'What is it then?'

'I'm frightened. I'm frightened that you will go away and come back a different person. I'm frightened I'll lose you to the navy.' They stopped. 'Yes, I was angry,' she said. 'I was angry because I love you. I want the best for you. I want to be proud of you.'

They reached the guest house where she was staying. He tiptoed up the stairs behind her and followed her into her room.

'We could,' he said. 'I've got something.'

'If only you knew how much I want to,' she whispered.

155

'Well why don't we?'

'It would be ... just wrong. And not because of using one of those things, either.'

'Why would it be so wrong?'

She spoke with utter assurance: 'When two people make love, they become one flesh. You can't stop it or lessen it. It's a mystical union – a sort of miracle. If we make love now, we shall be one flesh. We would be bound together in a way that nothing can ever change.' She reached up and touched his forehead with her fingers. 'And if it doesn't mean that, if making love doesn't make you as one ... then it isn't worth doing, anyway. It's meaningless.'

He told her, stumblingly, that he loved her and spent his waking hours thinking of her, that he would do anything for her – leave the navy for her if she wanted. 'I've had plenty of time to think about it,' he said. 'You say we would be one flesh. That's what I want. I want to share everything with you.' He smiled sadly. 'I just want to marry you, that's all. Is there anything wrong with that?'

'Wait just a year,' she said. 'Please. I won't run away. Promise.'

For a moment he wondered if he might seize her, force her to make love – wondered if perhaps that was what she subconsciously wanted him to do. He wished he understood her better. What she said always carried so much more weight than his clumsy, fractured sentences.

He said in a barely audible whisper: 'If we didn't make love then?'

'Can I trust you? Can I trust myself?'

He nodded. She whispered, 'All right, then,' and he undid the small velvet buttons that went down her back, letting the dress slip off her shoulders and down to the floor. She stepped out of it, shivering violently, but not from cold. He helped her off with her slip, released her breasts. She pulled back the bedcovers, hesitated, and stepped quickly out of her briefs before getting in and pulling the sheet right up to her chin.

'Come on then if you're coming,' she said. 'I'm cold. I want you to keep me warm.'

He sat on the bed to undress and she watched him, reaching out to take his hand for a moment. They had never done anything like this before; she had never seen him naked.

She lifted the sheet for him and he came in beside her. He whispered 'My darling, my darling,' and for the second time that day she knew that she could not trust herself at all, that she was his for the taking, all of her; but then he seemed to jolt three or four times, letting out a pathetic whimpering cry, and she felt a warm flood on her stomach.

They lay still, and the tears went silently from her eyes. 'All those babies,' she whispered. 'All those wonderful babies.'

'There's a going away present for you in my bag,' she said when he was dressing. She was sitting up with the bedside light on, her hair loose over her shoulders, her breasts white and pink. He handed her the bag, and she took out a slim packet. He wasn't sure what to expect: he thought it might be a cigarette case, and that's what it looked like for a moment when he was unwrapping it. But it wasn't a cigarette case. It was a leather bound New Testament.

She had written 'Catherine to Steven, May 1960' inside the cover, and there was a loose card with a verse on it. 'Read that later,' she said.

'It's smashing,' he said. 'I shall treasure it.'

The sun was rising. He walked quickly back through Devonport dockyard to HMS *Copenhagen*. As he approached the ship and heard the steady hum of its generators and fans he experienced a feeling of drab hatred.

'Good run sir?' the quartermaster asked knowingly as he stepped aboard, and he replied, 'Yes thank you,' and made his way for'd.

He carefully slid open the door to his cabin, which he shared with Wingrove, and having taken off his shoes hoisted himself onto his bunk.

It was impossible to sleep. He took out the New Testament Catherine had given him and looked at the card inside, reading the lines she had written in her neat, educated hand:

I would be true, for there are those that trust me;
I would be pure, for there are those who care;
I would be strong, for there is much to suffer;
I would be brave, for there is much to dare;
I would be friend to all – the foe, the friendless;
I would be giving, and forget the gift;
I would be humble, for I know my weakness;
I would look up – and laugh, and love, and lift.

When he had read these words, he lay on his back and thought of all that had happened since the moment he first met Catherine at Dartmouth. He thought about his father, about Alan, about his very earliest memories.

There had been a feeling of freedom, of choice, a long time ago. It was as if his life were a path that descended by imperceptible degrees into a cutting. He felt that he was becoming trapped at the bottom of this cutting, knowing full well that there was another sort of life, beyond the high banks on either side, but that it was impractical to try to climb up the banks to reach it.

The ship sailed at nine o'clock. The officers and ratings fell in for leaving harbour, and HMS *Copenhagen* exchanged salutes with other ships as she steamed down the winding Hamoaze and out past the breakwater.

Standing on the port side with his division, Steven Jannaway looked in vain for Catherine, who had promised to be waving from Plymouth Hoe: she was there, he was sure she must be there, but he could not see her.

There were plenty of others waving goodbye. Wives and parents, sweethearts, lovers and relations waved and cheered and screamed farewell as the destroyer turned the last corner and headed out towards the open sea. A puff of dark smoke came from the funnel as the propeller revolutions were increased; the sea bubbled and foamed under the stern, and the land diminished and slipped away beneath the horizon.

# 10

Peter Lasbury was pleased to be back in Malta. There was something about that barren island that never failed to heighten his self-esteem, in the same way as a landlord's sense of his own importance is enlarged by a visit to one of his properties.

There were a lot of old acquaintances to renew, and he began renewing them from the moment he stepped off the accommodation ladder into Salvo Borg's newly painted dghaisa.

'O Signore! Meester Lasbury sair!' Borg croaked, touching his cloth cap with one hand and holding the high prow of the dghaisa alongside with the other. 'What a pleasure to see you again, sir!'

Lasbury sat in the stern sheets and Borg propelled the boat across Sliema Creek. 'So how's the world treating you, Salvo?' Lasbury asked.

The old man rested on his oars, and while the dghaisa drifted on towards the landing stage he proceeded to tell a tale of woe: with the cut-backs in the fleet, fewer warships were visiting Malta and the dghaisamen were going out of business. His son Jo wanted to take over from him but there was hardly a living to be gained any more. 'You know what I have to tell him, sair? I have to tell him is better go and find work in a bar. No, sair, is no good these days, no good at all.'

Stepping ashore, Lasbury pressed a florin – four times the going rate – into Borg's gnarled hand and the old dghaisaman raised his cap and called, 'Thank you, sir! Thank you very much!' before manoeuvring the dghaisa back among the other dghaisas and settling down to sleep, his cap tipped down over his face to protect him from the blistering heat of the sun.

Lasbury's first call after landing at Sliema was on his tailor, a diminutive man called Mamo who worked eighteen hours a day in a cluttered room that gave onto the pavement of Old Mint Street, in Valletta. Mr Mamo had once been a cutter for Gieves, but had started up on his own some years before, and his order book now contained as many famous names as the visitor's book of the Commander-in-Chief. Peter Lasbury was made even more welcome by Mr Mamo than by Salvo Borg, and the tailor was gratified to take his measurements for a lightweight suit. 'So how long will you be in Malta, sair?' Mamo asked, passing the tape-measure round Lasbury's waist.

'A month or two yet, but we'll be in and out,' Lasbury said, aware of the importance of keeping the ship's programme confidential.

'Thirty-six, sair,' Mamo said. 'You have put an inch on the waist since you come to me last time.' Mamo knelt before him and measured his inside leg, muttering the measurement and noting it in his order book. 'Now how you like it, sir? Double breasted this time perhaps?'

'No, single breasted and a single slit up the back, if you would.'

'Hand stitching on the lapels, sir?'

'Of course. Four buttons on the cuff, no flaps on the pockets.'

'Very good sair.'

'First fitting by the end of the week?'

Mr Mamo wrung his hands apologetically. 'Oh sair. I have big order to do for Admiral Peebles, sair. Can you give me till Monday?'

'Without fail?'

'Without fail, sir. Monday evening, will be ready for first fitting.'

Lasbury walked down Old Mint Street and on to Straight Street, known in the navy as The Gut. He called in on Mr Zammitt the tattooist and drank a glass of beer with him for old time's sake before going on to sign the Governor-General's book. From there, he took a taxi to the Marsa club where he was meeting Paddy Railton, the captain of HMS *Zeus*, for lunch.

The club was quiet for a Saturday. In the old days the cricket and polo pitches would have been in use, but now they were deserted. He was on his way into the clubhouse when he heard his name called, however, and turning saw Julietta Braddle.

She almost ran to him, and before he knew what was happening she had planted a succulent kiss on his cheek.

She gazed up at him with her big fawn eyes.

'How super to see you, Peter! You're in *Copenhagen*, aren't you – Daddy's old ship? I saw you backing into Sliema this morning.'

At nineteen, she was still absurdly young for her age, and he had forgotten how like David she was. He had not seen her for over six years, but he had replied to one or two of her letters. She bubbled over with her pleasure at seeing him, looking up at him from under her eyebrows, twiddling a tennis racquet in her hands and shifting the weight of her suntanned body from foot to foot. 'Oh,' she said as another girl approached. 'Sorry. This is Penny Forden-Jones. She's staying with us for a bit. You only came out the day before yesterday didn't you?' She took in a deep breath so that her little breasts tautened the material of her tennis dress. 'It's really *super* to see you, Peter! I say – have you been invited for Sunday?'

'Not to my knowledge –'

She hardly gave him time to reply. 'Daddy's taking the barge out. Will you come?'

Lasbury bowed gratefully and rolled a pebble under his shoe like a sleek stallion pawing the ground. 'Well thank you kindly, Julietta. I'd love to.'

'I'll tell Flags then,' she said. Then another idea occurred to her. 'Are you having lunch here? Would you like to join us?'

'That's awfully kind of you, but I'm meeting someone,' he said.

'Well see you on Sunday then, if not before.'

'Yes indeed. Super.'

The girls returned to their table under the trees and Lasbury went on into the bar, where he was met by Paddy Railton, an officer almost as smooth as himself.

'Who was that little beauty you were talking to, Peter?' he asked.

'That was Julietta Braddle.'

'Henry's daughter?'

'That's right.'

'My God!' Railton said. 'Quite the little stunner, isn't she?'


'Isn't he gorgeous?' Julietta said. 'I haven't seen him for aeons. He used to come to the house when we were in Hampshire. Sarah was nearly engaged to him once but he dropped her. Oh – bugger,' she added. 'Have you got a ciggy? I'm out.'

Penny produced a pack of cigarettes. Julietta sighed suddenly. Meeting Peter again had started up all sorts of feelings. It was marvellous he was out in Malta. Just marvellous. They would have barge picnics and cocktail parties and midnight swims and silly suppers with lots of friends in that little place on the shore at Marsaxxlok. 'Don't you think he's got the most wonderful shall-we-dance eyes?' she said, and giggled suddenly, squeezing her thighs tightly together in excitement. 'I wonder if he's got a flat yet? I bet he'll be getting one.'

161

Penny Forden-Jones hardly listened, for she had already fallen in love with Henry Braddle's flag lieutenant, Charles Crivett-Smith, and had ambitions of her own. So she sat and sipped her fresh lime juice while Julietta prattled on and a caged canary sang under the trees and a starving bitch stole chicken bones from the rubbish bins at the back of the clubhouse.

In spite of Julietta's invitation to Lasbury, they had not planned to have lunch at the club, so when they had finished their drinks Julietta drove back through Valletta to the admiral's residence, which overlooked Sliema Creek.

'Charles!' she called as they entered the tiled coolness of the house, and the flag lieutenant appeared.

'Hello Julie, hello Penny. Good game?'

'Charles I've asked Peter Lasbury for the picnic on Sunday. I said we'd collect him from *Copenhagen* on the way.'

The flag lieutenant's face fell. 'But I've just invited the captain and one from *Copenhagen*.' He went into the hall and came back with the social diary. 'Here we are. Commander Tinnick and Lieutenant Jannaway.'

'Who's he? Do we know him?'

'No, but I gather from Peter Wingrove that he's a good guy, and your mother thought you might like –'

'Blow what Mummy says!' Julietta looked over Crivett-Smith's shoulder at the diary. 'Delete Jannaway, insert Lasbury,' she said, and giggled suddenly.

Crivett-Smith looked doubtful. 'Are you sure?'

'Quite sure. Mummy positively dotes on Peter, she'd much rather have him than Janner-whatever-his-name-is.'

'She invited him for you, not herself.'

'Well I want to invite Peter Lasbury.'

'If you say so, I suppose –'

She had already gone down the hall and into the big tiled kitchen, where a Maltese steward was stoning prunes for the evening cocktail party. 'I do say so!' she called back, and the bottles of tonic water, ginger ale and lemonade jingled as she opened the refrigerator door.

'Anyone for a Pimms before lunch?' she asked.

Steven Jannaway knocked on the captain's door and looked in. 'Barge in sight, sir!' he said, and a moment later Commander Tinnick emerged from his sleeping cabin, wearing khaki shorts and an aertex shirt. Jannaway held the curtain aside for him.

162

'Thank you Steven,' Tinnick said. 'Does Number One know?'

'He's manning the skimmer now, sir.'

'Hope the bloody thing'll start,' Tinnick said, and collecting his towel and swimming trunks stepped out into the June sunshine.

The admiral's barge was a sleek, twin-engined, thirty-foot launch, painted a glossy green, with white covers on its seats and sun-bleached fancy rope work on the polished brass handrails that ran along the top of the coach roof. It was normally used by the admiral for making calls upon ships and establishments in Malta, and complicated rules of etiquette governed the type of salute required by the admiral when he passed by. That morning, when Jannaway stood with his commanding officer at the top of the starboard after accommodation ladder, Henry Braddle was proceeding informally, and a white disc with five black crosses on it announced to the ships of the destroyer squadron that the minimum mark of respect – a hand salute – was all that was required.

It approached HMS *Copenhagen* at speed, planing on a white wave that looked like a walrus moustache at its bows. As it neared HMS *Copenhagen*, the Maltese petty officer coxswain took it in a gently curving turn, so that it made the last approach to the accommodation ladder at exactly the right speed and angle for a neat alongside. The engines roared for a moment in astern; the bow and stern men extended their boat hooks, and the barge lay, wallowing slightly in its own wake, exactly positioned beside the platform at the foot of the accommodation ladder.

'My first lieutenant is bringing the skimmer, sir,' Tinnick said, saluting Henry Braddle as he stepped aboard.

Jannaway stood on the top platform and looked down, ready to salute as soon as the barge departed. He had spent most of his forenoon ensuring that the ship was properly squared away for the admiral's brief time alongside, for however informal the occasion, Braddle could always be relied upon to spot a dirty scuttle or an Irish pendant, the signs of a slack ship. Below him were the members of the barge picnic: Rear Admiral Braddle, in voluminous shorts and a flowery shirt, his wife, looking hot in a print dress, the flag lieutenant, the two girls and Commander Tinnick. 'Permission to carry on, sir?' Jannaway asked.

Braddle waved an airy hand and said, 'Yes please!' The petty officer coxswain ordered 'Let go for'd, let go aft,' and with a roar, the barge accelerated away from the ship.

Seconds after the departure of the barge, Peter Lasbury let go the painter of the skimmer, and it too accelerated out of Sliema Creek. Jannaway watched the two boats depart from the fo'c's'le to HMS *Copenhagen*, and when he was satisfied that neither was returning, went into the wardroom and helped himself to a gin and tonic, and going to the corner under the fan settled down to read the Sunday papers, which had recently arrived from the airport.

He sipped his drink appreciatively and opened the *Observer*. It was not often that both the first lieutenant and captain were out of the ship, and for once he didn't have to worry about what he might have forgotten or what he might be doing wrong.

He settled back contentedly. He was not at all disappointed about the cancellation of the invitation to the picnic: he had even volunteered to do the duty of officer-of-the-day so that he could be free for a week-end when the ship visited Piraeus the following month. I shall have a quiet lunch, an afternoon zizz and then I shall write to Mouse, he thought, and found himself smiling at the thought of her.

Peter Lasbury caught up with the barge as it turned to starboard out of the creek and reached the open sea. The skimmer was the faster of the two boats, being capable of nearly twenty knots, and he throttled back to keep pace, maintaining station about twenty yards on the admiral's beam.

When the two boats had been proceeding side by side in this way for a few minutes, Lasbury saw the admiral turn and say something to the flag lieutenant. A moment later, Crivett-Smith raised his arms and made a 'J' in semaphore, indicating that he intended to pass a message.

Lasbury raised a hand in acknowledgement and the semaphore began. CLOSE – ME – FOR – TRANSFER he read. He waved to show that he had understood, and edged the skimmer in towards the barge. Henry Braddle, looking sun-pinked and jolly, opened a can of beer and held it out. The skimmer came closer, the beer was transferred, and when Lasbury was out to a safe distance again, he raised the can in a toast to his senior officer.

A few minutes later, the flag lieutenant was making more semaphore. STAND BY FOR OFFICER-OF-THE-WATCH MANOEUVRES, Lasbury read, and laughed as he waved back his acknowledgement. This was typical of Henry Braddle: he couldn't stop being a naval officer even when taking his family and friends for a picnic.

The first signal was made, and as Lasbury read it, he realised that Braddle intended to conduct these manoeuvres by the book. The barge was 'designated guide' and 'distance between ships' was laid down. Sequence numbers (one and two) were allocated and after a brief pause the first order was issued. IMMEDIATE EXECUTE, FORM COLUMN IN ORDER OF SEQUENCE NUMBERS. STAND BY ... EXECUTE. Lasbury laughed aloud and manoeuvred the skimmer rapidly into the new station astern of the barge. Immediately, Crivett-Smith began sending more semaphore: IMMEDIATE EXECUTE, TURN NINETY DEGREES TO PORT. After that, the signals came thick and fast. They did a search turn, reversed column from the rear, a turn of 180 degrees and then a 'corpen one-eight', wheeling 180 degrees back, so that they ended up in the same formation they had started.

The only person who did not enjoy these nautical fun and games was Commander Tinnick, who was terrified that his first lieutenant might make a mistake and let the side down, or that there might be some sort of accident that would put him in a bad light. He sat on the front seat of the barge beside Clara Braddle, clutching his can of beer, a fixed smile on his face, while Henry Braddle, resplendent in a Christopher Robin sun hat, discussed each new manoeuvre with his flag lieutenant as if he were directing fleet manoeuvres from the bridge of a cruiser.

'Daddy!' Julietta said after a particularly tight turn at half standard distance, 'Penny's feeling sick!'

'You'll be all right,' Braddle reassured Penny. 'Just keep your eye on the horizon!' He turned to Crivett-Smith. 'How about a gridiron to finish up with Flags?'

But the gridiron manoeuvre (which had caused the navy's most notorious collision) was never completed, for Penny threw up her breakfast on the immaculate coach roof, and it was decided that officer-of-the-watch manoeuvres were complete.

FLAG ECHO signalled the flag lieutenant. FLAG AND COMMANDING OFFICERS WILL HAVE TIME FOR THE NEXT MEAL. It was the signal sent traditionally at the end of intensive manoeuvres, and indicated to Lasbury that the game was over.

Ten minutes later, the barge dropped anchor in three fathoms of Mediterranean water that was as clear as the gin and tonic in Clara Braddle's glass. The skimmer came alongside, the cold box was opened and lunch began.

Henry Braddle was in a really excellent mood. He crossed his short legs and sipped his Chablis and forked cold swordfish steak and fresh green salad into his mouth, reminiscing to Johnny Tinnick (who listened intently) about a banyan picnic he'd once been on as a midshipman before the war. While this went on, Clara Braddle decided that she couldn't resist another gin and tonic and another helping of potato salad and another chicken leg; Penny Forden-Jones wondered if Charles Crivett-Smith would ever look at her again, and Julietta lay on her flat brown tummy and from time to time glanced lasciviously at Peter Lasbury. In the sternsheets, out of sight, the three Maltese crewmen ate lasagne and watermelon, murmuring to each other in their guttural language and passing unrepeatable remarks about the view they had of the admiral's daughter.

'Right!' Braddle said when the profiteroles had been finished and Clara was licking the cream from her red fingernails. 'Who's for water skiing?'

'Well not me, for a start,' said Clara, who was looking forward to a snooze and a swim and another snooze and another swim, followed by tea.

'I'm game,' Henry said. 'What about you, Johnny?'

'Honestly, Daddy, that's typical,' Julietta said.

'What's typical?'

'Well what about me? What about Penny?'

'You wait your turn, young woman,' Braddle said.

Clara closed her eyes and lay back. 'Age before beauty, dear.'

Lasbury got into the skimmer and prepared to start the engine. 'Are you going mono, sir?' he asked.

'I'll have a crack,' Braddle said, and sat on the gunwale to put on the ski.

'You're mad,' Clara said. 'You shouldn't go in so soon after eating.'

'Balls,' said the admiral, and slipped into the water.

'Charles, give us a hand will you?' Lasbury said, and Crivett-Smith stepped carefully down into the skimmer.

The engine was started and the skimmer went slowly away until the tow line was taut. 'Hit it!' roared the admiral, and a moment later he was carving a feathery wake back and forth across the bay. 'I wish your father had a little more *sense*,' Clara said without opening her eyes. 'He'll have a socking great coronary one of these days, and serve him right.'

After the admiral had had his five minutes' worth, they decided to give Penny a try. Penny had only tried once before, and she didn't really want to try again. Crivett-Smith had been ignoring her and she wasn't so sure she was in love with him after all. But she did try – for nearly ten minutes she tried and tried and tried again until she was finally heaved back aboard the barge, waterlogged and bleary eyed and secretly determined never to don another water ski as long as she lived.

It was Johnny Tinnick's turn after that. He had water skiied before but did not enjoy the sport, having been witness some years before to a fatal accident when a young officer was drawn into the screw of a minesweeper while skiing on a long tow from the sister ship. But water skiing was Henry Braddle's latest fad, and it would not look well to decline. Accordingly, he put on two skis and gave a mediocre demonstration, his knees and back bent, looking like a reluctant monkey on the end of a string.

'Me now!' Julietta called when Tinnick let go the tow rope and sank gratefully into the water alongside the barge.

Julietta weighed eight stone six pounds, and because they were out of sight of a public beach wore a red and white striped bikini. She popped up out of the water like a cork that has been held under. The flag lieutenant, who had taken over the wheel of the skimmer, made figures of eight round the bay and Julietta put on a dazzling performance, accelerating to amazing speed on the outside of the turns, jumping across the wake, letting go with one hand, and leaping right up out of the water.

After several minutes of this, Charles Crivett-Smith began to try to shake her off. He throttled slowly back so that Julietta sank into the water, then opened the throttle so that she popped up again. She went swishing across the wake, passing so close to the barge that a feather of spray soaked her snoozing mother, who leapt up with an angry shriek.

Then Peter Lasbury had an idea. He started hauling Julietta in. He knelt in the stern sheets of the skimmer and hauled the tow rope in, hand over hand, until she was skiing only fifteen or twenty feet from the stern.

Julietta shrieked with delight. Lasbury was wearing brief swimming trunks, which flattered his manly contours; she was face to face with him, separated by foam white water, joined by a nylon line.

When he let go of the tow rope, it looked as though Julietta must

167

fall: she sank deep into the water before the tow rope tautened again; but up she popped once more as the line came taut, and off she went, skittering over the blue-green water, laughing and waving delightedly.

'Pull me in! Pull me in!' she shouted, but her words were drowned by the noise of the skimmer's engine. Lasbury understood however: again she skiied close to the boat, again he let her go and again she popped up out of the water like a submarine-launched missile.

'Once more round and we'll have to stop!' Lasbury shouted to Crivett-Smith, who nodded in reply.

Julietta was waving and signalling to be pulled in again, so Lasbury obliged, heaving the tow line in over the stern and flaking it down between his legs, until she was barely ten feet from the transom, bouncing about like a suntanned aquatic nymphet.

She let out a shriek as he let the tow line go again, balancing on her skis as she slowed down and began to sink into the water. The boat accelerated, and she sank further: for a moment, Lasbury thought she must have let go the tow handle; but then the line went taut and she began to rise up out of the water again.

The line stretched and parted. The boat leapt forward. 'She's down!' Lasbury shouted, and Crivett-Smith took the skimmer in a wide, sweeping turn to head back towards her.

They thought she was laughing at first, but as they approached they realised she was not.

'Oh my God!' Lasbury said. 'Come on, sweetie, give me your hand.'

She made high whimpering noises as he helped her into the boat. She had already taken off the top of her bikini and as they lugged her in over the gunwale, she screamed with pain: the line had whipped back against her, and an angry red weal ran from her midriff, across her breast, and over her shoulder.

Jannaway woke with a start and knew immediately that something was wrong. He heard the rapid 'pip-pip, pip-pip' of the bo'sun's call over the ship's broadcast, the signal used to inform the officer-of-the-day that he was required on deck at the rush. He leapt off his bunk, cast round for his hat, realised that he had left it in the wardroom, decided to do without it, and ran aft along the main passage, onto the upperdeck and along the starboard side.

As he reached the quarterdeck, he saw that he was too late. The admiral's barge was already alongside. He had committed the heinous crime of not being on deck for its arrival, a crime that was aggravated by his hatless condition.

At the same moment, Tinnick appeared at the top of the accommodation ladder. Jannaway was caught.

'I apologise sir –' he began, but Tinnick cut him short.

'Your leave is stopped until further notice,' he said curtly, and walked briskly for'd to his cabin.

Julietta lay propped up in bed and listened to the evening bells. They bonged and jangled, echoing against the pocked buildings, and the sun's rays slanted in through the open window of her bedroom.

It was the Friday following the accident. Her temperature was back to normal and her bruise was less tender. The stream of visitors to her bedside had dwindled to a trickle, the flowers Peter had sent were beginning to look tired, and Julietta was bored.

She was a bit cross with Peter. He had been really sweet at first. He had lifted her in his arms, up into the barge, and had carried her down to the cabin and laid her on the seat. He had come to her room that evening after the surgeon captain had examined her and had sat with her on Monday evening. She had expected that he would call every evening, counting on it and looking forward to his arrival. She had prepared little things to say to him and had imagined how, when they were alone together, she might lead him into some little intimacy that would bring them closer. Each evening she had been disappointed, however, and now four precious days had passed and she hadn't seen him once.

Her parents, the flag lieutenant and Penny Forden-Jones were out at CINCAFMED's cocktail party that evening. CINCAFMED was one of these new NATO admirals that her father was so rude about in private. CINCAFMED meant Commander in Chief Allied Forces Mediterranean, and he was a small Italian with oily hair and about seventy medals. He had felt her bottom three weeks before at a dance and she had dug her fingernail into the back of his hand to teach him a lesson. She had felt well enough to go to this party but her mother had insisted she have just one more day in bed.

Boring, boring, boring, that's what it was. Penny didn't help either, coming in every morning to give a blow-by-blow account of her romance with Charles.

Julietta hopped out of bed and went to the long mirror. She wore

169

Chinese pyjamas, brought home from Hong Kong by her father two years before. She undid the top and inspected the bruise, a blue line that ran, like the order of the garter, from her brown tummy across her white breast to her shoulder; and while she was doing so, she heard people arriving downstairs.

She turned her head, listening. She heard Penny's laughter, the earnest voice of Charles and then, unmistakably, the gentle boomy tones of Peter Lasbury.

Quickly, she went to the dressing table to freshen her lipstick and add another hint of eye shadow. She guided her dark hair with her hands so that it curled up under her chin, and having done up the buttons of her pyjama jacket, she went onto the landing and called Peter to come up.

As he started up the stairs, she went back into the bedroom and went to the window. The sun had gone now, leaving the sky a pale turquoise behind the Sliema buildings. She heard him knock. She had taken ballet lessons as a child, and was hoping to start at drama school in the autumn: when she turned to look back at him over her shoulder, she spoke as eloquently with her body as her voice.

'Come in, Peter,' she said.

It had been a formal cocktail party, and Peter Lasbury still wore his 'ice cream suit' – the full white uniform with brass buttons to the neck and gold braid on the shoulders.

'What are you doing out of bed, naughty girl!?' he asked.

She smiled languidly and turned back to the window. 'Looking at the sunset. It's beautiful.'

He couldn't help being a little fond of her, in an avuncular way. She wasn't really looking at the sunset at all: all she was doing was creating a little romantic scene in which he was expected to play a part.

He moved closer. She pushed her top lip out, pouting in the Braddle way. 'Why didn't you come and see me?'

'I did come and see you.'

'No you didn't. You haven't been since Monday.'

'You don't expect me to see you every day, do you?'

She jerked her bottom sharply from left to right impatiently. 'Yes I do.'

Lasbury had already made up his mind about Julietta. He had half expected her to try and lure him into some sort of affair, but he was determined not to let her. He liked the Braddle family and valued Henry's friendship as a useful asset in his career. Clara had always been kind to him, too, and was almost an aunt. Sarah was now married to an extremely wealthy Dutchman and poor David was dead. The trouble with Julietta was that she was so like David to look at, and for that reason was worryingly attractive; but he knew enough about himself by now to be aware that it was quite impossible for him to enjoy any sort of sexual intimacy with a woman, and it was therefore necessary to make sure that Julietta wasn't given the wrong idea.

'Well you mustn't think that,' he said. 'See?'

'Don't you like coming to see me then?'

'Yes, but –'

They were interrupted. Penny came in and said, 'Oh.' She looked from one to the other. 'Am I interrupting anything?'

'Not at all,' Lasbury said.

'I just wondered if I could borrow that stripey sloppy joe of yours, Juju. We're going to a bistro party and I'm supposed to look Frenchified.'

'Second drawer down I think,' Julietta told her. 'Help yourself.'

Penny found what she was looking for. 'Super,' she said, and looked at Peter. 'You won't be long, will you?'

Julietta looked at him sharply. 'Are you going too?'

Lasbury nodded. 'I'm changing at Paddy's.'

'Paddy Maher's?'

'That's right,' Penny said. 'He's invited everyone back. Wine and onions, he's calling this one.'

'In that case I'm coming too,' Julietta said. 'I shall wear my cat-suit. You and Charles can go on ahead, Penny. Peter and I'll follow, won't we?'

'Steady on,' Peter said. 'Steady on. You're supposed to be in bed!'

'Peter! Don't be boring!'

'Well what'll your mother say if I let you go gallivanting off to a party when you're supposed to be tucked up in bed?'

'Pooh!' Julietta said. 'I don't care a fish's tit what Mummy thinks!'

'Well I'll leave you to fight it out,' Penny said.

'Right,' Julietta said when Penny had gone, 'That's got rid of her!' She took his hands and giggled. 'We don't have to go straight away, do we?'

He tried to let go of her hands, but she wouldn't let him. He felt a certain inner confusion: a small stirring of attraction. He looked down into those fawn eyes, and remembered an evening years ago when David had pretended to be asleep.

'Relax!' she whispered. 'You're all tensed up, aren't you?'

'I still think you ought to be in bed.'

'I feel perfectly all right. In fact I feel better than all right now you're here.' She reached up and touched his face. 'Peter! You're so gorgeous in that uniform! I wish you didn't have to take it off!' She slipped her hand round the back of his neck, and the sensation of her fingers running up and down his nape was pleasing, in a flattering sort of way. This was the peculiar difficulty Peter Lasbury had with women: he liked to be fondled by them, but sometimes experienced physical revulsion if required to fondle them back.

Julietta pushed her little tongue in between his lips, in and out, in and out, then moved her head back to look at him.

'We're off!' Penny called from the landing, having the tact not to come into the room because she could see what was going on through the crack. 'See you at Paddy's, okay?'

'Okay!' Julietta called back.

They stood together, listening as Penny and Charles drove off. More bells began to ring in the town, and a firework sputtered and exploded.

Julietta led him to the bed and sat down. He sat down beside her, not really sure what he was doing or why. She smoothed his white trouser leg with her hand, and then quickly undid the press-studs of her pyjama jacket, so that her small white breasts came partially into view.

'Now then, Juju,' he said. 'Put them away, they'll catch cold.'

'Not if you keep them warm,' she whispered, and taking his hand placed it over the unbruised Wilhelmina, pushing it to and fro across the nipple, until it rose and hardened under his palm. 'There you are,' she said. 'Now you know what to do next time.'

'This is very dangerous,' he said.

'I bet you've done more dangerous things than this before.'

'Dangerous for you,' he said. 'Not me.'

'That's all right then. I'm not frightened.' She started moving his hand down under the elastic of her pyjama trousers, but he stood up quickly and moved away. He didn't mind women's breasts all that much, but the Other . . . no, he couldn't.

172

'What's the matter?'

He shook his head. 'We mustn't,' he said. 'It's not fair on your parents.'

'Blow my parents! I'm a big girl!'

He shook his head. 'It can lead to all sorts of things.'

She laughed. 'So what? I want it to! I'm not a virgin you know!'

He backed to the door. 'I'm sorry. This just isn't on.'

'You're not going? Peter – wait –'

'I'm sorry, Julie. But yes, I'm going.'

Her face crumpled. 'What is it? What's wrong? Don't you like my body? Is it my bruise or something?'

'I can't explain,' he said, and repeated, 'I'm sorry,' before leaving the bedroom and going down the stairs and out by the front door.

She decided immediately to pursue him to the party. The iron was still hot, and she was determined to strike at it, bend it to her will. She hadn't had a man since coming out to Malta because Peter was the only one she had wanted. She had never been refused before, and wasn't prepared to take no for an answer now.

What was wrong with her? How could he possibly have been able to resist her?

She looked at herself in the mirror. She had always known she was pretty, always been aware of her body as near perfect. While sharing a flat in Kensington during her secretarial course, she had studied health and beauty magazines and spent two evenings a week at a gymnasium and sauna off the Bayswater Road. Her hair shone and her teeth were brilliant white: her toenails were neatly clipped, and every three weeks she had unwanted hair removed from her legs with hot wax. She was as perfect as she could possibly manage to be, and yet he had backed away from her as if she were dirty.

She blinked back tears, determined not to spoil her face. She opened her wardrobe and took out her catsuit. It had been made for her two years before, for the school production of Dick Whittington, and had seen good service at fancy dress parties since. It came complete with a mask and tail, but she decided to do without these this evening, using eye shadow to make her eyes look catlike instead. It still hurt to wear a brassière, so she did without that as well. She put on a pair of high heeled shoes and found a long cigarette holder in her top drawer. She took one last look at herself in the mirror, miaowed experimentally to herself, and was gone.

The party was on the fourth floor, and she could hear the accordion music as she climbed the marble stairs. The flat had been rented by a succession of submarine wardrooms, and was used by the young officers as an escape from the diesel-laden atmosphere of their boats.

Paddy Maher, at twenty-five, was one of the youngest submarine captains in the Royal Navy, and commanded a small black boat called *Sea Demon*. He was a surprising officer in almost every way: surprisingly young, surprisingly fertile (he already had three children), surprisingly successful and surprisingly full of good ideas. Most surprising of all, he was happily married, with a loving wife and a mongrel he called Hervey, which revealed that he was adequately, if not surprisingly, well read. He believed that life should be full of surprises and like Field Marshal Montgomery, to whom he was distantly related, he made sure that all his parties were good ones. During his time in Malta, he had organised pyjama parties, breakfast parties, instant parties and mystery parties, as well as the common-or-garden barbecue parties that everyone else organised on the rocky beaches up and down the island.

This evening was a French bistro, wine and onions party. The flat had been hung with fishing nets and green glass floats; there were red and white check table cloths on the tables and candles in bottles. Strings of onions hung from the walls, and the room seethed with men in berets smoking Gauloises and women in fishnet tights trying to look as if they had stepped out of a Toulouse-Lautrec poster. A tape-recorder blared 'Sous les Toits de Paris' and some of the clotted cream of Britain's youth swayed and sweated to the beat.

Paddy forced his way through the crush to welcome the latest guest. 'Bonsoir, Pussycat!' he exclaimed. 'Ow ze bloody 'ell êtes-vous?' to which Julietta miaowed in reply and melted into his arms, which she found particularly exciting that evening, because underneath her feline body stocking she wore nothing at all.

Lasbury saw her arrive and escaped to the kitchen under cover of darkness. He put on a blue and white striped apron and began chopping onions, which he took from a hanging chain by the door.

She found him when he was starting his fifth onion. 'What are you doing in here?' she asked crossly.

'Honorary acting unpaid chef,' he replied.

174

She watched him for a minute or two, in which he made no attempt at conversation.

'Am I going to have to watch you chopping onions all night?'

'No. Not if you don't want to. Plenty of spare blokes next door.'

'I don't want a spare bloke. I want you.' She found a glass and an opened bottle of wine. 'Do you want some, Peter?'

'I have some already thank you,' he said.

'What is it? What have I done?' she whispered.

He shook his head impatiently. Paddy Maher entered. 'Would you mind telling me what you're doing with those onions, sir?' he enquired.

'I am making soup, my dear sir,' Lasbury answered. 'That is what I am doing.'

'Well kindly desist. Those are decorative onions, God rot your size nine socks. Not soup-making onions.'

Julietta giggled. 'I knew you shouldn't be fiddling with other people's onions. Come along. Take that apron off, wash your hands, and join the party.'

She dragged him back into the darkened bistro. She put her arms round his neck and spoke directly into his ear.

'What's the matter with me for God's sake? Why am I so repulsive?'

'You're not repulsive,' he said.

'Well what is it then?'

'I can't tell you here.'

'Where can you tell me?'

He led her into the hall. It was necessary to finish things, once and for all, but it was also necessary to give her a reason she could repeat to her friends that would cast no slur upon himself. He closed the door on the noise of the party and stood with her outside the door to the flat, with the well of the staircase below them. 'Listen,' he said quietly, 'I'm very, very fond of you, Julie, understand?'

'Don't talk to me like that! You're treating me like a ten year old!'

'Well that's the trouble. You are still very young –'

'I'm nineteen for God's sake!'

'I don't mean young in years. Look, I don't want to hurt you, but the fact is, I can't really enjoy sex with a woman who doesn't stimulate me intellectually. Do you understand? I need a woman who is much more mature, do you see?'

'Well I've got four "O" levels!' she wailed. 'Isn't that good enough?'

'Sweetie I'm ten years older than you are! You can't see it, can you? You're just a silly little girl to me. A silly, spoilt little girl. Now do you get the message or don't you?'

He took a quick decision. He could leave now, that was the best way to do it. He could pick up his uniform in the morning. It would be better that way, neither of them would lose face, she would be able to go straight back into the party and find someone else. He took her face in his hands, kissed her quickly and uncomfortably on the lips, and ran away down the stairs.

'Bastard!' she shouted after him, her voice echoing in the stairwell. 'Bastard! Bastard! Bastard!'

He met a group of officers from *Copenhagen* as he came out into the street. It was Jannaway's first proper run ashore since the ship had arrived in Malta, the captain having recently released him from his stoppage of leave.

'Steve, just the man,' Lasbury said.

'What's that sir?' Jannaway had already visited several bars and was pleasantly oiled.

'There's a bird up there in a catsuit who's just been given the heave-ho by yours truly, so if you play your cards right, you'll be in like Flynn. FOFMED's daughter. Julie Braddle. Tell her I sent you.'

He walked off down the street chuckling to himself. All in all, he felt he'd handled that very nicely.

Julietta drank a lot that evening. She wandered about, glass in hand, trying to pretend that nothing had happened. She commandeered a number of young officers to dance with her, draping herself over them, laughing too loudly and too often, but turning coldly away from Steven Jannaway when he tried to engage her in conversation. She graduated to Bacardi and Canada Dry after a while, and some time in the early hours slumped down on a sofa. The candles had gone out and the only light in the room was the red pilot light on the tape recorder. She wasn't drunk because she never got drunk, but she was certainly the worse for wear.

She was just falling asleep when the ungainly Jannaway came and sat on the sofa beside her. She opened her eyes. She could just make him out. He seemed to be swaying like a large tree in a strong wind. He put his head in his hands and groaned.

'You're pissed,' she said. 'Aren't you?'

'Only in a very minor sort of way,' he said.

She lay back and went to sleep, awaking with a start to find that he was whispering in her ear.

'Do you mind?' she said.

'There's nowhere else, you see,' he said. 'And you've got this all to yourself.'

'What? What are you talking about?'

'Me,' he said. 'I want to lie down.'

'Suit yourself,' she said, and moved over for him. She dropped into another stupor, and woke up again. 'Now what is it?'

'Sorry,' he said. 'I don't know what to do with my arms.'

She turned over and found herself looking at him eyeball to eyeball. 'Have I seen you before?' she asked.

'Probably. Most people have.' His eyes moved. 'You don't look a very happy cat.'

'Nor do you.'

'I'm not a cat.'

'You don't look like a happy anything.'

He said nothing for a while. She could just make out his face. 'I'm not anything,' he said. 'I'm due to be shot at dawn.'

'What's your name?'

'Jesus Christ.'

'I knew I'd seen you before.'

'Everybody tells me that.'

He closed his eyes. She decided that there was something pleasantly animal about him after all. Earlier, she had discounted him as being too unsmooth, too much of a scruff in his rather ordinary shirt and ordinary trousers and ordinary tweed jacket. She examined his face in detail. He had a slightly squashed nose and thick eyebrows.

He opened his eyes and smiled. 'Would you like a sandwich?' he suggested. 'I've been thinking of making one for the past hour.'

They picked their way over prostrate bodies and fumbled for the light switch in the kitchen. She blinked in the harsh neon light.

'Ham?' he said, opening the fridge. 'Tomatoes? Onion?'

'Anything but onion. And I'll have a Seven-Up too.'

'Bright wheeze,' he said.

They couldn't find the bottle opener, so he took the top off with the palm of his hand using the edge of the marble work top.

She stuck the neck of the bottle in her mouth and drank

gratefully, looking at him while she did so, her dark hair falling away from her face. When she handed the bottle to him, she knew that she was having an effect on him. He didn't say much, but he looked. She looked too, deliberately, so that he would know she was looking. 'Come on, we'll go for a burn up,' she said.

She led the way down the stairs and out into the street. She collected the keys from under the tyre. 'This one?' he said. ' This load of rubbish?'

She put her finger to her mouth. 'Sshh!'

He stopped in front of her, swaying again. 'I think you should know that I am promised to another.'

'So am I. Get in.'

'Just for the ride, then. The fresh air.'

She got in behind the wheel and he sat beside her. She put the wrong key in the ignition and swore softly.

'Are you okay to drive? Am I taking my life in my hands?'

'I always drive better when I'm pissed.'

She started the car and they moved off, the wheels squealing on the cobbles as she let the clutch in too quickly. They plunged down through the back streets of St Julians to the coast at Tigne, and turned right through Sliema. She was an appalling driver: she drove in straight lines, making sharp alterations of course to miss obstacles at the last moment. Twice he covered his face with his hands.

'Have you ever driven before?' he shouted as they ricocheted down through Valletta.

'Not often!' she shouted, and they both went on laughing for a long time.

'Where the hell are we going?' he asked as they left all traces of civilisation behind, climbing up into the barren wastes.

'Wait and see!'

What seemed to be a long time later, she pulled up and switched off the engine. 'Okay, now what?' he said.

'I'm going to have a swim.'

'Where's the sea? I see no sea!'

Following her down the path, with the sky jammed full of stars and the night insects playing a crazy symphony, the thought of Catherine went through his mind like a bright, fast moving comet that caught his attention one moment and was gone the next.

Julietta attacked him with her mouth, her lips, her tongue. She pressed and squirmed against him, she breathed her breath down into his lungs.

'I can't see a pig's arse,' she whispered as they went on down the hill.

'I can't even see any pigs,' he said.

'You smell of ham.'

They stopped again. 'Ah,' he said. 'The sea. Thalatta.'

'The latter what?'

'Thalatta thalatta.'

'You're crackers.'

Going down a steeper bit, she slipped and nearly went down. He caught her by the upper arm. 'Okay?'

'Yes, okay.'

Below them they could see the natural pool, cut out of the sandstone by the sea.

'Where are we?'

'St Peter's Pool.'

'Quite a place.'

She led the way down over flat rocks to the water's edge. He turned back, looking at the dark slope, silhouetted now against the sky. He heard her say 'Last one in's a sissy,' and was in time to see her dive. She swam under water for several yards, her body pale and frog-like as it jerked along under the surface. He took off his clothes and laid them down beside the little black heap that was her catsuit. He dived in and surfaced beside her.

'It's perfectly safe,' she said. 'I only finished yesterday.'

'Finished what?'

She reached down and felt him, and the size of it made her cry out in anticipation and excitement.

'Careful,' she whispered. 'Careful of my poor breast.'

# 11

HMS *COPENHAGEN*
at sea.

Sunday 12th July

My darling Mouse,

I'm sitting up on B gundeck writing this. Almost the entire ship's company is sunbathing on the upper deck, many of them stark naked. There's not a breath of wind, and apart from a gentle swell the sea is flat calm – almost oily in appearance.

Well – we finished our inspection last Wednesday and came out of it better than anyone expected. I'm the 'GDO Blind' which means I have to sit in the ops room at action stations and direct the guns onto the target by means of radar. My faithful assistant and I 'shot down' (ie alerted the gunnery system in time to possibly shoot down) the BEA morning flight as it took off from Luqa, much to the inspecting staff's surprise, and Tinnick was actually seen to smile, so they told me later.

Anyway, now we have this visit to Piraeus and the Greek islands coming up, and I hope to do a little culture vulturing, though every time we go anywhere interesting it hardly seems worth making the effort to go sightseeing because you aren't here to share it.

I went for drinks on board *Nile* the other day and they were talking about Tim Whettingsteel who was in my term and left right at the end of our time at Dartmouth. Apparently he's doing very well: he was a languages alpha at Dartmouth and got into the Foreign Office on the strength of it. I gather he's now a Third Secretary in Madrid. I suppose the grass is always greener, but I compare what I'm doing (pushing bumph, pacing the deck, shouting the old warcries in the ops room and getting worked up about things no intelligent being should get worked up about ...) with what he must be involved in and well, there's no comparison. Feeling a bit uncertain about everything, you see Mouse. I *suppose* it's necessary to have all these comforting things like nerve gas and H bombs isn't it? Something disagrees somewhere, but provided we keep the brass-work shining no doubt it'll all come out right in the end. Thinking aloud. Sorry.

There was a party last Sunday. The usual thing, you know: cheap wine/loud music/jolly, gung-ho naval officers/even jollier debby females, each with their great big eyes and their tiny minds. Why do I go to these parties? This one was a French Bistro party and l'élève Jannaway was the only idiot not suitably dressed in stripey tee-shirt and black beret, so when I walked in in my dog-robbers some bright spark shouted 'Touriste!' (Do you ever get the feeling you don't belong?!) I ended up asleep on a sofa, dreaming of you. I spend a lot of my sleeping hours dreaming of you, Mouse. I won't go into details because you don't like sticky bits in letters do you? And you're right not to. But I dream – and think – so often of our last night together. Words fail me. Love . . .

A proposition: would you consider coming out to Malta for a week or two in August? We have our next maintenance period in the second and third weeks, and I hope to be able to get a bit of local leave. Apart from the fact that it would be wonderful to see you, there is another reason: I actually do need you, Catherine. There are things about this man's navy – temptations, difficulties, dangers – which I need to talk out with you. I have a sneaky feeling that if I had real courage I would ask for release from the service, but I also have a feeling that you would say, 'Don't be a quitter.' Also, I know what we said we'd wait until the end of this commission before becoming engaged, but I'm beginning to think it would be better to hurry things up a bit. Wouldn't it be a good idea to meet away from home influences, to be right away from everyone, to make our decision once and for all?

About your becoming a Catholic: the last thing I want to do is influence you. It must be your decision, and I already feel pretty bad about the battle you're having with your family. I can't say that I know what it feels like, but I went through something like the same thing with my Ma over joining the navy, as you know. I think all you really need to know from me is that I love *you*, Mouse, not your Protestantism or (if it happens) your Catholicism. (Which was Christ, I wonder?!)

These months away have been like a prison sentence. There doesn't seem to be any point in *doing* anything without you around. I have a sort of emptiness inside. I don't really feel good enough for you either. No, I'm not putting you on a pedestal, just feeling a little disgusted at this vile body. I'm a brutal and licentious sailor, you see.

There is an ever-so-slight breeze coming up now and I am having difficulty ensuring that these pages don't fly off over the Mediterranean on their own, so I think I'd better stop. I'm thinking of you all the time, Mouse – longing for you, living for you, hoping and praying for you. Come out in August – please. Keith and Jill have a flat out here and will willingly put you up. (Jill is pregnant – due in December.)

I don't want to stop but must.

Love you always,

Steve.

PS Just read this through. All I really mean is this – please marry me because I love you. Soon. Please.

It was not, as Steven had called it, a battle so much as a war of nerves: Catherine realised that quite quickly after arriving at her brother's house on the edge of Clapham Common. She had left Gainsborough House for the last time that morning, and on arriving in London had gone straight to Westminster Cathedral. Father Vincent, the priest in Brixham to whom she had been going for instruction, had told her to do that. They had been discussing her doubts about her motives for adopting Steven's faith and he had said to her 'Go to Westminster Cathedral, kneel down and say the Hail Mary aloud, my dear. When you've done that you'll know sure enough whether you should become a Catholic.' But now, here she was in her brother's house having followed Father Vincent's advice and still she did not know.

Her sister-in-law, Elspeth, ran the household to a strict routine and whenever Catherine went to stay there she always had the feeling that her presence was to be tolerated rather than welcomed. This time, she was more anxious than ever to get on well with her brother's family: she knew that her interest in Catholicism was causing her parents much distress, and she longed to be able to talk to someone who was prepared to listen without taking sides.

The days started at six forty-five when Phillip rose to make his wife's early morning tea. Breakfast was prefaced by prayers and a reading from the Daily Light, and when the children had been sent off to school and Phillip went into his dental surgery for the morning, Elspeth set about tidying and cleaning her already clean and tidy house. Catherine sometimes felt that she was in danger of being hoovered up into the little bag Elspeth emptied, her face averted, at the bottom of the garden; it also gave her a certain wicked satisfaction to note how many graven images in the form of glass giraffes and pottery elephants decorated her sister-in-law's mantelpiece in the front room.

As Sunday approached, the question of whether Catherine would attend the morning meeting was raised, and Elspeth told her of Phillip's concern. 'He is so worried about you,' she said. 'He doesn't show it I know, but he's desperately worried all the same.'

'There's no need for anyone to be worried,' Catherine said. 'Catholics do actually worship the same God, you know. I don't

182

think any of you would mind nearly so much if I just became an agnostic or an atheist. In fact I often feel that Catholicism is closer to the beliefs of the Brethren than Anglicanism.'

In the next door room, the drill hummed. Elspeth picked up a hand-carved gazelle and dusted it, replacing it among others of its kind on an empty bookshelf. 'Don't you realise what it will mean? If you become a Catholic? You will be separating yourself from the family. Phillip says that we shall be able to welcome you into this house only as we might welcome a neighbour. We shall no longer be able to embrace you as a sister in Christ.' Elspeth turned, appealing to her. 'I don't think you always appreciate how much you are loved, Catherine, do you? By your brother and by your parents. And I don't know if you have any idea how much you are hurting them.'

That argument had the opposite effect to what Elspeth had intended: Catherine knew that she was hurting her adoptive parents, but that could not be a reason for turning back. The only reason for doing that would be if she felt that she was being untrue to her own conscience, kidding herself that she believed one thing when she knew she believed another.

'You will be coming to the breaking of bread on Sunday won't you?' Elspeth said now, and looked at her expectantly so that Catherine could not help wondering if it was more a matter of saving face than of saving a soul.

The meeting was held in a plain brick hall. Outside, a notice board proclaimed the times of the Sunday morning meeting, the weekly Bible reading, the Prayer meeting and the Youth Fellowship. During her last term at Gainsborough House, Catherine had been attending Mass at the Roman Catholic church in Brixham, and returning to the atmosphere of the meeting was like going back to weak tea after your first taste of vintage wine.

Sitting in the front row with her brother, Elspeth and their two children, Catherine was conscious that her presence had been noticed with particular interest by some of the brethren and sisters. It was not so much a case of covert glances in her direction, though there were a few of these, as of a latent awareness, a watchfulness which she knew was not normally present at the Sunday morning meeting.

They sang 'Love divine all loves excelling' and Catherine,

standing next to Elspeth, received the benefit of her sister-in-law's powerful voice. After a few minutes' silence, old Mr Nash, who had been gassed in the Great War, stood up to give thanks to the Lord in his hoarse, cockney tones. Catherine listened to the strange mixture of seventeenth-century English and twentieth-century cockney which ascended from the lips of the old man to the ear of the Lord, reflecting that this stream of largely nonsensical prayer did more for old Nash's ego than for anyone else's edification.

They sang another hymn and another brother prayed. Then one of the elder brethren, Mr Sturges, stood up and opened his Bible, inviting the assembly to turn to the tenth chapter of the first book of Corinthians.

'Ye cannot drink the cup of the Lord and the cup of devils,' he read slowly. 'Ye cannot be partakers of the Lord's table, and of the table of devils.'

Where was the connection between this reading and what had gone before? She had no idea, but she was certain that Mr Sturges had chosen the passage for a reason.

'Whosoever,' he read, and repeated the first word for emphasis, 'Whosoever shall eat this bread and drink this cup unworthily shall be guilty of the body and the blood of the Lord.'

That was the moment that she knew finally what her decision must be. Mr Sturges was reading this passage with no other purpose than to drive her, an erring ewe, back into the flock; what he did not realise was that the words he read conveyed a quite different message, for the doctrine of transubstantiation had been one of the most difficult for Catherine to accept. Now, she was listening to the words of St Paul in a new way and she saw that the bread and the wine did indeed become the body and the blood; if not, how could a person be guilty of them by taking them unworthily?

She felt a great surge of relief. This was that moment of certainty she had been praying for for weeks, and it had been made possible by poor old Mr Sturges, for whom she had a great affection and to whom she knew she would never be able to explain.

She broke the news of her decision to Phillip and Elspeth after lunch when they were taking coffee on the swing seat in the back garden. They received the news in stunned silence and she realised that it would be impossible to stay on with them.

'Where will you go?' Elspeth asked when she told them she would leave the following day.

She smiled. It seemed impossible not to hurt them. 'To the

Jannaways. I was thinking of staying with them in any case.'

At the bottom of the garden, a thrush had found its way into the vegetable enclosure and was flapping about in a panic against the black netting, and somewhere in the distance a train hooted as it went through the main line station.

Alan was compiling an order list for new titles when Catherine walked into the library the following afternoon. His tweed jacket was slung over the back of his chair, his tie was loosened and he was controlling his left hand by hooking his thumb into the waistband of his grey flannel trousers. He had a copy of *The Bookseller* open on his desk, and as he noted another title down on a pad his face contorted and his knuckles whitened in the effort to string the jerky letters together across the pad.

'With you in a second,' he said without looking up, and then a moment later saw who it was.

She looked a little upset. It was a hot afternoon and she had brought a suitcase into the library with her. 'I've been trying to phone you at home but couldn't get a reply, Alan.'

'Well we were on holiday in Wales until yesterday. Got back late. Where are you staying?'

She knew Alan well enough not to pretend. 'Nowhere at the moment. I was wondering if you could possibly put me up.'

He grinned, glancing across at one of the library assistants, who was obviously intrigued by his visitor and listening to every word. 'Of course we can. No problem at all.'

She seemed to relax. He asked, 'Have you just come up from Devon?'

'Not quite. I've been staying with my brother for a week –' She broke off. 'It's a rather long story I'm afraid.'

He looked at his watch. 'Tell you what, I was thinking of knocking off early today and Sheila here can quite easily hold the fort, can't you Sheila?'

The girl nodded. Alan turned back to Catherine. 'Just give me a couple of minutes to sort myself out – no – I tell you what –' He felt in his trouser pocket and took out half a crown. 'There's a bakery fifty yards down on the other side. Could you buy a malt loaf? Otherwise Mum'll get into a panic because she'll think she isn't feeding you properly. I'll meet you out in the front. You can leave your suitcase here.'

When she had gone he turned back to the assistant. 'And

185

whatever you're thinking, you can just stop, Sheila, because that is almost certainly my future sister-in-law.'

He threw a few papers into a tray, locked up his filing cabinet and put on his jacket. By the time he had finished he saw Catherine coming back from the bakery.

They went round to the back to collect his tricycle, and after an unsuccessful attempt to balance her suitcase on the handlebars he agreed to let her carry it while he pedalled slowly along beside her.

'So,' he said as they went down Dollis Road. 'What news of Steve? We had a letter the other day, but he never says much. Isn't he off to Cannes soon?'

'He's there now, I think. They're due back in Malta at the end of next week.'

Alan grinned in his crooked way. 'Living the life of Riley, no doubt.'

'He's asked me to go out there.'

'Oh yes? Lucky you!'

'I haven't decided definitely whether I'm going yet.'

He looked at her quickly.

'What's the matter? Has something gone wrong?'

'No … just the opposite really. I've decided I want to become a Catholic.'

His brakes squeaked as he freewheeled down the hill beside her. 'I see,' he said. 'That's quite a decision.'

She smiled gratefully back at him. He seemed to have a knack of hitting exactly the right note: of listening without intruding his own opinion.

'Steven's asked me to marry him, too,' she said. 'I don't suppose I should have told you that, should I?'

'I won't repeat it,' he said. 'Unless you'd like me to.'

'I'm not going to dither much longer,' she said. 'I've made up my mind about joining the Church. Now I've got to make up my mind about Steven.'

'Aren't the two decisions linked? There's not much point in turning Catholic if you aren't going to marry him, is there?'

She looked surprised. 'Isn't there?'

He shrugged. 'Well – we're all Christians, aren't we? Sugar tastes the same whether you get it from Tesco's or Sainsbury's.'

'It may not cost the same though.'

He laughed. 'Ah. Now there you've got a nice point!'

They reached Chestnut Road and he wheeled the tricycle down the track between the two blocks of terraced houses, putting it in the shed before leading the way up the back garden to the kitchen door.

'Mum'll be back in about half an hour,' he said. 'I'll put a kettle on. You can butter the malt loaf if you're feeling energetic.'

He put the kettle in the sink and turned on the tap and while he did so noticed that she was watching how he managed it. 'If I tried to do it the usual way you'd be treated to a shower bath,' he said, and she remembered how Steven had once said that it was no good worrying about the way Alan did things or the way he spoke: you just had to accept him as he was and listen to what he said.

'So how long will you stay in Malta?'

'I didn't say I was going.'

'Oh you must! Never mind about Steve, think of the sunshine!'

They both laughed, and at the same time Mrs Jannaway arrived. 'Guess what, Catherine's here,' she heard him say in the hall.

Dora came into the kitchen looking hot and middle-aged. 'I've got nothing at all for tea,' she said. 'I'm sorry, but I had no idea –'

'We've saved the day,' Alan said, and showed her the malt loaf. 'Why don't you go and put your feet up for a change and leave everything to us?'

They walked along the cinder track at the back of the houses, and down the path that led between the allotments to the stream. She told him something of the difficulties she had had at her brother's and apologised again for arriving without notice. He sensed that she needed to talk, and he wanted to help her for Steven's sake.

'If only there was some way one could be sure what one was doing was right,' she said, when they had returned to the question of whether she should go to Malta.

'Well I'll tell you one thing that may help,' Alan said. 'Steven is very much in love with you, Catherine, and what's more, I think you're just the person he needs.'

They came to some children playing on a rope that dangled over the stream. When they were clear of them, Catherine said: 'I think I know that already, in fact it may be part of the reason why I'm hesitating. I feel that he may need me ... in the wrong way. Temporarily. That he will suddenly find that he can do without me, and we'll be left with nothing.'

They went in single file along a narrow stretch of path beside a pond. She went ahead, then waited for him to catch up so that they could walk side by side again.

'You were very close, weren't you? As boys.'

He nodded. 'Yes, we were.'

'But not so much now?'

'No, I'm afraid we aren't.'

'I suppose the navy's done that, has it?'

'Maybe,' he said, then after a hesitation added, 'Did Steve ever tell you how he decided to join?'

'Not in great detail, no. But I remember him saying that he would never have got in if it hadn't been for you.'

Alan laughed. 'Yes, that is just what he would say.'

'Was there more to it than that?'

To their right, beyond the wood, a golfer smacked at his ball, hoisted his bag of clubs on his shoulder and set off in pursuit.

'The reason he joined ... the real reason, was a convolution of reasons. It was a sort of accident.'

'Like Steve himself?'

Alan stopped. 'He told you that?'

She nodded. 'I was too. I'm adopted.'

'Kindred spirits,' he said.

'In a way. We felt we belonged together practically from the moment we met.'

'That must be a very good feeling.'

'Yes it is.' They walked on a little. Alan could not walk very fast, and they were overtaken by a couple out with their dog. 'Tell me about it,' Catherine said. 'I mean his reasons for joining the navy.'

'Well, he went through a difficult time. Everyone expected a great deal of him. Especially Mum. His school was partly to blame. They were convinced he would win a scholarship to university. I suppose we were all to blame to a certain extent. There were certain things that I could obviously never do, and Steve was the one who would do them. But I think Steve knew all along that he wasn't quite the high-flyer everyone thought.' Alan laughed.

'What?'

'I was just thinking: it must be quite difficult to have an elder brother who's a spastic.'

'I think he's very lucky to have you as an elder brother.'

He ignored that. 'Something happened. When he was fourteen.

I don't know what it was, but it must have been something quite big. He played truant from sea scouts, gave up the piano, stopped working at school. Has he ever told you that?'

She shook her head.

'Perhaps I'm telling you too much.'

'You aren't saying anything against him.'

They crossed another bridge and came to the end of the path, where it rejoined Dollis Road. The red brick arches of the viaduct towered above them. They turned and began to retrace their steps, walking in silence for some time.

'One day he came to my room and asked me what I would have done if I hadn't been a spastic.'

'What did you say?'

He frowned, the left side of his face contorting slightly as he did so. 'There was a complicated sort of telepathy between us. Still is, to a certain extent. It was a trick question really, we both knew that. We'd always been interested in ships, because of Dad, and I had a feeling he wanted to do whatever I wanted him to do.'

'What did you tell him?'

Alan laughed. 'I told him I'd have been a brain surgeon or a violinist. So he came out with it and said he was thinking of joining the navy. But he didn't want to be an officer then. He'd been reading T.E. Lawrence and he wanted to do the same sort of thing – commit intellectual suicide. Said he'd join as a boy seaman like Dad and work his way up.'

'Who suggested he took the Dartmouth exams then?'

'I did. I never thought he'd pass the interview, and as his only strong subjects were the classics he was unlikely even to get that far. But once he'd agreed to try, he became very determined to pass. We did a sort of joint project on it. I read up every mortal thing I could find about the navy and gave him sort of ... briefings. Neither of us realised until it was too late how much Mum was against him going in for it. I don't think she's ever forgiven Steven.'

'What about you, Alan? Have you forgiven yourself?'

He looked back into her grey eyes. 'Do I have to answer that?'

'It might help if you did.'

'Have I forgiven myself?' he repeated. 'That presumes I felt to blame, doesn't it? Which I did – do still to a certain extent. So I suppose the answer's no. When he asked me what I would have done we both knew that I would have gone into the navy. I didn't

189

have to tell him that. And we both knew that if he did join I'd always want to know what it was like, always be interested. And then ... when his uniform actually arrived and he put it on for the first time, I think I knew he was wrong for the navy. Maybe he did too. It's a sort of double deception that deceives neither of us. He pretends to enjoy the navy for my sake, and I pretend he's doing the best possible thing with his life for his. We put on an act every time he comes home. He's the keen naval officer and I'm the admiring brother.' They walked on a few more paces. 'That's why you're so good for him,' he added. 'He can open up to you, can't he? If anyone can save him from becoming the complete naval barbarian, it's you.'

She laughed. 'I get the distinct impression that you're trying to marry him off!'

'Isn't that what you want?'

She had never been able to be so open with anyone – let alone a man – before. Was it his disability that made him so approachable? She didn't know. It was as if the very speech defect which he had to fight in order to express himself clearly was the reason for the clarity of what he said.

'I want to do what's right for both of us,' she said. 'It's not a decision I intend to take more than once in my life, and I'm determined not to rush it. I've always been convinced that God has something special for me to do, and I'm still not completely sure that he wants me to be a naval officer's wife.'

'That's a very Protestant attitude,' he said. 'If you're going to be a Catholic you'll have to be more definite. God's quite capable of pushing you over onto the right path, you know.'

They walked back along the cinder track and paused to watch the tennis.

'Has talking helped?' he asked.

'A lot, yes.'

'I did quite a lot of the talking, too.' He smiled, and his eyes wandered down from her face and back. 'You know why I want you and Steve to get married, don't you?'

'No?'

'Because you'll make a smashing sister-in-law, that's why.'

Dora Jannaway peered out over the potted geraniums on the kitchen windowsill, looking across the next door garden to see if she could see Alan and Catherine on their way back.

No, there was no sign of them. Why were they taking so long? It was most unlike Alan to go for a walk in any case: he got quite enough exercise pedalling up to the library and back every day without tiring himself by walking.

She moved back from the window and looked about the kitchen, mentally promising herself that one of these days she would have a really good tidy up. If she had known Catherine was coming she would have made an effort to make the house look more presentable. Really it was a bit much of her, landing herself on them without warning and she couldn't help feeling annoyed at Alan for being so welcoming. Catherine had said that she only needed to spend a couple of nights, but Alan had insisted she stay as long as she liked without so much as a by-your-leave. She got on very well with Alan on the whole, but sometimes he did take things for granted.

She took a damp cloth from the sink and gave the kitchen table a wipe over. It didn't need a wipe, or at least the part she was wiping didn't; what she should really do was take all the storage jars, the breadboard, the bowl of odds and ends, the magazines and the tin of nuts and bolts off the table; she should remove the oil cloth and give it a good scrub, all over. But at the end of a day in the classroom she didn't have the energy to be as thorough as that any more.

'Here they are now,' she said aloud as she rinsed out the cloth and squeezed it dry at the sink. She watched Catherine and Alan come in through the gate at the bottom of the garden, smiling and talking together, and felt a little pang of jealousy. I needn't be here at all, she thought. I just get in the way.

'Good news,' Alan said as they came into the kitchen. He turned to Catherine. They seemed to have some secret that was making them smile. Dora felt a wave of anger.

'Go on,' Alan said. 'Tell her.'

Catherine smiled at him and turned to break the news.

'I'm going to see Father Longstaff tomorrow, Mrs Jannaway. I've decided to become a Catholic.'

There was something about her manner that unexpectedly melted Dora's heart. She saw in Catherine's face a look that touched some half-forgotten emotion of long ago – one that Dora had known herself when her elder brother had decided to go and make a life in New Zealand and she had found herself virtually alone in the world; one that said quite simply, 'Please trust me.'

'Bless your heart,' she whispered, and her eyes softened and filled

191

with tears. She reached out to Catherine and they embraced, both unable to express in words exactly why they felt the way they did, but both aware that the barrier which had separated them for so long was suddenly down.

She saw Father Longstaff the following morning at ten o'clock. She had a letter of introduction from Father Vincent, which the old priest had to hold out at arms' length to read, as he had mislaid his glasses. They sat in the presbytery, and the trolley buses hummed by on their way to Golders Green. It was not necessary for Catherine to be baptised, because the Roman Catholic Church recognised the form of baptism by immersion which she had already undergone; instead, when Father Longstaff was satisfied that her desire to become a member of the Church was a sincere one, he heard her first confession before saying Mass and giving her her first communion.

Afterwards, outside the church, Father Longstaff blessed her and held her hands. 'How lucky you are,' he said. 'Your soul is like a new born baby's, do you know that?' His voice wavered; he seemed to be holding onto her hands in order to prevent himself from falling over. 'All your sins, washed clean away.' He turned to Alan. 'And this is Steven's young lady, I hear? Are they going to be married?'

Alan grinned and stuttered. 'It's not beyond the b-ounds of possibility, I understand, Father!'

'Well I hope you do, my dear. Keep him on the straight and narrow, and give him a good big Catholic family.'

She laughed delightedly and said she would do her very best.

'I never thought I would feel like this,' she told Alan as she walked with him back to the library. 'I want to go to Mass again. Now.'

She left him at the library and went straight to the travel agent's. She booked herself on a night flight to Malta and then went to the Post Office and sent a telegram: LIEUTENANT JANNAWAY WARSHIP COPENHAGEN. ARRIVING BEA NIGHT FLIGHT FOUR A.M. SATURDAY 13TH AUGUST. ALL LOVE ALWAYS. MOUSE.

She decided that she wouldn't tell Steven about her conversion until she was out there with him: she was almost certain that they would get engaged, but she didn't want to hold a gun to his head by announcing her conversion first.

Walking down the hill to Chestnut Road she found herself smiling and her eyes filling with tears of happiness. I've done it, I've done it, she thought. I'm a Catholic, a proper Roman Catholic. I'm part of the oldest Christian tradition. Upon this *rock* I will build my *church*.

She clenched her fists and looked up at the clouds; she prayed silently, thanking God, asking His blessing on herself, on Steven, on Mrs Jannaway and on Alan. And my parents, she remembered; help them to understand what I have done. Bring all Catholics and Protestants closer together.

Just then it seemed to her that there was nothing that was not possible: all that was needed was faith, and if enough people believed and prayed and had faith, all the conflict and hatred of four centuries could be brushed aside and finally forgotten.

# 12

Steven Jannaway stood on the bridge of HMS *Copenhagen* and focussed his binoculars on the upper rim of the sun as it rose out of a misty horizon. The four destroyers, *Nile* , *St James*, *Matapan* and *Copenhagen*, were proceeding in column at the end of their passage back to Malta, the outline of which was a dark lump, fifteen miles distant on the horizon.

'Off navigation lights!' Jannaway ordered, as he saw the senior ship's lights go out. The bosun's mate pressed down the master navigation light switch, and Jannaway moved to the Pelorus to take a bearing of the sun. 'One zero nine and a half,' he whispered to himself, and noted the bearing in the log. He took the Stuart's distance meter from the bridge chart table and focussed it on the masthead of HMS *Nile*, bringing the image of it down to the waterline and reading off the range from the scale. 'Two and three quarter cables,' he muttered, and picked up the wheelhouse intercom microphone. He thought a moment, then ordered, 'Revolutions, one one zero,' and the man on the wheel a deck below repeated the order and reported, 'One one zero revolutions repeated sir.'

Jannaway replaced the microphone in its stowage and turned to the bosun's mate. 'Right Kingsbury. You can make a start on the brightwork.'

Ordinary Seaman Kingsbury swallowed the last of his bacon sandwich and said, 'Sir.'

'And no dribbles of Bluebell, either.'

'Sir.'

Jannaway watched Kingsbury take out the cloth and the polish, then went and stood on the upper platform. He had been on watch since four a.m. and was a little stiff with tiredness. Apart from that, all was well: the ship was in station, the log was up to date, the bosun's mate was polishing the copper voicepipes; the duckboards had been scrubbed by the morning watchmen, and a neat row of radar fixes on the chart would demonstrate to the captain, when he came up to the bridge, that his officer-of-the-watch had been keeping a careful check on the ship's position.

He heard a step behind him and turned. It was the yeoman of signals, in white open-necked shirt, white shorts, white stockings and white shoes, his cap cover clean and his cap badge central. He saluted. 'Morning, sir.'

'Morning yeoman.'

The petty officer crossed to where the signalman of the watch sat crouched over a well thumbed copy of *Kaywana Blood*. 'Come on, lad, put that away,' he said, and looked at the signal log to ensure no signals of importance had been passed since he was last on the bridge. That done, he glanced back at the signal halyards and immediately noticed something wrong. 'Permission to lower the emergency NUC lights, sir?' he asked Jannaway, to which Jannaway replied. 'Oh, Christ. Yes, thank you yeoman.'

The signalman scurried to lower the offending 'not under command' lights, which should have been lowered at sunrise, and the yeoman said, 'I'll be round at tot time, sir,' to Jannaway, with a small smile of satisfaction at saving the lieutenant from the captain's wrath or a rude signal from Captain D, or both.

Jannaway looked at the islands on the horizon. He could just make out the skyline of Valletta through his binoculars now.

'Excuse me, sir.'

'Yes, Kingsbury.'

'Permission to call the hands, sir.'

'Yes please,' Jannaway said crisply, and lowered his binoculars. Ordinary seaman Kingsbury blew the biscuit crumbs out of his bosun's call, and a moment later launched into that infuriating piece of noise that is used by the Royal Navy to awaken its servants: the pipe chirruped up and down like a starling gone berserk, and the bosun's mate intoned over the ship's broadcast a little ditty that went, ''Eave-o, 'eave-o, 'eave-o, lash up and stow. Wakey-wakey, rise and shine, you've had your time, I've had mine. Hands off cocks, on socks.'

A few minutes later, the first lieutenant appeared on the bridge, immaculate in his newly laundered whites and smelling of his elusive after-shave. 'All well, Steven?' he enquired, and looked aft to make sure that the NUC lights had been lowered, which they had. He crossed to the chart table, looked at the log and the chart. 'Worked out the gyro error?' he said.

Jannaway hadn't, but wasn't going to admit the fact. 'Half a degree high, sir,' he said.

'Stick it in the log, then.'

'Just about to, sir.'

Peter Lasbury stood on the upper platform while Jannaway entered his little piece of fiction in the log, and sniffed the morning air like a freshly groomed gelding. 'Are we in station?'

'Just about sir.'

'We look a bit close to me.'

Jannaway focussed the Stuart again and made an adjustment in engine revolutions.

'So we were inside,' Lasbury said.

'Fractionally, yes, sir.'

'Kingsbury!' Lasbury said.

'Sir?'

'What's all this about "hands off cocks on socks"?'

Kingsbury grinned. 'Makes a change from "don't turn over turn out", sir.'

Lasbury drummed his fingers on the Pelorus. 'Well I don't like it. It's vulgar. It'll give the junior seamen the wrong idea.'

The ship came gradually to life. The captain appeared on the bridge with a trace of egg on his lip and acknowledged the morning salutes of his first lieutenant, his yeoman and his officer-of-the-watch, looking back at the mast to make sure Jannaway had remembered the NUC lights, glancing at the ship ahead to check that *Copenhagen* was in station, glancing at the row of fixes on the chart, noting that there was a trace of Bluebell on one of the brass tallies. Kingsbury piped 'Hands to breakfast and clean,' and three quarters of an hour later, both watches of seamen fell in by the torpedo tubes and were detailed off to prepare for entering harbour.

Jannaway, relieved of the watch by the gunnery officer, snatched a quick poached egg in the wardroom before going down to his cabin to wash and change. While he was doing so, Lasbury's voice came over the loudspeaker in the passage. 'Special sea dutymen to your stations. Assume damage control state two condition Yankee.' Jannaway laced his lieutenant's epaulettes into a clean shirt and put it on. He put his best cap on his head, checked in the mirror that the seam of the cover was central, and went aft to the upperdeck.

Malta was a few miles off the starboard bow now. He walked out onto the irondeck and acknowledged the salute of the top petty officer, a weatherbeaten torpedoman from Cornwall. 'all squared away are we, petty officer Pascoe?' he asked, and walked along the deck with his hands behind his back, nodding good morning to the men in his division who were taking in the boat rope. He was not exactly playing a part so much as behaving in the way a naval officer was expected to behave: demanding high standards, thinking ahead, making sure and sure again that nothing had been overlooked. The awareness that he was doing so was oddly pleasing. He knew that he had learnt a great deal in the past two months, and was proud of the fact. He was at last beginning to feel like a proper naval officer; he was giving the captain fewer opportunities upon which to exercise his scorn and was beginning to carry out his duties as correspondence officer in the way that Commander Tinnick expected, presenting ready-drafted letters for his approval and writing suggested courses of action on the minute sheets that were attached to incoming correspondence.

He flexed his shoulders. The sun was well up now, and the sandstone harbours of Malta were bathed in its light. He paced up and down, looking out over the dark blue sea. Catherine was due out tomorrow on the morning flight. He had had a letter from Alan saying how well she and his mother had got on this time.

He thought of Julietta. He had seen her four more times after that first night at Paddy Maher's. She had been a lot of fun, and he was glad to have had the experience: part of him felt that a man should have a little experience before getting married, and he believed that to have had a brief flirtation like that was probably no bad thing. It had been quite difficult to break the friendship, too; but he had done it: he had come to his senses, gone to confession and written a letter to her explaining that he was as good as engaged and that he could not meet her again. She had written back a short, hurtful letter which he had immediately destroyed. It was an episode that was now over, in the past.

The members of *Copenhagen*'s wardroom, with the exception of Keith Parry, had agreed that he was crazy. Julietta Braddle was quite a catch, and anyone who threw her back into the pond must need his head seeing to. All the same, he felt that they were treating him with a little more regard: not many junior lieutenants captivated the heart of an admiral's daughter and then dropped her. Jannaway might be a bloody idiot in some respects, but at least he knew his own mind.

The first lieutenant's voice boomed out over the loudspeakers again. 'Close all screen doors and scuttles. Men out of the rig of the day, clear off the upperdeck.'

The four destroyers reduced speed, and each hoisted her call-sign flags at the yard arm. On the bridge of HMS *Copenhagen*, Commander Tinnick sat in his high chair supervising the special sea duty officer-of-the-watch, awaiting the moment when he would take over the con for the final stages of the arrival. A clean white ensign flapped from the ensign staff at the stern, and the ceremonial tompions with the ship's crest had been placed in the muzzles of the four-point-five inch guns. The first lieutenant had personally toured the upperdeck to ensure that no rope's end had been left hanging, no scuttle left open, no piece of armament left at the wrong angle of elevation or training. The radar aerials were trained fore and aft, the signal halyards made taut and the gash shute stowed away. HMS *Copenhagen* was ready for entering harbour.

The procedure for entering Sliema Creek was not a simple one. Tradition laid down that ships should berth with their bows pointing seaward, to facilitate a quick get-away if required. Because Sliema Creek was too narrow to turn in, each destroyer had to nose into Marxamxett harbour, lower her boats while turning at rest in the entrance and then, to give good steerage way, proceed backwards as fast as the captain dared down the creek to her berth between head and stern buoys. It was a test of skill for the whole chain of command on board – from the captain giving engine and wheel orders right down to the most junior rating in the boiler-room, manipulating the oil sprayers under the direction of the chief stoker. Split second timing was required, and mistakes could be expensive.

Another tradition – peculiar to Sliema Creek – was that when a destroyer squadron arrived, the Flag Officer Flotillas witnessed the arrival from the balcony outside his offices on Manoel Island, and Henry Braddle was there with his chief yeoman and flag lieutenant, watching as HMS *Nile*, Captain D's ship, turned at rest at the entrance to the harbour.

Braddle raised his telescope and examined the destroyer in detail as she passed in front of him, a white wave of foam at her stern, the voice of the first lieutenant barking over the ship's broadcast to call the men fallen in to attention, the bosun's call shrilling out over the water, a puff of black smoke emerging from the funnel as the boiler room connected another sprayer.

The water boiled harder under her stern as the engines were put ahead and the ship slowed and came to rest between her buoys; the ship's motor boat crew caught the heaving line thrown down to them from the destroyer's fo'c's'le, and a minute later the two buoy jumpers were scrambling over the mooring buoy in their blue overalls, heaving the wire picking-up rope through the buoy ring and passing it back to the fo'c's'le to be hove in. At the stern, a wire bridle was passed to the buoy, and this would later be covered in canvas and the canvas wetted and whitened so that it shrunk tight. The order 'out booms and ladders!' echoed across the water, and immediately the midships and stern booms swung out and the accommodation ladder was lowered.

Rear Admiral Braddle lowered his telescope. The evolution had been well but not perfectly carried out, and a moment later the chief yeoman was making rapid semaphore to the bridge of HMS *Nile*. BERTHING WELL EXECUTED. BOATS COXSWAINS FAILED TO PAY PROPER MARKS OF RESPECT.

*Copenhagen* was already turning at the entrance to the creek. Her boats were in the water, and each coxswain saluted smartly as his boat passed under the admiral's balcony. A cloud of black smoke shot upward from the destroyer's funnel as Tinnick ordered the engines astern; Braddle raised his telescope and smiled in approval. *Copenhagen* was his favourite ship: he had commanded her in '45 in the Pacific when she was brand new, and had never lost his affection for her. There was no doubt that Tinnick was using considerably more revolutions to make his sternboard than had the Captain D: the foam at *Copenhagen*'s stern boiled white, and spray came up over the quarterdeck, soaking the torpedo and anti-submarine officer's ankles as he stood to attention and faced aft.

That was the sort of dash that Henry Braddle expected of his destroyer captains. The trouble with 'Britain's New Navy' as Carrington insisted on calling it was that there weren't enough damn ships in it, and that meant that captains were for ever nervous of denting them or their careers. Tinnick was taking a risk by using such high speed to approach the buoys, but it was a risk of which Henry Braddle approved.

He watched as another cloud of oily smoke issued from the funnel, and the ship stopped dead between her buoys. Braddle turned to his chief yeoman. 'Make to *Copenhagen*, Bravo Zulu.' The chief yeoman raised his arms and made the 'J' in semaphore, which was immediately acknowledged. Braddle focussed his lens on the face of Tinnick and watched as the message was passed, so that

199

he could actually see the brief nod of the destroyer captain as the message was passed to him.

The letters 'BZ' meant 'well done' and a few moments after the signal had been sent, a brief cheer went up from the decks of HMS *Copenhagen*.

Four bags of mail arrived on board while the hands were spreading awnings. They were taken for'd to the coxswain's office where Postie and a couple of volunteer electricians who had nothing else to do sorted it into pigeon holes. At ten fifteen, the bosun's mate piped: 'Stand easy. Mail is now ready for collection at the coxswain's office,' and a queue formed in the passage to collect the bundles of letters.

The officers fell upon their mail with as much enthusiasm as the ratings. They sat on their chintz covered seats by the bar fender, cups of tea balanced beside them, ripping open envelopes and suppressing exclamations of surprise at the news from home. A wooden fan whipped round overhead, and for a while no one spoke.

Steven Jannaway had a bill from Gieves, a bank statement from Lloyds and a last minute letter from Catherine. 'Just a note to say I'm counting the minutes and that I love you,' was how it started, and although it covered three sides it said little more than that. She was due out on the night flight arriving at crack of dawn on Saturday; she was packing her dark glasses and her sun tan lotion, there were all sorts of things she had to tell him and she loved him and loved him and loved him.

He smiled to himself, put her letter back into its envelope and opened the last letter, which bore no stamp and had come by hand from the office of the Flag Officer Flotillas. It was from Julietta. 'We're having a barge picnic tomorrow, Sat, after the regatta, will pick you up soon after midday. See you. J.'

He looked at the note for several seconds without changing expression: he sat with his bare elbows on his bare knees under the rotating fan; and then, crumpling the note quickly and tossing it into a polished four-point-five inch shell case, he left the wardroom to go down to the ship's office.

'Out pipes,' announced the bosun's mate on the ship's broadcast. 'Hands carry on with your work.'

Catherine felt dazed. Her night flight to Luqa had been delayed several hours, she had been unable to sleep in the departure lounge at Heathrow, and sleep on the plane had been made impossible by the child in the seat next to her, who had cried almost all the way.

She stepped out of the aircraft soon after nine o'clock. A warm, southerly wind was blowing, making her regret the choice of a wide-brimmed hat for her arrival. She held on to it as she crossed the dispersal, and her pale green dress was blown against her legs.

She looked up at the spectators' gallery to see if she could see Steven, but he wasn't there, nor was he in the arrivals hall when she emerged from the customs check. She put her case down and looked round for him, and was just about to go across and have a cup of coffee while she waited when Jill Parry hurried up looking sun-pink and pregnant in a print dress and a bright blue hair band.

'Sorry!' she said as if she had been with Catherine only a moment ago. 'I got stuck behind a lorry. Steven's in a regatta so he can't make it. If we get a move on we may be in time for the first race. I'm parked just over there, can you manage that case?' She talked almost non-stop, giving Catherine little time to reply. 'Why they have to start at ten, goodness knows. Keith says it's because the sailors are full of rum in the afternoons. How are you? You're looking well. Here we are, this is our jalopy. Stick that in the back, that's it.'

They drove off.

'Ever been to Malta before?' Jill asked, and when Catherine said no, it was her first time, said, 'Oh, first of many I expect' in a knowing way, glancing across to smile at Catherine and then, having glanced back at the road, swerving to avoid a mule cart.

Catherine looked out at the dusty little fields and the crumbling stone walls. Jill guessed what she was thinking. 'It's looking a bit barren I'm afraid. Lovely in the spring, but the green soon goes. Do you play tennis? Because that's the place to play if you do. The Marsa. Very pukka sahib.'

'When's the baby due?' Catherine asked, breaking into the stream of chatter.

'Oh – first week in December. I'm afraid we got a bit carried away when I came out to Gib. Keith says Gib's a go mad place, and I have a feeling he's right. Everyone's either having their first fling after leaving UK or their last before going back. Something you should remember if you ever marry a naval officer. Always visit him in Gib!'

'What's this regatta?'

The tyres squealed on hot tarmac as Jill took a corner and accelerated up towards Valletta. 'Squadron pulling regatta. They have it once a year. You know – boat races. They all get rather worked up about it poor dears. See all the different colour buses?'

'Yes, I know all about that, they're different routes aren't they? I've been reading up my travel brochure.'

'You have, have you?' Jill lapsed into silence for a while and they sped down through Vittoriana. 'This is Msida Creek,' she said. 'Where the minesweepers and subs live. Sliema's the next one along. That's Manoel Island.'

They went along a straight road beside the water, and the four destroyers came into sight. Jill drove round to the far side of the creek and parked near the dghaisa landing stage.

The ships looked immaculately clean: they were berthed with their bows pointing away from the town, the scuttles polished, the mooring bridles painted white, the awnings spread and the guns all pointing in the same direction.

'I don't really feel as though I'm here!' Catherine said.

Jill had called a dghaisa alongside and they stepped into the sternsheets. A wizened Maltese began rowing them out to the second ship in the line; there was a loud report, and the creek was suddenly full of the sound of cheering.

'They've started!' Jill said. 'Look! Coming this way!'

The race had started at the seaward end of the creek: Catherine could see the four whalers almost head on, their oars dipping out of time, and a small following of ships' motor boats coming along behind them. On Jill's instructions, the dghaisaman lay on his oars so that they could have a close view of the race as it went by.

As the boats came along the creek, the cheering transferred from the first ship to the second and the second to the third. Each of the destroyer fo'c's'les was crowded with men, and officers looked down from the bridges and gun decks. Each ship had its own peculiar method of urging on its crew: there was chanting, cheering and a great deal of time shouting. 'IN ... OUT ... IN ... OUT ...' A hunting horn, property of the navigating officer of HMS *Nile*, tooted and bayed; bongo drums, owned by the skiffle group aboard HMS *St James*, sounded insistently. But all this shouting and noise seemed to do little to speed the four boats. Their crews swung back and forth, back and forth; the oars dipped, and dipped; the coxswains, standing in the stern with a spare oar poking out over the back, urged their men on, one swaying his body back and forth to give the time, another barking it out, holding his body rigid, and a third apparently brandishing an imaginary cat o' nine tails in his clenched fist with which to lash the sweating bodies of his five-man crew.

As they came past HMS *Copenhagen*, a new chant started: 'Co-pen-ha-gen! Co-pen-ha-gen! Co-pen-ha-gen! Oggy-Oggy-Oggy!'

'What's the Oggy-Oggy-Oggy for?' Catherine shouted to Jill, who shouted back, 'It's because she's a Guz ship. You know, from Devonport.'

Here they were now: only a few feet separating the first two boats, the second two having a private race of their own for third place. As they went past, Catherine had a blurred impression only. It was not that the boats went by at great speed but that the flying spray from the oars, the roar of men's voices and the sheer competitive aggression that was latent in the air had a mesmeric effect. Five men, faces red, teeth bared, singlets drenched in sweat; oars bending under the strain; a hoarse, Glaswegian voice which shouted 'PULL! – out! PULL - out! PULL – out!'; and then, when they were past, the sight of the boats going on to the finishing line and a feeling that the race was not nearly as important as it had seemed. All that shouting, all that tumult, and it ended with men slumped over their oars exhausted and sadly inglorious.

The dghaisa went alongside the starboard after accommodation ladder, and a midshipman saluted as Jill and Catherine stepped aboard. He led the way along the irondeck and up to the fo'c's'le, where he waited for them by a vertical steel ladder.

'Are you expecting me to climb that, Nigel?' Jill asked.

The midshipman looked apologetic. 'I'm afraid there's wet paint on the Bofors gun deck,' he said. 'So this is the only way up.'

'Are you sure we're supposed to be here?' Catherine asked when she had followed Jill up the ladder. 'We're the only females present!'

'Don't worry about that. It's "officers and their ladies". The fact that we're the only two is neither here nor there.'

The officers were wearing their white tropical shorts and shirts and looked like knobbly-kneed boy scouts. 'Peter, where's that husband of mine?' Jill asked Lasbury, who smiled, ignoring Catherine and saying: 'On the bridge, organising the tote.'

A Maltese steward brought iced coffee on a silver tray, and they were joined by Commander Tinnick. 'Now let me see you're . . .'

'Catherine Eagles.'

'Oh yes. Yes. Of course.' He looked her up and down and nodded, seeming for a moment to be listening to a voice no one else could hear. 'Arrived today, yes?'

'Yes.'

'Well young Jannaway's stroking the officers' whaler, so I don't suppose you'll see him yet awhile.'

Another race started. The officers leaned out over the guardrail and shouted. One jumped up and down. On the fo'c's'le, the ship's company yelled their chant again, and another quartet of boats came by, the oars digging into the water. Shortly after it was over, they saw Steven. He was standing in the bows of the ship's motor cutter looking serious. 'Why doesn't he look this way!' Catherine said, and waved furiously to no effect.

The next race was the officers' whaler. 'We'll walk this,' Wingrove told Jill. 'No trouble at all.' The starting gun fired and the oars dipped. Commander Tinnick watched through his telescope. 'Oh bloody hell,' he said in a matter of fact way. 'They've broken an oar.' The boats approached, the cheering rippled down the creek, echoing back off the sandstone buildings on Manoel Island, and quite unexpectedly, Catherine found herself swept away on the tide of cheering as the *Copenhagen* boat, creeping up from third place to second and then on to challenge the lead, came by. 'Come on! Come on! Come on *Copenhagen*!' she heard herself shouting, and when the race was over was as anxious to hear the result as anyone else.

'Second!' Tinnick said and punched the air in frustration. 'Not good enough,' he said, pacing up and down. 'Not good enough at all.' He shook his head as if something very serious had gone wrong. He smacked a fist in his hand, and when Jannaway came up to the gun deck, sweaty in shorts and singlet and gym shoes without socks, he beckoned him over immediately. 'Did you snatch at that oar, you miserable officer?' he asked, and Jannaway said good humouredly, 'No sir, I did not.'

'Well you may have lost us the cock.'

Jannaway came across to Catherine. 'You made it!' he said, but didn't touch her. A dribble of sweat was going down the side of his face; he seemed bigger, heavier, more muscular. 'We were bloody unlucky,' he said. 'We'd've had them in a few more seconds.' He looked back into Catherine's eyes. 'Good trip out?'

'She's exhausted,' Jill said. 'She hasn't slept all night.'

'I'm all right! Just feeling a little strange.'

'I'll grab a shower,' Steven said. 'Be with you in ten or fifteen minutes.' He went backwards down the ladder and blew her a secret kiss before his head disappeared below the level of the deck.

There was a dghaisa race for commanding officers after the whaler races were over. HMS *Nile* won the overall cup and hoisted a bright red rooster made of plywood to indicate that she was the cock of the squadron. Cold champagne was served in the wardroom of *Copenhagen*, and Jannaway came in wearing the lightweight suit Mr Mamo had made for him.

'Steven', said Commander Tinnick in Catherine's hearing. 'What about the punishment return?'

'Done, sir,' Jannaway said crisply, aware that Catherine was listening. 'Rudd will bring it up for signature tomorrow morning. I've checked it personally.'

Tinnick nodded and listened to his inner voice. 'Inputs for Captain D's report of proceedings?'

'Drafted, sir. Chief's added a paragraph about the diesel generator, and TAS has promised his squid firing comments by Monday.'

'Anything else before you go?'

Jannaway grinned confidently. 'No, sir.'

'Sure?'

'Hundred percent, sir.'

'Right.' Tinnick looked at Catherine. 'I suppose you want to drag him away do you? Go on, Steven, off you go.'

They went ashore in the officers' motor cutter. Catherine transferred her luggage into the car Steven had hired and unpacked her swimming things. They stopped in Sliema and bought cooked chicken legs, tomatoes, melon and wine for a picnic. 'What about a knife?' she asked, and he said, 'Got one; a seaman always carries a knife.'

They drove north along the coast past St Julians and St George's to St Paul's Bay. He left the main road and they bumped along a track that seemed to lead nowhere, parking by a ruined farmhouse where prickly pears grew and a herd of shoats grazed. He led the way down a narrow path to a small beach, and they spread their towels.

'How do you know about this place?' she asked, looking up at the cliffs on either side.

He winked. 'Local knowledge.'

'I feel very strange. As if I'm in a dream.'

He kissed her. 'Perhaps you are.'

She put her swimming costume on before taking off her dress, and turned away from him to put the straps over her shoulders.

'Last one in's a sissy!' he said, and dived from a rock. They splashed about; he duck dived and came up close to her. They kissed wetly and looked into each other's eyes. 'You make me feel randy,' he said. 'It's been a long time.' He pressed himself against her. 'It's all right. There's no one around.'

But she felt it was necessary to keep him at his distance. 'Perhaps *because* there's no one around,' she explained.

They lay on their towels and dried in the sun. 'Anyway, what's this surprise you were talking about?' he asked.

She hesitated before telling him. Lying almost naked with him on a beach seemed the wrong place to speak of such things. 'I've been accepted into the Church,' she said.

'That's wonderful!'

She smiled uncertainly. They sat side by side and she told him of her week with her brother and Elspeth, and the opposition of her parents.

'Shall we get engaged?' he said. 'Officially? Today? I'd like to. I want to. I need you.' He thought a moment. 'We could announce it tonight. At the party on board *Ausonia*.'

'What's *Ausonia*?'

'The support ship. They're giving a jump up. I thought we could go on there after dinner.'

He made it all seem very simple. Perhaps she should say yes, go through with it. She imagined how it would be: they would open champagne, it would be like winning a boat race.

'Let's keep it a secret a bit longer,' she said.

'Does that mean you've said yes then? Definitely?'

'All right.'

He held her. 'Don't cry, little Mouse.'

'I can't help it.'

'You are sure, aren't you?'

Was she? If only she knew! Everything seemed right: her body longed for him, they were friends, he needed her and goodness knew how much she needed him. But did she need him for the wrong reasons? Did she want to be an elder sister or a mother to him?

'Yes, I'm sure,' she whispered. 'It's just – been a bit sudden, that's all.'

He laughed. 'Not all that sudden! Over four years!'

'Let's be really close,' she said. 'Let's never hide anything from each other. All right?'

They swam again, lay in the sun again, and talked. She told him how, ever since learning that her parents were not her real parents, she had always prayed that one day she would be more important to someone than anyone else in the world. 'You are that to me now,' he told her.

'Am I? I don't know about that.'

'You are. I can't explain why. But you are.'

'You seem . . . more confident, Steve. You've changed.'

'For better or for worse?'

'I don't know.'

He rolled on his back and looked up at the sky. 'Yes, I suppose I have,' he said. 'I'm beginning to latch on to how the navy works. I thought I knew it all when I left *Syston*, but I realise now that I didn't. And I'm really quite grateful to Tinnick. He was a bastard to me when I joined *Copenhagen*, but it was necessary for him to be one. Commanding a warship isn't like organising a Sunday school outing.'

'Did you ever think it would be?'

'Not consciously.' He took her hand and lifted it so that her white arm was close up against his heavily suntanned shoulder. 'If we actually had to go to war, I'd rather have a Tinnick for a captain than some kindly old Father Christmas with twinkling blue eyes. Efficiency is what counts in the long run, and you can't run an efficient ship by being a nice guy to everyone the whole time.'

'Does that mean you're not a nice guy anymore?'

'I never was all that nice.' He rolled over towards her. 'You are making me feel very, very randy,' he whispered.

'Not the first day,' she said. 'Please.'

The sun edged down towards the cliff behind them, and they went up the path to the car. On the way back to Sliema, they stopped by a church and went inside. They knelt down side by side, their hands tightly clasped. Catherine prayed a jumble of prayers, asking for blessings, for forgiveness, for strength. In the middle of these prayers she felt a touch on her shoulder and looked round. It was the priest, pointing to her bare arms and shaking his finger. 'Not in the church please,' he said.

A dog jumped out of the way as they drove off. 'That makes me bloody angry!' Steven said.

'Steve! It doesn't matter!'

'It matters to me!'

'You don't have to defend the Church to me! I'm part of it!'

He drove fast back to St Julians, the low stone walls hurtling by on either side, a woman in black standing close in to the side of the road as he went past. Catherine was staying at the Parrys' flat and he dropped her there before going back to the ship to get changed. 'I'll be in a better temper when I've had a shower,' he said. 'Don't give up on me, will you?'

She leant across and kissed him. 'I'll never give up on you,' she whispered.

Jill Parry welcomed her into the flat. 'Have you had a super day? Where did you go? I should think you're scorched to a frazzle aren't you?' She padded about the tiled floors, the sound of her flip-flops echoing in the hall, and an aroma of fly spray pervading the front room where they sipped their iced colas and waited for Keith to finish in the shower.

Jannaway sat in the dghaisa and heard, all over again, how Salvo Borg had been dghaisaman to the battleship HMS *Queen Elizabeth* in the thirties. 'Oh yes, sair, those were some ships in those days, sair. All this creek – full of destroyers. All Grand Harbour – full of cruisers, battleships. Big ships, sair, with big guns. I remember my father he did one hundred seven trips in one day. I remember –' On and on he went, a steady stream of nostalgia issuing from his toothless head, his back to Jannaway as he pushed on the looms, the boat jerking forward, jerking forward across the calm water. Behind them, the evening sky erupted suddenly in a shower of explosions: another saint's day celebration had begun, another excuse for letting off countless more expensive and highly dangerous home-made fireworks.

They went alongside the accommodation ladder. 'Wait here Salvo, okay?' Jannaway said, and gave the old man a sixpenny piece as he stepped off the dghaisa. 'I'll be back in ten minutes to go ashore again.'

'Sair! Wait a minute! Oh sair!' Salvo Borg looked up at the grey hull of the destroyer in anguish. Sixpence wasn't enough these days, and you could never be sure, when an officer said that he would be right back, how long you would have to wait. He pushed the boat a few yards clear of the ship and sat down, breaking off a hunk of bread to eat with a piece of sausage he had gleaned from the petty officer chef that morning.

On board, the bo'sun's mate caught up with Jannaway just as he was about to enter the starboard screen door. 'Message from the flag lieutenant to FOFMED, sir,' he said. 'Will you please ring the admiral as soon as possible?'

'The admiral?'

'The admiral's residence, sir,' the bo'sun's mate said, correcting himself.

'Okay, Ringwood. Thanks.

That would probably be Julietta wanting to know why he hadn't been on the barge picnic. He went for'd, stepping over the high bulkhead coamings, and slid open his cabin door. He stripped quickly, wrapped a towel round his waist and went back along the starboard passage to the officers' bathroom. Lasbury was just finishing a shower. He came out of the cubicle naked and eyed Jannaway as he soaped himself under the cool water.

'You're in trouble,' he said. He dried between his buttocks and pulled the towel up, over the prancing panther. 'The Braddles were expecting you on their barge today.'

Jannaway turned and lifted his face to the rush of water. 'I never said I was going, sir.'

'Yes, but weren't you invited?'

'Only very informally.'

Lasbury dried between his toes. 'That doesn't matter, Steven. If you get invited to an admiral's picnic, you make bloody sure you answer the invitation. That's basic good manners, apart from anything else.'

Jannaway felt suddenly impatient. 'Sir – it was just a scruffy little note from Julietta. It wasn't a proper invitation at all.'

Lasbury looked at him and shook his head. 'What an idiot you are,' he said, putting on a silk dressing gown with a Chinese lion embroidered on the back. 'It doesn't cost much to keep on the right side of the admiral, and what it does cost is a bloody good investment. If I were you, I'd ring up and apologise right away.'

Lasbury left the bathroom and Jannaway returned to his cabin. He put on black evening trousers and a white sharkskin dinner jacket. He tied his bow tie rapidly, pulling the doubled ends out so that they were exactly equal in length. He put on patent leather shoes and a deep blue cummerbund. He pushed a freshly laundered linen handkerchief into the left sleeve of his jacket, ran an electric razor over his face and smacked his cheeks with Yardley after-shave. 'You are a handsome swine, Jannaway,' he muttered, looking at himself in the mirror. He bared his teeth, and looked at his tongue. His coal black hair, wet from the shower, was shot with reflected colour from the electric light. He checked his wallet, his identity card, his contraceptive and his cash; he filled a leather cigarette case with king size Rothmans, and departed rapidly, striding aft along the irondeck, stiffening to attention for a moment to acknowledge the bo'sun's mate's salute as he went over the side.

Moments after the boat had moved away from the side of HMS *Copenhagen*, able seaman Ringwood came to the stern and called to him.

'Lieutenant Jannaway, sir!'

'Yes?'

'Telephone for you sir. Miss Braddle.'

'Tell her I've gone ashore.'

'I can't do that, sir!'

'Why not?'

'She says she can see you from where she's phoning, sir.' Ringwood grinned. 'Sorry sir, but she's insisting like.'

Jannaway thought a moment. He didn't want to get involved in a conversation with Julietta. He didn't want to hear her voice, that low, sexy voice which had captivated him from the moment he had shared a sofa with her. He didn't want to speak to her ... and yet at the same time he did. He felt confused, tempted. He knew he shouldn't feel the way he felt, knew that he should not be in the slightest bit tempted. He knew, too, that if there was not the last vestige of affection left for Julietta, if there was nothing about her that he liked, that it would be all too easy to go back on board, pick up the phone and tell her, in the nicest possible way, to get lost.

'Tell her ... tell her I'm ... otherwise engaged,' he said. 'Have you got that? Otherwise engaged.'

Salvo Borg leant on the sweeps and the boat moved forward. 'That Admiral Braddle, Henry Braddle, I remember him when he was a midshipman, sair. He was cox'n of the officers' cutter the year *Devonshire* was cock of the fleet. He was in charge of a picket boat that year the gregale blew so hard one of the destroyers dragged her moorings...'

The sun was down now and the lights of Sliema were reflected in the creek. At the landing stage, other dghaisas lay alongside, their owners sitting on crates, smoking and talking.

Jannaway pressed half a crown into Borg's horny hand, and set off. 'Thank you sir! Thank you very much!' the old man called after him; and as he drove off through Sliema and up through the back streets, Julietta Braddle stood at her bedroom window, grimly determined that Jannaway would be forced to speak to her again before very long.

They sat at a corner table in the Phoenicia eating swordfish steaks and fresh green salad, Catherine looking pink from her first day in the sun, her hair loose about her shoulders, her grey-green eyes deep and serious when she looked up at him in the shy way she had. The waiter brought Asti Spumante in an ice bucket, and they toasted each other lovingly, aware how well they looked together, how right they were for each other and how strong was the bond between them.

After the meal, the wine waiter offered the liqueur list. 'We must have a cognac,' Steven said. 'The cognac here is rather special, isn't it Mario?' He smiled knowingly to the waiter, who offered him a cigar.

'Yes, why not,' he said, and pierced the end with a matchstick.

'I've never seen you smoke a cigar before,' Catherine said.

'Lots of things you've never seen me do, my lover,' he said in his Devon drawl.

The waiter poured the brandies. 'Watch this,' Jannaway said, and laid his glass on its side.

'Careful!'

'No, look. It won't spill.' The cognac came exactly to the rim of the glass. He rolled it round in a circle and the Maltese waiter looked on, beaming.

'It's amazing!' Catherine said. 'He measured it by eye, didn't he?'

'I've seen him do that for sixteen people at a lunch party, and he got every single one exactly right,' he said, and she was inwardly amused at the importance he attached to the waiter's trick.

'Let's dance,' he said, and took her confidently in his arms, steering her about the floor, avoiding other couples, his hand firm in the small of her back. She thought of the last time she had danced with him in Plymouth. She would hardly have believed it possible for him to gain so much more poise in so short a time. But it was a fact: she had known him first as a gangly teenager, gauche and tongue-tied; then a muddle-headed sub lieutenant, determined to get her into his bed and now – now he was a naval lieutenant in a white dinner jacket and sparkling patent leather shoes.

'What are you thinking about?' he asked, drawing back to look down into her eyes.

'Just that I love you,' she whispered, and he held her very closely, his chin against the top of her head.

The band played, they turned round and round and she thought yes, this is a moment that I shall remember.

Julietta was not inclined to revelry that evening and had not come to the party on board HMS *Ausonia* to enjoy herself. The band was playing 'Rock Around the Clock' and she watched contemptuously as her parents tried to demonstrate that there was life in the old dogs yet.

Henry was wearing his tropical mess undress. The good life of cocktail parties, barge picnics, mess dinners and beach barbecues was already taking its toll on his figure, and his brass-buttoned waistcoat was having difficulty in containing his belly. He was twirling Clara this way and that with great gusto, his face flushed and his heavy body jigging up and down out of time with the beat. 'Over here, over here!' he roared, 'No, your left hand, your left hand!' and Clara, wishing she were forty and pretending she was thirty, dashed about trying to obey and look feminine at the same time.

'Not dancing?' a voice shouted in Julietta's ear.

It was Johnny Tinnick, the captain of *Copenhagen*. She shook her head briefly and looked back at the band. The saxophone player – a Royal Marine corporal wearing a burgundy tuxedo – was swinging his instrument up and down like an elephant tossing its trunk; the drummer seemed to be hitting out at anything within reach.

Tinnick was attempting conversation. 'Splendid party!' he shouted. 'I must say your pa is doing exceedingly well! Quite sure you wouldn't like to give it a try?'

'Quite sure, thank you.'

Tinnick sat back in his chair and they watched the tumult. On the far side of the wardroom, a couple entered. It was Steven Jannaway and his girl friend who had come out from England.

Julietta watched them as they looked round for somewhere to sit. She saw Catherine nod in the direction of the admiral's table, and Jannaway shake his head. She saw another couple – Keith and Jill Parry – stop dancing, and the four go to a table and sit down. 'Rock Around the Clock' came to its shattering end, and the floor cleared, Henry returning breathless and laughing to his table.

'Most impressive sir!' Tinnick said, rising as Henry and Clara took their seats.

Clara took Julietta's hand. 'Are you all right, darling? Why aren't you dancing?'

'Because I don't feel like it,' Julietta said.

Charles Crivett-Smith came back to the table with the chief-of-staff's nanny. Penny Forden-Jones had gone back to Berkshire to treasure her memories.

The nanny, Carrie Dudswell, was freckled, jolly and capable. She was holding her arms away from her sides to allow the perspiration to evaporate.

The band began playing 'Blue Moon', and Julietta saw Jannaway and Catherine get up to dance. 'Charles,' she said, speaking to Crivett-Smith so that only he could hear. 'I've got to speak to Steven Jannaway.'

'He looks a bit heavily engrossed at the moment.'

'I don't care about that. He's been avoiding me, and I must speak to him.'

'What about?'

Her big dark eyes looked directly into his: she had done something to her eyelashes that made them look long and silky. The absurd thought occurred to him that her eyes would close automatically if you tipped her backward.

'That's my business,' she said. 'Now are you going to get him over here or am I going to have to ask my father?'

Charles Crivett-Smith looked back across the floor at Steven and Catherine. It was the end of a very long day for Catherine; her head rested on Steven's shoulder, and her eyes were closed.

Steven was glad Julietta was there. Catherine had not been very keen to go on to the dance in HMS *Ausonia* after her evening at the Phoenicia, but Jannaway had said that he wanted to show her off and be seen with her, so that even if they did not actually announce their engagement the likelihood of it would be apparent to all. Jill

213

Parry had already guessed as much. 'You're both looking very happy,' she had whispered to Steven. 'I wonder why?'

He had seen Julietta looking across at him, too, and was glad of that. Perhaps she would stop chasing him now. He moved his head more comfortably against Catherine's, holding her hand close under his chin as they danced. How soft and loving she was! She brought out all that was protective, gentle and – yes – good in him. He felt that with her he might be a better person. No, she was not the typical 'naval officer's wife'. She wouldn't prod him into promotion or woo his senior officers' approval with successful cocktail parties; but she would be 'there', his better half, the person he would love, honour, and care for above all others.

'Blue Moon' came to an end, and they returned to the table where Keith and Jill were sitting.

'I should think you're absolutely whacked aren't you?' Jill said to Catherine.

'Yes, but Steve's very good to lean against.' She took his hand. 'You're nice and solid, aren't you?'

'Thick as a short plank, more like,' Keith said, then glanced up as the flag lieutenant approached their table. 'Hullo, Charles. You coming to join us?'

'Not exactly.' Crivett-Smith bent and said quietly to Jannaway, 'Could I have a word?'

'Of course.'

Crivett-Smith glanced quickly at Catherine. Jannaway stood up, and they moved away. 'What is it?'

'Julietta tells me you've been deliberately avoiding her.'

Jannaway went on the defensive. 'Oh does she?'

'Yes she does, Steve.'

'Well I'd have thought the reason was fairly obvious.'

'Maybe. But you were invited to the barge picnic today, weren't you?'

'She sent me a note saying "see you tomorrow". I don't call that an invitation.'

'But you never bothered to reply.'

'No. I didn't. And she knows why.'

'Maybe she does. But she wants to speak to you.'

Jannaway pushed his thumbnail in between his front teeth. 'I don't care what she wants,' he said.

'You're being a bloody fool. Good manners don't cost much, and bad manners can cost one hell of a lot. If you've got any sense at all you'll get over to that table and make your apologies. Got it?'

Jannaway returned to his table.

'What was all that about?' Catherine asked.

He shook his head. 'Nothing much.' The band started playing a samba. 'Come on,' he said. 'I've had enough of this party.' He stood up. 'We're off,' he told the Parrys.

'Oh, shame!' Jill said. 'So soon! Wait a minute, you'd better have a key.'

They made their way out of the wardroom, and Catherine went into the officers' heads, which had been converted into a Ladies. When she came out into the cross-passage, she found Steven in conversation with Commander Tinnick. They turned as she appeared. Steven looked even more angry than he had while talking to the flag lieutenant.

'I'm afraid you'll have to excuse Steven for a few minutes,' Commander Tinnick said.

Steven shot a hostile glance at his captain and said to her, 'I'll be as quick as I can. Sorry about this,' and they left her there in the passage outside the wardroom.

She stood and waited, a stole round her shoulders. There was a glass-fronted cabinet on the bulkhead which contained a few silver trophies, and framed photographs of the Commander-in-Chief and the Flag Officer Flotillas flanked a ceremonial lifebuoy with the ship's crest mounted on a polished board. The brass ends of the fire hoses had been polished, as had the tallies on the electric switches by the door. While she stood there, a continual traffic went past her: stewards went to and fro taking piles of plates from the ante-room to the pantry, officers and their ladies went up on deck or returned to the party. She felt alone in an unfriendly world: people seemed to look through her.

She waited five minutes and then ten. What had happened? She had already heard that one of the ships in the squadron was being despatched at short notice to Cyprus to reinforce the naval presence there during the post-independence celebrations. Or perhaps it was this trouble in Kuwait. But surely Keith would have known about it already. She listened to the conversation of a lieutenant commander and a girl who looked ten years younger: a seducer and an obviously willing seducee. They went up a ladder holding hands and she heard the girl giggle excitedly at something he had said.

They belonged to a world of which she had little knowledge and felt afraid. She knew that Steven was being absorbed into that world and was adopting its mannerisms, its code of behaviour. Even now, there lingered a small thread of doubt about whether she should commit herself to him. It was as if she had given him the confidence to manage without her. Perhaps I'm being selfish, she thought. Perhaps I want him to need me too much.

She looked at her watch. He had been gone nearly twenty minutes. She was wondering if she ought to go and rejoin the Parrys when he appeared.

'Affairs of state?' she asked.

'No,' he said. 'No.' The light seemed to have gone out in his eyes. He looked as if he were haunted.

'What's wrong?'

He shook his head briefly. 'Let's get out of here,' he said, and she followed him up the double accommodation ladder, along the upperdeck and off the ship by the officers' brow. Saint's day fireworks exploded overhead. She almost had to run to keep up with him.

'What's wrong? What's happened? Where are we going?'

He laughed bitterly. 'I don't know where we're going, Catherine.'

She shivered. A motorbike went noisily along the Sliema waterfront; across the water, by the landing stage, drunken voices were singing 'Wonderful, wonderful Copenhagen.'

She caught his hand and held him back. 'You've got to tell me what's happened, Steven.'

They stood at the water's edge. The four destroyers were floodlit: their lights swam and shimmered in the water. A motor cutter chugged by, the coxswain blowing four blasts on a whistle for slow ahead.

'Can it be as bad as all that?' she whispered.

She looked up at him: she saw him struggle for control. She felt his hand tighten on hers. His voice broke in a sob; his eyes closed, and his mouth opened in a silent shout.

She reached out to him and took him in her arms, not caring any more who saw or what anyone might say. He wept bitterly and without restraint. Holding him, soothing him, she was aware of a feeling of great relief: for the first time since landing at Luqa that morning she knew positively that he was unchanged after all, that

216

he really did need her more than anyone else in the world, and that her decision to become a Catholic and to marry him had been right.

After a while, he was quiet. He drew back from her, gazing at her.

'Whatever it is, whatever has happened, I shall understand,' she whispered.

He released her and turned away. A rocket soared up into the night and burst into a shower of stars which drifted down, hissing as they fell into the waters of the creek.

He looked briefly into her eyes and then away. 'I've made a girl pregnant,' he said.

She didn't want to know how it had happened or with whom. He would have preferred it if she had broken down and wept, but she took the news in a frighteningly calm way. He wanted her to be angry with him, to condemn him, to let fly, but all she did was look down at his hands and shake her head. He explained about Julietta, how it had happened late at night, his first night ashore, his first real party. She didn't seem to listen. She looked away from him, seemed to travel elsewhere while he spoke. When he had finished, she was silent for a long time before she said, 'What are we going to do now?' He told her of Julietta's ideas about having the baby adopted, and immediately Catherine came back from where she had been. 'No!' she said. 'That is the one thing she must not do. Whatever else she does, she mustn't have it adopted! Your child, Steven. Your child, brought up by someone else. Never knowing who you are or who she is. Never knowing why – why –'

She broke off, controlled herself and finished: 'Never knowing why she wasn't wanted. Never knowing where she belongs. Always wondering. Always wanting ... someone ...'

They stood in silence. He heard Julietta's words again: 'I could have an abortion.' She had borrowed an officer's cabin in which to talk to him. Her parents didn't know yet but she was going to have to tell them soon. It was definite, too: a friend of hers, a surgeon lieutenant at Bighi, had done the test for her.

'Would you do that?' he had asked, horrified at the thought of it, and she had replied, 'Yes, if I had to.' And she, like Catherine, had said, 'What are we going to do?' She had not blamed him; she had simply put the facts before him: I am pregnant; I could have it adopted; I could have an abortion. What are we going to do?

She had looked up at him, her eyes liquid and pleading. 'So bloody silly,' she had said. 'I'd only just finished. I didn't think it could possibly happen.' Then she had sniffed and laughed and said, 'Well you could at least kiss me, you great big beautiful monster!' and she was in his arms again, her arms tight round him, her cheek against the lapel of his white dinner jacket.

'I think I'd like to go back, please,' Catherine said.

They walked to the car. He didn't know what to say. There was nothing he could say. 'Will I see you tomorrow?' he asked on the way back.

'I don't know. There isn't much point, is there?'

They stopped outside the Parrys' flat. He turned to her. She was staring ahead. He leant across to her but she put up her hands to stop him.

'No. Please don't kiss me, Steven.' She got out of the car and ran to the door. She struggled briefly with a key, and went inside without looking back.

Keith Parry arrived on board for Colours the following morning, Sunday. The ship's company was turned to for an hour, to clean the ship before having the rest of the day free.

He found Jannaway in the ship's office, staring moodily at the bulkhead. 'Steve! What's happened? Catherine's gone. She left a note saying she was catching the next flight back.' He produced a letter. 'She left this for you.'

He went up to the bridge to be alone. He opened the letter. She said that she would always love him and that because she loved him she felt she had to leave Malta. She was going to the airport straight away because she couldn't face Keith and Jill. She said she would take the first seat that was offered, but she didn't know what she would do when she got back to England. She said that whatever he decided to do, his decision must be his own, and not influenced by her. She said that if he had any love for Julietta she believed it was his duty to marry her so that their child would know its father and would have the security and love of real parents. She sent her prayers and her love. She said that her heart was breaking – had already broken for him. Wherever she went, whatever she did in her life, she knew that he would always have a place in her thoughts and her prayers.

While he was reading the letter through again, the bo'sun's mate piped: 'Lieutenant Jannaway – shore telephone call.' He put the letter back in its envelope and went down the ladder to the irondeck, and aft to the quarterdeck. He picked up the telephone, and put a finger in his free ear to exclude the noise of a ventilation fan nearby.

It was Julietta. 'Hullo? It's you is it?' Her voice was the voice of an accomplice, a partner in crime. 'Listen – when can we meet?'

They arranged that she would be at the landing stage in her car when he came ashore in an hour's time. They had to talk, yes, of course they had to talk.

As he replaced the telephone, the BEA flight to London flew overhead, climbing away to the north-east.

# 13

They sat outside a restaurant on the foreshore at Marsaxxlok. Brilliantly painted fishing boats with whitened thwarts lolled in the sunshine, and two dogs were taking it in turns, solemnly, to mount a bitch. In the bay, other boats floated at their moorings; the noon sun was making the wavelets look like rows of tiny sharpened blades.

Julietta was being grown up. She had put on a turquoise dress and white sandals. Her eyes were hidden behind a large pair of dark glasses. She inspected Jannaway through them, seeing him in a new light.

He had put on his dog's tooth suit, had shaved twice that morning and had plucked away the hairs that grew on the bridge of his nose. He was being grown up, too. Twelve hours of prospective parenthood had changed things.

Julietta delivered an olive stone into the tips of her fingers, and carefully placed it on top of a cairn of stones she was building in her ashtray.

'I don't feel pregnant at all,' she said.

He smiled. 'You don't look it.'

'But I am, all the same.' She gave a little sigh. 'Actually I do feel pregnant in a way. Sort of . . . expectant. Silly, isn't it?'

'If you say so.'

She slipped her hand over his, and he looked down at her slender fingers and the translucent nails that were like semi-precious stones, they were so perfectly honed and polished.

Her doll's eyes opened wide, the lashes curling outward. 'You weren't in love with her were you?'

He had difficulty answering. He shook his head and said he didn't know.

'I don't think she could have been very much in love with you.'

'Why do you say that?'

She pushed her hand gently back and forth over his. 'Well. Bombing off back to Mum like that. If that had been me –' Her fingers tightened over his. 'I'd have hung on for grim death. I wouldn't have let you go.'

220

He looked away from her, his mouth clamped shut.

'She wasn't like that,' he said.

Her hand went back and forth over his. She leant across the table. She had been fiddling with her white coral necklace and had tied it in a knot. It descended, out of sight, between the curves of her breasts. She made love to him with her eyes. 'Great big monster!' she whispered.

She patted his hand and became brisk. 'Let's decide what we're going to eat, and then we can talk.'

They lunched well, on fresh squid and almond tart. She twirled her wine glass back and forth in her fingers, sipping the sparkling liquid delicately, her lipstick leaving a neat, pink kiss upon the rim.

'You want me to have it, don't you?'

He frowned. 'Have what?'

'The baby! Clot!'

'Sorry.'

'Well you do, don't you?'

He turned away, blinking rapidly. A muscle flexed repeatedly in his cheek. 'Yes I do,' he said. 'I couldn't live with myself if you got rid of it.'

'That's just because you're a Catholic.'

'No. It's more than that.'

'I suppose I could have it adopted,' she said. 'Go to Switzerland or something.'

'I don't like that idea much, either.'

'We've got to decide.'

'What do you want to do? Really?'

'I want to be ... unpregnant again. I wouldn't mind getting rid of it.' She looked at him guiltily. 'Is that very sinful of me?'

'I'm not really in a position to judge, am I?'

'You're really rather sweet aren't you?' she said, and quickly touched her upper lip with the tip of her tongue.

'What the hell are we going to do, Julie?'

'It may be more up to you than it is to me.'

'What does that mean?'

'Well, if you really want me to have it –' She shrugged, letting him draw his own conclusion.

'I'm bewildered,' he said. 'I don't know where I am or what I'm doing.'

'You wouldn't be bewildered if you loved her.'

'Wouldn't I?'

'Of course you wouldn't. You'd be much more positive. You'd say, "Yes, let's get rid of it," and we'd go off and live our own lives. But you don't want that, do you? You want me to have it. I'm right, aren't I?'

'I don't know. Maybe.'

'Shall I tell you something? Yes, I will. There's someone else who knows. Peter, your first lieutenant.'

He stared at her. 'Why did you have to tell him?'

'I had to tell somebody! I had to!'

'But why him of all people?'

'He's a friend of the family – oh, what does it matter why I told him? I did, and he said that you and what's her name weren't in love at all. He said she was like a big sister to you. And when I saw you with her last night . . . well it was obvious. She must be about thirty isn't she?'

'She was very tired when you saw her.'

'Maybe she was, but she wasn't in love. Honestly.'

He felt as if she were pushing him ever closer to the edge of a crevasse, across which he would sooner or later be forced to leap.

He paid the bill and they walked together along the foreshore. They sat side by side on the gunwale of a fishing boat. 'Was I so desperately boring?' she asked. 'All those silly suppers and funny evenings we had? I thought we were hitting it off jolly well.'

'We were.'

'Well then. You couldn't have done all that and been in love with her at the same time. Could you?'

He said nothing. The sun glinted on the sea. The dogs had found some shade and lay side by side, panting.

'We've got to decide something,' she said. 'You can't have both of us, can you?'

He shook his head. 'I don't know what to think,' he said.

'You are funny. You look so serious!'

'I am serious.'

'No, but you *look* so serious! Like a sort of mongrel, gone wrong.'

She turned to him, leaning against him, her hands down at her sides. It seemed impossible not to fold her in his arms and comfort her. Her head went sideways against his chest and she breathed out in a long sigh. 'Oh!' she whispered. 'I could love you! I know I could!'

She moved gently against him and he felt her finger nails sharp in his back. He liked the perfection of her, the downy smoothness of her brown shoulders, her neck, the musky perfume that rose from her back. She began to tremble all over. Her breathing sounded as though she were shivering with cold. Dimly, he wondered if Catherine had been on that plane and whether she had now arrived in England.

They walked further along the shore, holding hands. 'I knew your brother, you know,' he said. 'We were the same term.'

'Really? Why didn't you tell me that before?'

He shrugged. 'We never actually got round to discussing our relations, did we?'

She giggled. 'Not those sort of relations anyway.' She stopped. She wanted to be kissed again. 'No,' she said. 'We mustn't. We've got spectators.' He followed her glance, and saw a man watching them from behind some rocks.

'Wait a minute,' she said. 'Were you the one they called "Shag"?'

'That's right.'

She laughed, biting her lower lip. 'I remember now! David used to talk about you. You were always doing things wrong, weren't you. Didn't you sink a boat or something?'

'Or something.'

'Shag Jannaway . . .' She laughed. 'David said you were an oik.'

'I am. I have humble origins.'

'And a spastic brother, right?'

'Yes.'

She threw a pebble into the sea.

'Does that make any difference?'

'Why should it?'

'It does for some people.'

She shrugged.

They sat on a stretch of rock. She took off her sandals and examined her toes. She asked him how well he had known David and if they had been friends. He told her that everyone had liked him, that he had been a sort of term mascot because he was so small and so full of enthusiasm.

'He would have done awfully well, you know,' she said. 'Mummy thought he was too young to go to Dartmouth, but he got marvellous reports from his House Officer.'

They talked about his death, and the enquiry that had followed

223

it. It had been believed that David had gone out alone onto the fo'c'sle to secure some gear that had broken adrift. 'Poor David,' she said. 'What a silly, typical, brave thing to do!'

He broke a long silence. 'We're still dodging the issue, aren't we?'

'I'm not. You are.'

He said they could always get married. She said yes there was always that possibility. 'I'm serious,' he said. 'I know you're serious,' she replied.

'Well? What do you think?'

'What am I supposed to think?'

'About marriage.'

'I told you. You said we could always get married, and I said yes, we could.' She smiled and raised her eyebrows, challenging him to fault her logic.

'Would you like to get married?'

'This is not fair,' she said. 'If you want to get married, you're supposed to say so, and if you want to get married to me, you'll have to ask.'

'I thought that was what I was doing.'

'Well you weren't. You were trying to get me to ask you.'

He took a deep breath and asked her.

She said nothing for some while, examining her toes carefully, one by one. 'Promise me one thing first,' she said. 'Promise me that you don't love her. And ... and that you *won't* love her. I couldn't bear that. I couldn't bear the thought of you ... remembering her. Thinking of her.' She faced him. 'Or *anybody*,' she added fiercely.

'Listen,' he said. 'I believe that when two people make love – especially when it's the first time for them – well, there's a sort of bond between them. They belong together.'

Her eyes hardened. 'Are you trying to tell me you've made love to her?'

'No – no, just the opposite. We never did. And you ... were the first person –' He stumbled over his words. They wouldn't come out in the right order. 'I'm trying to say that I feel I belong to you.'

She relaxed immediately. It was her moment of victory. He belonged to her, every inch of him. He was hers.

'So you never did love her at all.'

He looked down and shook his head. 'I don't think I could have.' It was the final betrayal.

She stood up and pulled him to his feet. 'All right then. Let's get married.'

'Just like that?'

'Just like that.'

'Are you sure?'

'I wouldn't say it if I wasn't, clot.'

'But I mean –' He needed reassurance that she actually loved him, but felt that he could not very well ask for it.

'What do you mean?'

'Nothing.'

'Come on,' she said. 'Let's go back and tell Mummy.'

She took him by the hand and they ran the length of the beach, back to the car. 'You drive,' she said. 'I'm all of a jelly.'

He got in behind the wheel and inspected the controls, never having driven a Morris before. The car bunny-hopped as he let in the clutch and accelerated away.

The leap had been accomplished: he was safe, if a little shaken, on the other side.


Clara was entertaining the wives of the minesweeper commanding officers to tea. They sat in the large drawing room of the admiral's residence and sipped Earl Grey from fluted cups.

'What you need are Moon Tigers,' she was telling the junior wife, who had only just arrived in Malta. 'You can get them in the NAAFI. I absolutely swear by them.'

'Don't you find they burn out at about four in the morning?' the senior wife said. 'And then its bzzzzzzz all over again and one gets bitten to death.'

Clara didn't enjoy this sort of entertainment but was good at it. She had a knack of putting people at their ease and making them feel they mattered. She modelled herself on the Queen (whom she had met) and tried to run the residence in the way she felt the palace was run. She had grasped that principle which she believed to be fundamental to success for a naval wife: that her ability to entertain and inspire respect was every bit as important to her husband's career as his ability to win the approval of his seniors.

She was not pleased therefore when Julietta burst in unexpectedly, trailing Jannaway behind her. They stood together in the doorway of the drawing room. 'Oh,' Julietta said. 'Sorry. I didn't realise.'

Jannaway was introduced. He stood with his hands half clenched, like a big bull mastiff which has been unexpectedly chosen as dog of the year at Crufts.

225

'The one who was supposed to come on the picnic,' Julietta explained.

He was offered a cup of tea and a piece of shortbread, and soon after choked, spraying crumbs onto the green and cream carpet. Julietta took him into the kitchen, and the petty officer steward gave him a glass of water. When he returned to the drawing room, the guests were departing.

Clara was rather sharp with Julietta. 'I'd much rather you didn't drop in like that,' she said. 'It was down in the social diary, so please remember in future. I'm afraid they may have left early.'

'I expect they were glad of the excuse,' Julietta said. 'Anyway we've got something to tell you.' She took Jannaway's hand and broke the news.

Clara wasn't as pleased as they had expected. 'This is very sudden,' she said.

'No it's not at all sudden,' Julietta contradicted. 'We've known each other for months.'

Clara looked at them and wondered how long it would last. August was a silly month in Malta, and a lot of troths were plighted only to be broken a few days later. She knew of Julietta's tiff with Peter Lasbury, and suspected that she might have taken up with this young lieutenant out of spite. Julietta was like that, unfortunately.

'We want to get married as soon as possible,' she said.

'I see.'

'Mummy you might try to sound just a little bit pleased!'

The petty officer steward came in to collect the tea trolley. It was Sunday, and he was anxious to get away.

'I am pleased,' Clara said. 'I'm delighted. But don't let's rush things.'

Julietta looked at Steven and raised one eyebrow. It was a trick she had developed while at school, and meant that she was cross. She sat on the arm of her mother's chair and tied her necklace in a knot.

'Mummy! You should be happy! If Daddy was here, we'd be getting out the champagne!'

Henry was in Naples for the wash-up of a paper exercise.

'You can have some champagne if you want, dear.'

Julietta pouted. 'I don't feel like any now.'

'Well there you are then.'

Julietta left her mother's chair. 'We want the wedding as soon as possible. We don't want a long engagement at all, do we?'

Jannaway shook his head obediently. Julietta had told him to leave her to do all the talking.

Clara didn't believe there would be a wedding. 'We'll just have to see about that,' she said.

'We thought the end of this month or the beginning of next.'

'That's just silly, Julietta.'

Jannaway sat with his fists on his knees and watched the argument go to and fro, like a long tennis rally. Clara said they would have to wait and hear what her father thought. Julietta said that wouldn't make any difference. Clara said it would be better to wait until they were back in England. Julietta said they couldn't possibly wait that long. Clara said, why the rush? Julietta said because we just happen to love each other. But why not have a nice wedding in Meonford? Julietta said she didn't want a nice wedding. Clara said that was silly, too.

Julietta paused, as if her mother had lobbed and she were positioning herself for a smash return.

'Oh Mummy!' she said. 'I'm expecting a baby, that's why!'

Game, set and match.

Things happened quite quickly after that. Steven was invited to lunch the following day and Julietta was sent out while Clara had a long talk with him. She was anxious to find out if he was suitable, and very thankful that Henry was away. Henry would have blustered and talked about obligations. Clara stirred her coffee slowly, and spoke of genuine affection.

Steven liked her: she was soft and motherly, in spite of her husband's rank. He told her that he thought Julietta and he would have wanted to marry in any case; that he loved her, and that he couldn't bear the thought of never seeing his child or of having it adopted.

Julietta had told her mother that Jannaway came from a naval family, so Clara asked him about that.

'My father was in mine disposal. He was killed in 1943.'

She warmed to him. He had had his hair trimmed and had obviously made an effort to impress.

'Julietta tells me you were the same term as David.'

'That's right. We were the same term and the same house. The same training ship, too.'

She smiled sadly. This boy was not a bit like David. He was much bigger, much tougher. But it was nice that there was this connection between them.

'Are you really sure?' she asked. 'Quite, quite sure?'

He leaned forward, clasping his hands round one knee. He had learnt, since joining HMS *Copenhagen*, how to convince. He looked her in the eye and said yes, he was absolutely certain.

Clara was sure she'd heard the name Jannaway before, a long time ago, but she couldn't for the life of her think when or where.

'Naturally I shall have to speak to the admiral,' she said, 'before any final decision is taken. There's also the question of education, isn't there?'

'Education?'

'I understood you were a Catholic?'

'Yes, I am, but –'

'Well I hope you're not going to make any stipulations about the child being brought up in the Catholic Church are you?'

He hadn't thought about that. He had not really thought abut the child being 'his'. It was an abstract thing, a responsibility that lay ahead.

Clara saw him hesitate and took the advantage.

'We shall have to think again if you are. The admiral wouldn't stand for that.'

He didn't feel he had much right to press the case. Having made the leap from Catherine to Julietta, it was impossible to leap back onto home ground again and demand what he knew the Church of Rome required him to demand; so he told Clara that he would not insist on the child going to a Catholic school, and agreed that it should be baptised into the Church of England.

They then discussed the date of the wedding. Clara was anxious that it should not be held in Malta, where the hothouse atmosphere was conducive to gossiping in the fleet. 'We'll have to see if we can get you back to England,' she said. 'A nice quiet wedding in Meonford.'

Henry arrived back from Naples the next day, full of bonhomie and Chianti. Clara broke the news to him before he visited his office, while he was still in a good mood. He took it remarkably well. He was fond of Julietta: she had more spunk in her than Sarah. The fact that she had got herself 'with sprog' as he called it, seemed to him to be in the naval tradition. One of his father's old captains,

Lord Beatty, had been born very much on the wrong side of the blanket, and that had done neither him nor his parents any harm at all.

Jannaway was invited to dinner.

They took a gin and tonic before the meal. Jannaway had put on his sharkskin dinner jacket and a set of new studs, with jet stones, which he had bought from Gieves. He was careful not to eat too many peanuts, and sipped his drink cautiously, anxious not to repeat his nose trick of the previous Sunday.

Henry Braddle had taken the precaution of sending for a draft confidential report upon the boy, in which Tinnick had described Jannaway as an officer of wide ranging interests and a good moral sense, who was inclined to muddleheadedness on occasion. Jannaway scored five or six out of ten for zeal, leadership and moral integrity, and four out of ten for tact and social qualities. Henry Braddle decided he was a bit of a rough diamond. He quizzed Jannaway about his father, and Jannaway had the prudence to avoid any mention of the Invergordon Mutiny.

'What about the rest of your family?' asked Henry, standing with his back to the mantelpiece. 'I understand you have a brother?'

'I did tell you about that, Henry,' Clara put in, trying to save Jannaway any embarrassment.

'Just one brother sir, yes. He's – er – slightly disabled.'

Braddle nodded and pulled his nose. The petty officer steward announced dinner, and they sat down to tinned cream of tomato soup from the NAAFI. Charles Crivett-Smith had been sent out to enjoy an evening with Carrie Dudswell, so they were just four.

'Well we all know why we're here,' Braddle said when the soup was finished, 'so I suggest we go ahead and discuss it.'

Jannaway helped himself to a slice of veal and waited for someone else to do the discussing. When the steward had withdrawn, Julietta said, 'We just want to get married as soon as possible, don't we?'

He nodded and said that was right.

'And where do you propose to live?' Braddle asked.

'Oh Daddy! In a flat!'

'Here in Malta?'

'Well we're hardly likely to rent one in Hong Kong, are we?'

Jannaway was amazed at Julietta's manner towards her father. It was a shock for him to see a man he had learnt to fear being treated as a bumbling fool.

'What do you think?' the admiral asked.

'I – I really don't know, sir –'

'Well you damn well should. It's your sprog.'

'Henry,' Clara said.

Braddle blew down his nose.

'I think we could find a flat quite easily, sir,' Jannaway said. 'And as long as I'm based out here –'

'Who says you're based out here?'

'Well I don't leave *Copenhagen* until March '62, sir.'

'We'll see about that,' Braddle said.

'It might be rather fun to go somewhere else,' Julietta said. 'I mean if we could wangle it.'

'We're not going to wangle anything,' Clara said.

When coffee had been served, Braddle insisted that Clara and Julietta withdraw. He dismissed the steward and took a box of cigars from the drawer in the sideboard. 'Do you use these?' he asked. Jannaway accepted, and was allowed to borrow the admiral's blade to slice off the end.

'Right,' said Braddle. 'Let's get one thing quite clear, Master Jannaway. If I wasn't convinced that my daughter wasn't besotted by you, I'd stamp on this from the start.' He blew a neat smoke ring, which shot upward towards the chandelier. 'I'll tell you what I propose to do. I intend to have you relieved of your duties in HMS *Copenhagen* and sent back to England, chop-chop. I'll have the banns read next Sunday and the wedding in four weeks. We'll see if we can organise some sort of job for you that'll allow you and my daughter to see something of each other in the first year of your marriage. Fair?'

'I can't say I'm all that keen on leaving *Copenhagen*, sir.'

'Maybe you're not. But you're in no position to pick and choose, are you?' Braddle compressed his lips and shot a shrivelling stare across the table.

'I suppose not, sir.'

The admiral looked at his cigar. He was never any good on these occasions. He felt there was much more he should be saying, more he should be finding out about the boy. 'Will you be a good husband to her?' he asked. 'Will you treat her well?'

'Yes, sir.'

'You'd better, boy.'

'I am in love with her sir.'

Braddle snorted. Then he sighed and pushed his chair back. 'All right. Let's go and put 'em out of their misery.' He held out his hand to usher Jannaway through the door first but Jannaway, seeing it extended, presumed that he was expected to shake it. Braddle saw what had happened. 'All right then, god dammit, shake my hand,' he said, and they did so.

They went into the drawing room. Julietta sat beside Steven on the sofa. She looked questioningly at him, and he signalled back that all was well. There was a lot to be discussed. The engagement would be announced in *The Times* and the *Daily Telegraph*, and Clara wanted Julietta's portrait to be submitted to the *Tatler*. The *Times* of Malta would want an interview, and she would have to telephone the Reverend Pringle, Vicar of Meonford, to have him read the banns.

'And there's something else,' she said, crossing to the bureau. She opened a secret drawer. 'There,' she said, and laid a ring in Steven's palm. 'What do you think of that?'

'It's beautiful!'

'It was my mother's engagement ring. I know she would have liked Julietta to have it as hers.'

He stared down at the amethyst set between two diamonds. The stones sparkled in the light of the standard lamp by his chair.

Julietta leaned against him. She was wearing a loose fitting dress with a high waist that made her look like a Greek goddess. 'Well go on, then!' she said, and held up her left hand. 'Put it on!' He slipped it on her third finger. She laughed in a way that was almost a sob. 'Do you mind if I kiss him, anyone?' she asked, and Clara gave a huge sniff and said no of course they didn't.

Henry Braddle braced back his shoulder muscles, then pulled at his nose. He didn't like the way, when his daughter kissed Jannaway, she did so with her mouth open, as if she were trying to eat him.

She spread her left hand and looked at the ring.

'It's lovely! It's beautiful!' she said, and went to her mother to embrace her.

He wrote to his mother the following day. He decided that it was not necessary to tell her about Julietta's pregnancy quite yet, feeling that to do so would hurt her unnecessarily. Instead, he told her that he had met the most marvellous girl and that they were to be married very soon. He said that he was happier than he had ever been before, that Julietta was 'a smashing person in every way' and that he knew she would like her. He regretted that his friendship with Catherine had had to come to such an abrupt end, but thought that it was better for it to do that than to drag on.

> We hope to be married in Meonford, Hampshire, where the Braddles live. I don't expect it will be a large wedding, but of course you and Alan will be right at the top of the guest list.

When he had written it, he read it over, aware of a vague feeling of discomfort deep inside him, which he suppressed immediately, licking up the envelope and sending it off by the next post to leave the ship.

Catherine was much more difficult. He started letter after letter, tearing each up after only a few lines. In most, he tried to dispel the feeling of undying love which he had once been at such pains to declare, though in one he told her that he still loved her and always would, that he was marrying Julietta out of a sense of duty and because he knew that was what she advised. He sat for a long time in his cabin, the light of his desk lamp on the writing pad, the draught of air cool from the punkah louvre over his head. Eventually he settled for a letter which said everything he felt obliged to say, but no more:

> My dear Catherine,
> This is to let you know, in case you don't see the announcement in the papers, that Julietta and I are to be married on the seventeenth of next month. I could say so much, and yet there is so little that I can say that will make any difference. I think you probably know me better than I know myself, so I won't try to describe what I think about all this. You have given me so much in the last four years, Catherine, that it seems almost impertinent of me to say 'I'm sorry' or even 'thank you'. But I *am* sorry as well as grateful . . . even that sounds terrible. Tongue tied as ever, you see. Is it any consolation at all to say that I have a feeling that I wouldn't have made you much of a husband? Perhaps not. I can't help feeling that you already knew that you were not suited to the life of a naval officer's wife. Perhaps it was a good thing you discovered that we are a brutal and licentious lot before it was too late.
> So – I suppose this is goodbye. I hope the wounds heal quickly, Catherine. Try to forget all about me, and find someone who will give you the happiness you deserve.
> With love – still,
> Steven.

This letter, he knew, was a necessary fake: he was engaged to Julietta and feelings of remorse or yearnings for what might have been had to be ruthlessly suppressed. Perhaps he was losing the ability to love deeply, just as he had lost his sense of perfect pitch – he didn't know, and it was easier not to think about it.

He sent the letter to Gainsborough House, presuming that Catherine would return there sooner or later because of her friendship with Miss Lucknell, the headmistress, and in this he was right. Having flown back to England, Catherine had gone straight down to Brixham, refusing to admit that the days of choking despair amounted to any sort of nervous breakdown. Instead, she volunteered to help with the redecoration of the cloakrooms, working furiously every day, sometimes blinded by her tears, sometimes numbed and drained of all feeling so that she would be found, paintbrush in hand, gazing vacantly into space.

She didn't blame Steven and she didn't blame herself. Like Steven, she decided that it was now necessary to make a leap away from her old life and into a new one. She was physically fit and positively aware of a vocation to help those in need, and knowing that she could never again face a class of well-to-do school girls, she decided that she should offer her services as a lay worker among children in need. Accordingly, after a week of thought and prayer, she went along to Father Vincent one Sunday evening after Benediction and told him what she wanted to do.

Henry Braddle paced rapidly up and down his office and stopped abruptly, his hands behind his back, the open collar of his bush jacket revealing an expanse of neck that was the colour of underdone roast beef.

'I'd lay a pound to a piece of cheese that if this happened to any other young officer under my command, he'd be shipped back to UK on compassionate draft. Agree?'

'Agree, sir.' Tinnick sat with his arms and legs folded and his back straight.

'Don't get me wrong, Johnny,' Braddle said. 'I don't want to make a special case out of him.'

'I don't think you are, sir.'

But this was not enough. Braddle knew that in fact he was making Jannaway into a special case, and he needed more positive reassurance that he was not. He picked up the brass cannon from his desk, weighed it thoughtfully, and put it back.

'Would you do the same in my place?'

'I would indeed, sir.'

Braddle went to the window and looked at the four destroyers moored in the creek. He flexed his shoulders, bared his teeth, and turned abruptly.

'All right then. Let's set the ball rolling. I'll make a personal signal to admiralty. Try and fix up a swap. Plenty of young officers who'd give their eye teeth to be in Jannaway's shoes.'

'Yes, sir,' Tinnick said, deliberately ignoring the admiral's unintended double meaning.

'Have a look at a navy list,' Braddle said. 'See if you can pick a few likely volunteers.'

'Will do, sir.'

Tinnick was dismissed, and Braddle made his signal. An answer came back the following day: approval in principle was given to an exchange of appointments between Jannaway and an officer of similar seniority serving in the UK, providing a volunteer could be found. After a further exchange of signals with several ships and establishments, that volunteer was found: Jannaway was summoned to Lasbury's cabin to be informed.

'You are a lucky officer,' Lasbury told him, sipping a cup of stand-easy tea.

'Am I sir?'

'Yes you are. How do you fancy being number one of an FPB?'

'Which one, sir?'

'*Bold Adventurer*. Based at Gosport.'

'Suppose it'll have to do, sir,' Jannaway said, grinning from ear to ear with delight.

'Cheeky young bugger.' Lasbury opened a file marked STAFF-IN–CONFIDENCE. 'Jeremy Harper. Know him?'

Jannaway remembered the cadet who had organised the Highland Games. 'Vaguely, sir. Yes.'

'What's he like?'

Jannaway loathed and detested Harper, but he wasn't going to prejudice his chances of being HMS *Bold Adventurer*'s first lieutenant. 'Good guy, sir,' he said.

'You'll be swapping with him,' Lasbury said. He flipped a page in the file and looked at a pink signal. 'You leave us on the 9th and join your new ship on the 22nd. That'll give you ten days for a honeymoon.'

'Four days, more like. We're getting married on the seventeenth.'

'Details,' Lasbury said. 'Count yourself lucky.'

He was dined out on the eve of his departure. The captain and officers put on their white mess undress and gathered in the wardroom at twenty hundred for twenty-fifteen. They sat down to Du Barry soup, which was followed by filet mignon served with portions of mashed potato which had been shaped into rounded domes, each with a red cocktail onion on top as decoration. The port, the madeira and the oloroso sherry were passed, and the loyal toast was drunk. After the captain had gone, the drinks circulated more freely, and the officers played games.

Peter Lasbury and Steven Jannaway were the mess champions. They played 'Are you there Moriarty?' and had one arm wrestling matches. They contended to see which could place a bottle furthest from a base line on the wardroom carpet, balancing the weight of their bodies with one hand on a Schweppes tonic bottle, and reaching out with the other to place the other bottle, upright, at arm's length. They sweated and grunted and accepted the cheers of their messmates; they patted each other on the back and bought each other drinks. It would be sad, very sad, to leave HMS *Copenhagen*. What a lot he had learnt, and how much of it was as a result of Lasbury's guidance! When the games were over, when the midshipman had been pushed through the scuttle for the last time, and Jannaway had demonstrated how he could stop the overhead fan with his head, they sat down side by side and had one last brandy.

'There's no stopping you now,' Lasbury said. 'You've got it made. Keep your nose clean, don't fart in church and you can't fail. Right?'

Jannaway was drunk. He had difficulty focussing, but was dimly aware that Lasbury was telling him something important.

'Mind you,' Lasbury was saying. 'You'll have to work for it. She'll be a handful.'

Jannaway laughed. 'I've got big hands.'

Tinnick gave him the same sort of advice, only more formally, the following morning. He told him to set himself the very highest of standards and never to be satisfied with second best. 'You have intelligence, and the beginnings of sound professional knowledge, my boy. Great things will be expected of you. Yes?'

They shook hands, and Tinnick wished him well. He went down

to the ship's office to say goodbye to Leading Writer Rudd, who looked at him gloomily and said it had been a pleasure to serve with him. He collected his luggage and went aft to the accommodation ladder, expecting that the members of his division would give him some sort of send-off.

He looked round to see if they were going to line the ship's side for him, or row him ashore in the whaler, but no such farewell had been organised; so he stepped down into Salvo Borg's dghaisa, and looked back at the destroyer with a sudden stab of regret that this stage in his life was over and could never be regained.

Julietta drove him to the airport. She and her mother were flying to England the following day, and her father five days later.

'A week tomorrow,' she said. 'It feels funny, doesn't it?' They stood in the departures hall, and she leant against him, the way she did, the way that never failed to make him feel older and more responsible. Two days before she had given him an engagement present: a framed photo-portrait of herself in evening dress, with pearls at her throat and her grandmother's engagement ring sparkling on her finger. The picture had been submitted to the *Tatler* for publication the following week.

She pressed her lips against his. 'You do love me, don't you?' she whispered.

He put his finger on her nose, as if she were a little girl. 'Of course I do.'

He turned and waved to her as he boarded the aircraft. He made his way to his seat, fastened his safety strap and noted where the escape hatch was. He hated flying: he had blacked out in a mock dog-fight during his air acquaintance course as a midshipman and on regaining consciousness had believed himself to be in hospital, having lost both legs. The whole business of flying seemed to him to be based on chance, aviators living by a fatalistic philosophy which held that if it wasn't your day there was nothing you could do about it.

The engines went up to full power and the wings vibrated. He tightened his safety strap again and looked out at the wing root, where streaks of oil emerged from the rivets. The aircraft accelerated along the runway; the sunburnt ground dropped away. They banked and headed for England.

He relaxed a little, and took out a small brown envelope given to him by Commander Tinnick that morning. It was his 'flimsy', the form given to each officer at the end of his appointment which is supposed to reflect the contents of his confidential report.

He opened it and read:

This is to certify that Lieutenant S.J. Jannaway R.N. has served as Correspondence Officer in HMS *Copenhagen* under my command from the 2nd day of February 1960 to the 9th day of September 1960 during which time he has conducted himself to my satisfaction. Jannaway has a pleasant manner and a smart appearance. His efficiency is continuing to improve and is now marred only by an occasional lapse of concentration. He has a high moral standard, a good strength of character and shows every indication of developing into a very useful officer.

He put it away in his wallet, along with the flimsy from HMS *Syston* and HMS *Diligence*. Coming from Tinnick, it was a very good report. He remembered how Tinnick had called him 'my boy' and how Lasbury, in his after dinner speech the night before, had referred to him as 'a good shipmate'.

I'm on the up and up, he thought, looking out as the aircraft climbed through a wisp of alto-stratus.

He began to think about his next job as first lieutenant of *Bold Adventurer*. He felt suddenly confident and ambitious. I shall demand high standards from the very first day, he decided. I shall start out the way I intend to continue.

London was wet and windy. He spent the afternoon in town to do some shopping and arrived home in time for supper. It was Friday again. Fish pie.

His mother opened the door to him and regarded him with thinly veiled disapproval. He kissed her warmly and played the conquering hero. 'How's Mum?' he asked. 'You're looking well. Alan in?'

She watched him put his coat over the bottom of the banister. He was healthily bronzed and his suit was tailor made. His hair waved behind his ears and was thick and shiny at the back of his head.

'He's upstairs if you want to see him.'

'Mum! Of course I want to see him!' He held her shoulders. She seemed to have shrunk since he last saw her. She always seemed to have shrunk. 'Well? You haven't congratulated me!'

She turned away from him and said, 'Congratulations.'

He hesitated a moment, then went upstairs. Alan turned down the volume of his record player and they shook hands.

'Well?' Alan said. 'What happened?'

He avoided Alan's eyes, shrugging. 'One of those things, you know. We just suddenly realised we were right for each other.' He grinned convincingly. 'She's a smashing girl. You'll like her.'

'What about Catherine?'

Steven shook his head. 'She was too good for me, Alan. It wouldn't have worked.'

'Mum's very upset,' Alan said.

'So I gathered just now.'

'I am too. I liked Catherine.' Alan crossed to the record player and switched it off. 'And this . . . Julietta. Is she a Catholic?'

'No. Does that matter so very much?'

'Who are you kidding, Steve? Of course it matters.'

Steven laughed. 'I can't very well be expected to choose a wife in order to please you two, can I?'

'I'm not saying you should. But Catherine was right for you. Wasn't she?'

Steven was prepared for this conversation but was finding it more difficult than he had expected. Alan seemed already to have guessed something of the real situation. It was necessary to act as if he were totally sure of himself in order to cover up his lingering feelings of uncertainty and regret.

'Maybe you don't know me as well as you think you do,' he said now, with a forced smile. 'I mean – maybe I'm not your little brother any longer. Maybe I've got a mind of my own.'

A gust of wind brought a spatter of raindrops against the window. 'Tell me more about Julietta,' Alan said.

'Her father's Flag Officer Mediterranean. A rear admiral –'

'So you said in both your letters.'

'Give us a break, will you? You ask me what she's like, so I'm telling you. She's nineteen. And her elder brother was the chap who got washed overboard when I was in the training squadron. She's got a married elder sister and the family lives in Hampshire. She's also a super girl. And I also happen to be in love with her. Satisfied?'

'And will she make a good naval officer's wife?'

'I'm sure she will.'

'Say all the right things and know all the right people?'

238

'Look – Alan – it's not like that!'

'Isn't it? Why else would you ... ditch a wonderful girl like Catherine? What's happened to *her*? And if you were so positive about Julietta why didn't you write and tell Catherine not to go out to Malta?'

'I wasn't sure about either of them then,' Steven said. 'And besides, Catherine hadn't said anything about becoming a Catholic.'

'Oh, I see. That would have made a difference, would it? That would have changed your mind.'

He had never known Alan use this biting sarcasm before. Part of him knew that Alan was right, but it was impossible to admit that. Had he guessed? Was some uncanny brotherly telepathy at work? He couldn't look him in the eye any more. The argument had gone too far already.

'I can't explain,' he said. 'You just wouldn't understand.'

He went into his bedroom and closed the door. The photograph of his father grinned confidently across the room at him. He took it off the wall, and there was a patch on the wallpaper where it had hung for so long. He stared down at the mischievous looking face.

'You would have understood,' he muttered. 'You would have known what it was like.'


They sat down to supper. Mrs Jannaway set the pie dish down on a wooden mat Steven had made during carpentry classes when he was a cadet. She sat down and nodded to Alan, who made the sign of the cross and prayed: 'Bless us, O Lord, and these thy gifts which of thy bounty we receive.'

Mrs Jannaway made the sign of the cross again and opened her eyes. She served the fish pie. 'Tell us all about her, then,' she said crisply.

'Not much to tell,' he said. 'You know how these things are.'

'I can't say that I do,' she said.

'We met last June. I've known her three months.'

'Really? That's the first we've heard of it, isn't it Alan?'

There was a silence.

Mrs Jannaway said, 'We've had the invitation. To the wedding, I mean.'

'Good. I was going to ask you about that.'

Mrs Jannaway rose from the table and searched among a sheaf of

239

envelopes behind the clock on the mantelpiece. 'Here we are. Her mother enclosed a letter with it.' She took out the letter, which was written on Clara Braddle's personal notepaper. 'There was something we didn't quite understand, did we Alan? Here we are. "... I do hope you will be able to come to the wedding and apologise for the very short notice, but I know that you will understand, in the circumstances..." ' Mrs Jannaway looked up. 'Circumstances? What circumstances?'

They stared at him across the table. There was no way out.

'She's expecting a baby,' he said quietly. 'I didn't tell you because I didn't want to hurt you.'

'Yours?' his mother asked.

He bowed his head. 'Yes.'

Bit by bit, she got it out of him. Where was Catherine? He didn't know. Why didn't he know? Because she hadn't said where she was going.

'Why?' she demanded. 'Why?'

He looked back at her and shouted, 'Because I am a human being, that's why!'

He calmed down. 'You don't understand a quarter of this. Either of you. You look at me like – like that, like the way you are now, you blame me, and you have no idea, either of you, what it's like. These are my private – my private affairs –'

His mother seized upon the word. 'Affairs. Yes. That is just what they are, Steven!'

'If you're going to deliberately misunderstand when I'm trying to explain, there's not much point in my trying.'

'I'm not misunderstanding you. I'm understanding you very well indeed. Why couldn't you tell us? Why did you have to deceive – Alan – never mind about me –'

'Mother,' Alan said. 'Please – don't –'

'Jesus Christ!' Steven said. 'Am I supposed to keep you two informed about my private life?'

Dora turned on him. 'If you want to blaspheme, go and blaspheme somewhere else. I'm not having that sort of language in this house.'

'Perhaps you'd rather not have me in this house then? Is that right?'

'I didn't say that, Steven.'

'Well you made it bloody clear that you thought it. You look at me like a nasty piece of – of shit.'

240

'I'm not listening to this!' Dora said quickly. She got up from the table, but he went immediately to the door.

'No, you will listen to this. Both of you. You accuse me of deceiving you. Well I have to. Everyone in the navy has to. That's what the navy's like, Alan, that's why I've never been able to tell you about it. You have to be protected from knowing that we keep a box of contraceptives on the gangway for anyone going ashore. You mustn't know that there are half a dozen people with gonorrhoea on board at any one time. Would you like to have heard about one of my captains who used to measure women's tits with a tape-measure after his cocktail parties? Should I have told you about that? What else am I supposed to tell you about? How else am I deceiving you? What else do you want to know?'

He stopped suddenly, shaking his head. His mother went quickly out of the room. He sat down at the table again and wept; and within a few days the gossip about the family row at the Jannaways' was being passed down the road, for the next door neighbours had heard raised voices through the wall, and everyone knew that Alan's younger brother was getting married to an admiral's daughter at very short notice.

The admiral's daughter met him on Monday in a brand new, scarlet Mini-Minor which had been delivered that morning, an advance wedding present to them both from her mother.

She whisked him off to Winchester and bought him five pairs of Y-fronts in assorted colours. 'I'm not having any husband of mine wearing those god-awful admiralty passion-poopers,' she told him. They lunched in the Royal Oak and shopped all afternoon. He stood about in boutiques, admiring dress after dress. She looked superb in all of them, but she reprimanded him for saying 'very nice' too often. 'Don't look at me, clot, look at the dress.' She sent him off with a load of purchases to put in the car and he sat in the passenger seat, watching as she ran towards him, her hair bouncing, her face alight with excitement. 'You're driving,' she announced, so they changed places. She got in beside him and opened a paper bag. 'Look,' she said, and fished out a pair of lacy black briefs and matching bra. 'I couldn't resist them. You'd better not either, Monster!'

They took the country road which undulates over the downs to Bishop's Waltham. They went under arches made by tall green-trunked beech trees; the first leaves were falling, and ploughing had

241

started: a flock of seagulls wheeled behind a tractor as it plodded across a field.

They drew up outside Meonford House and Julietta tooted the horn.

Clara was in the middle of wedding preparations. Mrs Hardesty was making the first of the canapés for the reception, and the telephone was ringing almost incessantly. Clara kissed Steven affectionately and admired Julietta's selection of winter dresses.

Julietta took him by the hand and showed him the house. She kissed him on the landing under the haughty stare of Bartholomew Braddle and took him into all the bedrooms. They stood in David's, which had been kept more or less as he had known it, with his school and Dartmouth photographs on the wall and his shotgun propped up in the corner. They looked out over the garden, the paddock and the water meadows beyond.

'It's a big place, isn't it?' he said.

She squeezed his hand. 'It's humble, but it's home.'

He spent the week there with Julietta and her mother, a week in which Julietta tantalised him daily and nightly with the prospect of passion to come. They all went up to London one day and lunched at Simpsons; Clara had invited Mrs Jannaway to this lunch but she had declined. She had also declined to attend the wedding, telling Steven that as it was not being conducted by a Roman Catholic priest he would not be married in the eyes of the Church. Steven telephoned her from the admiral's desk in the library and tried to persuade her to change her mind, but she was adamant.

Alan decided that he would attend and Steven at first wanted him to be best man, but Julietta said wouldn't it be much nicer to have an all-naval wedding, so he asked Barry Courtenay instead. Courtenay was on course at the submarine base in Gosport and brought some of his friends along to act as guard of honour. Apart from Alan, they were the only guests to attend on Steven's side, so the ushers decided it was better to ask the guests to sit on both sides of the church. A surprising number came: most of the men were in uniform and the ranks ranged from Julietta's grandfather, Admiral Sir Thomas Braddle, down to the two pages, aged seven and six, who wore old fashioned monkey jackets and buckled shoes.

The organ thundered and a gale blew; the officers of the guard of honour kissed the hilts of their swords and held them aloft. The happy couple walked beneath the arch of steel, and the confetti was caught by a gust and carried upward in a pink and blue cloud, the little heart-shaped pieces of paper fluttering among the sycamore branches and floating away over the meadows, to settle on the Friesian cattle that chewed the cud by the river.

Courtenay made a risqué speech about Jannaway at the reception and some of the officers sang a lewd song on the lawn. Alan, who knew no one at all, kept in the background, unperturbed at being ignored ('That's the brother,' he overheard an aunt say in a hoarse whisper) yet a little saddened by the uniforms and the splendour.

The couple emerged from the front door to depart on their honeymoon and the guests lined the gravel drive to wave them farewell. The best man had put a kipper in the engine of the new Mini and a balloon over the exhaust, which exploded with a satisfying bang soon after the engine was started. Off they went, streamers and empty cans fluttering and rattling behind the car; the guests turned back; Henry Braddle wiped his eyes secretly, and his sister said, 'What a lovely, lovely wedding!'

Soon afterwards, Alan slipped away by taxi. He caught the London train from Petersfield and sat looking out of the carriage window as the countryside fled by.

He didn't expect he would see much of Steven, now that he was married.

Part Three
DEAD SOULS

## 14

'Let's keep a jamjar and put dried peas in it,' said Julietta. 'No, I'm serious. We put a pea in the jamjar every time we make it during the first year, and after that, every time we fuck, we take one out.'

'I don't know about you,' Jannaway said. 'I thought you were a nice upper-class girl with a nice upper-class mind.'

'What about my body?' she whispered, mock urgently. 'Do I come up to scratch?'

He laughed. 'Not often last night anyway. You hardly came up at all.'

They were breakfasting in bed at the Savoy. Julietta had done her face and put on her baby doll nightdress.

'Waking me every twenty minutes!' he said.

She pouted. 'Well I wanted it.' She slid her hand under the bedclothes. 'What's the matter, can't you keep it up?'

He grinned, feeling pleased with himself. It had been an amazing night: she had turned from a bandbox bride into a she-animal. He had no idea how many times they had made love, and had not been aware of sleeping. She had made her demands upon him as if they were her right, and in a way they were. She had agreed to have his baby, her mother had provided the engagement ring, the car and the cost of the honeymoon. It was his privilege to sit beside her now, propped against lavender scented pillows.

'The idea is to fill the jamjar in the first year,' she said. 'I read about it in a magazine.' She lifted the tray of breakfast things off the bed and put it down on the floor. 'Think we can manage that?'

'No probs,' he said. 'No probs at all.'

She lay down beside him and pulled the sheet up to her chin.

'Now what do you want?'

'Can't you guess?'

'Are you trying to test me to destruction or something?'

'Just putting you through your paces.'

'You make me sound like a race horse.'

'Well you're a bit like one, aren't you? All hot and frothy when you break into a gallop.'

'One thing.'

'What?'

'What do we do when the jamjar's empty?'

'That's the point. This article says it never does get empty. But I'm going to make you the exception that proves the rule.'

He grinned. 'Sounds like the story of my life.'

She sat up and pulled her nightdress over her head, tearing it in the process. 'Bugger,' she said. 'Never mind.' She pulled him down. 'Come on, come on,' she whispered. 'Up funnel, down screw!'

They had been unable to find a flat that suited them in the short time before the wedding, and Julietta had persuaded her mother to let them have Meonford House for the time being. When they returned there, the admiral and Clara had gone back to Malta, and there was a letter of welcome on the big deal table in the kitchen. 'Darlings,' it said. 'Just a note to say we hope you had a wonderful honeymoon and that the years ahead will be filled with happiness and love ...' Instructions followed about how to run the house, when to pay Mrs Hardesty (who would be coming in twice a week) and how to manage the Aga.

Julietta read the letter then put her arms over Jannaway's shoulders. 'So,' she said. 'I suppose this is where we start playing mothers and fathers.'

They went upstairs feeling like naughty children. She led the way into her parents' bedroom. The silver and the family photographs had gone with the Braddles to Malta, but the atmosphere of a parental bedroom remained.

Julietta flopped down on her back in the middle of the double bed.

'I don't think we ought to use this room somehow,' Jannaway said.

'Don't be so boring! Why shouldn't we?'

He glanced about at the heavy oak furniture, and crossed to look at an oil painting of a young woman of the thirties.

'Who's this?'

'That's Anita Yarrow.'

'The actress?'

'Mummy was at school with her. They were great friends. That's how we know Peter Lasbury.'

'How does he come into it?'

'She's Peter's mother, clot. Didn't you know that?'

She got off the bed and they wandered from room to room. 'I feel I shouldn't be here,' he said. 'I feel like an interloper.'

She pressed him against the wall on the landing and unbuttoned his shirt. 'In that case you can interlope me.'

'Here?'

'Yes! Here!'

He looked up at the portraits of by-gone Braddles. 'Don't you feel as though we're being watched?'

'That's what I like about it!'

She lay back over a sixteenth-century coffer, and gave a little squeak as he entered her.

He put on his uniform the following morning and she came down to the kitchen to cook his breakfast. He sat down to bacon and eggs, toast and marmalade and real coffee. She had put a check tablecloth on the kitchen table, and the spoons and forks were solid silver.

'This is very nice,' he said.

She mocked him. 'Very nice? Yeah, in't it? Is it tasty? 'Ave you got sufficient, love?' Then she reverted to her real self. 'Bloody oik, aren't you? Where do you think you are? In a bloody British Rail dining car?'

'Sorry.'

'And don't say sorry like that. It annoys me.'

He raised two fingers at her. He was learning quickly.

'I suppose you want the car do you?' she said.

'That's what we agreed.'

'Well if I want it I'm bloody well going to have it.'

'We agreed that, too.'

He rolled up his table napkin and put it back in the monogrammed silver ring, one of a pair that had been given them as a wedding present from Peter Lasbury.

'Better go and fight the war, I suppose.'

'Christ, I love you in uniform!' she whispered.

'Sweetie I've got to go!'

She put her arms round his waist and clung to him. 'We'll be a success, won't we?' she said. 'We'll make it work.'

He drove down through the Meon Valley feeling full of determination. There were still bits of the old Jannaway left – witness that 'Very nice' remark at breakfast. But he would shrug all that off, cease to be an oik. Tinnick had said that Julietta would be good for him, and he knew already that she was. The knowledge that you had made very satisfactory love to the daughter of an admiral did wonders for the self-confidence.

He strode down the jetty at HMS *Hornet* and went aboard HMS *Bold Adventurer*.

'Lieutenant Jannaway come aboard to join, sir!' he said, treating the traditional report as something of a joke as he saluted Lieutenant Commander Trussel, the captain.

'You have, have you?' Sam Trussel had been passed over for promotion a long time ago, and had been given command of *Bold Adventurer* as a consolation prize at the end of a chequered career. His principle interests in life were horse racing and Plymouth gin, which he drank with water from a green dolphin jug.

He showed Jannaway the boat. HMS *Bold Adventurer* was an experimental gas turbine craft, with twin funnels, side by side. 'They go brown at any speed over thirty knots,' Trussel said. 'So we get through a lot of paint.'

They sat down to an excellent lunch, which had been bought and cooked by the cox'n, who hoped to go into catering the following spring, on leaving the navy. The only other officer present was a shy sub lieutenant, who excused himself to go and do chart corrections while Trussel and Jannaway sat over their coffee.

The following day, they took the boat out. Jannaway had drawn a white polo-necked sweater from the store, and wore it under his reefer; Trussel produced an antique hat with a king's crown on the badge and wore that. The boat headed out between HMS *Dolphin* and HMS *Vernon*, the submarine and anti-submarine schools which glowered at each other across the entrance to Portsmouth harbour.

Trussel stood at the throttles on the port side of the bridge and the cox'n stood at the wheel. The formalised method of passing engine and wheel orders was ignored.

'Take her down to Gillkicker,' Trussel said, checking a transit bearing on the Southsea foreshore astern as they took the shallow water channel to the westward. He opened the throttles and the engines whined. A pale blue smoke rose from the twin funnels; the boat lifted onto the plane, leaving a bar of white water behind her. Jannaway's hat blew off, to the amusement of the crew. 'Are we flat out?' he asked Trussel.

Trussel glanced at the Pitometer log reading, which was showing thirty-eight knots. 'Not quite. She'll do over forty.'

They dropped a marker buoy over the side, and the new first lieutenant practised going alongside it, getting used to handling the throttles. An able seaman brought up cups of tea and ginger biscuits, which Trussel softened in his tea before eating.

'Like to take her alongside?' Trussel said as they entered Haslar Creek.

Jannaway could hardly believe it. 'Thanks, yes,' he said, concealing his delight.

'Just take it nice and slowly,' Trussel told him, lighting a briar. 'She's like an overgrown picket boat, with thin sides.'

Jannaway took the throttles. The boat was approaching the bend in the creek just after the submarine base. 'Starboard ten,' he said.

'Cox'n knows the creek,' Trussel said. 'Leave the steering to him until you start your approach.'

Jannaway reduced the throttles.

'Not too slow, or we'll be blown sideways,' Trussel said.

They made the last turn to port and began the approach to the jetty. On the foredeck, an able seaman stood by with a heaving line.

'Aim for the centre of the berth,' Trussel said. 'That's nice. I'd stop engines now. Keep her like that. Astern on the port engine now. Touch more. Stop her there.'

They were alongside, and the heaving line was not necessary. The head and stern ropes were handed up to the jetty and the springs passed.

'Not too difficult was it?' Trussel said.

'You did most of it sir.'

'Well ... first time.' Trussel relit his pipe and threw the match to leeward.

'Double up and secure?' the cox'n asked.

'Ask the first lieutenant,' Trussel said.

As soon as Trussel was satisfied that Steven could handle the boat, he was left to do so more and more. He was twenty-two, and virtually in command. He awoke at six in the morning, made love to Julietta, ate a good breakfast, went to work, drank gins at lunch time, developed his power of command and drove home to tea and toast by the fire. From time to time, but not too often, the boat went out on night exercises with the Special Boats Section of the Royal

Marines: nameless reservists would arrive from the city, blacken their faces and be taken at high speed to exercise covert landings on a hostile shore. Trussel, Jannaway and the sub lieutenant worked as a team, conning the boat in total darkness about the waters of the Solent, making rendezvous with rubber dinghies full of people who were never introduced when they came down to the wardroom for a drink. The boat would slip back into Portsmouth harbour and up Haslar Creek, and the whisky bottle would be opened; and the following day, when Jannaway returned to his child wife, the twenty-four hour absence would have made her heart grow fonder.

They gave a party: Julietta rang up her friends in London, Petersfield, Winchester and the Meon Valley, and their cars crunched on the gravel in the drive one Friday night at seven. They arrived clutching bottles of wine, which were mixed in large quantities with brandy and lemonade. Mrs Hardesty grilled sausages and baked potatoes, and the cellar echoed with the new pop music of 1960. Jannaway was introduced like a tame gorilla, and Julietta made it clear to all, by the way she danced with him, that they were very much in love. The female guests cooed over the wedding presents (which were kept locked up in the library until the Jannaways had a place of their own) and said how well Julietta was looking. The male guests took it in turns to kiss, dance and on one occasion fondle the bride, but as that one occasion caused the first tiff between the newly-weds, the experiment was not repeated. As Christmas approached, they were invited to a succession of parties; the presence of the scarlet Mini outside some Petersfield flat or Meon Valley house became a guarantee of a good party. 'Oh good, the Jannaways are here,' people would say, and there they would be, usually holding hands, Julietta talking animatedly while young women came up to Steven and told him how much they liked his tie.

The secret of Julietta's pregnancy was carefully guarded, and she was determined that the baby would make as little difference as possible to her vital statistics. She did ante-natal exercises by the double bed every evening and refused to go into maternity clothes.

'Are you quite sure you are pregnant?' Steven asked her one evening.

'What's the matter, are you wondering if you need have married me after all?' she giggled. 'It would be rather a hoot, wouldn't it – I mean if Number One turned out to be a large belch after all. Would you be dreadfully upset?'

'Well – a bit. Yes.'

Julietta lay on her back and raised her legs. 'I wouldn't mind not having it. I think I'd buy a horse.'

She sat on the bed and asked about his early life. She wanted to know all about his girl friends and was fascinated by his childhood experiences of sex. She told him about her first orgasm, which she said she had achieved trotting on a donkey along Southsea beach.

One evening she wanted him to make love to her in his uniform with his cap on. She opened the door to him wearing only a towelling bathrobe and promptly poured an egg cup full of crushed ice down his back. This was the signal for him to chase her all over the house, catch her and spank her, which she liked. He picked her up, giggling and screaming, and took her into David's room. He put her down on the bed, being gentle with her but pretending he was being rough. 'No!' she screamed. 'Not in here! Please! No Steve!'

He had pinioned her wrists to the bed and was holding her down. Her head went from side to side. 'No!' she whimpered. He thought they were reaching a new height of sexual sophistication: she liked him to dominate her, had said once that he should treat her like his slave in bed.

'I said *no*, damn you!'

Suddenly he realised that she meant it. He let her go and she ran out of the room.

'I didn't realise,' he said. 'I thought you were enjoying it.'

'I said no.' She was sitting on her parents' bed, her shoulders hunched and fear in her eyes.

He went to her. 'Sweetie ... I'm sorry.'

She shook her head. 'It wasn't your fault.'

'What went wrong? Did I hurt you?'

She shook her head.

'What was it then? It must have been something.' He had never seen her looking like this before. 'Are you feeling all right?'

'Let's have a drink,' she said.

He brought up two horses' necks. He tried to get her to talk about what had gone wrong, but she wouldn't. They had a sleepless night and didn't make love. When he came back the following day she said very little, staring at him as if he were a stranger.

He awoke in the middle of the night. She was crying. He took her in his arms and comforted her. 'Listen,' he said. 'I'm your husband. I love you. Why can't you tell me?'

She switched the bedside light on and looked down into his eyes.

'You were the one who always wanted us to have no secrets at all,' he said.

'I know.'

'Probably help to talk about it.'

'I know that, too.'

She lay back beside him. 'You thought I was a virgin, didn't you?'

He laughed indulgently. 'I didn't really believe that!'

'Well I wasn't,' she said.

'All right. It isn't the end of the world. I forgive you. Why couldn't you have told me before?'

She rolled over onto him and sobbed until the tears ran down over his chest. 'Oh Jesus!' she whispered. 'I feel so guilty!'

'Well tell me about it then. If it'll help.'

'It happened in there,' she whispered.

'You don't mean at that party?'

'No, of course not. Ages ago. Ages and ages ago. When I was eleven.'

He stared upward. 'Who then?'

'David.'

He said nothing. There was nothing much he could say. He didn't feel shocked, just sickened.

'Do you want to know any more?'

'If you need to tell me. Not otherwise.'

She told him how it had happened. It had been her fault. 'I liked playing ... games with him. We always had. He was very small, the same height as me. We used to swap clothes and things. Then ...' She sighed. Things had got out of control. Once they started, they couldn't stop. They didn't talk about it at all, didn't even admit to each other that it happened. But it did. Every afternoon for nearly a week. 'Then Sarah found us. She walked in on us. She threatened to tell Mummy if we didn't promise never to do it again.'

He put the light out. She curled up against him and sucked her thumb. Her sobs died down, and some while later she asked, 'Are you very cross with me?'

'No,' he said, his eyes wide open in the darkness.

'And it won't make any difference, will it?'

He shook his head.

'I'm a good girl really,' she whispered, and a little while later her breathing became more regular and he knew that she had fallen asleep.

She lay beside him, curled up like a foetus, snuffling from time to time as she breathed. His thoughts went back to that night Catherine had allowed him into her bed, the night before HMS *Copenhagen* sailed for the Mediterranean. It seemed a long time ago, but it was under a year. He was deeper into the cutting and he knew that he would never be able to climb out.

Thoughts of Catherine brought him quickly to the edge of tears. She had seen through his act – that was why he had loved her and loved her still. Neither Alan nor his mother had known him as well as Catherine: only she had held the key to the real Jannaway. He smiled bitterly in the darkness. The real Jannaway, the quintessential Shag.

But there was no getting away from what had happened. He was married to Julietta and she was going to have his baby. Yes, he thought, and I am playing a part. I am not myself.

Was it possible to live your life like that? To be divided into two people? Provided I don't deceive myself, he thought, I can survive.

His thoughts became confused as he dropped into a doze. Memories of Catherine swam in and out of his consciousness. He fell asleep, and some time later became dimly aware of Julietta reaching out to him. In a semi-dream state he was able to believe that it was not Julietta at all, but Catherine. Time had slipped: these small, firm breasts were not Julietta's but the fuller, softer breasts of Catherine. This hair was Catherine's long, fine hair, not Julietta's fashionable bob. He willed the dream to continue as they began to make love: he suspended the reality of Julietta's urgent lips and darting tongue and assisted the dream of Catherine's gentle, loving kisses. He didn't force the pace and allowed the release to come of its own accord without holding it off or bringing it on.

After it was over, Julietta sat up in bed and put on the light. 'That was different, wasn't it?' she said. 'We haven't had it like that before.'

He made a pact with himself: he admitted to himself that he did not love Julietta, but at the same time swore never to admit it to anyone else. He determined to be a good husband and a good naval officer. He counted his blessings: he had married well, Julietta was already being good for his career. She was attractive, often amusing and very good in bed. He convinced himself that it would be possible to lead an agreeable life provided he understood his own inward rationalisation and kept a small part of himself true to Catherine, believing that one day, he didn't know how or when, they might be reunited. Very occasionally, when making love to Julietta, he was able to repeat the phantasy of making love to Catherine. He felt his situation to be unique: he had never heard of anyone who had lived in this way. Sometimes in the middle of a cocktail party or when he was seated at dinner with Julietta's friends, it was as if he caught a glimpse of himself, the outward self, the large lieutenant with a jolly manner and a carefully nurtured naval accent. He saw this individual eating and talking and drinking and conversing; he heard his short, confident laugh, noticed the way he had of pulling his chin and and bracing his shoulders back. He saw this person and was content, in the way you can be content with a coat that fits and looks well, although it may have been rather expensive and not exactly what you wanted.

Mrs Jannaway and Alan came down by train in the first week of December. Steven met them on Saturday afternoon and drove them down the A32 to Meonford. Dora was fifty-eight now, still teaching at Mill Hill Primary, but due to retire in two years. Alan, at twenty-nine, was as thin as a rake and looking a little more affluent in a tweed suit.

'Here we are, this is the mansion,' Steven said as he drove the Mini in through the green gates.

'Very nice,' his mother said.

Julietta came out to welcome them. She was six months pregnant now and looking it: there was a certain sleek placidity about her.

'Mum,' he said. 'Julietta.'

'Mrs Jannaway,' Julietta said. 'How lovely to meet you.'

He saw his mother looking with awe at the oil paintings, the Persian rugs. She was clearly petrified.

'Well,' she said. 'This is *very* nice.'

'Isn't it?' Julietta said. 'We love it.'

Steven took them upstairs and showed them to their rooms. 'There you are, Mum, you've got your own bathroom through here.'

She looked in at the green marble and the tiles. 'Steven!' she said. 'It's palatial!'

He took Alan into David's room. 'How are you?' he asked.

'Well, thank you,' Alan said. 'You're putting on weight, I see.'

He laughed. 'Julietta's an excellent cook.'

Alan studied one of David's old term photographs, taken on the fo'c's'le of HMS *Gazelle* only a few weeks before his death, then he moved to the window and looked down upon the walled garden, the paddock and the meadows beyond the river.

'You've really fallen on your feet, haven't you Steve?'

Steven felt uncomfortable. 'It's not ours of course. We're only here temporarily.'

Alan turned. 'That's true,' he said, and Steven felt that his brother was making more of a philosophical observation than any sort of comment about the house.

'What's this about *Argosy*? I gather you've had a story accepted.'

'That's right.'

'What's it about?'

'You'll have to read it, won't you?'

'Well... Good news, isn't it?'

'I suppose so.'

'Come on, Alan! You've been trying to get into print for years! It's a breakthrough!'

Alan laughed, relaxing. 'Maybe it is. I hope so.'

'There'll be no holding you now,' Steven said. 'Let it all flow. Be another Proust.'

For a fleeting moment, it seemed as if the old rapport was there again. They faced each other, both wanting to talk as they had once talked, to voice their hopes and fears. But the moment passed: Alan said that perhaps he'd better have a wash, and Mrs Jannaway came in and said would it be all right if she went downstairs.

Julietta waited for them in the sitting room. She was determined that Mrs Jannaway should have no cause for criticism whatsoever. She had brought tea in on a tray, and a log fire roared in the inglenook. She had cut the hot buttered toast into fingers so that Alan would not have difficulty. She sat on the floor by the fire and arranged the skirt of her maternity dress around her.

'You don't mind if I don't get up, do you, Mrs Jannaway?' she said when they came in.

Dora clutched her bag and wondered where to sit.

'Plonk yourself down, Mum,' Steven said, as anxious as Julietta to appear at ease and in command of the situation.

'Well this is *very* nice,' Mrs Jannaway said yet again, and Julietta stared at Steven, her eyes wide and shining with suppressed laughter.

Steven felt as if they had split into teams, and he knew that he was on Julietta's side. He felt that if his mother said 'very nice' once more he would roll about and bite the carpet. He had never realised just how genteel she was until now, nor had he realised how obviously spastic Alan was. They sat together on the sofa, and he thought: there they are, my private life, my darker side, the ones we don't mention. He raged inwardly, listening to Julietta chattering away, putting them at their ease, being the perfect daughter-in-law and hostess. He sat in the armchair and consoled himself that it was only one weekend and they would soon be gone.

'So what happens after this job?' Alan asked at dinner. The question was directed at Steven, but Julietta answered.

'We're hoping to get to Greenwich,' she said. 'There's a new course they've started for lieutenants.'

'I'm a bit junior for it,' Steven said. 'But my appointer thinks he can wangle it.'

'I should think you're a bit junior to be a first lieutenant of a fast patrol boat aren't you?' Alan asked.

'Oh – not really,' Julietta said.

'What's this course for?' Alan said. 'Are you going to be a gunnery officer or something?'

'It's a sort of poor man's staff course, isn't it?' Julietta said. 'They do staff papers and have political briefings.' She rose from the table to collect the plates and put them through the hatch. Dora Jannaway held out her hand for Steven's plate, intending to pile it on hers.

Julietta gave a little laugh of condescension. 'Oh no, Mrs Jannaway,' she said. 'We don't stack.'

'Beg your pardon,' Dora said.

Julietta went into the kitchen.

'I heard from Catherine last week,' Mrs Jannaway said. 'She sent you her love.'

Steven ignored her.

'Sorry I spoke,' she said.

Julietta came in with the coq-au-vin. 'You're all very silent in here!'

'It's an angel passing over I expect,' Dora said.

'We don't get many of them round here,' Julietta said lightly. She lifted the lid off the casserole. 'Now then. Mrs Jannaway?'

'Lovely,' said Dora. 'That looks very tasty.'

'We do our best, don't we Steve?'

'When do your parents come back from Malta?' Alan asked.

258

'In about six months' time,' Julietta told him. 'Then we'll have to find somewhere else to live.'

'That's right,' Steven said. 'Can't stay with the in-laws!'

He realised what he had said and saw Julietta laughing at him with her eyes from the other end of the table.

'Gracious no!' she said. 'Perish the thought!'

'Now tomorrow,' Dora said later when they were having coffee in the drawing room. 'What time is Mass, Steven?'

'There's a ten o'clock at Bishop's Waltham.'

'Is that where you go?'

He nodded. 'It's the closest one, yes.'

Julietta could contain herself no longer. 'You're a flaming liar, Steven Jannaway!' she laughed. 'You haven't been there once, to my knowledge!'


Soon after Christmas (which they spent in Malta with her parents) Julietta welcomed Steven in great glee when he arrived home from his day in *Bold Adventurer*.

'Remember Penny Forden-Jones?'

'No?'

'Sweetie you do! You met her at that party. The one that played the trumpet. Horsey face, straight blonde hair and a flat chest.'

'Oh her. What about her?'

He followed Julietta into the kitchen. She lowered herself carefully onto a stool. Now that her pregnancy was no longer a secret, she made no attempt to restrict her size.

'I rang her up this morning for a womanly chat, you know, and guess what? She's got herself a job working for the advertising agency that's handling the Senior Service contract.'

Jannaway took off his greatcoat and hung it behind the door in the boot room.

'Anyway,' Julietta went on. 'She says they're casting round for subjects for another of those "Senior Service Satisfy" ads, and I said, why not do one in *Bold Adventurer*? And she said ...' Julietta came to him and put her arms round his neck. 'Guess what she said?'

'How should I know what she said?'

'She said she might be interested.'

'She might be. She's probably only a secretary.'

'I know that, but she does happen to be sleeping with Jeremy Delacroix, darling, so snooks to you.'

'Who's he?'

259

'He's the artistic director, clotface. Anyway, I told her I'd get you to ring their office, okay? Penny said she'd see what she could fix.'

'This sort of thing has to go through admiralty!'

'Bugger the admiralty! Can't you see? If you fix it up with Penny's lot first, the admiralty can't say no!'

He made a face. 'It's not as easy as that.'

'Don't be so boring! Why shouldn't it be as easy as that? Make it happen!'

She persuaded him to broach the subject to Trussel the following day. Trussel was suffering from the onset of lethargy, prior to leaving the service, known as 'greasing the end prior to letting it go'. 'I don't give a fish's tit, Number One,' he said. 'If you're determined to get your name in lights, then by all means go ahead.'

'I'm sticking my neck out,' Steven told Julietta that evening when he finally agreed to ring Penny.

'No you're not, you're coming out of your shell, tortoise.'

Penny's voice was excited at the other end of the line. 'Absolutely super, Steven!' she said. 'Listen, I'll get Jeremy to ring you in your ship, okay? I know he'll be interested.'

Julietta took the phone from him.

'Penny? It's me. Look – I had an idea. What about beards? Wouldn't it be rather super if they all grew beards? What do you think?' She giggled and listened to Penny's voice for some time, and a few minutes later, when she had rung off, said, 'Right. She thinks its a marvellous idea, too. You're all to grow beards.'

'But does anyone else know about it?'

'Of course they do, darling idiot!' She stroked his chin. 'I think you'll be rather sexy in a beard, anyway.' She held his hands. 'Do you love me?' she demanded.

He nodded.

'Say it then. Tell me.'

'I love you.'

She gave a short, sharp sigh. 'You're very unromantic sometimes, aren't you?'

'Doing my best.'

To his surprise, the idea to use *Bold Adventurer* for a new Senior Service advertisement was taken up. Trussel was persuaded to inform the admiralty by signal, and a commander in a fawn British Warm came down from London on the day Jeremy Delacroix and Penny Forden-Jones arrived in an Aston Martin.

Jeremy had floppy hair and yellow suede boots. He picked his ear with a biro and looked at his shot list. 'I want a rapid montage,' he explained. 'Nice long shot establishers of the boat at speed, aerial shots from a helicopter if we can get them, close-ups of the skipper giving orders on the bridge, the gun firing. Action action action. Then right at the end, we'll have a nice dreamy sequence with the boat coming in at the end of the day, the trill of those whistles, you know –'

'Bosun's calls,' said the commander.

'Yes, those as well, why not? And then we'll bring out the pack of Senior Service, zoom in really tight on the skipper lighting up –' Jeremy held his hands up, palms forward, as if directing the shot. 'And *freeze*.' He looked round. They were having drinks in the cramped wardroom, and he and Penny had made do with gin and tonic because there was no Campari. 'What do you think?'

The three naval officers, Trussel, Jannaway and the commander from London, looked at each other, not sure what to think. Penny, in furs by Dior, was in no doubts. 'Wonderful!' she said. 'Simply wonderful! I really love that, darling, I really do!'

'What about beards?' Jannaway asked.

'Well you're all going to have them aren't you?'

'Are we?' Trussel said. 'First I've heard about it.'

'Can do,' Jannaway said. 'Will fix, sir.'

The idea was a personal success for Jannaway. He allowed Trussel to believe that the whole concept had been his, and when word went round that the entire ship's company of HMS *Bold Adventurer* was being required to grow beards, he won renown in the navy as a young officer of verve and imagination. A short column appeared in the *Portsmouth Evening News* a month later, with a photograph of the newly bearded Jannaway and his piratical crew. THE BOLD AND THE BEARDED ran the caption, and there followed a short piece about the boat and its go-ahead first lieutenant, who, it was noted, happened to be the son of Frank Jannaway, the mine disposal winner of the George Cross.

He cut out the article and started a scrap book with it. Suddenly he realised that Julietta was right: it was necessary to push oneself forward relentlessly. It was possible to make things happen. He began to feel that he was walking with destiny.

The first day of shooting involved filming the boat from a helicopter, as she pounded at speed into a head sea. It took place on a bitterly cold afternoon in late February, and Jeremy Delacroix arrived in sheepskins and suedes. The boat sailed from Haslar Creek soon after a roast beef lunch cooked personally by the coxswain and served with an excellent Macon wine. Contact was made with the helicopter from the navy air base at Lee-on-Solent, and Trussel took the boat up to forty knots for the first run.

Delacroix decided that the water was too calm to achieve the effects he wanted. 'Awfully sorry, dears,' he said to the bridge in general, 'but I'm afraid this is going to look boring.'

'It'll be a lot less boring out at sea,' Trussel said.

'Will it? Are we allowed out to sea?'

Fifteen minutes later, the boat was heading out through the Needles Channel into Poole Bay. The bows lifted over the first wave and smashed down, making the spray fly upward on either side. 'Wonderful!' Jeremy said, and immediately threw up his lunch.

When the boat arrived back alongside the jetty of HMS *Hornet*, there was an urgent message waiting for Steven. Julietta had gone into premature labour, and was in Haslar naval hospital. Without bothering to change out of his coastal forces sweater, he raced ashore and drove the short distance into the hospital grounds.

'She's in theatre now,' he was told by a wardmaster lieutenant.

'Theatre?' For a moment he wondered if Julietta had arranged some sort of publicity stunt for herself.

'They're doing a Caesar,' the wardmaster explained. 'Nothing to worry about, just a few last minute complications, that's all.'

He sat and tried not to think of them cutting her open. He wondered how they managed to make the cut without hurting the baby inside. In his mind's eye, he kept seeing the scalpel, opening her up, flaps of flesh falling apart, the foetus, huddled there in her womb. O God, he prayed silently, make them both be all right.

Her room was full of flowers, cards, chocolates, telegrams and assorted tropical fruit. She lay propped on four pillows, and careful use of eye shadow gave him the impression that she had deliberately made herself up to look ill.

'I've just been in to see her,' he said. 'She's fine.'

Her eyes watched him but she said nothing. She had been bubbling with high spirits on the day after the delivery. They had opened champagne in her room and shared it round with the nurses.

She had made him read all her cards and telegrams out to her and had to be kept from getting up immediately. Three days later, her wave had broken. She had complained about the nurses and made a scene with the surgeon rear admiral when he came to visit her. She had become hysterical, had been sedated, and had not talked since.

The staff nurse had advised Steven to pretend that all was normal. He kissed her lightly on the cheek and sat down by the bed running his fingers through his new beard.

'How's things then? Are you feeling better?' He gave her enough time to reply but showed no surprise when she did not. 'Had a phone call from Jeremy this morning,' he told her. 'He's seen the rushes and he's pleased with them. He wants a couple of retakes next week, then I can shave this off.'

Sleet pattered on the sash window. He went and looked out. He could see across the cemetery and the submarine base. Below him, two nurses walked across the car park, their red and blue capes billowing.

He turned. 'What are we going to call her then? Have you thought any more about that?'

She was pouting in that peculiarly Braddle way: pushing her top lip over her bottom one. It made her look singularly unattractive, and she knew it. Her eyes swivelled round and fired off a black beam of hatred.

'Juju!' he said. 'Come on! It's not as bad as that!'

He returned to the bed and took her hand. She pulled it away from him, but he held on to it.

'No,' he said. 'I'm not letting you go.'

She stared in front of her, and breathed as if gasping for breath. He felt panic rise inside him: women could lose their mental balance after childbirth, and he was afraid that this was what had happened to Julietta.

'I want to help you,' he said, looking down at their joined hands. 'That's what husbands are for, isn't it?'

The sound of a bugle call – or rather a recorded bugle call, played over the loudspeakers in HMS *Dolphin* – reached them through the window.

'Stand easy,' he said, and looked round to try and catch her eye.

'Shall I tell you something? I'm proud of you. I love you. I love you both.'

She spoke at last: 'Nobody loves me,' she said. 'Not in the way I need. No one ever has.'

Her tears overflowed and spilled down her cheeks.

'Go on,' he said. 'Tell me. Give.'

She shook her head.

'Well then let's talk about names,' he said.

'I don't know, and I don't care.'

'Yes you do.'

'Catherine then.'

'I'm not going to call her that, Juju.'

'I think it would be most appropriate. It would remind us, wouldn't it? Of when and where and how. Did you know ... did you know it was supposed to be impossible under water? Did you know that? But you managed it.' She faced him. 'With your great big bloody ... dick. You managed it.'

He tried not to listen, discounting what she was saying. He told himself that whatever she said was caused by the chaos of post-natal depression. It was a form of hysteria, he knew that. Perhaps it was a good thing that she was saying these terrible things; perhaps it was necessary for her to get it out of her system. He reassured himself that she would be over it in a few days. He had booked a Norland Nanny to look after the baby for the first four weeks, and teach her how to care for her. Her mother would be coming over in a fortnight's time. People in Meonford village – retired naval people, the vicar, were rallying round.

He put his arm round her shoulders and she leant against him, accepting his comfort.

'That's the way,' he said. 'That's the way.'

He sat with her like that, and realised that the act of comforting her in this way helped him, too. He needed to comfort, he needed to be leant against. He felt tears in his own eyes, and was surprised at the sudden onrush of love for her.

'Listen,' he said. 'You'll feel so much better in a few days. I know you will. We've got a smashing baby, too. Everyone's saying she's just like her Mum.'

She shook herself free of his arm. She seemed to gulp back her anger, clenching her teeth against it as if it might spill out on the sheet like some evil fluid. She scrabbled at the bedclothes, pushing them away from her. She lifted her nightdress and ripped away a dressing to reveal the fresh wound and the row of black stitches. 'Just like her Mum? Is she? Has she got one of these? I bet she hasn't, has she?'

264

# 15

They arrived at Greenwich in their new Morris 1000 Estate on a Saturday morning in May the following year. After a fruitless search for a flat near the college during the previous weeks, Julietta had finally found one in a Georgian house close to Greenwich Park. The rent was twice as much as Jannaway could afford, but as the Lieutenants' Course lasted only three months, they took it.

Julietta had gone into the flat and Steven was unloading the brake when a familiar voice called, 'Shag! You old devil! What the bloody hell are you doing in this neck of the woods!'

It was Chas Tomkins, looking like a bookmaker in a twill jacket and a yellow waistcoat with brass buttons.

They shook hands firmly. Steven had not yet shaved off his beard after the Senior Service advertisement, and he was taller and broader than Tomkins. The latter introduced his wife Wendy, a pert blonde with suitably thrusting breasts to match the image of intrepid aviator which Tomkins was building for himself.

'Oh!' she said. 'I know who you are. "Senior Service Satisfy".'

'Seldom before lunch,' said Julietta, coming out of the house.

Tomkins kissed her warmly on the cheek.

'I didn't know you two knew each other,' Jannaway said.

'Dartmouth ball '55,' said Julietta. 'Before you were even thought of.'

Tomkins looked into the carry-cot. 'And this is your son and heir is it?'

'Heiress,' corrected Jannaway. 'Looks as though she's just been sick.'

'Don't be so beastly!' said Julietta. 'Her name's Anita and she's blowing very beautiful bubbles.'

'Look, why don't you come and have a noggin when you're sorted out?' Tomkins suggested. 'We're just down the road. Number eighty-four, flat three.'

'No, you come to us,' Julietta said. 'Otherwise we have to drag the sprog along.'

'Well very nice to meet you,' said Wendy when they had agreed a time. She had only been married two months: Tomkins had found her behind a bar in Lossiemouth.

'My God!' Jannaway said when they were out of earshot. 'It would have to be Tomkins we bump into first.'

'I rather like him,' Julietta said.

'He's a crashing bore, like most aviators. "There I was in a ball of flame, nothing on the clock but the maker's name." '

'You're jealous.'

'Not at all. They can keep flying, so far as I'm concerned.'

'She fancied you.'

'I didn't notice.'

'Oh yes you did, you bloody liar. She kept pointing her tits in your direction. I expected you to start panting at any moment.'

He grinned and felt her bottom. 'Well I fancy you a lot more.'

'In that case you can go and fix me a drink.'

'Good thinking,' he said, and went off in search of the cardboard box in which he had stowed Julietta's special store of low calorie tonic water and Gordon's gin.

The course started the following week. The fifty lieutenants were lectured to on the nuclear balance, leadership and the political situation in Europe. They discussed the relevance of the convoy system in modern warfare and embarked upon special projects.

Working in syndicates, they were presented with problems designed to develop their ability to plan, and heated discussions took place about the wisdom of taking the imaginary Hill 456 before establishing a company headquarters, or the feasibility of providing air cover for the logistics train. They delved deeper and deeper into naval staffwork: they learnt the difference between a loose minute and a docket and studied the intricacies of indented sub-paragraphs; they became acquainted with how to define the Aim, draw a Conclusion and list their Recommendations.

Jannaway and Tomkins drove to work each morning and brought work home to do each night. They ate their lunches under the magnificent ceiling of the Painted Hall, whose Baroque grandeur provided a fitting backdrop to the casual splendour of the brass buttons and gold lace of the officers who sipped their Brown Windsor soup and arranged games of tennis or rendezvous for Derby Day.

There was ambition in the air now. Standard issue items of

uniform were being discarded: freshly starched, cut-away collars were *de rigeur* for an officer who wanted to get ahead; highly polished mess boots from Gieves were preferred to shoes, and a knitted black tie with one's number five uniform was an advantage.

Jannaway returned to his flat one Friday evening and announced: 'I have to write a paper on the role of the navy. I thought I might do a sort of Jules Verne version. Submersible aircraft carriers and monster hovercraft.'

Julietta was laying the table for a dinner party they were giving that evening for her parents and the Sykes-Morrises. Freddy Sykes-Morris was now the Director of Naval Officer Appointments, and Henry Braddle was an Assistant Chief of Naval Staff, working in the admiralty.

'You'll be an idiot if you do,' she told him, setting a silver bowl of roses in the centre of the table. She inspected the place settings carefully, making sure the dolphin candlesticks were precisely placed and the cut glass and silver immaculate.

'I thought it might be interesting to do something different,' Jannaway said, following her into the kitchen. 'Everyone else will be writing what we've virtually been told to write – the old brush fire contingency force, commitment to NATO, fishery protection. Very boring.'

'Keep your ear to the ground and you might pick up a few ideas tonight,' Julietta said. 'You could even sound out Freddy on your next job while you're about it.'

He laughed. 'He doesn't have anything to do with people as junior as me! He's vastly superior!'

Henry and Clara arrived early so that they could see the flat. Now that his tour of duty in Malta was over, Henry looked more of a prosperous businessman than an admiral; while Clara, having plunged back into village life at Meonford, looked more relaxed and homely.

'I think you've done wonders darlings,' she told them. 'It feels really warm and welcoming, doesn't it Henry?'

Steven came in with the gin and tonics and Julietta fetched Anita, causing an immediate effusion of grand-parental admiration. In the middle of this the Sykes-Morrises arrived and there was the usual long-time-no-seeing, back slapping, cheek kissing and mutual reassurances of how well everyone looked.

At dinner, Mrs Sykes-Morris asked Steven about his career. She was a small, determined lady who looked older than she was, and who was well versed in the art of dinner party conversation.

'What do you expect to do when you leave Greenwich?' she asked. 'Or is that a secret?'

'I've been tentatively offered a coastal minesweeper in Singapore,' he said, spreading duck pâté on fairy toast and being careful not to finish first.

'That sounds as though it might be fun.'

'Yes, doesn't it? Julietta's very keen. Have you been out East?'

'Many times,' said Jane Sykes-Morris. 'Freddy was out there just after the war. That's how we met. I was working in the British High Commission and we used to go for glorious banyan parties on one of the islands off the east coast.'

He listened as she continued her reminiscences. Not for the first time, he had the impression that the navy he had joined was somehow not the 'real' navy, the navy that had once been, the Navy with a capital N.

'So I don't suppose you've specialised yet have you?' she asked.

He took a careful sip of his Yugoslav Riesling and said no, he didn't expect to specialise for another three or four years.

At the other end of the table, the conversation had stopped. 'Are you asking Steve about his choice of specialisation?' Julietta asked. 'That's a real saga! He simply cannot make up his mind, can you? First it was gunnery, then it was communications, then it was submarines and now it's what? Navigation?'

Jannaway didn't think it was all that funny. 'I was considering navigation and direction, yes.'

'Perhaps you ought to consider aviation,' Sykes-Morris suggested. 'We're crying out for observers these days.'

'Not really my scene, sir,' Jannaway said. 'I'm a small ship man myself.'

'We'll be having plenty of small ships with helicopters in the next ten years,' Sykes-Morris said. 'Right Henry?'

'Absolutely,' Henry agreed.

'I should think flying helicopters would be rather fun,' Julietta said.

'Maybe you ought to volunteer, darling,' Steven countered suavely.

The guests laughed politely, and Julietta shot a warning look across Steven's bows. She rose to take the plates into the kitchen and he went to help her but was rounded on immediately. 'Get back in there, clot!' she hissed. 'They'll think you've come in to apologise!'

Later, when the cigars had been lit and the ladies had withdrawn, Henry asked how the course was going.

'Really excellent value, sir,' Jannaway said. 'I'm enjoying it tremendously.'

'I think it's a damn good idea, don't you Freddy? So much better than those subs' courses we had to endure.'

'We're all sweating over our papers on the role of the navy at the moment,' Jannaway went on. 'I suppose I'd be cheating if I asked your ideas on the subject?'

Braddle took his cigar out of his mouth and looked at the smouldering end. He glanced at Sykes-Morris, who was twirling his brandy glass back and forth by the stem.

'Depends what you want to know.'

Jannaway grinned confidently. As Braddle's son-in-law, he was in a position of privilege: he enjoyed a certain gruff comradeship with him, playing Othello to Henry's Brabantio. 'I'm trying to come up with one or two new ideas,' he told them. 'As straw men rather than concrete proposals of course. Hovercraft for instance. Have they got a future? For amphibious operations or mine-sweeping?'

'Undoubtedly, but not yet-awhile,' Sykes-Morris said. 'It's the submarine that still has the greatest potential for development in my book, don't you agree Henry?'

Braddle still owed an allegiance to the gun, but as a rear admiral was expected to put such preferences behind him. He nodded and pulled at his nose, wearing the solemn expression he used for briefing the Chiefs of Staff.

'And aircraft carriers?' Jannaway asked.

'Sitting ducks,' Braddle observed.

'But can we do without them sir?'

'I think you would find that the Soviets were exceedingly grateful to us if we did,' Sykes-Morris said.

Braddle laughed. 'Trouble with the navy is all these damn ships, what?'

When the laughter had subsided, Jannaway said, 'But what about the *role* the navy has to play. Is it going to change? Are we going to be cut back to a coastal force?'

'I shudder to think what Messrs Wilson and Healey might do if

Labour gets office,' Sykes-Morris said, and Braddle shook his head weightily and muttered 'Heaven forbid!'

'What would have to go first?' Jannaway asked. 'If the navy had to be halved, say?'

Braddle and Sykes-Morris looked at each other. Braddle waved his cigar. 'You can't do it that way, Steve. We must retain a balanced navy. Can't lop off an arm or a leg, so to speak.'

'What I was wondering was – couldn't we design a completely new class of ship – perhaps a hovercraft – that can do everything a frigate can do and sweep mines as well. And land troops for that matter. These new Leander frigates are all very well, but they can't *do* very much can they? They can't detect submarines as well as a helicopter, they're not all that hot at shooting down aircraft and they can't sweep mines – or lay them for that matter. They haven't got any torpedoes and they're so overcrowded with radar and communications equipment that there's no room left for any real hitting power in the way of guns. And what's more, they cost one hell of a lot of money.'

Henry Braddle punched his son-in-law playfully in the solar plexus as they rose from the table. 'You put that load of rubbish in your paper,' he said. 'See what kind of a raspberry you get back!'

He started work on his paper a few days later. He decided that he would write it with the aim not of voicing his opinions but simply to please the staff. He remembered Tim Whettingsteel's counsel that afternoon at Dartmouth when he had explained the rules of the Need to be Seen club. The panel of judges that would be reading the papers and deciding the prizewinners included an aviator, a submariner, a Royal Marine officer and a naval historian, so it seemed advisable to lay particular emphasis on the importance of aircraft carriers, submarines, amphibious operations and the lessons of the past. After some weeks in which he made quantities of notes but had failed to get anything else down on paper, when the deadline for submission of essays was only a few days off, he sat down one evening and made a start.

Throwing caution to the winds, he decided on the broad sweep, the grand view. He crossed his fingers and hoped that no one would recognise Clausewitz's words which he paraphrased and used as his own: 'War is never waged for its own sake,' he wrote, 'but for the purpose of furthering a nation's political intentions. War is not an exact science, but an art. It is not merely an act of violence between nations, but an alternative, an option, a tool in the workbag of a national leader. Thus military organisations are in turn tools, and to be efficient they must be sharp, effective and obedient to the wishes of their masters. The purpose of this paper is therefore not merely to theorise upon the Role of the Navy, but to put forward what that Role might be in the context of war as an extension of politics...'

He was pleased with this grandiose introduction. I'll really make them sit up, he thought. He even began to think that he might hold inside himself the seeds of greatness.

Three nights later, with only a day to spare before the deadline, he completed the last paragraphs of conclusions and recommendations. He brought it into the bedroom in triumph.

'It's nearly six thousand words!' he announced.

Julietta was fresh from her bath. She sat at her dressing table examining her skin for blemishes.

'I'd like to read it to you some time. See what you think.'

'Read it to me now then, if you like.'

'Okay, here we go.'

Julietta bent close to the mirror and looked very closely at her eyelashes.

'Are you listening?'

'Yes of course I'm listening.'

He started out. After the first page, Julietta knelt on the bed in her baby doll nightdress and looked over his shoulder.

'There can be little doubt that in terms of cost-effectiveness, the anti-submarine frigate comes a poor third to the anti-submarine helicopter and the long range maritime patrol aircraft,' he read, turning to page five. Julietta undid his shirt buttons and began tickling his chest.

'I can't concentrate if you're doing that!'

'Yes you can, it makes it more interesting.'

He returned to his paper. 'With the advent of nuclear hunter-killer submarines, the speed, range and endurance advantage once held by the surface escort is reversed: in the coming years, more and more submarines will be able to evade and outstrip all but the air or air-cushion borne pursuer.'

'Go on!'

'Thus – thus –'

'I won't do it if you keep stopping, Monster. I'll leave you all up in the air.'

He made an effort. 'Thus it seems logical to propose ... oh! ... to propose a fleet of ships or cushion vehicles capable of uniform ... oh Juju! ... of uniform high speed ... ee-ah! ... not reliant on low speed surface escorts for air and anti-submarine defence ... aargh! ... but upon pocket carriers ... with their own organic – organic – multi-role aircraft ... ahhhhh!'

The Role of the Navy fell to the floor.

'It's rather heavy isn't it?' Julietta giggled. 'When do we get to the exciting bit?'


There was a mess dinner a few evenings later. It was the usual sort of affair: everyone trooping into the Painted Hall to the tune of Roast Beef of Old England, the bang of the mess president's gavel for Grace, the long rows of seated officers in their mess undress, the silver trophies on the tables and the throwing of peanuts and knotting of table napkins at the end. After the loyal toast, which was drunk seated, a Royal Marine bandsman played the Post Horn Gallop on a trumpet. The notes of it echoed against the frescoes, bouncing off the Baroque pillars and steps, which looked real until you approached to within a few yards. The applause lasted and lasted, the officers banging their hands on the tables so that the glasses of port and madeira jumped and rang. The bandsman played the Gallop again, and the applause thundered again; and after the speeches, down in the lower ante-room, the officers gathered in a smoky atmosphere to drink pints of draught bitter while the world was put to rights and the inevitable Tomkins leapt up on a table and conducted the inevitable songs. Then it was time for mess games: High Cockalorum, Cardinal Puff, La-di-da, during which Jannaway had to be taken off to the sickbay for attention to a gash in his hand caused by a broken bottle.

There was a letter for him the following morning. It was a Saturday: Julietta was giving Anita her breakfast and the radio was on. They sat over coffee and newspapers, Steven nursing his bandaged hand and a king-size hangover.

The letter was from the admiralty and the 'Dear Jannaway' and signature were hand-written:

Dear Jannaway,

I am writing to you privately to say how pleased I am to see that you have been provisionally selected for aircrew duties under the provisions of AFO 733/59. Providing you are found to be physically fit, I would expect you to start your Observer training on or about the 9th of August this year. No doubt you will wish to ask a lot of questions about your future career as an aviation specialist, and to this end I shall be visiting the Royal Naval College, Greenwich to deal with your queries.

In the meantime, let me assure you that you will find your new specialisation to be a most rewarding and challenging one, which offers excellent career prospects, as well as the knowledge that you will belong to the most élite fighting force in the world.

Yours sincerely,
Douglas Larman
Commander, Royal Navy.

'There must be some mistake,' he said. 'I just can't believe this.'

Julietta had had a postcard from Peter Lasbury. 'He can come to the ball after all but he wants us to fix him up with a partner. Isn't that super?'

He handed her his letter. She started laughing before she had finished it. 'Well at least they've made up your mind for you, haven't they?'

'I don't think it's at all funny, and I don't see why I should go along with it, either.' He took back the letter and stared at it. 'I know why they're doing this. They lost two Gannets last month. Mid-air collision. Two pilots, four observers. So now they've started press-ganging again.'

'Do you know, I think you're scared?' Julietta said, playing with her necklace and looking challengingly at him across the kitchen table.

'I'm not scared. I just don't want to be a woolly bear.'

'Woolly bear? Is that what they're called? I rather like that! You're a bit of a woolly bear anyway, aren't you? Sort of dark and grizzly.'

'I dislike flying, I dislike big ships and I dislike aviators,' Jannaway said. 'And I also dislike the thought that I've probably been volunteered because of what you said at that dinner party last month.'

'I thought you said you were far too junior for Freddy to have anything to do with you?'

'Yes, I am, but I'm not so sure about you.'

'Well if you think I had anything to do with this you're wrong.' Julietta took the top off a boiled egg for Anita, who conducted her own personal pre-egg celebration, beating a tattoo on the arm of her high chair.

'It's a bloody betrayal,' Jannaway said. 'It's unethical. It's like telling a coalminer he's got to be a steeplejack.'

'He's chicken,' Julietta said confidentially to her daughter, and clucked like a hen. 'Chicken, chicken, chicken!'

'It'd be nice if you were on my side for a change.'

'I am on your side! But you can't take on the admiralty, can you? If they say jump, you jump, and if they say be a woolly bear, you bloody well get up on your hind legs and dance.'

He put his head in his good hand, staring down at the letter. 'If I'd wanted to fly, I'd have joined the Crabs. Have you any idea what observers do? They spend their entire lives gazing at radar sets while some teenage pilot drives them unreliably about the sky. I don't want to go cross-eyed in the back of a Vixen, thank you very much.'

Julietta lifted Anita out of her high chair and put her on her pot. 'I suppose I could always give Daddy a ring and ask him to get on to Freddy for you. Would you like me to do that?'

'You mean pull strings? And get labelled as "lacking in moral fibre"? No thanks. I'll sort this out for myself.'

Major Vogel was a tall, wiry Royal Marine officer, whose brass buttons shone and whose Sam Browne had that deep, leathery glow that can only be achieved by hours of dedicated attention. He wore parachutist's wings on his tunic and campaign medal ribbons for service in Cyprus and Malaya. He sat at a clear desk, without in and out trays, taking a pride in dealing with all paperwork as it arose. Sitting in the armchair by the desk was Commander Larman, a small, rounded man of nearly forty, who wore pilot's wings above the three gold rings on his left arm, and Korean campaign medals above the silk handkerchief in his breast pocket. He was one of the few pilots in the fleet air arm to have shot down a Russian Mig fighter, but he did not look the part of the flying ace. Saliva gathered easily at the corners of his mouth; he looked as though he would be more at home behind the counter of a sweet shop than at the controls of a supersonic jet.

'You know who he's married to, don't you?' Vogel was saying. 'Henry Braddle's daughter. ACNS Policy.'

'Never heard of him,' Larman said.

'You will, sir. He's heading for the top.'

'What about Jannaway? Has he shone in any way?'

Vogel opened Jannaway's personal file. 'Hasn't done at all badly here. Played a bit of rugger. He's not brilliant, but he's a useful guy to have around.'

'Well if he's out there, we may as well have him in,' said Larman, and Vogel went to the door and beckoned Jannaway to enter.

Jannaway had had his beard trimmed and his hair cut. He shook Larman firmly by the hand, sat as directed in the upright chair, crossed his legs and folded his arms.

'So how do you feel about becoming an observer?' Larman asked him.

Jannaway unfolded his arms and put on his determined look. He had spent some time preparing his line of argument and was confident that he would emerge with honour, free of all commitment to aviation. 'I'm not sure that you've picked the right bloke for the job, sir,' he said.

Larman laughed. 'That's our problem, not yours. You can leave us to worry about that.'

'I must say I'd like to feel enthusiastic about the idea,' Jannaway said, 'but I joined the navy because of the ships, not because of the aircraft.'

Larman smiled reassuringly, displaying a thin line of saliva on his lower lip. 'Don't worry about that,' he said. 'We find that a lot of chaps come to the course with misgivings, but by the time they've finished it they're keen as mustard. I've seen it happen dozens of times.'

Jannaway wondered if all those dozens of times had applied to officers who were volunteered to fly against their will. 'The trouble is, I've never been interested in aviation. I've never had any desire to fly, and I have none at this minute.'

'Look at it this way,' Larman said. 'You won't be doing the flying. You'll be exercising a vital tactical role. You'll be taking responsibility for a highly sophisticated aircraft.'

'From the back seat of a Vixen?' Jannaway said, and regretted it immediately.

Larman's eyes narrowed, and a dottle of saliva slid to the corner of his mouth. 'Yes, from the back seat of a Vixen, or a Gannet or one of the new Buccaneers. Or a Wessex helicopter for that matter.

You could be in command of an aircraft with more hitting power than the heaviest battleship. You can't really say that that won't involve responsibility can you? Or does the thought of so much responsibility make you apprehensive?'

Jannaway sat back and tried to relax, but there was sweat under his arms, and he was conscious of Major Vogel watching him closely. This was more of an interrogation than an interview. He recalled Julietta's warning about taking on the admiralty, and he recognised in the steely confidence of this commander and the deceptively placid silence of the major the tip of a huge iceberg: the iceberg of naval authority.

'No, sir, it doesn't,' he said. 'But I can't say that I feel particularly well motivated towards observer duties. It's as simple as that.'

'What have you actually done in the way of flying?' Larman asked.

'Well, I did the acquaint course at Brawdy while I was a midshipman sir –'

'Well there you are. Just wait until you've got forty thousand pounds of thrust strapped to your arse, then you'll know what flying's about.'

There was a silence in which Jannaway began to realise that unless he threatened to resign from the navy or told them blatantly that he was terrified of the thought of flying, he would end up as a trainee observer.

Vogel was looking at his confidential file, and he now spoke for the first time. 'You see you've already demonstrated that you're unsure which sub-specialisation you want,' he said. 'You put down gunnery when you were in HMS *Syston*, then changed to communications. Then you volunteered for submarines, and when you didn't get that you changed to navigation and direction.'

'Well there you are,' Larman said. 'We're virtually giving you your first choice, aren't we? As an observer, you'll be navigating and directing aircraft. And you'll find it a damn sight more challenging in the back seat of a Buccaneer than you will in the air direction room of a carrier.'

Larman and Vogel smiled at each other. Jannaway was cornered.

Their victim looked up. 'Well,' he said, 'If I've got to fly, I'd rather be a pilot than an observer.'

'Now you're talking,' Larman said, and licked his lips.

'A helicopter pilot, that is,' Jannaway said. 'Could I do that?'

'Can I use your phone, William?' Larman asked. 'I can probably get an answer on this from admiralty straight away.'

He dialled the admiralty. 'James,' he said. 'I've got a volunteer here for rotary wing pilot duties!'

Jannaway listened to Larman in a semi-daze. He didn't want to be a helicopter pilot at all, but it seemed a lesser evil than being pressed into flying as an observer. Perhaps he would have done better to be honest and admit that he was terrified of the idea of flying from an aircraft carrier: plenty of people did, after all, and with good reason. Landing an aircraft on a ship's deck had for a long time been recognised as a high risk occupation. Helicopters, he felt, were at least a little safer than the fixed wing aircraft. At least they did not have to be launched by catapult or recovered by arrestor wires.

Larman had rung off. 'They can't give you a definite answer right now,' he said, 'but they'll be ringing back this afternoon when they've done their sums. They hold out every hope they'll be able to fit you in.' He beamed. 'So there you are. And don't say we don't look after you.'

'Glad that's sorted,' Vogel said, and turned to Jannaway. 'Happy?'

Jannaway found himself out in the corridor a few minutes later. Vogel had promised to let him know the answer on his request for helicopter pilot training as soon as it came through.

He stood outside the office, feeling disorientated, and while he stood there, Chas Tomkins came paddling along in his cut-away collar and knitted tie.

'Shag!' he exclaimed. 'Have you seen the noticeboard? You've got a life subscription to the *Naval Review*!'

'What for?'

'What do you think, you idiot! You've won the Role of the Navy prize!'

'Guess what,' Julietta said. 'Steve's going to be a Woolly Bear!'

'Shag!' said Tomkins. 'You dark horse! You never said anything about this to me!'

They were having a glass of champagne before going on to the summer ball: the Jannaways, the Tomkinses, Peter Lasbury, a large Third Officer Wren called Mary Lomax-Yately, Jeremy Delacroix, and Penny Forden-Jones.

277

'What in heaven's name is a Woolly Bear?' asked Penny.

'Same as an RAF navigator, only he can read and write,' Tomkins said.

'Well good for you mate!' Lasbury said to Jannaway.

Jannaway had not told Julietta of the outcome of his interview with Larman yet, nor had he heard confirmation that he would be accepted for helicopter pilot training.

Third Officer Lomax-Yately gave a moan of delight. 'Oh!' she said. 'I think men are so lucky! I'd love to fly, I really would!'

Julietta held Steven's hand and leant against him. 'There you are, darling, you'll have all the girls falling over themselves to get at you now.' She looked up at him, then across at Peter Lasbury. She had not seen Peter for nearly two years, and this was only a fleeting visit. Julietta had asked Mary along because she was the least good looking spare female she could find, and had made a particular effort to look well herself: she had piled her hair in a knot on top of her head, and wore a close fitting, crimson sheath of a dress that flattered her newly regained figure.

They arrived at the ball rather late. There was a Royal Marine band in the Painted Hall, and a rock group in the lower ante-room. They collected their bottles of wine from the bar and gathered at the table they had reserved in the marquee, the officers in mess dress, and Jeremy Delacroix in white tie and tails. The occasion should have been a triumphant one for Steven: he had won his prize, and here he was, showing off his wife to all the people he needed to impress; but he could not catch the party mood that Julietta was now bent upon creating. He danced with her and with Wendy; he collected his shrimps in aspic from the buffet and sipped his Niersteiner, and the officers and their ladies cavorted and joked and showed off and roared, repeatedly, with laughter.

Towards ten o'clock, when he was pressed against the bosom of Mary Lomax-Yately, he saw Vogel trying to catch his eye. He finished the dance with Mary, and excused himself to speak to the major.

'I've been trying to find you all evening,' Vogel said. 'Had a phone call from admiralty just after you'd left this afternoon. They say they're delighted to take you on for pilot training. So that's good news.'

'Pilot training?' Jannaway said. 'That is helicopter pilot training?'

'No, that's fixed wing. They're topped up with chopper pilots right now. They say you'll start your course at Linton in the second week of August.'

'Fixed wing,' Jannaway said.

'That's right, fixed wing.'

The band had started playing a Charleston, and Jannaway saw Julietta taking to the floor again with Peter Lasbury. Lasbury's patent leather shoes flashed back and forth, and his fair hair flopped over his face as he danced, while Julietta jigged about moving her shoulders up and down seductively.

'Well anyway,' Vogel said. 'Just thought you'd like to know.'

He wandered off the floor and out of the college. He descended the wide stone steps and stood looking out over the River Thames. Behind him he could hear both the rock group and the Royal Marine band, and the two jarred against each other and made a cacophony.

He remembered the small boy he had once been, the boy who had wanted to join the navy because his father had been a hero, the boy who had gone off to Dartmouth promising to come back and tell Alan what it was like. How had it been possible that he should change – and lose – so much?

Am I condemned to spend the rest of my life stumbling from crisis to crisis? he wondered. He stood with his back to the college buildings and stared down at the moving water, and while he was there, heard Julietta's laugh somewhere behind him.

He turned. She had come out of the building with Chas Tomkins, and they were walking hand in hand. He stood quite still, not knowing whether to make them aware of his presence or not. They descended the steps he had just descended, and Tomkins put his arm round Julietta's waist.

Jannaway turned his back to them and coughed deliberately. There was silence for a few moments, and then he heard Julietta call, 'Steve?'

He turned. She was alone.

'Hullo,' he said, and started back up the steps.

'You are an idiot,' she said. 'I've been searching for you everywhere!' She looked up into his face and took his hand. 'They're going to have an Eightsome any minute, so we need you.'

They went back into the marquee, and the party assembled in the Painted Hall for the Eightsome. They set and joined hands, they danced six hands round and six hands back; they figure-of-eighted, whooped and did the teapot, and afterwards, out of breath and cheerful, they returned to their table.

The band started a slow foxtrot. 'Let's dance again,' Jannaway said.

Julietta made a face. 'Do we have to?'

'I'd like to, yes.'

'Darling you are a bore.'

'I know I'm a bore, but I'd like to dance.'

She got up reluctantly. On the way to the floor he said, 'I like people to see us dancing together.'

She looked at him quickly. He took her in his arms and they moved slowly about the floor. She put her head sideways against his chest, and he rested his chin upon her sleek, chestnut hair.

The silly thing is, I do love her, he thought. Catherine had been right: making love actually created a bond, and the birth of Anita had strengthened that bond. This small, svelte body, these slender hands and delicate fingers had become almost a part of him.

He must have sighed. She looked up. 'What was that for?'

'I have a small piece of news,' he said, and was again aware of that sensation of being outside himself, of watching himself and listening to his own words. 'I'm not going to be an observer after all. I've volunteered to be a fixed wing pilot.'

He saw the pupils of her eyes dilate with excitement, and experienced that rare, heady feeling that can be brought on only by a woman's unbridled admiration.

'Sweety that's wonderful!' she breathed, and pulling his head down kissed him open mouthed, thrusting her tongue right in between his lips. 'That's really wonderful!'

They moved slowly round the Painted Hall, and as they did so, the implications of becoming a fleet air arm pilot began to dawn on him. It occurred to him that he would almost certainly be killed, sooner or later. It would therefore be necessary to live his life on a higher level, at a faster pace. He would wear golden wings on his sleeve and receive flying pay; he would become more attractive to the opposite sex.

Suddenly, things that had mattered considerably only minutes before – like his career, and Julietta's flirtation with Chas Tomkins – were of little importance.

# 16

He drove down to Lee-on-Solent the following week for a medical examination at the Central Air Medical Board at Seafield Park. After rigorous tests, he was made to sit on a calibrated floor with his back to a calibrated wall so that his spine and legs could be accurately measured.

'What's all this for, Chief?' he asked the sick berth attendant.

'We just like to make sure you'll fit into the cockpit, sir.' The chief petty officer looked at the card upon which he had noted Jannaway's statistics. 'And I reckon you're right on the limit.' He left Jannaway sitting there in vest and underpants and returned with the surgeon commander, who looked equally doubtful.

'Get your arse well back against the wall, laddie,' he said, and checked the measurements again. He looked at Jannaway over his glasses. 'You're a volunteer, I take it?'

Jannaway nodded eagerly. There was no question of going back now.

The surgeon commander pursed his lips. 'Well if you weren't, I could quite easily make a recommendation that you shouldn't fly. You're right on the borderline.'

'Borderline what for sir?'

'You've got an exceptionally long femur, laddie. If you ever have to eject from a Venom, you could be in problems.'

The surgeon commander left him to get dressed, and the chief petty officer remained to finalise some paperwork.

'What sort of problems would those be, Chief?' Steven asked.

The sick berth attendant finished noting details on a medical card before looking up. 'That's just the surgeon commander, sir,' he said. 'He passed someone fit a couple of years ago, and then when he banged out from a Venom, he lost his kneecaps.'

Starting flying training was like plunging back into adolescence. Naval pilots were being trained at the RAF station of Linton-on-Ouse in Yorkshire, and the Jannaways moved into a small terraced house in York. Julietta joined the Conservative Club, the local hunt

281

and the English Speaking People's Union, and set about the business of getting to know people who would assist Steven in his career.

Steven found himself one of twelve student pilots, and as the only lieutenant was appointed 'course leader'. Within three weeks of starting flying, four of the students had been withdrawn from training, and this ruthless weeding out heightened the feeling of belonging to an élite among the eight who remained. Commander Ottram, the Senior Naval Officer in charge of the naval contingent, took Jannaway into his office one day and emphasised the importance of high morale. 'There are good courses and bad courses, Jannaway,' he said. 'The good courses have energetic, enthusiastic course leaders, who give flying all they've got, and they're the ones that succeed best. Morale is easy to establish early on in the course, but damn difficult to get back once it's been lost.'

Jannaway took these words to heart, and abandoning thoughts of career and promotion set about enjoying the beer and the barrel rolls. He knew that he was not a natural pilot, but was determined to survive the course. He invited the other student pilots back for drinks in his house and introduced them to Julietta, who enjoyed the adulation she received from two of the younger sub lieutenants. In the crew room, he found himself enjoying humour that he had abandoned when he left HMS *Syston*, and the shared challenge of flying bound him closer in friendship to the other students than he had at first expected.

He discovered that the Fleet Air Arm was split into two sorts of officer; the General List officer, who had been trained at Dartmouth and considered himself superior, and the Supplementary List officer, who had joined the navy with the specific intention of flying, and consequently regarded himself as even more superior. SLs were usually regarded by the GLs as 'gits' the GLs were regarded by SLs as 'twits'. It was possible, though about as difficult as getting a camel through the eye of a needle, to turn an SL into a GL, and if this happened, the officer concerned took on all the outward appearances of being a gentleman, discarding his knitted waistcoats and Hush Puppy shoes in favour of tweeds, brogues and knitted ties. Steven Jannaway was at pains to bridge this chasm between the SL and the GL, and abdicated some of his GL habits, to Julietta's disgust. He went on drinking sessions with his course mates and returned to his marital bed smelling of Threlfall's ales. He purchased another 250cc BSA motorbike, upon which he rode back and forth between York and Linton-on-Ouse at high speed.

If the young aviators were divided by class, they were certainly united in their low opinion of the Royal Air Force, whose members they referred to as 'Crabs' (they themselves were called 'Fish-heads' by the RAF). Enmity between the two services was deeply rooted, and went back to the days before the Royal Air Force existed, when army and naval officers had formed the Royal Flying Corps and the first aircraft had been launched from the catapults of cruisers. Naval aviators considered themselves superior to those in the RAF, regarding anyone who had not landed on the deck of a carrier as an inferior being. There was also the question of the replacement building programme for Britain's ageing aircraft carriers, and the lines were already being drawn up within the two services for a political battle, in which the navy insisted upon retaining its own air arm and the Royal Air Force saw its chance of doing away with its detested rival once and for all. This battle was to leave both sides deeply scarred, and if there was a victor at all it was the politicians in the Tory and Labour parties who succeeded in using senior officers to argue the case for cutting each other's services.

The aircraft Jannaway was training on was the Jet Provost Mark Three, a small, toylike plane that had originated from a design for a pilotless target aircraft and was therefore not difficult to fly. Sitting side by side with a dour, Liverpudlian flying instructor called Algy Purbright, he was introduced to the art of setting the power, selecting the altitude and adjusting the trim. He did his stalling and spinning, his aerobatics, instrument flying and circuits, and within weeks was beginning to think, speak and behave like all those aviators he had once detested.

You couldn't really help it. It was impossible to attend the morning briefing in your flying overalls, sip your coffee in the crew room, where model aircraft hung from the ceiling and nudes decorated the walls, or walk back after a flight with your instructor, discussing handling techniques and not absorb, as if by osmosis, the jargon, the catch-phrases and the élan.

At first, he was a little ashamed of telling Julietta about his day, and would let slip such small items of news as, 'I went solo today' or 'We did a stall turn this afternoon.' Later, he became wrapped up in what he was doing, and told her about it whether she liked it or not.

Though he would never have believed it possible a few months before, he found himself beginning to enjoy the crisp January mornings when he walked out alone to the line of silver aircraft and strapped himself into the cockpit. He enjoyed the feel of the control column in his gloved hand as he checked the controls for full and free movement. He liked the whine of the engine as it ran up to idling revs and the puff-puff of oxygen in his face when he tested it on high flow. He liked the anticipatory feeling of power he experienced as he taxied the aircraft slowly to the runway threshold, completed his TAFFIOH checks and requested take-off.

Then there was the opening of the throttle against the brakes, the muted roar of the engine, and the acceleration along the runway, the centreline dashes coming faster and faster under the nose; the lifting of the nose wheel at sixty-five knots and the unsticking at ninety; the dropping away of the runway, the fields, Yorkshire, England, the World, beneath him, and the darkening blue of the sky above him as he climbed on towards it.

Yes, it was good up here at twenty thousand feet. You could hear your own breathing if you switched on the intercom, could talk to yourself, calling yourself Jannaway, ordering yourself about, reminding yourself of your checks, humming the overture to 'Carmen' as you did a couple of wing-overs to check the airspace beneath you.

'Closing the throttle,' you say, and then say the same thing again but in your instructor's adenoidal accent. You lift the nose as the speed dribbles off, maintaining height until all you can see out of the canopy is blue sky and the condensation trail of a V bomber somewhere up at thirty-five thousand feet. Stick centrally back, right boot progressively forward until the rudder is right over, and the aircraft wallows neatly onto its back. The world comes into view. The nose pitches up; another wallow, more blue sky.

'Rolling right needle right,' you say, a little hoarsely now, because no one pretends that spinning solo is a doddle. 'That's one turn. That's two. That's three.' The Vale of York spins round beneath you. You put on hard left rudder, pause, push the stick forward, pray, see the world stop, centralise and come out of the dive. Your heart is going ga-dunk-ga-dunk-ga-dunk-ga-dunk, and your vision is blurred and speckled because you pulled four 'g' recovering from the dive and weren't ready for it.

In the afternoon you ride back to York and park the bike under its cover in the lane at the back of the house. You pick up Anita and kiss your wife.

'I did my first solo spin today.'

'Oh yes?' says Julietta, looking up from the ironing board. 'I ironed my millionth pair of knicks.'

He graduated to the Vampire in the spring of the following year, and changed instructors. The Vampire was a very different customer to the Jet Provost: it was a vicious little fighter like an arab stallion that is only partially broken. Don Goodson, his new instructor, was an outgoing, Mars bar-eating, rollicking, tub of a man whose wife had left him to be a Mormon and who lived in the officers' mess bar. He introduced Jannaway to a new attitude towards flying, arranging private rendezvous with other instructors for dog-fights and hair-raising reciprocal passes. In the air, he could not resist singing, and on one occasion Jannaway inadvertently pressed the transmit button while his instructor was giving one of his performances, and Goodson's baritone rendering of 'Cwym Rhondda' was transmitted on channel B.

The pace quickened now: Jannaway was taught flying in close formation, turning the aircraft at maximum rate and high 'g' loading. Goodson took him on low level navigation exercises, during which they skimmed over the Yorkshire moors, the sheep running outward in all directions as they roared overhead at three hundred knots. Later, there were formation take-offs and landings, high level aerobatics, and tail chases.

The tail chases were an introduction to air-to-air combat, or dog-fighting, and took place during formation exercises. You took off in a three-ship formation usually, keeping station on the leader for the take-off run and climbing all the way up to twenty thousand feet with him. You practised changing stations, line astern and echelon and then the leader would call 'Line astern, go. Follow me for tail chase' and would immediately bank away from you, diving for speed.

You dive after him, keeping him high in your windscreen in order to avoid losing him under the nose. You see him pulling out of the dive, his aircraft silver against dazzling white cloud. The game's on: you pull up to follow him, automatically tensing your stomach muscles to counteract the 'g'. You have no idea where the horizon is, but the horizon doesn't matter: all that matters is that you keep your leader in the windscreen, match his angle of bank with your own, roll when he rolls, dive when he dives, loop when he loops. The sun glares suddenly through your visor and you almost lose him; but there he is, going away from you, so you add power, steal a glance at the instruments to make sure you haven't got a fire. You see that your speed is falling off rapidly and make the mistake of adding more power, and at the top of the climb find yourself suddenly overtaking the leader and he seems to come rapidly backwards towards you so that you can see the shimmer of heat from his jet pipe and the dull oily sheen of his belly. You put out the airbrakes and the aircraft vibrates. You close the throttle and immediately he starts going away from you again. In airbrakes, add power. You're diving again and he's going into a steep turn. He's tightening it up: you brace thigh and stomach muscles and clamp your teeth, feeling a trace of judder as the aircraft approaches a high speed stall. Your leader rolls rapidly into a maximum rate turn in the opposite direction and you almost lose him, and have to use rudder as well as aileron to roll the aircraft and match his angle of bank. He reverses the turn again and you snap round with him, refusing to be thrown off. This is the 'scissors'. He's trying to get on your tail and you're trying to stay on his. 'Stick with him, stick with him,' you tell yourself. You lose all sense of time: there is a ghastly delight in it: it is a death dance, the 'tumult in the clouds' of Yeats's Irish airman. For a few brief minutes you are more than just a human being: all that matters is that you stay behind that small silver aircraft, the jet pipe sticking out between the tail booms, the sun flashing momentarily on the canopy as he rolls to reverse the turn, your own breath coming in grunts and gasps as you roll with him.

The leader levels out and calls you to join up in echelon: you slot in on his wing and check your fuel, oxygen and engine. You descend through cloud and level at a thousand feet, the ground dark beneath you and you change radio frequency and run in for the break. The leader calls, 'Thirty seconds!' and you see the airfield ahead out of the corner of your eye, and as you cross the boundary you hear 'Breaking, breaking, go!' and the leader peels away to port and three seconds later the next aircraft follows him. You count: 'A thousand and one, a thousand and two, a thousand and three,' then immediately roll the aircraft into a sixty degree banked turn, putting out the airbrakes and closing the throttle at the same time. You check the speed, bring in the airbrakes, put down the undercarriage, check the speed again, lower flap, retrim and call downwind, making sure the two Vampires ahead are on the horizon and not above or below it. You roll out of the final turn behind them and line up for a left-right-left landing on the runway. You see the leader touching down and the second aircraft making his approach. You come in over the hedge, closing the throttle, flaring the aircraft, holding the landing altitude, keeping the nosewheel off the runway as the main wheels yelp on the tarmac. You squeeze dabs of brake as the aircraft decelerates and at the end of the landing run turn off the runway, stop the aircraft, complete the after landing checks.

In dispersal, you lift the canopy, put the ejection seat safety pins in, unstrap. You carry your silver flying helmet under your arm as you walk back to the line hut, and your leg restraint buckles click with every step you take. You're drenched in sweat and there's a mark round your face where the oxygen mask has been. You sign up for the flight: DCO, duty carried out.

You're Shag Jannaway, you're an aviator, you're a god.

'I have to state a preference for which operational aircraft I want to fly – Vixens, Scimitars, Gannets or Bananas.'

'Bananas?'

'Buccaneers.'

Julietta was cooking the Saturday lunch. She held the lid on the saucepan, rattled the partially boiled potatoes about inside, then tipped them into a tray of sizzling fat and began basting each potato. 'Here we go,' she said. 'It's make your mind up time again.'

'I'm going to ask for Scimitars,' he said. 'Stacks of air-to-air combat and very little night flying.'

Julietta put the potatoes on the top shelf in the oven and turned the thermostat up to seven. 'So long as you're happy dear,' she said, mimicking his mother.

He grinned cheerfully. 'Oh I shall be. I'll probably do one tour on Scimitars then go on to Buccs. That'll be good, too. Fifty feet above the sheep, all cool and deadly. They can carry the Bomb, you know.'

Julietta turned to him and made an exaggerated gesture of awe. 'Cor!' she said.

He grinned and felt her bottom. She put her arms round his neck, and when they kissed, Anita, who had been riding a plastic trike, ran to her mother and clutched at her skirt. Steven picked her up and held her on his arm, and there they were, the three of them, with the lamb roasting and the newly fledged pilot clasping his wife and daughter to his chest.

'Time we had another one,' Steven said. 'Don't you think?'

'Thanks very much! Yes, I'd love to be split open all over again!'

'Maybe you won't have to be.'

'No, but you don't have to have it, do you? All you have to do is sit and drink cups of coffee.'

He put Anita down. 'You said you wanted lots.'

Julietta snorted. 'That was a long time ago.'

She began chopping mint leaves on a board. She held the knife blade in both hands and see-sawed it up and down. 'You know what I really wanted to do when I first met you? I wanted to get into television. I wanted to direct. And look at me now. The little woman.'

He held her waist, putting his head over her shoulder. She chopped away at the mint, venting her frustration on it.

'Don't you feel we're over the difficult part?' he asked. 'Can't we start being close? Properly close?'

She gave him a frosty little smile. 'You mean as if we were really in love?'

He kissed her neck and said, 'I do love you.'

'No you don't. You may kid yourself that you do, but please don't try to kid me.' She scooped the chopped leaves up and put them in a pottery jug. 'You don't even know what love is,' she went on, adding sugar and vinegar to the jug and stirring the mixture briskly. 'The only reason you married me was because you were a Catholic. You didn't love me, did you?'

She busied herself, ignoring him completely, as if he wasn't there. She cut up the broccoli and washed it, and put plates to warm under the oven.

She was remembering the meeting she had had with Peter Lasbury one afternoon in Malta, the afternoon before the dance in HMS *Ausonia*. She had told him about being pregnant and had ended up begging him, imploring him to marry her.

'Why? Why can't we?' she had sobbed when he said it was impossible, and he had taken her in his arms and said that he couldn't explain why and that it would be far better for her to marry Steven, who would make her happier than he, Peter, ever could. He had told her that he didn't expect to marry, that his career in the service was everything to him and that in any case he would not be able to be a proper father to someone else's child. So she had forced herself to accept Steven, had made believe that she really did love him and had sought to compensate for the lack of emotional feeling she had for him by being ambitious for him and pleasing him in bed. But the memory of Peter Lasbury never faded: it had been refreshed that evening at the Greenwich Ball; they exchanged Christmas cards still – had done ever since she was thirteen. She knew that if she belonged to anybody at all it was to Peter, and the knowledge of Steven standing in the kitchen behind her, like a big Catholic dog, caused a sudden revulsion in her, like a belch of bad wind, so that she had to get away from him as quickly as possible. She left the kitchen and ran up the narrow staircase to the bedroom. She closed the door and leant her back against it in the way she had seen heroines do in old movies; and when Steven came to the door and tried to push it open, she pushed it shut again and told him to leave her alone.

Steven went downstairs and looked at the paper. Julietta was like this from time to time: he supposed that all women were. She would be down again in ten or fifteen minutes and they would have a small reconciliation. They would kiss and hold hands, and agree that perhaps they did love each other after all, and that night they would have oral sex, which Julietta liked especially and which Steven secretly found distasteful but cooperated because it gave her so much pleasure and helped her to sleep well and wake up in a good mood the next morning.

Night flying was different again. There was apprehension in the air at night. Great emphasis was placed on the preservation of night vision, and a white light in the line hut or the crew room brought forth howls of anger from the pilots.

They mustered in the briefing room at 2100, for a 2200 take-off. They sat in a line of eight in their jungle green flying suits, noting wind and weather details, runway direction, active danger areas and call signs on the perspex pads set into their knee pockets. They set their admiralty issue stop-watches at the time check and noted soberly that there was eight-eighths cloud cover at three thousand feet.

Afterwards, the students on the second sortie played liar dice in the crew room, where a water heater sounded off a plaintive note every time it came to the boil. They munched the free issue of chocolate bars and mixed more cups of coffee. They watched their course mates taxiing out into the darkness and awaited the summons, via the squawk box from the instructors' crew room.

'Jannaway!'

'At the dip!' Jannaway said, using one of the old fish-head expressions he had learnt in HMS *Copenhagen*.

'On your tricycle,' Goodson said that evening, and Jannaway left the crew room and went to the locker space to collect his mae west and helmet.

Goodson bit into a Mars bar, lit a cigarette, sipped his cup of coffee, yawned and settled his largest feature on the windowsill of the briefing cubicle.

'Okay, Steve. Night famil. All same as a general handling exercise except it's all dark and spooky, right?'

'Right.'

'So we leaps off into the bundu, climbs up to shall we say fifteen or so, have a shufti at the night sky in August, do a few steep turns and then call for a QGH and GCA. We'll roll off that into the circuit and shoot as many as we've got time for. Normal, flapless, low level, high level, glide. Get it?'

'Got it.'

Goodson drained the last of his coffee. 'Right me old. Let's go and dice with death.' He led the way out to the line hut and pored over the aircraft log. 'Dear old bloody XE 890, my favourite hairyplane,' he remarked to the line sergeant, who sucked on a home rolled cigarette and assured him it was top line. 'Okay, I'll believe you, thousands wouldn't,' Goodson said, and they went out across the dispersal to the line. Jannaway did the external checks, running his gloved hand along control surfaces, examining the creep lines on the tyres, checking the hydraulic leads and pausing at the tail to ensure that the elevator and rudder would not mutually interfere at maximum deflection. He climbed up to the cockpit and shone his torch over the ejector seat, checking that the pins were in and the drogue withdrawal line and gun were properly connected.

Taxiing out, with the amber and blue airfield lights going slowly by on either side, he went through the taxiing checks: 'Turning left, needle left, ball right, artificial horizon erect, compass decreasing.

Turning right …' Yes, there was a feeling of apprehension at night that was not present by day. But he had learnt to deal with fear now, knew that it was a necessary thing, that a fearless pilot was a dangerous one.

He rolled the aircraft onto the runway and said a small, silent prayer: 'O God, keep us safe.' That prayer was becoming something of a habit with him. It was his equivalent of the mascots and talismans other pilots kept in the pockets of their flying suits or hung round their necks.

He ran the engine up to full power, read out the jet pipe temperature, the revs, checked the fire warning light out, and accelerated down the runway, lifting the nosewheel, transferring his attention to the instruments, flying the aircraft off and applying the brakes momentarily before raising the undercarriage. At full power, the aircraft buzzed and trembled and the darkness of the night seemed to make the vibration sound all the louder – at least, that was what he was telling himself when Goodson said, 'I have control, Steve,' and Jannaway realised at the same time that they had an emergency on their hands.

The aircraft shook violently and the jet pipe temperature went up into the seven hundreds. At the same time, the fire warning light burned and Goodson transmitted very calmly, 'Victor four four, mayday, mayday, ejecting.'

'Shall I get rid of the canopy?' Steven asked, and it was as if they were sitting side by side in a small, darkened room. 'Yes, jettison,' Goodson said.

He pulled the handle, and immediately was buffeted by slipstream. His intercom lead must have become disconnected: he looked at Goodson, who pointed sharply up with his finger, indicating that he should eject.

Even now, it seemed safer to stay in the aircraft than to pull the handle above his head. He hesitated a moment longer, then felt Goodson hitting him and gesticulating at him. He put his hands up in front of his face, grasped the face blind handle and pulled it sharply out and down, exactly as he had practised on the ejection seat rig down at Lee-on-Solent.

There was an immediate explosion, a moment of unconsciousness, and then he was out in the night, tumbling, being snatched out of the seat by his parachute, flying feet first over dark buildings and trees for no more than three seconds before the

291

ground came up at him, snapped bones and hit him in the face.

He lay very still for what seemed a long time. He went in and out of consciousness, and was then aware of a torch beam, bouncing up and down over the field, coming towards him.

The light shone full in his face, and a gruff Yorkshire voice said, 'You all right?'

'Yes I'm fine,' said Jannaway, 'But I'd rather not be moved, because I think I may have broken my back.'

When he woke up he could hear people shouting. He recognised the shouting but couldn't remember what the shouts meant. A whistle blew from time to time, and gradually he remembered: they were playing rugger. He listened to the shouts, and began trying to guess when a penalty was being awarded or a try had been scored.

There was something ridiculous about the shouting and the blowing of the whistle, and he wanted to laugh. He tried a tentative laugh, and his voice sounded as if it belonged to someone else.

The door opened and an RAF nurse appeared. 'You're awake,' she said, as if he needed to be informed of the fact. She was blonde, and pleasantly tarty. 'How are you feeling?'

He didn't know how he felt.

'Hungry?' she suggested.

'Thirsty.'

She poured water into a glass. He enjoyed the noise it made, liked her hand as it held the glass for him to sip. 'Have I broken my back?' he asked.

She smiled and took the glass away. 'No. What made you think that?'

'I don't know what's making me think anything at the moment.'

She stood by his bed and he longed suddenly for her to hold his hand.

'When's breakfast?'

'Supper's the next meal.'

He gazed up at her. She smiled a little sadly and said, 'Your wife's here to see you. She's been waiting all day for you to wake up.'

He had forgotten that he was married until that moment. He had simply been himself, Steven John Jannaway, unconnected with other people, pleased to be alive.

'Would you like to see her?' the nurse asked.

He nodded, and immediately cried out in pain.

292

Julietta came in. 'Clot!' she said. 'What did you want to go and do a thing like that for?'

It was frightening how weak he felt. He hadn't felt little-boy weak like this before. Julietta's brisk, contrived optimism frightened him, too. He didn't want her here at all. He wanted ... he wanted Catherine. She would have held his hand and pressed it to her cheek; she would have thanked God he was alive.

'Well thank God it didn't happen next week,' Julietta said.

'Why?'

'Well – right in the middle of your Ma's stay. She'd have done her proverbial nut.'

He began to weep. He didn't want to, but he couldn't help it. The tears flowed silently, of their own accord. 'I'm sorry,' he said. 'I'm sorry.'

She patted his hand. 'Shock, I expect.'

She pulled up a chair and sat beside his bed for a while. 'Poor old you,' she said. 'What hard luck.'

The shouts outside the window rose to a crescendo, and died down.

'I rang them this afternoon,' Julietta said. 'I got through to your brother. He sent you his love.' She lit a cigarette, inhaled deeply and looked down at him.

'Are they still coming next week?'

'Well there's not much point, is there? I mean we won't be able to do anything.'

He tried to remember what day it was. He felt as though he were lying in a mist of faces, voices and memories.

Julietta got up and went to the window. 'They've asked me to break the news to you,' she said, and took a breath before going on. 'Don Goodson ejected too late. He was killed.'

He closed his eyes, and immediately relived those few seconds when Goodson gesticulated to him in the cockpit to eject. How long had he hesitated? A second? Two seconds? Or had it been much longer than that? He tried to remember clearly what had happened. They would want to know. They would ask questions, a report would have to be written.

He felt Julietta's hand over his again. He didn't want her there with him any more. He felt that the knowledge of Goodson's death should have caused him more distress, but all that mattered to him was that he was alive.

The nurse came in and whispered to Julietta. They looked down on him in a kindly way. Outside, the game of rugger came to an end, each team giving three abrupt cheers.

'I'll be in first thing tomorrow to see how you are,' Julietta said. She kissed him on his cheek and squeezed his hand. It was a relief when she went. He relaxed, listening to her footfalls going away along the corridor. The nurse smiled a little conspiratorially, and he had the impression she knew exactly what he was thinking.

He had fractured his thigh and pelvis, and had compression fractures of two vertebrae, the latter injury caused by the impact of ejection. He gave evidence to the accident inquiry, and was absolved of any blame for Goodson's death: they had ejected below the minimum height and speed for a Vampire and Jannaway was considered to have had an almost miraculous escape.

He made it clear from the start that he would continue flying, and after several weeks in hospital and a course of physiotherapy, he reported once again to the Central Air Medical Board to be passed fit. After further X-rays and a careful examination, the surgeon commander decided that it would be inadvisable for him to fly operational aircraft with ejection seats. 'So it's helicopters or Gannets,' he was told.

Although he was not aware of it at the time, Steven found himself in the masculine dilemma – that of needing approval and love, but believing that this can only be achieved by proving that he was not afraid. Gannets were the last aircraft he wished to fly. Heavy, unarmed, ungainly and slow, they were used to provide radar cover for the fleet against low flying aircraft, and their role required Gannet pilots to fly in the most appalling weather conditions. Jannaway's instrument flying was not his strongest point, and the craggy, pipe-sucking image of the Gannet pilot did not appeal to him. On the other hand, he now regarded helicopter pilots as a lesser breed: having become part of an élite, he was loathe to leave it. So he chose Gannets, and after returning to Linton-on-Ouse for a month to complete his training and qualify for wings, he reported to the Royal Naval Air Station of Culdrose in the early spring of 1964 to start operational training in the airborne early warning role.

# *17*

Dear Admiral,
You said . . . start at the beginning,
go on until you reach the end
and then stop.
I don't know where the beginning is.
Perhaps it's at the end.
I will begin at the end.
The end of this mighty vessel.
There is a small boat deck, right aft.
You get to it from the quarterdeck.
It is my bolt hole.
I go there 'to be alone'.

Yes, I come here to be alone.
I open this book.
E (crown) R
Supplied for the public service
S.O. Book 444
And I begin to write.
Faces and places, you say.
Pretend I'm an admiral, you said.
But which admiral?
And how hard should I pretend?

I have been on board three weeks now.
It's no good saying 'it isn't worth it'.
It must be worth it.
And this is a start, isn't it?

*

So here we are, Dear Admiral,
sitting in our cabin, number Four X-ray Twelve. That's not the
royal 'we', either. I share with Dave Holden who, at this very
moment, is lying on his back, on his bunk, his hands clasped upon

his chest as if laid out for burial. But he is not dead – not yet, at any rate. He snores lightly from time to time.

His bunk runs athwartships and underneath it is his desk unit and drawer space. Mine runs fore and aft and I have a scuttle to look out of from which I can see the sea. I sit here with the flap of my tinny desk down, penning these immortal lines. I have a small desk light and a small personal safe. Above me, the air conditioning punkah breathes cold air, a muted roar of it, laden with cold and flu germs which are circulated endlessly about the ship and sealed in by quickly swinging doors that close with a rubbery bang behind you.

We have little metal washbasins with taps that come on when you lean on them. We have narrow wardrobes which contain fuel pipes. Overhead, other pipes with cryptic band markings in blue or green criss-cross our ceiling.

At ten to seven our steward, Graves, comes in with an aluminium teapot. Fitted into the side of our bunks, we have little teacup shelves with fiddles to stop the cup sliding off. Dave Holden always allows his tea to cool completely before drinking it. He sits up in his bunk at half past seven, reaches for his Stuyvesants, groans, lights up, coughs and sips his cold tea. He will not drink hot tea in the mornings because he says it causes cancer.

*

The ship is thundering down the Red Sea.
As it rolls I can hear the screws thumping round beneath me, making it difficult to get to sleep.
I need my afternoon sleep.
I am an over-fed, over-paid, indolent, old-school-tie officer. I have three gin and tonics before lunch. I feed on mushroom soup, chilli con carne and green ice cream. I drink evil tasting coffee and sip a Drambuie to counteract the caffeine. A couple of aspirins on top, and that should do the trick. I open the flap of my desk and step on it to get into my pit. I have put on my pyjamas and we have hung a DO NOT DISTURB notice on the sliding door.
It's Sunday afternoon at sea.

Just as I am falling into a deep and satisfying zizz, I am disturbed by the rattle of a gong over the ship's main broadcast and I am jolted back into wakefulness. 'Hydrogen danger,' says a voice from Aberdare. 'No smoking or naked lights, echo, foxtrot golf sections, all decks.' Thank you very much, I mutter. I really wanted to know that.

I turn my pillow and try again, but the officer-of-the-watch has different ideas. He says something like, 'Port thirty, stop port inner, half astern port inner,' and our steel box tilts and jumps up and down. A wave comes up and slaps at my scuttle. All the books in my bookcase at the foot of my bunk fall on my feet. I put them back, pausing to sniff the leather of this beautiful, pristine, empty journal you would like me to keep.

Ten minutes later, there's another announcement. 'The Post Office is now open for normal business.' I don't like the sound of that. What do they do the rest of their time? I imagine grotesque philatelic orgies, strange practices with rubber stamps and lead seals amid a welter of surface mail and registered letters, and when it's all over a telephone call to the bridge. The Post Office is open for normal business.

Sleep drifts towards me like smoke on an autumn evening. Outside in the wardroom flat, a Scouse voice is telling a silent listener about how he laid a brigadier's wife in Beirut. I hesitate to include this, Admiral, as it is hardly believable. He says: 'Fucking essence, she was, I tell yer. I never had it so fucking good.'

Rule Britannia, marmalade and jam.

Suddenly everything goes quiet. No announcements, no sudden manoeuvres, no sexual narratives. I sink slowly and blissfully into oblivion.

And wake with a start. It's Aberdare again. 'Hydrogen stowed, hydrogen stowed,' he chants. I fling off the bed clothes, leap down via the flap of my desk. It is a quarter past three. I have indigestion and my head aches. My fillings are full of chilli con carne.

So I come out here again, under that part of the flight deck which is called the 'round-down'. I sit and watch the wake stretching out in front of me, and have deep, metaphysical thoughts.

∗

I need to explain to you this business of deck landings. To attempt to tell you 'what it's like' would only result in one of those 'There I was, nothing on the clock' pieces which you could probably make up for yourself. No, what you want is a recipe for a deck landing.

The ingredients.
Take one Gannet, preferably serviceable, and add a pilot in the front cockpit and ballast in the back (two observers if preferred). Place them on a long, smooth runway, add power and allow them to rise to five thousand feet.

Transfer them as rapidly as convenient from their land base to a pre-arranged position out at sea.

Now take an aircraft carrier and place it approximately into wind. The best sort of aircraft carrier to use is a British one, though the American ones are larger. Be careful not to use a carrier which does not have the latest British inventions: an angled deck, a projector landing sight (or at least a mirror sight) and adequate radar. Also remember that you will probably need to leave the carrier again, so make sure it has all those British invented loading arrangements and steam catapults for an easy departure.

Take your Gannet, and stir it slowly round and round as it loses height over a low carrier. Give the Gannet the Flying Course and the correct pressure setting and tell it to Slot.

The Gannet should then be ready to overfly the carrier at four hundred feet, calling 'Slot' as it does so. Try to keep the carrier moving in a straight line, and if possible keep the funnel smoke turned down and not blowing in the pilot's eyes. Funnel smoke is very bad for deck landings.

At this stage you should let the deck landing get on and cook itself, under the direction of the pilot. It goes without saying that you should have chosen a good, young pilot, free of blemishes if possible and firm, but not over-fleshy. Avoid very tall, thin pilots and very small fat ones: the former are inclined to introspection and instrument hypnosis; the latter to feelings of inferiority and manic-depression.

You also want a pilot that will make tight circuits. There is nothing worse than a pilot who drags his arse round finals. The best pilots fly their circuits so tight that they make a complete circle, rolling out of the turn for only a few seconds before they land with a bump on the deck.

Unfortunately such pilots are rarely found and do not last long. They are also prone to use up your precious supply of Gannets.

Remember that the pilot is quite busy when he's in the circuit, so don't ask him to comment on the weather or the appearance of the carrier from the air. Remember that the average pulse rate in the final seconds before touch down is a hundred and fifty to the minute. He is not really flying at all, but balancing the Total Drag of his ungainly aircraft against the power being produced by his co-axial, contra-rotating, constant speeding, variable pitch Double Mambas. He is trying to keep a white light between two horizontal green lights and the note of his audio air speed indicator from changing from a high steady note to a high beep-beep, which would mean he was too fast and would float over all the wires, or a low burp-burp, which means he's too slow and is in danger of stalling or hitting the round-down or losing your Gannet, or all three.

He is also dealing with lining up the aircraft to the centreline of the deck, flying through the funnel smoke (which you forgot about, didn't you?) and counteracting the effects of wind shear and cliff edge effect. In fact as he comes in over the round-down you may be inclined to think Oh Dear, but don't worry: all deck landings are like this. There is no such thing as a normal deck landing.

Crash. He's down.
The hook's caught Number Three Wire, and in one and a half seconds his speed is reduced from a hundred knots to nought.

Always make sure that he raises his hook, raises his flap, taxies forward and folds his wings as quickly as possible. You want him out of the way, because forty-five seconds behind him is another aircraft.

The best deck landings end like that.
Some deck landings aren't deck landings at all, and these are called 'bolters'. Bolters are annoying. The Gannet misses all the wires and goes flying off again provided the pilot remembers to put on the power in time. People scream and fire red lights, and the search and rescue helicopter, which is hovering just off the stern throughout deck operations, gets ready to hoik the crew out of the water.

No, it isn't as bad as that, but it's nice to pretend, isn't it? The steely, intrepid aviator image must be maintained. You trudge manfully back over the flight deck between the parked Buccaneers and Scimitars, and in the evening you all get pissed and sing the fleet air arm song. It's embarkation day: the captain makes an eloquent speech to the ship's company in which he likens the arrival of the Air Group (that's us) to the arrival of the bride at the church. We are the *raison d'être* of the aircraft carrier, and Britain's aircraft carriers are the *raison d'être* of her navy. (The navy is Britain's *raison d'être*.)

You see, Admiral, I am IT.
I am at the very tip of the patriotic spear. Well, almost, anyway. Let's not talk about all these noisy jet-jockeys who think they're the bees' knees.

*

Julietta.
Bloody hell, she makes me wild sometimes. A few weeks ago, she had a go at my family. You, Admiral, in particular, because you were foolish enough to ring up and ask if she'd heard from me. I was foolish enough to attempt a mild defence on your behalf (there'd been a postal delay) and now here's her reply, the pages stained with the black venom of her sarcasm.

Just to make me a lot happier, she tells me about a wardroom party she's been to and how one of the chopper pilots tried it on. This

300

is not entirely a surprise to me. There was a party nearly two months ago at Culdrose on the evening after I'd done my first deck landings and catapult launch. We took Anita and put her in one of the officers' cabins to sleep. I had to go and make sure she was all right half way through, and on my way back stumbled upon the said chopper pilot with Julietta behind a privet hedge. Giving her a lecture in experimental philosophy as Voltaire so eloquently puts it.

She doesn't know that I know. I try to make myself believe that the incident was of no consequence. So what? I say to myself. Your wife has allowed a chopper pilot to squeeze her tits.

But even putting this down on paper now makes me feel queasy: damp under the armpits with infantile anger.

I see him arriving at the back door of our gaunt little married quarter on the hill above Helston. He knocks and she opens it to him immediately, having already tarted herself up for him. He comes in and she kisses him with those little shooting kisses that land between his lips; she gets hot and squidgy for him and her neck flushes and he can smell the musky smell of her desire. They stand in the hall where they cannot be seen through any window and he 'comes the verbals' which she likes, all that pseudo soft porn fab-buzz-vibes and hard-on rubbish that turns her on like a neon light so that she goes flick, flick, flick. Then there'll be the carefully planned afternoons at Godrevy, the secret meetings in Redruth, the romantic rendezvous, the billets-doux. And when I arrive home in four months time (D.V.) there she'll be, flushed and adulterous and no doubt anxious to try out some 'new way' she has 'read about in a magazine'.

I am shaking. I mustn't do this again.

*

My first whiff of the Far East.
We have disembarked to Seletar.
Orioles in the morning and bulbuls in the afternoon.
Royal palms and Tamil caddies.
The RAF live here. They run an Operational Golf Course.

301

We are doing 'operational patrols'. We take off at about nine in the evening and wreck the officers' film show at the Terror Club as we go overhead. We fly up the east coast, dodging thunderstorms and searching for nasty Indonesians who are trying to Confront the nice Malaysians. This is my first taste of Confrontation.

In the afternoons we sit in cane chairs and contemplate the RAF school teachers, who are known as tool-screechers. At night, when we're not flying, we rush off to Bugis Street for a Chinese Nosh, or to Johore Bahru for a Massage or a Short Time.

Dave Holden is having a deep and lasting relationship with a school teacher called Audrey. He says she likes his body. He's getting all of two hours sleep a night and comes into our living quarters, where we sleep eight to a room under mosquito nets, waking everyone up at five in the morning.

I am having a lightweight suit made by Mr Shafi, the station tailor. Being in the far east heightens the self-esteem wonderfully. I walk about in shorts and desert boots and in the evening I have a tall glass of fresh lime juice or, if I'm not flying, a Tiger and lemonade which is known as a Tiger Tops. This is the land of contrasts: teeming rain and glorious sunsets, almond eyes and syphilis, sky-scrapers and little wooden shacks built on stinking mud.

Here is my amah. She has done my ironing. She doesn't actually go down on one knee to me, but it's a damn close run thing.

*

I have your letter.
I'm sorry to have to say this, but I don't want to hear news of Catherine. It stirs me up, I lie awake at night, I start worrying about life and death and God and where the hell we're all going. So – all right, fine. She's in Mombasa. Why did you have to tell me that Alan? I didn't want to know where she was. Don't you realise we may go to Mombasa sometime in the next year?

302

We are in Hong Kong.

I disembarked this morning, at dawn. It was not a pleasant experience. I was catapulted into a six hundred foot cloudbase and spent a long time on the wing of my revered C.O. while he warmed up his radar in the lead aircraft. I was nearly wiped off on a passing island, and I had a feeling that no one knew where we were until we actually saw the Kowloon skyscrapers. All extremely dodgy. I do not wish to be snuffed out through someone else's incompetence. That would be annoying and inconvenient.

We are now in the Philippines.

The pock-marked hill sides of Olongapo. Five of us – Dave Holden, Brian Shelcock, Cy Keeler (no relation to Christine), Lou Venables and myself went on the traditional Run Ashore, and missed the curfew when they close the gates on the city, so we ended up ever-so-respectably in a Philippino brothel. The ladies were so kind – told us all about their American husbands, showed us photographs, gave us one-thousand-year-old eggs. A little bit strange, waking up with an almond-eyed lovely on one side of you and Lou Venables's ugly mug on the other. The ladies brought us a nice cuppa in the morning. It was a very comfortable night, free of charge, and we're all as innocent as innocent can be, except perhaps Shelcock, who tarnished his image with a little late night negotiating that came to nothing. We marched back through the early morning streets to the ship, and when I was back in Four X-Ray Twelve, the duty air petty officer came along to see me. 'Sorry I couldn't find you last night, sir,' he said. 'But we coped with that little fire in the lower hangar quite quickly. If you'd just sign the log, sir ...' So I signed, and when he'd gone and the door had slid closed behind him, Dave Holden began to laugh. I'd forgotten I was air officer of the day, you see. I don't know what the hell they'd do if they found out I'd been ashore all night. I think I'd be court-martialled. In fact I'm sure I would be.

On our way home. Thundering back up the Red Sea. We're all still alive. In the four months since we embarked, I've flown less than eighty hours and made only twenty-three deck landings. Pathetic.

The banks of the Suez Canal slip by and evil-looking natives give us the privilege of seeing their private parts. On the flight deck, the aircraft are ranged in neat rows and the Royal Marine band plays selections from the shows. In three weeks from now, I shall be holidaying in France with Julietta. I am a little apprehensive of meeting her again. We have both changed, I know. I don't want to have any big confession sessions nor do I wish to hear what she's been up to. So it looks as though we have a nice, taut little marriage.

Are many naval marriages like mine? And is my marriage the way it is because of the navy, or does the navy attract people like me who make lousy marriages? Or am I just being very naïve?

Here we are again. A few subtle changes. A new, fresh-faced pilot called Ron Hurley. A new C.O. who does extremely steady approaches to the deck. Our first fatality. Not a Gannet, but a Sea Vixen. He got the power on too late after a bolter: flicked and went straight to the bottom of Lyme Bay. The observer's name began with a K and I share his letter pigeon hole in the mess. There were six letters from his newly wedded wife when the Wessex brought the mail off from Gib. Six. It quite put me off my Stand Easy cup of coffee.

A cocktail party in Malta. Pilot's wings are like an aphrodisiac to some women. The young things pulsate with sexual yearnings, and we young bloods make the most of it. After an hour or two of horses' necks and mutual admiration, you take your new-found companion up to the flight deck. There's Valletta: all spit and sandstone in the star-flung night. The Royal Marine band appears as if by magic, playing 'A Life on the Ocean Wave' as it comes up on the aircraft lift. It marches and countermarches up and down the flight deck and your teenage lovely holds your hand and leans against you. The bandsmen break into a slow march, then six drummers step forward, separating themselves from the rest. The drummers stand in line and beat the retreat. A spotlight falls on the White Ensign, hoisted after dark specially for the occasion. And then – O Henry! – they play that tear-jerking bugle call, 'Sunset', with the band crooning 'The Day Thou Gavest' in the background. It's powerful stuff. She puts her hand inside your bum freezer and you think, my God, I'm proud to be British. The White Ensign slips slowly down into the arms of an obedient servant, and the band marches away into the night.

Julietta is pregnant. She is also moving out of our married quarters. She has found a place in Meonford. Thatched, begorra. Handy for Mummy and Daddy. Will I stump up thirty pounds a month for a mortgage? Yes, I suppose I will. But to be honest, I don't really expect to see the baby or the house. We have started night flying. I have done my first night deck landing.

I think back to the flight commissioning ceremony last October. We stood in a hangar and the wives and families and hangers-on sat opposite in their knickers and gloves. A C of E chaplain led us in hymns and prayers. 'What do ye fear seeing that God be with you?' he asked and we, rehearsed and briefed beforehand, roared back: 'We fear nothing!'

But in those last seconds at night when the deck looms up out of the blackness and the audio airspeed indicator blurps in my ears, I am afraid.

We are all afraid, in our own ways. Cy Keeler plays organ requiems on his Akai. Dave Holden goes to sleep as if laid out for burial. I have developed an annoying habit of clenching and unclenching my fists. We gather in the wide, chintzy wardroom to play Mah Jong or Crib; we huddle together for mutual reassurance, dipping potato chips into Daddy's sauce and playing games of Spoof or Horse to determine who will stand the next round or buy the wine with supper.

*

'Flyco' is short for Flying Control. It's a compartment where a gentleman called Little F sits, and it has a sun roof which overlooks the flight deck. The top of Flyco is known as Goofers, as are those who Goof (watch, stupidly) the flying operations. Only officers are allowed on top of Flyco, and it gets quite crowded on a sunny day. It's pleasant to chat to pilots and observers of the other squadrons, watch the launch and recovery of aircraft every hour and the comings and goings below you between times. The Buccaneers are practising toss-bombing on a splash target at present. They pull up into a loop and roll off the top – a manoeuvre designed to take them clear of the flash of a nuclear explosion.

305

The voice of Little F booms out: 'On shirts on the funnel deck and on top of Flyco. Stand by to start the Vixens. Stand clear of intakes and jetpipes. Start the Vixens.'

The afternoon is shattered by the whine of palouste starters and Avon engines winding up to idling revs. A Wessex helicopter lifts off the stern and wheels round the ship. The sunbathers on top of Flyco have put on their shirts. They jostle for position to get a good view as the carrier heels heavily, turning into wind.

The aircraft taxi up the deck, forming an orderly queue, to be squirted one by one off the bow and waist catapults. They are positioned, tensioned, wound up to full power and ejaculated into the air, the heavy wire towing strop falling into the sea as each aircraft parts company with the deck. As the last one launches, three Buccaneers fly overhead at five hundred feet, slotting into the landing circuit. A Vixen, found unserviceable at the last moment, taxies rapidly out of the landing area, folding its wings and shutting down. The arrestor wires are raised one foot off the deck. A Buccaneer appears through the funnel haze looking like a goose coming in to land on a lake: its neck outstretched, its wings held rigidly out, its webbed feet held slightly forward, its tail feathers flared to act as brakes. It thunders onto the deck: the Buccaneer engines are so underpowered that pilots have a standard procedure of putting on full power whether or not they catch a wire, so this one ends up at full power within feet of the end of the deck, the wire pulled out as far as it will go.

Four Vixens in the slot. They fly tighter circuits than the Buccs. They're like overgrown Vampires, almost delta winged. I know the pilot of this one – a large, frightened sub lieutenant, whose observer walks round with death in his eyes. The pilot's having difficulty hacking the deck landings, and the observer doesn't know what to do about it. I cannot help thinking that I might have been that observer. I wonder what Brian Shelcock and Cy Keeler (my observers) think of me. Brian seldom relaxes these days. He has a cruel, sardonic sense of humour and is interested in psychoanalysis. He goes regularly to the church services held on the quarterdeck, claiming that he enjoys the fresh air and the hymns.

We have been doing night exercises off Gan, in the Maldives. Everyone is worried about the Indonesian 'FPB Threat' and the Gannets are practising experimental tactics to direct strike aircraft onto these impossibly small targets, which can evade at the last moment and are exceedingly difficult to hit. We use helicopters to act as fast patrol boat targets, so end up with a mixture of Buccaneers, Gannets and helicopters all whirring about in the gloom. Grey hair and ulcer country.

Of course the RN has given up the idea of small, fast, manoeuvrable warships, developed in the days of Drake and used to good effect against the Armada. Now we specialise in building status symbol ships for senior officers to pace up and down upon, and for tinpot nations like the Indonesians to threaten with their little forty knot boats, supplied in kits by Soviet Russia.

Another dash down the Malacca Strait, and a disembarkation this time to Changi. But now we are housed in a hotel. We travel to 'work' every morning in a naval bus. We come back to our hotel and drink Tiger beer. Holden is screwing Audrey again.

A Buccaneer flew into the water in the Singapore Strait last night. Disorientation, probably. You get interesting reflections of the night sky sometimes. He may have thought he was the right way up when he wasn't. We were sharing a crewroom with the Bucc aircrew. They just didn't come back. In a strange way, I envy them.

✽

We are thundering back across the Indian Ocean having been sailed at twenty-four hours' notice for an unstated destination. The ship did a very rapid replenishment (of beer mainly) alongside in Singapore dockyard, and all the squadrons flew back on board this afternoon. The only possible reason for this sudden dash to the west, we think, is that Ian Smith is doing a South Africa with Rhodesia, and Harold Wilson doesn't want to let him.

We meet in cabins to discuss what might happen. Dave Holden and I sit high up on our bunks, and Shelcock and Keeler sit in our red, tubular chairs. As the ship rolls, the propeller vibration makes Holden's eye lotion and after-shave bottles rattle in his wash cabinet.

'If we keep up this speed, we'll hit Africa in four days,' says Keeler. He is an ungainly merchant who ties his legs in a knot when he sits down. 'Momboozer,' says Shelcock. 'Bloody good-oh.' Holden yawns and says he fancies Aden. He had a nurse in Aden. He had arranged for his wife to come out and spend a fortnight in Hong Kong while the ship was there, but this change of plan has forced him to cancel her visit. I envy Dave Holden's placid promiscuity: he ambles about the world taking his pleasure where he can find it, and spends all his free time on board contemplating the deckhead, harbouring his powers.

*

We think we may be going to War. There has been a mass briefing for squadron commanders and senior pilots and observers, as well as some of the planners and spare commanders. They came away from it with their lips sealed and Looking Serious, and it has been announced that there will be compulsory PT on the flight deck every afternoon at 1600 for the whole ship's company off watch. Shelcock, who was a midshipman observer during the Suez crisis, says that as soon as they start having compulsory PT, you can bet your flying boots they mean business.

We have arrived somewhere, but very few people know exactly where. We steam aimlessly about, waiting. It is almost certainly Rhodesia, but I for one don't see what we can do about it. Attack Salisbury? One of the pilots who is of South African origin says he'd refuse to fly if called upon to do anything like that. It's quite a strange feeling to know that the rest of the world doesn't know where we are: this aircraft carrier has simply disappeared into thin air.

There is a nasty, fake pre-war atmosphere on board. There are ominous signs that Harold Wilson is about to make some bold, ignominious show of weakness. It makes me realise how un-political I am. I don't *know* what I think Britain should be doing over Rhodesia. Does anyone?

But I do know, now, what it's all about. We were all assembled ('we' being all pilots and observers in the Gannet flight) in the main briefing room this morning. We sat in our adjustable arm chairs and were given the low down. We are now on standby to fly into

Zambia (ex-Northern Rhodesia) in support of Mr Kaunda, who is feeling nervous about his Kariba Dam. The plan is for the Gannets to fly in to Ndola, and then provide radar cover and a sort of do-it-yourself air traffic control for the Vixens, which will be armed with rockets and bombs to give I. Smith hell if need be. Whether there's a fall-back plan to use Ndola as a springboard for some sort of take-over of Rhodesia I'm not sure, but 'one has that impression'. But the really good news is that (a) I have been selected as one of the pilots to go and (b) I have been issued with a Browning automatic! It's a really neat little weapon, and Dave Holden and I take ours to pieces and put them together again in the evenings. Now thrive the armourers, and honour's thought lies solely in the heart of every man. On the flight deck, the Vixens are being armed up with live ammunition and our Air Engineer Officer is flapping about tinkering with the two Gannets and three spares to make sure they're all serviceable and he gets his OBE.

It is very nice to be In The Know. I have a new-found, cool and deadly swagger, an élan, a tight-lipped walking-with-destiny look. Behind this haughty, veteran-warrior mask, there lies an ever so slightly frightened me. What if we arrive over Ndola and there's one of those god-awful thunderstorms, no radar let down and not enough fuel to get back? What if the natives aren't friendly when we arrive? What if it all gets nasty and the Rhodesian air force intercepts?

*

We are still waiting for the off. We had a mammoth 'Ras' today. 'Ras' stands for Replenishment at Sea. We steam along for hours side by side with the stores ship. The Royal Marine Band plays selections from the shows. Long canvas shutes are rigged from the flight deck down into the hangars, and the cartons of beer go zipping down. Helicopters do an endless shuttle service with loads slung in netting beneath them. When the solid stores have been transferred, an oiler moves up and takes over position, about two hundred feet from the carrier. They fire a gun line between the ships first, and then string a lot of knitting out to support the fuel hoses, which pulsate a little obscenely as the fuel oil or AVTUR or whatever is pumped through. I stroll up and down the flight deck with nothing to do. We shall be going to Mombasa for Christmas, almost certainly. I am trying not to think about that, but it's difficult. I really wish you hadn't told me.

We have been briefed that we shall only be allowed to take 'one loosely packed grip' when we go, and I am wondering whether to take this book with me. It has turned into something of a compulsion. If I didn't make these little paragraphs I'd go even crazier than I have already gone. But the trouble is, it already contains things 'what it didn't ought to'. I have taken to keeping it in my combination safe. How ridiculous it seems to be thinking of the danger of it 'falling into enemy hands'. The Rhodesians are not my enemies.

It makes me angry at myself. This pseudo-war situation. This blowing up of a tiny wrangle into a monumental, world crisis. We go up for final briefing in half an hour. We have FOAC on board. (Stands for Flies Off At Christmas). He's a nice, grandfatherly man with twitchy eyebrows and a pipe. I should think he's good at pruning roses. A jolly sort of admiral with a twinkle in his eye.

I am changed and ready. My Browning is in the left shin pocket of my flying overalls and the bullets in the right chest pocket. Crossing the coast near Quelimane, and straight up the Zambesi. Six hundred miles, approx. I feel I should be writing some immortal last lines, some 'If I should die' crap. But that's what it would be. Crap. This whole thing is a crater made out of a pin prick. It makes me feel ashamed of my nationality. All I hope is that no one gets killed as a result of this. But maybe these unpatriotic feelings are a commonplace among those who set out to solve arguments by force. The trouble is, I feel completely divorced from the militaristic attitude. I have no desire to kill – anybody. I think I understand the need for national defence, but what we are doing now has nothing to do with that. (Actually, I haven't a clear idea of what we are doing now. Is Ian Smith really likely to think of bombing the Kariba Dam?) I shall be *very annoyed* if I'm killed. There are a lot of things I want to do.

The game's afoot:
Follow your spirit; and, upon this charge
Cry 'God for Harold Wilson! England and Saint George!'

---

310

And how foolish and presumptuous of me to rule that neat little line, for here I am, back in my cabin.

Well, Admiral, it was like this.
There was an expectant hush in the briefing room as the Great Man walked in. The OPs Officer swallowed his adam's apple and began. We knew it all, or most of it. Climb out to fifteen thousand feet and go straight there. Land, refuel, take-off immediately and talk the Vixens in. Natives friendly, living conditions spartan.

Then the met brief. Sea state, wind, cloud, thunderstorms, weather inland over Africa. I began to feel a strong need to laugh. You don't really believe it'll happen, that's the strange thing. Your mind refuses to look further ahead than the immediate future.

The Great Man stands up, his jowls quivering gently with emotion. He does a sort of unconscious parody of Horatio Nelson, telling us that he has every confidence that the Royal Navy and the Fleet Air Arm in particular will live up to all the finest traditions of the service. While he speaks, I think of the clapped-out Gannets and Vixens we shall be taking into darkest Africa. Last year, when we did a detachment to Lossiemouth, we had difficulty maintaining two aircraft serviceable for a week, and that was with the full support of our maintenance team. Now, we are being expected to fly and maintain our aircraft with virtually no technical back-up at all. Well really!

Anyway, Flies Open After Church has nearly finished. It's a tense moment in the briefing room. Will he actually burst into tears or not? No, he doesn't. His spiel over, he moves for the door, then stops dramatically to add one last word. 'And ... good luck!' he says, a tear dropping to the corticene deck with a splash.

The aircraft are ranged on deck, one Gannet on each catapult, the Vixens behind the island. I hand my loosely packed grip to Messrs Shelcock and Keeler (they sound like a firm of solicitors, don't they?) who have already packed themselves into their dark little hole at the back by the time I've done the externals. I climb up the green cliff and into my cockpit. Below me, the flight deck crews stand around and wait. I strap in, complete all my checks and then sit there, sweating gently, waiting for the order to start up.

An hour later, I am still sitting, still sweating, still waiting, and do not feel like laughing. Every ten minutes we hear that a decision is likely to be taken in the next ten minutes. The cabinet is in emergency session. Harold Wilson is trying to decide what he ought to decide. I realise, sitting here looking out over the flight deck, the ocean and the sky, that I do not really want to be involved in either course of action. I don't want to go and I don't want to stay. I recall something I wrote in that Role of the Navy paper I did at Greenwich, the one that won such acclaim. Something about the military being the tools of the politicians. That is the real quandary, isn't it? They give you a smart uniform to make you feel good, help you hook the birds, so that you won't mind bouncing on your head when they tell you to. You have got to be obedient. I have the *honour* to be, sir, your *obedient* servant. We write it every time we acknowledge an appointment, and what we are saying in effect is that whatever government comes into power and whatever they order us to do, we shall do it without question. Yes, yes, yes, yes, yes, yes, yes, yes, yes.

And now the decision comes through. Unman aircraft. It is not just the aircraft that will be unmanned, Mr Wilson. You cannot psyche two thousand men up like this, shoot them across the Indian Ocean, tell them to prepare for war, for the wielding of the Big British Stick, and then calmly change your mind. If only you could see the expression on the faces of ordinary naval airmen as we climb down, figuratively and literally. You have not merely unmanned our aircraft, you have unmanned this aircraft carrier, all fifty thousand tons of her. You've snipped her balls off with a pair of political nail scissors.

So I am back in this creaking and groaning cabin, with the water gurgling in the pipe under the washbasin and Dave Holden prostrate in a pair of Y fronts on his pit.

And we are going to Mombasa for Christmas.

I look back on my life and see myself, years ago, like one of those cars you see in movies which are taken in long shot through a telephoto lens. You can see that the car is coming towards you at high speed, but although its image fills the silver screen, it gives a curious impression of lack of progress. Its wheels are going round, it is eating up the miles, and yet it is getting nowhere. It hardly seems real, and because of this unreality, this lack of progress, you are aware of the telephoto lens. It is this telephoto lens which is giving me difficulty. I look back on my own life and I can hardly believe that I have existed except in this point of time. Did I really go to Dartmouth? Those chestflats, those corridors that smelt of polish, those extraordinary rules about how to wear your lanyard and when to salute – was I really part of them?

Even if I look back only three years to my flying training in Yorkshire, to that little terraced house by the Minster, those afternoons by the Ouse, those days in the clouds and Sunday evenings watching 'Doctor Findlay's Casebook' ... I can hardly believe in them. I wonder sometimes if I really am a little crazy. A trifle schizophrenic perhaps.

But I am a 'good pilot'.
My S.226 says so.
'A good pilot, day and night qualified.'
It is nice to be told what you are every so often. Very reassuring. Perhaps we should have similar reports written on us for other walks of life. 'A good husband, day and night qualified. Limited experience in adultery only, but making good progress.'

She was there, I know she was there.
I ran away from her, went fishing at Malindi. Sampled the fleshpots, sipped my mess of potage. And now we are back again, with our snapshots of giraffes in Tsavo game park and those little haunting memories, snatched moments of ersatz happiness, the little death. The ship bumbles along again, and Dave Holden and I sit at our desks, writing letters of fake affection to our distant wives.

❊

I have a small patch of incipient baldness at the back of my head.

I have recently started pulling out grey hairs. There is a sort of anger inside me. I am a rat, caught in an experiment. I shall never get out.

*

Haven't been bothered to put anything into this for a long time. We spent a long time doing 'Flyex's' off Aden. Then back across the I.O. to Singapore and now … would you believe it? … we are on our way back westward again to take over this Beira Patrol. We lost a Gannet the other day, or rather the other night. Ron Hurley lost an engine shortly after launch and couldn't maintain height so he swished into the sea. They all got out in good time and were back in the wardroom within the hour, unscratched. There was then the usual Air Group Piss Up to celebrate. This has become something of a ritual. It starts off with bottles of wine at dinner and choruses of abuse between the squadrons. Buccaneers drink milk, Vixens go home, Hold My Hand, it's a Brown Hatters' Paradise. Suitably enraged with cheap red wine, we add pints of beer, Scotch mist, brandy etc afterwards and gather for song. The Fleet Air Arm song, in particular, is a period piece:

> They say in the air force a landing's okay
> If the pilot gets out and can still walk away
> But in the Fleet Air Arm the prospects are grim
> If the landing's piss poor and the pilot can't swim
>
> Cracking show! I'm alive!
> But I still have to render my A.25!
>
> We beat up the Warspite and Rodney a treat…

Yes, I'm afraid we still sing that. Then there are all the others, mainly of the gung-ho rugger variety. 'Dina, Dina, Show Us a Leg'; 'Life Presents a Dismal Picture'; 'The Dogs They Had a Party'; and the 'Crow Song':

> Once two black crows sat on a tree
> They were as black as black could be
> Said one black crow unto another
> You are a black enamelled bugger!

314

We sing these songs in a sort of hysterical fury. That night, after Hurley & Co ditched, I found myself doing a Tomkins: conducting the hooting mob, standing on the bar holding a pint of beer in one hand and conducting with the other. This was my finest hour. Then, after some choruses of 'Hold Him Down You Zulu Warrior', Shelcock led a break-away group in a rendering of 'A Stands for A' which is a long, repetitive wallowing in a particularly obscene piece of anality. The words (A long strong black sausage sticks up my sister's cat's arsehole twice nightly) take about twenty minutes, more or less, to intone and they seem to reflect much of what is worst about the navy. It starts off reverently, almost religiously (it's sung like a C of E psalm); it becomes humorous, saucy, 'cheeky' and daring; it is ritualistic, requiring its own special discipline and mental agility; it stimulates ésprit de corps and is by degrees phallic, lavatorial, incestuous and bestial. It also involves almost endless repetition, and a sort of fascinating boredom, those who can last out to the end achieving satisfaction more from the fact that they have stayed the course than from having achieved anything positive.

Sad really.

*

We have started the patrol.
It's autumn here in the Mozambique Channel. Great long twenty foot waves, streaked in foam, and as you approach the deck you can see the ship moving around, the perspective of the deck changing as she pitches, the round-down rising up towards you and then falling away and the ever present knowledge that if you spear in, things will get Very Interesting.

We are doing two sorts of sortie, 'Ship Plot' and 'Ship Search'. On a ship plot sortie, we climb to fifteen thousand feet and the observers report back all the contacts to 'Mother'. On a ship search, we have a happy time (for me) flying at low level positively identifying the various ships that have been detected on radar. The Buccs, Vixens and Scimitars are also flying by day, but only we rugged Gannet pilots are sent up by night.

We have been having great excitement with a ship called the Joanna V, which is said to be trying to break the blockade. It is almost as

315

if Harold Wilson is deliberately degrading the Royal Navy. We are using a fifty thousand ton aircraft carrier, armed with nuclear bomb dropping Buccaneers, highly sophisticated radar, heavily armed Vixens etc etc to intercept and waylay an unarmed, clapped out, oil tanker. But Wilson has got us exactly where he wants us. He, and his henchman Healey, have decided to scrap the aircraft carriers and provide the navy with air defence from 'island bases'; they know that Their Lordships dare not squeal about this gross misuse of naval power, for if they do, they will cut the ground from under their own feet: Wilson will be able to say – 'Even you can't find a use for the carriers.' So the British Lion is being made to stand on its hind legs, do backward somersaults and piddle in public. Everyone knows that the job we are doing could be done just as effectively by a single frigate, stationed just outside Mozambique territorial waters. And because the navy can be relied upon to be the 'Silent Service', the carriers are kept out of the way at a time when their future is being decided. Pah!

I seem fated to see service in the last of everything. The navy is a declining industry. My term was nearly the last of the sixteen-year-old 'Dart' entry, the entry of chestflats, cuts and silly lanyards; HMS *Copenhagen* was one of the last 'real' destroyers, ships with proper guns and rivetted hulls instead of the new fully-automatic-never-works welded ships that you can open with a tin opener; my course at Linton was the last to train on Vampires, and now I am in this Rogue Male of a carrier, the last of its breed.

People are already beginning to say that if the navy loses its carriers, it won't be worth belonging to. They are collecting names for the ship and squadron command examinations, and it is about time I put mine down. I am twenty-eight. A lieutenant commander in only two years' time. At the moment I'm too worried about surviving the next night deck landing to worry very much about my future career.

I have another daughter. I can't say how I feel or what it's like, only that all the time there is the awareness that time is running out. Zero must come up soon, I know it must.

*

316

I am not sure how long it will go on. I hope that there will be an ending but I am afraid of the nature of the ending. What annoys me above all is that I should find myself in this situation. I tell myself that if there were a real enemy, someone to shoot at, or at least shooting at me, then there would be a motive for the stiff upper lip and a reason for the gnawing disease which is spreading among us.

Symptoms: I am writing at my desk and the door slides open. I 'jump' visibly. I have difficulty in sleeping because I drink black coffee during the night sorties to keep alert. The less I sleep, the tireder I become, the more I need the black coffee, the less I sleep. When I do sleep, I am assailed by the most sensual dreams which end in massive ejaculation and sudden awakening. My fist clenching has given way to almost permanent finger twitching. Now that Ron Hurley is off flying with a cold, I blame him and rage inwardly, because we are now one in four instead of one in five. I have become a compulsive Goofer. I go up to watch the land-on at every possible occasion. There are other pilots who are experiencing a similar compulsion. We grin at each other a little shame-facedly, and stand in the night wind watching the aircraft loom up out of the darkness and hurtle onto the deck. There is great relief to be gained from witnessing a bolter, especially a night bolter. But what we really want to see is the accident, the fatality that everyone is waiting for.

Harold Wilson has said this business will be a matter of 'weeks, not months'. It is already months. There are rumours going round that Rhodesia is getting refined oil products from South Africa and Mozambique. This knowledge causes a bitterness against Wilson and politicians generally that is difficult to describe. You foresee your own death, and you know that it will be a completely futile one.

In a strange way, I find our situation degrading. However hard I try, I cannot develop that fatalism pilots are traditionally believed to possess, so I am behaving – on these pages at least – like a WW1 pilot in the Royal Flying Corps who has what they used to call a touch of the vertical breezes.

I suspect this is true of all of us. What is worrying however is a sort of superstition that fear *causes* death. We are all in touch with death.

317

And we're all afraid, and come short of the glory commonly attributed to the Fleet Air Arm pilot.

I think it would be easier if there were some honour in what we are trying to do, but there is none. This is not a worthy cause, and Harold Wilson is making sure that we are kept out of the public eye. Instead, he is billing the RAF as the heroes, the boys in blue who are going to enforce this blockade and prove that two or three island bases can do the work of any number of aircraft carriers.

The words 'aircraft carriers' and 'Fleet Air Arm' have become politically obscene.

*

There is a ghastly sameness about it all. I feel as if I am part of a very long tradition: a tradition of disillusionment and distrust. Did Drake's sailors feel the same after the Armada? What was morale like in the navy after the death of Nelson? Weren't there mutinies just after the First World War? Perhaps it is in the nature of navies to be discontented. Our discontent has spread from Wilson downwards. Admirals like Flies Off At Christmas are reduced in our eyes to figures of fun: people who are clambouring on their promotion ladders, hanging on for their knighthoods, becoming ever more mandarin like, the higher they get.

And yet ... the loyalty goes deep. We all believed in the Andrew when we joined.
The spark still glows.

*

An interesting sortie today: we have intelligence that petrol is getting to Rhodesia by rail from Lourenço Marques, and we are to be used to guide a Buccaneer in over the port on a photo-reconnaissance mission. This is a bit of a vain hope, because any rail traffic to Rhodesia must surely be moved by night. They're certainly getting their petrol from somewhere, that's for sure: if this blessed blockade of Beira had worked, Rhodesia would by now be on its knees. Instead, Zambia seems to be suffering the effects far more. What a laugh. I don't think I really care any more. The only important thing is to get back onto the deck. Every time.

318

### JANNAWAY DOES IT AGAIN!!!

Only yours truly could fly backwards into the sea!

But we didn't actually fly. We trundled. I am laughing inside, writing this. The relief is tremendous. I am all in one piece except for a couple of stitches where I caught the back of my hand on something getting out.

Oh, sweet Jesus, thank God it's finally happened. We went backwards over the edge. The ship was turning fast into wind, and some bloody idiot took the chain lashing off. Trundle, trundle, trundle, bang, tip, splash.

It was a visit to Hades. And I didn't panic. 'There was no panic.' Oxygen to emergency, jettison canopy, release harness, take a breath, release oxygen, kick clear, inflate Mae West, and up we go.

Coming up, into the sunshine and seeing bloody Keeler and bloody Shelcock bobbing up beside me . . . I dunno, I dunno . . .

I'm sitting in my bolt hole writing about it, laughing and sort of crying at the same time. We are going to get so pissed tonight you wouldn't *believe* it. I am going to get so smashed, so smashed. I won't fly this fucking patrol again. It's all over in three days, and the medics say I have ear damage – not serious – but enough to keep me off the flypro.

I feel so weak, like a jelly. I am an old fool who is going bald and grey before he ought to. Christ, Christ, Christ . . .

I am *alive*!

# 18

Stocks Cottage, which Julietta and Steven had bought the previous year, was one of those beamy, whitewashed buildings that look as if they have thrust their thatched roofs up through the Hampshire meadows with the summer mushrooms. It stood a few yards back from the main road, at the southern end of Meonford village, about half a mile from Meonford House. A brass dolphin clung to the black front door, and as you entered you had to duck your head to avoid bumping it on the eighteenth-century lintel, which had once been a timber in Admiral Lord Howe's battle fleet. Inside, there was a pleasant glow of old oak, whitewash and quarry tiles. A small, lattice-windowed dining room overlooked the road at the front, and a larger sitting room with an open fireplace and french windows gave onto a small walled garden at the back. The kitchen was well stocked with dishwasher, spin-dryer, cooker and Key-matic; copper-bottomed saucepans hung in a rack on the whited brickwork, and Anita's kindergarten artwork was on display on the walls. Upstairs, there were more exposed beams, whitewash and opportunities for cracking your skull.

The telephone was lemon yellow. It squatted on a seventeenth-century oaken coffer in the hall, and when it rang that afternoon in late August, Julietta was making chocolate cake in the kitchen, Anita was watching cartoons on television and Penny, now five months old, was blowing spit bubbles in her pram on the lawn.

Julietta came quickly out of the kitchen, wiping her hands on a cloth before lifting the receiver. She heard the rapid pips of a phone box call and then Steven's voice loud in her ear. 'Juju? It's me! I'm at Waterloo!'

Dust particles floated in a diagonal shaft of light, which fell in a bright trapezium on the Persian rug. Julietta twisted her pearls round her little finger and said yes, okay, she'd meet him at Petersfield.

'How are you?' he asked, his voice breaking with excitement.

'I'm fine.'

'And Nita? And Penny?'

'Fine too.'

'Well... see you in just over an hour, okay?'

The pips went.

'I haven't any more change!' he shouted. 'I love you!'

They were cut off, and she replaced the receiver. Now that Steven was actually about to arrive home, she wasn't so sure that she wanted him back. For two years she had bewailed her lot as a naval wife whose husband was away at sea. She had taken pride in keeping the stiff upper lip, in managing the household single handed. She had bought this house, had it renovated, given birth to Penny, written to Steven regularly and welcomed him back during his period of disembarkation and his mid-tour leave. She had developed her own organisation for the running of Stocks Cottage and her two daughters, and she knew that with Steven's arrival that organisation would be disrupted.

She telephoned her mother to borrow Mrs Hardesty, and then went upstairs to prepare herself for her husband. Although it would be inconvenient having him untidying her tidy nest, there were compensations. Her affair with a helicopter pilot in Helston had been dangerous and unsatisfactory: it had been part of the reason for moving to Hampshire, and since her arrival in Meonford she had been careful to avoid any repetitions that might sully her reputation. In consequence, she was badly in need of a man, and Steven would do very nicely.

She stepped out of her everyday trousers, removed her everyday shirt, and took from the wardrobe a frothy blouse and mini-skirt she had bought in Carnaby Street the week before. She felt enjoyably daring, showing so much of her legs, and stood sideways to the mirror to check her tummy, buttoning the yellow blouse and slipping her feet into high heeled shoes. She pouted a little and stuck out her bottom like a drum majorette, and while she was doing so Mrs Hardesty knocked the brass knocker on the front door.

Mrs Hardesty was a Methodist, the widow of a Royal Marine. It wasn't her place to tell Julietta that she looked like a tart, but she still thought it. She acknowledged her instructions and assumed command, and when Julietta had driven off with her customary panache, went into the garden and lifted Penelope from her pram, allowing herself the small indulgence of holding the baby's cheek to her own, recalling those brief, happy years of motherhood which could never be regained.

Julietta hardly recognised Steven when he stepped down from the train. He was thinner, deeply bronzed and his hair was going grey. She stood at the ticket barrier and watched while he put a suitcase under his arm, a cardboard box under the other, his ticket in his teeth and finally picked up his grip and two plastic carrier bags full of duty-free goods. He struggled with this load and grinned at her as he stood in the queue of passengers, waiting to give up his ticket.

She went on tiptoe and kissed his cheek, said 'Hello Sweetie,' and led the way out of the station to the car. She got into the driver's seat, waited for him to load the luggage.

He looked at her legs. 'So this is the mini-skirt.'

'Do you like it?'

'I like you in it.'

She crashed the gears and drove off.

'Well?' she challenged as they went out of Petersfield.

'Well what?'

'Glad to be back?'

'What do you think?'

'Depends, doesn't it? I mean you might be pining after some glorious geisha for all I know.'

'Well I'm not.'

'Glad about that!'

'How's Nita? And Penny?'

'Fine. I told you on the phone.'

'Nita still doing well at Wickham Hall?'

'Yes.'

'Juju! What is it?'

She pulled off the road and cut the engine. They smiled sadly, searching each other's eyes, each wanting to love and be loved, each unable to fulfil the other's expectations. This was the moment they had built up in their imagination: the homecoming, the relocking of souls; but their souls had never locked in the first place and could not lock now. It was therefore necessary to pretend, for Julietta to slide her hand to the back of his neck and pull his head forward, kissing him on the mouth, and for Steven to touch her breasts through her blouse in a tentative way, as if to inform her that he had not forgotten what to do, and to reassure her that he would do it when required...

When she started the car and drove off, she crashed the gears again, and he winced visibly.

'Now now!' she said. 'Let's have none of that!'

They arrived at Stocks Cottage, and Mrs Hardesty, having said how nice it was to see Steven safely back, changed out of her fluffy slippers and went back to Meonford House.

Steven lifted Anita and kissed her on the cheek; Anita looked coolly back at her father and asked him if he had brought her a present.

He put her down and picked up Penny, who immediately began to cry and had to be handed over to her mother.

'Come to Mum,' she said. 'That's the way. What a big frightening Daddy!'

Anita was examining the cardboard box. 'That's for you,' Steven said. 'You can open it.'

They stood in the drawing room and Anita insisted on doing everything herself. The box was opened and a large, grey donkey revealed.

'Her name's Modestine,' Steven said. 'You must be kind to her because sometimes she feels lonely.'

Anita lifted the donkey out and put her arms round its neck. 'It's not a her, it's a he,' she said.

'In that case you'll have to think of another name,' Julietta told her.

Anita fondled her donkey lovingly. 'Jesus,' she said. 'Grey Jesus.'

Steven laughed, 'You can't call her that!'

'It's not a her it's a he!' Anita insisted.

He appealed to Julietta. 'She can't go calling a toy Jesus!'

'Why not? Why shouldn't she? You can call it anything you like, can't you Sweet?'

The donkey was called Grey Jesus. Steven accepted it with a pang of regret, aware that the buying of this soft toy had meant more to him than it should: perhaps its large, liquid eyes were a token of love he wanted to show, or perhaps the name Modestine reminded him at one remove of a wife and a family he might have had. Anita's insistence upon changing its sex and its name had seemed almost instinctive, as if she had known immediately that it was necessary to contradict her father and put him in his place.

'Well?' Julietta said. 'What about me? Where's my present?'

'That comes later.'

Julietta's lips moved in the beginnings of a smile. 'You bet your sweet life it does,' she said in a low voice.

323

'Mummy!' Anita said. 'It's rude to whisper!'

They went on a tour of the house. Julietta had whitewashed the hall, stairs and landing walls, and had hung Morris wallpaper in the main bedroom. 'And what about this?' she said, showing off what had been a boxroom.

He looked in. She had had it converted to a tiled shower room, one wall of which was a mirror. They looked at their own reflections, Steven in tweed jacket and grey flannels, Julietta looking as if she had been recently plucked from a fashion show and dropped down into this bijou naval officer's cottage.

'We'll christen it tonight,' she said. 'Okay?'

'What's christen?' Anita demanded. 'Mummy? What's christen?'

Steven looked round the room. 'Where's the door?' he asked.

'I've sent them off to be stripped,' Julietta told him. 'Two quid a go. Much nicer, plain wood.'

He went onto the landing. 'But you've sent them all to be stripped! Even the loo and bathroom!'

'Well it seemed a bit pointless to do them one at a time. They're due back next Tuesday.' Julietta saw his disapproval and shot him a warning look. 'Nobody minds about that in this house!'

'Silly Daddy!' Anita said.

'That's right. Silly old Daddy.'

He read *Paddington Bear* to Anita, who corrected him when he missed out a paragraph. Sitting on her bed, surrounded by her assortment of stuffed tigers, elephants, kangaroos, rabbits and the latest addition, Grey Jesus, he found it difficult to believe that only twelve hours before he had woken for the last time in cabin number Four X-Ray Twelve and watched Dave Holden roll over onto his back and light a Stuyvesant. The carrier had been in Gibraltar, and Steven had been one of the pilots flown home by British European Airways. It was all over: two years gone, plucked out of his life and dropped into the stream of time, and all he had to show for it were a few pages of jumbled impressions that would arrive, in a few days, at the bottom of his black tin trunk.

Julietta grilled fillet steak and mushrooms for him, and they opened a bottle of Nuits St Georges. They drew the curtains in the dining room and lit the candles, and Anita had to be shooed back to bed when she came down halfway through and said she couldn't get to sleep because they were talking so much. Steven tucked her back in her bed and brought Julietta's present down.

It was an opal ring he had bought in Singapore. She gave a little gasp of surprise when she saw it.

'Lover!' she said. 'It's beautiful!'

'Aren't you going to try it on? It's an L. You take an L, don't you?'

'Sweetie – I know this sounds terrible, but opals are frightfully bad luck, didn't you know that? I mean – it'd be all right if opal was my birth stone, but it isn't. I am sorry.' She put the ring back in its box and closed it with a snap. 'Perhaps we can part exchange it, okay?'

When she brought coffee in, he was staring vacantly into space. She snapped her fingers to awake him from his thoughts.

'Sorry,' he said. 'I'm just feeling a bit disorientated that's all. I don't quite know where I belong.'

'Old grey haired monster!' she breathed. 'I'll show you where you belong!'

He smiled obediently and wished that she could stop acting and be herself; but he wasn't sure what her real self was like: it seemed to him that he had never known her when she was not behaving as if for the benefit of some hidden gallery.

She pushed her hand over his. 'Come on. I can't wait any longer.' She pulled him to his feet and led him upstairs, and in the bedroom became oddly businesslike. She stepped out of her skirt, hung it up in the fitted wardrobe, and with a downward movement of her hands over her hips, rolled off a pair of flowered pants. 'I'm just starting the dear old blessing,' she told him, 'but I don't mind if you don't mind, okay?'

She took him into the shower and did those things that she had planned to do when she had had it fitted. 'This is what I've been waiting for,' she whispered, 'This.' Looking down at her, he could not help feeling that all she wanted of him was the exclusive use of one part of his anatomy – that part which she had wanted from her earliest childhood, one that fascinated her, one that she wanted to make entirely her own. She towelled him dry and led him back into the bedroom. She organised and stage-managed him, progressing towards her all-important climax. 'Slowly,' she whispered, 'Slowly. Don't you dare come yet, don't you dare!' She lay back and pointed her short, muscular legs at the whitewash. The organs thundered and the piccolos trilled: her whimperings rose to a crescendo and died away, and in the silence that followed there was a soft patter of feet as Anita ran quickly back to her room and got into bed.

'Do you think she saw?' he asked, horrified.

'Of course she saw! She was standing out there the whole time!'

'You mean you knew?'

'Sweetie, she knows all about it. I've explained it to her. I was reading in a magazine that it's a jolly good thing for them to know what happens right from the beginning. Providing we don't get hung up about it, it can't do anything but good.'

She curled up against him. 'Old prude,' she said, and slipped her hand between his legs, grasping him as if reclaiming a piece of lost property. 'Never mind. It's nice to have you back.'

For the six weeks of his foreign service leave, he behaved as most good naval officers behave after an extended time abroad: he enjoyed the blessings of the land, the fruits of his labours. He pottered about the house and the garden, mending some things and breaking others; he learnt to change, pot and wind Penny, and annoyed Julietta by explaining to her the awful implications of the Labour party's decision to scrap the Fleet Air Arm's aircraft carriers.

'I don't see why you get so het up about it,' Julietta said one afternoon when she was ironing in the kitchen. 'I mean – you didn't have much time for aviators before you became one yourself, did you?'

'It's not a question of whether I like aviators or not,' he explained. 'It's what's good for the navy that matters. The navy without aircraft carriers would be like the army without tanks. Or an air force without fighters.'

Julietta folded Anita's pyjamas and put the iron over them. 'I thought the RAF were going to take over the flying side.'

'That's the theory, yes, but they won't be able to. I mean this swing-wing F111 they say they're going to get – it won't be able to do half the things they claim it will. And what about AEW? What about organic all-weather fighters?'

'It's no good saying this to me, Steve. You ought to talk to Daddy about it.'

He laughed. 'Fat lot of good that'd do.'

She looked at him quickly. 'Oh yes? I suppose you think you know more about it than he does, do you?'

'Gracious me, no!' he said sardonically. 'You don't realise, do you? Half of our senior officers don't give a damn whether we have

326

carriers or not. All they're interested in is getting to the top and getting a knighthood.'

'That's just sour grapes. Daddy isn't a bit like that. He's absolutely dedicated to the navy.'

'Sure he is. But he's never accepted that aircraft are an indispensable part of the fleet. He still thinks in terms of guns or missiles.'

'Of course you could always be wrong I suppose?'

'Look – what were the major battles – naval battles – in the last war?' He counted them off on his fingers. 'Battle of Britain. Fought in the air –'

'By the RAF.'

'*And* by the Fleet Air Arm. People don't know that. Pearl Harbor. Carrier-borne aircraft. Taranto. Carrier-borne aircraft. Battle of the Atlantic, would have been lost but for the pocket carriers. All the Pacific battles – fought out by carriers. *Bismark* – disabled by a single Swordfish. And look at the disasters. Narvik. No air support.'

'Wasn't there?'

'Not much, anyway. *Repulse* and *Renown*. No air support. The *Hood*. No air support.'

'Daddy,' interrupted Anita. 'Why are you always *arguing*?'

Julietta laughed. 'Here blooming here!' she said, folding up the ironing board. 'Anyone would have thought this was the naval staff course!'

The issue of the scrapping of the aircraft carriers became a central part of his life. He had reached the stage in his career when he felt himself to be part of the navy, and although he knew it had its faults, he believed passionately in the necessity of Britain retaining her sea power. He, and many other officers of his age, despaired of the naval leadership, who had apparently washed its hands of responsibility for maintaining balanced forces, acknowledging defeat to the planners in the RAF who redrew the world atlas in order to ensure that their radii of action supported their arguments.

He joined the Fleet Air Arm Association, and began writing impassioned letters to admirals and captains, receiving replies which said that all was not lost and encouraging him to remain in the service in order to get to the top and change it. In late October, he started a course at the RAF Central Flying School of Little

Rissington to become a flying instructor. When he had completed it successfully the following spring, the Jannaways moved north, back to Linton-on-Ouse, where Steven began training what were believed to be the last of the fixed wing pilots in the navy.

The new house was another married quarter. They made it into their home by transferring their ornaments and pictures from the mantelpieces and walls of Stocks Cottage to the mantelpieces and walls of the three-bedroomed semi that they had been allocated. Anita was sent to a new school; Penelope began to toddle, and Julietta accustomed herself to the daily noise of aircraft taking off and landing.

He was in the thick of his career now, and knew from his annual reports that he was doing well. He learnt not to be too outspoken in his views about the shape and direction of the navy, and consoled himself that the new 'through deck cruisers' would at least keep the navy's foot in the door and retain access to the art of naval aviation.

After a year of teaching people to fly, he began to think it was time to get back to sea, and when he went to visit his appointing officer in London, he was pleasantly surprised to be offered his first command.

He travelled north to York in a state of near elation. 'They're giving me a ship,' he told Julietta as they drove out of York station. 'How about that?'

'Sweetie!' she said. 'Wonderful!'

He laughed, and had to brake suddenly to avoid going into the back of a lorry. 'HMS *Plumpton*. Coastal minesweeper.'

'Where?'

'Yes, that's the only trouble. Rosyth, I'm afraid.'

'Oh – bloody hell! Why did it have to be Rosyth?'

'I asked for Malta or Hong Kong. But I'm one of the most junior officers being given command, so beggars can't be choosers.'

'Shitty death!' said Julietta.

'It's not all that bad. Handy for Edinburgh.'

'Rosyth isn't Edinburgh.'

'Twenty minutes by road. Over the bridge. Or we might be able to get a quarter in Cramond. There's a nice little pub there, I seem to remember. Does excellent seafood.' He looked across at Julietta. 'It's a bloody good job, Juju. My appointer says he's grooming me for stardom. It isn't everyone gets command as a lieutenant.' He accelerated out of Clifton, doing mental calculations. In six months he would be automatically promoted to lieutenant commander, and three years after that he would be eligible for further promotion. 'Four years from now, and I could have my brass hat.'

Julietta lit a cigarette and sucked at it hard. 'You'll be lucky.'

'Well. It's something to aim for, isn't it?'

'Why don't you start aiming for it then?' she said, suddenly angry. 'Instead of farting and moaning about your precious carriers all the time?'

'All right,' he said. 'I will.'

HMS *Plumpton* was identical to HMS *Syston* with the exception that the former had an enclosed bridge. For Jannaway, taking over command was like stepping back into the past, only this time, instead of being welcomed aboard by a tea-drinking able seaman in a polo necked sweater, he was formally greeted by the outgoing commanding officer, a large, freckled overgrown schoolboy called Nigel Calder-Young. Together, they went aft along the fo'c's'le and down the accommodation ladder to the sweepdeck. In the wardroom, the new captain was introduced to his officers: one lieutenant, one sub lieutenant and two midshipmen, all of whom called him 'sir' at least once per sentence, and who laughed unconscionably at his slightest attempts at humour. He stood among them in his best number fives, his violet and green medal ribbon (earned during his Malacca Strait patrols) and his pilot's wings adding indefinably to his self-esteem.

The hand-over between captains took four days, and as soon as Calder-Young had departed, Jannaway had his ship's company assembled on the fo'c's'le. Lieutenant Goatling, the first lieutenant, reported them fallen in to his new commanding officer, and Jannaway put on his cap and left his cabin, walking importantly for'd to the eyes of the ship, from where he could look down upon the thirty-six members of his crew.

'Right,' he said when Goatling had stood the men at ease. 'You will be pleased to know that I have now formally taken command of this mighty vessel, and I thought you'd like to hear from me how I intend to turn her into the ship you will one day look back upon with pride and affection.'

He looked round at the attentive faces of his officers, petty officers, leading hands and junior rates. Behind him, the Jack fluttered at the Jackstaff. He folded his arms and turned a little sideways, so that he spoke to his audience slightly over the left shoulder, being careful to allow his gaze to travel about their faces and trying to look each one of them exactly in the eye.

'Let's start off from that basis,' he said. 'We want to be proud of this ship, don't we? We want to be proud of ourselves. We want to feel that we aren't wasting our time. So how do we go about that? I suggest it's a bit like going out to win a soccer trophy, which I understand this ship has already done. We have to work as a team. We have to know our stuff, and every individual, from myself right down to the most junior of you, has to pull his weight. And it's no good having a team if there isn't a feeling of comradeship among the members of that team. Let's work at this. Let's mould ourselves into what a ship's company should be – a company. Let's be all of one company. Let's be loyal to each other, help each other out, respect each other.'

He stopped, and was suddenly aware of a glazed look in the eyes of some of his listeners. He felt a moment of panic. Was he saying all the things that every new commanding officer always said? Why was he failing to reach these men? Had they heard it all before?

'Listen,' he continued, deciding to cut his planned address short. 'I want this ship to do well under my command. I want you to do well, and *I* want to do well. So I'll just leave you with this promise. Give me all you've got, and I'll give you all I can.'

He stepped down from the scrubbed wooden beading upon which he had been standing. 'Thank you, Number One,' he said, and returned to his cabin, where he sat on his bunk and cursed himself for speaking like a newly appointed prefect at a public school.

He stared at the framed photograph of Julietta, the one that had been taken before their wedding, and which had appeared as the frontispiece of the *Tatler*. He remembered how he used to deride all those other married officers who kept similar photographs of similar wives. He wished he could have caught a glimpse of himself, standing up there on the fo'c's'le doing his make-way-for-a-naval-officer act.

There was a knock at the door and the first lieutenant, a small, wiry officer with deep set eyes and a Roman nose, put his head in.

'Damn good, sir,' he said. 'They loved it.'

He was surprised how easy it was to assume the role and authority of command and how quickly he came to take for granted the respect of his officers and the laughter which greeted his humour in the wardroom. He heard himself saying 'Let us start off in the way we intend to continue,' and using the same old exhortations, cajolings and reprimands at his weekly sessions of Captain's Requestmen and Defaulters which he had heard used by his previous commanding officers. On Saturday mornings, he conducted Captain's Rounds, making a tour of the ship, flashing a service issue torch into corners, examining lavatory pans and expressing his disapproval at the new style of unshaven nudes that were pinned up in the messdecks.

When the ship was detached to pay courtesy visits, he buckled on his sword and pinned on his medal, saluting as he was piped ashore, proud of the naval tradition of which he found himself a part. He lunched at civic centres in Whitby, Aberdeen, Fleetwood and Milford Haven. He gave cocktail parties and attended cocktail parties in return. He bullied the midshipman for running out of tonic water and handed out stiff punishments to the ratings who broke their leave or returned on board drunk. At sea, sitting in his high chair on the bridge, he held court among his officers and senior ratings. A steward brought him a cup of tea, his yeoman brought him a signal pad, and the midshipman brought a carefully fudged magazine log for his signature. Three months after taking over command, and two and a half months after his thirtieth birthday, he rose automatically to the rank of lieutenant commander, and he found himself on a par with the other commanding officers in the squadron. He began to laugh as heartily as they and enjoy the late night drinking sessions in their wardrooms. He developed a certain panache in the handling of his ship, and deliberately indulged in eccentricities of behaviour and speech. 'Stuff a chocolate pig!' he would say in mock annoyance, and playfully beat his first lieutenant on the head with the Gangway Wine and Spirit Book; and at the end of his first year in command, was gratified to be told by his senior officer that he led his ship's company with flair and imagination, and was being earmarked for early promotion to commander.

'Have you heard the news?' Julietta asked.

'What news?'

'About Daddy. He's going to be FOSNI.' FOSNI stood for 'Flag

Officer Scotland and Northern Ireland' and Julietta pronounced it 'Fozny'.

'Really? Splendid!'

She had collected him on the ship's arrival an hour before, and they were driving over the Forth bridge.

'It's not at all splendid,' Julietta said. 'He's terribly upset about it.'

'Why, for God's sake?'

'Isn't it obvious? It's a retirement job. He's being passed over. Mummy says he's awfully depressed.'

Jannaway slowed to a stop and handed over three shillings at the toll gate before accelerating away. 'He can't exactly complain, can he? I mean he's made Vice Admiral, hasn't he?'

She snorted. 'You have no idea what it means to Daddy. He's got a tradition to follow. He wanted to get to the very top. He should have, too.'

'He's not the only one with a tradition! We can't all be happily married First Sea Lords!'

Julietta said nothing for a while, pushing her upper lip out in a pout.

'There's something else,' she said at length. 'I was looking for one of your old shirts today to make into an overall for Anita, and I found that journal of yours.'

'What journal?'

'The one you kept while you were at sea.'

He turned left towards Cramond. Ahead of them, as the car topped a rise, they glimpsed the Firth of Forth and beyond it the Fife hills.

'Did you read it?'

'I read enough of it.'

They arrived at their married quarter, the usual bleak semi-detached building with metal framed windows and nondescript shrubs in the garden. The next door neighbour brought Anita and Penny back, and Steven unloaded his dirty washing into the Keymatic. Julietta set the programme and regarded him with tight-lipped disdain.

When the children were in bed and she and Steven were eating supper in the sitting room, she resumed the attack.

'I hadn't realised you had such a filthy mind,' she said matter-of-factly.

332

'I don't think I do have a filthy mind.'

'I think you must have. To be able to write that sort of stuff.'

'You don't have to have a filthy mind to report facts. I was just putting down what was happening to me, that's all. I wasn't imagining anything.'

'You imagined enough about me.'

'Well you did give me one or two hefty clues, didn't you? It wasn't very nice, getting letters saying how difficult it was to say no.'

She coloured down to her neck. He had never met anyone who coloured so extensively: when she did so, it was a sign either of anger or sexual arousal, but never – to his knowledge – embarrassment.

'What about you then? What about the brothel? What about that bit about adultery?'

He shrugged. 'You shouldn't have read it, Juju. It wasn't written for your eyes.'

'Who was it written for then? Your brother?'

He shook his head. 'They were just rough notes. Letters to myself, if you like. They were an outlet, no more than that.' He added a shovel of coal to the fire: it was April, but still cold. He had not looked at what he had written for over a year. That part of his life was half forgotten. It was necessary in the navy to put what was past behind you, to live in the present and plan for the future.

'And that horrible thing about a sausage. That was disgusting. Was it necessary to put that down?'

'It happened,' he said. 'I was trying to be objective.'

'Well I'm not having it in the house,' Julietta said, pushing the remains of her chicken and mushroom pie to the side of her plate. 'What if Anita found it? How would you like her to read it?'

'She's unlikely to.'

'I would say she's very likely to. She was asking all about the instructions on my Tampax only last week.'

He shrugged. 'All right, I'll destroy it if you feel like that.'

Julietta immediately put her plate to one side. 'Right,' she said. 'I'll get it now.'

He sat and listened to her going upstairs and coming down again. If I had any balls, I'd stop her, he thought, watching as she bent at the fireplace and fed the individual pages into the fire. The flames leapt in the chimney, carrying the ashes with them. Julietta became engrossed in what she was doing, appearing to forget that he was there. When she had finished, she stood up and gave him what remained of the notebook. 'Still a good few pages in it if you want it for anything else. Or I could give it to Penny to scribble on.'

'By all means give it to Penny,' he said.

She sat down beside him on the sofa. He had finished all he wanted of his supper. 'It's much better that way,' she said. 'Isn't it?'

He felt angry with himself more than with her. She had twisted him round her finger and tied him in a knot. What was worse, they both knew she had. He felt continually obliged to play the gentleman for her, accede to her requests, give way to her foibles and humour her carefully orchestrated tantrums. He told himself that he gave in to her in order to keep the peace, but there was a nagging doubt that this was just another brick in his wall of rationalisations.

He followed her out to the kitchen and helped put away the supper things. When they had finished, she turned to him and put her hands up to his face. She pushed her lips briefly against his, and invited him to make love; she took his hand and led him upstairs, and when the telephone started ringing halfway through, insisted upon her moment of rapture before allowing him to put on a dressing gown and answer it.

'It's for you!' he called from downstairs. 'Your mother!'

She ran down to him, naked, and crouched on the bottom stair. He raised his eyebrows in mock disapproval, and she put out her tongue in reply.

'Hello Mummy?' she said.

She pressed the receiver to her ear, and for one of those rare moments ceased to act a part. Her mouth opened in surprise and then shock; suddenly she took his hand and held it against her breasts, interlocking her fingers with his.

'We'll come down,' she said into the telephone. 'Tonight. We'll drive down tonight.'

Henry and Clara had been invited to a cocktail party and dinner on board HMS *Eagle*, the aircraft carrier which was paying off to be scrapped. Henry had breakfasted in his Kensington flat, lunched with the Secretary of State and returned to his office to attend to the flood of paperwork that threatened to break the dam each

Friday afternoon. He had travelled to Petersfield in his first class railway compartment and had been met by a flustered Clara, who informed him that the Rover was out of action with a faulty clutch and that they would have to use the Triumph that evening. He had changed hastily into his tin legs and boiled front and had then had a silly argument with Clara about who should drive. Clara knew that he was upset and worried about his new appointment. Since its announcement, he had become increasingly morose, brooding upon a past career which he now looked upon as a failure. She had insisted upon driving the Triumph because it was hers, and Henry had behaved like a spoilt child because she had said he should wear his safety strap. Going through Portsmouth, they had been held up in traffic and he had told her that if she had gone through the Unicorn gate instead of the main gate, they would have arrived at the ship before Sunset. Arriving after Sunset meant that he would not be piped over the side. He was not concerned about that on his own account, he said, but on the ship's. By arriving ten minutes late they detracted from the occasion. 'I'm sorry, I'm very sorry,' she had said. 'But how was I to know that?' 'I would have thought, after all these years, that you might have gained at least some insight into naval ceremonial,' he had replied, and had walked up the brow to the aircraft carrier's quarterdeck ahead of her, pausing as he went on board to return the stiff salutes of the commanding officer, executive officer, officer of the watch, midshipman of the watch, quartermaster, bosun's mate and Royal Marine bugler. He had deliberately kept apart from her during the reception on the quarterdeck. This was not unusual, for they had long ago accustomed themselves to circulating separately on such occasions. Standing and being talked to by a succession of officers and their ladies, she had looked across the quarterdeck at Henry from time to time, secretly a little relieved that he was not to be promoted and that they would be able to settle down to life in Meonford in two years' time. She had accepted more gin-and-tonics than she would normally have done, and had enjoyed a frivolous conversation with the Flag Officer Royal Yachts, a young, forceful Rear Admiral whom she found unusually attractive and who managed, with his mischievous eyes and clean cut features, to make her feel twenty again. All around her, people were talking about the reason for this party: the terrible 'damn shame' of paying off so fine a ship, and the slender hope, if the Tories got in, that the decision would be reversed. It seemed to her that she had listened to such conversations all her life; the war had provided a brief interlude, but looking back on it, only a very brief one. How sad it was that naval officers should be condemned to this eternal battle in time of peace, the battle for survival in the face of determined politicians, bent upon wielding the axe. No, Henry was lucky to have got as far as he had: he had survived the war, survived the Golden Bowler redundancies of the fifties, survived the internal convulsions caused by Britain's abandonment of her colonies, as well as the crisis of confidence caused only a few years before by Wilson's government. If she was honest with herself, and a fourth gin and tonic was good for being honest with herself, she had to admit that she was glad he was being passed over, glad that he would not become a full Admiral, glad that he would not be forced, all over again, into planning a campaign to achieve the last, most difficult ascent to the final peak, the five golden rings worn by an admiral of the fleet. She was content with what they had: Henry would spend two years in Scotland, which would be nice because Steven and Julietta would be up there for a month or two yet, and at the end of his time he would be awarded a knighthood, accept a pension of over three thousand a year, take on a lucrative directorship of some prestigious firm and *retire*. It was at the very moment that this last, wonderful thought occurred to her that she became aware of a disturbance on the other side of the quarterdeck, and some instinct or sixth sense told her immediately what had happened: she went quickly through the throng of guests and came upon what might almost have been a tableau, for Henry was kneeling on the quarterdeck having been violently sick. When he saw her, he looked up, crossed his gold braided arms across his chest as if he had been shot by a sniper and said, 'Scallops for lunch,' before a vast convulsion shook him, the colour went from his face and he fell, writhing in agony, to the deck.

That crisp, awesome, naval efficiency had then come to the fore. A fifteen-second argument had ensued between a surgeon commander and a surgeon rear admiral, the former overruling his senior officer and insisting that Vice Admiral Braddle should be taken by the fastest possible route to Haslar hospital. The captain had then ordered a helicopter to be scrambled. White-faced officers ran hither and thither, knowing exactly what to do, where to go, each thinking ahead, each aware that if the vice admiral's life could be saved their contribution to the saving of that life might later be remembered and rewarded. An announcement had been made over the ship's broadcast: 'D'you hear there. Scramble the Wessex. Standby for Casevac.' A surgeon lieutenant came running onto the quarterdeck with a case of hypodermics and drugs. He knelt by Henry Braddle, gave him a massive injection and immediately started cardiac massage. The guests were ushered away; a commander tried to get Clara to go with them, but she insisted upon staying. 'There is nothing to see, madam,' the commander said. 'Please cooperate –'

'I am his wife!' she screamed at him.

She had stayed by his side, staring down into his grey face in disbelief and horror. The helicopter had started with a whine on the deck above them, and sick berth attendants had arrived with a stretcher. She had followed them along polished corridors and through swing doors, into an aircraft lift, which rose, a bell clanging, to the flight deck. She had insisted upon going with him in the helicopter: it had risen into the air above Portsmouth dockyard, and as it turned and headed across the water, she had caught a glimpse of Nelson's flagship, HMS *Victory*, floodlit. They had landed in the gardens of Haslar hospital and had moved at the run into the long, tiled corridors. They had taken him into the emergency treatment room, and she had been kept outside and given a cup of sweet coffee which she didn't want. Gradually, she had become aware of what had happened and what was happening, and when the surgeon captain came out to her in his white coat, she was ready for what he had to tell her.

'We've lost him,' he said. 'I'm sorry.'

She did what she had been doing all her life. She began to cope, on her own, immediately. It would be just like it was when he was sent off to sea at short notice. There would be a lot of things to do, a lot of arrangements to be made. She would accept help when help was offered, but if it wasn't offered, she would get on and manage, somehow, by herself. She felt she owed it to Henry to behave with dignity and control: he was, after all, the last of the Braddles, and it was now her duty to honour his name and prolong his memory.

Peter Lasbury drove the five miles from the shore establishment of HMS *Dryad* to Meonford House the following afternoon, and was shown into the big drawing room at the back of the house, where the Braddles were assembled.

Sarah and Willy Keuning had flown over from The Hague that morning, and Julietta had driven down from Edinburgh with Anita and Penny. Steven had had to remain behind: his ship was to have her sea inspection on the day of the funeral, and his presence was required.

Peter had not seen Julietta for some years, and was struck by how much she had matured. She had chosen dark navy stockings, a dark navy skirt and a simple blouse and pullover set in a pleasing blend of natural colours. She sat on the sofa by the french window that overlooked the sloping lawns and the river, and her smile was welcoming and relaxed. Sarah, he felt, had let herself go rather. She was into her thirties now, the mother of four children who had been left behind in the huge Wassenaar mansion Willy had inherited from his father.

'Peter, how lovely to see you,' Clara said, and kissed him warmly on the cheek. Julietta did likewise, and Willy and Sarah shook his hand. He accepted a seat at the other end of the sofa where Julietta was sitting, and they discussed the funeral arrangements.

'I don't see how it can be a small one,' Julietta said. 'We can't very well forbid people to come, can we? And I could list a hundred without having to stop to think.'

'What I'd like to do,' Clara said, 'is to give Henry the sort of send off he would have liked himself.'

'In that case let's have a *big* wedding,' Julietta said. 'Don't you agree Peter?'

'Funeral,' he said. 'You mean funeral.'

The colour came to her neck and stayed there for several minutes.

'There's an awful lot to be done,' Clara said. 'I hardly know where to start.'

'We'll help,' Sarah said. 'Don't worry, Mummy.'

'I can type and use a phone,' Julietta said. 'If you're prepared to take charge, Peter, I'd be very happy to act as your sort of – well – first lieutenant.'

They looked to him for an answer. 'I'd be very honoured to take it on,' he said.

'There you are, Mummy,' Julietta said. 'You can leave it all to us.'

Lasbury set about the task with the same meticulous care he would have used had he been planning a naval operation. Assisted by Julietta, who set up headquarters in her father's study, he drew up the guest list, the form of service, car parking arrangements and a seating plan. He approached the mess president of HMS *Dryad*, and arranged a reception to be held in the wardroom mess after the funeral, and when it was learnt that a member of the Royal Family had expressed a wish to attend, Julietta spent an hour on the telephone to Buckingham Palace discussing protocol and security arrangements.

'Now is there anything we've forgotten, Peter?' she asked him on the eve of the funeral. 'Anything at all?'

He took the question seriously: Julietta was no longer the silly little girl he had known ten years before in Malta: she had developed an authority which he admired. They sat side by side at Henry's teak desk and went through the whole schedule for the last time. There had been a little difficulty in persuading the local vicar to give up his pulpit in favour of the fleet chaplain, but Julietta had ironed that out by calling personally on the vicar and agreeing that he should be allowed to say a few words at the beginning of the service.

'You've done quite marvellously,' he told her. 'I couldn't have asked for a better staff officer.'

She turned her brown, liquid eyes on him, pushing her forefinger under the loop of her pearls and twisting it once. 'I think we make a very good team,' she said.

The day dawned. After a brisk, heavy shower which might almost have been sent by the Almighty to add one last sparkle to the village of Meonford, the glistening staff cars began to arrive and the sun shone on their polished bonnets. Each new arrival at the church door was told exactly where to sit by the four uniformed ushers. The church filled to capacity: lieutenant commanders and below in the rear six pews, captains and commanders in the next six, commodores and above in the front six. They sat, jammed together, the broad, dark superfine uniforms intermingled with the slenderer bodied but wider hatted wives. The organ played Bach in the background, and a gentle murmur of muttered conversations rose and fell under the fourteenth-century rafters like the lapping of wavelets upon a shore. Royalty arrived, a hush fell, and finally the principal guest himself: Henry Braddle – or at least his temporal remains – lying at peace inside his walnut box with brass handles, covered with the white ensign, upon which, like decorations on a cake, rested his sword, his hat and a small brass cannon.

With that flair of imagination that set him apart from other

339

officers of his rank and seniority, Peter Lasbury had decided that the organ should be used only to set the key for each hymn: thus, the congregation sang without accompaniment, just as officers and men sing on church parades at sea.

Fight the good fight with all thy might!
Christ is thy strength and Christ thy right;
Lay hold on life, and it shall be
Thy Joy and crown, eternally.

'Henry Bartholomew Macey Braddle did indeed lay hold on life,' said the fleet chaplain, leaning out over the golden eagle, whose spread wings supported the lectern under his elbows. 'And his life is indeed his joy and his crown . . .'

Clara had insisted that Peter should sit in the front row with the family and he wondered, listening to the eulogy, what form his own funeral might take. He had recently purchased a property in the Dordogne, where he planned to seek sanctuary from the condemnation of the world with a friend who shared his inclinations, but he could not help feeling, with Julietta tense at his side, a little wistful about what might have been.

The funeral service drew to a close. They sang 'Eternal Father Strong to Save', and remained standing for the naval prayer.

'O Eternal Lord God, who alone spreadest out
the heavens, and rulest the raging of the sea;
who has compassed the waters with bounds until
day and night come to an end; be pleased to
receive into Thy Almighty and most gracious
protection the persons of us Thy servants
and the Fleet in which we serve . . .'

The chaplain of the fleet beckoned to the pall bearers: two rear admirals, two captains and two commanders, each proud to carry Henry to his last resting place. They lifted the coffin onto their shoulders and bore it from the church; Clara, with Julietta on one side and Sarah on the other, followed behind, and behind them walked HRH and Peter Lasbury, Willy Keuning and other close relations, followed by the First Sea Lord, the chiefs of staff, the aides de camp and the formal representatives from the Royal Air

340

Force, the Army and the Royal Marines. Swaying gently from side to side, Henry was borne along the path between the lichen-covered stones and the rain-washed daffodils; his hat, his sword, his cannon and the ensign were removed, and the last rites spoken. The coffin was lowered and the Last Post sounded.

It was over. The cars moved out of the paddock and nosed into the road, heading across country to HMS *Dryad*, where smoked salmon and sparkling white wine awaited; two grave diggers came out from their hiding place behind the church and began spading the heavy lumps of clay down upon the polished walnut box, so that its brass handles and the brass plate were quickly lost to view. A gust of wind blew a few petals off a nearby almond tree, and in the meadow on the other side of the Meon, a Friesian cow bellowed repeatedly for the calf that had been taken away from her that morning.

Julietta found herself to be pregnant the following month, and Steven received his next appointment: he was to return to flying Gannets at the squadron headquarters, which had recently moved from Cornwall to Brawdy, in west Wales. When Julietta learnt this, she announced that she had no intention of moving to yet another married quarter, especially as the naval air station was due to close down and the squadron would have to move to Lossiemouth after a year. Instead, she moved back to Stocks Cottage with Anita and Penny, and Steven went to live in the mess at Brawdy, taking advantage of his rank and position in the squadron to fly from Brawdy to Lee-on-Solent in a training Gannet at the weekends.

The arrangement suited Julietta well: she was able to see a lot of her mother, and help her through the first difficult months of her bereavement, and this gave her a legitimate excuse for seeing a lot of Peter Lasbury, who became a regular visitor to Meonford House.

Peter had never had the opportunity to meet and talk to Julietta on a platonic footing before, and as the months passed, he became fascinated by her pregnancy; aware that he would never father a child himself, he was moved and intrigued by the extraordinary change in Julietta as her physical health blossomed, her hair shone and the child in her womb grew. When Steven returned on his weekends and Peter was visiting, the latter made no attempt to hide his fascination, and Steven, who enjoyed Peter's urbane humour and was stimulated by his informed conversation, was touched and amused.

'You don't mind Peter visiting do you?' Julietta asked him one afternoon, and he replied 'Not in the slightest.'

For Julietta, this time of pregnancy was one of the happiest of her life: she was quite sure that the baby would be a boy, and in a strange way could sometimes convince herself that he would not be Steven's son at all, but Peter's; she welcomed the latter's attentions and interest, and encouraged them.

One Sunday evening in early December, when Steven had departed to return by train to Brawdy and Clara had gone up to bed, Peter and Julietta found themselves alone together in the drawing room by the last of the log fire. Julietta sat at the end of the sofa. The baby was due the following month. She gave a little gasp.

'What is it?'

She laughed. 'He's kicking.'

They had been listening to a tape recording of a Liszt sonata. Peter sat in an armchair, his legs stretched out towards the bar fender. He was getting on for forty now and had thickened considerably. 'More music?' he suggested.

'No. Come and sit beside me.' She patted the sofa.

He moved across and they sat side by side, Julietta resting her back into the corner of the sofa against cushions, Peter nearly but not quite at ease, a safe distance away from her.

'Oh!' She said. 'That was a goal!' She turned to him and sighed.

He looked briefly back and then away. There was no getting away from it: he was very fond of Julietta. In recent years she had ceased to 'pursue' him, and as a result he felt more at ease with her than with any other woman. He felt safe with her: she was married, she was pregnant. He knew that there were rumours in the navy that he had never married because Julietta had become Mrs Jannaway, and he felt that such rumours were useful to him: they provided him with a cover, and brought a certain wistful tragedy to his personal life which added to his popularity with senior officers. Lasbury was the chap who would never marry: a confirmed bachelor, a man's man, better to have loved and lost than never to have loved at all … He could almost believe the myth himself.

She had slipped her hand over his. 'What are you thinking about?'

He shook his head. 'Nothing of great consequence.'

She gave a little squeak. 'Really, Thomas! It's time you were asleep!'

'Will you be terribly disappointed if it's a girl?'

She shook her head. 'I won't be disappointed. It isn't a girl. I know it isn't. I feel quite different with this one. Sort of – bouncy.' She lifted his hand. 'Feel,' she said, and he allowed her to guide his hand between the buttons of her maternity dress and onto the smooth dome of her belly. 'If only he were *yours*,' she whispered, her eyes filling with tears.

'You mustn't say things like that.'

'Well. Don't you wish the same?'

'Perhaps. But I could never have married you, could I? Much better this way.'

'I'm not so sure about that.'

He tried to remove his hand, but she held it where it was. 'No. Don't go. I like it there.'

'It's not entirely proper is it?'

'Bugger what's proper!'

He smiled. 'Ah. Yes, I can feel him now.'

'You're to be godfather. Will you?'

'Providing Steven agrees.'

'Oh he'll agree. Steven always agrees.'

'Luckily for you, perhaps.'

She made an impatient sound.

'I wouldn't have agreed nearly so much. We would have fought cat and dog, darling.'

She tightened her hand on his and breathed in quickly.

'What is it now?'

'You. Calling me darling like that. Lovely.' She laughed. 'That means I can call you darling back, doesn't it?'

'Listen,' he said. 'I'm not in love with you, see? I'm very, very fond of you, and I also happen to like Steve a lot. I think you're very good for him, and he isn't a bad husband for you, either. You could have done a lot worse.'

'I should never have got married,' Julietta said. 'If I could have my time again, I'd have Anita and keep her, and I'd talk you into being my lover. We could have been like Penny and Jeremy, couldn't we. A nice easy come and go relationship.' She giggled. 'Lots of come, and not much go.'

'That was very naughty,' he laughed, and at the same time the door opened and Clara, who had come downstairs in her bathrobe and slippers said, 'Oh!'

'Peter was feeling the baby kicking,' Julietta said, immediately on the defensive. 'Weren't you?'

343

Clara looked nonplussed. 'Don't get up, Peter,' she said. 'All I came down for was to remind you to put the fire guard up when you go to bed, all right? Night-night then.'

As the door closed behind her, Julietta collapsed into silent giggles; and just for once Peter Lasbury did something that he very seldom did: he kissed a woman on the lips, and enjoyed it.

Thomas Henry Jannaway was born five weeks later, on the fifth of January. He was a boisterous seven pounder, with a red face, almost black hair and a grin like his father's. He was christened in his great-grandfather's christening gown, and his godfather presented him with a silver egg cup, a silver saucer and a silver spoon, each inscribed with his initials. His uncle Alan sent a small crucifix, but this was banished to the loft by Julietta, who warned Steven that if his brother thought he was going to muscle in and turn her son into a bloody Left Footer, he had another think coming.

Steven was the proudest possible father. He threw a champagne party for his squadron to celebrate Thomas's arrival, and when he came home at the weekends actually volunteered to bath him and change his nappies, feeling that it was important for his son to get to know him from his earliest months. When Anita and Penny had been born, there had been a tiny pang of disappointment; only now did he realise how much he had longed for a son. Thomas was the baby he had imagined that Malta midnight when Julietta had announced her first pregnancy, the night the fireworks had hissed into the water, the night Catherine had told him he must marry Julietta in order to give his child the love and stability that every new-born baby deserves. This was the baby who would carry on the name of Jannaway, the son who would make the ten uneasy years of marriage to Julietta worthwhile.

## 19

Peter Lasbury's villa stood on rising ground a mile or so south of Echourgnac, on the edge of the St Emilion wine district. Since acquiring it three years before, he had transformed a collection of grey stone buildings into a cleverly unified cluster of tiled roofs and whitewashed walls. Bougainvillea flowered brilliantly over the arched verandah; geraniums flourished in earthenware pots and hanging baskets, and a vine was growing over a trellis on the eastern patio, where Peter was wont to take his breakfast in the sun. Below the patio, a swimming pool in the classical Roman design had been installed, and passion fruit grew up the wooden windbreaks on two of its sides. Below that, to the south and west, the escarpment dropped sharply away, giving a breathtaking view of the Dordogne valley.

He invited the Jannaways to stay for a week at the end of the August following the birth of Thomas Henry, along with Penny Forden-Jones and Jeremy Delacroix, who were mutual friends. Julietta left the children at Meonford House in the care of Clara and a nanny, and she and Steven arrived in the late afternoon when Jeremy, who was now one of Lew Grade's up and coming producers, was reading a television script in the shade of the verandah and Penny was lying on her back on a sun bed with her bikini straps tucked into her cups.

Lasbury came round the house as the car approached down a dusty track and pulled up in the drive. He wore a pair of flowered Bermudan shorts and a brilliantly coloured Indian shirt, both of which were particularly fashionable now that the days of flower power had arrived.

'Finally made it!' Julietta said, looking hot and flushed as she stepped from the car.

'What kept you? The others have been here for nearly an hour!'

'My mega-clot of a husband was reading the map upside down,' Julietta replied, and offered her cheek to be kissed.

Steven was by now so used to Julietta's little sallies that he seldom bothered to answer them.

Lasbury led the way round to the verandah, where there were more kisses and welcomes. Jeremy raised a hand and looked up from his script, and Penny, sitting up quickly without thinking, lost the top of her bikini. There was general amazement and applause. 'Oh – who cares!' she said, having struggled for a moment to retrieve it. 'I've hardly got anything worth looking at, so why bother?' She flung the cups to one side and Jeremy, returning to his script, observed that small was beautiful.

'Stop staring, you,' Julietta told Steven. 'Go and unload the car.'

Peter was an ideal host. He seemed to know all the shopkeepers in the village by name, and enjoyed catering and preparing al fresco meals for his guests. He could talk amusingly on a wide range of topics, too, and in the evenings, sitting outside by the dying embers of the barbecue, he discussed the plight of the British film industry with Jeremy, the fashion world with Penny and mutual naval acquaintances with Julietta and Steven.

This latter topic occupied much of their last evening. There was mention of Johnny Tinnick, now retired as a commander (everyone had thought he would go higher) and working in the Central Office of Information, of Charles Crivett-Smith, who had been promoted to commander at his very first shot; of poor old Peter Wingrove, who was struck by lightning while playing golf in Singapore, and Chas Tomkins, who had earned a Queen's Commendation for dealing with a Phantom aircraft that jumped its chocks during an engine run.

'What intrigues me, Peter, is how exactly do they choose who to promote?' Jeremy said. 'I mean – take you for instance –'

'Darling,' Peter said. 'I didn't know you cared.'

They giggled happily: they had consumed three bottles of St Emilion between them that evening, and the world was an extraordinarily pleasant place.

'You're a commander, aren't you? Isn't that right?'

'For far too long,' Julietta said. 'Peter should have been promoted ages ago.'

'That's what I'm getting at,' Jeremy said. 'I mean – do you suddenly wake up one morning and say – "Oh gosh, I think I'm going to be a captain!"?'

Steven leant across the table, playing with the candlewax, something he could seldom resist doing. 'We have things called "zones", you see. It's a bit like the Peter Rabbit Race Game. Every

346

six months they put the names of all the officers in the promotion zone in a bowler hat, and then they invite the Playmate of the Month to come and pick out the lucky few.'

'It isn't *quite* like that,' Lasbury said. 'We have rather nasty things called "half-yearly reports".'

'Chaps get put under the rotten old microscope rather,' Julietta said, swaying gently from side to side.

'So they take the ones with the best reports do they?' Jeremy said.

'Not quite,' Lasbury explained. 'They have meetings, you see. At flag officer level, then at command level, then at admiralty level, when the final list is agreed.'

'That's right,' Steven said. 'A large collection of white haired captains spend an afternoon up in admiralty getting woozy on South African Sherry –'

'Why South African?' Penny said.

'Tradition of the service. They all sit round getting woozy on Paarlsack, and at the end the boss man knocks their heads together and tells them what he's decided. Then the one with most Brownie points is "It" and they all play tig till it's teatime.'

Julietta turned on him, punching his shoulder as hard as she could. 'Why do you have to be so bloody anti the whole time?'

'Joke darling. You know. Humour. Ha, two-three, ha.'

'And this zone,' Jeremy said, 'How long does that last?'

'Five or six years. Depends on your rank.' Peter offered another bottle of wine. 'You must be just about to enter your zone aren't you Steve?'

'Next year, for my sins, sir,' Steven said, slipping the 'sir' in by mistake as he had done twice before during the week.

'And I'm already in my zone,' Peter explained.

'So I suppose you're beginning to sweat a bit are you?'

Penny linked her arm with Peter's and rested her head against his shoulder. 'Peter never sweats, do you darling? You glow.'

'Put him down, you don't know where he's been,' Jeremy said.

Julietta accepted more wine. 'It's not where he's been that counts, it's where he's going.' She looked at the candlelight through her glass. 'I will make a prediction. I predict that Peter will be a captain this time next year. Anyone like a bet on that?'

'Juju's the person the Chief of Defence Staff asks when he can't make up his mind,' Steven said, 'so I wouldn't recommend taking her on.'

'Piss off, you.'

'I only wish I shared your confidence, Julietta,' Peter laughed.

'Well they're bound to give you your fourth stripe at the end of your time in *Fleetwood*, aren't they?' Julietta said, opening her eyes very wide in an attempt to sober up.

'Fleetwood?' Penny asked. 'I didn't know you were going up north, Peter?'

'Not the place, the ship,' Lasbury explained. 'Type twelve frigate conversion.'

'I think it was rotten hard luck they're not giving you a Leander,' Jannaway said.

'That's another sort of frigate, just in case you were wondering,' Julietta added.

Lasbury slapped his shoulder with his hand in an attempt to trap a mosquito. '*Fleetwood*'s not a bad ship,' he said. 'And she's got a good serviceability record.'

'What about your officers,' Jeremy asked. 'Are you allowed to pick your own?'

Penny giggled. 'Like raspberries.'

'It's all very complicated these days,' Lasbury said. 'We have something called "trickle drafting", you see –'

Jeremy turned to Penny. 'Do you believe a word they're saying, darling?'

'I'm totally boggled,' she said.

'It's like this, see,' Steven started, putting on his yokel accent. 'In good old days of yore, everyone joined the ship on commissioning day and left on paying off day. Everyone got to know everyone else very well and you ended up either with a superlative ship or a hell ship. These days we do it differently. There are people arriving and leaving the whole time, so that the captain can never quite get his act together and the underlings can never quite get organised enough to mutiny.'

'It sounds rather horrifically like socialism, doesn't it?' Julietta remarked. 'I mean everyone has to be mediocre these days. We're not even allowed to have outsize eggs.'

'Oh I disagree with that,' Jeremy said. 'I can't possibly let you get away with that.'

'Now you've really done it,' Penny said. 'You'll never stop him now!'

They sat round the table, arguing into the night while the cicadas clacked in the bushes and a pale moon rose behind the hill. They discussed the differences between totalitarian regimes, authoritarian regimes, communist regimes and fascist regimes, and whether it was right that eggs should be stamped with the emblem of a lion.

'What an absolutely blissful holiday,' Julietta said the following morning when they were having croissants and coffee under the vine trellis.

'Here here,' Steven said. 'I shall return a new man.'

'Back to your Gannets,' Peter said.

'That's right – if they haven't all fallen into the sea by the time I get back.'

Penny and Jeremy had a plane to catch from Bordeaux, and had to leave straight away. They packed their matching leather luggage into the back of the hired Renault, kissed Julietta and Peter on both cheeks and departed up the track, sounding the horn in a syncopated farewell as they reached the main road and drove away.

Julietta went up to change and pack, and Steven and Peter sat out on the patio.

'So,' Lasbury said. 'How much longer are you going to stay in the flying world, Steve?'

Jannaway pushed his chair back from the table and rested his right foot on his left knee. 'Until next spring at least, I should imagine. I'm rather hoping to get on the staff course after that.'

Lasbury nodded. 'Yes. You don't want to get stuck in a backwater too long, do you? I'd have thought number one of a frigate might suit you next.'

'Bit early isn't it?'

'Not at all, Steve. You need to think ahead a bit. If you went to a frigate next spring, you'd be – what – something like two years into the zone by the time you leave. I'd say that would be about the time you should expect to get yourself promoted.'

Steven smiled uncomfortably. Now that he was on the brink of the promotion zone, talk of being selected for commander was inclined to embarrass him; he had difficulty in being as blatantly ambitious as some of his peers, preferring to believe that promotion came to those who served well and waited patiently rather than scrambled in undignified haste up the ladder.

They strolled down the terraces and stood looking out over the escarpment to the Dordogne valley. Below them, a grey Citroën van rattled downhill, sounding its horn at each corner.

Peter Lasbury had been considering inviting Jannaway to be his first lieutenant for some time now, and was on the point of making the proposal. He was due to take over command of HMS *Fleetwood* in late November, and the present first lieutenant, Brian Wiggins, was due to leave the following April. Although captains were not officially allowed to pick their officers, it was sometimes possible to arrange these matters, providing you put the wheels in motion well in advance.

Peter Lasbury liked Jannaway. He had a certain bluffness of manner, an economy in his conversation and a healthily tolerant sense of humour. He was something of a punch-bag for Julietta certainly, but Julietta needed a punch-bag for a husband, and Steven seemed big enough to take her little darts of sarcasm and condescension. He would need training up of course, but Lasbury enjoyed moulding his officers and men into what he considered to be right for them and right for him.

He looked at Steven now. He was squinting up into the sky at a jet aircraft that was leaving a condensation trail far above them. 'I thought it might be Concorde,' he said, 'But I don't think she flies as far south as this.'

Yes, he liked Jannaway. But would he make a good first lieutenant? The next eighteen months were of vital importance for Lasbury: if he was to achieve what he wanted to achieve in his career, he had to get himself promoted to captain as a result of this command. He must make no mistakes, and he must be required to take no blame for the incompetence of others. He needed a first lieutenant who would lead a strong wardroom and run an efficient, happy ship. What he did not want was some ambitious lightweight who was trying to outshine him – such combinations were frequently disastrous. Jannaway would not be like that: he would do what he was told, he would be loyal and he would be well liked.

There was another good reason for inviting him, for Lasbury felt indebted to the Braddle family. Clara had treated him as a second son; Julietta had loved and lost him; Henry had patronised him, and David . . . poor David. He preferred not to think about him.

'Steve,' he said, and for a moment felt as if he were proposing marriage. 'Tell me. Would you view the prospect of being my number one with great dismay?'

Jannaway's thick eyebrows went up in surprise. That was what Lasbury liked about him: he really was rather delightfully ingenuous. Any other officer of his rank and seniority would have been hoping for such a suggestion.

'Not at all, sir,' Jannaway said. 'In fact WMP, if that's an invitation.'

They walked back up the steps towards the house. 'Wouldn't do you any harm,' Lasbury said. 'Might even do you a lot of good.' He allowed his hand to rest momentarily on Jannaway's shoulder. 'Who knows, Steve. We might make quite a good team.'

The Jannaways left half an hour later. They said their thank yous and their goodbyes and drove off up the track, leaving a small cloud of pale dust behind them.

When they were gone, Lasbury returned to the verandah. He stood beneath the hanging baskets of geraniums and the bougainvillea, his bathrobe a dazzling white in the morning sun, and watched as a boy in his late teens, suntanned all over, appeared from his hiding place behind the filtration shed, dived neatly from the springboard and began to swim up and down in the brilliant water.

Brian Wiggins, the first lieutenant of HMS *Fleetwood*, was thirty-nine years old and had been in the Royal Navy since the age of thirteen. He was a tall, quiet, introspective officer who had married late in life and who had been converted to Seventh Day Adventism a few years before. Earnest and well meaning, he considered himself to be a conscientious officer and an efficient one; he also believed that it was possible to run a ship in accordance with Christian principles, and could never understand why things went wrong.

He had taken over the ship eighteen months before, at the end of her major conversion to a helicopter-carrying anti-submarine frigate, and since the moment of his arrival had struggled daily to turn her into a clean, operational fighting unit. He had driven himself hard, telling his wife that it was necessary to make sacrifices as a first lieutenant for the good of the service. He sacrificed his home life and his health; he gave up alcohol, except for a very occasional can of beer, and urged his officers to do likewise. Two captains had come and gone during his time on board HMS *Fleetwood*, and both had been promoted: Wiggins was too humble a man to believe that his efforts had contributed to their promotion, but this was most definitely the case.

The last captain, who had been relieved by Commander Lasbury just over a month before, had informed Wiggins that he was recommended for promotion, and this had buoyed him up and given him hope. Every six months, for six years, he had eagerly scanned the promotion lists when they arrived in signal form at the end of June and the end of December, and every six months he had been disappointed. Now, he was waiting to hear if patience had finally been rewarded: this was his 'last shot' for promotion.

The arrival of Peter Lasbury as his commanding officer had caused him considerable pain: he had been on the same sub lieutenants' courses as Lasbury, and the two officers had virtually nothing in common. Wiggins regarded Lasbury as a flamboyant symbol of evil, and Lasbury regarded Wiggins as a sanctimonious weed. Wiggins was aware of Lasbury's complete atheism, and Lasbury had to be careful not to sneer openly at Wiggins's fringe religiosity. Each consoled himself that they would only have to serve together for six months.

The letter from the Director of Naval Appointments arrived on a cold, blustery day a week before Christmas. When Wiggins saw it in his pigeon hole in the wardroom, his heart seemed to turn over, and as he slit the envelope open with a table knife, he still believed that it might be early advice of his promotion.

Dear Wiggins,

I am writing, with the authority of the Second Sea Lord, to tell you that you have not been selected on this, your last occasion for normal in-zone promotion.

2.    It is thought you would prefer to have advance notification of this disappointing news by private letter rather than await the official signal. It is intended for your own personal information and you should preferably not disclose it (other than to your own family of course) before the promotion selections are officially promulgated. You may, however, tell your commanding officer if you so wish.

3.    You will realise that competition for promotion is strong and that not all officers who have given excellent service in their present rank can be promoted even though they may have many years of valuable service still to give.

4.    As far as the future is concerned, I would like to reassure you that there still remains a range of interesting and worthwhile appointments open to you, and I hope that in due course you will visit your appointer and discuss with him your preferences for these.

He stood in the wardroom of HMS *Fleetwood*, deaf to the chatter of officers who stood about him sipping their stand easy coffee. Suddenly he needed to be alone. He left the wardroom, went along the main two-deck passage and up a ladder to his cabin, just below the bridge. Inside, he slid the door shut and, because he was already in tears, locked the door.

'Out pipes,' announced the bosun's mate on the ship's broadcast. 'Captain's requestmen and defaulters muster in the wardroom flat.'

Peter Lasbury sat at his desk and listened while his correspondence officer briefed him on the various ratings' requests which were to be brought to him that morning. His first lieutenant had already briefed him on the disciplinary charges that were being brought, and a few minutes after the pipe had been made, the master-at-arms knocked on his door, pulled aside the curtain and reported that requestmen and defaulters were mustered and correct, and that all officers required were present with the exception of the first lieutenant.

'Let me know as soon as you're ready to start,' Lasbury told him, and remained seated at his desk, using the spare minutes to complete the remaining three clues of the *Daily Telegraph* crossword, which he did without great effort.

While he waited, a midshipman searched the ship for Lieutenant Commander Wiggins and reported back, rather breathlessly, that he was not to be found.

'He's definitely not in his cabin,' he said. 'I knocked, and the door's locked.'

Lieutenant Arborfield, the correspondence officer, decided to have him piped for. 'First Lieutenant is requested in the wardroom flat,' the bosun's mate announced a little illogically, but with no result.

Lasbury became impatient. He particularly disliked delay, and when a quarter of an hour had passed and the first lieutenant still had not been found, he ordered that requestmen and defaulters be dismissed.

A buzz went round the ship that the Jimmy had gone missing, but within half an hour the mystery had been solved: Lieutenant Arborfield had peered in through Wiggins's forward facing scuttle and had seen his first lieutenant kneeling by his bunk, striking the heels of his palms against his forehead.

Arborfield reported to Lasbury, who sent for the surgeon lieutenant. A duplicate key to the first lieutenant's cabin was taken from the keyboard, and the door was opened.

Wiggins became hysterical, insisting that he wanted to be left alone. The surgeon lieutenant suggested a sedative, but he refused to take one; and while this was going on, the number two diesel generator tripped and went off line, plunging the ship in darkness. The ventilation fans ran down with an eery sigh and silence fell between decks, so that the sound of the first lieutenant weeping and shouting, 'I can't go on! I can't go on!' was heard throughout the ship.

One of the advantages of being a pilot was that you had time to think, and it was on occasions such as these, when the observers had switched to a separate intercom and the Gannet was bumbling along in cloud that Jannaway sometimes made an effort to do so.

He conducted conversations with himself in the manner of Alice in Wonderland, ruminating on matters over which he felt he should have control in the hope of being able to sort out his thoughts, rather as he might go up to an attic and sort out the bric-a-brac that can be given away for jumble.

Item one, he thought. Family. Bag and baggage.

I should love them equally but I can't. Julietta has formed a small, female mafia. I can see it in Anita's eyes. She watches you, and if you put a foot wrong, she reports back to Mummy.

Tom is not part of their mafia, and I don't think he ever will be. When I make my faces to him or whistle and hum at the same time or carry him up to bed or sing 'Deedle Deedle Dumpling', or place my hat on his head or cover my face with my hands and peep out at him through my fingers, he gives me his special laugh and we know that we are father and son and that there is something special between us – even though he is only eleven months old and I, God help us, am nearly thirty-three.

My mother (Your Mother).

Well okay. What am I supposed to do? See her more often I suppose. Make the effort. Write long, newsy informative letters about how well her little boy is doing in the sea scouts.

Sometimes when I visit her ... when did you last visit her? ... I feel we have not progressed at all since I was fourteen. We have never resolved that argument, have we? She is still waiting for me to say, all right, little mother, I'll go back to sea scouts for you, so that she can let me go on with my piano lessons, study my Xenophon, translate my 'Aeneid', write my essay on 'Sohrab and Rustum'; so that Alan and I can live on happily with her, the sons of a hero gallantly looking after their widowed mother. That is what she wants and has always wanted. It is this stifling possessiveness, which swirls out of the front door as she opens it to you that stirs me up and chokes me the minute I step into that house. I become unreasonably antagonistic, and that makes me feel guilty, and the guilt angers me further, and so on and so forth until we have to break, like wrestlers in an arm lock.

Alan.

He probably knows me better than anyone. Last Easter, when I saw them, and Mother was playing her long playing record on the Loss of Values and the Abandonment of True Excellence by the modern generation, I saw a gleam of understanding in his eyes as if he were saying all right, Steve, I know what you're thinking.

The trouble is, I don't really know what I think myself. The trouble is, I've taken the soft option, haven't I? I've chosen to be a good naval officer, instead of taking arms against the sea of troubles.

Being the good naval officer is the old standby, the cure for all ills. The good naval officer has the finest excuse in the world for being a bastard at home and a shit on the bridge: all he has to ask himself is, 'What is in the best interests of the Service?' Total commitment is the softest option of all. It's the *simplest* way of living, the final solution. If you put the Service first (or the Party, the Family, the Fatherland, God or IBM) everything falls neatly into place.

Time to turn round. 'Okay to turn one-eighty onto one five zero?'

'Okay!' say the observers, and round we go: a gentle fifteen degree banked turn so that they won't lose their radar picture. Steady on the new heading, check the hydraulic pressure and engine instruments and then back onto the scan of the flight instruments as this machine buzzes on and on through the clag.

Where are we? Nowhere in particular. Strange how it is possible to lose a sense of reality. You wonder if you are you, sitting here (where?) in this heavy rubber suit, gloved masked and booted, or whether you are just part of the machine, as the silk worm is part of the moth.

She was wrong about becoming 'one flesh'. If we had made love properly that night in Plymouth, it would probably have ended everything between us. I would have 'had' her and she would have 'had' me, just as Julietta and I have had each other. We would have indulged in the same form of mutual destruction.

But we didn't, so she is always there, intact, in my mind, and now it is dangerous even to whisper her name inside my mind, dangerous to think about her – is she still in Mombasa? – doing whatever she is doing, 'working with children'. We are still part of each other, nothing can change that. She is with me, in my thoughts, and she is happy to be here, she is a willing prisoner; and I know that I am over there with her, in exactly the same way. Suddenly, day or night, we are aware that we are thinking of each other. Very occasionally, when I am making it with J (we make *it*, not love) she (She) is suddenly there, I am inside her, we are joined. Sometimes, too, I dream dreams in which I am with her, under a single sheet in a room with mosquito netting at the windows and we are making love. And it is real love: it is a giving and a receiving, not a taking and a surrendering. It is so perfect that I am afraid that it will never happen except in my dreams, but I still hope.

So there you are. There is a real person underneath all these layers, after all.

Wouldn't it be nice (pleasant) to be a regular guy? A good chap, an honest cove. Wouldn't it be satisfactory if you could be exactly what you really were, or are. You see, Jannaway, you are like a sort of inaccurate navigational fix. A jumble of bearings, which make a confusion of cocked hats on the chart. You are a tangle of knitting, a pie, a mess of potage.

How long to go? An hour and a half. Time to change the engines round. 'Changing the engines!'

'Okay!'

HP cock on. Press the relight button. JPT rising. Open the throttle to flight idle. Constant speeding. Match the throttles. Yus-yus-yus. Change the rudder trim. Okay. Temperatures and pressures look good. Pom-pom-pom-pom-pom. And close down the other one. Press the feather button. And the prop stops. Bit more rudder trim. And there we are, buzzing along again in this great grey green greasy monster, which is (so inevitably) like life. That is the trouble with life. It is so like itself, so lifelike. We bumble along through it, making a lot of inconsequential noise for what seems a very long time and then we stop. Bonk. The party's over.

356

What erudite, penetrating thoughts you do have, Jannaway!
(Why thank you, Steven, thank you!)

You see? you *do* exist, because you even have the courtesy to
reply to yourself, though unfortunately you cannot be awarded a
prize, because someone thought of it before you. About – what –
three hundred years ago? And still it seems like a discovery. I think
therefore I am, yes, but I am not necessarily what I think I am, nor
what others may think I am.

I am 'a most competent pilot who sets a good example to his
subordinates by his own high standard of airmanship and
professional skill'.

A sharp cookie, you see, because my S.226 says so. Destined for
great things, doubtless.

Pom-pom-pom-pom-pom.

All you need is love!

(La la-la-la-la)

All you need is love

(Love)

Love is all you need, love is all you need, love is all you need . . .

Bit out of date, that one. Out of the mouths of babes and
sucklings. Is that Shakespeare? Dunno. You're a bloody barbarian,
Jannaway, you really are. A cultural fink. An intellectual –

'Steve?'

'Yup?'

'Where are we going?'

'Hang on. I've got a small problem.'

'What sort of problem?'

Voices in my ears. It's the artificial horizon, that's the trouble.
Must have gone bananas. One thing is quite definite. We are not in
a thirty-five degree banked turn to port. Or starboard for that
matter.

'Steve!'

Shit. Something is wrong. Maybe it isn't the artificial horizon.
The engine sounds different.

Throttle linkage gone? Has it jammed on full power? Why is the
speed building up? Is there a partial blockage of the static vent?
Water in the pitot tube?

'Steve! Steve! For fuck's sake!'

Holy Mary Mother of God. I've lost it. Rate of descent two
thousand feet a minute plus quite a lot. Altimeter unwinding, speed

357

building, turn and slip indicating a rate two turn to port . . .

'Disorientation! Steve! You're disorientated!'

They are screaming in the back. They are locked into a dark hole and their pilot has lost control in cloud because he was contemplating his naval navel.

Jesus, Mary, Joseph, I give you my heart and soul. Level the wings, close the throttle to flight idle, pull – out – of – this – fucking – dive!

And there is the sea, white flecked and heaving: Cardigan Bay, and you can hear heavy breathing from the back.

'Sorry about that folks!'

'You all right now?'

'Yeah, I'm okay. No problem.'

Silence.

'Steve?'

'Yup?'

'You reckon we might call it a day?'

(That was Death, that gentleman in the long grey coat who came and sat behind me on the way down. I felt his fingers grasp my shoulders, I caught a glimpse of his cadaverous face in the rear view mirror. He had come to collect me. I saw the coffin with the Union Flag on it, my cap, the flowers. I heard them singing that bit that goes, 'Time like an ever rolling stream bears all its sons away/They fly forgotten as a dream dies at the opening day.')

'Sorry about my momentary lapse,' he said when they were walking back to the squadron buildings.

The staff observer, an ex-scrum half for the navy who had once parachuted from a Skyraider at night, shrugged. 'We're all in one piece, aren't we sir?'

He signed up the flight and went along the passage to his office at the end of the block, then changed his mind and went into the crew room to make himself a cup of coffee.

'A very nasty touch of the leans, I had,' he announced to the senior observer. 'It got young Danby quite excited.' He wanted to make sure the senior observer knew before he heard anything through the grapevine. It was also important not to show any sign of being twitched. If the senior pilot got twitched, everyone else did too.

He mixed instant coffee, tinned milk and sugar in the bottom of a pottery mug and added boiling water from the heater. He collected a few chocolate bars and took them and his coffee back to his office.

On his desk was a note asking him to ring Colin Elderman, his appointer. He bit into a Mars bar and dialled the number. He had still not taken off his rubber goon suit, and the neck seal was making his skin itch. Outside, drizzle continued to sweep off the Atlantic and over the airfield. Just under his window, a seagull was stamping its webbed feet on the grass. Colin Elderman's resonant voice came on the line.

'Steve! Thank's for ringing back, you've just caught me. Look here, old fruit, how would you like a pier-head jump?'

'What sort of pier-head jump?'

'First lieutenant of a frigate.'

Jannaway looked out of the window. The seagull had stopped marking time and was cocking its head on one side. Suddenly it plunged its beak into the turf and withdrew a worm, which elongated considerably before leaving home.

'Which frigate?'

'*Fleetwood.*'

'*Fleetwood*? I thought Brian Wiggins was staying on until April!'

'So did we, mate. But he went round the twist at the end of last week. Cracked. Your friend Peter Lasbury's thumping the table and saying he wants Jannaway and he wants him now.'

## 20

Being Peter Lasbury's first lieutenant was like being the son of a hero all over again. It made him feel as though greatness were being thrust upon him.

'HMS *Fleetwood*?' Virginia Alton said. 'Surely that's Peter Lasbury's ship, isn't it?'

The Jannaways were giving a Boxing Day drinks party, and their sitting room was crammed with naval acquaintances. Virginia Alton was a riding friend of Julietta's. She was married to a chartered accountant, and bred English setters.

Jannaway beamed happily, stooping a little in order to avoid hitting his head against a wrought iron lamp bracket. 'That's *right*,' he said, using a new method of emphasis which he had noted among media people and was now developing for himself.

Julietta, talking in another group nearby was saying at the same time: 'He was hand picked for the job of course. Peter Lasbury's in command, you know.'

Anita came round with a tray of canapés. 'Mummy says you're not to hog the devils on horseback,' she told her father.

'My goodness, don't they grow up quickly!' Virginia said, and smiled, showing an extraordinary expanse of gum over her front teeth. 'So I suppose we won't be seeing much of you in the next two years, Steven?'

'Probably not. *Fleetwood*'s based in Guz, so I'll only be home for the odd weekend.'

They were joined by the local doctor and his wife, and Jannaway excused himself to replenish drinks. He went into the kitchen and made another large jugful of hot wine cup, pausing to talk to Thomas, who crawled in from the hall. He hoisted him up onto his shoulder and jigged him up and down until he gurgled with laughter.

'Daddy,' said Anita in the doorway. 'Mummy says everyone's dying of thirst and will you please hurry *up*?'

'I'm not going to preach any sermons to you Steve,' Peter Lasbury had said that first afternoon when Jannaway had been ushered into his cabin. 'We both know what we're after in this ship, so let's just go out and get it, right?'

Lasbury had put on a little weight in the past few years but he was by no means fat. His blond hair had thinned a little too, but it was still blond, and although small pouches were forming under his eyes, he still retained an air of youth and vitality. Of the two, Steven might have been mistaken for being the elder, with his grey hair and bald patch.

They sat in chintz-covered armchairs sipping cups of tea and planned their campaign. 'We should count ourselves lucky,' Lasbury said. 'We're starting off together. neither of us has got himself used to some other captain or first lieutenant's ways.' He placed the tips of his fingers carefully together. 'What I want to do in this ship is regain some of that feeling of pride and excellence we seem to have lost in this modern navy of ours. Do you know what I mean?'

Jannaway sat back in his chair, his clenched fists on the arm rests. 'I think I do, sir, yes. The trouble is, fleet commitments being what they are, there isn't the time for excellence, is there?'

Lasbury smiled through pursed lips. 'There'll be time for it in my ship, Number One, believe you me.'

Jannaway was as anxious as Lasbury to make the commission a success. He made it clear to his officers that he intended to demand the highest standards of professionalism and smartness from the start. He also made it clear, after being told several times that his ideas conflicted with those of the departed Brian Wiggins, that he wanted no further harking back to the ways things had been done by previous captains or previous first lieutenants. He dug out the old catchphrase he had used in HMS *Plumpton*, dusted it off and used it again: 'Give me all you've got, and I'll give you all I can,' he told the fourteen officers who assembled in the wardroom to hear him give them his views.

He found these officers to be an interestingly mixed bunch. The engineer officer, Bob Pangbourne, was a fairly typical Cambridge University and Manadon product: intelligent in a technical way but quite hopeless at getting the members of his department to work amicably together, so that his Chief POM(E) and his Chief ERA were continually at loggerheads and the ship seemed to stagger from mechanical breakdown to mechanical breakdown. The engineer's chief enemy was the Weapons Electrical Officer (known as the Wee-o). This was Douglas McDermot, a small, acerbic Scot who had joined the navy as a Junior Electrical Mechanic many years before and who organised his department entirely to his own satisfaction, even to the extent of giving them a different stand easy time from the rest of the ship's company. McDermot was the oldest member of the wardroom and knew very well that he would be promoted no further. He had served as WEO in a number of ships, and regarded Peter Lasbury's demands for excellence with a dour, jaundiced eye. The wrangles between Pangbourne and McDermot seemed to dominate the life of the wardroom when Jannaway joined the ship, and after a few weeks he put a stop to them, banning professional arguments in the mess except during the weekly planning meetings which took place every Thursday afternoon.

McDermot, Pangbourne, their two deputies and the supply officer, Roy Kemble, formed one unit within the wardroom: a unit whose members loved to hate each other, the officers who actually made the ship work, kept it fed, fuelled and moving. The other clique was made up of those officers who were required to 'fight' the ship – the gunnery officer (Cyril Morris), the Torpedo and Anti-Submarine Officer (Mick Delaney) and the Navigating Officer (Vince Chilbolton). Of these, Morris and Chilbolton were Darmouth products, while the mad Irish Mick Delaney was an 'SD' officer, about the same age as Jannaway, who had been promoted to the wardroom from the rank of petty officer some years before. Jannaway found that of all his officers, Delaney knew most about the running of the ship, and during Brian Wiggins's latter months had acted as a sort of unofficial first lieutenant. Although Jannaway had no possible way of knowing it, Delaney enjoyed the same sort of popularity and trust among the members of the ship's company as had Frank Jannaway forty years before, in HMS *Winchester*. Such officers are not common specimens; they are quirks of nature, unexpected examples of leadership that is born in the blood rather than swotted up from books and self-consciously practised. Finally, there were the 'players' of the wardroom: Arborfield, Clough-Davis and Lester, the three sub lieutenants, whose primary interest in life, as is common among sub lieutenants, centred on sleep, food and sex. Beneath them, hurrying about the ship from department to department with their huge navy blue task books under their arms, were the two midshipmen under

362

training, who lived together in a cramped cabin permeated by hard rock, full frontals and sweaty underwear which no officer in his right mind ever cared to visit.

'My philosophy,' Jannaway told all these officers, 'is to work hard and play hard. And my pet hates, which you may as well know about straight away, are disloyalty, discourtesy and disinterest. I would like HMS *Fleetwood* to get a name for herself – not only of being a ship which is clean and efficient, but of being one whose ship's company is known for its good manners and its sense of humour. That reputation, as I am sure you are well aware, starts right here, among us officers in the wardroom.'

Jannaway set about living by his philosophy of working hard and playing hard from the moment he had stowed away his kit in the polished wooden drawers beneath his bunk. Freed from the need to stop work at five o'clock every afternoon, he lived his job as a first lieutenant should: twenty-four hours a day, seven days a week. In the evenings, he set about 'playing hard' with as much determination as he drafted temporary memoranda, attended planning meetings or urged his senior ratings on during the day. He became a staunch member of the run ashore club, and indulged in wide ranging activities, from beery evenings with McDermot to cultural visits to the concert hall with Roy Kemble, or lustful nights at the Groin Exchange with the three sub lieutenants.

Within a few weeks of his arrival, he made written application to the Herbert Lott Trust Fund (known, inevitably, as the Herbert Trott Lust Fund) for a grant of one hundred pounds to purchase a stereo record player for the wardroom. To his officers' amazement, his request was granted, and *Fleetwood*'s record player became the envy of other wardrooms. Jannaway put it to almost immediate use: the sub lieutenants were despatched to the Plymouth city centre with the wardroom mess fund and told to come back with a selection of the best and latest pop records. That done, Jannaway organised his first wardroom party, to which local nurses, teachers and secretaries were invited by the half dozen, to be plied with duty-free drinks, and clutched at in the darkness behind the curtain which could be drawn across the wardroom to screen off the dining area.

Thus were the old inhibitions of the Wiggins era sloughed off, and thus was the wardroom spirit of HMS *Fleetwood* distilled.

363

Peter Lasbury did not attend the wardroom parties, though he would occasionally put in an appearance. He approved of them, however: HMS *Fleetwood* had been, until only a few months before, a ship based at Rosyth, and many of the families had been left behind up there. Thus several of the officers were, like Jannaway, separated from their wives by the exigencies of the service, and were happy to indulge in the occasional mild affair. Peter Lasbury obtained a certain vicarious enjoyment from seeing his officers cavorting in their mess and provided no rules were broken or scandal caused believed it could only benefit the morale of his ship's company, who liked to think of the officers as red-blooded and lustful rather than the pale, tired professionals the wives were led to believe them to be.

From time to time, Lasbury invited Jannaway to lunch with him in his cabin. They sat at the small table by the polished brass scuttle, and Lasbury would have a bottle of St Emilion opened to go with the roast beef. On these occasions, they discussed the running of the ship and the personalities of their officers, and Lasbury occasionally took the opportunity to give his first lieutenant advice.

'One aspect I think you might do well to look at a little more closely is the question of cleanliness between decks,' he told Jannaway one day. 'Two-deck passage, for instance. Grotty, don't you think? Definitely grotty.'

Two-deck passage was the main corridor which ran the length of the ship, and its cleanliness was a much discussed topic among first lieutenants. A few days after Lasbury's gentle hint, the commanding officer and officers of HMS *Fleetwood* invited their opposite numbers in HM ships *Ganymede* and *Persephone* to lunchtime drinks; and while the supply officers talked new potatoes and permanent loan lists, the gunnery officers shouted to each other about boarding parties and Seacat firings and the engineer officers muttered about their evaporators and condenseritis, the three first lieutenants, Courtenay, Tomkins and Jannaway, discussed their respective two-deck passages, and the merits of Gleam.

Gleam was a special preparation applied to deck tiles between decks to make them look as though they had been polished, and the first lieutenants were divided on whether it should be used.

'If I were you, I wouldn't touch the stuff,' said Courtenay, who had now been a first lieutenant for nearly a year. 'If you don't get it absolutely right, it peels off in six weeks and looks the most god-awful mess. Personally I don't think you can beat the good old fashioned scrub out at oh-six by the morning watchmen. Scrub your two-deck passage, and you know it's clean, don't you?'

'And look at the state of it an hour later when the entire ship's company has tromped up and down it a couple of times,' Tomkins said. 'We've got better things to do in *Ganymede* than spend our time on our knees scrubbing passages.'

'You've Gleamed then, have you Chas?' Jannaway asked.

'My predecessor did,' Tomkins told him, allowing the midshipman to top up his glass of horse's neck. 'And I'm bloody glad he did, too.'

Courtenay laughed shortly and helped himself to a handful of peanuts from an EPNS tray. He threw them into his mouth with a quick backward jerk of the head. 'Yes, but you've even painted your spurn-water beading, haven't you, Chas?' he remarked, with a thinly veiled sneer.

'So bloody what! It saves a lot of man hours, and it looks one hell of a lot better.'

'We don't waste time in *Ganymede*,' Courtenay said. 'We're just more efficient, that's all.'

'Shitty but happy, eh?' Tomkins said, and changed the subject abruptly. 'So what do you think of this Pee-woe concept?' he asked Jannaway, and stared intently into his eyes while awaiting an answer.

'Pee-woe concept?' Jannaway laughed. 'What the hell's a Pee-woe concept?'

Courtenay and Tomkins were astounded. 'Shag!' Tomkins said. 'Where have you been for the last year? Haven't you heard of the Pee-woe concept?'

Jannaway had to admit that he hadn't.

'It's Ashmore's brainchild,' Courtenay said, referring to the Vice Chief of Naval Staff. 'PWO. Principal Warfare Officer. We're going to do away with the specialisations and train lieutenants to be all-rounders instead.'

'Sounds like the old swing of the pendulum to me,' Jannaway said. 'Change in the name of progress.'

'Not at all,' Tomkins told him. 'It's a bloody sound scheme. It'll sort out all the prima donna argy bargy between gunnery officers and TAS officers, once and for all.'

At that moment they were interrupted by Christopher

365

Arborfield who, as officer-of-the-day, wore a sword belt with his uniform. He made his way through the crush of officers and told Jannaway, 'Looks as though the captains are making a move, Number One.'

The party immediately broke up. Courtenay and Tomkins spread the word among their officers that it was time to go, and there was a scramble to collect the hats from where they had been hung, perched or crammed on the hooks, fire extinguishers and overhead piping in the wardroom lobby. Jannaway was first out: he took his cap from the hook reserved for him and went up the ladder and out onto the upperdeck, walking briskly aft to the flight deck in order to be ready to salute the guests as they went over the brow and back along the dockside to their ships.

Following close behind them came the captains, who had been drinking in Lasbury's cabin. Lasbury strolled with them along to the flight deck, exchanged a little friendly repartee with them and saluted briefly as they departed.

'Steve,' he said as they made their way forward past the funnel. 'A small suggestion.' He paused by the motor cutter davit and reached up to turn the motor boat's propeller. 'Might it not be a nice touch of the fancy waistcoats if we polished our boats' screws? Can fix?'

He became increasingly absorbed in the life of his ship, the morale of his men and the social commitments of his wardroom. Inevitably, his family took second place to his work, and thoughts of Julietta and the children had to be driven back into a small corner of his mind. It was not that he did not care for them or feel responsible for them, but simply that he had very limited time available to play the role of husband or father.

He came and he went: he snatched week-end leave, arriving after the children were in bed on a Friday evening, and departing when Julietta was giving Thomas his evening bath two days later. At first he expected Julietta to welcome these brief visits, but it quickly became apparent that they were more of an inconvenience to her than anything else. Like many naval wives, she had been forced to accept that if anything went wrong in the household, it was up to her to get it put right, and that the upbringing of the children must be her responsibility. It was unsettling to have Steven breezing back as if he owned the place, and having bright ideas about not allowing

Anita quite so many sweets, or not letting Thomas stand too close to the television set. And it was no good expecting him to mend the tap or change the back door lock because something or other always conspired to prevent him. Thus his arrivals and departures tended to disrupt the smooth running of the home, and there were occasions on which both breathed a sigh of relief when Sunday evening came and it was time for him to return to his ship.

There was a tacit agreement between them now that they were bound by circumstance and a sense of responsibility to remain married, but neither pretended that their marriage meant more than that. Having largely caused the difficulties between them, the Royal Navy now assisted in keeping their marriage afloat: had Steven been working from nine to five in an office, it would have been likely that they would have split up quite soon.

Julietta had decided that she would definitely not have any more children, and was taking up riding seriously again. She had bought a hunter called Business, which she stabled at Meonford House and occasionally rode to hounds. After she had taken Anita and Penny to school and left Thomas with her mother, she changed into her riding things, saddled up Business and rode off, trotting through the village and away along the bridle path that led over farmland to Old Winchester Hill. Cantering along frosty lanes when the cobwebs hung over the hedgerows like silver veils, Julietta found time to be herself. She would ride for miles, her boots highly polished, her hacking jacket immaculate, her back ramrod straight as she moved with the horse and gripped with her knees. Although she often went out with Virginia Alton, she preferred to ride alone. Business became for her a compensation for the man she needed in her life, and the love she seemed destined never to receive. The smell of him in the mornings and the velvety exhalation with which he welcomed her when she went into his stable became her substitutes for the intimacies shared with a lover; and in a way, Business was indeed her lover: very occasionally, she would urge him forward over a flat stretch of common, and leaning forward as his powerful legs gathered and extended beneath her, she would allow the movement of him between her legs to raise her up to that moment of ecstasy which she needed so desperately, and which she so seldom achieved.

So the months passed: three wintry months at the bottom of a dry

367

dock; a month of Hats and Sats, of trials and of setting-to-work; six weeks of purgatory at Portland followed by a Families Day to which Alan was invited, but which was cancelled at the last moment when HMS *Fleetwood* was required to stay at sea in order to trail one of the new Soviet guided missile destroyers. After the summer leave came the annual autumn exercises off the north of Scotland; after that came a succession of courtesy visits to European ports; and a fortnight after Christmas, having said their goodbyes to families and friends, the officers and men of HMS *Fleetwood* fell in for leaving harbour and the frigate sailed out past Plymouth Hoe, bound for the Far East, on what was called – sadly, perhaps – the Foreign Leg.

# 21

Pippa Lane was the sort of girl who has difficulty shaking off the attentions of older men. She had naturally curly hair, very fine, white teeth and a useful sense of the ridiculous; she also had ambitions in investigative journalism and a nose for a good story, so when she caught wind of the Royal Navy's embarrassment over the Beira Patrol she was quick to persuade the British Naval Attaché in Capetown to put her on the guest list of visiting British warships.

Her first invitation to a ship's cocktail party arrived soon after: the pleasure of her company was requested at 1830 on Saturday the 12th of February 1972, for cocktails on board HMS *Fleetwood* in the Simonstown naval base, and now here she was, driving south along the coast road from Muizenberg, with the evening sun glittering on the South Atlantic to her left, and the tyres of her yellow Volkswagen Beetle humming on the smooth, South African tarmac.

Midshipman the Honourable Henry Bean saw her first. 'Bloody hell,' he said. 'Take a look at this one, sir!'

Christopher Arborfield took a look. 'Very nice,' he said. 'Very nice indeed.'

They watched Pippa approach along the jetty. She wore white shoes and a dark blue dress with white broderie anglaise at the neck line and sleeves. She carried a leather bag over her shoulder and wore no stockings – or, for that matter, knickers, though Arborfield, Bean and the bosun's mate weren't to know that.

'Man the side!' Arborfield ordered as she came up the brow, and the three of them saluted as she stepped down onto the flight deck.

Pippa was determined not to be nonplussed, so she saluted them back.

Christopher Arborfield laughed a little nervously. Ladies weren't expected to salute. 'Would you like to go with the midshipman?' he asked, and for a moment Pippa felt as if she were in the middle of some as yet undiscovered operetta by Gilbert and Sullivan.

'This way,' Bean said. 'And mind the eyebolt, it's easy to trip.'

He led the way forward, past the burnished brass bell, the ship's name board and the battle honours board. 'Shall I go up first?' he said when they came to a ladder. 'All right,' she said. 'Unless you want to look up my skirt,' a reply which turned Bean a dull red.

They arrived on the fo'c's'le. A steward in a high necked tunic stepped forward with a silver tray. 'That's whisky and soda, Ma'am,' he said in a thick Glaswegian accent. 'That's horse's neck, that's gin and tonic and that's white wine cup.'

A lieutenant approached. 'Ah,' he said. 'Are you being looked after? Ah. Good. Shall we join the merry throng?'

The merry throng consisted largely of colonial-looking couples in their middle age, jammed together under the striped awning, stepping awkwardly over the chain cables, ducking under the twin gun barrels, balancing their drinks on the cable holders and flicking their ash into the potted plants.

'Roy Kemble,' the officer said. 'I'm the Purser for my sins.'

They were joined by another officer, who had a large, pulsing vein that ran down the centre of his forehead. 'Nick Robson,' he said, shaking her hand so firmly that her drink slopped. 'Beg pardon,' he added, producing a used handkerchief with yellow snot on it to mop her wrist.

'Buck up, Robson, for God's sake!' Kemble said, and added for Pippa's benefit: 'He's the flight commander – you know, pilot type. Explains everything, doesn't it?'

Robson put away his handkerchief. 'So what do you do?' he asked. 'When you're not making our fo'c's'le a much more beautiful place?'

Kemble groaned.

'I'm a nurse,' Pippa told him, which by a small stretch of the imagination could just be true.

'Ah,' said Kemble. 'Good for you. Have you specialised?'

Robson grinned widely and the vein in his forehead throbbed. 'Isn't your wife a nurse, Roy?' he asked, as if confidentially, but making sure that Pippa heard.

'Belt up you bastard!' Kemble replied, and turned to Pippa. 'We're all bachelors south of Gibraltar.'

This conversation continued in a similar vein for some time, until Midshipman Bean, released from his guest-welcoming duties, joined them.

'This is Hairy,' Robson said. 'His full name is the Honourable

Hairy Bean, but you don't like to put on airs, do you Hairy?'

Bean blushed and his eyes watered. He swallowed three times and gazed at Pippa's cleavage.

'So what are you all doing in Simonstown?' she asked them, deciding that if they insisted upon behaving like prep school boys, they would probably like to be treated accordingly.

They grinned at each other and made in-jokes for their own amusement.

'I suppose you're on your way to do this Beria Patrol are you?' she asked.

'Ah,' said Kemble. 'We don't talk about that.'

She fluttered her eyelashes deliberately. 'Why not?'

'It's no good,' Robson said. 'Our lips are sealed.'

'We hope yours aren't though!' said Bean, who then realised exactly what he had said and turned scarlet.

Robson beat him over the head. 'Go away you horrible midshipman!'

A tall, blond commander turned and frowned, and the laughter ceased immediately. Pippa found herself being handed over from one group to another.

'Peter Lasbury,' he said, and she looked back into his glittering blue eyes and took an immediate dislike.

He started talking smoothly and confidently to her about what his ship had been doing, making it quite clear to her that he was the captain, touching the corner of his mouth with the knuckle of his forefinger from time to time and licking his lips between sentences in a way that gave her gooseflesh. After a few minutes, when his conversational flow was beginning to falter (she had fixed him with her clear, green eyes in a way that had that effect on certain men) she asked him, 'What will the weather be like when you get up into the Mozambique Channel?'

The eyes stopped glittering in an instant, and went icy. This is a man I do not like, she told herself.

He laughed lazily and changed the subject, and later introduced her to another officer, the deputy engineer officer, who smelt of diesel oil and who wanted to tell her about his turbo-generators; and having made the introduction, Lasbury quickly turned his back on her and moved away across the forecastle to speak to a ferocious-looking lieutenant commander with grizzled hair that was going thin on top. Pippa saw them talking together and glancing across

371

at her, and a few minutes later the ferocious-looking officer, who didn't look nearly so ferocious at close quarters, came up and introduced himself.

'Steve Jannaway,' he said. 'I think you must be Miss Lane, right?'

The deputy engineer officer melted into the background: he had obviously been making a great effort to continue a conversation with her, and was glad to get away.

'I thought you looked as though you needed rescuing,' Jannaway said. She decided that she liked the look of him. He was like a mongrel at a dog show. One of those comfortable scruffy mongrels, with bushy eyebrows and grey round the muzzle. He had rather doggy eyes too: browny-green, with flecks of orange.

'How did you know my name?' she asked.

He took out a sheet of paper from his inside pocket (the officers were wearing their dark blue reefers, though the weather was hot enough for whites) and opened it up. It was a guest list. 'There you are. "Miss Pippa Lane, Journalist". What sort of a journalist are you, Miss Lane?'

She remembered the way he and the captain had glanced across at her as if they were talking about her. She suspected that he had been detailed off to chat her up. It seemed absurd, but then both the captain and those prep-school lieutenants had reacted sharply to questions about the Beira Patrol. She began enjoying herself. If they were playing cloak and dagger games with her, she could play as well, and if they weren't, this Jannaway man was a nice hulk of horseflesh, even if he was a naval officer.

She smiled at him, enjoying catching his eye. Men really were so easy!

'Travel, mostly,' she told him. 'But I'll write anything that'll sell.'

'Anything?'

'Anything within the bounds of good taste.'

He smiled and went to the guardrail, peering out over the harbour between the coloured pennants which had been rigged as a decorative windbreak.

'So are you going to write an article about us? Or aren't we sufficiently newsworthy?'

'What a pity,' she said. 'I thought for a moment you were going to be less pompous than the others.'

That took him aback. He seemed a little annoyed at first, then he relaxed and grinned quite disarmingly. 'Yes, maybe you're right there.'

She caught his eye again, and this time felt she had actually made contact. Behind his naval officer mask there was a human being, trying to get out.

'Too many cocktail parties,' he said. 'One slips into the patter rather easily.'

They looked at the chattering crowd. Robson and Kemble were laughing and talking with two embassy secretaries. Kemble was rubbing his stomach in a circular motion and patting his head at the same time, while Robson held his drink for him.

'He's explaining how to hover a helicopter,' Jannaway said, answering her unasked question. 'He does it every single time.'

'How boring of him.'

'It's a great little icebreaker.' The embassy secretaries had started trying to do the same, amid peels of diplomatic laughter. 'See what I mean?'

'Jealous?'

He managed not to be pompous this time. 'Yes, probably.'

'You're married, I take it?'

He nodded. 'You?'

'No.'

'And ... let's see. You come from Liverpool, right? You're a Scouse.'

'Half Scouse, half bog-Irish.'

'That explains the colour of your hair.'

She felt herself blush and was annoyed. Men didn't usually make her blush. And what's more, he had seen her blush and was admiring it with gentle amusement. Damn.

'How long does this go on for?' she asked.

He looked deliberately at his watch. 'Not much longer. You arrived rather late, didn't you?'

'You saw, did you?'

'I think we all did.'

'And what happens after this?'

He shrugged a little. 'Well, some of the really experienced soaks will hang on for as long as we are foolish enough to keep the drinks going, and when we've finally herded them off the ship, there'll be a jump up for the bloods down in the wardroom.'

'A jump up?'

'Smooch session. Disco night. Groping in the dark. Would you like that?'

373

'Not much.'

He looked at her gravely for a few seconds. 'What would you like?'

'What's on offer?'

'You might be able to persuade someone to take you out to dinner.'

His nostrils trembled. He was laughing inside. She looked round at the babbling crowd. 'Yes, I suppose I might. But it's difficult, isn't it? I'm not sure I like the look of anyone here.'

'We're a pretty rough lot, I must admit,' he said. 'Mind you, I wouldn't take much persuading. In fact if you said you'd wait five minutes I'd be changed and ready and raring to go. If you could bear to put up with me, that is.'

'One condition,' she said.

'What's that?'

'That you tell me why the navy's so frightened of talking about this Beria Patrol thing you're doing.'

He laughed. 'I thought so,' he said. 'I thought so! You're not just here for the beer, are you?'

'Nor are you. You were detailed off to come and talk to me, right?'

She held his eyes, and this time knew she had him on the run. She rather hoped that he would deny it, because she felt sure she could make him admit it later.

But he did not deny it. Suddenly he was even more a human being and even less a naval officer. 'All right, games over,' he said. 'Let's go and eat somewhere, and I'll tell you all I'm allowed to. Okay?'

'Okay,' she said, and watched him go away down the slope of the fo'c's'le, feeling unexpectedly pleased at the way things had turned out.

Driving out of the naval base thirty yards behind the yellow Volkswagen, Jannaway felt even more pleased. He had liked the look of her the moment Lasbury had pointed her out and suggested that he go and find out what she was up to. 'Do a bit of James Bonding,' he had said. 'But don't do anything I wouldn't enjoy.'

He had had the impression that she had hoped to be asked out almost as soon as they met. He gripped the wheel and laughed aloud, following her out of Simonstown on the coast road to Fishoek and Capetown. They hadn't said a great deal to each other in words, but those looks of hers had spoken volumes.

He had heard some time ago that the visit to Simonstown was likely to be good value, and so far it had exceeded his expectations. They had arrived two days before, and waiting for him at the end of the jetty had been this Volvo estate, placed at his disposal free of charge by the ship chandlery firm which was contracted to clean and paint the ship during her ten-day stay. Within hours of arriving, a work force of black Africans had arrived under the supervision of a coloured African and had set about the task of painting the ship's side. Invitations to the officers and ratings had flooded in: to dinner parties, braais, coach tours, golf, tennis and swimming matches. Nowhere else had the ship received such a warm welcome and such generous offers of hospitality.

Admittedly, he had felt a small prick of conscience, seeing the negroes starting work with the pots of grey paint and the long-handled brushes. Nobody was prepared to call these people second-class citizens, but there was something about their manner that gave the game away: it was impossible to forget that the blacks did not enjoy the same privileges as the coloureds, and that the coloureds did not enjoy the same privileges as the whites. He had never before felt so conscious of the colour of his skin: on the way south, he had sunbathed along with the other officers and had become deeply suntanned. This, together with the fact that his nose was not quite as aquiline as it might have been, made it just possible for him to be mistaken for a coloured, and he was amazed to find himself inwardly justifying his looks, and wondering what he would say if he were prevented from entering a restaurant.

It was dark now. There were pin-pricks of light along the coast to the east, and ahead, as he followed the Volkswagen out of Muizenberg, the lights of the Capetown suburbs sprawled beneath the slopes of Table Mountain to his left.

Pippa had suggested they go first to her flat in Claremont so that they could leave one of the cars and go on to Capetown together. He had changed into cords and a dark red shirt, bringing with him a lightweight jacket and a tie. He had a wad of rands in his wallet and that pleasant expectation one experiences at the beginning of an evening with a new woman in a foreign port.

Pippa wasn't the first woman he had taken out since sailing from Devonport. There had been that QARNNS nursing sister in Gibraltar, and the cabaret singer in Funchal, but neither had been as attractive or as apparently willing as this one. Perhaps it was the cloak and dagger aspect which added a certain piquant flavour to it all: he had never actually been given a carte blanche to seduce a woman in the service of the crown before, and the idea of it amused him considerably.

Peter Lasbury was very keen on what he called overt intelligence work. Since the work-up, HMS *Fleetwood* had developed a name for the accurate reports she had made on sightings of Soviet shipping, the photographs Jannaway had taken from the Wasp helicopter of a Kresta guided missile cruiser and an amusing article, written by Lasbury, about the occasion on which the skipper of a Soviet intelligence trawler had been entertained to breakfast, to the west of Cape Wrath.

And now there was this girl. Jannaway didn't believe for one moment that she was any sort of spy or agent, but as the ship's intelligence officer he had personally briefed the ship's company two days before their arrival at Simonstown that they must not discuss the Beira Patrol with civilians, and that if any civilians showed an unusual interest in it, they should be reported to him personally.

She was slowing down and indicating left. They were entering the Capetown suburb of Claremont. He followed her off the main road and up a side street, parking immediately behind her.

He lifted his jacket off the passenger seat, got out and locked the car, and noted with great satisfaction the movement of Pippa Lane's buttocks beneath her dark blue dress as she led him to the door.

It was strange how people changed in different surroundings. Now that he was out of his uniform, out of his ship, he was no longer a naval officer, just a bloke in a red shirt.

'I've only just moved in,' she explained. 'That's why the place looks a bit like a prison cell.'

'Don't apologise,' he said, and looked round at the bare walls, the rush mat on the floor, the gonk toy that dangled on a spring, and the big blow-up of an African woman, weeping outside a concrete hovel. This latter he admired: she had stuck it up at the end of the hall so that it was the first thing you saw when you entered. 'That's good,' he said. 'Not very pleasant, but good. Where did you get it?'

'In a slum, about five miles from here.'

376

'You mean you took it?'

He followed her into the kitchen, and saw all the other photographs. 'You took it,' he repeated, and grinned in that mongrel way of his. He examined some of the photographs closely: nearly all of them were of natives.

'Is that your subject? Black Africans?'

'Their predicament, yes. Do you want a coffee?'

'Are you having one?'

She smiled. 'That is a very – "married" – response.'

'All right, I'll have a coffee. Thanks.'

She kicked off her white shoes and went barefoot. He leant against the fridge, moving quickly aside when she wanted to open the door for the milk. 'It's only instant,' she said.

'Suits me.'

She switched on the electric kettle and looked back at him. He went to the sink and peered out of the window at the back garden and the line of houses beyond it. She found herself watching him, half expecting an advance, and a little annoyed with herself for being disappointed that it didn't come. She made the coffee in two mugs and they stood sipping it. 'I haven't got any furniture yet,' she said. 'Silly isn't it?'

'Where do you sleep? Or are you like a horse, do you just doze, standing up?' And now he did make an advance: he carefully traced a pattern on her bare shoulder with the tip of his forefinger.

She left him in the kitchen and went into the only bedroom, where there was a card table with her typewriter on it, a few open suitcases, a scattering of clothes and a mattress on the floor. He came to the door.

'This is my stable,' she said. 'Would you like to sit down?'

He lowered himself into a cross-legged position, being careful not to spill his coffee.

'Didn't quite expect this, did you?' she remarked, sitting down beside him.

He stirred his coffee. 'We learn to be ready for anything in the navy, you know. "Ready aye ready", that's our motto. Pretty close to the boy scout's motto really, isn't it?'

'Were you a boy scout?'

He glanced at her. 'I was a sea sprout. It was ever so jolly.'

'Do I detect a note of irony?'

'I don't know. Do you?'

She decided she was beginning to like him. They sipped their coffee and chatted inconsequentially. When he had finished his coffee, she took his mug and put it, with hers, against the skirting board.

'So,' he said. 'What would you like to do? Go out to dinner?' He took her hand. 'Or would you like to play silly games?'

They drove in his car to the city. They had showered together and she had changed into a white dress.

'I feel all set for the Assumption in this,' she had remarked, and he had asked her if she was a Catholic.

'Yes I am,' she said. 'But not exactly a shining example, as you probably gathered.'

He laughed. 'Join the club!'

'So you are as well? I knew there was something about you!'

They went to the Café Royale. 'Ever so posh,' Pippa said. 'You'll have to put on your tie.' She looked at the menu. 'You've given me an appetite,' she said. 'I am extremely hungry.'

She began telling him about herself. She spoke rapidly and intimately, in contralto Liverpudlian. He enjoyed listening to her voice and watching the slight movements of her nearly plump body so much that he scarcely took in what she was saying.

She had lost her parents in one of the Comet crashes when she was eight and had gone to live with an uncle and aunt in Kirkdale, a suburb of Liverpool. They had no children of their own and tried to buy her affection. She was smothered in presents, and when she left school to start at a commercial art college, her uncle gave her an allowance on condition that she complete the course.

'It was hopeless,' she said. 'I just floundered about knowing that I wasn't any good, or at least not good enough. Then I was caught with a boy friend in his room, and his landlady actually pushed me out onto the street in my underclothes and threw my things after me. Can you believe it?' She shook her head, laughing at the memory of it, and finished her wine at a gulp. 'Anyway, the word went round as they say, and when Uncle Cyril got to hear of it he stopped my allowance. He said I was a tart. Maybe he was right.'

'And?'

She shrugged. 'Well, it was summer, so I went to Blackpool and joined one of those formation swimming teams, you know, lots of lovelies all diving in together and doing fancy strokes. I didn't actually get round to soliciting, you know. Money didn't actually change hands. But I earned the odd bed and breakfast. Am I shocking you?'

He shook his head. 'Shaming me if anything. As a member of the male sex.'

She went on. She told him how she had been taken on as a photographer's model, and had become interested in photography herself. 'But I wanted to travel, you see, and I wanted to travel *respectably*. So I gritted my teeth and went in for nursing.'

She launched into a long, complicated story about a German patient with Hodgkinson's disease with whom she had become emotionally involved. He had escaped into Russia during the war and had later escaped again from Russia to the west.

She paused while the waiter served T bone steaks. 'Why on earth am I telling you all this?' she asked.

'Go on, I like listening to you.'

'Well, when I met him, he thought he was dying. He was very sweet, but very muddled. He kept asking me to take him back to Germany in a taxi. He said he could pay me in gold coins. I thought his brain was going – he'd been on barbiturates. Anyway, I came on duty one morning and his bed was empty. He'd discharged himself. Gone.'

She stopped.

'You felt you'd let him down?'

She nodded. 'I felt terrible about it. He'd been – sort of relying on me to help him, and all I'd done was play him along. I suppose he was a bit of a father figure in a way. I still feel bad about it, even now.'

'Did you ever see him again?'

'No. I chucked nursing and tried to break into photography again. Then I found I was better writing the captions than getting the pictures –'

He smiled. 'I doubt that.'

'No, I was. Am, I hope. I got myself taken on as a cub reporter with the *Sunday Pic*. Yes, okay, I slept with one of the editors, and then he went out to Bahrain of all places to start up a newspaper there, and I went with him. That didn't work for long, so I trotted off to Kenya. I needed some money by then, so I did a bit more nursing, saved a bit of money and then actually got a bit of a break. I did an article on the new face of Kenya which was accepted by the

*Observer*. Marvellous! Then I went up to Ruanda and did another piece about what's going up there, then I got interested in the Rhodesia business, and did a trek with a friend all the way south.

'From Kenya?'

'From Kenya.'

'That must have been quite a journey.'

'It was.'

'And this is why you're interested in the Beira Patrol?'

'It could be.'

'You're doing an article on it?'

She shook her head. 'Not necessarily.'

'You don't want to talk about it.'

She laughed. 'Maybe not.'

They finished their coffee, and he paid the bill. Outside, she took his hand. 'Let's go up a mountain,' she said.

The parked on the slope of Table Mountain and looked out over the glittering lights of Capetown and the pale sea beyond.

'This is the best time to come up here,' Pippa said. 'If you come up in the daytime you either see too much or too little.' She took his hand and held it between her own. 'Well, Mr Jannaway. And how often have you done this sort of thing before, I wonder?'

'Once or twice, certainly.'

'I keep thinking about your wife,' she said.

'I try to avoid doing that.'

'You don't sound as though you're passionately in love with her.'

He paused a moment or two, looked at her, then looked away. 'No,' he said eventually. 'I'm not.'

He kissed her. She said: 'I'm a lost cause.'

'We all need someone to lean against.'

'Are you making excuses for me?'

'No, for myself, more likely.'

'So who do you lean against?'

'You at the moment.'

'What about your wife? Doesn't she help prop you up?'

'Julietta?' he laughed. 'No.'

'Julietta. She sounds like quite a swinging person.'

'She was once.'

'But you've given her a fridge and three children and now she's a frustrated housewife, right?'

380

'Not exactly. She rides.'

'Horses?'

He laughed. 'And people.'

They got out of the car and strolled across a slab of black, volcanic rock.

'You're a nomad, like me,' Pippa said quietly.

'All naval officers are.'

'Are you typical of the breed?'

'I hope not.'

'How long are you here for?'

'We sail Monday week.'

She looked up at him. 'Things like this shouldn't happen, should they?'

He just shook his head, staring down at the traffic that crawled about the streets below them.

'Ridiculous, isn't it?'

He enfolded her in his arms and held her.

'Maybe we can share a tent or something,' he whispered. 'Isn't that what nomads do?'

She arrived on board for a drink at noon the following day. He met her on the flight deck and took her down a steep ladder and into the wardroom, which reminded her of a cocktail lounge, with a dining table set for lunch at one end. She sat beneath a polished brass scuttle and accepted a glass of rum and coke.

A number of officers came and went, and there was a holiday mood among them. She sat in her safari dress, aware that she was pigeon holed as 'the first lieutenant's bird' and was a source of mild interest.

He had spent the night with her, leaving at six in the morning to get on board for breakfast. Nothing was said about that, but Pippa sensed that everyone knew.

She finished her drink, and Steve led her off to show her the ship. They went along a tiled corridor, and an anonymous wolf whistle came up from one of the messdecks.

'Pantless today?' he asked.

'No, but my bikini bottom's got zebra stripes.'

They went up a ladder to the operations room. 'This is where it all happens,' he said. 'It looks impressive, but most of the kit's at least ten years out of date.' He explained what some of the radar sets and plotting tables were for, and while they were in there, the captain entered from his night cabin. He was dressed in a beige suit with a scarlet handkerchief in the breast pocket. He nodded good morning to Pippa and turned to Jannaway.

'Number One – have we resolved the question of numbers for Spinoza's braai?'

'Fixed, sir,' Jannaway said. 'Chief, Pilot and Wee-o are going.'

'Not yourself?'

'No, sir.'

Lasbury's blue eyes turned their pale beams upon Pippa. 'I see,' he said abruptly, and went back into his cabin.

'What on earth was he talking about?' she asked when they were up on the bridge. 'Who's Spinoza?'

'Senior Naval Officer South Africa. It's a sort of nickname. Father's cross because he wanted me to go to the braai.'

She sat in the captain's high chair, and they looked out over the bay. 'It must be very romantic up here at night on watch,' she said. 'All on your own and the stars up above.'

'Oh it is. Definitely.'

'Show me your cabin, then. I want to see where you live.'

They went back down the ladder and he slid open a door. He had a small teak desk, a bunk with drawers under it, a folding table and a brass scuttle that looked out over the fo'c's'le.

She picked up a framed photograph. 'This must be Julietta.'

'Yes.'

'I'm not exactly in her league, am I?'

'I don't put people in leagues.'

She put the portrait back on the desk. 'You're quite a complicated person really, aren't you?'

'Am I? I didn't think I was.'

'One moment you're the naval officer and the next you're –'

'What?'

She came to him and linked her hands at the back of his neck. 'I think you're a bit like me. You're someone who needs a lot of love.'

They were interrupted by a knock on the door, and the curtain was drawn aside by a grinning able seaman.

'Beg pardon, sir,' he said. 'But is there any chance of you signing daily orders?'

He stepped into the cabin and placed a duplicating skin on the desk, and when Steven held out his hand, gave him a stylus for signing it. She noticed that he was left handed: he signed his name with neat, jagged letters and a strong line underneath. 'Thank you, Hatton,' he said, and the able seaman withdrew.

'What are you smiling at?' Steven asked.

'You. I was enjoying watching you being a first lieutenant.'

'One man in his time plays many parts.'

She laughed. 'I know, that's what's so fascinating.'

They spent four evenings, three afternoons and five nights together. Both felt rootless, and because of their rootlessness were pessimistic about being able to prolong the friendship.

'It's the bloody navy that does it,' he said on their last afternoon when they were lying on the beach. 'It's impossible to be a real person and a naval officer at the same time. The two aims are mutually incompatible.'

'It's a bit like prostitution isn't it?' Pippa said. 'I mean you get given smart clothes and good money for doing something which is basically immoral.'

'It isn't exactly immoral,' he said. 'It's sort of... destructive.'

'So's prostitution. It destroys love.'

'The navy destroys *people*. It takes away their souls.'

She linked her hand with his. 'I'm going to find it quite difficult to forget you, Mr Jannaway.'

'We could always write, I suppose. Keep in touch across the sea. Look at the new moon every month and think about each other. And then ... one of these days ... I'll see you high on a steep and windy hill.'

'We'll run to each other. We'll sail away into the sunset.'

He rolled onto his back. 'The trouble is, I sort of mean it.'

'I do too, my love. But it won't happen, will it? You'll go back to your county wife, and I'll go back to my typewriter. And maybe we'll remember each other. Just occasionally.'

'I expect you'll find yourself a hulking blond Yapi for a husband one of these days, and all your ideas about African liberation will be quietly forgotten.'

'In that case I expect *you'll* be nauseatingly successful in your career and end up all smooth and glittery like that slithy tove of a captain of yours.'

'Some 'opes.'

'Why don't you leave then? There's not much point in staying on if your heart's not in it.'

383

'It's not as simple as that. They've got me by the short and curlies, you see. I can't afford to leave. There's nothing I could do outside –' He stopped. 'You see? We even refer to the real world as "outside". We live in a sort of blue cocoon. Besides. There's always that argument about staying in in order to get to the top and change the system. I mean – that's roughly what you're doing in South Africa, isn't it?'

'I have no ambitions about getting to the top.'

'No, but you're here. You're living within a system you don't approve of.'

'Do you approve of it?'

'Not at all.'

She sat up, and he brushed off the sand that had stuck to her back. She was wearing her zebra bikini. The pleasant thought crossed his mind that in an hour or so they would leave the beach, return to her flat, shower together and make love. He was quite certain of this: the week they had spent together had brought him closer to her than he had ever been to Julietta. Pippa had turned all his thoughts about life upside down. He knew inwardly that he was in love with her, but he also knew that he must not admit the fact. He wasn't sure how he might keep in contact with her, but he was determined to try.

'I'll tell you something,' she said suddenly.

He sat up beside her. 'What?'

'This Beira Patrol thing of yours is a complete and utter waste of time.'

He laughed. 'Oh we all know that!'

'Do we? Why are we continuing it then?'

He shrugged. 'Wasn't there some UN resolution? Back in '66?'

'Yes there was. And Harold Wilson was going to bring Rhodesia to its knees within six months, wasn't he?'

' "Weeks not months" wasn't it? Something like that.'

'And it's now six years.' She looked at him for an answer. 'Well? What's gone wrong?'

He shrugged. 'I don't know. Haven't they been trundling oil up by road or something? What's the name of that bridge?'

'Who's "they"?'

'Wait a minute. Is this the conversation we were going to have on the first evening? Are you trying to pump me?'

'I'm not pumping you, Steve. I'm spoon feeding you. Come on, tell me, who do you think's sending lorry loads of petrol to Rhodesia?'

He blinked, having a feeling that he was being led somewhere he didn't want to go. 'The people here,' he said. 'Can't be anyone else, can it?'

'The white South Africans. Agree?'

He nodded.

'And is that the reason you people are so cagey about talking about oil sanctions while you're here?'

'Possibly. It's an embarrassing subject, isn't it? It wouldn't be exactly diplomatic to talk about it in a country we know isn't observing the United Nations resolution.'

'*And* one that's providing much needed bunkering facilities while the Suez Canal's closed.' Pippa opened the cold box and took out a can of lager. 'Last one. Shall we share it?' She drank some and handed the can across. He sipped from it and looked at her.

'What are you trying to tell me?'

'We'll come to it. Next thing: why isn't the Royal Navy allowed to admit that it exercises with the South African navy?'

He grinned. 'Who says we exercise with them? First I've heard of it.'

'I know it happens, love. You can deny it if you want to, but I know it happens. I've seen the Buccaneers flying out to meet you.'

'Okay, so we do. Any more questions?'

'Plenty. So far we've agreed that British warships are coming in here to get themselves painted and fuelled and entertained for ten days before going on up the Mozambique Channel to make as if they're enforcing the oil sanctions, right?'

'We are enforcing them! There hasn't been a single tanker shipment of crude oil through the pipeline to Umtali since the sanctions began!'

She knelt in front of him, her legs tucked neatly under her, heaping up the sand on either side with her hands. 'So where's Rhodesia getting her crude oil from? Would you think?'

'Didn't we agree it was going up by road?'

She laughed gently. 'Have you any idea what Rhodesia's consumption of oil is? Have a guess.'

'I've no idea. But presumably they're on strict rationing –'

'I'll tell you. It's about fifteen thousand barrels a *day*. You reckon that's being convoyed up over the Beit bridge?'

'I don't see how else it's getting in.'

'Christ, Steve, you amaze me! Don't you people ever think about this? What do you do all the time you're bobbing about out there off Beira?'

'Oh, you'd be surprised,' he laughed. 'We have kite competitions. Beard growing competitions. We fire our squid bombs and catch fish. We have open air cinema shows and sods' operas on the flight deck –'

She was suddenly angry. She jumped up and made a shower of sand. 'Don't you realise there's a guerilla war going on in Rhodesia? Haven't you ever heard of ZAPU and ZANU? Don't you realise you're not doing anything to end the Smith regime? Can't you see that if anything this farcical so-called blockade of Beira is prolonging white rule in Rhodesia, not shortening it?' She turned, and faced out to sea. 'You really have no idea, have you? You really think you're doing a great job.'

'I don't see how we can be doing any harm.'

'Okay I'll tell you. These oil sanctions are a massive piece of international deception. They give the world the impression that the UK is trying to stop oil getting to Rhodesia, when the UK is one of Rhodesia's principal suppliers.'

'Don't believe it,' Jannaway said. 'Sorry. But whoever's told you this has given you duff gen –'

'Steve, I *know* it's happening. Shell and BP are shipping crude oil into Lourenço Marques, and it's being railroaded straight into Rhodesia. Mobil and Sonap and Caltex are in on it as well. It's very big business.'

He lay back in the sand, propping himself on one elbow. 'Proof?'

'Yes, that's the trouble. I haven't got any.'

'So how do you know?'

'I was in Lourenço Marques last month. There was … bar talk. And a large tanker called the British Flag unloading. And I took the trouble of spending a night with a particularly objectionable Portuguese who thought it was very funny that the Brits were breaking their own embargo and lining his pockets in the process.' She sat down beside him, sifting sand through her fingers.

He said: 'Jesus.'

'You mean you really didn't know?'

'Well, would I?'

'I'm not so sure. What I'm trying to find out is, does the British

Government know? Does the Foreign Office know? Do the intelligence services know? Because if they don't, they ought to be told.'

'Write your article about it. Send it to the *Guardian* or the *Observer*.'

'I haven't got proof. I haven't got any hard evidence. But I *know* it's happening.'

'Wait a minute, I've just remembered something.' He stared at her. 'We had a feeling they were using Lourenço Marques when the blockade first started. In fact I nearly directed a photo recce mission to take photographs of the railway line.' He held up his hand and showed her a thin white scar on the back of his left hand. 'I got this instead. We rolled overboard by mistake.' He took both her hands and smiled guiltily. 'Now I definitely shouldn't have told you that.'

'So naval intelligence may know something about it.'

He nodded. 'I should think they suspect, at least.'

'They've probably been told not to look too hard. After all, it'd rock the boat, wouldn't it? Maybe HMG wants Ian Smith in charge for the time being.'

'I don't suppose we'll ever know.'

She said nothing for a long time. They sat side by side, watching some surfers trying to make the most of an inadequate swell.

Pippa sighed impatiently. 'Don't you feel you want to do something about it?'

'What can I do?'

She considered a moment: he admired how self-contained she was, how quietly confident in her own ability to think something out and then take action.

'Make a report,' she said. 'You needn't disclose your source. Just say that –'

'Go on.'

'Say that conversation with civilians ashore ... something like this ... indicated that certain British oil companies are deliberately shipping oil to Mozambique in the knowledge that it will be passed on via a South African agency to Rhodesia.' She raised her eyebrows. 'Well you could, couldn't you? At least it might stir someone into trying to prove you wrong. And it isn't just a game, Steve. There are lives at stake as well as livelihoods.'

'I'll think about it.'

She laughed. 'Yes I bet you will. But you won't do anything will you?'

'I might.'

'I wonder. I mean – it might not do the old career much good, might it?'

'Maybe my career isn't quite so important to me as all that.'

She laughed again. 'I'll believe it when I see it.'

They collected together their things and walked back along the beach to the car, stopping at the top of a dune to look back at the surfers.

'I wasn't going to tell you about it you know,' Pippa said.

'So why did you?'

She slipped her hand into his and held it. 'I just had a feeling that you might be the sort of person to take it seriously.'

'Perhaps I am,' he said, and looking down was surprised to see her eyes filling with tears.

'Oh – hell!' she whispered. 'It doesn't often happen does it? But my God, it's bloody painful when it does.'


While the ship was on the Beira Patrol, mail was delivered by RAF Hercules aircraft operating from a temporary base at Majunga, in Malagasy. It was dropped by parachute into the sea and picked up as an evolution, Lasbury manoeuvring the ship and Jannaway lowering the seaboat so that the floating waterproof bags remained in the water for as short a time as possible.

Pippa's first letter arrived after the second week of the patrol, and was handed to Jannaway by Roy Kemble when the officers were having tea in the wardroom.

'Wey-hey, Number One!' he said. 'A letter from La Belle Dame Sans Merci!'

There was also a letter from Julietta, which Steven opened first. It covered two sides and told him very little that he did not already know. 'I gather you'll be having a maintenance period at the end of June,' she wrote. 'Would you object violently if I got myself an indulgence flight out to Singapore then? RSVP, as I have to get the application form to the RAF pretty soon. I hope it won't upset your social programme or anything, but I would like to see the sun again, just for a change, you know.'

He put the letter away without finishing it and opened Pippa's. She had enclosed a photograph of herself which he had taken one afternoon when they had picnicked on Cape Point, and the sight of it caused a flutter of excitement and affection.

388

Steve, love –

No, I don't know what to do about it, either. I read your letter about six times a day – hadn't realised you'd been hit so hard (hadn't realised I'd been either, for that matter). Love's a bleeding soufflé, isn't it? Not easily achieved and so easily collapsed. I'd hate to think I was just a temporary relief in your life, though I suppose, if we're strictly honest that's what we were to each other. And I did *not* enjoy the little simile you made of yourself bouncing obediently like my poor Gonk. You didn't bounce for me did you? You may be a bouncy toy for Lady J, but you are not that to me, so please let us have no more of this ridiculous bouncing.

Pause. Is there *any* hope of us getting together ever in the future? No, you'd better not answer that question. But promise that if ever you see me across a crowded bombshelter you'll come on over and say 'hi'. Also please answer this letter. I can't let go quite yet. Tell me how you are and whether you have done anything about you-know-what. I am terrified that you will have reverted to being the true blue officer, that you weren't the 'real' person I was so sure you were/are. You will do something about it won't you? I can't put much more than that in a letter for obvious reasons . . .

Why does life have to snatch away the best people all the time? I feel lousy all over without you. And I don't care if that does make you feel swollen headed either, I should think you could do with a bit of appreciation, couldn't you? I want you *so much* Steve. I want you here *now*, I want you to walk right in through the door and lift me up and plonk me down and love me all to bits again. Bloody navy! (No, no, we mustn't say that, must we? Beautiful, kind, benevolent, all-wise navy.)

Here's a photo of me – the one that got away. I've blown yours up and have covered it with that Fablon you so kindly pinched for me. I now have you leering cheerfully at me every time I take a shower.

Ah well, Sir Jannaway, I'm not a great dab hand at chatty letters and all I really have to say is that the flame still burns, the torch still glows. If you find me perplexing, don't worry because you were too. It takes a muddle to love a muddle, doesn't it?

Send me snaps of your children will you? Especially Thomas?

Love you always –

Pippa.

He found this letter both moving and frightening. While longing to love Pippa and be loved by her, he shrank from the final betrayal of his family. Her request for a photograph of Thomas in particular, caused an inner scream of protest, and this in itself seemed to be a betrayal, for if he could not bring himself to send Pippa the photographs she had asked for, how could he possibly claim to love her?

The matter of writing an intelligence report on the breaking of oil sanctions had already caused him a lot of thought: at first he had been inclined to let it drop, aware that it might rebound adversely against him. Now, knowing that he had been unfaithful to Julietta and was likely to end his affair with Pippa, he began to view the writing of it as a way of buying back a little of his self-respect, reasoning that it must be his duty as the ship's intelligence officer to report what he had heard, and that if Britain really was breaking her own embargo and the Royal Navy was being used to preserve a front, not to call attention to the fact would amount to a betrayal on a far larger scale.

Late one night, he was called to Lasbury's cabin to discuss what he had written. The ship had been meandering along all day: the whaler had been lowered in the morning for some of the senior rates to go shark fishing, but they had returned hot and sun blistered with little to show for their efforts. In the ops room, the radar plot ratings had spent their day as they spent every other day on the Beira Patrol: laboriously plotting the radar contacts as they crawled up and down off the east coast of Africa and reporting them to the bridge, where a bored officer-of-the-watch sat in the captain's chair sipping cool drinks and whiling away the hours in conversation with anyone who was kind enough to visit him.

In the evening, the officers had rehearsed the skit they were planning to stage for the Sods' Opera, which was due to be held at the end of the week, and when the captain's steward came down to ask the first lieutenant to go up to the captain's cabin, Jannaway was in the middle of a rousing chorus of 'Hand me down that can of beans'.

He excused himself and went up the accommodation ladder, tapping on Lasbury's door before pulling aside the curtain and going in.

Lasbury sat alone in his mess undress, a glass of lime juice at his elbow. He bade Jannaway sit down, offered him a drink, and when the steward had withdrawn took out his keys and opened a drawer in his desk.

'Now then,' he said. 'This intelligence assessment of yours. Are you seriously suggesting that we submit it to MOD? Or is it some sort of joke?'

Steven cradled his glass of brandy in his hands and replied that he had not intended the report to be funny in any way.

'My dear Steven!' Lasbury said, patting his knee. 'What you've implied here is that the Royal Navy has been wasting its time for the past six years!'

'I'm not the first to, sir. Everyone knows this patrol's a farce. I just thought it was about time someone put it in writing, that's all.'

'It may be a farce, I grant you,' Lasbury said. 'But it is a necessary farce, just as the United Nations is a necessary farce. I thought everyone on board this ship appreciated that. In fact I seem to remember your briefing the ship's company on the subject before we even arrived at Simonstown.'

'The point I'm trying to make sir – and I thought I made it in that report – is that by doing this patrol we're actually providing a cover for the shipment of oil to Lourenço Marques. By British tankers, what's more.'

'Yes, I don't believe that for one moment,' Lasbury said. He stood up and went to the scuttle, looking out into the darkness. 'Do you know what I think?' he said after a while.

'No, sir?'

'I think you've been got at, first lieutenant. I think you've been fed a subtle piece of disinformation. And I think you've swallowed it whole.' Lasbury turned back from the scuttle and sighed deliberately. 'Of course that's the drawback of having a weakness for a pretty face, isn't it Number One?'

Jannaway felt a pulse of anger in his stomach. 'This has nothing to do with any pretty face,' he said thickly, and regretted his words immediately. It would have been more dignified to keep silence.

'Come off it, Steve,' Lasbury laughed. 'She had you trailing round after her with your tongue hanging out! Every single member of the ship's company knew very well that the Jimmy was having it off every night. I nearly spoke to you about it, but I don't like making an officer's sex life my business unless he makes it mine. And you have now, haven't you?' He shook the stapled manuscript under Jannaway's nose. 'With this.'

A small loudspeaker crackled for a moment beside Lasbury's desk, and the voice of Lieutenant Delaney said, 'Captain sir, officer-of-the-watch.'

Lasbury dropped the sheets of paper on the coffee table by Jannaway's chair and picked up his microphone. 'Captain?' he said, and Delaney began to report details of a new contact which appeared to be heading for the port of Beira.

Jannaway sat and tried to order the turmoil of anger and resentment Lasbury had already caused. So far, they had made a success of their time as captain and first lieutenant: the ship's inspection had earned Lasbury a glowing report for leading a most efficient, clean and happy ship, and a tithe of this effusion had seeped in Jannaway's direction. A few months before, Lasbury had informed him that apart from a slight shortfall of professional knowledge in operational matters, he was thoroughly satisfied with him and would be recommending him for promotion to commander; but although their relationship had remained cordial, they had not 'clicked' as some naval captains click with their first lieutenants. Jannaway was aware that he was not, and could never be the obedient, loyal and admiring first lieutenant Lasbury had hoped he might be, and there was something about Lasbury's sheer perfection as a naval officer which he only now realised was distasteful. Pippa had called him a 'slithy tove' and he now knew exactly what she meant.

Lasbury had finished his conversation with the officer-of-the-watch and had resumed his seat. He licked his lips and touched the corner of his mouth with his knuckle. 'I suppose you thought you were in love with her, is that it?'

Jannaway clenched his fists instinctively, then deliberately relaxed them. 'Could we confine ourselves to discussing the contents of that report, sir?'

Lasbury lifted one leg over the other and revealed a few inches of black silk sock as he pulled up the leg of his trouser. 'No, I don't think we can. I don't think you appreciate the seriousness of this, Steven. I should think Miss Pippa what's-her-name's had a very good laugh at your expense by now. A lieutenant commander! Falling for a story like that! I should not be in the least bit surprised if your name was now noted in some Kremlin file as an officer who can be very easily persuaded by a pretty face and a pair of tits. Had you thought about that?'

He felt the colour rising to his face.

Lasbury saw, and continued. 'Have you any idea what sort of reaction I'd get from DIS if I forwarded this? Can't you see that it is very much to the Soviet advantage to sow distrust between South Africa and Britain? What if we lost our bunkering facilities at

Simonstown? Wouldn't we look a bit stupid? And isn't this sort of mischief exactly what might bring that about?' He picked up the offending sheets of paper, tore them in two and dropped them into a small sack he kept by his desk for classified waste. 'That's what we'll do with that little piece of subversion,' he said. 'And while we're about it, I think a short signal to Spinoza might be in order.'

He reached for his signal pad and took a silver propelling pencil from his desk. He paused a few moments, licked his lips, then began to write the signal in neat, staff college capitals, glancing at Jannaway before starting the second paragraph.

When he had finished, he surveyed his work and saw that it was good. 'There we are,' he said, and handed the pad over. 'I think that says what we want it to say, doesn't it?'

Jannaway read:

EXCLUSIVE
SECRET

FROM: HMS FLEETWOOD
TO: SENIOR NAVAL OFFICER, SOUTH AFRICA

1. MISS PIPPA LANE, GUEST AT MY COCKTAIL PARTY IN SIMONSTOWN 12 FEB 72 APPEARS TO HAVE USED INTRODUCTION TO PROPAGATE SUBVERSIVE DISINFORMATION CONCERNING CURRENT OPERATIONS.
2. RECOMMEND COMMANDING OFFICERS OF SHIPS VISITING SIMONSTOWN BE MADE AWARE OF THIS WOMAN'S ACTIVITIES, AND THAT LANE BE EXCLUDED FROM GUEST LISTS IN FUTURE.

Jannaway looked up and returned Lasbury's harebell gaze.

'It's for your own good, Steven,' Lasbury said quietly. 'And I say that both as your commanding officer and as a friend of the family. I suggest you regard this whole episode as a very useful lesson. Fair?'

For a moment, Jannaway was tempted to retaliate – either in verbal abuse or physical violence. What sweet relief it would be to call Lasbury a 'slimy bastard' and slam a fist into that bland, condescending face, but also what foolishness! Eighteen years in the service had taught him that such puny displays of insubordination were quickly crushed by the weight of the Naval Discipline Act.

Suddenly he saw that he had never truly belonged to this navy of cultivated leadership and scrambling ambition; that he had joined for naïve, idealistic reasons, and that the last thing he wanted to be was an admiral.

He stood up, and the dam burst. 'I wrote that report because I genuinely believed that this embargo is being broken by British oil companies,' he said. 'I wrote it because I believed it was my duty to write it, because I thought the navy would not want to be part of this sort of deceit. I'm prepared to accept your criticism of my personal behaviour, but I don't accept that I was "got at" and it disappoints me that you have such a low opinion of my judgement.' He crossed to the door. 'That signal is a misrepresentation and a libel,' he said finally, and went out onto the deck, where he stared westward at the lights of Beira, wondering at the emptiness and futility of his life as the ship steamed slowly on through the night.

# 22

Julietta and several other wives of officers and men serving in HMS *Fleetwood* flew out to Singapore three weeks later. Eighteen hours after taking off from Brize Norton (which one wife explained stood for 'Be Ready In Zealous Expectation, Nickers Off Ready To Open Nees') they stepped out into the humid heat of Paya Lebar airport and braced themselves to meet their men.

Julietta was well prepared. She had spent a day in Knightsbridge and had kitted herself out with new dresses, shirts, jeans, bikinis, sandals and a pair of sunglasses with rose-coloured frames which, if you looked at her quickly and half closed your eyes, made her look like a Nabokov nymphet.

She had chosen tight red jeans and a cheesecloth shirt in which to arrive, and as she emerged from the customs hall she spotted Steven before he saw her.

He turned, and she looked quickly away to delay the moment of mutual recognition. Now that she had actually seen him, she felt that she would have been quite happy to get back on the plane and go somewhere else. She pushed her trolley of luggage out into the arrivals hall, aware of him striding towards her, and feigned surprise when it was no longer possible to ignore him.

He had hired a Mercedes coupé of which he seemed rather proud. 'I think we'll be all right to have the hood down,' he said, and glanced southward at the line of clouds over Sumatra. 'We don't usually get the storm until about four.' He packed her suitcases into the boot, kissed her again, opened the passenger door for her, insisted that she fasten the safety strap, and drove off.

'Right, I expect you'd like to know what the programme is, wouldn't you?' he said. 'Well Peter hands over to the new captain at the end of this week, but he's taking four days off before that so I'll have to be temporary acting unpaid captain while he's away. Then as soon as the new captain arrives, I leave them to it, and we can take off somewhere. I've wangled six days' station leave, so we might be able to get up to Penang. How does that grab you?'

'Super!' she said. 'Anything you like!'

He drove fast down the Thomson road through Nee Soon and on to Chong Pang. She had been in Singapore when she was six years old, but could remember very little of it. They hurtled along, overtaking an elderly woman pulling a handcart, narrowly missing a head-on collision with a green city taxi, screeching to a halt as a crocodile of neat, blue and white uniformed schoolgirls wound its way across the road. 'Do we have to drive quite so fast?' she asked, after an exchange of horn-blaring with a lorry that refused to move over.

He grinned. 'It's the quick and the dead in this place. You're either quick or you're dead.'

They slowed, entering Sembawang village. Smoke billowed up from foodstalls, and pop music jangled from loudspeakers. They turned right, off the main road, and bumped over a track to a small bungalow. 'Well this is it,' Steven said. 'I thought we could park your stuff first, and then go down to the Terror Club for a bite of lunch, okay?'

A girl of eighteen or so opened the front door to them. 'This is Annie,' Steven said. 'The amah. You speak excellent English, don't you Annie?'

'Yes please,' Annie said. 'Okay?'

Steven carried the luggage into the bedroom. A fan idled round overhead, and sunlight seeped in through venetian blinds. There was a smell of fresh fly spray.

'Okay, I go now,' Annie announced. 'Okay?'

'Okay,' Steven said, unable to refrain from using a slight sing-song intonation himself. 'Come late tomorrow, okay? Late. Not early.'

Annie laughed a clear, tinkling laugh. 'Okay. Late tomollow.'

The door closed behind her. Julietta looked round the bare little room. A pink house lizard scrambled quickly up the wall behind the bed and clung motionless, upside down, to the ceiling. 'That's a chik-chak,' Steven said. 'Nothing to worry about. They're supposed to be good luck.'

'I know. I have been here before.'

'Sorry.'

They stood on opposite sides of the bed. 'Well,' he said. 'Shall we go to the pool? Or do you want to rest for a bit?'

'Rest? Why should I want to rest?'

'Isn't it six-thirty in the morning for you still?' He smiled apologetically, the way he had so often smiled, the way she hated. She opened a suitcase and took out a towel and a bikini. She filled her leather cigarette case and set out her cosmetics on the dressing table. She brushed her dark, bobbed hair rapidly, and retouched her lipstick. While she was doing so, he came and stood behind her. He placed his hands on her shoulders. She finished her face, looked sideways at herself to the left and to the right, and stood up.

'Hullo,' he said.

She said hullo back, but in a different way. He gazed at her with dog-like eyes.

'It's wonderful to have you out here.'

She gave a little snort. 'Is it?'

'Juju. Come on. Try a little.' He took her hands. 'Would you like to make love?'

'Now?'

'No time like the present.'

'I've just done my face! Couldn't you have thought of it a bit sooner?'

He let go of her hands. 'Just a thought. Sorry.'

'Oh – come on, then, I don't mind.'

'No,' he said quickly. 'Not as a duty.'

She laughed. 'Well that's why you asked me in the first place wasn't it? As a duty?'

'Christ!' he said. 'Christ! How did we get into this?' He shook his head. 'Okay. Forget it. Let's go to the pool.'

Singapore had been undergoing radical changes in the previous year: in October 152 years of British military presence – ignominiously broken by the Japanese occupation – had come to an end, and the once busy naval base was now in use as a commercial dockyard where Soviet merchant ships were frequent customers; only a small corner of the base was now available for the repair and maintenance of warships, and the accommodation blocks, clubs and swimming pools that had once been part of a naval shore establishment known as HMS *Terror* had been taken over and renamed by the allied forces of ANZUK – Australia, New Zealand and the United Kingdom.

The Terror officers' club, as it was still known, was situated on the north coast of the island, overlooking the Johore Strait. It consisted of a large clubhouse with bars, restaurant, kitchens and changing rooms, two swimming pools, one for adults and one for paddling toddlers, a steak bar, golf course and wide expanse of paving where officers with nothing better to do sat at tables and whiled away the afternoons with their wives or mistresses. Here, day after day, the bulbuls chirruped in the palm trees and time went lazily by. Chits were written for steak sandwiches and Pimms No.1, and Singaporean waiters ambled to and fro between the clubhouse and the tables by the pool. In the evenings, there were dances or open air cinema shows; when a big ship arrived the bar would fill with loud, heavy drinking lieutenants, and the school-teachers and nurses would be put into a frenzy by the influx of fresh male faces. Marriages would be made, and marriages would be broken; Tiger beer was drunk in large quantities, and at the end of the evening the pent-up aggression, fuelled by too much beer and not enough women, was sometimes released in an outburst of violence. An officer would appear in his ship with a black eye at breakfast the following morning, or a brand new suit, hand made by the tailor in Nee Soon, would be ruined when its owner was thrown into the pool.

When Steven and Julietta arrived at the poolside, several of the officers of HMS *Fleetwood* were already established round tables, having finished work on board the ship at midday. They had had their first swim, and pools of chlorinated water were forming under their chairs. The wife of the engineer officer, an intellectual looking person who had flown out with her three daughters, all under five, was lying face up on a click-click bed; Melanie Kemble, Roy's wife, had come straight to the club with him and was dabbing Ambre Solaire on her shoulders. Two Third Officer Wrens were being entertained by the flight commander and the navigating officer, and Peter Lasbury lay on a golden towel, his panther glistening as it dried in the sun.

Julietta had changed into a lamé bikini. She caused a few curious glances as she walked across to join the *Fleetwood* group, and was conscious of her white skin, her Caesarean scar and a vague hostility in the manner of some of the officers which she could not understand – unaware that wives east of Suez were among the least popular of individuals among married officers because of their habit of seeing too much and reporting back to the wives at home.

There were a lot of introductions. Peter Lasbury rolled over, opened his eyes, got to his feet and kissed her on both cheeks.

Steven found a chair for her and other officers moved theirs to make room. She had slept for little more than three hours in the previous twenty-four, and their voices seemed far away.

The sun beat down. She agreed to a steak sandwich and a glass of fresh lime. Peter lowered his weight into a chair beside her. A pair of orioles swooped overhead, and the officers sprawled in their chairs, their knees apart, their Tigers close at hand.

Julietta had not been surrounded by so much masculine thigh and torso for a long time. Suddenly she saw that she might enjoy her holiday more than she had expected to. Steven arrived with the steaks from the self-service bar. Meonford, Hampshire, Business, her children and her friend Virginia seemed to exist in a separate world.

She gave a little sigh, arching her back sensuously and spreading her arms out over the sides of her deck chair, so that the tip of her little finger accidentally touched Peter's shoulder.

'This is bliss,' she murmured. 'Sheer bliss.'

But it was not bliss. Something had gone wrong, and she didn't know what it was. Steven was much quieter: he talked of 'trying to get close again' but there was no magic left in their lovemaking which somehow managed to turn into a chore. She saw far less of Peter than she would have liked, too: he was busy preparing to hand over his command, and she guessed that he was worried about promotion. Julietta began to feel restless.

'I feel like a spare prick at a wedding,' she told Steven. 'I mean you don't want me here at all, do you? I'm just getting in the way. What is it, am I fouling your pitch? Are you madly in love with someone else or something?'

He shook his head. 'No. I'm not in love.'

She laughed. 'No, you bloody well aren't, are you? Not with me, anyway.'

She was lying under a single sheet: it was her third day in Singapore, and Steven was about to leave for his morning's work on board before meeting her – yet again – for lunch at the Terror club. He picked up a battered brief case and a Chinese umbrella he called his Wan Chai Burberry. 'See you about midday then,' he said, and bent to kiss her.

She turned her face away impatiently.

'What's wrong with you?' he asked.

'Nothing's wrong with me. I'm bored, that's all. I'm bored with this smelly little village. I'm bored with being treated by you as a sort of bloody nuisance.'

He stood by the double bed looking down at her. 'It does take two, doesn't it? I am trying.'

'Funny sort of bloody trying!'

'Do you have to use the word "bloody" in every single sentence?'

'Why? Does it offend you? Your lily white conscience?'

He went to the door, looked back a moment and repeated, 'I'll see you about midday.'

'Don't bet on it!' she called after him.

She got up an hour later, padding about with a sarong round her waist while she made herself a cup of coffee and cut a slice of papaya. The door bell rang: she hoisted her sarong up over her breasts and opened it to Annie, who set about flooding the bungalow in half an inch of water before scrubbing the floors. They carried on a conversation in pidgin English. 'Tree chidren,' Annie said. 'Okay. Annie like chidren a lok.'

She put on a dress and walked out into the heat of the day. She wandered along by the roadside stalls where smoke billowed from charcoal kitchens and music jangled and blared from the shop that sold pirated tape recordings. She browsed in a book stall and came across a book in a plain white cover. She read a few pages at random while a sleepy Tamil regarded her and tapped a sandalled foot to the music from his transistor radio.

'I'll take this one,' she said, and handed over five dollars, meeting the Tamil's eyes defiantly, telling herself that she didn't care if he did despise her: if she couldn't get any satisfaction out of Steven, she might as well get some out of a book.

She wandered about, pausing to watch an elderly Chinese couple doing slow motion eurhythmics under a flame tree.

She went to a stall and ordered a cup of tea. She sat down at the rough table, noticing a dead rat in the monsoon ditch at her feet, and began to read her book. She had never read one of these books before and she found herself becoming impatient when a paragraph of commonplace description held up the action. When she had finished it, she took it back to the stall where she had bought it and dropped it on the pile. 'You can have this one back,' she said. 'It's no good at all.'

She walked out, not bothering to ask for her money back. It was time to go down to the Terror pool – at least, it wasn't time to go there, but it wasn't time to do anything else. She summoned a taxi, and it rattled her down the hill to the ANZUK gates.

She was early. She changed into a white bikini, which flattered her newly acquired suntan. She sauntered out among the empty tables, glancing about at the few people who had already arrived.

'As I live and breathe,' a familiar voice said behind her. 'It's the fair Julietta!'

It was Chas Tomkins, sleek, bronzed and muscular in a pair of swimming trunks that laced up at the sides. 'Chas!' she said. 'What a surprise! I didn't realise you were in Singapore!'

'Nor did we until yesterday evening,' he said. He led the way to the other side of the pool, where half a dozen officers lounged about or lay on towels. 'We graunched our boat,' Tomkins explained. 'Awfully boring because we were due in Bangkok tomorrow and now we're stuck in Singers for a week. Can I get you a noggin?'

She hadn't met Chas for ages, but she had heard about his divorce. People said that he had beaten his wife but she didn't really believe that and anyway, she thought to herself, if he had, the silly cow had probably deserved it.

Chas Tomkins's wardroom officers were a livelier bunch than Steven's. They dressed outrageously in batik shirts and stripey trousers and were quite convinced that HMS *Persephone* was the finest ship in the fleet. Because of their unscheduled stop in Singapore, they were untrammelled by the inconvenience of having to entertain their wives and felt at liberty to commandeer any nurse, schoolteacher, embassy secretary or visiting daughter they could lay their hands on. They threw each other in the pool; they did spectacular dives off the top board; they tore around the island in a large, jointly owned Cadillac, and they sat in the back row during the open air cinema shows at the club, making risqué remarks.

The day after HMS *Persephone* put in for repairs was a Friday, the all-important thirtieth of June. This was the day on which the half-yearly promotions were announced, and to take people's minds off the subject Peter Lasbury had suggested a water skiing banyan on the Johore Strait. Jannaway was directed to borrow one of the last remaining picket boats in the Far East for the afternoon, and Roy Kemble ordered the petty officer steward to arrange a dozen chicken salads. Duty-free drink was smuggled off the ship and loaded aboard the picket boat at the Terror landing stage, and the party set off in company with a hired ski boat at about noon.

Julietta had invited Chas to come on this floating picnic at the last moment, without referring to Steven first, and the matter had caused one of their frosty little arguments in which Jannaway had pointed out that it was good manners to ask the host before inviting a guest and Julietta had apologised with all the searing sarcasm at her command.

The ski boat broke down after half an hour and the afternoon was swelteringly hot. Steven and Julietta managed to keep at opposite ends of the boat, while Tomkins began making increasingly blatant overtures to Julietta as the boat proceeded down the strait with Singapore island to starboard and the Malay mainland to port.

Everyone was disappointed at not being able to ski, but then the flight commander, rummaging in the stern locker, came upon an old aquaplaning board, which was quickly fitted out with a tow line and put into use.

Julietta stood on the bridge of the picket boat and watched the goings on with disdain. She couldn't help comparing this picnic with a picnic almost exactly twelve years before, in her father's barge. How much had changed in those twelve years! She remembered the dazzling white decks, the polished brass, the fancy ropework and the smart Maltese crew; she looked across the strait at the old naval base and compared the two frigates berthed in the basin – one elderly and the other broken – with the proud grey destroyers that used to lie in Sliema Creek; she looked at the shabby decks of this picket boat and listened to these Grockle naval officers talking to their Grockle wives, who were actually getting excited about being pulled through the water on an old board when she had skimmed along on skis.

'Ah there you are!' Chas said, coming up to the bridge. He had a hard, hairless chest which she found extremely attractive: his skin was tanned to a deep copper colour and his swimming trunks left nothing of great importance to the imagination.

She turned away from him and lifted her face to catch some of the breeze made by the boat's forward speed. He stood behind her so that his body just touched hers. He had been signalling to her on every possible occasion since they had met at the pool the day before: the tropical heat, her difficulties with Steven and the contents of the book she had read the previous day had combined to make Chas's approaches extremely attractive. She didn't move away therefore, and a moment later felt his finger push inside the back of her bikini bottom. 'We might get it together one of these days don't you think?' he said, his chin over her shoulder, and in reply she pushed back against him and moved gently from side to side, until he found it necessary to take a running leap off the picket boat and, surfacing some yards off, to bellow, 'Man overboard!'

They anchored the picket boat at the end of Seletar island and sat on a small beach to eat their picnic. Julietta and Chas pretended to ignore each other, but neither were in any doubt of the other's intentions. On the way back to the Terror landing stage, he said casually, 'I could come up to your place tomorrow morning if you like,' and she replied, 'That would be nice. I'll give you a cup of tea or something.' He smiled and said, 'Or something,' and moved away.

As they approached the landing stage, they saw that Lieutenant Arborfield was awaiting their return. He held in his hand a lengthy piece of teleprinter paper. 'Oh my God he's got the signal,' Kemble said, and from then until the picket boat went alongside no one said a word.

Lasbury stepped off the boat first. He acknowledged Arborfield's crisp salute and took the signal from him, looking more like a wealthy tourist in his Bermudan shorts and flower-power shirt than a naval commander. He studied the signal for some seconds before looking up. 'Chas!' he said.

Tomkins had been making the stern rope fast. 'Sir?'

Lasbury handed him the signal. 'This may interest you.'

Tomkins took the signal and a moment later began to laugh. 'I don't believe it!' he said, and laughed louder. 'I don't bloody believe it!' He clenched his fists and shook them at the heavens in joy.

The news broke: Peter Lasbury had been selected for promotion to captain, and Tomkins to commander.

Julietta was almost overcome. She couldn't decide who to kiss first. 'Wonderful!' she kept saying. 'Simply wonderful!'

'What would you say,' Tomkins asked Lasbury. 'One crate of champagne or two?'

'Two, I think, don't you?'

'Each!' said Tomkins.

They set out in a group, up the path towards the club, Julietta walking between her two favourite men, in love with the gentle

403

hugeness of Peter Lasbury and in lust with the bulging muscularity of Chas Tomkins.

Jannaway remained behind to lock up the picket boat, collect a few empty beer cans that had been left in the after cabin, and return the keys to the boat shed.

He had known already that he would not be selected for promotion: Lasbury had informed him, after the incident during the Beira Patrol, that he was no longer prepared to recommend him; but in spite of this foreknowledge, he could not help feeling let down. He had guessed that something was brewing between Julietta and Tomkins, and however hard he tried to separate his feelings of jealousy from his loyalty to the service, he could not help feeling that the navy had been in some way devalued, telling himself (as so many officers before him had told themselves) that if that was the sort of person who achieved early promotion there might be some consolation in the fact that he had not been promoted himself.

The celebration started quietly enough at about seven o'clock when Peter, Chas, Julietta and Steven met in the Terror club bar to open the first bottles of champagne. The officers of *Fleetwood* and *Persephone* arrived in twos and threes, raising their glasses to toast Lasbury and Tomkins with a certain reverence, as if they had been recently beatified or had metamorphosed into a higher life form.

Julietta twiddled her glass back and forth, turning her back on Steven in order to exclude him from her conversation with Lasbury. 'Well Peter, what next? Do you know what your next job is?'

Lasbury presumed that it would be the Ministry of Defence. 'That's where they send the baby captains usually,' he said.

Julietta moved her bottom from side to side in one of her excited wiggles. 'Oh that'll be super,' she said. 'I shall come up to town and we can have nice lazy lunches together.'

'I don't expect I'll have much time for lazy lunches,' he laughed.

He was beginning to think it was time to leave Julietta behind. She had served her purpose as the reason why he had never married, and as her marriage to Steven looked as though it might be going wrong, he was anxious not to be associated with her in any way that might lead people to suspect him as the cause.

'Anyway now you can relax, can't you?' she was saying. 'I mean maybe we'll see something of you this weekend for a change?'

'No, I'm off at crack of dawn tomorrow, and I'll be pretty busy with the hand-over to Mike Cobbold when I get back on Wednesday.'

'You mean you're going away? Where for God's sake?'

'I told you about that,' Steven said. 'If you remember.'

'I'm going to go and contemplate the turtles,' Lasbury said. 'Have a real break.'

Tomkins breezed up with more champagne. He had put on a pair of sky blue trousers and was wearing a loud batik tie. 'Come on, folks, drink up! This is a celebration, not a bloody conference!'

'Chas what a perfectly spectacular tie!' Julietta said. 'It's a kipper, isn't it? You really do pick them, don't you?'

Tomkins flashed his smile and fingered the symbolic object of her admiration. 'We're all going to get smashed tonight, by order. Isn't that right, Steve?'

Jannaway managed a laugh. 'Not so sure about that,' he said.

'Our Steven is being very boring this evening, aren't you Steven?' Julietta put on a capable nanny voice. 'I think we've got a touch of the green eyed monsters, haven't we dear?'

The party gathered momentum. The bar filled to capacity and the temperature rose quickly into the nineties. The champagne gave way to Tiger beer, and towards eleven o'clock, when there had been a minor scuffle between some of the younger officers from the two ships, Tomkins leapt on a table. 'Everyone to Bugis Street!' he announced, and there was a rush to commandeer taxis and get to the car park.

'This is where I bow out,' Lasbury said. 'I'm getting an early night. You're happy are you Number One? Got the weight?'

'Affirmative, sir,' Jannaway said.

Julietta kissed Lasbury warmly on the mouth. 'Many many many congratulations again, darling,' she said, not caring any longer what Steven or anyone else thought.

The officers of HMS *Persephone* were cramming into the white Cadillac, which was to be driven by their captain, a senior commander who had already been passed over for promotion. Julietta ran across. 'Room for a small one?' she asked.

She was pursued by Steven. 'It's a stag party,' he told her. 'You can't go.'

'Bugger that!' she said. 'Just watch me.'

In the back of the Cadillac, Chas Tomkins pretended to be unaware of the marital argument going on outside, but he saw

Steven take Julietta's arm, and Julietta snatch it away; and then Julietta launched herself into the back and settled herself on his knee, and while the car sped out of Sembawang and across the island to the city, he shifted her weight carefully onto his hand, and returned the compliment she had paid him that afternoon.

The people of Bugis Street recognised an officers' celebration when they saw one, and as the cars and taxis arrived and the British spilled out into the road, the food stall owners, the street vendors, the violinists, photographers and beggar boys – as well as the drug pushers, whores, catamites, pickpockets, pimps and purveyors of blue films – braced themselves for an evening of brisk business.

Tomkins led the way between the jumble of tables that filled the street, and his officers chortled to each other, mimicking the pidgin English of the Chinese to each other and saying 'Ah, so!' They inspected the food stalls and prodded the fruit, brushing aside the hag who clutched at them and offered them a short time.

Julietta had heard of Bugis Street but had never visited it. Now that she was here, and as far as she could see the only white woman, she was anxious not to get lost and stuck close to Chas, feeling a mixture of guilt at walking out on Steven, nausea from the motion of the car and sexual excitement at what had happened on the journey.

They sat down at the round metal tables and a Chinese brought an armful of Tiger, setting a bottle and a glass down before each customer. Julietta accepted a challenge to play noughts and crosses for half dollar stakes with a small boy who crouched by her chair with a small blackboard and a fistful of chalk. 'How does he do it?' she laughed. 'I've lost three dollars fifty already!'

An older youth was whispering in Tomkins's ear. Tomkins leant back in his chair and said loudly, 'No thank you kindly, I do not require a blue movie, exhibish, massage or short time.'

The transvestites appeared. 'You mean that's a *man*?' Julietta asked Tomkins, looking across at a particularly seductive specimen.

'It's a catamite,' he told her.

'Aren't they well named?' Julietta said earnestly. 'I mean even tom cats look female, don't they?'

They ordered their shark's fin soup, their egg rolls, their sweet and sour pork and their fried rice. While they ate, an ancient Chinese with a long grey wisp of a beard came to their table and

406

performed what he called a 'Hong Kong Oppla,' his voice wavering up and down the scale as he accompanied himself on a one stringed violin. 'You give me money for pot?' he whispered urgently when the applause was over, and limped away to try his luck elsewhere.

'Don't look now,' Julietta said to Chas when they were finishing their meal, 'But here's my ever-so-boring husband.'

They looked across the sea of tables. Jannaway was standing by himself at the head of the street, obviously searching for them. He spotted them and came across. He made an effort to be jovial, but was clearly soberer than anyone else.

'Lost my city road map!' he said. 'Took me half an hour to find this place.'

'Bloody typical,' Julietta said.

'Can I squeeze in?' he asked, bringing a chair. He made room between her and one of the *Persephone* officers so that she was between him and Chas. He caught her eye and smiled a little apologetically. Part of her wanted to respond but another part felt impatient with him.

'I've come to look after you,' he mumbled.

'I was perfectly all right on my own,' she replied.

They were interrupted by the sound of singing. A crowd of ratings from *Fleetwood* had arrived. They weren't in uniform (ratings seldom wore uniform ashore these days) but Julietta could tell they were ratings by the sort of shirts they wore, the tattoos on some of their arms and the cheery, half-insubordinate way they greeted their officers. 'Evening, sirs!' one shouted, and another did a recognisable impersonation of Lasbury by saying, 'Hello Number One!'

Julietta never knew how to treat ratings. They were like another species to her, and she usually found it easier to ignore them.

This crowd was difficult to ignore: the fo'c's'le petty officer of HMS *Fleetwood* was due to fly back to England before leaving the navy a month later, and they were giving him his last run ashore. He was a stocky man from Devon, one of the last of the old salts, with a lot of memories to take back to his wife and his terraced house in Bideford. He stood on his table and announced to the entire street that the drinks were on him, so everyone cheered and banged their fists on the tables and sang the Oggy song:

Half a pound of flour and rice
Makes lovely clacker
Just enough for you and me
Oh, bugger Janner!
So we'll all go back to Oggy land,
To Oggy land,
To Oggy land,
So we'll all go back to Oggy land,
Where they can't tell arse from
Tissue paper, tissue paper,
Marmalade and jam.

The petty officer was persuaded to sit down after this and have his photograph taken in company with two of the transvestites who hung about like sleek leopards waiting to pounce.

'Why don't we do that?' Julietta said when she saw what was going on. 'Come on, Chas, have your picture taken!' She turned to Steven. 'Go and ask that one to come over!'

'I'm not asking that creature to do anything,' he said.

'God, you are a bore, aren't you? You really are!'

He shrugged. 'It's the way I'm made. Sorry.' He lowered his voice. 'Do you really want to have your photograph taken in the company of a transvestite? These people aren't glamorous. They're sick.'

'Why don't you piss off back to your little bungalow,' she said, and turned away from him while Tomkins posed for a photograph with a young man who draped himself over his shoulders and pouted seductively as the flash bulb exploded.

The glasses were replenished with more Tiger, and at the adjoining tables the old petty officer climbed up on his table again to perform. He danced a jerky parody of The Stripper, undoing his shirt buttons one by one and coyly revealing a glimpse of a hairy, black nipple, writhing his muscle-knotted stomach to the whistles and cheers of his messmates. Urged on, he began to unbuckle his leather belt. His trousers dropped suddenly to his ankles and he stood there in the middle of Bugis Street, swaying slightly and drinking Tiger from the bottle, clad only in a long, baggy pair of service issue underpants. Then, while the assembled officers and ratings gave a mass rendering of the sunset bugle call, he lowered this garment slowly to his knees, and Julietta pretended she wasn't looking as his humble glory was revealed.

After that, when the petty officer had pulled up his trousers and got down from the table, Chas Tomkins led them all in 'Bread of Heaven' and 'Life Presents a Dismal Picture', ending with repeated choruses of 'Land of Hope and Glory' which whipped up a drunken fury of patriotism among the singers, who swung their glasses of beer from side to side with such fervour that Julietta felt a great swelling of pride in the knowledge that she was part of so fine a tradition.

She awoke to the sound of the front door closing, and for a moment didn't know where she was. Then her headache, her dry mouth and her feeling of nausea brought back the taste of those last brandies she had had at the end of the party in Bugis Street, and she remembered everything. She lay curled up in a foetal position, sucking her thumb and squeezing her hand between her thighs. It had been the brandy that had caused the trouble, almost certainly. She had wanted to travel back with Chas but Steven had insisted she go back to the bungalow with him. There had been a public argument between them, there in the street with the Chinese looking silently on, and it had ended when Steven had dragged her away by the arm. They had driven back in silence, and in the bungalow, with the refrigerator vibrating noisily in the kitchen and a tok-tok bird punctuating his sentences, he had told her she was his wife and that he happened to believe in trying to keep their marriage intact. He had appealed to her and like a bloody fool she had given in to him and wept on his shoulder; they had begun to make love and because of everything that had happened that day, and the things she had read in that book and what it said in the *Sensual Woman* and the fact that she had done it once, a very long time ago, with David, she had rolled over and asked him to take her 'the other way', that's what she had said, and he had leapt off the bed looking sanctimonious in the way he could sometimes, saying that that was something he would never be prepared to do; he had taken his pillow and gone to sleep on the sofa in the living room and she had wept a little because everything was in such a mess: she had wept, aching inside for Chas or Peter or anyone at all, and the light had crept into the room, the bulbuls had started, and gradually she had fallen asleep.

Tomkins was in the changing room when Jannaway entered.

'Steve!' he said, being deliberately hearty. 'How are you today?'

'I'm fine,' Jannaway said. 'I didn't drink as much as some people last night.'

Tomkins stepped into his swimming trunks and laced up the side. 'I think Juju was just a *touche* sloshed, wasn't she?'

'Was she? Maybe.'

Tomkins lowered his voice. 'Look, sport, I hope there are no hard feelings? I mean – it was nothing to do with me, you know. I didn't invite her along, she invited herself.'

Jannaway turned away to hang up his shirt. 'Quite all right,' he said. 'No hard feelings.'

'Glad about that,' Tomkins said, and flinging his towel over his shoulder, sauntered into the sunlight.

Outside, he was faced with a decision. Julietta was lying on a sunbed by herself, looking delicious in a one-piece bathing suit and a pair of dark glasses, and he was either going to have to ignore her and go and sit with his officers, or brazen things out, pretend all was well and speak to her. It was all a bit awkward, but he decided it might look worse to ignore her, so he strolled over and pulled up a chair.

'Good morning,' he started.

She rolled over. 'Is it? Some nasty little brat has crapped in the pool.'

'Thought things were a bit quiet. What about you? Did you get a hard time last night?'

She lifted her head, scanned the surrounding tables, then lowered it again. 'No comment.'

'So things aren't exactly sweetness and light, eh?'

She didn't answer that, but asked instead, 'Why didn't you come and see me this morning?'

'Were you expecting me?'

'You did say you'd drop in, didn't you?'

'Yes, well.' He put his hands together between his knees and looked at them. 'It's all getting a bit dodgy, isn't it? I mean I've got a lot to lose, haven't I? Hell hath no fury like a passed over two-and-a-half.'

'He's not passed over yet.'

'You know what I mean.'

'So you're saying... the party's over.'

'I think so. Don't you?'

'Bastard.'

'You sound like my ex-wife,' he said and then, glancing across at the clubhouse, added: 'Uh-oh. Stand by your beds. Here comes your old pot and pan.'

The afternoon dragged slowly by. Julietta lay on her sunbed and Steven sat at a table beside her. The Malay waiters ambled to and fro, the children hurled themselves from the springboard, the sun beat mercilessly down, and a turbanned Sikh called people to the telephone over the loudspeakers in a mournful voice.

'Don't you want to improve things between us?' he asked.

'Yes of course I do.'

'All right then. Let's try. Shall we?'

'You have said that four times in ten minutes! Okay, if you want to, we'll try. I've got the message. Happy?'

He returned to his book, moving his chair round to keep in the shade of the parasol.

'You talk about trying,' Julietta said. 'You weren't trying very hard last night.'

'I thought I explained. I'm not prepared –'

'I don't mean that. I mean yesterday. In the bar here. And after. Talk about "life presents a dismal picture". You were wandering round like a ghost.'

'Do you think it was easy for me? Seeing you slobbering over Chas? And Peter for that matter?'

'I didn't slobber over anyone. Aren't I allowed to congratulate my friends when they get themselves promoted, or are you so choked on your sour grapes –'

'This has nothing to do with promotion.'

'This has everything to do with promotion, Clotface.'

'I may just hit you one of these days when you call me that.'

'I should be so bloody lucky!'

They were silent for a few moments. On the other side of the pool, a group of *Fleetwood* officers glanced across at them.

'Listen,' Steven said. 'We've got another ten days together. Everyone knows what's going on. Couldn't we at least put on a pretence of enjoying ourselves? Couldn't we at least try to sort ourselves out?'

She stretched a little and rolled onto her back. 'I don't give a shit,' she said.

411

'No, you may not. But I do.' He stopped, sighing deeply and putting his head in his hands. 'Can we stop this, Juju? Please?'

She was about to reply when the Sikh's lugubrious voice boomed out over the pool. 'Lieutenant Commander Jannaway, sir, please. Telephone. Lieutenant Commander Jannaway.'

She watched him walk away in his tartan swimming shorts, glad to be rid of him if for only a few minutes. This bickering was very draining: she would have liked to have stopped it, but it seemed to carry its own momentum. She was tired of his condescending way of talking down to her like a schoolgirl, tired of his repeated pleas to make a fresh start. She didn't want a fresh start, not with him at any rate, not after what happened last night. Everything was such a mess now between them that the only thing to do was throw it all away and start again.

He was coming back. He looked as if he had had some sort of argument. She watched him covertly from behind her sunglasses. My God, he looks miserable! she thought. Why can't he relax a bit?

'What's happened. Has the ship sunk?'

He stood by the white table and shook his head.

'What then?'

He looked down at her then away. 'It was a telegram from Alan,' he said. 'My mother's had a stroke. He's asking me to come home.'

It always annoyed her that he referred to that grotty little house in Mill Hill East as 'home'.

She sat up and took off her sunglasses.

'Sweetie,' she said. 'I am sorry. When will you go?'

It wasn't as simple as Julietta had presumed. Steven was in temporary command of the ship, and considered it necessary to recall Lasbury from his east coast tour before departing. Lasbury had stated, before taking his leave, that in an emergency he could be contacted by ringing the various government rest houses. Accordingly, Christopher Arborfield was set the task of ringing these establishments in turn.

He was not successful. None of the government rest houses he managed to contact knew anything of Commander Lasbury, and two appeared to have telephones that were out of order.

Jannaway became increasingly aggravated. He consulted the Defence Council Instructions concerning the granting of compassionate leave, and found that in the case of an elder brother being

412

present at home it was not obligatory to grant leave, nor was it likely that the crown would meet the cost of a compassionate flight back to the United Kingdom. He was also in the awkward position of having to judge his own case. If he had been dealing with a junior rating whose mother was dying, there would have been no question about whether he should be flown home: he would have been put on the first available plane. The chief of staff to the ANZUK commander was not of great help when consulted, either: 'Your decision, fella,' he said, dangling his Australian legs into the pool. 'But if the ship blows up while you're away, don't ask me to defend you at your court-martial.'

Julietta lay on her sunbed while he went to and fro, finding out the times of flights from Paya Lebar, booking an international call to his brother and discussing with the engineer officer the possibility of his taking over temporary command.

'Why don't you just go?' she asked. 'I mean is it really likely that anything'll happen? Can't you just risk it?'

'I am responsible,' he said. 'Perhaps you wouldn't understand that. And anyway, this could rebound on Peter. If this were a real emergency, all hell would have been let loose by now.'

'For God's sake! He's almost certainly lying on a beach somewhere! The poor man's supposed to be having a holiday!'

He was called to the telephone again. When he returned, he sat down at the table, looking suddenly old and tired.

'That was my call to UK,' he said. 'She's in and out of a coma. She may last a week and she may go tonight. They can't say either way.'

The afternoon was almost over: the sunbathers were leaving the pool surrounds, to shower and change before returning to the club bar. Julietta sat up on her sunbed and took off her dark glasses.

'So now what?'

'There are spare seats on the Cathay Pacific flight at twenty-two hundred. I told Alan we'd take them.'

'We?'

A single oriole flew low over the pool, and a moment later began its oily smooth call from a nearby tree.

'Don't you want to come then?'

She gave a little laugh, examining her painted toenails. 'I presumed you'd want to go on your own.'

He watched her for a few seconds. 'I presumed you'd want to come.'

'What about Peter?'

He shrugged. 'I've decided I must risk that. Bob Pangbourne's perfectly capable of looking out for me. Besides, I expect they'll manage to contact him.' He hesitated a moment. 'Will you come with me?'

She stopped the examination of her toes and reached out to cover his hand with hers. 'Steve,' she said. 'Wouldn't it be very much better if you went on your own? I mean it is awfully expensive, isn't it, and your mother won't want to see me, it's you she wants. I'll only be in the way, I know I will.'

He put his head in his hand, and his shoulders seemed to sag. 'All right,' he said eventually. 'You stay here, I'll go on my own.'

The oriole warbled in the tree by the pool, and Julietta breathed a little sigh of relief. Peter would be back tomorrow, almost certainly. She would be left on her own. She would be free.

There was a skittles match going on in the Terror club annex when Julietta arrived back from the airport. The officers of HMS *Fleetwood* had challenged those of the infantry battalion garrisoned at Nee Soon barracks, and the evening was approaching its alcoholic climax. The wooden bowls went thundering down the alley; cheers and groans alternated as the pins went down or did not go down and Arborfield, perspiring heavily, was flourishing a piece of yellow chalk and trying to keep the score.

Released from the authority of both captain and first lieutenant, the *Fleetwood* officers were in a party mood, and an end-of-term feeling prevailed: when Julietta entered, Nick Robson had interrupted proceedings to perform his special imitation of a Wasp helicopter conducting an anti-submarine attack, whirling his arms round his head to simulate the helicopter blades and reciting – to the half-horrified amazement of his fellow officers – the cosmic-top-secret checks used before dropping a nuclear depth charge.

Julietta sidestepped neatly to avoid being soaked by a fast moving Tiger and made her way through the crush to speak to Arborfield.

Arborfield had let the end go. He had had a long and frustrating day and his relief was due to join from England the following morning. He had been the correspondence officer of HMS *Fleetwood* for far too long and was now looking forward to six weeks' leave before starting one of the first of the new Principal Warfare Officer courses at HMS *Dryad*. 'Oh shit!' he mumbled half to himself and half to Kemble. 'It's Juicy Julie!'

There was no getting away. He was cornered. 'Any joy finding your skipper?' Julietta said in that slightly piercing, senior officer's wife voice she had inherited from her mother.

Arborfield swayed forward and back, trying to focus. 'Well yes and no,' he said. 'By a process of elimination we reckon he must be at Rompin.'

'What? Romping?'

'Rompin. It's a . . . place on the coast. Before you get to Kuantan.'

'How do you know he's there?'

'We don't know he's there, but we don't think he can be anywhere else. I've phoned every bloody – er – single government rest house on the east coast, and that's the only one we can't get through to.'

'So what are you doing about it?' Julietta had to shout to make herself heard: the army had had another strike, and there was a lot of cheering going on.

Arborfield shrugged. 'I dunno. I guess we'll have to wait for him to come back. It's only three days.'

'Are you sure he's staying at a rest house?'

'Positive,' Arborfield said. 'He said that quite definitely.'

'What about asking the police to contact him?'

'Yes, we thought about that, but we don't think Father would be too pleased.' Arborfield grinned. 'Captains aren't supposed to go missing.'

'So you don't expect him back until Tuesday?'

Arborfield shook his head. 'No. Short of going to collect him, there's no way he'll be coming back before then.'

Julietta considered a moment. She imagined Peter on his own at Rompin, sitting by himself having his breakfast, or wandering out alone along a palm-studded beach. And then she saw herself arriving by car, stepping out onto the hot sand – seeing him, going after him.

'Rompin, you said?'

Arborfield belched inadvertently and nodded. 'Grompin,' he said. 'That's right.'

'I've got nothing to do tomorrow,' Julietta said. 'Except sit by this bloody pool. I'll go up and find him myself.'

Arborfield watched her make her way out of the annex. 'Yes I bet you will,' he muttered, and accepting a battered wooden ball, proceeded to roll it down the alley so that it slipped into the trough

415

at the side and trundled down, missing all the pins at the end.

Julietta set out very early the following morning when the sun was huge and watery above the horizon and mist still hung about over the mangrove swamps on the mainland. She drove the Mercedes along the causeway to Johore Bahru and on through undulating country planted with rubber trees and oil palms. She passed through Kota Tinggi and Mersing, and sped on along the straight, flat coast road, with the sea glinting like dull metal beyond the line of coconut palms.

As she drove, she imagined what she would do when she found Peter. They wouldn't have to return to Singapore immediately, she decided. No, they would at least be able to have lunch together, and perhaps a swim. They would drive back in convoy, and when he had been to the ship she would insist upon taking him out to dinner in Singapore. They would go to that new Russian restaurant and have borsch and steak tartare; perhaps they would find somewhere to dance. She would open her heart to him, tell him all about Chas and Steve and how unhappy she was and how she needed him and only him. How much time they had wasted all these years, and how foolish she had been to agree to marry Steven! Looking back, she was sure that she could have persuaded Peter to marry her, if only she had had patience. Her parents would have been on her side, it would have been the best possible solution; and if she had, she would now be the wife of a captain, instead of a lieutenant commander who looked dangerously as though he might go no further.

Nearly four hours after setting out from Sembawang, she arrived at Rompin. She found the government rest house, parked and stepped out of the car, looking round for any sign of Peter's Peugeot.

It wasn't in the car park, but that didn't worry her. It was quite possible he had moved on by now; if he had she would simply go in pursuit, up the coast to the next rest house at Kuantan.

She went into the house and found a Malay receptionist sitting under a Sanyo fan eating a banana fritter. Indian music wailed out of a small transistor radio, and a girl walked past barefoot, her arms full of laundry.

The receptionist paused in mid-fritter. No, he told her, no one called Lasbury had stayed there either last night or the night before last. No, the telephone was not out of order. He smiled, revealing golden teeth and golden fritter. 'Mistake in telephone directory,' he said. 'Sorry.'

She asked to use the telephone and spoke to the officer of the day in HMS *Fleetwood*. 'I'm at Rompin,' she told him. 'Commander Lasbury is not here, will you tell Lieutenant Arborfield? He's missing, do you understand? Missing.'

A lazy voice replied: 'I shouldn't worry too much, Mrs Jannaway. I'm sure he can look after himself.'

She went back to the car and wondered what on earth to do. She pictured Peter lying injured in a wrecked car somewhere, or even being held by communist guerillas. Things like that happened out here, didn't they?

But what was she to do? Go on up the coast? What point was there in that? Was she making a fuss over nothing? Had he perhaps chosen to stay in an hotel instead of a rest house? She couldn't believe that. Peter was a meticulously careful person, a man of his word. That was what she admired about him so much: if he said he would do something he would do it. He was utterly reliable.

Her mind went round and round, and the more she thought the more convinced she became that he had had some sort of accident. Perhaps he had gone swimming alone and had suffered a heart attack or cramp. The thought of it sent a shiver of fear through her: she looked out at the dully glinting sea, and imagined him floating face down.

There was nothing for it but to drive back to Singapore. At least by doing that she might stir those indolent officers into taking some sort of positive action. She got back into the car, turned and accelerated back along the coast road.

She stopped in Mersing. Her bladder was full, and she thought she might buy something to eat. She parked the car near the harbour and walked along a shabby side street, where dogs lay panting in the shade and children played in the dust. She found a small bar-cum-café with faded advertisements for Brylcreem and Pepsi-Cola in the window and went inside, asking permission of a seedy-looking Indian to use the lavatory. There, she saw the biggest cockroach she had ever seen in her life, which decided her against buying any sort of food in that establishment. She nodded her thanks to the Indian, who regarded her with thinly veiled hostility, and went out into the street.

It was then that she saw Peter's car. It was parked a few yards down the road. It was definitely Peter's. She recognised the rush mat he used on the driver's seat, and the Chinese umbrella on the shelf under the rear window.

She could hardly believe it. What would he be doing in Mersing of all places? The least attractive town, probably, on the east coast?

She went back into the café. 'That car,' she said to the Indian. 'Do you know where the owner is?'

It was not an unreasonable question: the presence of strangers in a town like this was quickly noted among the locals, who had a way of finding out a great deal about you within a few hours of your arrival.

The Indian regarded her suspiciously.

'You speak English?'

His eyes travelled slowly down from her turquoise sun hat, to her Thai silk blouse, her brilliant white trousers and her leather sandals.

'Yes,' he said. 'I speak English. And Malay. And Urdu and Chinese. And Arabic.'

'He's my husband you see,' she said. 'He's looking for me, I believe. Is he staying here in Mersing?'

The Indian opened his mouth and revealed a surprisingly pink tongue. When he laughed, he made a gargling sound that sent goosepimples down her back.

She opened her bag and took out a fifty dollar note. 'There you are. Now will you please tell me where he is.'

'Perhaps I don't know?' he said, and his eyes still held a cruel humour.

'You know all right. Don't you?'

He took the note and slipped it into a purse. He pointed with his chin. 'Pulau Tioman,' he said.

She stared at him. Pulau Tioman was a large island, thirty miles off the coast.

'Are you sure?'

He shrugged, and stared back at her, then swatted a fly accurately with his hand so that it was left crushed on the wooden counter where nondescript cakes and biscuits went stale in a glass case. 'You can go by boat if you want,' he said.

'Is there anywhere on the island I could stay the night?'

He nodded. 'Government rest house.' He took out a pocket watch, opened it, then closed it again with a snap. 'You can take

418

the boat,' he said. 'But hurry. It goes very soon.'

She ran down the pier carrying an overnight bag and caught the ferry as it was about to cast off. Within minutes, she had paid the fare, stepped aboard and was sitting on the bench seat on the foredeck as the boat chugged out between the stakes that marked the deepwater channel.

She was the only passenger. The boat was skippered by a white haired Chinese-Malay and crewed by a boy of fourteen or so with spiky black hair and a wide grin. When the boat was clear of the channel he set up a butane cooker and began to fry onions and peppers in oil with a large quantity of paprika, mixing it with cooked rice he kept in a muslin bag. He grinned and offered her some: she accepted eagerly, feeling ravenously hungry. She sat in the bows with the plate on her knee, feeling like a tourist on a trip round the bay. The boat chugged on and on. An island floated on the horizon, and a line of small fishing boats under tow went by.

The boy produced a bottle of lemonade for her. She took a drink and pointed at the island. 'Pulau Tioman?' she asked. He shook his finger. 'Another two hour,' he explained.

A little while later, the tip of Kajang, the single mountain on Pulau Tioman, appeared above the horizon. Slowly, the island took shape. It was far bigger than she had expected, and she wondered if the boat would take her to the same part of it that Peter had gone to. She had heard of Pulau Tioman some time ago: it was the island where South Pacific had been filmed, and was sometimes used by the navy as a recreation beach for ships taking a day off from exercises in the South China Sea. Why Peter had chosen to visit it, she couldn't imagine, unless it was his way of getting right away from civilisation.

The boat chugged on and on. She sheltered from the sun under a canopy over the stern, dozing from time to time and waking with a start as her head nodded forward.

As they approached the island, the boat was overtaken by a squall. A black cloud appeared from nowhere and a flash of forked lightning made contact with the wooded peak. Within minutes, the wind was whipping up the sea, and heavy rain was lashing down. She sheltered under the canopy and looked out at the palm trees on the shore which bent right over, as if bowing in worship to a greater power.

The Malay boy grinned. 'Soon over,' he said. 'Not last long.'

He was right: when the boat went alongside a small jetty ten minutes later, the storm had passed; the sun was out and the wooden pier was steaming as she stepped ashore.

She carried her holdall to the beach and stopped to look about her, feeling quietly triumphant at having actually arrived and being about to track Peter down at last.

The rest house stood right on the beach, facing west to the mainland. She walked in through the main entrance, smiling a greeting to an elderly Arab in a sarong who was sipping a cup of tea on the verandah.

She found the manager, who confirmed that there was a room available and invited her to sign the visitors' book. She took it from him with trembling hands, and was relieved to see Peter's signature on the last entry but one.

'Is Mr Lasbury here at the moment?' she asked the manager.

'Gone for walk,' he replied, and took the book back from her.

He showed her into a simple but clean room, with a single bed and a mosquito net tied in a knot over it. Left on her own, she inspected the damage of the sun's glare that afternoon. She effected a few running repairs to her make-up, changed into a bikini, put a loose shift dress over it and brushed her hair. Then she went out again in search of Peter.

She followed a path that took her into the main village on the island – *kampong Tekek* – and walking along under tall palms found herself in surroundings reminiscent of a painting by Gauguin. Swarthy, copper chested natives eyed her curiously as they passed, and girls with melting eyes and coloured sarongs moved gracefully among the trees.

She wondered if perhaps one of the latter might be the reason for Peter's presence on the island, but dismissed the thought quickly. Peter wasn't like that.

The path led through the village and back to the beach, so she took off her sandals again and walked along at the water's edge.

Quite soon, she found that she was completely alone. It was as if she were in a dream: the sea broke gently on the white sand, and the palms swayed in the breeze. She saw a coconut fall with a thud. She came to a small promontory of rock, and picked her way carefully out to the point, drawing back suddenly as hundreds of slimy lizards plopped into the water at her approach. She clambered further out and sat down, deciding not to go any further, as it only meant longer to walk back. Instead, she stared down into the rock pools and poked at a sea anemone with a stick.

While she was doing so, a movement caught her eye. She looked up: something had moved at the tree line some hundreds of yards away. And then she saw a couple standing at the head of the beach. Both were men, and both were naked. She froze. Was it? Yes, one of them was almost certainly Peter. Slowly, her heart beating and thumping against her rib cage, she sank down behind a boulder. She saw them look right and left, as if about to cross a busy road. The coast was clear: they ran down the beach and into the water.

They were playing together. Fighting? No, not fighting. She realised that she was trembling all over: they were playing in a way that told her something terrible about them, and there was now no doubt that one of them was indeed Peter, for as he turned away from her, she saw the prancing tattoo on his back.

Bending double to keep out of sight, she scrambled back over the rocks, jumped down to the sand and ran as fast as she could along the beach, keeping the promontory between herself and them. When she was well clear, she left the beach for the cover of the interior. She did what she did entirely by instinct, taking the first path she found and following it uphill, away from the sea.

She slowed, becoming out of breath. The path climbed steeply among huge trees. A monkey crashed noisily somewhere to her right, and a lizard scuttled away almost under her feet. Insects buzzed and droned, and a huge butterfly flapped about overhead.

She squatted down on her haunches, covering her face with her hands and sobbing bitterly. 'Oh Peter!' she whispered aloud. 'Oh Peter darling, how could you? How could you, how could you, how could you?'

Somewhere high above her in the trees a bird squawked mockingly as if in reply.

She returned to the rest house an hour later when the light was going, and Peter and Miles were sitting with drinks on the verandah overlooking the beach. She had wept for a long time, and knew that she must look terrible, but she behaved as normally as she could and told Peter the whole story of Steven having to go to England and the efforts they had made to contact him, and her journey up to Rompin and back to Mersing.

'If young Arborfield had done what he was told and rung all the numbers on the list I gave him, none of that would have been necessary,' he said.

She was introduced to his friend Miles who, they claimed, happened to have been staying at the rest house when Lasbury had arrived. Miles was an RAF flight lieutenant, a smilingly ceremonious man of about thirty whose eyes never stayed still. He said very little, leaving Peter to do all the talking.

They ate supper together – biriani and fresh fruit – and afterwards were joined by the old Arab Julietta had seen earlier. This was Mr Hamid: he had been the headman of the island during the war, and he regaled them with stories of the Japanese occupation. He was an old friend of Peter's, who had met him nearly twenty years before while serving as flag lieutenant to the Commander-in-Chief, Far East Fleet.

They sat out on the verandah late into the night, the insects ringing and chirruping around them and the mosquitoes dancing in the light of a paraffin lamp. Towards midnight, when the moon was above the mountain and Mr Hamid had returned to his house, his goats and an ailing wife, Julietta turned to Miles, putting her hand over his and looking into his beady eyes.

'I'm going to be very rude and take Peter away from you now,' she said. 'I hope you don't mind, but we are very old friends.'

She rose from the table. 'Come on, Peter. You can take me for a walk in the moonlight.'

They went in silence along the beach towards the pier. When they had gone a hundred yards or so, she said, 'I saw you together this afternoon, Peter. So I know.'

They stood side by side, the waves lapping gently at their feet. Behind them a cicada trilled loudly.

'What I wanted to say,' Julietta started. 'What I want you to know, is that it doesn't make any difference. No, that's wrong. It does make a difference.' She grasped his hand tightly. 'It makes every difference. It means –' She stopped, leaning against him. 'I *thought* I loved you before,' she whispered. 'But now I *know* I love you. And I know that nothing can stop that love, not after this, now that I know.'

He stared out over the sea. She looked up into his face, aching for him.

'You must feel so *lonely*!'

'Yes,' he said, and his mouth clamped tight shut.

They walked on. 'In a way I'm relieved,' she said. 'Now that I know. Now that I can understand.'

They stopped again at the pier. 'Are you in love with him?' she whispered.

He shook his head. 'Not really.'

'Do you think you could ever love me? I mean as a person? Not necessarily as a woman?'

He breathed out through his mouth. 'I don't know,' he said. 'Perhaps.'

She pressed his hand to her lips, holding it there reverently. She looked up at him, worshipping him.

'I will do anything,' she whispered. 'Do you understand that? Do you understand what I am saying? I will do anything at all for you. I am yours. I belong to you, I am part of you. I always have been and I always will be.'

He looked down at the sand for a long time. 'Promise me one thing,' he said. 'Promise you will never tell anyone. Will you?'

She felt the sudden thrill of possession. It seemed to her that everything that had happened had been pre-ordained. She reached up and pulled his head down to hers, pressing her mouth over his lips and promising that she would never tell a living soul.

# 23

Dora Jannaway could not understand why she could hear the sea. She was too tired now even to open her eyes, but she knew that she was nowhere near the sea, so why was it that she could hear waves gently swishing up a sandy beach?

She could see them in her mind's eye: there was a long, empty beach of perfect, golden sand, and the water was crystal clear. The waves were hardly more than ripples: they tumbled onto the sand with a gentle hiss.

She was a little girl again, running along beside the water. She could feel the sand between her toes as she ran, and stopped to look at the line of neat footprints she had left behind. She was seven years old; it was August, she had made her first communion and her father had called her his little angel. She was the baby of the family, the only daughter. She ran on and on until she saw ahead her father and her four brothers, Phillip and Dan, Arthur and Billy. They stood in a row in their Sunday best looking down at her, and she stopped, feeling suddenly shy of meeting them and of her bare feet and of her hair loose down her back.

Their faces melted away and the scene changed. She was twelve years old, sitting on the school roof with her friends and listening to Mother Dorrity reading from 'The Lives of the Saints'. She was excited because the war was over and soon it would be Christmas. It was a clear day, frosty, and the country was blue and brown. Rooks followed a plough. Her father, Phillip and Dan were in heaven.

And still she could hear the sea.

Here was Alan. She had not opened her eyes but she sensed his presence as he stepped inside the screen, and a moment later she felt his hand slipping gently into hers.

He whispered to her, unable to prevent his voice breaking through from time to time.

'Hullo darling,' he whispered. 'I'm here. It's Alan.'

She tried to speak, tried to indicate to him that she knew his voice, but she was too tired even to return the slight pressure of his hand.

'Don't try to speak,' he said. 'I understand.'

Did anyone understand? She listened to the waves that swept gently up and down that beach and began to hear new voices, children's voices, Welsh and excited. She was walking at the head of a crocodile, down to the Cardiff docks. She heard her own voice speaking firmly and confidently to the children. She saw their faces, upturned, excited, some of the little boys wearing those big, flat caps, the girls in black stockings and gym slips, their hair in plaits and ribbons. And here were the sailors dressed as pirates, and a lieutenant with rounded ends to his stiff white collar, and a fresh, weatherbeaten look: a vigour and a vitality in his humorous eyes that entranced her from the moment he welcomed her and her charges to the party.

The sea paused, held its breath. Another wave gathered itself, broke, and swept up the beach.

She saw little glimpses of Frank as he had been in that first year: saluting to her as she accompanied the children off the ship at the end of the party; waiting for her outside a church to go in to Mass with her; kneeling beside her to receive the Body of Christ; walking with her in Alexandra Park, ordering tea and toast for two before he had to go back on board.

There was a babble of voices. She was an officer's wife. She walked with him along a shore and an aeroplane flew overhead; she stood on a tower and ships slid away into the mist. She walked alone over pebbles; the waves tumbled and broke; out of the corner of her eye she caught a glimpse of her baby as he slipped out of her grasp, and then a moment later she was holding out her hands to him, crouching a few feet away, saying 'Come on, Alan, that's the way, you can do it, try, try ...' and he staggered towards her and fell into her arms and she hugged him, sobbing, 'Well done, well done!'

She heard the wail of the siren and saw Frank again, wearing his uniform for the first time in years, and she was proud for him because of that uniform, in spite of what it meant, in spite of his having to leave her to manage on her own. She felt the brass buttons hard against her when they kissed, and it was so real that she thought she could hear his voice and smell that mixture of soap and tobacco that was peculiarly his. She looked into his face: it was real. He was here.

'Frank?' she said. 'Frank?'

Alan smoothed her hand, and the vision faded. She listened to the waves: they were bigger now; they swept up the beach and rushed back down again, swishing on the pebbles, gathering, breaking again. In a strange way, these waves were a part of her: it seemed that as she grew weaker, they gained in strength and size, breaking harder upon the shore, reaching white fingers higher and higher over these thick, smooth stones.

And now the light was going: the sea became dark against a paler sky. She heard her own voice. 'Let's talk about Daddy. Do you remember that morning when he came home? No, Alan, let Steven see if he can remember. What did we do? We went toboganning, didn't we?'

They walked beside her, one on each side, holding her hands. They went slowly forward together, they spoke to the King.

'Mummy? Mummy? Was *that* the King?'

'Can we have the little boy on his own with the medal? That's the way, look up here, sonny! That's it!'

She saw him on his first bicycle, head down, pedalling furiously. She stood at the window covering her mouth with her hands, thinking that he had not seen the parked car, breathing a prayer of thanks as he swerved to avoid it at the last moment.

He was sitting at the piano, playing his first piece to her, a gavotte by Bach. He frowned and his dark hair fell over his forehead; the notes came out with a firmness, a precision and a confidence that made her gasp: she had played the piano once, and she knew he had a talent for it.

She heard his voice, saying his prayers. 'God bless Mummy and Alan and the soul of my father; help Alan with his difficulties, help me to work hard and use my talents, thank you for a lovely day and help me to be a good boy tomorrow, in the name of the Father and the Son and the Holy Ghost . . .'

Crash . . . That was a big wave. It swept up over the beach, reaching a new height, and as it receded again the stones and pebbles tumbled noisily with the undertow.

He was coming downstairs in his cadet's uniform, still so much a little boy, so innocent of the life he had chosen, and she was weeping because it was her fault, her fault that he had turned away from the excellence that she had always known was in him.

She heard her own sob: it stopped the sea for a moment and her eyes opened. Alan was bending over her. He smoothed her brow with his hand: she looked up into those deep, serious eyes and saw

426

reflected in them the face of an old woman, toothless, her mouth open.

'I'm here darling,' he whispered, and his voice broke through with a croak. 'I'm here.'

He had taken her hand again. The storm was gathering force. It was moving in from the sea: she could see the darkness of it, the whirling rain and cloud; the waves became shorter and steeper; they crashed upon her shore and retreated in a mass of foam and falling stones.

The faces and voices, sounds and memories fused into the crashing of the surf, and these waves were her own, they were breaking inside her with every breath she took; dimly, she was aware of a new voice at her side. It was a man: she sensed him beside her, on the other side from Alan. He had taken her other hand, whoever he was, and was holding it in his.

She tried to say, 'Who is it?' but was unable; she could see a wave coming, and she knew that this was the wave she had known all along must come. She saw it far out to sea, gathering strength as it approached, a huge grey mound of water that travelled swiftly and relentlessly towards the shore. She saw its crest outlined against ragged clouds: it rose up, peaking and curving. It towered above her until the light was blotted out.

She heard a voice whispering urgently in her ear. It was a voice she did not know, the voice of a stranger. 'Mum?' the voice said. 'Mum? It's me. It's Steven.'

She heard a rattling of stones as the wave broke. There was a thundering in her ears and she felt herself caught by the undertow. She was swept out and down: suddenly the voices were silent, the sea became calm, and the darkness and fear were gone.

The funeral three days later was not memorable in any particular way, but just another laying to rest of an elderly mother who has left her sons behind. The congregation in St Phillips numbered sixteen, and that included the server, the organist and Father Dreyfus, the new priest who had replaced Father Longstaff the previous year.

At the end of the Mass, they sang a hymn which caused Alan visible distress:

Now thank we all our God,
With hearts and hands and voices,
Who wondrous things hath done,
In whom this world rejoices;
Who from our mother's arms
Hath blessed us on our way
With countless gifts of love,
And still is ours today.

The undertakers – two of whom looked little more than teenagers, with soft collars to their shirts and hair that seemed disrespectfully long – lifted the coffin easily to their shoulders and slid it into the back of a polished hearse. The Jannaway brothers rode in a black Humber, and the cortege threaded its way smoothly through the streets of north-west London, gliding to a halt among the rhododendrons and sloping lawns of an Edgware cemetery. The last prayers were said, the holy water sprinkled, and the coffin lowered into the ground. Alan and Steven stepped forward to look down upon it and say farewell, then turned, to go slowly up the gravel path to the car.

They returned to Chestnut Road. It was high summer. The birch trees, planted over twenty years before, were in full leaf. The front gardens blazed with colour. Neighbours trimmed their privet hedges, and an electric lawn mower whined fitfully opposite number fifty-nine.

They sat at the table in the front room, listening to the silence, sipping cups of tea, the cuffs of Steven's shirt white against his suntanned wrists, the teaspoon with which he stirred his tea ringing gently in the cup.

'Orphans,' he said. 'Do you realise that? We're orphans.'

They went through their mother's papers. There was a copy of her will in a sealed envelope which they put to one side, neither feeling inclined to open it straight away. They sorted the jumble of letters into piles, wondering what to keep and what to destroy. There were letters from forgotten uncles in New Zealand, Steven's first letters from Dartmouth, their father's letters, written hastily from Portsmouth during the early years of the war. They found a picture postcard signed 'Roland', and two miniature envelopes, one marked Alan and the other Steven; each contained a small curl of silken hair, one light brown, the other almost black. They found the George Cross in its dark blue box, with the name of their father inscribed on it, and the words FOR GALLANTRY.

'Poor old Mum,' Alan said. 'She didn't have much of a life did she?'

Steven put the medal back in its box. They seemed to be walking on the very edge of a precipice of grief into which either might fall at any moment. 'What with the two of us,' he said, and managed a smile.

'What about these?' Alan asked, and held up a sheaf of airmail letters from Catherine. She had written twice a year since 1960. Steven glanced at one: it was full of news about children, 'my family' she called them.

'We'll have to write to her,' Alan said.

Steven nodded. 'Yes. You can.'

They returned to the will. Alan handed it across the table, and Steven opened it. He read it in silence for a few moments, then came to the sentence which conveyed its essential meaning and read it aloud:

'If my son Alan Francis Jannaway shall survive me for the period of one calendar month then but not otherwise I give devise and bequeath all my estate of whatsoever kind and wheresoever situate to him absolutely and beneficially without any sort of trust or obligation and appoint him sole Executor of this my Will.'

He looked again through the typed paragraphs and the witnessed signature, feeling a dull sense of hurt.

Alan took the will and read it for himself.

'She shouldn't have done it this way,' he said.

Steven made light of it. 'What does it matter? There's damn all money, after all, and you're the one who needs the house.'

Alan's face twisted inadvertently. 'It's not that. She should have trusted us. It's as if – as if she were trying to punish you. It makes me feel terrible.'

Steven laughed. 'Well I don't feel punished.'

'I'll put this house in our joint names,' Alan said. 'And we'll split the money fifty-fifty. No, I'd prefer that Steve, I really would. And if there's anything you'd like – Dad's medal, or the piano –' He stopped. 'Why did she have to do this?' he demanded. 'Why did she have to put us in this situation?'

Steven felt a slow-burning anger. He had caught the first available plane. He had travelled six thousand miles. He had sprinted to the taxi, sprinted up flights of steps and sprinted along hospital corridors to her ward. He had been convinced, all the way from Singapore, that he would be in time. He had prayed that she might last out until he arrived. And he had been in time: she had been alive, she had still been just conscious. He had slipped his hand into hers and she had lain there, her sons sitting on either side, in the way she would have wanted to die. He had whispered to her, sure that there would be a reconciliation between them, some glimmer of love and recognition before she slipped away. But that recognition had been withheld: he had felt that she had deliberately not recognised him, deliberately allowed herself the final satisfaction of bringing him to her bedside only to leave without knowing him, without saying goodbye.

He regretted going to confession now, aware that he had done so for the wrong reasons. He had knelt and whispered the synopsis of sins going back twelve years: absence from the sacraments, lies of convenience, selfishness, anger, avarice, adultery, pride. It had been a false reconciliation. He should have emerged from the confessional feeling clean and washed, he should have taken joy in the saying of the Stations of the Cross which Father Dreyfus had given him as a penance; but there was no feeling of atonement, no feeling of renewal. Perhaps it had been the memory of Pippa that had caused this inadequacy, for although he had not written to her for some time, he could not forget or regret his week with her. Perhaps it was the knowledge that soon he would have to return to Julietta, or perhaps it was because he knew that spiritual repentance was in a complicated way tied up with another reconciliation yet: a reconciliation with authority and with the Royal Navy.

He had said those words again: O My God, because thou art so good . . . He had received the Body of Christ. But the saying of those words had been with his lips only, and the acceptance of that host an outward sign more of a temporary suspension of disbelief than of inward grace. For either sacrament to have any meaning, he knew that he would have to embrace that state of unquestioning obedience, that childlike trust he had never – even from his earliest childhood – quite attained, whether in the Catholic Church, God, or Their Lords Commissioners of the Admiralty. He would have to abdicate another sort of birthright; he would have to become an obedient servant.

The lawn mower on the other side of the road had stopped its electric buzzing and whining. Children looked in at them over the privet hedge as they went past on their way home from school. He was aware of a new maturity: his parents were dead, he had stepped up into the older generation.

He smiled sadly, shaking his head. 'Alan,' he said. 'There's no need to feel bad about it. I don't want the piano. Or the medal. I don't want anything at all.'

But that was untrue, he reflected later, for he still yearned inwardly for love and approval and that feeling of belonging which seemed destined to remain just beyond his grasp.

Flying back to Singapore, he experienced a familiar sensation of being in transit between one world and another, and of having time on his hands to think out where his priorities lay.

Superficially, it seemed that the task was simpler than it had been a week before. Now that his mother was gone, he felt a release from the guilt feelings she had always caused him: they could be packed away and put into the attic of his mind. Alan would be all right, too: he was capable of looking after himself and already full of plans to write a book. And Catherine: reading her letters to his mother had shown him how far their lives had diverged. The links between them were tenuous now: she was engrossed in the wellbeing of her children and he enmeshed in his love-hate relationship with the navy and Julietta.

Ultimately, everything hinged upon Julietta. If he belonged anywhere, it must be with her, and with the children she had borne him. It was possible to imagine himself being separated from her and from Anita and from Penny, but the thought of losing Thomas caused a fierce, primordial ache inside him even at that moment, as the Boeing flew on through the night and the stewardesses made their way between the seats collecting the plastic trays.

Whether he liked it or not, Julietta was the key to the whole puzzle. If he had been in tune with her before the ship had sailed from Devonport six months before, he would not have become involved with Pippa. If he had not become involved with Pippa, he would not have written that ridiculous report about the breaking of oil sanctions – and he saw now that it was ridiculous: could Her Majesty's Government, the Foreign Office, the Intelligence Services and the Royal Navy all be hoodwinked so blatantly? It was impossible! Peter Lasbury's snub and his refusal to recommend him for promotion had been well deserved.

431

He dozed, and awoke as the stewardesses served breakfast. An hour later, the aircraft landed at Colombo to refuel. He stepped out, blinking in the sunshine and paced about the dispersal, resuming his self-analysis.

It was no good blaming the navy for his marriage to Julietta any more than it was for the fact that it had turned sour. Nor was it any good sneering at the promotion rat race while at the same time secretly longing for promotion. Such attitudes were puerile and destructive. He must be bigger than Julietta, bigger than the navy, bigger than the rat race.

Pressed against the boundary fence, several Tamil women were calling out to the passengers for alms, thrusting their hands through the wire. On an impulse, he went over to them, took out a few pound notes and put them at random into the outstretched fingers. He walked quickly away, aware that he had been seen and feeling foolish as a result. Why had he done that? Was it some sort of conscience money? He suspected it was, and was angry with himself. Pippa was right, he reflected. I'm a muddle.

The plane took off again and he opened a newspaper he had bought in the airport building. Dr Kissinger had been to Peking for talks on Vietnam, and there was further comment on the break-in at Watergate which had taken place three weeks before.

He could not forget those Tamil women and their pitiful, imploring hands. An article heading caught his eye: A GENERATION THAT HAS LOST ITS WAY, it read, and he thought Yes, and I'm part of that generation. Then he made an effort. It was no good being pessimistic just because your mother had died. That was why he was feeling like this – it was mother guilt, plain and simple. I must plunge back into the mainstream, he thought. A little bloodied perhaps, but still unbowed.

He called at the bungalow in Sembawang to change before going on to the Terror club. As he paid off the taxi, he heard the Sikh make an announcement over the loudspeakers: the pool was out of use until further notice, owing to contamination of the water.

Julietta was in her usual place, lying on a sunbed, but there was no sign of any of the *Fleetwood* officers. He walked over to her, determined to make a fresh start.

'Hi,' he said cheerfully, and kissed her on the cheek.

'Hi,' she replied. 'How was your funeral?'

He looked down at her: she lay with one leg straight out and the other bent, and was lazily stroking her inner thigh with the tips of her fingers. He pulled up a chair and sat down beside the round, white table.

'Quiet,' he said. 'But dignified. What have you been doing?'

'Nothing much.'

He looked round. 'Where's the *Fleetwood* crowd?'

'On board *Fleetwood*, presumably.'

'Has she sailed or something?'

Julietta shook her head. 'The new captain's making them work in the afternoons.'

'Where's Peter?'

'Gone. He left yesterday.'

'I didn't think he was going until tomorrow.'

'Nor did he. But he changed his mind.' Julietta reached for her bag and took out an airmail letter. She handed it to him, and he recognised Pippa's handwriting and the Capetown postmark. 'I brought you this,' she said, and lay back again to watch his reaction.

'Thanks,' he said, folding the letter and putting it in a pocket.

'Aren't you going to read it?'

'Later. Tell me what you've been doing.'

She snorted and pushed her top lip out. 'Wouldn't it be better if you told me what you've been doing?'

He sighed. 'Not much to tell. I arrived ... just too late. She didn't know me.'

Julietta stopped stroking her thigh and examined her toenails instead. 'I didn't mean that. I meant in Capetown.'

'Who said anything about Capetown?'

She shrugged. 'Open your letter.'

She knew. Somehow she knew. He wasn't sure whether to call her bluff and open the letter in front of her, or to ignore her altogether.

'Look – Julietta –' he started, unsure even then what he was going to say.

'Don't "Julietta" me. Read your girl friend's letter.'

'She's not a girl friend.'

'Lover, then. Concubine. Bint.'

He handed the letter back. 'Okay – go ahead, read it yourself if you want to.'

'No thanks.'

People were aware that there was something happening. A few

heads turned, a few conversations stopped, then started again.

He opened the letter, feeling detached from his own crisis, able to watch himself, his elbow on the table, the bronzed people round the pool in the background. He saw himself rip open the envelope and unfold the letter inside. But it was not the original letter. It was a photocopy. The handwritten words occupied one side only:

> Steve love,
> In haste. They've ransacked my place. All films, equipment, mss, notes, research etc – including your letters – gone. Expecting the big knock any minute. Will send this out via a friend if poss. Will write again when I know where I am. Don't try to contact me at this address whatever you do. Hope none of this rebounds on you, Steve. I don't think they'll do anything drastic – just chuck me out of SA I guess. The bloody walls have ears, Steve, so be careful. See you one day. Keep the flag flying. Still love you, as ever, P.

'Bad news?' Julietta asked.

He shook his head and put the letter back in its envelope. She said nothing for some time. He felt relieved. Perhaps she was letting it pass. After all, her behaviour hadn't been immaculate with Chas, had it? Perhaps she had a guilty conscience, too. Perhaps she had misbehaved in his absence. Well, he wouldn't press her on that subject. He wondered who had told her about Pippa. Someone had. Someone in the ship. Peter? Surely not. That sort of thing was beneath Peter. He might be an oily toad in some respects, but he didn't break the unwritten rule in every ship that you didn't talk about other officers' affairs. But if not Peter, who? He had never got on well with Robson, the flight commander, but their mutual dislike was not as strong as all that. Then he had another thought. Who could have made the photocopy of her letter? Had it been intercepted by the South African authorities?

'Tell me about her,' Julietta said.

He decided to play it straight. 'Look, sweetie,' he said. 'There's not a great deal to tell. Surely you realise we're not all angels. Okay, yes, she was a girl friend. I met her at a cocktail party in Simonstown, we went out to dinner a couple of times. What else can I tell you? She was a journalist.'

'A journalist.'

'Yes. As a matter of fact Peter *asked* me to get to know her. We thought at first that she might be doing a bit of overt information gathering, if you know what I mean.'

'But she wasn't?'

He shook his head. 'No. She wasn't up to anything.' He had an idea. 'Look – this letter doesn't mean anything to me, see? I'll show you.' He crossed to a waste bin, tore up the letter and dropped the pieces in. 'There,' he said, returning to the table. 'All over bar the shouting, okay?' He reached out his hand to take hers. She allowed him to hold it for a moment, then withdrew it.

'The trouble is, there may be some shouting,' she said.

'Does there have to be? It's all over, I've said that.'

'How many letters did she write you, Steve?'

He shrugged. 'Two, counting that one.'

'I made it five,' she said. She reached for her bag again and took out all the originals of Pippa's letters. She held them up for him to see, like a hand of Solo. She counted them. 'One two three four five. Yes. I thought so.'

He called her a bitch, very quietly.

She said, 'I could say the same of her.' She looked through the letters, found the one she wanted and took it out. 'Sorry to do the dirty on you, Steve, but a girl has to protect her interests, doesn't she? Let's see now ... "Come and find me on that hill my love ... I want you to love me to bits again." Again? how many times did you shag her to bits, "Mr Jannaway"?'

'We had an affair,' he said hoarsely. 'All right. I admit that.'

'How very kind of you.'

'Those letters were locked up in my drawer –'

'Yes I know that. I had a devil of a job persuading some silly little wetnosed midshipman to give me the keys, too.' She smiled. 'But the photostats are good. You can have them free of charge, but I may be needing the originals.'

She put the letter back into its envelope and all the envelopes back into her bag. She picked up her towel, took off her sunglasses and put them in their case. She tossed her hair back into shape and stood up, slipping her feet into a pair of leather thong sandals.

'There's a dent in the wing of the car,' she said. 'But it wasn't my fault, it happened when it was parked. I'll leave it at the airport, okay? Oh, and I'll leave the keys somewhere – British Airways information desk, okay?'

'Listen – this is ridiculous –'

'Yes, isn't it? That's exactly what I thought when I read those letters. I thought – well, who's been had, had for a great big sucker, then?'

Her voice rose shrilly in the sullen heat of late afternoon. To the south, the sky darkened, and a growl of thunder announced the approach of another storm.

'Keep your voice down,' he said quietly. 'If you don't mind.'

She looked round to make sure she had left nothing behind. 'I don't know when I'll see you again,' she said. 'I hope you have a safe voyage back.' Her voice trembled and her lips went out of shape. 'I didn't want this Steve, I promise you I didn't want this. But I did tell you, didn't I? Once. I warned you.'

'Listen – Juju – please –'

He felt as if every word they spoke could be heard by all the officers and wives and children and nurses and teachers who sat about round the white tables or lay on towels by the pool.

'It's over,' he said. 'I promise you it's over. She doesn't mean anything to me.'

She looked straight back into his eyes, and he knew that what he had said was not true. Pippa still meant a great deal to him.

'Bloody hypocrite!' Julietta whispered.

'Maybe I am.' He turned his head left and right. 'Can't we talk somewhere else?'

'There's nothing to talk about as far as I'm concerned. I'm booked on the night flight. I only stayed on so that I could tell you to your face. Quite good of me in the circumstances, I thought. This is the end of us, Steven. Finito, do you understand?'

He felt his heart beating as fast as it used to during a night deck landing. Another clap of thunder echoed about in the Sumatran hills: it made a noise like a cannon ball being rolled slowly along a wooden floor.

'For Christ's sake,' he whispered. 'Please.'

'No it's not for Christ's sake. It's for my sake. And Nita's and Penny's and Thomas's. It's too late, Steve. I've seen the whole lot. All the photographs of Catherine you kept, that letter of hers telling you to marry me. I know what you are now. You're a hypocrite and a shit and I don't want to be married to either of you.'

She moved to get past him and he tried to prevent her. 'Get out of my way!' she said, and heads turned in their direction. 'Get out of my fucking life!'

Then she was walking away from him, her leather sandals slapping on the crazy paving.

He sat down again and watched her go into the changing rooms. Perhaps it was better to let her go. She was very wayward in some respects: he knew that the more diligently he sought to resolve an argument, the more determined she became to prolong it. He was not sure whether he believed that she had actually booked a flight. Would she really do that? The contents of Pippa's letters were loving, and they referred to lovemaking as well, but he didn't think they warranted quite such an outburst. He decided to let her get away and then go after her immediately. He would catch her in the bungalow, he would explain. He would make love to her, he would persuade her that they could use this last week together to start again.

'Steven Jannaway, I presume?' a voice said at his side.

It was the newly promoted Commander Cobbold, Peter Lasbury's relief, a small, neat man with curly ginger hair, his eyes bright with leadership and officer qualities.

They shook hands.

'I tell you what,' Cobbold said. 'It's going to rain fire and brimstone any second. Why don't we grab a table inside and talk?'

The first heavy drops fell as he followed his new captain into the clubhouse. Within minutes, the downpour was torrential. Bolts of orange forked lightning cracked and roared, and the monsoon ditches filled with swift rivers of brown water.

Commander Cobbold ordered two pints of Tiger and set them down carefully to avoid spilling the froth. 'Now then,' he said cheerily. 'You're the bloke who knows all there is to know about HMS *Fleetwood*, so let's hoick all the old skeletons out of the cupboard from the start shall we? Or perhaps I should tell you what my philosophy is first. Right. Yes. I'll do that.' Cobbold was like a robin redbreast: he hopped from subject to subject, spying a worm, making sure it was safe to take it, snatching it quickly, flying away. 'In my book, there are no bad ships' companies,' he declared, as if announcing a brand new concept upon which he alone had had the good fortune to stumble. 'Only bad wardrooms. Let's be clear about that from the start.'

While they talked, a waiter brought a folded sheet of paper and gave it to Jannaway. Commander Cobbold watched as his first lieutenant looked at it. He had not been pleased to discover that

Jannaway was in England when he arrived to take over command, and had already decided that it would be necessary to sharpen him up.

The note was from Julietta: I MEANT EVERYTHING I SAID. GOODBYE.

He crumpled it quickly and put it in his pocket. Outside, the rain teemed down. He stared out of the windows at the deserted tables and chairs by the pool.

'I'm not having any passengers, right?' Cobbold was saying. 'You can tell the wardroom from me, that if anyone thinks he's on a pleasure cruise, he's in for a nasty shock.'

Julietta ran past the window.

'I say,' Cobbold chirruped. 'Wasn't that your wife?'

Part Four

WAR AND PEACE

# 24

Something was extinguished, something was dead. He made believe that nothing mattered except the efficiency of the ship, convincing himself that because he was separated he could be a better first lieutenant.

The ship sailed from Singapore and took part in exercises with Australian and New Zealand frigates in the South China Sea. Commander Cobbold, intent upon making the best possible use of his time in command, set about sharpening up his first lieutenant. There was no time for remorse and no opportunity to salvage the wreck. It was necessary to put all thoughts of family out of his mind.

In some ways, being separated was a relief. He no longer felt obliged to compose letters to Julietta and was seldom faced with that feeling of dread when a letter from her appeared in the rack. It seemed that by separating from Julietta he was also separating himself from the female sex. He no longer pursued women at the ship's cocktail parties as he had once pursued them, no longer felt any need to go ashore with the randier members of the wardroom for a massage in a Bangkok bath house or a short time after dinner in the No Hands restaurant in Yokohama.

He began to turn into what he had once thought he would never become: the ruthless bastard, the efficient first lieutenant, the 'taut shit'. He drove his officers and his petty officers hard, and they quickly began to detest him. He revelled in their hatred. He persecuted the new correspondence officer to such a degree that he actually managed to reduce him to tears. That was a triumph. What use was an officer who couldn't stand up for himself?

Weeks passed. HMS *Fleetwood* rescued a lone yachtsman in a typhoon and rendered assistance to the civilian population of Hong Kong after a flood. In early September, she headed west again for Mauritius and another month of the Beira Patrol.

During that patrol, he took to staying up late in the wardroom and forcing the younger officers – it didn't matter which – to drink with him. He mixed McWhirters and threw the empty bottles out of the scuttle. If an officer decided to turn in before Jannaway considered the evening to be over, he would be pushed back into his seat.

'Have another bloody drink,' he would be told. 'You haven't bricked up for the fourth oasis.'

Later, at one or two in the morning, the first lieutenant would lock up the bar, go along the main passage (the Gleam was breaking up now and some of the tiles were lifting) and up the vertical ladder to the ops room flat. He visited the ops room, studying the tracked radar contacts, said goodnight to the plotters on watch and went across the flat to his cabin.

Sleep did not come easily, and when it did it brought strange dreams. One was of a fire consuming his ship, another was of a new jet aircraft which he was required to fly without any previous experience or handling notes; and one morning when the first grey light was filtering in through the scuttle above the head of his bunk, he woke up drenched in sweat and shaking with fear. His mouth had been full of rotting teeth, his eyes had turned to granite, and a voice – his own voice – had cried out, 'Is Christ God?'

He wanted to fight now, he longed for a bloody war. On passage north, up the west coast of Africa, he insisted on holding exercises in damage control and protection against nuclear attack. Sitting in the cramped space of the damage control headquarters, and assisted by the weapons electrical officer and the engineer officer, he planned detailed programmes of simulated damage, fire, flood and machinery breakdown. An imaginary H bomb exploded twenty miles away; the ship was shut down, every hatch and door and intake closed and every clip and pin hammered down. The ship's company was ordered to shelter stations and a skeleton crew left to operate the machinery and con the ship. Up on the bridge, Jannaway wore his action working rig and his anti-flash gear and made broadcasts about the imaginary situation, while the pre-wetting fountains drenched the ship and the bridge windscreen wipers banged to and fro.

But there was no war. When the exercises were over, the ship's company stretched out in the sun to put the finishing touches to their suntan before returning to the British winter. The ship stopped at Gibraltar, and the correspondence officer's virginity was lost to a predatory army nursing sister who was due to get married in

442

three weeks' time and who wanted to have one last fling.

Six hours after sailing from Gibraltar, a large container was sighted that was considered to be a danger to navigation. Commander Cobbold sent for Jannaway and together they hatched a plan. A signal was sent to the Flag Officer Gibraltar requesting permission to fire the four point five inch guns, the Oerlikons and the anti-submarine mortars. As soon as permission was granted, the plan was put into effect. Jannaway strolled onto the bridge and pressed the polished brass push to sound action stations. The klaxon blurped urgently. 'Hands to action stations! Hands to action stations!' Jannaway announced. The officer-of-the-watch stared at him aghast.

'Is this for real, sir?' he asked.

Jannaway sneered, but otherwise ignored him. Between decks, men ran along corridors, up ladders, down hatches. Magazines were opened, shell hoists started, emergency pumps and generators run up and tested. In the sonar control room, ratings donned headphones and began to operate the range and bearing recorders. The fire control dish aerial spun, the four point five gun mounting swivelled in unison with the director. Telephones yodelled and intercoms buzzed. Commander Cobbold strutted back and forth slapping his hands together. 'Come on, come on, come on!' he cried. 'Not fast enough, first lieutenant! Not fast enough!'

'Do you hear there,' Jannaway said over the main broadcast. 'First lieutenant speaking. For exercise, I say again for exercise, information has been received that a Soviet submarine is in our area and that a massive conventional attack is underway across the West German border. We have been ordered to immediate readiness and have clearance to attack unidentified submarine contacts in our area.' He continued to explain that 'for our purposes' the semi-submerged container was the submarine they were looking for. His voice bellowed out along corridors, in messdecks, in the helicopter hangar and on the Seacat deck. Although some eyebrows were raised and teeth were sucked, the officers and men took it in good part, for most of them needed the simulation of war as much as did Jannaway: you cannot herd men together and provide them with weapons and not expect them to want to fire them once in a while.

The ship made several passes at the container (which was full of kitchen units being exported from Portugal to Angola) and when the captain was satisfied that the sonar team had been sufficiently exercised, he authorised the firing of the anti-submarine mortars. For a few minutes, as the transducers sent their pings out through the water and the hushed operations team listened for the tell-tale echo, the ghosts of *The Cruel Sea* and *In Which We Serve* returned. A hooter sounded, and moments later the mortars fired in two lots of three. Bump-bump-bump, bump-bump-bump, they went, and six bombs soared high over the mast, to explode in a pattern several hundred yards off the port bow.

'Not very impressive,' Jannaway announced from the bridge. 'Missed by a good hundred yards.'

Then it was the gunnery department's turn. The submarine had been 'forced to the surface' and was to be engaged with high explosive.

'Excuse me sir,' the bosun's mate said quietly to the action stations officer-of-the-watch. 'But do we know what's in that container like? I mean it might be chemicals or poison or something, mightn't it?'

The officer-of-the-watch raised his binoculars and said that that was extremely unlikely.

The ship slowed to eight knots and a few minutes later the first shell whistled away and sent a plume of spray into the air. Voices barked orders over intercoms and another shell went on its way, sending another plume of spray into the air a little closer to the target than the first.

The gunnery officer explained the difficulties to the captain. The gun mounting was having to be operated in 'local' rather than in 'remote' and the visual aimer was having difficulty seeing through the armoured window, which was badly scratched and inclined to mist up. It was difficult to lay the guns accurately in the swell that was running, the container was too close to use fire control radar and yet if the ship moved further off it was unlikely that the fire control radar would be able to pick it up.

Another shell was fired, and this time a massive spout of water rose into the air not fifty yards away. HMS *Fleetwood* had nearly shot off her own foot. Two more shells were fired, with little more success, and the awful inability of the gunnery department to hit a stationary target at five hundred yards became apparent to all. The weapons electrical officer came onto the bridge in a white overall and anti-flash gear to explain to the captain that the gunnery system was not designed to operate against this sort of target, and that poor design or incompetence could be completely ruled out. Commander Cobbold sighed and ordered the twenty millimetre Oerlikon to open fire, which took a little while because the magazine had been incorrectly loaded.

The captain lost his temper. His lips went white and a vein throbbed in his neck. Hands fell out from action stations. The shells and bombs were returned to their magazines and the helicopter allowed to fly twice round the ship.

Half an hour later, when the officers were queueing up to fill their crested cups with tea from an aluminium pot, and the ship's company were seated in the dining halls eating Marmite soldiers, the navigating officer made an announcement over the broadcast. He had joined at Gibraltar and was anxious to make a good start.

'It may interest you to know that we are now passing twenty-one miles west of Cape Trafalgar,' he announced, and the hoots of derision coming up from the messdecks could be heard in the captain's cabin, where Commander Cobbold was already quizzing his first lieutenant on exactly what had gone wrong and why.

A fortnight's leave was granted to each watch when the ship arrived in Devonport. Jannaway bought a secondhand Ford and drove to Hampshire. He rang Julietta and broached the idea of a reconciliation. She told him that there were a lot of his clothes and books in the house which she intended to sell if he didn't collect them by the end of the year.

She was alone when he arrived at Stocks Cottage. She looked chic in a Fair Isle tank-top and a creamy blouse. She stood at the door and looked at him as if he were a Jehovah's Witness. 'I suppose you'd better come in,' she said.

He asked where the children were and she said. 'Out.'

'Can we talk?' he asked.

'As far as I'm concerned, there's nothing to talk about.' She told him to collect his things and go. She said she didn't want him in the house any longer than was necessary.

He went into the children's bedrooms. Thomas had pictures of Paddington Bear and the Magic Roundabout on his walls. He carried his suitcases and a cardboard box full of books to the car. He had brought a dozen roses for Julietta and had left them on the driving seat. He had no one else to give them to, so he decided to give them to her in spite of her attitude.

He went into the kitchen with them. Julietta was shaking flour onto a board. He offered the roses, but she hardly bothered to look at them.

'Please take them,' he said.

She shook her head. 'I've taken all I'm ever going to take from you.'

She rolled pastry, ignoring him. He looked at the children's drawings and scribbles she had pasted up on the walls.

'When am I going to see the children?' he asked.

'What makes you think they want to see you?'

'You must let me visit them,' he said. 'I'm entitled to that at least. Thomas in particular.'

She looked back at him for a moment and snorted. 'You'll have to ask my solicitor about that.'

There was a gentle explosion as the gas central heating boiler came on, and a roaring of gas jets.

'Have you any idea what this is doing to me?' he asked. He held out the roses again, gulping back tears.

She took the roses from him, looking at the half opened blooms and the tight buds. Then she brought them down sharply against the edge of the sink, severing some of the heads from their stalks.

'That's what you've done to me,' she whispered. 'Now will you please leave.'

He drove through Meonford, Droxford, Meonstoke and Corhampton and then, because he was half-blinded by his own tears, pulled into a lay-by where he remained for nearly an hour.

He wondered where he could go. He had not yet admitted to Alan what had happened, and couldn't face him now. The only possible place he could go – apart from staying in an hotel – was back to his ship; so he went back: he spent his leave on board, taking occasional trips out of Devonport into the country, walking great distances over Dartmoor, visiting cinemas and watching the programme twice through, sitting alone in public houses, returning on board late at night and opening the bar with his personal key in order to sit in the wardroom with a glass and a bottle of brandy for company.

There was another cod war, that winter. HMS *Fleetwood* was sent north into the arctic circle to defend the British fishing fleet against the Icelandic aggressor. Trawlers were having their gear severed by

446

the *Thor* and the *Odin*; frigates braved the storms and suffered such bad collision damage with the Icelandic gunboats that they had to be armed with pieces of railway line, to protect their thin sides. Ice clung to guardrails and hung from gun barrels. The ship plunged and reared through a force eleven storm. The chairs in the wardroom had to be lashed into one corner; the captain was flung out of his bunk one night, and a chef scalded by cream of mushroom soup. In the evenings, the first lieutenant did his rounds with the master-at-arms, starting right for'd in the paint shop, where the smell of white spirit and cordage turned weaker stomachs. Steadying themselves with both hands, clinging to handholds as the bows lifted over a wave and then plunged, juddering, into a trough, they visited every bathroom and urinal, every messdeck, every office, bunk space and dining hall. A smell of vomit pervaded the ship. In one of the messdecks a mixture of seawater and diesel oil sloshed back and forth as the ship moved. The bulkheads creaked and groaned.

One afternoon when the upperdeck was out of bounds because of the ferocious sea that was running, one of the glass reinforced plastic liferaft containers broke loose on the Seacat deck, and the first lieutenant and chief boatswain's mate went to secure it. The sea was a mass of spindrift and leviathan waves which from time to time smacked at the ship's side and exploded into white spray.

They made their way aft, making a rush for the vertical ladder to the Seacat deck between waves. While they worked to get the heavy white container back into position and lash it down, a sea lifted the ship and put her almost onto her beam ends. Jannaway went sliding across the deck and would have gone straight overboard had he not managed to fling himself against the lee guardrails; the chief petty officer slid down after him and they ended up holding on to each other and the guardrail in a life-or-death embrace.

'Bit dodgy, that,' the chief boatswain's mate remarked when they were back in the safety of the enclosed bridge. 'Thought we were going to get rid of you at long last, sir.'

Jannaway laughed, his face reddened by the wind. 'You don't get rid of me that easily, Buffer!' He stood and looked out through the bridge windows at the mountainous seas, warming his hands on a mug of coffee brought to him by the bosun's mate. 'All good stuff, isn't it?' he said. 'What we joined for, after all.'

He saw Thomas four weeks later, soon after leaving HMS *Fleetwood* for the last time. He was just three years old: like his father to look at, but very shy of him. He clung to Julietta's skirt and pressed his face against her leg. Steven squatted down and held out his hands, but the child refused to go to him.

Julietta put her arm round her son and held him protectively to her side. 'Well are you satisfièd now?' she hissed. 'Is this what you wanted?'

'This needn't be happening,' he said. 'We could have sorted it all out. I wanted to. Do you think I enjoy this? Why won't you talk? Why?'

She shook her head and turned away from him.

He became calmer. 'I've heard from your solicitor. He'll be hearing from mine. I'm not giving up without a struggle, Juju –'

'Don't call me that, please.'

'What about Nita and Penny? When am I going to see them?'

'They don't want to see you. They're as disgusted as I am.'

'You mean you've made them disgusted.'

'Not at all.'

He stood up. They had nothing to say to each other, and he didn't want Thomas to associate his visits with argument and bitterness. Julietta went into the hall and opened the front door, waiting for him to leave. At the last moment, he turned back and picked up Thomas, holding him in his arms. 'Be a good boy, Tom,' he said. 'And don't forget your old Dad, will you?'

Thomas gazed back into his eyes. He left quickly.

The Joint Maritime Operational Training Staff, short title JMOTS (pronounced J-mots), was housed in a suitably whitewashed building on the edge of Turnhouse airport, eight miles west of Edinburgh. The bars on the ground floor windows gave it an air of a select place of detention that was not entirely misleading. Neat beds of roses flanked the two flag poles, where the RAF ensign and the white ensign flew side by side, hoisted when a whistle was blown at eight thirty and lowered again at five.

The Director (RN) arrived in a black Vauxhall and the Director (RAF) in a blue one; the deputy Director (RAF) arrived on a moped, and the deputy Director (RN) in a Ford Cortina. The staff officers, all of the rank of lieutenant commander or squadron leader, arrived in shared cars which they parked at the back of the building. Most of them were placed together in offices on the ground floor, light blue with dark blue, in mating pairs. There were staff officers responsible for air defence, long range maritime patrol, submarine warfare, attack, operations, air direction, communications, electronic warfare and finally airborne early warning, and nearly all of them had reached that stage in their careers when promotion or non-promotion was regarded as success in life or failure.

Jannaway took over the duties of Staff Officer (AEW) on a blustery day in late March, soon after the publication of the Defence Estimates. He was ushered along a polished corridor on the first floor and shown into the Director (RN)'s office.

This new commanding officer of his was a senior captain, whose hopes of promotion to rear admiral were fading. Like every other officer in the building, he had not been a volunteer to serve on this particular staff, and like nearly every officer in the building, he pretended the opposite.

He rubbed a pair of meaty hands together and twirled a signet ring round and round on the little finger of his right hand. He was not unlike Jannaway himself to look at: a little large, a little ponderous and a little puzzled. His name was Holt. Jannaway liked him.

'And have you been dragged here screaming by the heels?' he asked.

'Not exactly, sir,' Jannaway said. 'But I can't say it was my first choice.'

Holt looked quizzically round the room, as if he had only just arrived there and was getting his bearings. 'Three years in the zone, right?'

'Nearly, sir. Yes.'

'Getting a bit pregnant, eh?'

'Perhaps a little expectant, yes sir.'

Holt looked at his personal file. 'Separated from your wife I understand?'

Jannaway looked at the carpet. This was the part that hurt. 'Yes, sir. I'm hoping that's not a permanent state of affairs.'

'You'll be living in the mess?'

'For the time being, yes sir.'

Holt twirled his signet ring, took it off, spun it like a top on his desk and put it back on. 'And your last appointment? Number One of *Fleetwood*, wasn't it? Did you rate that a success?'

'Not too bad, sir. I got a reasonable flimsy, if that's anything to go by.'

Holt sighed a sigh that spoke volumes. There was a short silence. 'Permit me to give you some advice, Jannaway. You'll be lecturing to large audiences here, you appreciate that?'

'Yes, sir.'

'Speak with conviction, yes? Deliver your lectures as if you actually believe in what you're saying. Sounds obvious, but is often forgotten.'

'Does that mean I'm going to be invited to say things I don't believe, sir?'

Holt stopped twirling his ring and looked up sharply. 'Why do you ask that? Did I give you that impression?'

Steven was one of the few officers on the staff who had an office to himself, and at first he enjoyed working alone, going through his lecture scripts, watching the Wrens go back and forth between the main building and the visual aids hut, and chatting with the staff officers who came in to ask his opinion on matters on which he was expected to be an expert.

The awfulness of what his duties involved took some time to dawn. One of his responsibilities was to deliver lectures on the new concept of Tactical Support for Maritime Operations. This involved a complicated organisation in which the Royal Navy made signals to the Royal Air Force begging for air support, and the Royal Air Force made other signals back saying what was available, what would be allocated and when it might be expected to arrive. Gradually, Steven discovered that he had fallen into a hornet's nest of inter-service politics, for what everyone knew but few were prepared to admit was that this new system was so ponderous and the RAF resources so reduced that, in time of war, Tactical Support for Maritime Operations would be a shambles. Standing in a darkened hall, with slides and vugraphs appearing on a screen, Jannaway found himself having to describe the king's new clothes to audiences who could see for themselves that the king was stripped to his combinations.

It was also his duty to lecture on airborne early warning, a subject of which the Royal Air Force had but slight knowledge at the time. It was necessary to explain in simple terms how unless a radar set were put into the sky to look down, enemy aircraft could slip under the cover of surface radar and catch its target unawares; how a fleet of warships was highly vulnerable to such an attack and how, without carrier-borne AEW aircraft, the navy was dependent upon the air force to provide radar cover.

There was worse to come: the RAF had recently formed a squadron of World War Two Shackleton bombers which were being converted to carry AEW radar that was thirty years out of date. It was Jannaway's duty to attempt to keep a straight face and suggest that this small squadron might be sufficient to provide worldwide radar cover for the Royal Navy.

Sitting in his office, he conducted arguments with himself on the morality of what he was being required to do. Much of his lectures was wishful thinking, and parts of them were criminally misleading. He found himself going right back to the fundamental rationale for the maintenance of armed services. Did it matter, after all, if they were inadequately equipped? Did it matter that the navy – and for that matter Britain herself – was vulnerable to low level air attack? Was it of any consequence that the navy and air force chiefs had been at loggerheads with each other for decades and that their in-fighting had actually caused each others' services to be cut and cut again? Was it perhaps better to allow the politicians to whittle the services away to nothing? Was there an argument for believing that Christian principles should apply on a national scale, that Britain should disarm altogether and announce to the world that if attacked, she would turn the other cheek? Would not money spent on guided missile destroyers and nuclear submarines be better spent on hospitals and schools?

He found himself in a dilemma of conscience. If Christian principles did apply on a national level, pacifism was the only logical answer: no amount of rationalisation could change the meaning of 'love your enemies, bless them that curse you, do good to them that hate you and pray for them which despitefully use you and persecute you'. That was an absolute: to follow it on a national scale must mean abandonment of weapons not only of vengeance or deterrence but also of defence, even at the risk of being overrun by Soviet communism; if he believed it, he must leave the navy as soon as possible. On the other hand if he did not believe it, how could he justify lecturing about a system of defence which he knew to be flawed and inadequate? How could he remain loyal to all those

451

senior officers who seemed happy to accept such dangerous doublethink? What if Britain actually had to go to war? What if men's lives were lost through the military incompetence of staff officers – himself included – who had propounded the myth that the Royal Air Force was capable of defending the fleet against air attack?

His predicament was not a new one. It is to be found in every military organisation and is as common as bacteria in a healthy body – indeed, if it were not present, the military body would be prone to far worse diseases.

Nevertheless, bacteria must be destroyed when it is discovered, and when it became clear to Captain Holt and his deputy director that there was an infection present within the sanitised walls of the Joint Maritime Operational Training Staff, measures were taken to eradicate it.

Jannaway was given more to do. He was invited to re-write his lecture scripts in more formal prose, organise parties in the mess, take on the duties of liaison between the staff and the civilian population of Edinburgh and assume custody of the secret and confidential books.

1973 passed: Mr Heath's Conservative Government slid on into crisis; the price of oil doubled; the miners refused to accept Stage Three of the pay policy, and the Wilson-led Opposition rubbed its hands in glee, laughing at the suggestion that there might be any reds under the beds. In the new year, the miners carried out their threat and Britain ground to a crawl: the fifty-mile-an-hour speed limit was introduced, the three-day working week instituted and television transmission times shortened. It seemed, that winter, that the whole of society was about to break up. The share market was tumbling, trade union leaders were jostling for more and more power, and private armies were being raised by retired colonels.

In the middle of all this, Steven was going through his own crisis. He objected to the mundane tasks he was being given to keep him busy and railed at the hair-splitting amendments that were made to his lectures. He was like a germ that has been treated with an insufficient dose of antibiotics: he wilted for a time, had second thoughts, suffered from self-doubt, and then emerged stronger and more convinced in his rejection of the credo he was expected to preach.

Soon after the General Election, when Wilson had formed his

minority Government and Foot had surprised even Arthur Scargill by meeting the miners' demands in full, Captain Holt tried a new approach to bring Jannaway back into the fold: he gave him an article to read entitled 'A View of the Royal Navy' published in a literary magazine called *Encounter*. In it, he found all that dark blue nostalgia and Britannic patriotism that lures and has lured so many sons to serve under the white ensign. It was all there: the history, the grandeur, the dash, ceremonial and heroism of centuries, eloquently contained in thirteen pages. 'I have loved the Navy all my life,' the author declared, and sitting in his little office beside the barred window, with the radiator honking by his desk and the tea lady gossiping in Midlothian accents down the corridor, Steven paused and wondered.

How was it possible for anyone to 'love the Navy?' What was the 'Navy' with its capital N? Had the author fallen in love with those hard, rusting hulls? Or the merciless guns? The huge, white, phallic missiles that were launched from submarines to devastate civilisations? Or had he been captivated by all that he had read about the navy – books like *We Joined the Navy*, *The Cruel Sea*, *Naval Occasions* and *Mister Midshipman Easy*? It was all very well for a civilian to love the Navy, but that civilian had not eaten and breathed and drunk the navy for twenty-five years. What he loved was not 'the Navy' but the outward image that the navy found it convenient to present to the world. His love was not a direct love, either, but a vicarious one: it was a love of bloody battles fought and won, of rough weather endured, of appalling living conditions – all experienced at second hand. This was the Navy that Alan had wanted to be told about, the Navy that did not exist in reality but in the imagination of those who are prevented from joining it. It was the Navy of Nelson's Column and the Admiralty Arch, the slow marching ratings drawing the king's coffin on a gun carriage; it was the cheering at Earl's Court when the field gun crews compete: the flash and the swank, the proud ensigns, the Hearts of Oak, the Rule Britannia, the Marmalade and Jam.

Steven was not impressed. He was receiving curt letters from Julietta's solicitor. He was living alone in the mess, turned in upon himself, wandering disconsolately about Edinburgh in the evenings, often to be seen sitting by himself in a corner of the Jolly Carter or the World. He did not love the navy, had never loved the navy. He despised the way senior officers still managed to make-believe that it was a credible force. Why was it, he wondered, that leaders of nationalised industries were prepared to resign when in disagreement with the government of the day while Their Lordships always rationalised their way into agreeing with and supporting the next round of cuts? Why was it that First Sea Lords were so ready to stretch the navy ever further in order to meet the demands of successive prime ministers? When (if ever) would the day come when a commander-in-chief turned round and said, 'No can do?'

He ceased to attend the midday gatherings of mandarin officers who pawed the mess carpet at their masters' feet and took it in turns to buy the drinks. He ceased to deliver his lectures on joint operations or airborne early warning with conviction, and he regarded with a jaundiced eye the morale-boosting gimmicks the navy was using to convince its servants that all was well. All was not well: the stickers that were appearing in the rear windows of cars which said FLY NAVY or SAILORS HAVE MORE FUN or THINK DEEP, THINK SUBMARINE seemed to him to be symptoms of a draining away of confidence, a creeping sense of bewilderment and lack of direction.

He was called to Captain Holt's office.

'Two-oh-six time,' Holt said, looking at him over a pair of gold-framed semi-focals.

Jannaway sat and waited. He was just thirty-seven now: the mischief had gone from his eyes and some of the confidence from his smile. He had been on the staff nearly two years, and now, if ever, was the time that he should receive a positive recommendation for promotion.

'Most disappointing,' Holt said, glancing at the confidential report on his desk. 'I feel that you are not making the most of your talents.' He paused to take off his spectacles. 'And I've said so. You are capable of creative, original thought, but at the moment you are failing to make use of your ability. I don't know if this is the way you are made, or whether this is the effect that JMOTS has had on you.'

They sat in silence. Outside on Turnhouse main runway, a British Caledonian jet rolled for take-off.

Holt sat back in his chair. 'You appear to have lost interest. Is that the case?'

Jannaway felt a gentle pounding in his chest.

'I'm thinking of leaving, sir,' he said.

'Ah,' said Holt. 'Well that explains it. When can I expect to have your letter?'

Back in his office, he stared at the wall in bleak despair. He had expected more surprise, more alarm at his announcement, but the captain had received it with barely a lift of the eyebrow. He was filled with a terror of the unknown. He was a naval officer, he had always been a naval officer. How could he survive as a civilian? What could he do? He had failed in his career, there was no getting away from it. He had failed as a naval officer and failed as a husband. He was failing as a *person*. It seemed that there was an inevitability about what was happening to him. He knew that he might have won himself promotion from this job: all that would have been necessary was to silence those doubts, go along with the policies that were laid down and fulfil his social obligations with a smile. Why had he been unable to do that? What force inside him had broken the circuit of obedience and loyalty to the service?

He gazed out of the window at a Wren who ran prettily across to Visual Aids, holding her hat on with one hand as she went. Perhaps I should not put in my letter after all, he thought. Perhaps I should struggle on, try again, force myself to win promotion in order to get to the top, in order to change the system. But that was the trouble: it was a mistake to believe that you could get to the top in order to change the system, because the process of getting to the top changed you, as a person. It required you to accept and embrace the system, to believe that it was good.

He took a sheet of foolscap paper from his drawer and began to write the letter. It was a letter he had known for a long time that he would have to write sooner or later, and the writing of it caused a numb, detached feeling, a drooping of the spirit:

Sir,
I have the honour to request retirement from the active list of the Royal Navy on completion of sixteen years' reckonable service.
I have the honour to be,
Sir,
Your obedient servant,
S.J. Jannaway
Lieutenant Commander, Royal Navy.

He looked at the words for some time; then, remembering that line in the *Encounter* article – 'I have loved the Navy all my life' – was suddenly gripped by an awful nostalgic remorse and a longing for what might have been.

## 25

'It's not really for me to say,' Alan remarked, 'But I have a feeling you're being a bloody fool.'

They were sitting on the lawn behind number fifty-nine. Tennis noises came to them over the wooden fence and recently fallen apple blossom made a pink and white carpet at their feet. It was early summer: Steven had come south for a couple of days to visit his appointer.

He laughed rather too loudly. 'Oh, but I've been a bloody fool for a very long time!'

Alan found his false bonhomie unnerving. 'I thought you were bigger than this sort of thing, Steve.'

Steven lolled in a deck chair and stirred his tea. 'I've been in the Andrew over twenty years, Alan. Don't you reckon it might be time for a change?'

'If you were doing it for the right reason, yes. But I don't think you are.'

'Why do you think I am then?'

Alan considered. He sensed in Steven a feeling of bewilderment and despair. That was what lay beneath his over-jolly exterior.

'Are you sure you're not just venting your feelings about your marriage on the navy?'

'What if I am? My marriage is part of the navy. The navy is part of my marriage.'

He had arrived back from his visit to the admiralty half an hour before, and still wore his city suit. Of the two, Alan looked the younger and the more prosperous: there was a spare, wiry look about him that contrasted with Steven's heavy frame and thickening waistline.

'Anyway,' Steven said. 'It looks as though you've been as busy as ever.'

Alan looked round at the neatly clipped lawn, the weeded flowerbed and the new rockery he had planted with alpine flowers and mosses. Yes, he had been as busy as ever: he had had the house redecorated, the partition wall between the sitting room and the dining room knocked down and the back bedroom converted to a study. He had made a start on the novel for boys he had been planning for years, and he had recently accepted a post as senior librarian in Hampstead, travelling to work in an invalid car which he could drive himself.

'Yes I suppose so,' he said. 'I jog along, you know.'

'What about the writing? How's this book of yours?'

Alan didn't like talking about his book or about writing. There were times when he became carried away of course, but those occasions always resulted in a vague feeling of dissatisfaction, of having boasted that he could spin gold from straw. And there was no question of talking about this book: based on his early memories of his father and holidays in Dorset before the war, it would have been like making a public confession.

'I wrote a short verse the other day,' he said. 'Would you like to hear it?'

Steven inclined his head. 'I should be deeply honoured.'

Alan recited:

'When asked "How goes the writing?"
Say – not "Damn and blast, confound it," but
"Left to right across the page, and
Top to bottom, down it." '

Steven laughed obligingly.

'I thought I might call it "Memorandum to Myself",' Alan said.

'In that case I shall look out for it in the Complete Works.'

The tension between them had eased a little. 'So what now?' Alan asked. 'Have you any idea what you'll be doing for your last year?'

Steven finished the last of his tea and set his cup and saucer down on the grass beside his chair. 'Have a guess,' he said. 'Just have a guess at what sort of job they're giving me.'

Alan shrugged. 'How should I know, Steve? Some sort of shore job I suppose.'

Steven seemed to be gaining a grim amusement from something. 'It is and it isn't,' he said. 'I'll give you a clue. What would be the last sort of job you'd give an officer who's fed up and disillusioned? Any ideas?' He laughed almost cruelly, extracting some sort of bitter catharsis from his situation. 'No, all right, I'll tell you. They're putting me into recruiting. Can you believe that?'

'I'm beginning to believe anything about the navy.'

'Well that's something, isn't it? All these years haven't been entirely wasted after all. But you haven't heard the whole of it yet. You may just have a little difficulty believing the next bit. Some genius has dreamt up a gimmick to get the kiddy-winkies interested, you see. They've bought up some old canal barges, had them converted to look like miniature warships and they're sending them up and down the inland waterways manned by regular RN crews who have to play toy sailors and spread the hot gospel about hunter-killer submarines and sea-skimming missiles to the little children. And you know who they're putting in charge of this lot? Me! Yours truly!'

They faced each other, sitting there on the lawn, with conversations going on in the next door gardens on either side and a ripple of applause from the tennis courts beyond the cinder track.

'I've arrived at last, Alan! They're giving me my flag!' Steven laughed, that hard, soulless laugh which Alan was beginning to hate. 'I'm the Flag Officer, Canal Fleet – short title FLAG OFF CAN FLEE. Well smile, damn you! I am trying to be funny!'

Steven started his new job at the Directorate of Naval Recruiting four weeks later. His office was in the basement of Spring Gardens, just off Trafalgar Square and adjacent to the Admiralty Arch – six floors below the board room where Their Lordships met to administer Her Britannic Majesty's Royal Navy.

He had originally intended to find digs in London, but Alan insisted that he move into number fifty-nine, so he unpacked his cases in the small front bedroom where the novels by Henty and Buchan and Kipling still stood in the shelves and the photograph of his father still hung on the wall.

Alan was up every morning at six to work for an hour on his book before breakfast, and on three nights of the week arrived home after seven. At first, the two brothers were a little awkward together, but when each discovered that the other was prepared to respect his privacy, some of the closeness they had known as boys grew up again; ironically, now that Steven was at the end of his career and Alan on the brink of a new one, Steven needed to talk about his job. He brought back cautionary tales of naval bureaucracy – of budgets that had to be used up in order to ensure that they were not cut the following year and of warehouses full of surplus goods. They saw most of each other at weekends. On Sundays, Steven cooked the lunch while Alan was at Mass (Steven having lapsed long ago) and in the afternoon they would sit out on the lawn with cups of coffee and let the world go by. Steven talked of the people with whom he worked. Most of them were retired officers and senior ratings who had been re-employed by the Ministry of Defence: still living their careers, stumbling on towards retirement, wondering where they had gone wrong.

'This is the backwater navy,' he explained. 'It's where sailors come to die. They bury us in offices under Trafalgar Square so that the good Lord Nelson can keep his eye on us. We spend our time brewing instant coffee and wondering how much of our pensions to commute.'

'What worries me is, what'll you do when you find yourself out in the street this time next year?' Alan wanted to know.

Steven was vague about that. He had ideas about going into politics, becoming a teacher, a civil airline pilot or a merchant navy skipper, but his enquiries did not produce encouraging results. Inflation was roaring, unemployment rising and rumours of corruption in high places multiplying. Alan had a feeling that his brother had tendered his resignation in haste and might regret it at leisure.

'You don't understand,' Steven said. 'I want to find myself again, before it's too late. I want to get my soul back from wherever they put it twenty-one years ago. I want to metamorphose back from a naval officer to a human being.'

A few evenings later, Alan arrived home to find his brother at the keyboard playing two-handed scales. The sound of it took him back to the early fifties. He stood at the door and looked on as Steven descended rapidly in E flat.

'No nasty cracks,' Steven said. 'This is strictly therapeutic!'

He started reading again and took Alan's paperback copy of *War and Peace* in his brief case to work each morning. He read it almost continuously for two weeks: in the crowded tube train to Charing Cross, at his office desk near Trafalgar Square and in the evenings after supper. One night he burst into Alan's study with it open in his hands.

'Listen to this, just listen to this,' he exclaimed, and read aloud:

Not only does a good army commander not need any special qualities, on the contrary, he needs the absence of the highest and the best human attributes – love, poetry, tenderness and philosophic enquiring doubt. He should be limited, firmly convinced that what he is doing is very important (otherwise he will not have sufficient patience) and only then will he be a brave leader. God forbid that he should be humane, should love, or pity, or think of what is just or unjust.

He looked up, laughing. 'What have I been doing all these years? Why didn't anyone ever show me this?'

He was required to visit his Canal Fleet during some of the summer week-ends, and motored to the north of England in a Royal Navy Mini-Minor. At the end of August, he took Alan to Henley where the boats were on show to the public, and Alan saw them for himself: miniature versions of the guided missile destroyer *Sheffield* and the nuclear submarine *Dreadnought*. There was something oddly shameful about seeing Steven in his lieutenant commander's uniform, talking to the holidaymakers as they stepped carefully aboard, that caused Alan a pang of anguish and embarrassment on his brother's behalf. It was as if the navy had achieved the ultimate humiliation by forcing Steven to play at sailors.

They sat over coffee one Saturday morning a few weeks later. The radio was on and Alan was reading the *Guardian*. Steven looked round the kitchen, which had recently been fitted with matching units.

'Do you realise that the only room in this house that you haven't changed is mine?'

Alan looked up. 'Would you have wanted me to?'

'Not really. I rather like it. It's a bit like sleeping in a museum. Sometimes when I wake up in the morning I half expect to hear Mum calling, "Ten to eight!" the way she used to. Remember?'

Alan smiled. 'And then she'd turn up the wireless so we could hear "Lift Up Your Hearts".'

The mail arrived. Alan had recently submitted a short talk to the BBC, and was anxious to receive a reply, but that morning there was a letter from Catherine. He came back into the kitchen and read it without comment.

'Well?' Steven said when he was putting it back into the airmail envelope. 'How is she?'

It was the first time Steven had acknowledged Catherine's existence since their mother's funeral.

460

'Very busy,' he said. 'As far as I can see she administers practically every children's home in East Africa.'

Steven pulled the *Guardian* across the table and read the front page. Alan saw that his mouth was clamped tightly shut. After a minute or two he mumbled something and went upstairs.

Alan raised the subject again a few weeks later. 'I'll be writing back to Catherine shortly. Can I send her your love?'

'Not love,' Steven said. 'Send her my regards.'

Alan hesitated. 'Is that how you feel towards her Steve? With regard but not with love?'

He turned away. 'Unfair question,' he said. 'No comment.'

Alan was not sure why he continued to write to Catherine. Perhaps he felt it his duty, perhaps he felt responsible. Although her letters were interesting, full of news and often amusing, he suspected that she was a lonely person and had never fully recovered from her broken engagement. He was not even sure if she wanted to continue the correspondence and often wondered if she wrote to him out of a similar sense of duty, or out of kindness because he was a spastic. Once he had experimented by failing to reply to a letter, but after a few months she had written again to ask if he was all right and why he had not written. So they had continued to exchange letters – three or four a year – in which she kept him up to date with the crises she had to deal with in East Africa and he gave her his everyday news and confided his hopes of publication. He had also told her of Steven's separation from Julietta and of his difficulty in visiting his children.

He gave her more news of Steven in this latest letter, telling her with pleasure how his brother was discovering a new interest in the arts, how he was reading and playing the piano for pleasure. 'Perhaps this is a dangerous thing for me to say,' he wrote at the end of the letter, 'but I am quite sure that he still thinks about you a great deal, Catherine, and has never quite been able to –' He came to a full stop. What could he say now? How could he complete the sentence?

He tore up the page and started again. It was better to keep right off that subject, however much he would like to see Catherine and Steven reunited.

Towards the end of the year, Alan put the finishing touches to his children's novel and sent it off to a publisher. 'It'll be at least six weeks before we hear anything,' he told Steven, 'and when we

461

do it'll probably be the thump of the manuscript as it lands back on the doormat.'

Secretly, he hoped otherwise. He had spent nearly two years writing just over sixty thousand words and had driven himself to shape each sentence and paragraph and chapter to fit his carefully planned outline. He did not believe in 'letting the book write itself' or in 'allowing his characters to make their own story'. He was in charge: his characters were his own creation and they did precisely what he wanted them to do, within his plan. Nevertheless, he had learnt a great deal from the writing of the book, not least that as far as writing was concerned, his paraplegia could be turned to advantage. All his life he had been struggling to achieve abilities that most people took for granted. He was used to struggle, he accepted it. But his brain – as he had discovered some years before when he gained admission to Mensa – was as agile as anyone's, and he saw that literary success would be within his grasp if he could struggle with his brain as hard as he had struggled physically all his life.

That success came unexpectedly early. Seventeen days after sending off his typescript, a slim envelope with a Bloomsbury postmark was delivered to number fifty-nine, and Alan opened it in haste, tearing the letter inside as he did so.

'What are you looking so pleased about?' Steven asked.

'I can't believe it!' Alan said. 'They've taken it. Just like that!' He handed the letter across.

Steven frowned as he read the immaculately typed lines, and then his face broke into a smile. He read out part of the letter half to himself: ' "... have now had the opportunity to read your novel *Sons of the Waves*, and want to tell you how much I enjoyed it and that we are delighted to make you an offer for publication ..." ' He looked up. 'That's fantastic! Wonderful!'

Suddenly – almost eerily – Alan was aware that their roles had been reversed, for he saw in his brother's eyes and heard in his voice the same wonderment and vicarious triumph that he himself had experienced when Steven had first learnt that he had won a cadetship to Dartmouth.


The months passed and Steven's retirement date approached. In the new year, after an angry scene with Julietta at the end of the nativity play put on by Thomas's school, he decided that it would be kinder to his son to give Julietta the divorce she wanted and to end the acrimony once and for all. But having taken this decision, he was faced with the prospect of high maintenance payments, and his search for profitable employment became increasingly desperate.

Alan, caught up in the business of re-writing sections of his book for a demanding editor, was aware that Steven was worrying about the future but was powerless to help. He was pleased – naturally – to have had his book accepted, but he could not help feeling that this success of his must be like salt in Steven's wounded self-esteem. He was careful not to talk about the book unless asked, but was nevertheless very gratified when Steven asked to read the typescript.

The story, about two brothers who rescued their kidnapped father by teaching themselves to sail an old fishing lugger in the treacherous waters of the Channel Islands, was firmly based on Alan's memories of his father and of a sailing holiday that he had once planned but had had to cancel because of the war. He handed over the pile of pages to Steven and was quite unable to work that evening while his brother read them.

He was sitting at his desk under the pool of light cast by a gooseneck lamp when Steven came in, having read it all the way through.

'It's smashing,' he said simply. 'I can see why they jumped at it.'

Bruch's violin concerto was playing quietly on the stereo. Alan grunted his thanks shyly.

'Was Dad really like that?' Steven asked.

'Well, I've embellished a bit. But it's the way I remember him.'

Steven put the typescript down on Alan's desk by the typewriter. He laughed. 'You realise you had me crying buckets, don't you?'

'It isn't supposed to have that effect.'

'I know. It won't on anyone else, either. It's just … that it made me realise what it would have been like to really know your father, be friends with him. To do things with him, the way they did.' He shook his head, swallowing. 'Maybe it's because you've called the younger brother Tommy, I don't know.'

'Steve …'

'I feel as if my whole life has been a waste, do you know that? Nothing I've done has been of any value at all. Everything I've touched has turned to mince.'

He bowed his head for several seconds and his lips bunched tightly. Then, recovering control, he said: 'Sorry, I'm being

463

embarrassing aren't I. Stupid old fool. Pull yourself together.'

'Would it help if I changed that name?' Alan asked. 'I could. They don't have to be called Frank and Tommy. I only used those names because they seemed right for the period.'

Steven shook his head. 'No, don't change them. They are just right. It's a smashing book, Alan, and I hope it sells a million.'

He was very quiet for several days after that evening and then announced that he had found himself a job. Alan said that was marvellous, but there was an odd look on Steven's face that told him the job he had found wasn't really what he wanted.

'What sort of job?' he asked.

'Mainly office work, but that could change. Pay roughly what I'm getting now, with increments every two years. Not over-taxing, and I won't need any special training.'

'But what is it for goodness sake? It sounds just what you're after.'

'Yes, that's what I thought. In fact I'd be crazy not to take it.' He looked out of the window. Drizzle was falling steadily. It was late February. He was due out of the navy in two months. 'I've seen the light, Alan,' he said quietly. 'I'm staying in. Withdrawing my resignation. Don't look so shocked, you said I was a bloody fool to leave in the first place. I'm trapped, aren't I? I've got a family to maintain and I want Tom to go to a decent school. I can't afford to leave. They've got me by the balls.'

Alan said: 'I think if you've said you're leaving, you should leave.'

'I am in a way. I've thought it through. The only reason I'm staying in is for the money. I'm not selling my soul to them again. The navy's going to work for me this time round. It's a living, nothing else. And you never know, I've got another year in the zone. They might even promote me. That'd be a laugh, wouldn't it?'

'You can't live like that, Steve.'

He laughed. 'Can't I?' Just watch me.'

His commanding officer was very pleased. A lot of lieutenant commanders were applying for Premature Voluntary Release at that time, and there was a joke going round that someone had scrawled LAST ONE OUT TURN THE LIGHTS OFF on the back of a lavatory door somewhere in the Ministry of Defence main building. Getting Jannaway back was a small victory for the service. He was known as a likeable sort of chap 'of considerable experience' in the confidential report jargon used to describe officers who had been in their ranks too long. Once his letter withdrawing his resignation had been logged in, docketed, circulated for comment and forwarded under a covering letter to the Naval Secretary, he was encouraged to submit himself for a Career Prospects Interview. This was a new scheme designed to give lieutenant commanders some idea of their promotion chances, and when Jannaway walked round the corner from Spring Gardens, under the Admiralty Arch and in through the courtyard of the Old Admiralty Building in his best blue suit, he felt a cautious optimism.

He waited in a waiting room for fifteen minutes, reading back copies of the International Defence Review until summoned to his appointer's office. As it was after midday, and as his return to the fold called for a small celebration, he was treated to a South African sherry in a smeary glass.

'How would you fancy a sea command?' asked his appointer, a tall, bald man with sun blisters on his head from a recent holiday in Tunisia.

'I'd be very interested,' Jannaway replied. 'What sort of sea command?'

'HMS *Tribute*. She's earmarked for the new oil rig patrols. Might blow the cobwebs away, eh?'

Jannaway was flattered. He had presumed he would never go to sea again, and he wondered if perhaps this might be a way back onto the promotion ladder.

'HMS *Tribute*,' he said. 'Not that old salvage ship?'

'That's the one.'

'I thought she'd been scrapped yonks ago.'

His appointer looked put out. 'Not at all, not at all.'

'Well can I think about it?'

'My dear chap by all means. But don't think too long, because we've got people queueing up for sea commands these days.'

He was ushered through two offices into the holy of holies. The Director of Naval Officer Appointments was a small, neat captain behind a wide, neat desk. He folded his hands on the edge of this desk and looked quizzically at a sheet of paper that lay upon it. The interview did not take long.

465

'Your term at Dartmouth was a particularly strong one,' he began, and Jannaway had a feeling he said this to every lieutenant commander he interviewed. 'And you tendered your resignation at a very bad time. I'm afraid we can't in all honesty put your promotion chances much higher than negligible, Jannaway. If you'd just sign there would you? To indicate you have understood the content of what I have told you. Have you any questions?'

'No questions at all, sir, thank you very much.'

In the evening, he told Alan what had happened.

'But this ship – surely you'd like a command wouldn't you?'

He shook his head. 'HMS *Tribute* is forty years old. She's held together with string. I'd spend half my time rolling about in the North Sea and the other half at the bottom of a dock undergoing repairs. I'd see very little of Tom or Penny, and I'd have to con my ship's company into working their butts off to keep the ship serviceable. I'm not prepared to do that. I told you, I'm not going to sell them my soul again. They can find some other fool to commanded their clapped-out ship.'

'Are you sure it's not a sort of death wish?'

Steven looked away. 'I don't know what it is. I don't know anything any more. Yes, maybe I've got a death wish. At least that'd solve a few problems, wouldn't it?'

Soon after he had been passed over for promotion and had received a letter identical to the one Brian Wiggins had received six years before, Jannaway was sent to a new appointment in the Directorate of Naval Equipment, part of the ship design and procurement bureaucracy at Bath. His new office, which he shared with two senior commanders and a retired lieutenant commander, was in one of the many utility hutments that sprawl down the slope of Foxhill, above the old Roman city; his duties involved visiting shipyards up and down the country and inspecting warships that were being built under admiralty contract. He travelled to Barrow-in-Furness to inspect a guided missile destroyer being fitted out for Argentina; Portchester where gunboats were being built for the Arab states, and Southampton where frigates were on the slip for Brazil. He attended line-out inspections, preliminary inspections and final inspections; he learnt how to read drawings and compare them with accommodation spaces, corridors and the upperdecks, and saw for himself the appalling problems of middle management in industry.

'I'm a sort of travelling inspector,' he told Alan when he returned to number fifty-nine for a weekend. 'I spend my time living out of suitcases, and when I go back to the office to write up my reports we have jolly beer and sandwich sessions after which the passed-over and two-and-a-halves wash up the dirty beer glasses for the yo-ho up-and-coming commanders. No one's got enough to do, so everyone rings up their friends in other offices in order to look as if they had. And the ships they're building these days – you wouldn't believe it. There's so much panelling in the accommodation spaces that they've got a topweight problem. All the priority goes on communications and radar sets, so there's hardly any room for weapons. The new oil rig defence vessels can't do more than about fifteen knots flat out, and the *Sheffield* class is so top heavy they've had to restrict them to one anchor!'

'You should write it down,' Alan told him.

'Ha! Write it down! Where have I heard that before!'

He was living in a bedsitter halfway up the hill to Combe Down, cooking curry and butter beans for his supper and living like a rogue male, thrust out from society. Sometimes in the middle of the night he would awake in tears. He would make coffee and sit on his bed sipping it and weeping without restraint. That at least was one advantage of living on your own: there was no one to see your distress, you could give it full rein.

Alan's book did well for a first novel. It sold nearly three thousand copies in under a year, and his publisher spoke optimistically of reprints and sales of subsidiary rights. Steven felt loathe to visit him now, aware that he brought a cloud of depression and the smell of failure with him wherever he went. Julietta continued to make it as difficult as possible for him to see the children, blaming him for Thomas's dyslexia and lack of progress at school. Anita's seventeenth birthday celebrations were broken up by the police, who discovered a small quantity of marijuana on one of the guests; Penny won the school music prize for the second year running.

Then one evening, Steven saw Pippa Lane. He was sitting in the lounge of a guest house in Newcastle watching the News at Ten, when a report on the troubles in the Congo came on, and there she was speaking confidently into the camera about the refugees making their way out of the country and the atrocities committed by the advancing guerilla forces.

467

He went out and walked about the empty streets, wondering if he might try to contact her but quickly realising that it would be futile to do so. She was clearly still climbing her ladder and he had fallen off his; and even if he could still find her attractive, he was honest enough to realise that she was unlikely to feel the same way about him.

The following year, the year after the Jubilee celebrations, the autumn before the Winter of Discontent, the *Sunday Times* broke the news of the breaking of oil sanctions against Rhodesia. Filled with hot rage, Jannaway sat down in his bedsitter one evening and began writing down what he thought of politicians, the Foreign Office and senior officers of the Royal Navy. He vented his spleen upon them. He poured a long stream of invective onto the page. He accused successive administrations of 'either deliberate deception of the electorate or culpable incompetence on a monumental scale'. He accused successive First Sea Lords of being more interested in their knighthoods and index-linked pensions than in the maintenance of a properly balanced fleet. He accused captains and admirals of being weak-kneed and unwilling to put their careers on the line in order to ensure the country got the sort of navy it needed.

'Why is it,' he asked, 'that when the head of the steel industry is in disagreement with the government about how his industry should be run, he resigns, while the white haired gentlemen in the Ministry of Defence content themselves with puny whisperings down Whitehall corridors? Could it be that they have reached their ranks by saying 'yes' so often that they have forgotten how to say 'no'? Could it be that the British nation is being led to believe – not least by propaganda television programmes like 'Sailor' and 'Warship' – that the Royal Navy is far mightier than is the case? Could it be that if Britain were required actually to go to war, these gentlemen with quantities of gold braid on their sleeves might rue the day they allowed the fleet to be emasculated?'

It was a foolish outpouring, but it was even more foolish of him, instead of sending it straight off to the *Observer*, to address it for the personal and private attention of the First Sea Lord; but he did so, and within a week he was standing on his commanding officer's carpet.

His letter had been returned under the cover of a curt note from the Chief of Staff to the First Sea Lord, and Jannaway's commanding officer was understandably annoyed that one of his

468

officers should commit such a gross indiscretion as to by-pass all the usual service channels and write direct to the top.

'I would have expected an officer of your experience and seniority to know better,' he said.

Jannaway was a little surprised at the fuss. If he had been the First Sea Lord, he would have torn up the letter and forgotten about it, knowing that it came from a passed-over time-server with not enough to do. 'Am I not allowed to write a personal letter to an admiral sir?' he asked. 'I marked it private, after all. I don't see why it was necessary for him to respond to it officially.'

'Writing to One SL like that is like the ordinary seaman who writes to his MP behind his captain's back,' he was told. 'It's just cheap and disloyal. You should have informed me of your intention, and had the courtesy to show me the letter before you sent it.'

'I apologise sir,' Jannaway said. 'I didn't realise that the First Sea Lord had to be protected in that way, I thought he might appreciate a little feedback that was uncensored for a change. I felt that what I said represented what a lot of officers of my seniority are thinking.'

He felt surprisingly calm and in control of the situation, realising that it really didn't matter at all what he said, because promotion was no longer at stake. He pursued the point, noting with pleasure the flush of anger in his commanding officer's cheeks. 'Does this mean I should ask your permission to write to the First Sea Lord to congratulate him on his promotion to admiral of the fleet when he retires next year? Will you require advance notification of that, as well?'

His commanding officer, speechless with anger, left his own office with Jannaway sitting in it and feeling puzzled; and a week later, when Jannaway was washing up the dirty beer glasses in the officers' and senior civil servants' lavatory, he was called back into the Director's office to be told that if he was again thinking of applying for early retirement, such a request would be viewed favourably by Their Lordships.

# 26

Catherine came to England in late April the following year. She was forty-six: matured but not aged, Alan thought when he caught sight of her coming out of the customs hall at Heathrow. It was twelve years since they had last met, and when she had written to say she was coming over he had replied immediately, inviting her to stay. She had had reservations about accepting the invitation: it was one thing to exchange letters with Alan every few months, but another to sleep under his roof.

But here she was in the bustle of the arrivals hall, and there was Alan, looking surprisingly fit in grey flannels and blazer. He kissed her warmly on the cheek, took over her baggage trolley and led the way out to an awaiting taxi.

It was a Saturday morning: her flight had arrived in the middle of a heavy shower, but the sun had now appeared and the roads glistened and steamed. They drove through the tunnel and joined the M4 motorway, leaving it again to take a route through Hayes, Harrow and Edgware.

'So how are you, Alan?' she asked. 'What's all this about a television programme?'

His second children's novel had been published a few months before, and he was now working on an adaptation of *Sons of the Waves*. She asked him when she would be seeing his name in lights, and he laughed and said that nothing was certain in television until the credits rolled.

'But you must be tremendously pleased aren't you? After all it's what you've always wanted to do, isn't it?'

'Yes, I suppose it is,' he said, and glanced back at her, smiling. 'But the grass always looks very green until you actually arrive in the field. Then, like as not, you find yourself ankle-deep in mud.'

'I've never arrived in any field,' she laughed, 'so I wouldn't know.'

The taxi went under the tall brick arches of the Mill Hill East viaduct, and a minute later they were drawing up outside number fifty-nine.

'They've cut down all your beautiful birch trees,' Catherine said.

'Yes, they came down last autumn. They were too big for our little road.'

He led the way into the house and she admired the white paint and natural pine. 'You've done wonders, Alan!' she told him. 'It's lovely!'

He was obviously pleased and proud. In the living room, there were pots of geraniums on the windowsill, and the knocking down of the partition wall had produced a feeling of space and light. Catherine realised that his flair for interior design must have lain dormant – or perhaps frustrated – for many years. Now that the house was his, what he had done to it revealed an Alan she had not known before, one that his mother must have unwittingly prevented him from becoming while she was alive.

'I'm putting you in Steven's old room,' he said, carrying a case for her upstairs. 'Hope you don't mind, but now I've turned my room into a study, I'm left with only two bedrooms.'

There were clean towels on the bed and a bunch of narcissi in a Delft vase on the bookcase. 'You know where everything is, don't you?' he said. 'Plenty of hot water if you want a wash. I expect you'd like to unpack.'

She was left alone.

The room had been redecorated recently, but it was still something of a memorial to Steven's boyhood, and she would have preferred not to have been put in here, not to sleep in this bed and awake in the morning to see that photograph looking down at her.

She went into the bathroom for a wash and returned to brush her hair, take out her night things, do her face.

Well here I am, she thought. I've done it, I've come here, after all. If I meet him I meet him and if I don't I don't. We'll just have to see how things turn out.

She went downstairs. Alan was in the kitchen shaking mushrooms about in a pan.

'I've brought you a present,' she announced, and unrolled a woven mat, umber and dark red, that she had chosen for him in Nairobi.

He put the pan down and turned off the heat. 'How very, very kind,' he said, and took the mat straight into the sitting room, where he laid it before the hearth. 'There. Look at that. Perfect!'

Lunch was mushrooms in a delicious sauce, green salad, wholemeal bread and butter, a glass of white wine. She could not help comparing Alan as he was now, in his new surroundings, with the Alan she had known who had lived in an atmosphere of cooking cabbage, cluttered rooms and crowded mantelpieces. She remembered how much Steven had changed during the time she had known him and wondered if literary success was the cause of Alan's new-found confidence.

'Now you must use this house as if it were your own,' he was saying. 'I'll give you a key, so you can come and go as you like.'

She had planned a full programme for her stay: she would spend five days in London first, then go on a tour, visiting friends and relations and attending conferences and seminars up and down the country. She would be travelling to Brixham, Exeter, Llandudno, Edinburgh and Whitby before returning for her last week in London.

'So it doesn't sound as though I'll be seeing a great deal of you at all,' Alan said when they had moved through to the sitting room with their coffee.

'Well I didn't think you'd want to be lumbered with me for too long,' she said.

She looked out of the french window at the trees by the stream. The allotments no longer existed: they were completely overgrown. She glanced at Alan: from this side he had a most distinguished profile – deepset eyes, a straight, Celtic nose and an immensely determined chin. There was a question she knew she would have to ask him sooner or later, so she asked it now.

'What news of Steven?'

He paused a moment before answering. 'Not very good news, I'm afraid. He's not exactly a happy person these days.'

He left it at that, as if giving her the opportunity to drop the subject; but she felt that it had to be aired if only to show that she wasn't afraid to speak of Steven and take an interest in him as a friend.

'How much longer has he in the navy?'

'He's due out in July,' Alan said. 'Always provided he doesn't withdraw his resignation again.'

'Is he likely to?'

Alan shook his head. 'I wouldn't have thought so. Not this time.'

'Has he any idea what he'll do yet?'

'No,' Alan said rather abruptly. 'He hasn't. I've tried to talk him into taking a teacher training course, but he won't do that. He won't be told any more. I think he's ... given up, in a way. Maybe he's been spoonfed for so long that he's lost the will to go out and earn his living.'

'What about his family?'

Alan saw that she was already a little upset but felt that it was better to tell her the truth than to make out things were rosier than they were.

'They seem to be very nicely thank you as far as I can make out. Julietta's taken him to the cleaners and seems to have done a skilful job in alienating him from the children. He tells me that Anita's gone punk.'

'Gone what?'

He laughed. 'Oh Catherine you really are out of touch, aren't you? Remember that creature we saw with pink hair standing up on end on the way here? That was a punk. I understand Anita's hair is bright orange.'

Perhaps it was the long journey, perhaps it was the jet lag, perhaps it was the coming back into this house, or some complicated feeling of guilt; whatever it was, Catherine found herself staring down into her cup, and her tears overflowing.

They went to the eleven o'clock Mass the following morning. There was room for one passenger in his invalid car, and sitting behind him as they went up Dollis Road, Catherine was reminded of an afternoon when she had sat behind Steven on a motorcycle called Modestine.

She wondered if she had been entirely honest with herself over her reasons for coming to England. Kneeling after receiving Communion, she joined her hands beneath her chin, staring up at the effigy of Christ, and recalled the sudden surge of emotion caused the previous afternoon when Alan had spoken of Steven's broken family and his daughter who had turned into a punk.

She suspected that all these doubts and self-searchings might mark the approach of her climacteric: quite suddenly, over the past year, she had become aware of a need for change, of a feeling that time was running out. Each month that passed seemed to be one more chance lost, another perceptible ebbing of the tide. Such feelings were foolish and irrational of course, but part of her was also foolish and irrational. It had been foolish and irrational to allow herself to be captivated by a midshipman five years younger than herself, and it was even more foolish of her now to hold out that small, slender hope that she might marry yet, might have a child, just one child, of her own. Was this the reason for her return to England? Were all these visits and conferences and seminars merely excuses for a deeper need that she had failed to admit to herself?

They returned down the hill to Chestnut Road; Alan busied himself with the basting of the leg of lamb; she laid the table, poured two glasses of sherry and took them into the kitchen where Alan was making thick gravy from the juices of the meat.

After lunch, he left her in the sitting room with the *Sunday Times*, and a few minutes later the sound of his typewriter came down to her from the room above. Some time after four, when the clatter of the typewriter was continuing, she took a cup of tea and a piece of sponge cake up to him. She found him hunched over his desk, touch typing one-handed, deep in concentration.

'I was going to come down,' he said.

'I don't expect you would if you were alone would you?'

'Well, perhaps not. I weaken occasionally though. I'm not always this disciplined.'

He worked on until supper and again after that until after eleven. The following morning he was up at six for another hour's writing before going off to work. He apologised for having to leave her so much to her own devices, but she insisted she was quite happy and didn't mind at all.

The five days passed rapidly. She went up to London, shopped, had lunch with friends, contacted Save the Children, LIFE and the NSPCC and made arrangements to spend a day with her brother when she returned to London. She had not realised until now how much she had needed this break, and to get away from the continual demands made on her in Kenya. She discovered all Steven's old music in the piano stool and amused herself at the piano in the early evenings.

On her last evening, she took Alan out to dinner. He put on a suit for the occasion and she a grey dress with a high neck. 'I shall wear a tie in your honour,' he told her, 'but I'm afraid I shall have to ask you to tie it for me.'

'Stand still then,' she ordered, and knotted it for him with practised hands.

'You did that very efficiently,' he said. ' Who have you been practising on?'

She blushed. 'Eight-year-olds mostly.'

'A likely story,' he laughed.

They went to a small, friendly Italian restaurant in Highgate where the management knew Alan and presented each dish he ordered in such a way that he could eat it without difficulty. They worked their way through a bottle of Asti Spumante, and on their way back to the car Alan remarked, 'I don't suppose you've ever been driven by a drunken spastic before have you?' and they were on such good terms by then that she laughed and took his arm.

'What would you say to an Irish coffee?' he asked when they arrived back.

'Glory be, he'll be getting me drunk next,' she said in pure Dublin.

He was delighted. 'I didn't know you were a mimic.'

'I'm not really. But you can't work with the Sisters of Charity for twenty years and not pick up some of the accent.'

They went into the sitting room. She had talked at some length about her plans for the future over dinner, and now the conversation turned to his earliest memories. He talked about his father, saying that he had always been full of bounce and enthusiasm. She saw that he needed to talk about him so she led him on. 'Wasn't he mixed up in the Invergordon Mutiny?' she asked.

'That's right, they virtually booted him out because he was a bit too friendly with the lower deck, at least that's the story we got from Mum. He refused to name names. The usual thing, I suppose. I've sometimes wondered what would have happened if he had lived, what difference it would have made. The whole idea of Steve going into the navy in the first place was to … not exactly exonerate, but make up for Dad's death. To complete his unfinished career. A sort of folk memory almost.'

'Hamlet.'

He smiled. 'Yes, but I hope Steve doesn't get quite as bad as that!'

He spoke of his mother. 'I can't be sure, but I've always felt that she was almost a different person after Dad's death. Maybe it's wishful thinking, but I remember her as warm, and funny, a bit muddled, but very loving. When Dad was killed it was as if – I don't know – as if something died inside her.'

He admitted that after she had died he had been plagued by intense depression and feelings of guilt for several months; he explained the reasons for it – how his mother had cut Steven completely out of her will and how on her death bed she had appeared deliberately to fail to recognise him.

'And then from that moment – or so it seemed – Steve started going downhill and I started on the up and up. I don't think anyone appreciates what happens – in psychological terms – when a parent dies,' he said. 'I don't think Steve's ever quite got rid of his bitterness over Mother, and I don't think he'll be happy until he does. At times I feel he *wants* to fail, to rub my nose in his failure, to prove to me how wrong I was about the navy.'

'And were you?' she asked. 'Were you wrong?'

He considered a moment before answering. 'I don't know. I think Steve has had a raw deal along the way somewhere, but I also have a feeling he brought it on himself. He's no good at toeing the party line, that's the trouble. He argues the toss instead of keeping his mouth shut. Like his Dad, probably. Am I boring you?'

'Not at all.'

He looked at her, hesitated then said: 'I know this may be a delicate subject, but when you come back, would you like to meet Steve?'

She took a breath, sighed out. 'Alan … I don't know. Would it be wise? Opening old wounds? And I don't suppose he wants to see me very much, either.'

'I'm not so sure about that. You may be just what he needs.' He smiled sadly. 'For the second time in his life. It might help both of you. It might be a sort of release.'

She wondered what it would be like, actually to meet him, speak to him. She was afraid: that they might feel nothing for each other, that they might feel everything for each other or that one would love and the other would turn away.

Alan offered the coffee pot, and when she shook her head helped himself. She said, 'Yes, it might be a release, but it might also be, well, dangerous.'

'Dangerous? Why dangerous?'

'Isn't it obvious? What if we were to fall in love all over again –'

'Do you think you would?'

She coloured. 'I don't know. But what if we did?'

He said gently, 'If you two were to fall in love again, that would be the best possible thing that could happen for both of you.'

'How can you say that? We couldn't marry – not without an annulment. And I doubt if he could get one. All that agony and pain –'

'What does he need an annulment for?' Alan asked. 'He doesn't need any annulment, he's free to marry.'

She was amazed. 'How can you say that? He's a divorcee!'

But Alan was shaking his head. 'Not in the eyes of the Church he isn't. In the eyes of the Church, he was never married in the first place, so he couldn't have been divorced.'

She was completely nonplussed. 'I never realised that.'

He laughed. 'Well it's a fact. If you and Steven wanted to get married there'd be no bar at all. The Church doesn't recognise a mixed marriage if it's not witnessed by a Catholic priest. And Steven and Julietta were married in a C of E church by a C of E vicar – I saw it happen. That's no marriage as far as the Vatican is concerned. It's a meaningless ceremony. There's nothing to annul.'

She was silent for a long time. 'Does Steven realise this?'

'Of course he does. Why do you think he's lapsed?'

'Are you absolutely sure you're right, Alan?'

'Positive. I had Father Dreyfus to dinner – oh, some years ago. He said that there are occasions, if he's ninety-nine percent sure that a marriage won't last more than a few months, when he'll tell a couple to go away and get married in a registrar's office rather than in the Church. At least that way it can all be dissolved and their lives aren't wrecked.'

'I think that's terrible,' she whispered. 'And cynical, too. I mean – anyone can administer the sacrament of baptism can't they? So why not marriage?'

He shrugged. 'Well it's the rule, that's all I can say.' Alan finished his coffee. 'Does it help you to make up your mind?'

'Make up my mind about what?'

'Well ... meeting Steven again.'

She shook her head. 'If anything it makes it more difficult. It changes everything doesn't it?' She laughed at herself. 'Do you know I thought it ironic that my conversion to Catholicism was a bar to my marrying Steven. But it's quite the other way round. I don't think I can agree with the Church on this. My conscience tells me that he was married and is a divorcee, and my conscience tells me it would be wrong even to meet him.'

Alan pushed himself up from his chair. 'Sleep on it,' he said, and smiled wickedly. 'Maybe your conscience won't be so active tomorrow morning.'

If she slept at all that night, she was hardly aware of it. However hard she tried, she could not stop thinking of the possibility of meeting Steven again, the possibility of getting to know him, learning to love him ... all over again. She felt as if she were being pulled, relentlessly, in opposite directions. If Alan was right, and she was convinced that he was, there was no reason why she should not agree to meet Steven again, hope for a reconciliation; indeed, there was no reason why they should not be joined in matrimony as she had once expected they would be, with the full blessing of the Church at a high, nuptial Mass. Did she want that? And did what she wanted matter? Might it perhaps be her duty at least to try again with Steven and to help him out of his slough of despond?

But there was the opposite side to the argument, the instinctive side, the Protestant side. In her heart of hearts she knew that marriages were not made on earth but in heaven, and it was for no man to say whether God had joined two people as man and wife or not. This argument went much deeper into her, it touched her soul. When she had converted to the Catholic faith, she had been aware of the necessity to make a conscious step away from the beliefs in which she had been brought up. She had been obliged to embrace new beliefs and a new set of moral standards, both of which were very similar to those of her childhood, but subtly different in certain respects. Now, unexpectedly, she discovered that she could not, after all, have stepped away from those Protestant beliefs as completely as she had thought. The old conflict between the authority of the Roman Catholic Church and the voice of her conscience had re-emerged, and if her conscience was right, then the Church of Rome must be wrong. If her conscience was right, then Steven and Julietta had indeed been married in the eyes of God, whatever the Church of Rome decreed, and if they had been married in the eyes of God, then they had indeed been divorced.

And if she believed that ...

She lay on her back and turned her head from side to side in desperation. On the wall at the foot of the bed, the photograph of Frank Jannaway grinned cheerfully down at her: she could just make it out in the darkness. She dozed, had a strange dream in which she tried unsuccessfully to mount a horse, and when she awoke it was getting light. She listened to the sparrows chirping under the eaves, and the rumble of the first tube train going over the viaduct. She heard Alan getting up and going to the bathroom, and later the clack of his typewriter in the study.

They breakfasted together. He was going straight off to work, and she would leave the house later to catch the morning train down to Devon. She would be travelling back along that same railway line upon which she had once struggled to decide whether or not to become a Catholic. She was still alone, still having to make her own decisions, still without that one person she had always longed for: the person who would be the most important person in the world to her, who would need her and love her more than any other.

Alan interrupted her thoughts. 'Well? How's your conscience this morning?'

She relaxed and smiled. 'A bit better, I think.'

'Does that mean you'd like me to ask Steve over some time when you're next here?'

She felt her mind being made up for her. She had blown the whole thing up out of proportion. Just because she met Steven didn't mean to say she was going to marry him.

'Yes do,' she said. 'I'd love to see him again.'

'Splendid. I'll fix something up.'

'But only if he'd like to, Alan.'

He looked at her across the table, his eyes smiling in that very intense way of his, and she felt that he had guessed something of what she had been thinking. 'Of course,' he said. 'I'm not playing cupid or anything. It's not compulsory.'

She went out into the hall with him, thanking him for the days she had spent with him, telling him how much she had enjoyed her stay and what an ideal host he had been. He picked up his brief case and opened the front door; she kissed him on the cheek, and he looked embarrassed.

'See you in about four weeks then,' he said. 'Take care.'

She went back into the dining room and watched him go out to the pale blue invalid car parked outside the front gate, and when he was gone she stood there for a long time, feeling confusedly happy and sad.

*

So here it was at last:

MINISTRY OF DEFENCE
Main Building, Whitehall, London SW1A 2HB

NAVSEC 11/2/2/963                19th June 1979

Sir,

I am directed to inform you that approval has been given to your request to be placed on the Retired List with effect from 4th July 1979. You are entitled to full pay up to and including 3rd July 1979.

2.   The Secretary of State for Defence has it in command from Her Majesty The Queen to convey to you, on your leaving the Active List of the Royal Navy, her thanks for your long and valuable service.

I am, Sir,

Your obedient Servant

Illegible Signature

He sat at one of the long mahogany tables in the officers' mess of the Portsmouth naval barracks, breakfasting beneath a portrait of Lord Nelson. Around him, wall paintings depicted Nelsonic victories: the flash of cannon, the broken masts, ripped sails, smoke-filled sunsets, drowning French matelots.

Mess waiters, white coated, stood discreetly in a group behind him ready to remove a plate, take an order or place the butter within reach.

Mister Jannaway, he thought, smiling to himself as he put the blue letter back in its blue envelope.

He finished his egg, and a mess waiter darted forward to remove his plate. He helped himself to toast and butter and marmalade. Up and down the table, using alternate places in order to isolate themselves from each other, officers breakfasted in total silence: commanders, lieutenant commanders, lieutenants. Not many of them – a dozen or so, no more. The barracks mess was fuller of ghosts from the past than it was of serving officers. He wondered how often his father had sat here under this high ceiling; he wondered what he had thought of it all and what he would think now if he were alive and could see what sort of mess his son had made of his career.

Musing on these things, he became lost in his thoughts, until a mess waiter, bending down behind his chair, murmured in his ear: 'Is there anything you require, sir?'

He shook his head briefly and rolled up his napkin, putting it in the numbered pigeon hole as he left the mess. He collected his cap from the long row of hooks in the corridor between the ante-room bar and the heads, and walked out of the main entrance, nodding good morning to the hall porter on his way.

He was in the second week of his resettlement course; he was learning to lay bricks. It was all part of leaving the service: you could

choose from a variety of courses to prepare yourself for civilian life
– business management, interior decoration, carpentry, bricklaying.

He crossed the road and went in through the main gate to the
barracks, returning the crisp salute of a sentry in white belt and
gaiters. He walked on between redbrick Victorian buildings and
modern blocks of concrete and glass, entering a caboose at the side
of a shed where the building course took place.

'Morning all,' he said, falsely cheerful, to the eight others, all
ratings, who were on the course with him. They looked up from
their copies of the *Sun*, the *Mirror*, the *Daily Mail*. He was the only
officer doing this course, but he sensed in these men the same
indefinable feeling of rejection, of disappointment and disillusionment that leaving the navy was causing in himself.

He helped himself to a cup of tea from the aluminium pot and
sat down on a chair among them. He had noticed on starting this
course that ratings were in one respect more honest in their
relationships than were officers. If these men had all been officers,
this caboose would have been full of chat and gung-ho repartee. It
would have been 'Where did you get to last night?' all over again.

After a while, the civilian instructor came in, a phlegmatic master
builder in a brown overall coat, who had the ability to talk about
the history and art of bricklaying for hours at a time.

'Well, gentlemen, shall we make a start?' he suggested.

They put their overalls on and went into the shed. They had been
split up into pairs, but as they were nine and he was the only officer,
Jannaway worked alone. That morning, they were to build a cavity
wall in English bond. They collected their trowels, their wheel-
barrows, their spot boards, levels and gauges. They mixed up the
mortar and set to work. At ten fifteen, the instructor emerged from
his office and announced ceremoniously: 'Gentlemen, the tea.'
They went into their caboose where cups were laid out on a tray,
together with a bottle of milk, a tin of sugar, the eternal aluminium
teapot. They drank their cups of tea, they returned to their walls.

Jannaway was having difficulty. The mortar kept dropping down
between the courses; he had forgotten a row of ties; his quoin was
off the vertical and he was missing a queen closer. He worked alone,
raging inwardly at his own inability to place bricks accurately, one
upon the next.

They stopped for lunch; he sat again at the long table, was waited

481

on again by the white-coated pensioners; he was served with braised lambs' hearts in thick gravy, bread and butter pudding, cheese and biscuits, coffee. He returned to his wall, he drank another cup of tea.

The master builder inspected his work. He pursed his lips at the bulging rows of Flettons, not bothering to check the horizontal and vertical with his level for fear of embarrassing the officer in front of the ratings. Officers were seldom as quick to learn as ratings, in his experience. They didn't have the patience or the skill with their hands.

At the end of the day the walls were dismantled. The bricks were cleaned and stacked in a pile. The trowels, spades and spot boards were washed down. The levels, gauges, lines and corner blocks were returned to the cupboard, and all the mortar collected and returned to a heap in the corner.

It was a special sort of mortar which never set, so that it could be used time and time again.

There was a message for him when he returned to the mess that afternoon. From Alan: a request to contact him by telephone.

He knew what it would be about. Alan had written to him two weeks before and had invited him to come for a meal one evening during Catherine's last week in England. He had not yet answered that letter, and time was running out. 'I'm not trying to bring you two together or anything like that,' Alan had written, 'but I know Catherine would like to meet you again and it does seem time you buried the hatchet.'

He went along corridors, upstairs, to his single room. He changed out of his uniform trousers, his woollen pullover. He showered and went along to the television room to watch the early news.

Mrs Thatcher was putting her hand on her heart again, and Britain on her feet; she was paying the police, paying the services, promising prosperity, leaning forward earnestly, appealing to commonsense ('You know –'), speaking for the people. She was repeating and repeating her credo, drilling it into these doltish reporters who asked their doltish questions, who had to be told, *ex cathedra*, exactly why her policies were right, exactly why they would work.

How pleasant it would be to be so sure, so confident that you were *right*.

He suspected, when he rang Alan, that Catherine might be listening in to that end of the conversation.

'Steve,' Alan said. 'Thanks for ringing. Have you got my letter? What's the answer? You know Catherine leaves on Monday?'

He knew. 'Does she?'

Alan made an impatient sound. 'Look – why don't you come up for the weekend? Why don't you drive up this evening?'

'I can't. I'm going for an interview tomorrow.'

'Not all day, surely? What about tomorrow evening?'

He thought rapidly, couldn't think of an excuse. 'No, booked. Sorry.'

'Well Sunday. Come for lunch and stay the night.'

'It's Thomas's exeat. I'm taking him out.'

There was a silence at the other end, then Alan said, 'Well come on here after that. You'll be halfway here.'

He hesitated further. Perhaps it might be an idea to see Catherine again, after all. Perhaps. But he didn't want to meet her like this, with Alan looking on, with Alan keeping his fingers crossed, with Alan enjoying their reunion at second hand. It seemed that his whole life had been lived for Alan's benefit, so that Alan might enjoy, through him, what Alan could not enjoy for himself.

'All right, good,' Alan said, as if Steven had already accepted. 'When can we expect you Sunday night? Sevenish? Earlier if you like. Come on here as soon as you've left Craybourne.' He laughed. 'I've got Catherine here with me now. She says she'll cook the supper!'

Alan, Alan. He was doing it all over again: taking charge, urging him on, refusing to take no for an answer.

He agreed; they rang off. It was still early: he had nothing whatsoever to do except sit in the mess, consume more food, watch more television; and he was now terrified of meeting Catherine. He needed to get out of the fusty atmosphere of the mess, leave all these history-laden rooms behind. He went out into the summer evening and walked through old Portsmouth to Southsea. He went along the shingle beach, stopping from time to time to look across the Solent. The yachts, tilting in the evening breeze, the hovercraft skittering along in a howl of spray, the forts, solid, Victorian.

He went down to the shore and stood there for a long time, throwing pebbles into the sea.

The exeat started at midday on Sunday, but if your parents came to matins, you could leave with them immediately afterwards, provided they didn't want to talk to old Sparrow about you, in which case you had to hang about outside the common room waiting for them while everyone else went off with their fathers and mothers and sisters. That Sunday morning, when he went into chapel, he saw his mother and Peter sitting side by side in the back row, which was surprising because he had thought his father was taking him out. His father had written to him and had said he could bring a friend, so he had invited Buzz Remington, whose parents lived in Portugal. He wasn't sure if his mother and Peter would want to take Buzz out as well and he thought about it all the way through matins. Peter was an admiral. He was allowed to call him Peter because he and his mother had talked about it and said that it would be silly to call him 'Uncle Peter' because he wasn't an uncle and Peter didn't want to be called Captain Lasbury or Admiral Lasbury, not by him at any rate, and his mother wouldn't hear of Mr Lasbury, so it had to be Peter. When the news that he was going to be an admiral had come, his mother had got all excited and had rung up all her friends and been in a good mood. That was last holidays, at Easter, when Nita and Penny were at home and they had had a birthday party for Granny Clara, who had surprised everyone by suggesting that they should swap houses, she move into Stocks Cottage and they into Meonford House. Thomas wasn't sure he wanted that, but his mother and Nita and Penny said it was a fabulous idea, so they were going to at the end of the summer when Granny Clara had had one more season of raspberries. His mother had shown him the room he would have for his own. It was bigger than the one he had in Stocks Cottage and had a big old-fashioned basin with brass taps, and a huge chest of drawers with a bow front and knobs; it was the room his mother's brother, the one who died, had had, and his shotgun, the one he would have when he was fourteen, was always kept propped up in the corner underneath all the photographs of cricket teams and naval cadets all crowded together under a gun. Thomas didn't know why but he didn't really like that room as much as his own but Penny said he was jolly lucky and she wished she could jolly well have it for her room, so he didn't complain.

He was glad, in a way, that his mother and Peter were taking him out, because that would mean that they would go to a restaurant called The Drum, down by the Thames. That was what they always did when his mother took him out. With his father it was different. Sometimes they went to Henley and saw a film, sometimes they went and visited Uncle Alan, who he liked in a shy sort of way because of the way that he was, and other times they went for walks in the rain and ended up having a Wimpy and chips. When his mother took him out she always wanted to know exactly what he had done and where he had been when his father had taken him out; when his father took him out, they never even talked about his mother. His mother gave him a lot of presents and sweets, but his father very rarely gave him either. He liked his mother because she was so smart and he could be proud of her when she arrived at the school, especially when she arrived with Peter, because Peter was very large and had a boomy voice and everyone knew he was a Senior Officer in the Navy. He liked his father because once he had told him, sort of secretly, that whatever happened, whatever happened (Yes, he had said it twice like that) he would always be his father and would always love him in a very special way, always be interested in him, not just how he was doing at school but how he was doing as himself, how he was growing up, turning into a person; and he had explained that that was why he didn't give so many presents, because he wanted them to be friends as well as father and son, and friends didn't have to be giving each other presents all the time, did they?

He sort of understood and he sort of didn't. When he was with his father he liked his father best and when he was with his mother he liked her best. It was muddling and difficult, especially when they came to the school together, to talk to old Sparrow or Mrs Nailor about him, because he didn't know how to talk. When he was with his mother he talked in one way and when he was with his father he talked in another; but he didn't have a way for talking when they were both together, so he said hardly anything at all, and once he had overheard his mother say, 'He's not like this with me, you know, he's perfectly natural with me.' That was the day last term when they decided he would have to have extra coaching. He hated that because it made him different from everyone else and he knew that if his mother and father had been happy, like Buzz Remington's, he would have been better at reading and writing and not dyslexic at all, because he had overheard old Sparrow talking about it when the common room door opened: he had been saying that nobody knew what went on in the mind of a child when their

485

parents split up and that might well be the cause of his dyslexia.

That's what his parents were, split up, and he hated them both in a way, for being split up. That was the funny thing: he loved them when he was alone with one or other of them but he hated them when they were together because they were together in the wrong sort of way. Sometimes he had a wonderful dream about them being properly together when they were all having tea in Stocks Cottage, all of them, Mummy, Nita, Penny and himself, and Daddy came in and everyone was laughing and talking and Mummy and Daddy kissed each other and they were all joined up, all of them, in a sort of circle; that was his best dream but he didn't often have it nowadays. More usually he had a nightmare that he couldn't explain to Miss Underwood the matron because it was just a sort of grey eye that got larger and larger, an eye like the eye of that horse they had to shoot at the point-to-point they all went to, the horse that fell and broke its legs. When he saw that eye he usually woke up everyone else in the dormitory because he couldn't help screaming.

No, he didn't know why his mother and Peter had come to take him out, but he didn't mind all that much. Sometimes they did change their plans like this. So long as it was one or the other, not both, he didn't mind. So they sang the last hymn, 'City of God How Broad and Far', and when they were outside he introduced Buzz Remington and his mother said 'Yes of course Buzz can come out, can't he Peter?' and Peter said ' The more the merrier,' and laughed so that his shoulders went up and down. 'Now you've got everything you need, haven't you, because we're in a bit of a hurry,' his mother said, and off they went in Peter's T registration Volvo Estate, between the rhododendrons and over the sleeping policemen, and he was glad, after all, that his father wasn't taking him out because his car had rusty mudguards and no acceleration.

So they went down the hill through Craybourne village with Peter's and his mother's heads in front of them against the high headrests, and he knew that Buzz was impressed, especially when Peter started talking to him as if he were a grown up, asking him where he lived and saying 'Is he indeed?' when Buzz said that his father was a director of a firm that made port wine. They went along the road towards Henley and parked behind The Drum, and they sat outside by the lock gates and the weir and had Coca-Cola and peanuts, which they threw to the swans, and inside the restaurant there were tables with crisp white tablecloths and a mynah bird that talked. They had melon and steak and wrinkly chips and mushrooms and peas and after that the waiter brought a trolley along with meringues and chocolate gateau and fruit salad, and he chose a very creamy thing called a profiterole and his mother put up her eyebrows and said 'You wouldn't be having this if your father was taking you out, would you, Thomas?' And he said no, he wouldn't, more like baked beans, and his mother glanced at Peter and they were laughing inside but not out loud.

After lunch, when Peter had paid with an American Express Card (Buzz said, 'My Dad's Diner's Club') they went for a walk along the tow path by the Thames, and it was so hot his mother suggested they take everything off except their pants and go in for a swim, so they did, and had to dry in the sun because no one had a towel, and when he was sitting on the bank with his toes in the brown water, Peter sat beside him and put his hand on his shoulder, saying encouraging things about working hard and playing hard and how these years at prep school were important years and he must really try his best and join in and have a go at everything.

Then there was tea, in the Tudor restaurant at Craybourne, and he asked for baked beans and sausages and his mother said, 'Really, Thomas how could you?' but he was allowed to have it, and Buzz told them all about Henshaw, who had been blinded in one eye by a golf ball, and they went on talking, taking as long as possible to drink their Coca-Cola because you always tried to get back to the school a little bit after six thirty, which was when the exeat ended.

On the way back, as they drove up the hill under the beech trees, a car came the other way, and his mother said, 'That was him,' and she and Peter laughed about something Peter said in French which he didn't understand. His mother gave him a bag full of Mars bars when they got out of the car and said he was to share them with Buzz because she hadn't known Buzz was coming. 'Mind my lipstick,' she said when she kissed him goodbye, and at the same time he saw the car bumping over the sleeping policemen. 'Here's Daddy,' he said, but his mother said he'd better go straight inside in case he was late for roll call, so he went in with Buzz, partly because she told him to but also because he knew there was going to be a fight. When he got into school house, he ran along the corridor, through the tuck box room and the boot room along between new block and school house, back towards the main drive, and crept in under the rhododendron bushes to where Peter's Volvo was parked; he went stealthily on all fours until he was so close he could have reached out and touched the polished black heels of his mother's shoes, but he was too late to hear what they were saying because they had already said it: his mother was getting into the Volvo and the engine was starting; the door was slamming and immediately the Volvo was reversing, turning and driving off, and then, looking up, he saw his father watching it go; and his face was frightening, horrible: he was crying without making any noise, something Thomas had never seen him do before, so he stayed there, quite still, hardly daring to breathe, and it was a relief when his father got back into his car, and the engine just managed to start and he drove slowly away.

Steven drove to Alan's in a mood of anger and frustration which had abated only slightly by the time he drew up outside number fifty-nine. He remained behind the wheel a few moments after switching off the engine, looking at himself in the driving mirror, brushing a wisp of hair over his head with his hand, straightening his tie and thinking well, here we go.

He went down the path to the front door and knocked, tapping his foot while he waited, already imagining Alan's welcome and the bluff act it would be necessary to adopt when he met Catherine. No, he would not kiss her – not even on the cheek. He would shake her firmly by the hand. He would look her in the eye and say how well she was looking, how little she had changed – whatever she looked like, however much she had changed. He would keep his guard up, give nothing away. He would sit down to supper with them and leave at eleven however much they wanted him to stay. He would do his duty, no more, no less. The hatchet would be buried, that would be that.

He knocked again, looked through the letter box and called, 'Hullo? Anyone at home?'

Probably in the garden, he decided. It was that sort of evening, a peaceful summer evening, when people sat in their gardens and tried not to think about Monday.

He let himself in with his own key and went through the hall to the kitchen. There was a note on the fake marble work-top. 'Steve: we've gone to watch the tennis. Come and join us. A.'

He crumpled the note, and went into the garden. The sound of clapping came from the direction of the tennis courts: the local club must be holding one of its summer tournaments. Beyond the wilderness of disused allotments, children pursued each other on bikes by the stream.

He went back into the kitchen, putting off the moment of meeting. Not that I'm scared of course, he told himself. No, not at all. Just that I don't want to rush into her arms, that's all.

He noted the preparations for supper: a plate of cold meats covered in clingfilm, a wooden bowl of salad, with tomatoes and radishes cut into rosettes and placed in a pattern among fresh lettuce hearts.

That would be Catherine's work: Alan could chop tomatoes (just) but he couldn't turn them into rosettes. He wasn't sure why, but it annoyed him that Catherine had been involved in the preparations. He wondered what else she had done for Alan and opened the refrigerator to investigate. Yes, here was more evidence of the fatted calf: a bottle of Liebfraumilch in the freezer, a summer pudding, a jug of clotted cream. He closed the door and the coolant pump started up with a hum.

The woman's touch was even more apparent in the living room. He noted the new hearthrug and wondered where it had come from; the room had a cosiness about it he had not known when he had last been here. There was a pink cardigan on the back of the sofa.

The piano was open with music on the stand. Chopin preludes, his old music. That annoyed him too. And the table: laid for three with the best glass, the best cutlery; a dark green table napkin on each sideplate; a white vase in the shape of a swan, filled with sweet peas and violas. He smiled grimly, almost desperately. Could he actually sit down with them? Alan and Catherine and himself? What could they possibly talk about?

He felt the beginnings of panic. He went into the hall and up to his bedroom. When in doubt, go up to your room and hide.

He opened the door and stopped dead. She was in here, of course. Not her physical being, but her presence. Her shoes were under the bed. Her night cream was on the small dresser. He was horrified actually to recognise her brush and comb. She had kept them for nineteen years!

He caught a glimpse of himself in the mirror: a grey intruder with baggy eyes that seemed to accuse and confess at the same time.

Turning back, he saw her nightdress, a pair of tights, a silk blouse, things draped over the back of the upright chair, on hangers behind the door. He touched the blouse as if to prove to himself that it existed. Then he noticed that the photograph of his father had been taken down. Perhaps she was a little beset by the past as well; perhaps she had not enjoyed using this room or sleeping in this bed.

He went out to the landing and listened for sounds of their arrival.

In Alan's study at the back of the house, sunlight was sloping in through the open window and a bowl of flowers – more sweet peas – had been set on the desk by the typewriter. He glanced down at the pile of typed sheets, the box of unused paper, the rack of pencils, the notepad. He looked out over the garden to the chestnut trees, heavy with foliage.

Julietta had ignored his outburst entirely. She had laughed at him with her eyes, the most effective way she knew of belittling him. She had stood beside Peter in a flame red dress, polished shoes with pirate buckles, a gold chain about her neck, her tinted hair stiff with aerosol spray.

'Bit late aren't we?' she had said.

He had faced them, shaking with anger. 'We agreed the dates, Julietta. You know that damn well. We agreed that I would take him out this week.'

Lasbury, large and opulent in check shirt, brass buttoned blazer and silk Etonian square, poured his particular brand of oil on the waters. 'Never mind, Steve. If you can't take a joke you shouldn't have joined, eh? Them what's keen gets fell in previous.'

He was an admiral now. Admirals could get away with such verbiage, such overweening self-satisfaction.

They had laughed, and re-embarked in their Volvo. The doors had slammed, they had driven off, enthroned in their status symbol, totally secure in their superiority.

Another burst of applause, prolonged this time, came from the tennis courts. The match had ended: he looked diagonally through the window towards the pavilion and saw hands being shaken across the net, backs slapped, people in whites.

He saw Alan and Catherine.

They were walking along the side of the court and out through the gate to the cinder track, Alan in his usual white shirt and grey flannels, Catherine in a grey-green dress with no sleeves, a white cardigan over her shoulders.

Suddenly all the cynicism about meeting her was gone. He stared at her. From this distance at least, she seemed unchanged by the years: as graceful, as gentle and as timorous as he had imagined her so often when seeking mental refuge from Julietta's feline malice.

They had paused to talk to a neighbour who had been watching the match over his garden fence. He saw Catherine smiling as she spoke, her head moving in a way he had forgotten but now remembered and recognised. He began to feel a breathlessness, a slipping away of control.

He whispered: 'Mouse ...!'

It was no good. He could not face her. He could not allow her to see the person he had become in these years without her; he could not bring himself to risk having to look again into those hazel-grey eyes and see in them the hurt that he knew would still be there, the hurt he had caused that summer night in Malta.

He went quickly downstairs and out to the car. He drove off along Chestnut Road, right into Gordon Road and right again into Dollis Road. Going under the viaduct and up Bittacy Hill past the gas works and the tube station, he felt a sort of hysteria rising in him: he was on that same circuit he had once pedalled on his bicycle, the night he played truant from sea scouts. He was running away, all over again.

He pulled up by a telephone kiosk. It was quite simple. A white lie was called for, that was all. A white lie that was so nearly the truth that it was hardly a lie at all.

He dialled Alan's number, and when Catherine answered, inserted a coin.

It was necessary to walk a little slower than normal with Alan. Catherine had found this difficult at first but now rather liked it.

As they went along the cinder track, he said, 'That went on longer than I expected. I hope you weren't bored.'

'Not at all,' she said. 'It was a good match.'

He glanced at her. She had been much more relaxed this last week and he had genuinely enjoyed having her to stay. He was beginning to wonder how he would feel tomorrow evening, when he came back to an empty house. Living on one's own had great advantages, but there were moments of loneliness. The weekends were the worst times, and Saturdays in particular.

'Wonder if Steve's turned up yet,' he remarked.

'Yes. I wonder.'

491

They went in through the back gate and up the path to the kitchen door, ducking their heads under the lower branches of the apple tree before going up the four steps by the coal bunker.

Entering the kitchen, he said: 'Ah. He's here.' He picked up the crumpled note on the work top. Catherine smiled quickly.

He lowered his voice. 'Don't be frightened, Mouse!'

She looked down. 'Please don't call me that, Alan.'

He went into the hall. His voice echoed briefly about the house. 'Steve? You upstairs?'

He lugged himself up to the landing and she heard him going into the rooms. He said: 'He's not up here.'

She was in the dining room looking out of the windows to the road when he came downstairs. He stood behind her.

'Well that's very odd,' he said.

She turned back: their eyes met briefly, and she tried to smile.

'I know what's happened,' he said. 'He's arrived here, seen the table, had a conscience, and rushed out to buy a bottle of wine or something.'

She seemed to accept that explanation, but Alan wasn't sure that he did himself. His brother wasn't as reliable as he had been.

'Anyway, don't let's wait for him,' he said briskly. 'If we've finished the plonk by the time he gets back, that'll be his hard luck, won't it?'

He went into the kitchen and a moment later called to her. 'Cat! Would you be very kind and open this for me? I'm feeling lazy.'

She came into the kitchen and accepted the corkscrew from him. 'You're not feeling lazy at all,' she said. 'You're keeping me busy. It's occupational therapy.'

He grinned sheepishly.

They took their glasses of wine into the sitting room. The sun was almost gone. They stood side by side at the window and waited. The silence slipped on, lengthening.

'Can I tell you something quickly before Steve arrives?'

She smiled uncertainly. 'Yes? What?'

'He'll be too shy to say it, but it needs saying.'

He glanced at her: she held her wine glass in both hands. There was a defencelessness in her expression which he had seen before; she had a very smooth, clear brow, steady eyes, a widow's peak. He knew that she was far more keyed up about Steven than she had admitted or allowed herself to show; he knew that she was badly in need of a boost to her self-confidence.

'All I want to say is – just – you look smashing. And I'm not just saying that to reassure you, either. You really do.'

She smiled and frowned in her confusion. 'I'm not used to people saying things like that to me, Alan.'

'All the more reason for my saying it then.'

'Well. Thank you.' She laughed. 'I don't know what else to say.' Her eyes travelled up and met with his, then moved quickly away. 'May I return the compliment?'

He gave a little laugh in reply and raised his glass to her. Then he said, 'Where the devil is that brother of mine?'

'You're as jumpy as I am,' she said.

He put his wine down on the low table and went into the hall. She asked where he was going. He said: 'See if I can see him coming.'

She watched him go up the path and stand at the latchgate looking up and down the road. He raised his hand to someone she could not see and walked out of sight. At the same moment, the telephone rang.

It was a call from a telephone box. She heard the rapid pips then:

'Catherine? It's me. Steven.'

She caught her breath. 'Oh! We were just wondering where you'd got to.'

He went on hurriedly: 'Look I'm afraid I've had a breakdown, I don't think I'm going to make it.'

For a moment she believed him, but only for a moment. He was too confident, too bland.

'Isn't it a bore? I am sorry.'

'So am I,' she said.

There was an awkward pause.

He said: 'How are you anyway?'

'Very well. Alan's looked after me very well.'

'Good. Splendid.'

'And you?'

He laughed. 'Oh – fair to middling you know. Surviving.'

She saw Alan coming back down the path to the front door. Steven coughed. 'So – er you go back to Kenya tomorrow, right?'

'Yes that's right.'

'Any idea when you'll next be over here?'

She shook her head then whispered. 'No, no idea.'

There was a silence. Alan entered the room. She glanced up at

493

him. He frowned then mouthed the question, 'Steven?' She nodded. He held out his hand, offering to take over the receiver from her. She shook her head.

Steven coughed again. 'Well I'm sorry to miss you,' he said. 'Maybe it's for the best though, isn't it?'

'Yes,' she agreed. 'Maybe.'

'Is Alan there?'

'Yes –'

'Well give him my apologies will you?'

'Would you like to speak to him?'

He laughed in a voice she didn't know at all. 'I'd rather speak to you!'

There was another pause. 'Catherine?'

'Yes?'

His voice broke. 'Look – I've never said this properly. But I am sorry. For everything.'

She saw Alan watching her and turned away.

Steven said: 'Did you ever manage to forgive me?'

'Yes,' she whispered. 'Everything.'

He was silent again. She felt that they were saying more to each other in their silences than in their words.

'And I am sorry about tonight,' he said. 'Really sorry.'

'It's all right, Steven. I understand.'

She heard him breathe out twice. He said, 'Bless you Catherine. I never deserved you in the first place.'

The pips went. In the last few seconds he said, 'Goodbye then. Goodbye Mouse.'

They were cut off. She put the receiver gently back on its rest and turned to Alan. He said: 'That was Steven.'

'Yes,' she replied. 'That was Steven.'

He was angry at first, that Steven had presumed to deceive Catherine with his excuse about a breakdown. There was no doubt of that deceit: it was not just a suspicion based upon the crumpled note he had found in the kitchen; he had spoken to Mrs Groves in her front garden and she had confirmed that she had seen Steven drive away only five or ten minutes before.

'Surely you must have known he was lying?' he said, staring at the row of books on the shelf by the fireplace, and swinging back to face her. 'Why didn't you ask him where he was? That would have put him on the spot.'

'It doesn't matter, Alan. I'm not at all hurt by that.'

'Well I am. That was my brother you were speaking to. Trying to get away with little fibs of excuse. I'm ashamed of him. And for him.'

She unlaid the third place on the table and put the cutlery and glass in the sideboard.

He said: 'You've been cheated by both of us. I talked you into agreeing to meet him and now he's gone and done this. We've let you down all over again. I talked you into becoming a Catholic and I talked you into going out to him.' He laughed. 'It's about as close as you can get to eternal recurrence, isn't it? What was that bit about a gateway called Time, "this slow spider"?'

'I've no idea what you're talking about,' she said quietly.

His face worked: grotesquely, she would have thought had she not known him as well as she did. He said: *Thus Spake Zarathustra.*'

'Yes, but we know about Nietzsche, don't we?'

He made no reply. She went into the kitchen and brought in the cold chicken and the bowls of salad, which she set on the table.

'I don't feel cheated,' she said. 'You heard what I said to Steven. I've forgiven him. Everything. We needed to have that conversation. I needed to. It unlocked something. Not just for me, for all of us.'

'It doesn't alter the fact that he was lying, and it doesn't alter the fact that he didn't have the guts to face you. I can't forgive him for that.' He picked up the bottle of Liebfraumilch. 'Have some more.'

'A little, thank you.'

He poured the wine, spilt it, swore. She said. 'I'll get a cloth.' He said, 'No. Leave it.'

He sat down heavily in an armchair and stared out of the window. She remained standing. There was a long silence, then she said, 'He told me he had had a breakdown, that was all. I know that implied a car breakdown, but does it matter what sort of a breakdown he had? I understood what he was saying, and he knew I understood. Does it matter whether it was his carburettor or his confidence, really? He needed to save face, didn't he? Can't we be big enough to let him do that?'

She explained, quietly, what she had meant by the release Steven had unknowingly achieved for them. 'I know my own mind now,' she said. 'I know why I came over here, and I know why I'm going back. It'll be easier for Steven, too: I think I've relieved him of a sort of weight, a responsibility he felt towards me.'

They sat down to eat, but neither was hungry. They said very little for a long time; he wondered what she had meant by saying that it could be a release for him as well, and she seemed to read his thoughts and began to explain.

It was painful for both of them. She said that from now on he need not feel so closely responsible for Steven, nor would he have to lead any part of his life at second hand through him. He sat stock still, listening to her words but not taking them in fully nor seeing exactly what they implied. She said that Steven must be left alone to find his own way and that he, Alan, must no longer expect to share in his triumphs or disasters.

'You mean I should no longer think of myself as his brother,' he said.

'No, I don't mean that. I mean you should no longer think of yourself . . . as his keeper.'

She told him that she wasn't sure, but that sometimes she had felt that Steven might have felt stifled by his brother's expectations. She said she thought part of it was that Steven had felt he had been playing the part of a proxy. She looked back into his eyes and wept a little, recovering quickly, telling him that she didn't want to hurt him but that she felt these things needed to be said.

'It's time to let him lead his own life,' she said. 'And it's time to lead yours, too – completely, independently.'

She stood up from the table and drew the curtains across the front windows. She put on the standard lamp by the piano: the shade of it was the colour of gold and its light warmed the room. He was beginning to understand what was happening now; he could see that Steven had unwittingly started something which Catherine was unwittingly assisting: something he was afraid of, something so frightening and so impossible that he could scarcely acknowledge it to himself; it was an impossibility, he knew it was an impossibility, because he was a spastic and that sort of thing, real love, love not imagined nor dreamt about nor written down nor experienced at second hand was not for spastics, not even for the luckier ones like himself. And yet he was being driven towards it, caught in a tide that swept him along, onwards, out to that impossible horizon: he was looking with new eyes at her hands, her arms, her neck, her chin, the gentleness of her breasts; he was listening with new ears to her voice, he was looking back with a new awareness into her eyes, frightened that his thoughts might appear to her, written in his expression; for there were phrases running in his mind: words he had used in the past to replace the first hand experience: Tread softly, for you tread on my dreams ... Such long, swift tides stir not a landlocked sea ... Love is not love that alters when it alteration finds, or bends with the remover to remove ... He fought to keep check on it all, and he won his battle for he had been fighting for other sorts of control all his life; he was an old campaigner, a veteran. He watched her – covertly – for any sign that she might either suspect what he was thinking or be experiencing a similar turmoil; but he saw none. Perhaps he was afraid of seeing it, perhaps he closed his eyes to it. From being at ease with each other all week they were suddenly at a loss for words, and when she had helped him clear away the dishes, she said she would have an early night. He held away from her so that she should not feel at all obliged to kiss him on the cheek as she had the night before; he listened to her going up the stairs and he understood more clearly yet what she had said about something being unlocked, and in a panic he wondered if she had been keeping something from him all the time she was speaking, wondered if there might be someone in Kenya, someone she loved and had come away from in order to think clearly about, someone to whom she would now return and give herself, confidently and with all her heart.

Of course: that must have been what she had tried to say, what she had tried to tell him. That explained why she had wept and quickly regained control, that explained her long silence during the meal.

In the morning, he carried her cases down, one by one, to the hall. They breakfasted together and he was unable to say anything of what he wanted to say beyond 'I shall miss you,' which he muttered embarrassedly and which she appeared to ignore.

When they were waiting for the taxi she said, 'I'm sorry I gave you that lecture last night, Alan. I didn't mean to hurt you.'

'You didn't, it needed to be said.'

'Don't let it make any difference between you and Steven, will you? I'd hate that.'

He wondered if she herself understood the full meaning of what she had said the night before, and guessed that she did not; in consequence it became even more necessary to keep one particular implication – the most important implication – a secret. She must not know what had happened to him, she must not be allowed to feel beholden to him, to take pity on him. She must not be burdened with him as she had been burdened by Steven. She must be set free.

The taxi arrived. He was not accompanying her to the airport because he had an appointment in town that morning. The driver took her cases, all four at once, and loaded them into the boot. He stood by the car and waited while his passenger and her spastic friend came out of the house and up the path to the car. He watched them say goodbye, standing to one side like a referee.

She kissed Alan briefly on the cheek before getting in. She wound down her window and put out her hand, touching his left hand, the one that curled in upon itself. Her eyes filled with tears: she whispered, 'Thank you for everything,' and suddenly he wondered if he had been wrong, if perhaps she did feel something for him after all.

But it was too late now. The driver was getting in behind the wheel and starting up; the car was moving away down the road between the saplings planted on either side, and Catherine's face was turned back towards him and her hand raised in farewell.

He raised his right hand in reply and watched until the taxi was out of sight; then he turned, and went back into the house.

# 27

'Number twenty-three, ladies and gentlemen,' said the Sotheby's auctioneer, a diminutive man in a grey flannel suit. 'Campagne Saint Marc, Echourgnac, signed with monogram and dated 1936, Lucien Pissaro. Shall we make a start at fifteen hundred pounds?'

A lady in a purple dress, butterfly brooch and ear pendants raised a finger and nodded. Two more bidders joined in and the price went steadily up. It was an important sale of Impressionists and Post Impressionists, and the room was full to overflowing.

'Four thousand five hundred ... Five ... Five and a half thousand ... Six ...'

Some of the dealers glanced down at the illustrated catalogues on their knees. This small painting of an obscure part of the Dordogne was going to be yet another one to fetch an inflated price. It was not even a particularly fine specimen of Pissaro's work, but two bidders at least seemed quite determined to own it.

'Seven thousand. And a half. Eight. Eight thousand five hundred.' The auctioneer waited, looking back at the lady in the ear pendants, who shook her head and sat back in her chair, closing her catalogue with a snap.

'Eight thousand five hundred pounds. For the last time –' The gavel rapped briefly. 'Thank you, sir.'

The purchaser, an elegant man in a dark blue suit, pale blue shirt and polka dot tie, left his seat and made his way across to register his purchase.

'Captain Lasbury, isn't it?' a woman in blue stockings asked.

He bent forward and said mock-conspiratorially: 'Rear admiral now!'

'Oh!' she whispered. 'Many congratulations!'

He wrote a cheque and signed it with his neo-Baroque signature, which occupied the entire width of the slip of paper, and having given instructions for the delivery of his purchase to his apartment in Cadogan Square, he collected his umbrella and raincoat from the cloakroom and went out into the March wind and away down New Bond Street, taking steps that might have been considered a little too short for a man of his stature.

He was in his fiftieth year now. His mother had died alone in a Los Angeles hotel room six months before, and as the sole beneficiary of her will, he had become one of the wealthiest officers in the Royal Navy. Since his promotion to rear admiral, he had had a most successful tour as the flag officer of one of the navy's two remaining flotillas and had spent nearly a year as an Assistant Chief of Staff. He had been made a Companion of the Bath in the New Year's Honours List, and had recently received his first approach from *Who's Who*. Particularly pleasing to him was his entry in the pages of the Navy List, showing as it did all the triumphs of his career: the award of the Robert Roxburgh prize and King's telescope, his interpretership in Russian, his qualifications at the International Defence College and the Joint Services Staff College.

He regarded his private life as being similarly successful. His circle of acquaintances and friends remained large and his newly acquired Knightsbridge apartment was a delight. He had installed a very dear friend called Terry Rubbock – an ex-Royal Marine colour sergeant – in his villa at Echourgnac and returned there for brief weekends of sunshine and love. The advantage, he had discovered, of having an ex-serviceman as one's lover was that you could rely upon him to be discreet. When friends came to stay, Rubbock metamorphosed into a manservant, a retainer, and when they had gone he reverted to the role of master. They slept in a huge bed on the first floor, and their window looked out upon the very countryside depicted in the painting by Pissaro Lasbury had bought that morning. Lasbury treated Rubbock with the sort of affection one might lavish on a well loved dog, and Rubbock, knowing which side his bread was buttered, did whatever Peter required of him with energy and skill.

In spite of his easy circumstances, the promotion motive was still strong in Peter Lasbury. Being promoted to rear admiral had been like moving up from the sixth form to university: he became, once more, a 'junior boy', a freshman. The wide golden ring on the sleeve of his uniform represented for him all the dedication, planning and hard work that had gone into hoisting himself up the ladder from sub lieutenant to captain, and the single thin ring above it represented the first rung of a new ladder, the final ascent. If he could climb this last ladder, these last three steps from rear admiral to vice admiral, from vice admiral to admiral and from admiral to admiral of the fleet, he would achieve that one goal he had always set himself: he would be knighted, perhaps given a peerage. He would win a mention in the history books; he would attain a small immortality.

He was not thinking of these things as he walked down New Bond Street, however, but was pondering whether to hang his new purchase in his London apartment or to take it out to Echourgnac, when a not quite familiar voice called his name and he found himself face to face with his old captain from HMS *Copenhagen*, Johnny Tinnick.

'Sir!' he said automatically, though Tinnick had been retired in the rank of commander many years before and was some sort of civil servant. 'What a surprise!'

Tinnick looked his old protégé up and down and hesitated as if listening to instructions only he could hear. 'Isn't it indeed?' he said. 'How very pleasant to see you. Are we going in the same direction?'

It appeared that they were, and after an exchange of pleasantries, Tinnick said, 'Look – would you be free for lunch by any chance?'

Lasbury was free. A few minutes later they were entering the white portals of Brown's, and a few minutes after that Peter Lasbury raised a glass of Campari and soda to his lips.

They spoke of old times. Tinnick was a member of the Association of Retired Naval Officers, the Naval and Military Club and the Greenwich Forum, and he had followed Lasbury's career with interest. Lasbury did not find this at all odd: Tinnick was one of several of his old commanding officers who continued to achieve a certain satisfaction in his success, members of that breed who regard themselves as part of the Royal Navy long after they have retired, and who cannot hear enough about the latest promotions, the latest commands, the latest ships to come off the slip.

As their conversation progressed, it became apparent that Tinnick had an unusually firm grasp of naval politics. He knew the names of every up and coming captain and rear admiral, and Lasbury began to have the feeling that he was being treated to an unusual glimpse into his own chances of promotion.

'What about you, Johnny?' he asked eventually. 'Weren't you in the Central Office of Information at one time?'

Tinnick laughed. 'That was some years ago, Peter. No, I've moved on from there.' He smiled enigmatically, stretching his neck muscles a little and lifting his chin in an unctuous way. 'But tell me, what are the feelings about the Defence Estimates on the sixth floor? What do you think of this man Nott?'

Lasbury did not think a great deal. The new Secretary of State for Defence was threatening to wield yet another axe and cut the surface fleet by twenty-five percent. That a Tory government should contemplate further cuts in seapower, when the Soviet fleet was being built up at an alarming rate seemed to him something of a betrayal; but on the other hand he was aware of the importance of not shouting his objections too loudly: if one did that, one was liable to receive a golden handshake and a curt farewell.

They moved into the dining room and ordered sole meunière.

'I tell you who I bumped into in Hamley's the other day,' Tinnick said. 'Clara Braddle. We were choosing birthday presents for our respective grandchildren. Didn't have much time for a chat, but I gathered Julietta's marriage broke up?'

'Yes indeed I'm afraid it did,' Lasbury said, looking suitably downcast. 'Not entirely surprising, though. You remember young Steven of course?'

'How could I forget! He was the idiot who broke his oar in the officers' whaler. We'd have won the cock but for young Jannaway. What's happened to him?'

'Been outside for a couple of years now,' Lasbury said. 'Last time I heard of him he was managing a yacht marina on the Hamble. I see Julietta from time to time though. She's very well. Put on a bit of weight, mind.'

Tinnick chuckled. 'To my dying day I shall remember the look on your face, Peter, when you brought her back in the skimmer after that accident.' Tinnick went on chuckling, somewhat to Lasbury's annoyance.

'I must be on my way shortly, Johnny. I've got a conference with VCNS at three.'

'You'll have time for a coffee,' Tinnick said, and there was something in the way he said it that made Lasbury glance quickly at his old commanding officer. Not for the first time since meeting him in New Bond Street, he had the feeling that something had been pre-arranged.

They rose from the table, and Tinnick led the way into a corner of the lounge where they could talk in private. When the coffee had arrived and the waiter had withdrawn, Tinnick said, 'Peter I have a delicate matter to raise with you.' He paused, listened to his private voice, then continued: 'It concerns your PV form.'

PV stood for Positive Vetting, and in making this simple statement Tinnick was revealing to Lasbury something that should not normally be revealed, namely that he was a member of the security organisation involved in vetting senior officers for the posts they held. He was also revealing that their chance meeting that morning had not been a chance meeting at all.

Lasbury touched the corner of his mouth with the knuckle of his forefinger and licked his lips. 'Johnny!' he said quietly. 'This sounds highly irregular!'

'It is highly irregular,' Tinnick replied, 'But I think we know each other well enough to keep it to ourselves, don't we?'

'Depends what "it" is.' Lasbury added a small spoonful of multicoloured sugar to his coffee. 'What about my PV form?'

Tinnick lowered his voice further. 'I'm concerned about one of your referees.'

The form Lasbury had completed was a long, complicated one in which facts about parentage, education, interests and social and political connections had to be revealed in detail. Aware of his Achilles heel, Lasbury had always been scrupulously careful in the filling in of this form, required every five years, choosing as his referees people of good standing and impeccable reputations. He knew that they were interviewed personally by retired officers who were re-employed by the crown, and he knew also that the two most important questions, always asked, probed into the possibility of an officer having homosexual or left-wing tendencies. He had never been aware of any problem over passing this security test, and over the years had had access to war plans, orders of battle, papers on experimental tactics, and details of electronic and cryptographic systems that were very highly classified.

'Which referee?' he asked.

Tinnick then surprised him again. He took from his inside pocket the form Lasbury had so carefully completed two weeks before, unfolded it and spread it out on the low table between them. 'That one,' he said, indicating the name of a QC who had acted as Lasbury's referee for many years and whose public reputation was spotless.

Lasbury was amazed. 'Douglas?' he whispered. 'Why?'

Tinnick consulted his private oracle, glancing at the ceiling with a pained expression. 'Do you know the name Denis Manchester?'

'I can't say I do.'

'Well he and your man ... Douglas ... are known to have been close friends some years ago.'

'I'm none the wiser,' Lasbury said.

Tinnick seemed to go off on a new tack. 'You must appreciate that there's been a lot of activity in my line of country these past two years, Peter. Mrs T's been putting the pressure on, and a lot of nasties are crawling out of the woodwork.'

'Maybe so,' Lasbury said, 'But surely Douglas –'

'Douglas and Manchester were on close terms in the mid-sixties, Peter, and we've also discovered that Manchester was at the same time on remarkably close terms with friend Anthony.'

'Anthony?'

'Blunt,' Tinnick said, almost inaudibly.

'My God!'

Tinnick laughed a little. 'I hope not, Peter!'

Lasbury looked decidedly white about the gills. He had not had the first inkling that his friend Douglas was that way inclined, and the revelation of it caused in him an illogical resentment at being deceived. He also had cause to feel frightened: he knew that there had been rumours going round about the Royal Navy being infiltrated at a high level, and the slightest whiff of suspicion could bring about a witch hunt and end his career very rapidly. It also struck him that Tinnick probably knew of his interest in fine art and that he was a friend and benefactor of the Royal Academy. What a fool he had been! Such associations, seen in this context, could quite easily prejudice his promotion chances, and he determined, then and there, to take up polo again.

'What do you suggest I do about it, Johnny?' he asked.

Tinnick nodded contentedly as if Lasbury had asked, 'What shall I do to be saved?' He put his hand once more into the inside pocket of his grey pinstripe suit, and brought out another surprise: a blank PV form. He looked into Lasbury's aquamarine eyes and said, 'Write me out another form.'

'Now?'

'Now.'

Lasbury looked at his watch. 'I shall be late for VCNS.'

Tinnick spread the blank form on top of the first. 'I'm the only person who has read your form in detail, Peter, and I'm required to pass it on to my superior with my comments this afternoon. Which would you prefer, a flea in your ear from the Vice Chief of Naval Staff or a knife between the shoulder blades from the Director of Intelligence?'

Lasbury took out his Schaeffer and began to write. When he came to the box which had contained the offending name he stopped and asked, 'Got any suggestions?'

Tinnick shrugged. 'I wouldn't have thought you would have any difficulty, Peter. He has to have known you at least five years, that's all we stipulate.'

Lasbury considered a moment and then had a brainwave. Charles Tomkins had left the navy as a commander some years before and had won a seat in the House of Commons in the '79 election. He would no doubt be happy to act as a referee and, what was more important, as a staunch heterosexual Conservative his opinion would carry weight with the security services.

Tinnick recognised the name and smiled. 'Just the chap,' he said, and when the form was complete looked it over carefully. 'I'm most grateful to you, Peter,' he said. 'That's saved us both a lot of unpleasantness.'

They strolled through to the hall, Tinnick refusing assistance in the putting on of his coat before going out to an awaiting taxi.

'A word of advice,' he said as they shook hands. He glanced upward at the racing clouds, listening for any last minute instructions from on high. 'Might it not be a prudent move to find yourself a wife one of these days?'

Then the taxi door was open and it was Goodbye Peter, Goodbye Johnny, Nice to see you again, and Very nice to see you too; and as the taxi went along Piccadilly, round the statue of Eros and down the Haymarket to Trafalgar Square, Peter Lasbury thought yes, perhaps it would be very prudent indeed to find myself a wife, or, to put it more strongly, perhaps it would be madness not to.

It had been a very close shave, there was no doubt of that. He lost a night's sleep thinking about what the consequences would have been if his form had landed on someone else's desk, if Tinnick had not warned him, if the matter had been taken up and further enquiries made. The thought of it sent cold shivers down his spine.

He telephoned Chas Tomkins at the House the following evening, to give him notice that he had used his name as a referee. 'You don't mind, do you old boy?' he said, and Tomkins's boyish voice came back down the line saying, 'Why of course not, Peter, absolutely delighted. You must come and have lunch one of these days.'

He returned to his flat. Sothebys had delivered his Pissaro, and he occupied a few minutes choosing where to hang it, eventually putting it in a place of honour on the wall opposite his desk in the study. He drew the blue velvet curtains and put on the wall lights, pleased with the effect, then he sat down in his leather armchair and thought about Julietta.

She was the obvious – virtually the only – choice. They were still good friends, and he had last seen her at Thomas's carol service three months before. He would enjoy playing father to Thomas, there was no doubt of that, but he felt apprehensive of some of the other obligations that marriage would bring. Terry would present a difficulty, too: he would have to play that very carefully. It would be necessary to explain to Julietta that his years of bachelorhood had formed habits that he could not break, and that he found it necessary to get away on his own from time to time. Perhaps he could keep Echourgnac to himself, perhaps he could have it both ways, Julietta as a wife and housekeeper and his beautiful colour sergeant as a manservant and lover. Why not? Both of them were devoted to him, so why should he not keep both happy?

Could he do that? Yes, he could: there was so much to be gained by the arrangement that the effort must be worthwhile, and the thought of actually going to bed with Julietta stirred his imagination: it seemed almost a 'naughty' thing to do, and for that reason it was attractive. Think of it! Him! Married!

He laughed to himself and soaped his armpits under the shower. Tinnick was right, of course he was: it would obviously be a huge advantage to him to be married, and especially *newly* married, with a wife who shared his ambition, a wife from a naval family herself, who would be immediately welcomed wherever she went. And how fitting, too, that he should marry in this, his fiftieth year!

But he was galloping ahead. He towelled himself dry and thought about courtship. He had told Julietta that he would never marry, but he knew her well enough to be able to convince her that things had changed. What was important was that she should not suspect any ulterior motive. She must believe that he was genuinely in love with her.

He began to plan his campaign. If he was going to be sure of persuading her to marry him, he may as well do the job properly, which as far as she was concerned meant romantically. He must woo her; and because he could understand how she would want to feel, he would woo her better than any other man ever could. He would make her wildest dreams come true.

He mixed a Campari and soda and went and admired his Pissaro. It wouldn't be very difficult, after all: Julietta had often made it clear to him that she believed they belonged together, and now that she had turned forty she was suffering those romantic yearnings which seemed to assail women in their early middle age.

Very well, he decided, sipping his Campari and listening to his Vivaldi; she shall have her romance, and I shall be the person who provides it.

He reached for the telephone and dialled Meonford House. 'Hello?' said Julietta's voice a little guardedly. She had been the victim of a number of obscene telephone calls until changing her number and going ex-directory a few months before.

'Julie, it's Peter.'

'Peter! I was just thinking of you!'

'Oh well isn't that nice,' he laughed. 'Listen, I've had a sudden thought. I have to go to Brussels – one of these NATO conferences – at the beginning of next week. It occurred to me that you might possibly like to come along too?'

He heard her catch her breath. 'Peter! Darling! What a perfectly fabulous idea!'

It happened so unexpectedly and perfectly that Julietta was at first afraid that it could not possibly last. She feared that by its very nature Peter's affection for her, so suddenly reawakened, was too fragile a thing to live more than a season: for they were not a Darby and Joan but super beings, whose love must be pursued not for its permanence but for its sheer ephemeral beauty, its single moment of ecstasy. When his huge, polished Daimler came nosing up the drive between the laurel and rhododendron bushes she felt herself spirited back to a time when she had been thirteen years old and he a glorious lieutenant. Driving away with him, she became the heroine, the super-star, the princess she had so often imagined herself on lonely nights when she was trying to sleep. How wonderful to walk at his side, he in full mess dress, the broad golden stripe down the side of each trouser leg, the decoration at his throat! How wonderful to be Rear Admiral Peter Q. Lasbury *and his Lady* on the gold embossed NATO invitation. Yes, she knew that he towered over her in many ways, but she felt no need to dominate him or boss him as she had with Steven. Peter was the man she had been delivered into this world for, the man she had kept herself for, the man to whom she had belonged in spirit since her childhood.

She knew, too, that it had taken courage on his part to invite her for those days in Brussels, and she was determined to be a credit to him and make him feel that next time he could not do without her at his side. Going into that reception with him, being introduced to the Supreme Allied Commander and the Chief of the Defence Staff and the Secretary General, she felt she had been mixing in such company all her life. These moments marked the beginning of a new existence for her, an emergence as her real self, the true Julietta. She captivated the Secretary General and she told Peter she thought the Chief of Defence Staff was dishy, to which he agreed, his blue eyes dancing with a special amusement, one which only she could understand and share. 'Was I all right this evening?' she murmured when they returned to the hotel and she went into his room to say goodnight, and he replied, 'You were superb, you are always superb.' Hearing him say that, and other things too, things she had so often longed to hear him say, sent a liquid warmth through her that made the blood tingle in her veins; and when she kissed him she parted his lips with the tip of her tongue, quickly, experimentally, drawing back to look at him, her own lips wobbling in an uncertain smile. 'You're trembling, Peter, aren't you? You're trembling.' And he smiled shyly, beautifully and the thought went through her mind like a bullet that if something really was beginning, she might be his very first woman and, in a sense, he her very first virgin. Yes that was the beginning of it because the next day they crossed in the ferry to Folkestone and drove all the way along the bottom of England, and when they arrived back at Meonford House after snails and chateaubriand in Botley, she said, 'Stay the night,' not believing for a moment that he would and so amazed and excited when he accepted that she blushed all over and went squidgy down there, having to pretend to be very busy putting out the king size bar of Imperial Leather in his bathroom, taking towels out of the airing cupboard, turning back the duvet in the spare room, plumping his pillow. 'Am I allowed to come and kiss you goodnight?' she asked outside his door when she knew he had had his bath, and he said, 'I should be desolate if you did not, Juju,' in that deep, melodious voice of his that made things jump up and down inside her. So she went in to him, knowing that she looked wonderful, little-girlish, with her hair loose and her breasts pretty, hiding under her nightdress; she went in to him, leant against him, felt the smooth warmth of his chest through his paisley pyjamas;

and for a moment she thought that it might happen then and there: she saw indecision in his eyes and she wanted to whisper yes, yes, go on, I'm yours; but she managed not to; they kissed, the moment passed. Early next morning, at six o'clock, she gave him toast and coffee. He was an admiral again, smoothly shaved, fragrant and distinguished. 'Perhaps we ought to do this more often,' he said when she went out with him to the car, and she replied, 'I'm sure we ought.' His Daimler slipped out through the gates and she was left in her porch wondering if it could ever happen again, ever be so fine, so restrained, so full of promise; but she was not disappointed: he rang her that evening and asked, 'How are you feeling?' making it clear to her in that way that something had happened and that he was acknowledging it. They didn't want people to talk or her mother to know, so when he came down the following Friday he parked the car by the church and came to her along the path by the river and up through the walled garden, over the lawn to the french windows, and he brought her a glorious red white and blue silk scarf and told her, out of the blue, that he had tickets for the ballet. How marvellous to have to telephone Mummy and make a silly excuse about not being able to go for Sunday lunch! And how satisfying too, to drive away with him out of the village, to wave airily to Virginia, who was now divorced herself and who had been making approaches, trying to get her to go riding again, trying to forge a womanly relationship; how pleasing to know that she could do without Virginia, need not respond to her advances or get involved in her personal distress.

In the morning after the ballet, they had a lazy breakfast and walked in Kensington Gardens; and she still did not ask Peter what was happening because she knew that he was not yet ready to tell her. It was necessary to let the seedling grow of its own accord, not dig it up in order to examine its roots. She went back with him to Cadogan Square; he put blissful Wagner on the record player: so grand, so proud, so full of cosmic meaning. She admired his paintings and his books and his Persian rug; she sipped his Muscadet and savoured his fresh prawns, and right at the end of that perfect day they rushed down the motorway with the speedometer needle touching a hundred and twenty miles an hour. 'Come in for a while,' she said when he delivered her to the door, and when she brought him coffee she sat on the arm of the sofa and stroked the back of his neck with her fingers, having the confidence now to ask,

509

'Do you like that?' and feeling that surge of happiness and expectation when he responded, smiling and saying yes, it was lovely, his lashes dark and irresistible and his eyes saying things she could not quite understand so that when the moment came she did not dare ask him to stay the night. She knew she should have as soon as he drove away and was suddenly terrified that she might have missed that one vital chance, or that he might have an accident or that whatever had happened inside him might dissolve or evaporate as mysteriously as it had appeared. But it didn't go away, it lasted and lasted and she could hardly believe, from one week to the next, that it was true. She felt like one of the heroines in the books she had been reading lately to escape the awfulness of life, who were virtuous in the way she had always been really, but for the things that had gone wrong, the things that weren't her fault. Peter was like one of those heroes, too: the real, impeccable, loving, thoughtful, romantic gentle man who gave her new reasons for being even nicer, even better than before. He gave her new reasons for taking care of her body, her skin, her hair, her teeth. She went back to her diet, she drank honey and lemon instead of coffee, she cut down on her cigarettes and took a course of beauty treatment with a local lady. She pulled back from the abyss of middle age, she refused to give up her youth just yet. So as the tulip tree by the gate burst forth and apple and peach blossom appeared, Julietta Jannaway found herself anew, living through each week for the Friday when Peter would appear at her back gate. But how difficult that last stage was, and how determined she was that he should be the one to make the final approach! She thought about him, went to matins and prayed about him, dreamt about him and read his horoscope with avid attention. April passed and most of May; she began to feel a growing desperation, a premonition that unless something happened soon, all his kindness and tentative courtship, all their evenings out, all their dinners and visits to the theatre would go to waste. In a strange way, their new intimacy was also an estrangement. She often had the feeling that Peter was trying to say and do things only to discover, at the last moment, that he was unable. Sometimes she thought she saw in his expression a pleading for help, and eventually she realised that if their love was to flower and bear fruit, she would have to be the one who brought it about. She was frightened of taking that step, but also frightened of not doing so, so finally, one night in early June when a half moon was

510

shining in through the lilac, she took her decision. The house was quiet: she slipped her nightdress over her head and tiptoed along the landing to his room, pushing his door open and going in to him, pulling the duvet back and sliding fearlessly in beside him; and she felt him trembling: she covered his face with her kisses, took his hand, pressed it over Elizabeth, took it on an expedition to the South. 'I can't,' he sobbed, 'I can't!' but she said 'Yes, you can, you can Peter, I'll help you.' 'I'm so small!' he whispered. 'It doesn't matter, I don't mind, I like you small!' and she helped him, on and on, and at first she was terrified because it didn't work and she was afraid of the growing disappointment inside her that had to be rejected and replaced by a determination to believe that this was what she wanted, that she really didn't mind. That was what she had to make herself believe because if she didn't, if she was disappointed, he would sense it and everything would be wrecked; so she did things for him, things she had daydreamed about doing with Steven or with Chas or with anyone. She did them and eventually, miraculously, it began to work: it became a battle that she knew she was winning; she worked at it and worked at it, doing it as well and as thoughtfully and cleverly as she possibly could until suddenly he succeeded, crying and whimpering in a voice she loved, a voice she had never heard; and she came back up to him, kissing him, sharing it with him, and it was for them both a great and glorious victory. After that she put on the bedside light and they faced each other, he proud in a shy, funny way, she hot, flushed, triumphant: she rolled back the duvet so that he could see all of her and she could see all of him. She ran downstairs and brought back a bottle of champagne which they took in turns to drink, frothy from the bottle; they lay there and talked and talked, because suddenly the barriers were down and there was so much to say, he to explain far off things about his school days and she to tell him about the emptiness inside her after David died. She confessed to him how she had always longed to be a boy and how that had been part of the reason for what had happened that week when David and she had been left on their own so much and had played together, he thirteen and she eleven, how they had swapped clothes, how it had happened; and telling him all about it was even more wonderful than she had imagined it might be because he wasn't at all shocked, he *understood* in a way she had never dared hope that anybody would ever understand; and now that they knew all about each

511

other and there were no secrets left on either side, it was possible to be like children together, which they both wanted. It meant that he could call her his Juju and she could call him Peterkin. It meant that she could tell him that she had meant every word she had said to him that night on the beach of Pulau Tioman, the night she had told him she would do anything for him, anything. When she said that he looked at her in a special way, a new way, his eyes glittering and his lips wet from her champagne kisses, and each knew immediately what the other was thinking; and she was the one who was trembling now, because they started playing a game in which she had to dress up in David's cadet uniform and he had to pretend she was a naughty boy who deserved a special punishment.

It worked, it worked. She was his Juicy-Ju and he was her Peterkin, her Mister Glorious, her Admiral.

# 28

Steven kept his boat moored out between the piles on the Hamble River. She was an old pre-war Hillyard, and her name, *Spindrift* was emblazoned in white letters on the dark blue spray dodgers either side of the cockpit. He had bought her with his gratuity and had lived on board for just over a year now, going to work in the brokerage office by rowing across in his rubber dinghy which he tied up among the scores of yachts, berthed alongside at pontoons.

He looked the part of an ex-naval man. Usually he wore a dark blue reefer with black buttons, grey trousers, rope soled shoes and a yachting cap with the Royal Naval Sailing Association badge. His brisk manner and gruff good humour, the grizzled hair, crow's-feet and that unmistakable Dartmouth accent marked him out immediately, but the effect was at least partly intentional: as yachtmaster for Acecraft Yachts, it was desirable that customers should see that he was something of a salt, and he fostered the image.

Mornings aboard the *Spindrift* began with a cup of strong coffee at seven o'clock drunk – if the weather was fine – sitting up in the cockpit listening to the calls of the terns and the tap-tapping of loose halyards against aluminium masts. This was the time when he let his thoughts wander or go blank, absently looking out over the forest of masts while the tidal stream gurgled quietly round the double-ended hull.

Now that he had been out of the navy for a couple of years, most of the old bitterness and frustration had gone, replaced by a wistful interest in naval matters which flared up into anger if a remark or a newspaper headline touched a nerve. Some months before, he had had a letter published in *The Times*, in which he decried the decision to build leviathan Trident-firing submarines, saying that when a weapon became so powerful as to be able to ensure the end of civilisation, it ceased to be a deterrent but became instead an added incentive to conventional war, with each side tacitly acknowledging to the other that they would never use the ultimate means of destruction. He had received a number of letters from people agreeing with him as a result, and among them a letter from Commander Tinnick, inviting him to come along to a meeting of the Greenwich Forum, in the House of Lords. The Forum, he discovered, consisted of a number of retired senior officers, politicians and industrialists interested in naval matters who met from time to time to discuss Britain and The Sea. The subject under discussion on the day when Jannaway went up to Westminster and entered those historic halls was The Navy's Essential Roles in Peace and War and Britain's Unchanging Maritime Interests Worldwide, a title that effectively summarised the entire proceedings of a stuffy morning and a stuffier afternoon. Metaphorically wringing their hands in despair at the government's proposal to cut the surface fleet by twenty-five percent, the Forum wrangled lengthily over the wording of a letter to the Prime Minister, while representatives of the media grew impatient as their deadlines approached. Towards the end of the day, Jannaway also lost patience: the old anger flared up again, and he caught the chairman's eye. He spoke nervously, self-consciously, passionately: 'The only way to persuade Mr Nott, Mrs Thatcher or for that matter any other politician not to make further cuts in seapower is to convince them that it would be politically dangerous to themselves to do so. I need hardly remind anyone here that this year is the fiftieth anniversary of the Invergordon Mutiny, when the Atlantic Fleet refused to put to sea over a cut in pay. The government of the day was forced to change course as a result, as is well known. Now while I'm not for one moment suggesting that anyone should consider mutiny –'

'I'm very glad to hear that,' put in the chairman, a peer of the realm in a red check shirt, and the meeting dissolved into nautical chuckles.

Jannaway sat down. It was no good: he was making a fool of himself, all over again, just as he had for the twenty-five years of his service career. That, he promised himself, must be his swansong, positively the last impotent rebellion against the massive self-satisfaction of the naval establishment.

After the meeting broke up, he visited the public gallery of the Commons, where a few dozen members of parliament lounged and dozed on padded benches while a debate concerning the modernisation of the railways dragged on through the summer afternoon. He wondered if old railwaymen suffered the same pangs of nostalgia as did old naval officers – the same anger, the same bitterness. Probably. He left the Commons and walked away over Westminster Bridge to Waterloo, feeling ashamed both of himself and of his country.

That had been nearly a month ago now, and he had heard since then of Julietta's engagement to Peter Lasbury. He received the news with mixed feelings: he would be released from maintenance payments and would be considerably better off, but he knew that he would also be distanced even further from his family, and Thomas in particular.

Thoughts of Thomas still engendered in him fierce feelings of paternal love, and the thought of losing him to Peter Lasbury was especially painful. In the long reaches of the night, lying in the quarterberth with the water rippling under the hull and the berthing ropes squeaking rhythmically in the fairleads, he sometimes wondered if Thomas might be happier if the link between them which he had been so careful to preserve, should now be allowed to part.

Lasbury would give Tom all the things he had been brought up to expect: there would be holidays in the Dordogne, skiing every winter, family Christmasses, disco nights, cellar parties. He would grow up as a good public schoolboy should grow up, no doubt of it, and if his academic failings prevented him from joining the navy, then his parental and step-parental influence would no doubt secure for him a bright future in some other sphere.

It was time to go to work. He finished his coffee and went below to tidy the cabin, collect his cap, button his reefer; and a few minutes later he stepped carefully down into the rubber dinghy and began to row with short strokes across the river to the landing stage.

His secretary, Ros Penfold, looked up from her desk as he entered the Acecraft brokerage office. Ros was twenty-three, fresh from her university degree in business management, a pleasantly wind-blown girl in a russet guernsey, a pleated skirt, a pair of wide-lensed spectacles.

'I had a call yesterday afternoon just after you'd gone, Steve,' she said ( she had insisted on Christian names from their first day). She consulted a desk diary. 'Mr Whettingsteel would like a test sail in a Thirty-Two.'

Jannaway hung up his yachting cap and went into his own office. 'He would, would he?'

'I said yes, I hope that's all right. If you can't do it I don't mind standing in myself.'

Jannaway came to the door. 'Did he sound like a potential buyer?'

'No idea. He's coming down from London, said he'd be with us about eleven.'

'Sounds keen.'

'Would you like me to organise packed lunches?'

'Yes, will you? Nice day for a sail.' He went back into his office and picked up the telephone. He needed to speak to the sailmakers about the new cruising chute for the Thirty-Eight. 'And Ros?' he said, waiting for the call to be answered. 'Make it six cans of beer this time, eh? I nearly died of thirst the other day.'

There wasn't a great deal to do that morning. The boat building and yacht brokerage industry was as depressed as any other, and Acecraft Yachts was struggling to keep afloat. After a couple of hours, Jannaway strolled out into the sunshine and went down to the pontoons to check out the Thirty-Two before the test sail. He connected the batteries, put fresh water in the freezer and switched it on, checked the electrics, the fuel, the fresh water. He left the mainsail cover on deliberately: it bore the Acecraft logo on it, and along with the four other Acecraft boats stood out as an eyecatching advertisement among the hundreds of other yachts in the marina. He was cleaning a smear of oil off the white hull when a voice behind him said, 'Mister Jannaway, I presume?'

He straightened. A man of about his own age, grey haired, suntanned, lean, with an intelligently humorous look was watching him from the pontoon. 'Tim Whettingsteel,' he said, and advanced to shake hands.

'It didn't even occur to me, when I saw the name, that it might be you,' Jannaway said. 'I gather you're after a test sail?'

'That was the general idea, yes.' Tim Whettingsteel looked him up and down. 'What is it, twenty-two years? Twenty-three?'

'Something quite horrendous!'

They stepped aboard and stood in the cockpit of the Acecraft, each amused at meeting a face from the past.

'You went into the Foreign Office, didn't you?'

'For my sins, yes,' Whettingsteel said. 'When did you leave the Andrew?'

'Couple of years ago.' Jannaway saw the question forming in

516

Whettingsteel's mind, and answered it in advance: 'As a very senior, passed over two-and-a-half, I'm afraid.'

It was surprising how quickly the gap of years was bridged and they returned to the easy terms on which they had been as midshipmen. Jannaway showed him round the boat – 'I'll give you the whole sales spiel, Tim, may as well' – and then set about taking the mainsail cover off.

'Can I single up?' Whettingsteel suggested.

Jannaway grinned. 'Thanks, if you would.' He watched Whettingsteel casting off the springs, coiling them and making them into neat hanks. 'Haven't lost the touch, I see,' he said.

Whettingsteel laughed. 'I don't think I could if I tried!'

Jannaway demonstrated how to start the diesel, and a few minutes later the boat went slowly astern from the pontoon, turned, and headed down the Hamble River towards Southampton Water, while Ros waved and called to them in vain to come back alongside and collect their packed lunches.

Jannaway realised what he'd done as they passed the last dolphin marking the entrance to the Hamble, when Whettingsteel was hoisting the mainsail.

'I've gone and forgotten the lunch!' he shouted, and Whettingsteel laughed. Jannaway hadn't changed much, over the years.

'Tell you what, we'll nip across to Cowes if you've time,' Jannaway said when the genoa was set and the engine shut down.

Whettingsteel agreed, and took over the helm. It was an ideal day for sailing: the Solent was dotted with yachts and dinghies, beating and running and reaching in the sheltered water between the mainland and the Isle of Wight. With the main and genoa set, the Acecraft heeled over until the lee gunwale was just under water, leaving a foaming wake astern. Tim Whettingsteel put the boat through her paces: they went down Southampton Water past Calshot, sailed close hauled up to the entrance of the Beaulieu River, then bore away for a fast reach across to Cowes.

'You've got a very nice little number here, haven't you Shag!' Tim said, and Jannaway, his yachting cap tipped down over his eyes laughed and said he supposed he couldn't grumble.

Towards one, they sailed in past the Prince Consort buoy and berthed alongside in the Groves and Gutteridge marina. 'Lunch,' Jannaway said, and they walked out of the yard and along the narrow main street to the Fountain Hotel.

Over ploughman's lunches and pints of best bitter, they caught up on each other's past. Whettingsteel had just returned from three years as First Secretary in the British Embassy at Santiago, and was now set for a tour in Whitehall. 'You caused quite a stir, leaving like that,' Jannaway told him. 'There were all sorts of rumours going round. One of the wilder ones was that you'd been specially selected as a double-oh-seven.'

'Nothing as melodramatic as that, I'm afraid,' Whettingsteel said.

'Why did you leave in fact?'

'Oh – reasons. Like another pint?'

They returned to the subject of the navy, and Jannaway gave vent to some of his old frustrations. 'What seems so tragic to me,' he said, 'is that an organisation can recruit so many idealistic young men, so much enthusiasm and determination and loyalty, and leave them at the end of their careers with so little.'

'Is it as bad as that really?'

'Show me a retired N.O. and I'll show you an embittered man,' Jannaway said.

Whettingsteel raised one eyebrow in surprise. He had that slightly lethargic urbanity to be found in many successful diplomats. 'I could tell you things about the FCO that would make your hair curl, Steve. Bureaucracy. Incompetence. In-fighting. It's the times we live in I'm afraid. We're part of an eroding civilisation.' He smiled wryly. 'And before you run the navy down too much, perhaps I ought to tell you that my son Richard passed out of Dartmouth as a sub lieutenant last April.'

'Did he now!' Jannaway exclaimed. 'Well good for him!'

'You see?' Whettingsteel laughed. 'You're not quite so anti as you make out, are you?'

Jannaway wanted to know all about Whettingsteel's son, what specialisation he was in, what ship he was serving in. 'He's in a minesweeper called *Ashton* at the moment,' Tim said. 'Hopes to start training as a helicopter pilot next year.'

'I was a pilot.'

'Really? I thought you were a seaman to your finger tips, Steve!'

Jannaway laughed. 'So did I until they press-ganged me. I enjoyed the flying, though. That was probably the best part of my time, the flying.'

They walked back to the boat. The wind had dropped right away now, so they bent on the ghoster and left harbour under power, hoisting the sails when clear of the entrance. The boat crept along, just making up over the tide. It was suddenly hot. The hydrofoil from Southampton sped past in a cloud of spray and in the distance the hovercraft howled back and forth between Southsea and Ryde.

'Did you ever go back to the college?' Whettingsteel asked.

'Never. I flew over it once in a Gannet, but I've never re-darkened those doors. Don't intend to, either.'

'I went to Richard's passing out parade,' Whettingsteel said. 'It hasn't changed all that much, considering. Still stinks of floor polish. They've got Wrens living where Hawkins chestflat used to be. I tell you one thing that annoyed me though. Remember the chapel? All those brass memorial plates? They've been taken down. Some ruddy little chaplain apparently – took 'em down and sold the brass for scrap. I could hardly believe it. One of them was a memorial to a distant relation of mine. I was quite angry about that.'

'So much for "We will remember them", eh?'

'Exactly.'

Jannaway heaved in a fraction on the mainsheet. 'Oh well. I suppose it'll make room for the next lot, won't it? And they'll need the room too, the way things are going.' He had a thought. 'I suppose David Braddle's memorial went as well did it?'

'That poor little poof?' Whettingsteel said, 'No, I didn't see it. There were a few left, but not his.'

'You realise I married his sister, don't you Tim?'

Whettingsteel grimaced as if in pain. 'Steve! I had no idea! I do apologise!'

'Don't worry. We had a rather messy divorce quite a long time ago. I don't exactly hold the name Braddle in the highest esteem.'

'Wasn't exactly diplomatic of me, all the same, was it?'

'I must say I'd never thought David was a poof,' Jannaway said. 'Wet as a scrubber maybe, but not a five bob note.'

Whettingsteel brought the boat slightly into wind to meet the wake of the Isle of Wight ferry bows on. When it had passed, Jannaway said: 'Why did you leave in fact?'

Whettingsteel seemed reluctant to answer. 'Water under the bridge, Steve,' he said eventually.

'I know that,' Jannaway said quietly. 'I wouldn't have asked if it hadn't been.'

Whettingsteel said nothing for some while then appeared to have a sudden change of mind. 'All right, I'll tell you,' he said. 'I didn't like it. It was a mafia. Boy scouts in long trousers. David Braddle was part of it.'

'Because he was a poof?'

'No.'

'What then?'

Whettingsteel shook his head.

'Let's keep out of the main channel,' Jannaway said. 'We can leave this buoy to port.'

Whettingsteel smiled. 'Aye aye, sir,' he said softly.

Jannaway said: 'It's not just idle curiosity on my part, Tim. I rather admired what you did. It was something I should have had the courage to do myself. In fact I suspect quite a lot of people may have felt the same way.'

Jannaway had spread himself out along one side of the cockpit, and Whettingsteel sat at the helm, from time to time peering under the big ghoster to make sure it was clear ahead. Scattered about the Solent, other yachts, many with coloured spinnakers, floated mirage-like in the distance. It was an extraordinary conversation they were having, but it was an extraordinary reunion and an extraordinary day. Jannaway reflected that if he had remembered the packed lunches they would have been out and back within the space of two hours, and Whettingsteel would by now be on the motorway back to his office in King Charles Street.

'Remember that run ashore we had in Gibraltar? When he was sick outside the Governor's residence?'

Jannaway laughed. 'Not really. You forget I've been on more than a few similar runs ashore since, Tim.'

'Well I remember it very clearly,' Whettingsteel said, 'because the day after that was Sunday and we all marched off to a church parade.'

'Not me. I was a Holy Roller. Still am, technically.'

'Doesn't matter. It was that afternoon –' Whettingsteel stopped, remembering. The jib flapped suddenly as he allowed the boat to come too close to the wind.

'May as well go about now anyway,' Jannaway said.

When they were on the other tack, Whettingsteel continued. 'In the afternoon, some of us went up the Rock, some people were shown round that cruiser –'

'*Durham*, that's right. Because Peter Lasbury was on board at the time, and David Braddle went to lunch with him. This is all part of the Braddle folklore, Tim.'

'In that case I'm not sure I ought to tell you any more.'

'Go on!'

'It's not very nice.'

Jannaway laughed. 'It'd take a great deal to surprise me, Tim, I can assure you of that.'

'All right. Well, a few of us, myself included went on board a very smelly little diesel submarine. *Sea Devil*, I think it was. And we were given the usual Cook's tour of the boat ending up in the control room looking through the periscope. High magnification, as you know, and big laughs all round when the Chief of the Boat tells blue stories about watching ladies revealing their all in upstairs windows. Anyway, when it was my turn at the periscope I focussed in on something I saw moving up on the Rock. It was Daisy Braddle sixty-nining with a matelot.'

A small speedboat shot past, bouncing with a succession of smacking noises over the wavelets.

'Are you sure it was David?'

'Quite sure.'

'What did you do?'

'Defocussed and pretended to take an interest in the sheerlegs.' Whettingsteel looked across, shaking his head. 'But that wasn't all. I didn't know what to do. I thought he ought to be warned. So that's what I did. I warned him.'

'Personally?'

Whettingsteel blinked quickly in embarrassment. 'Anonymously. I left a note in his hammock. And regretted it ever since.'

'And twenty-four hours later . . .'

'Yes, twenty-four hours later he was being hailed as the hero who went out alone to do battle with the elements.'

'But you haven't any proof that he committed suicide, have you? I mean it might have happened the way we believe it happened.'

Whettingsteel laughed sadly. 'I was in the same part of the watch as David, Steve. Every time we went away in the seaboat or across on the jackstay, he was terrified. It just wasn't in him to go onto the fo'c's'le like that, and I'd lay good money the board of inquiry knew it, too. No, he was a captain's son and they had to preserve the family reputation, didn't they? Heroes mustn't be allowed to fall, must they? If heroes fall, we fall with them.'

'And was that why you left?'

'It was part of it. I told my father I wanted out at the end of that term, and he said he'd consider it provided I finished my training at Dartmouth. So I did, and he very decently kept his promise and bought me out.'

The wind died right away as they approached the entrance to the Hamble River, so they started the engine and lowered the sails. Steven took back the helm and they stood in the cockpit as the Acecraft proceeded up the entrance channel between the red and green stakes.

He had no idea why he asked the question when he asked it. It seemed to come out of its own accord.

'How did you know it was a matelot?'

Whettingsteel glanced at him for a moment then looked ahead at the crowded harbour. 'I didn't know for sure,' he said. 'But I was pretty certain it was. He was tattooed, you see. One of those big prancing leopards all over his back. That's what caught my eye in the first place. This ... animal moving in the bushes. Not quite the animal I expected though. More of a two-backed beast, in a very nasty way.'

Steven Jannaway stood at the helm and steered the boat in towards the marina. He was glad to have something positive to do at that moment, something upon which it was necessary to concentrate.

'Could you get a couple of fenders out, Tim? We'll be going port side to the pontoon.'

He aimed for the centre of the berth, slowed, stopped and went astern, stopping the engine again at exactly the right moment to leave the boat alongside, motionless in the water.

Ros came out of the brokerage office. 'You forgot your packed lunches,' she said. 'And your precious beer.'

'Yes,' Jannaway said. 'Sorry about that.'

She came down the ramp to the pontoon looking relaxed, cheerful, and refreshingly feminine. She watched them stowing the ghoster, pushing it down into its bag. 'I don't know, Steve. You men. Honestly!'

It was one of those calm, warm evenings when voices carry long distances over the water, and seabirds swoop low for insects.

He knew that he would have to make a decision one way or the other, very soon. The wedding was only ten days off: he must either take action quickly, tomorrow, or he must keep silent and accept the risk.

He sat on the coach roof of *Spindrift* and wondered what to do.

At first, he was tempted to dodge the issue altogether. What if Tim Whettingsteel had not come down that day? What if he had not forgotten the lunch and they had not had that long, slow conversation about the navy and why Whettingsteel had left it? And what if he had not asked that last question – 'How did you know it was a matelot?'

This dilemma would not have arisen.

But Whettingsteel had come down, he had forgotten the lunch, he had asked that question, and there was no doubt in his mind that the 'matelot' on the slopes of Gibraltar had been Peter Lasbury. It was as if the last infuriating piece of a jigsaw had been found and fitted into place – as if Whettingsteel had been used as an unwitting messenger of Fate, sent to warn him, sent to challenge him. How amazing and incredible that he had never recognised Peter for what he was over so many years! And how many gestures, remarks, incidents this explained! He wondered if Julietta's affair with her brother had caused David's homosexuality, and understood a little more now of her penchant for sexual deviation which he had finally found so repulsive and which lay at the root of their divorce.

Thomas: he was the only person who mattered now. Whatever he decided to do – or not to do – Thomas must take precedence over all other considerations. And however hard he tried to rationalise about the financial benefits of allowing Lasbury to become Thomas's step-father, he could not escape the knowledge that if he did so, he would be placing his son at risk.

He considered consulting Alan about it. He had seen little of Alan in the past year. Since Catherine's visit two years before (and that night he had sat in the pub, got drunk, been breathalysed, fined £50 and banned from driving for a year) contact between the brothers had been limited to the very occasional weekend in London.

And if he consulted Alan, would he take Alan's advice? Alan was shrewd and Alan knew him well – too well in some ways; but he didn't know the whole story, and any advice he gave would have to be based, yes, on second-hand experience.

A priest perhaps? He dismissed the thought immediately. His experience of the Church told him that the average priest was usually as muddled in himself as the flock he was supposed to lead.

He thought about the risk itself, of allowing Thomas to become Peter's step-son. Was he perhaps being very old-fashioned about the whole thing? Did it really matter that Peter was a homosexual – or for that matter if his homosexuality caused Thomas to go the same way?

He had heard from Thomas a week before: Julietta and Peter had decided to take him and Penny on their honeymoon with them. They were going to the Seychelles, would be staying in a house with a private beach.

He felt a sudden wave of nausea: real nausea, a heaving of the stomach and a watering of the mouth. The image of Peter Lasbury rose in his imagination: that heavy, fair body, those sapphire eyes, that repulsive, faded tattoo. Hatred burned inside him: hatred with the white hot intensity of magnesium. It flared up without warning, out of control. It left him breathless, terrified at his own malicious, murderous intent.

He threw the remains of his beer over the side and went below. He should make himself some supper now, fry up chicken and mushrooms and rice, eat it alone in the cabin, ploughing on through the fourth volume of Gibbon, the work Alan had told him he must read if he wanted to understand the foundations upon which the British Empire had been built. But it was impossible to consider food or history until a decision had been reached. He peered out of the brass porthole, still thinking, still wondering.

A confusion of recollections and muddled thoughts drifted through his mind. Does it matter, does it matter? he kept asking himself. He remembered those British Bulldog evenings at sea scouts; he remembered a boy called Lutt, a misty night in November, hands pinning him against a wall, fumbling at his flies. That was where the murder came from, yes, that was part of this pattern which he was only now beginning to understand. He remembered lying in his bed, the night it had happened, the night his mother had asked him if he had been running the marathon. He remembered trying to make his father come back alive, shouting silently for him, longing for him, stifling tears for him in his pillow. He would have understood, he would have understood. And even now, at this very moment, he knew that the only person he could consult was his own father, who had lifted him up out of the icy water, who had rubbed his hands and run with him back to the top of the slope, ignoring his mother's pleas for caution. He remembered his mother's voice, so confident in her own rectitude, her Catholic infallibility: 'You're lucky to be able to go to sea scouts, aren't you? Life isn't all roses, you know. Money doesn't grow on trees. You've got to learn to take the rough with the smooth...'

He remembered, also, an afternoon when he had walked by the River Thames with Tom, when he had held his hand and told him that whatever happened, however bad it was, Tom could always tell him about it and that he would always understand, because he had been nine years old once, and hadn't completely forgotten what it was like; and later, when they were sitting in the car before it was time to go back to the school, Tom had unexpectedly turned to him saying 'Oh Daddy!' and bursting into tears. He had held him in his arms, comforted him, told him that he was on his side and that so long as he kept on trying, doing his best, he would be all right. He had said, too, that he understood that you couldn't do your best all the time but that what was really important was that you didn't give up, you kept trying. What a devilish thing a boys' prep school could be! But that breakdown of Thomas's had served its purpose: it had bound them together as father and son. It meant, too, that he must not now fail Thomas. Whatever he did, whatever action he took, he must take out of carefully considered and mature judgement; it must not be coloured by financial or social expediency. It must not be vindictive in any way, but nor must it shirk the responsibility he had as a father, however difficult it might be to fulfil it.

Quite suddenly his mind cleared, and he knew what he must do. There was no longer any doubt left. Whatever anyone said – any sociologist, psychologist, Tory, Socialist, Liberal, Social Democrat, Marxist or Quack – he knew that part of his duty as a father lay in protecting his son against the misery and despair of homosexuality. His duty as a father was to bring his son up to be a man. And he saw – as if it had been revealed to him by a sudden insight – exactly what homosexuality was: not something to be condoned or condemned but something to be treated as a disability and struggled against in the same way Alan had struggled against his paraplegia, fought against it, learnt to overcome so much of its handicap. This was the parent's duty: this was why a child must have two parents, real parents, who complimented each other as man and woman rather than attacking each other from opposing stockades.

He went up on deck again and stood by the shrouds, watching

525

a tall ketch, its sails hanging limply, motoring in on the flood. A tern wheeled above him and swooped along the water, skimming the surface and uttering a plaintive cry.

For the first time in many years, he felt a clear sense of purpose, and an inward calm.

He took the train up to London the following morning and rang the Ministry of Defence from a call box on Waterloo station. He experienced a strange feeling of déjà vu, hearing the voice of the operator and encountering the old hostility of a civil servant who believed it her duty to withhold the number of Rear Admiral Lasbury if the caller did not know what post he held.

'I don't need to know what post he holds,' he said. 'I want to speak to him personally.'

'In that case you should ring his private number.'

'I don't know his personal number, and he's ex-directory.'

There was a note of triumph in her reply. 'We don't divulge official extension numbers for the purpose of private calls.'

He stood in the phone box and thought. There was another way. He dialled again, this time the only number he could remember: his old office in the Directorate of Naval Recruiting.

A cheerful voice answered, a voice trained to welcome enquiries invited by advertisements in the national press. 'Ministry of Defence, good morning, can I help you?'

He imagined a neat Wren sitting at one of many desks, picture postcards and wall charts, cooling coffees, the hum and banter of office conversation.

'Ah, damn!' he said crustily. 'I think I've got the wrong number. Is that Main Building or OAB?'

'It's OAB, sir. This is DNR.'

He continued in his senior officer's voice. 'Well I'm speaking on an outside line. I want to speak to A/COS to VCNS. Could you heave out the directory and look him up?'

'Er – who is speaking sir?'

'Gibbon!' he shouted impatiently.

He could very nearly hear her heart beating faster.

'Could I have your rank, sir?'

'Captain!' he barked.

'I'm sorry, but we do have to make sure –'

'That's all right.'

'If you could just hold on a second, sir –'

He waited.

'Did you say A/COS to VCNS, sir?'

'Yes. Rear Admiral Lasbury. It's just possible he may have moved across to another office in the last month or so. May be easier to look him up by name.'

'Oh, thank you, sir. I'll do that.'

'My pleasure!' he shouted.

'Here we are, sir. Would you like the external number or the internal extension?'

'Both, please.'

She gave them; he thanked her gruffly and rang off, grimly pleased to have used the system to penetrate its own bureaucracy.

When he rang Lasbury's number, a secretary answered: probably a Third Officer Wren, fresh from her honours degree in English at Exeter University.

'May I speak to the admiral please?'

'Who is calling?'

'Mister Jannaway, Acecraft Yachts. He knows me.'

There was a click, then: 'Lasbury.'

'Good morning, Peter. Steven Jannaway.'

'Steve! My dear chap!'

He ignored the condescension. 'I have to speak to you urgently, Peter. I can't talk on the phone, we'll have to meet.'

There was a pause. 'Well this is a surprise, Steven. What is it, you want to give me some sort of hand-over?' Lasbury chuckled.

'It's about Thomas. Something's cropped up. If we could meet today I'd be grateful.'

Lasbury said: 'I'm a bit pressed for time, old boy.'

'It won't take long. Five or ten minutes.'

'All right, well look, I'm going down to Meonford this evening but I've got to call in at my flat first. If you like to be there at five you'll probably catch me, would that suit?'

'I'll be there. It's Cadogan Square, isn't it?'

'That's right.' Lasbury gave the number.

'At five then.'

'Look forward to it,' Lasbury said, and rang off.


The naval Vauxhall drew up alongside Lasbury's flat a little before six, when Jannaway, who looked a bit like a chauffeur in his reefer and grey trousers, was beginning to wonder if Lasbury had stood him up.

Lasbury told the Leading Wren driver to wait then ran up the flight of steps to his front door.

'Well, well, well,' he said. '*Ave fratre*. Come you in.'

He ushered Jannaway into a spacious drawing room and excused himself to pay a call. He emerged a few minutes later from his marbled bathroom, having freshened his cologne. 'I must say it's very good to see you,' he said. 'Will you have a gin and tonic or something?' Jannaway refused, so he mixed himself a St Clements in an Edinburgh crystal glass. 'I rather hoped we might be able to meet before the wedding. After all, no hard feelings on either side, are there?' He spread himself on the sofa, stretching out his legs so that his ankles showed through his silken socks. ' So what can we do for you?'

Jannaway clenched and unclenched his rope hardened hands, feeling out of place and wary of Lasbury's bonhomie.

'It's about Thomas. I want custody.'

Lasbury frowned and laughed at the same time. 'Oh come come, old lad! That's out of the question!' He played a syncopated rhythm on the piecrust table at his elbow. 'And besides, it's a case of "Not me Chief, I'm radar." Tom-Tom's Juju's part of ship, you know that.'

'Yes, but this concerns you more than it does Julietta.'

'In what way?'

Jannaway hesitated, bracing his shoulders back. 'I don't regard you as a suitable person to have charge of a young boy, Peter.'

Lasbury's eyes narrowed momentarily, then he laughed. 'Well that's very nice of you I must say! Thank you very much indeed! May one ask why?'

'I think you already know the reason,' Jannaway said. 'If you're honest with yourself.'

'Why don't you help yourself to a drink and sit down, Steven? You look like Marlowe's ghost.'

Jannaway ignored that. Now that the moment had come, he did not savour it. This was no triumph, no victory. He would have liked, even now, to back away from what he had to say. That would have been much, much easier.

He said, 'I've found out – by accident – about you.'

Lasbury seemed to squirm slightly. 'I must confess I have not the first idea what you're talking about, Steven.'

'Yes you have, Peter. I'm sure you have.'

Lasbury touched the corner of his mouth with the tip of his finger. 'I think if you're trying to make some sort of accusation, you had better come right out with it.'

'Yes, perhaps I had,' Jannaway said, 'I'm talking about your homosexuality, Peter. That's why I want custody of Thomas.'

Lasbury froze. Only his eyes moved, and they seemed to swivel like a reptile's. It was as if he might gradually merge with his background and then, when Jannaway was least expecting it, shoot out a long tongue and gobble him up.

'I think perhaps you ought to tell me exactly what you've heard,' he said eventually.

'I'd rather not. I don't want to embarrass you. All you need to know is . . . that I know.'

Lasbury made an excellent pretence of relaxing. 'Need to know? You sound like the security manual! Of course I need to know! I'm intrigued, I really am! You must tell me who has been saying what, and I shall take great pleasure in dragging them through the high court for defamation.'

'I doubt if you'll do that, Peter.'

Lasbury was thinking fast. As an expert in naval communications and electronic warfare, he was well versed in naval security and in methods of interrogation. He was also aware that it was just possible that this encounter with Jannaway might be linked with the interview he had had with Tinnick: curiouser things happened at sea after all, and Jannaway's sinecure with Acecraft Yachts could be a cover for some other activity. It was necessary to tread extremely carefully.

He took a sip of his St Clements and set the glass carefully back on a mother-of-pearl mat. 'You can't make an unsubstantiated accusation like that, Steven,' he said. 'After all, what's sauce for the goose. I might be able to dream up a few nasties about you, might I not?'

Jannaway's jaw went out and his fists clenched. He said, 'David Braddle, Sunday the nineteenth of June, 1956. On the south-facing slopes of Gibraltar in the afternoon.' He breathed out then added: 'Gross indecency. Do you want any more detail than that?'

He turned quickly away, going to the window – partly to contain his anger, partly to give himself time to think. Whatever happened, he must not lose control. That white hot anger must not, on any

529

account, be allowed to ignite. He watched a brown Rolls-Royce coupé edge backwards into a reserved parking slot.

"All I am saying is that I want custody of Thomas. And I want it now. I'm not prepared to let him go to the Seychelles with you.'

'You're up a gum tree,' Lasbury said behind him. 'Or a Jannaway tree, more likely. Who's going to believe you? Obviously you want custody of Thomas. You've been campaigning for that for the past six years to my knowledge. So now you resort to this. A malicious smear. A concoction, a fiction. But of course this always was your forté, wasn't it? The big rebellion. What is it, some sort of Oedipal throwback?'

Jannaway came back from the window. 'I'll give you the week-end to think about it,' he said quietly. 'I've got your office number, so I can ring you direct on Monday. I don't want Julietta to be involved in this, but if you force my hand she may have to be. If I can't get custody by private agreement, I'll go to my solicitor and we'll get a court order. And if I can't get that, I'm prepared to go further. I've got nothing to lose. I'm not blackmailing you, I'm telling you. Thomas is my son. I'm not having him driven to suicide as well.'

Lasbury looked up quickly. 'Who said anything about suicide?'

He had not intended to mention that. It had slipped out by mistake. Lasbury got to his feet. They faced each other.

'The person who saw you with David sent him an anonymous note. I personally saw him in tears that evening, and he went overboard the following night. It may not have been suicide, but I'm inclined to think it was.'

There was nothing else to say. Suddenly he needed to escape from this drawing room with its individually illuminated oil paintings, its priceless carpets, its piecrust tables. He needed to get out before something boiled over inside him, before he was tempted to strike out, do damage. So he left abruptly, letting himself out at the front door and going quickly down the steps into the square; and as he reached the corner of Pont Street, he was overtaken by the naval staff car with Lasbury sitting in the back, and for a moment, a split second, their eyes met, and he knew that what he had said had struck home.

Julietta was waiting on the down platform at Petersfield when Lasbury's train arrived. She was wearing a frothy blouse and tight white jeans, and the sight of her caused him a pang of dismay.

She ran to him and hugged him as if he had just arrived back from the antipodes; she pushed her tongue between his lips when she kissed him, a habit of hers which he did not enjoy.

'Peter-Pooh, darling,' she said. 'How are you? You look a bit ragged. Have you had a ghastly week?'

She bubbled with excitement all the way to the car. Nita and Penny and Tom-Tom were all at home, and Granny Clara was coming to supper. She squeezed his hand tightly. 'Only nine days to go!' she reminded him.

They drove out of the station car park, taking the West Meon road. She held the steering wheel in one hand and teased him with the other, patting his thigh, swerving to avoid an oncoming motorbike.

Going up a steep hill under an arch of beech trees, she said: 'Peterkin is something really the matter? I mean really really?'

She glanced at him, and for a moment the nearside wheels ran over the grass verge.

'There is something isn't there?'

'I can't talk about it while you're driving,' he said.

'We'll stop then. I want you in a good mood when we get home. I've got a little surprise for you.'

He had half expected some sort of surprise. It was his fiftieth birthday on Monday, and this weekend was the obvious choice to celebrate it.

He had thought hard about what Jannaway had said. Instead of doing *The Times* crossword as he usually did on the journey down, he had gazed out of the window weighing the risks and advantages of various courses of action. Trained to tackle problem-solving in a logical way, he had identified the aim and mentally listed the factors affecting the achievement of that aim. It had not been difficult to do the former: promotion was his aim and always had been. Marriage to Julietta had been a way of improving his reputation and furthering that aim; now that decision had to be re-examined. He knew, for a start, that nothing would persuade Julietta to give up custody of Thomas – whatever he told her, however much he admitted. Thomas was hers, Thomas was the symbol of her victory over Steven: she would as soon give him up as re-marry Steven himself. Nor was there any doubt in Lasbury's mind that Jannaway had been in deadly earnest. The details of that incident with David Braddle, resurrected so unexpectedly, had frightened him far more than he had shown. The thought of them being brought out in court literally terrified him. He had considered having Jannaway silenced, dealt with: such things were possible. But that was too dangerous. Jannaway was the sort of person who might lodge a statement in writing to be opened in the event of his death. No, that was out of the question; but there was one alternative way out, and he prepared to take it now.

Julietta had swung the car off the main road and was accelerating it up a narrow lane that led to Old Winchester Hill. She pushed the speed up to eighty along the flat, then braked sharply to a halt.

'Come on,' she said brightly. 'You can tell me all about it.'

They walked along a path at the top of the escarpment. The rolling countryside, fields, copses and farms of southern Hampshire stretched out into a blue distance, and the chimneys of the Fawley oil refinery were just visible on the horizon. Overhead a hawk hovered, moved over and hovered again.

He looked down into her face. Since their engagement she had had her hair cut shorter and had changed her make-up, accentuating the cheek bones in order to make herself look younger.

'I want you,' she whispered. 'Can't we find a bush or something?'

He disengaged his hand from hers and stopped, shaking his head.

'What's the matter Peter-Pooh?' she asked him as if he were five years old. 'Tell a Juju.'

'I can't go through with it, Julie. I can't marry you.'

'Oh rubbish! Rubbish, rubbish, rubbish!'

'I'm serious.'

She stared at him, breathing out through bared teeth, fire slowly kindling in her eyes.

'Why?'

He seemed to swallow something distasteful. 'Do I have to explain? Can't you understand?'

'Yes you do have to explain. I don't understand.'

'I don't want to hurt you.'

She laughed shrilly.

He said: 'I love you as a person, Julie. But I can't love you as a woman.' He closed his eyes. 'It revolts me.'

The terrible thing about it was that it was true. It was not an act at all.

She began speaking in a low, choking voice. 'I thought you

enjoyed it. You said you enjoyed it. It did work. I know it worked. I *made* it work. Didn't I? Didn't I?'

He looked down at the turf, her bright red toenails. He mumbled something about not being able to explain.

She began to panic. 'What about the wedding? We can't call it off, Peter, we simply can't!' She mentioned names: names of admirals, politicians, royalty. 'And what about Penny? What about Tom-Tom? They love you! They need you Peter!'

She gripped his arms and began whispering promises to him, begging him, telling him what she was prepared to do, what she would let him do. She told him they could make arrangements, that he could have anyone else he liked. 'I wouldn't mind. We could have a triad if you want. Would you like that? Wouldn't that be fun?'

He turned away from her in disgust.

Her tears gave way to anger. She clutched at him, she cursed him, she abused him. She snarled at him like a cat, gathering spittle at the back of her throat; and as the stream of invective reached full spate, like a bore rushing downstream, he was suddenly aware of a great relief: that this outburst would soon be spent and that when it was over he would be finally rid of her, unchained, uncommitted.

She stood before him finally, panting and grunting like an animal. In a last demonic gesture of contempt she opened her blouse and thrust out her breasts at him, threatening him with them as if they were secret weapons.

He watched her walk away, back to the car; and as the MG started up with a roar and hurtled off down the hill between the trees, Peter Lasbury sighed briefly, and turned to begin the long walk back.

She drove at breakneck speed, the hood down, the wind in her face, her blouse open. She didn't care, she didn't care. She put her foot hard down coming out of the bend after Warnford and the tyres screamed as the car skittered across the road, recovered and snaked on along the straight towards Exton and Corhampton. She knew what she was going to do and nobody would stop her. She didn't care who knew about it or what anyone said; in fact she wanted everyone to know about it and say as much as they liked. She ran over a dog on the way past Meonstoke; she saw it fly upward in her mirror and flop into the middle of the road. She accelerated as hard as she could at the automatic caution lights outside Meonford, laughing at the SLOW DOWN PLEASE and flashing lights. She braked hard as the green gates of Meonford House came into view, and hit the far post with a crash as she turned into the drive. What did it matter? Nothing mattered. She accelerated at the house, slammed on the brakes again, arrived in a hail of gravel and stones.

And there was Thomas, as planned, all dressed up in his best school suit at first smiling and then, when he saw her and saw that Peter was not with her, frowning.

'Mummy!' he said urgently. 'Mummy, your blouse isn't done up!'

She strode past him into the hall, the house quiet and apparently deserted, the surprise for Peter organised by Nita and Penny working perfectly. She flung open the door to the library and stood before them, enjoying the horror in their faces and the way one or two began singing Happy Birthday to You only to stop in numb embarrassment. She looked round at them and laughed at them: the Crivett-Smiths, the Tinnicks, the Railtons, the Sykes-Morrises, the Dudswells, the Keunings, the Tomkinses, Jeremy and Penny, her mother, Nita, the vicar.

'Well have a good look,' she said. 'It's all off, you see. He's chickened out. Just thought you'd like to know. But don't run away. Do finish the champers.'

She heard her mother's voice: 'Darling! Julietta!' She saw the men turning away, playing gentlemen, not looking. She heard Nita saying, 'Spectacular, Mummy, perfectly spectacular!'

Back in the car, she slammed the door hard and reversed as fast as she could, straight out into the road. She raised two fingers to the driver of the Fareham bus as his wheels locked and he skidded to an emergency stop, just missing her. She kept her thumb pressed on the horn all the way through Meonford village, touching ninety as she passed the HOUNDS PLEASE notice outside Droxford, and nearly rolling the car as she turned down the track that led to the big converted barn where Virginia now lived alone.

She sat in the car, feeling out of breath, looking at herself in the mirror, buttoning her blouse. She went to the door and rang the bell, waiting for a long time until Virginia finally answered it.

They looked into each other's eyes.

'Julie!'

'Hello,' she whispered. 'I've come – I've come –'

Then she was in tears, and Virginia was helping her in, comforting her, holding her and encircling her with strong, protective arms.

# 29

The real reason Alan was up so early was that he still hoped that *Spindrift* might come in on the flood tide, but the excuse he made to himself was that he wanted to see the sun rise over the Beaulieu River.

Whatever the reason, he was glad to have made the effort. He closed the door of the hotel quietly behind him and stood for a moment enjoying the cool bite in the air and the silence of early morning.

It was not yet six o'clock. There was dew on the wide stretch of grass between the two rows of artisans' cottages, and mist hung in patches between the high mud banks. Swans, drifting on the slow moving water, were perfectly reflected and the boats moored at piles below Buckler's Hard were like models set upon a mirror.

He loved this place. He had been here twice before: once while researching for his second novel and once, the previous autumn, when it was being televised. Even at the height of the tourist season it was still redolent with history but now, with only the solitary cry of a seabird breaking the silence, the effect was magical. He felt that if he stood quite still and listened intently, he might hear echoes of the shipyard which had once thrived at the head of this long, winding inlet: the voices of Hampshire workmen, the hammer blows, the steady thud of adze on oak.

He went down to the water's edge, comfortable in corduroys and polo-necked sweater, a pair of binoculars slung about his neck. Here on the shore line were the two large indentations that marked where ships had taken shape on the stocks two hundred years before: ships like the *Euryalus*, the *Agammemnon*, the *Gladiator*. They had been launched and fitted out here before being towed out to the Solent and handed over to captains who were the contemporaries of Howe and Nelson; they were ships that had been a part not only of the greatest navy ever built but of something more: a tradition that became the oaken heart of Britain.

Standing there alone at the water's edge, he paraphrased Wordsworth to himself: 'This river now doth like a garment wear/

The beauty of the morning; silent, bare ...' and his thoughts began to turn – inevitably – upon the events of the past months.

He had been too busy with his scriptwriting to delve into the scandal that had rocked the Meon Valley the previous July. All he knew for certain was that Julietta had called off her marriage and gone to live with a friend, and that Steven had received a plea from Mrs Braddle to take Thomas away from the centre of the family crisis.

They had come to him for Christmas: father and son, drawing up outside number fifty-nine when the snow was whirling down Chestnut Road. It had not been an easy time. Thomas, unsurprisingly, was disturbed by his mother's rejection of him, and the absence of a woman in the house had rendered the Christmas celebration strangely barren and meaningless. There had been an argument between himself and Steven over whether Thomas should be encouraged to go to the midnight Mass on Christmas Eve, and in the event Alan had gone on his own, returning to find his brother and nephew watching a film on the video recorder.

He had plunged back into television work in the new year. He was still working as a librarian in Hampstead and he found it necessary to work flat out to keep up with the deadlines set by his producer. Quite unexpectedly, he had found himself on a lucrative treadmill. the Rumplestiltskin comparison was often in his mind: each evening, entering his study and sitting down at his desk, he saw the blank sheets of paper as a pile of straw which had to be spun into gold before morning.

He had spun much gold that bitterly cold winter, but success carried the usual penalties. Now that his name had appeared on the small screen, many of his friends regarded him in a new light: he was no longer the kindly spastic librarian to them but the up and coming TV writer who no longer needed friendship because he had found success. But however many television credits he earned or books he published, he knew that nothing could heal the jerking muscles in his face and arm and leg; nothing could uncurl his left hand, nothing could stop his voice breaking out unexpectedly of its own accord. The battle for physical control continued and would always continue; it was one that he fought alone, one that he knew could never be won outright but one which he must never give up. It was a battle that brought its own particular kind of loneliness. Far back, there had been a day on which he had tried to play the pianola with his one good hand, pumping at the pedals in a frenzy of effort to keep the roll unwinding steadily, and there had been a terrible evening when he, Steven and their mother had wept in separate parts of the house. Later, his mother had spoken to him at some length about coming to terms with his disability. He had been seventeen and she had told him, 'You must accept that there are some things that you will never be able to do.' Hearing those words, and knowing that Steven was being brought up to believe the exact opposite, that he had all his faculties and a good brain and that there was nothing that he could not do, planted inside Alan an iron determination to succeed, to achieve, to show them.

And it was still there. It was still there.

He strolled along a path and through a gate to the boatyard, pausing to look up at the sleek fibreglass hull of a yacht under construction. There was the faintest stirring of a breeze now, and the sun was a pale disc above the wooded river banks. People were beginning to stir in the boats moored in midstream: he saw a hatch lift and a man put his head and shoulders out, looking round sleepily.

What an extraordinary year it had been! The Falkland crisis was over now – or at least, most of the ships had returned and most of the bands had stopped playing 'Land of Hope and Glory'. Steven's reaction to it he had found both perplexing and sad. Instead of wishing the task force well or wishing that he could be with them, he had conducted another battle of his own, one that he seemed to have been fighting for many years.

While the task force prepared to sail and the people of Great Britain were being jerked back into an awareness of the importance of seapower; while names like Lewin and Fieldhouse and Woodward leapt into the public eye as once had those of Fisher, Jellicoe and Beatty; while *Hermes* and *Invincible* sailed out through the narrow entrance of Portsmouth harbour to the cheers and wavings of the families on Southsea Round Tower, Steven was insisting that this expedition was no more than a huge and dangerous gamble. Mrs Thatcher and her admirals were, he said, cold-bloodedly risking a fleet which they knew to be inadequately protected against air attack.

He had fired off letters by the salvo: letters to admirals, letters to politicians, letters to the Foreign and Commonwealth Office. He had claimed that the rulers of the Queen's Navy were successfully holding a gun to the head of the Prime Minister, using the crisis to buy back the Royal Navy's self-respect which they and their predecessors had allowed to be so severely eroded over the post war years. That prestige, he said, was being bought back with men's blood.

When the news of the sinkings came in, of the *Sheffield*, the *Ardent*, the *Coventry*, *Atlantic Conveyor* and *Antelope*, it was as if Steven felt personally responsible: one day when he was staying the weekend, Alan had found him weeping in front of the television set at a film of the bombing of the *Sir Tristram* and the *Sir Galahad*.

Even when it was over, and the heroes and widows of heroes were being called to Buckingham Palace, he had insisted that the victory had been an empty one.

'It is the most dangerous outcome possible,' he had said. 'All that's happened is that the British people have been conned into believing that their armed forces are as powerful as ever, still able to cope with any threat, when in fact by saying "Can do" yet again, the admirals and generals have had to stretch their resources to the limit in order to achieve a skin-of-the-teeth victory. And it also means that the politicians have been reassured that failures of foreign policy can be patched up and turned to glory by acts of war.'

Had he been right? Alan strolled along the pontoon between the boats berthed in the marina and wondered about it. Yes, in a way he had, but then similar arguments could be used against the waging of any war in history. To say that the war had been a face saving exercise on both sides was merely to provide a blinding glimpse of the obvious.

The rights and wrongs of it all were intermingled like salt and sugar in a bowl: it was virtually impossible to separate them. In an outburst of anger against so much death and tragedy, Steven had attacked the British tradition itself, that slow turning wheel which over and over again seemed to thrust the nation out, forcing her to stand alone. He had said that this war had been a convenient war, a needed war, a 'lovely' war. Britain had had her Jubilee, her street parties, her eightieth birthday celebrations and her royal romance, and having wallowed in every sort of nostalgia ('including your sort, Alan') the time had come to complete the British Dream, to sail off to war again and prove her masculinity.

How obliging of Argentina to fit in with the dream, to play the

538

role of fascist aggressor and cooperate with this national urge for battle! How fitting that Albion should be given the opportunity to be perfidious, all over again! How deliciously, Britishly ruthless to launch an old torpedo at an older ship and sink her in waters she had been led to believe were safe! How splendid to pretend that old wounds were healed, to give the Pope a rapturous welcome, while at the same time giving the world a demonstration of how to organise an armada! How splendid to take on the Spaniard again, to play Waterloo at Goose Green and the Normandy Landings in San Carlos Water! And wasn't it the Best of British Luck not to have sold *Invincible* to the Australians and not to have scrapped *Fearless* or *Hermes*? To find an enemy whose navy conveniently funked the battle?

'So you're a pacifist,' Alan had said.

'I prefer the term "peacemaker".'

'What should we have done then? Given in to them?'

Steven had thought a long time before answering. 'We had already given into them. We had already given them the nudge and the wink that the Falklands were theirs for the taking. We should have had the courage to admit to the world that we'd made a huge diplomatic mistake. And we should have had the self-confidence in our own greatness to rise above the military solution.'

'And the next time?' Alan had asked. 'When the Soviets walk into Norway, or Iceland, or the Shetlands?'

Steven had smiled sadly, and admitted that he didn't really know, that part of him knew instinctively that it had been right to fight and that another part knew, with equal certainty, that it had been wrong. 'You were asking me questions like that thirty years ago, I seem to remember,' he had said. 'And I still don't know the answers, do I? I still need to learn them by heart!'

He walked back along the shore to Buckler's Hard. The tide had been making for nearly two hours now, and by his calculations there was enough water for Steven to bring *Spindrift* up the inlet to the visitors' moorings. He raised his binoculars and scanned the masts which could be seen beyond the marshes to the south-east. No, there was no sign of movement. Really it was silly of him to think that they might come in this early. What they would do – if they were coming at all – would be to anchor in the entrance and have a leisurely breakfast before weighing and motoring in.

The holiday had been Steven's idea. They had often talked of going sailing together, and now that Thomas was twelve and spending most of his holidays on the boat, it was possible. The previous month, having finished the last re-write of the last script, Alan had travelled down to the Hamble and spent a weekend with his brother on board. They had spread out the charts on the cabin table and planned a cruise to the Channel Islands. It was in a way the Jannaway dream, the holiday their father had talked about before rejoining the navy in 1939. At last it had seemed possible. 'Fresh air and navigation!' Alan had said. 'Just what I need!'

Steven had tempered his enthusiasm with caution. *Spindrift* was a good seaworthy boat but not rigged to be sailed single-handed, and Alan, guessing the reasons for his brother's reservations about sailing across the Channel with him had suggested taking on another pair of hands. A week later, Steven had telephoned to say that his ex-secretary, Ros Penfold would be coming along.

Alan had put two and two together, but Steven had insisted that he was making five. 'The only reason I've asked her is because she's the sort of person I know I can trust on her own in the shipping lanes at night. And besides, it'll be much better for Tom, having her around.'

As the holiday approached, Alan had become quite childishly excited about it. He kitted himself out with sailing boots, sweaters and foul weather gear, and invested in his own hand bearing compass and these Zeiss binoculars. What he was doing was putting into practice all the preparations he had once written about and dramatised: for once in his life he was going to experience something at first hand.

Just a few days before they were due to sail, Catherine had rung up. She was in England again, had been for several weeks. Would he like to meet?

He had almost lost touch with Catherine. After her return to Africa, he had been convinced that she was making it easy for him not to prolong their friendship. Remembering what she had said that evening three years before, he had told himself that it was better not to think about her, better to let her go her own way, better not to hope.

Hearing her voice and carrying on that extraordinary conversation in which each had seemed as tongue-tied as the other had opened the floodgates all over again.

Would he like to meet her? Of course he would! When? Where?

She had suggested any one of four days, and all of them lay in the time he was going to be sailing with Steven. He had agreed to the last one on the spur of the moment, realising as soon as he put the phone down that he should have consulted with Steven first.

Steven was not amused, and they had had one of their brotherly arguments over the telephone. Couldn't they return from the Channel Islands a few days early? No, they could not. What about trying to get Catherine to come out to Alderney or Guernsey and sailing back with them? No, Steven wasn't at all keen on that, either. Sailing across the Channel in a Force Eight wasn't the same as slipping across to Bembridge on a sunny afternoon.

'Look,' Steven had said eventually. 'If you want to meet Catherine, go and meet Catherine, and if you want to come sailing, ring her up and tell her you can't make it.'

Suddenly, Alan had known that he was up against the biggest challenge he had ever faced. He knew that Catherine need not have rung up and he knew that the only possible reason she had suggested they meet was because she wanted to meet him – not Steven or anyone else. Those words rang again in his ears: 'There are some things you will never be able to do ...' Was this one of them? He was afraid of meeting her, yes, but he was terrified much more of missing this one last chance.

He had rung Steven back and told him that he had decided not to accompany him on the sailing holiday after all.

The sound of a diesel engine came to him over the water: the unmistakable thump of a Volvo Penta. He raised his binoculars. Yes, a mast was moving along behind the trees, coming up river. He felt a surge of hope: if only it could be them! He had expected them yesterday and had been disappointed, but he was sure that if Steven had received one of the messages he had telephoned to the harbour masters at Alderney, St Peter Port and St Helier, he would make an effort to fulfil this rendezvous. The boat came into view round the bend in the river. It was difficult to identify at this distance because it was bows on, a wrinkled wake spreading out in a V over the calm water.

Yes: that was a boy standing on the foredeck; yes, it did look like a Hillyard; yes, he could see the dark blue spray dodgers. It was *Spindrift*.

541

He lowered the binoculars. The boat came on up the river, slowing as it approached the visitors' moorings. Thomas stood ready with a head rope. Steven was in the cockpit at the helm. Ros was standing by the mast in faded denims and a russet guernsey, ready with fenders.

He saw Steven raise his hand, and waved back an acknowledgement, watching as the boat made its approach, stopped, went astern and berthed alongside another boat that was tied up between the wooden piles twenty yards off shore.

He heard a step behind him and turned. Catherine was coming down the slope from the Master Builder's House, the hotel where they had been staying. She slipped her hand into his and kissed him good morning.

Steven had finished making the stern rope fast. He straightened and spoke to them across the water without having to raise his voice. 'Got your message. Many congratulations!'

Alan felt Catherine's hand tighten. 'Thank you!' he called back.

Ros had gone below. Steven bent to speak to her, then straightened, and said, 'Ros says come on board and have some breakfast!'

'We'd love to!' Catherine said.

'I'll send Tom over in the boat.'

They walked round to the landing stage while Steven and Thomas put the rubber dinghy in the water. 'Frightened?' Alan asked quietly.

'No. Not now. Not with you here.'

Alan laughed quietly. 'Well I can tell you, I'm terrified!'

Thomas rowed across with short even strokes of the oars. He held the dinghy alongside for his uncle to get into the bows and for Catherine to get into the stern.

It had been a good holiday, very rough at times, but he had enjoyed even that. Ros had been very funny, teasing his father and making him laugh; they had been to Alderney and Sark, and on the way back the topping lift had got caught in the radar reflector and Thomas had been hoisted in a bosun's chair to clear it. Now that he was getting on better at school, he was beginning to think that he would like to join the Royal Navy, but he hadn't said anything about that to his father.

Rowing back to *Spindrift* with his uncle and Catherine, he felt proud of being able to handle the dinghy so well. He pulled in the oar closest to *Spindrift* as they approached, and back-watered with the other one in the way his father had taught him, so that the boat went gently alongside with a rubbery squeak.

'That was very neatly done,' Catherine said.

There was a smell of bacon and eggs coming from the cabin, and the sun was beginning to break through the mist. His father had come out on deck to help them aboard.

'Glad you made it,' Alan was saying.

'Glad you did, too,' Steven said back.

He reached down to help Catherine. 'Give me your hand, that's the way,' he said, and pulled her up.

Then – suddenly, unexpectedly – they were hugging and laughing and crying too, and there was a happiness among them that Thomas had never known before. He knew that his uncle and Catherine were going to be married, but it wasn't just that, it was as if all three of them, Alan, his father and Catherine, were sharing something very special, something he couldn't possibly ask about because it would take a very long time to explain.